SHORT FICTION OF THE MASTERS

SHORT FICTION

Edited by LEO HAMALIAN

Second Edition

OF THE MASTERS

and FREDERICK R. KARL

Capricorn Books

G. P. PUTNAM'S SONS NEW YORK

COPYRIGHT © 1973 BY G. P. PUTNAM'S SONS

All rights reserved. No part of this book may be reproduced in any form, by mimeograph or any other means, without permission in writing from the publisher, except by a reviewer, who may quote brief passages in a review to be published in a magazine or newspaper. Published on the same day in Canada by Longman Canada Limited.

SBN: 399-30023-6

Library of Congress Catalog
Card Number: 72-87641

Fifth Impression

PRINTED IN THE UNITED STATES OF AMERICA

Acknowledgments

The editors wish to thank the following individuals and publishers for their permission to use copyrighted material:

"The District Doctor" by Ivan Turgenev, from the Story Classics edition, by permission of Thomas Yoseloff, Inc.

"Il Conde" by Joseph Conrad, from *A Set of Six*, by permission of J. M. Dent and Sons, Limited.

"Tit for Tat" by Sholom Aleichem, from *The Old Country* by Sholom Aleichem, translated by Julius and Frances Butwin. Copyright 1946 by Crown Publishers, Inc. Used by permission of the publisher.

"The Madness of Dr. Montarco" by Miguel de Unamuno, from *Abel Sanchez and Other Stories* by Miguel de Unamuno, by permission of Henry Regnery Company.

"The Soft Touch of Grass" by Luigi Pirandello. Copyright © 1959, from *Gli Eredi* di Luigi Pirandello. Reprinted by permission of Simon and Schuster, Inc.

"The Melancholy Summer of Madame de Breyves" by Marcel Proust. From: *Pleasures and Days* by Marcel Proust. Reprinted by permission of Librairie Gallimard and Doubleday and Co., Inc.

"Little Lizzy" by Thomas Mann, reprinted from *Stories of Three Decades* by Thomas Mann, by permission of Alfred A. Knopf, Inc. Copyright 1936 by Alfred A. Knopf, Inc.

"Within and Without" by Hermann Hesse, by permission of Marie Rodell and Joan Daves, Inc., on behalf of Suhrkamp Verlag.

"A Man Without Character" by Robert Musil, translated by E. M. Valk. Used by permission of the translator and Franz Horch Associates, on behalf of Rowohlt Verlag.

"Counterparts" by James Joyce. From *Dubliners* by James Joyce. Reprinted by permission of the Viking Press, Inc.

"The Judgment" by Franz Kafka. Reprinted from *The Penal Colony* by Franz Kafka, copyright 1948 by Schocken Books, Inc., New York, translated by Willa and Edwin Muir, by permission of Schocken Books, Inc.

"The Man Who Loved Islands" by D. H. Lawrence, reprinted from *The Woman Who Rode Away* by D. H. Lawrence, by permission of Alfred Knopf, Inc. and William Heinemann, Limited. Copyright 1927, 1928 by Alfred A. Knopf, Inc.

"The Children's Campaign" by Pär Lagerkvist. From *The Eternal Smile and Other Stories* by Pär Lagerkvist. Copyright 1954 by Random House, Inc. Reprinted by permission.

"In a Grove" by Ryunosuke Akutagawa. From: *Rashomon and Other Stories* by Ryunosuke Akutagawa. By permission of Liveright, Publishers, New York. Copyright © 1952, by Liveright Publishing Corp.

"My First Goose" by Isaac Babel, Copyright 1955 by Criterion Books, Inc. Reprinted by permission of the publisher from *The Collected Stories of Isaac Babel* (New York: 1955).

"Brother" by Graham Greene. From *Nineteen Stories* by Graham Greene. Copyright 1947 by Graham Greene. Reprinted by permission of the Viking Press, Inc. and Laurence Pollinger, Limited, on behalf of William Heinemann, Limited.

"The Wall" by Jean-Paul Sartre, translated by Lloyd Alexander, from *Intimacy*, translated by Lloyd Alexander. Copyright 1948 by New Directions. Reprinted by permission of the Publisher.

"Yellow" by Samuel Beckett, from *More Pricks Than Kicks*. Used by permission of the author and Grove Press, Inc.

"The Ruin of Humanity" by Alberto Moravia. Reprinted from *Roman Tales* by Alberto Moravia, by permission of Farrar, Straus and Cudahy, Inc. and Secker and Warburg, Limited. Copyright © 1956, 1957 by Valentino Bompiani and Co.

"Big Black Good Man" by Richard Wright, reprinted by permission of *Esquire Magazine* © 1957 by Esquire, Inc.

"The Children's Campaign" by Pär Lagerkvist, reprinted by permission of Albert Bonniers Förlag.

"The Judgment" by Franz Kafka, reprinted by permission of Schocken Books, Inc.

"The Secret Miracle" translated by Harriet de Onis from Jorge Luis Borges, *Labyrinths and Other Stories*. Copyright © 1962 by New Directions Publishing Corporation. Reprinted by permission of New Directions Publishing Corporation.

"The Battler" is reprinted by permission of Charles Scribner's Sons from *In Our Time* by Ernest Hemingway, Copyright 1925 Charles Scribner's Sons; renewal copyright 1953 Ernest Hemingway.

"Dry September" Copyright 1930 and renewed 1958 by William Faulkner. Reprinted from *The Faulkner Reader,* by William Faulkner, by permission of Random House, Inc.

"The Guest" from *Exile and the Kingdom* by Albert Camus. Copyright © 1957, 1958 by Alfred A. Knopf, Inc. Reprinted by permission of the publisher.

Introduction

IN attempting to give the reader an anthology of short fiction distinguishable from the numerous other collections of its kind, the editors have been guided by three basic principles. First, we sought to include only the story which is continuous with the author's major work, not the isolated or bizarre piece. For the student who is fresh to these writers, the stories should provide an introduction to their longer and more involved fiction, which he may study later in his college career. For the general reader who enjoys good literature, the stories should reward him with insights into his favorite authors and perhaps suggest aspects of their art that he missed in their novels. For each author in question, our selection presents, in small, what great literature is about.

Second, we considered the intrinsic worth of each piece. We did not choose a story simply because it was representative of the author's work or because it illustrated some principle of the craft: it had to be as well one of the short masterpieces of that writer. In selecting the best, we tried, moreover, to avoid the over-anthologized story, not because the too-familiar piece is necessarily poor but because it often perpetuates merely an accepted or stereotyped view of the author. We have embraced stories which, while central to the writer's canon, are also slightly divergent from the usual run of selections. Thus, instead of Kafka's "The Country Doctor" or "In the Penal Colony," we have included "The Judgment"; instead of Conrad's "The Secret Sharer" or "Youth," we have the relatively unknown "Il Conde"; instead of Greene's "The Basement Room," we preferred "Brother." These selections, we feel, suggest quite successfully somewhat different ideas and views from those in the more common choices. When we had no alternative, either because of a publisher's restriction or because no other piece by the author approached his most famous story (with Balzac), we were not reluctant to represent him by the favorite.

Third, we made our selections from authors (with the exception of the Japanese master, Akutagawa) whose work stands at the center of

[7

major Western literature and whose reputations are established or growing into major dimension. Hence, authors usually not available in such anthologies—such as Musil, Beckett, Proust, Silone, and Moravia—make their appearance here. As with the older masters, the themes and conflicts in their stories lead into the themes and conflicts common to all great literature. These are not stories merely good of their kind but insignificant or thin when measured against weightier fiction. These stories stand by themselves as literature.

A successful short story shares the substance of all great literature. These thirty-three stories are concerned with the nature of man's existence, with his ability or failure to grapple with the problems of life and to resolve his conflicts. Since great literature is "moral" simply by virtue of the author's honesty with character and theme, these stories are "moral" entities because they create a world of real life. Whether the author is realistic, poetic, or symbolistic in his methods, whether for him a bird is a creature who chirps on a tree or a symbol of freedom and flight, the artistic success of his work depends upon his creation of a world in which *his* view is possible. The moral resolution of our own conflicts—the catharsis that Aristotle spoke about—occurs when the author, for that moment, raises us to his level of insight and imposes his values. At that moment of pity and terror, no matter what the method for seducing us, we recognize the moral justification of all great literature.

The stories in this collection are serious, sometimes even morbid, but most important fiction is serious and often morbid. Serious writing, however, does not preclude the possibility of some leavening, and many of the authors in this collection are in the best sense witty. Nevertheless, any collection of short fiction that pretends to serve as an introduction to the masters must concern itself with the heights and depths of human behavior. These stories, accordingly, raise and lower us, make us respond to the best and worst in man, and, finally, give us a sense of the world with which all of us must come to terms.

Although these stories can speak ably for themselves, we believe that as editors we would be irresponsible if we left the learner rudderless and the instructor empty-handed. We have therefore provided a brief critical biography of each writer before his story and a series of questions after his story. These questions attempt to make the generalizations above less abstract, to show how each writer achieves the atmosphere one associates with great craft. The terminology and method the sensitive student needs to approach and appreciate these stories we have tried to work unobtrusively into these questions. Thus, we hope to induce the student to read closely and carefully, without controlling his response, and to offer the instructor several means of approach without restricting his direction or interfering with his own interpretation of the story.

LEO HAMALIAN
FREDERICK R. KARL
The City College of New York

Contents

INTRODUCTION	7
PREFACE TO THE SECOND EDITION	12
HONORÉ DE BALZAC (1799-1850)	
A Passion in the Desert	15
NATHANIEL HAWTHORNE (1804-1864)	
My Kinsman, Major Molineux	28
IVAN TURGENEV (1818-1883)	
The District Doctor	46
GUSTAVE FLAUBERT (1821-1880)	
A Simple Heart	55
FEODOR DOSTOYEVSKY (1821-1881)	
The Grand Inquisitor	84
LEO TOLSTOY (1828-1910)	
Alesha the Pot	102
HENRY JAMES (1843-1916)	
Europe	109
GUY DE MAUPASSANT (1850-1893)	
Little Louise Roque	127
JOSEPH CONRAD (1857-1924)	
Il Conde	160
SHOLOM ALEICHEM (1859-1916)	
Tit for Tat	176
ANTON CHEKHOV (1860-1904)	
The Bet	191
MIGUEL DE UNAMUNO Y JUGO (1864-1936)	
The Madness of Dr. Montarco	199
LUIGI PIRANDELLO (1867-1936)	
The Soft Touch of Grass	213
MARCEL PROUST (1871-1922)	
The Melancholy Summer of Madame de Breyves	219

THOMAS MANN (1875-1955)
  Little Lizzy — 231
HERMANN HESSE (1877-1962)
  Within and Without — 244
ROBERT MUSIL (1880-1924)
  A Man Without Character — 255
JAMES JOYCE (1882-1941)
  Counterparts — 262
FRANZ KAFKA (1883-1924)
  The Judgment — 272
D. H. LAWRENCE (1885-1930)
  The Man Who Loved Islands — 283
PÄR LAGERKVIST (1891-   )
  The Children's Campaign — 307
RYŪNOSUKE AKUTAGAWA (1892-1927)
  In a Grove — 318
ISAAC BABEL (1894-1940)
  My First Goose — 327
WILLIAM FAULKNER (1897-1962)
  Dry September — 331
ERNEST HEMINGWAY (1899-1961)
  The Battler — 343
JORGE LUIS BORGES (1899-   )
  The Secret Miracle — 352
IGNAZIO SILONE (1900-   )
  The Trap — 359
GRAHAM GREENE (1904-   )
  Brother — 380
JEAN-PAUL SARTRE (1905-   )
  The Wall — 388
SAMUEL BECKETT (1906-   )
  Yellow — 405
ALBERTO MORAVIA (1907-   )
  The Ruin of Humanity — 417
RICHARD WRIGHT (1908-1960)
  Big Black Good Man — 423
ALBERT CAMUS (1913-1960)
  The Guest — 436

Preface to the Second Edition

IN our introduction to the first edition, we explain the threefold criteria that guided us in the selection of the short fiction by the masters. Briefly recapitulated, they are: (1) the story should be continuous in theme or style with the author's major works; (2) the story should be among the author's outstanding work without being overanthologized; (3) the story should be chosen from writers who stand near the center of "the great tradition" in Western literature.

Ten years later, as we prepare a second edition of this book, we find our allegiance to those standards remains unchanged, and we believe this collection continues to represent in miniature the masters of fiction in the Western world. To know these writers, even at their briefest, is to be educated.

However, anthologists have a responsibility to their audience as well as to themselves, and, whenever possible, they should respond to whatever feedback they are fortunate enough to receive from the readers of their anthology. Now that the first edition has had the benefit of trial by teaching, we feel certain improvements have accrued to the second edition. Apparently, some stories were less successful than others in exciting the student's imagination, and we have proceeded to drop those which have been so reported: Machado de Assis' "Midnight Mass," Giovanni Verga's "The Orphans," Henry James' "The Death of the Lion," and Maxim Gorki's "Twenty-Six Men and a Girl." No doubt some teachers will miss one or more of these stories, and they may, if they wish, continue to order the first edition. The right to reprint "A Clean, Well-Lighted Place" was withdrawn by Hemingway's publisher, and, in its place, we have used "The Battler," which many Hemingway admirers regard as his greatest short story. The theme of the aging artist in "The Death of a Lion" did not seem to catch the fancy of student

Preface to the Second Edition

readers, and we have chosen in its stead a story that deals with an experience more familiar to this generation of college students, the American in Europe.

We have added two American writers who were conspicuous in the first edition by their absence, William Faulkner and Richard Wright. With Faulkner, his publisher's requirements kept us from including him, and with Richard Wright, our own oversight. Omitting Flaubert was another oversight which we have corrected by representing him through a story of novella length, "A Simple Heart." We have also represented a South American writer, Jorge Luis Borges, whose reputation as a major writer has been undeniably confirmed by his creativity of the past decade. His story will clearly indicate why he deserves to be among the present company even though his name is perhaps less familiar than that of his contemporaries in this volume. Finally, we have added Albert Camus, the French Algerian writer, whose reputation, since his death, deservedly remains higher than ever.

The reader may be curious to know why the editors have excluded the work of women writers and black writers with the exception of Richard Wright, a suspicious pair of omissions, it might be argued, in this age of liberalism in all things. The major women writers of the past such as Jane Austen, George Eliot, the Brontës, Edith Wharton, Willa Cather, and Gertrude Stein either did not practice the short story form or did not excel in it. Among contemporaries, Doris Lessing, like Virginia Woolf and Isak Dinesen, is at her best in somewhat longer forms. Flannery O'Connor, together with Katherine Mansfield, excels in the short form, though we think of both of them as minor writers next to such powerhouses of productivity and enormous creativity as Tolstoy, Balzac, and Faulkner. To call them "masters" would deprive the term of its rigorousness of meaning.

The black writers—many of them unquestionably of great promise—have not yet achieved the status of "master," although Willard Motley won E. M. Forster's admiration as the best living American novelist some years ago, and both Ernest Gaines and Ronald Fair appear to have imaginative powers and the mature craft to make their work lasting. James Baldwin and John Williams may still go on to become Richard Wright's successors, but at present they appear to be seeking a great theme. LeRoi Jones sometimes strikes off a memorable story, but his forte is drama and poetry. Ed Bullins, Douglas Turner Ward, Lonnie Elder, and Charles Gordone, among the Americans, and Wole Solinka and Athol Fugard have so far confined their considerable talents to the theater. But there is little doubt, as anyone acquainted with black and women's writing will agree, the next edition of this book will have to be expanded to include both black and female writers if the book is to represent the "masters" sure to develop during the future decade.

LEO HAMALIAN
FREDERICK R. KARL

Honoré de Balzac

A PASSION IN THE DESERT

> One of the most prolific of novelists, Honoré de Balzac was born in 1799 in Tours, France. Before he died of apoplexy in 1850, he had attempted to complete an all-inclusive panorama of the French society of his day. The dozens of interconnected novels and stories which constitute this great vision were grouped under the title The Human Comedy and were to occupy him for sixteen years. In the process of describing and analyzing the passions which have a devastating effect on men's lives, he used realism and precise documentation to transform fiction and make the modern novel a comprehensive literary form. "A Passion in the Desert" is one of his most effective accomplishments, for in the relationship between the man and the beast, Balzac has dramatized the mystery of a man forced to face his inner self.

"The whole show is dreadful," she cried, coming out of the menagerie of M. Martin. She had just been looking at that daring speculator "working with his hyena"—to speak in the style of the program.

"By what means," she continued, "can we have tamed these animals to such a point as to be certain of their affection for—."

"What seems to you a problem," said I, interrupting, "is really quite natural."

"Oh!" she cried, letting an incredulous smile wander over her lips.

"You think that beasts are wholly without passions?" I asked her. "Quite the reverse; we can communicate to them all the vices arising in our own state of civilization."

She looked at me with an air of astonishment.

"Nevertheless," I continued, "the first time I saw M. Martin, I admit, like you, I did give vent to an exclamation of surprise. I found myself next to an old soldier with the right leg amputated, who had come in with me. His face had struck me. He had one of those intrepid heads, stamped with the seal of warfare, and on which the battles of Napoleon are written. Besides, he had that frank good-humored expression which always impresses me favorably. He was without doubt one of those troopers who are surprised at nothing, who find matter for laughter in the contortions of a dying comrade, who bury or plunder him quite light-heartedly, who stand intrepidly in the way of bullets; in fact, one of those men who waste no time in deliberation, and would not hesitate to make friends with the devil himself. After looking very attentively at the proprietor of the menagerie getting out of his box, my companion pursed up his lips with an air of mockery and contempt, with that peculiar and expressive twist which superior people assume to show they are not taken in. Then when I was expatiating on the courage of M. Martin, he smiled, shook his head knowingly, and said, 'Well known.'

"How 'well known'?" I said. "If you would only explain to me the mystery I should be vastly obliged.

"After a few minutes, during which we made acquaintance, we went to dine at the first *restaurateur's* whose shop caught our eye. At dessert a bottle of champagne completely refreshed and brightened up the memories of this odd old soldier. He told me his story and I said he had every reason to exclaim, 'Well known.' "

When she got home, she teased me to that extent and made so many promises, that I consented to communicate to her the old soldier's confidences. Next day she received the following episode of an epic which one might call "The Frenchman in Egypt."

During the expedition in Upper Egypt under General Desaix, a Provençal soldier fell into the hands of the Mangrabins, and was taken by these Arabs into the deserts beyond the falls of the Nile.

In order to place a sufficient distance between themselves and the French army, the Mangrabins made forced marches, and only rested during the night. They camped round a well over-shadowed by palm trees under which they had previously concealed a store of provisions. Not surmising that the notion of flight would occur to their prisoner, they contented themselves with binding his hands, and after eating a few dates, and giving provender to their horses, went to sleep.

When the brave Provençal saw that his enemies were no longer watching him, he made use of his teeth to steal a scimitar, fixed the blade between his knees, and cut the cords which prevented using his hands; in a moment he was free. He at once seized a rifle and dagger, then taking the precaution to provide himself with a sack of dried dates, oats, and powder and shot, and to fasten a scimitar to his waist he leaped onto a horse, and spurred on vigorously in the direction where he thought to find the French army. So impatient was he to see a bivouac again that he pressed on the already tired courser at such speed that its flanks were lacerated with his spurs, and at last the poor animal died, leaving the Frenchman alone in the desert. After walking some time in the sand with all the courage of an escaped convict, the soldier was obliged to stop, as the day had already ended. In spite of the beauty of an oriental sky at night, he felt he had not strength enough to go on. Fortunately he had been able to find a small hill, on the summit of which a few palm trees shot up into the air; it was their verdure seen from afar which had brought hope and consolation to his heart. His fatigue was so great that he lay down upon a rock of granite, capriciously cut out like a camp-bed; there he fell asleep without taking any precaution to defend himself while he slept. He had made the sacrifice of his life. His last thought was one of regret. He repented having left the Mangrabins, whose nomad life seemed to smile on him now that he was afar from them and without help. He was awakened by the sun, whose pitiless rays fell with all their force on the granite and produced an intolerable heat—for he had had the stupidity to place himself inversely to the shadow thrown by the verdant majestic heads of the palm trees. He looked at the solitary trees and shuddered—they reminded him of the graceful shafts crowned with foliage which characterize the Saracen columns in the cathedral of Aries.

But when, after counting the palm trees, he cast his eye around him, the most horrible despair was infused into his soul. Before him stretched an ocean without limit. The dark sand of the desert spread farther than sight could reach in every direction, and glittered like steel struck with a bright light. It might have been a sea of looking-glass, or lakes melted together in a mirror. A fiery vapor carried up in streaks made a perpetual whirlwind over the quivering land. The sky was lit with an oriental splendor of insupportable purity, leaving naught for the imagination to desire. Heaven and earth were on fire.

The silence was awful in its wild and terrible majesty. Infinity, immensity, closed in upon the soul from every side. Not a cloud in the sky, not a breath in the air, not a flaw on the bosom of the sand, ever moving in diminutive waves; the horizon ended as at sea on a clear day, with one line of light, definite as the cut of a sword.

The Provençal threw his arms around the trunk of one of the palm trees, as though it were the body of a friend, and then in the shelter of the thin straight shadow that the palm cast upon the granite, he wept. Then sitting down he remained as he was, contemplating with profound sadness the implacable scene, which was all he had to look upon. He cried aloud, to measure the solitude. His voice, lost in the hollows of the hill, sounded faintly, and aroused no echo—the echo was in his own heart. The Provençal was twenty-two years old;—he loaded his carbine.

"There'll be time enough," he said to himself, laying on the ground the weapon which alone could bring him deliverance.

Looking by turns at the black expanse and the blue expanse, the soldier dreamed of France—he smelt with delight the gutters of Paris—he remembered the towns through which he had passed, the faces of his fellow-soldiers, the most minute details of his life. His southern fancy soon showed him the stones of his beloved Provence, in the play of the heat which waved over the spread sheet of the desert. Fearing the danger of this cruel mirage, he went down the opposite side of the hill to that by which he had come up the day before. The remains of a rug showed that this place of refuge had at one time been inhabited; at a short distance he saw some palm trees full of dates. Then the instinct which binds us to life awoke again in his heart. He hoped to live long enough to await the passing of some Arabs, or perhaps he might hear the sound of cannon; for at this time Bonaparte was traversing Egypt.

This thought gave him new life. The palm tree seemed to bend with the weight of the ripe fruit. He shook some of it down. When he tasted this unhoped-for manna, he felt sure that the palms had been cultivated by a former inhabitant—the savory, fresh meat of the dates was proof of the care of his predecessor. He passed suddenly from dark despair to an almost insane joy. He went up again to the top of the hill, and spent the rest of the day in cutting down one of the sterile palm trees, which the night before had served him for shelter. A vague memory made him think of the animals of the desert; and in case they might come to drink at the spring, visible from the base of the rocks but lost farther down, he resolved to guard himself from their visits by placing a barrier at the entrance of his hermitage.

In spite of his diligence, and the strength which the fear of being devoured asleep gave him, he was unable to cut the palm in pieces, though he succeeded in cutting it down. At eventide the king of the desert fell; the sound of its fall resounded far and wide, like a sign in the solitude; the soldier shuddered as though he had heard some voice predicting woe.

But like an heir who does not long bewail a deceased parent, he tore off from this beautiful tree the tall broad green leaves which are its poetic adornment, and used them to mend the mat on which he was to sleep.

Fatigued by the heat and his work, he fell asleep under the red curtains of his wet cave.

In the middle of the night his sleep was troubled by an extraordinary noise; he sat up, and the deep silence around him allowed him to distinguish the alternative accents of a respiration whose savage energy could not belong to a human creature.

A profound terror, increased still further by the darkness, the silence, and his waking images, froze his heart within him. He almost felt his hair stand on end, when by straining his eyes to their utmost he perceived through the shadows two faint yellow lights. At first he attributed these lights to the reflection of his own pupils, but soon the vivid brilliance of the night aided him gradually to distinguish the objects around him in the cave, and he beheld a huge animal lying but two steps from him. Was it a lion, a tiger, or a crocodile?

The Provençal was not educated enough to know under what species his enemy ought to be classed; but his fright was all the greater, as his ignorance led him to imagine all terrors at once; he endured a cruel torture, noting every variation of the breathing close to him without daring to make the slightest movement. An odor, pungent like that of a fox, but more penetrating, profounder—so to speak—filled the cave, and when the Provençal became sensible of this, his terror reached its height, for he could no longer doubt the proximity of a terrible companion, whose royal dwelling served him for shelter.

Presently the reflection of the moon, descending on the horizon, lit up the den, rendering gradually visible and resplendent the spotted skin of a panther.

The lion of Egypt slept, curled up like a big dog, the peaceful possessor of a sumptuous niche at the gate of a hotel; its eyes opened for a moment and closed again; its face was turned toward the man. A thousand confused thoughts passed through the Frenchman's mind; first he thought of killing it with a bullet from his gun, but he saw there was not enough distance between them for him to take proper aim—the shot would miss the mark. And if it were to wake!—the thought made his limbs rigid. He listened to his own heart beating in the midst of the silence, and cursed the too violent pulsations which the flow of blood brought on, fearing to disturb that sleep which allowed him time to think of some means of escape.

Twice he placed his hand on his scimitar, intending to cut off the head of his enemy; but the difficulty of cutting the stiff, short hair compelled him to abandon this daring project. To miss would be to die for *certain*, he thought; he preferred the chances of fair fight, and made up his mind to wait till morning; the morning did not leave him long to wait.

He could now examine the panther at ease; its muzzle was smeared with blood.

"She's had a good dinner," he thought, without troubling himself as to whether her feast might have been on human flesh. "She won't be hungry when she gets up."

It was a female. The fur on her belly and flanks was glistening white; many small marks like velvet formed beautiful bracelets round her feet; her sinuous tail was also white, ending with black rings; the overpart of her dress, yellow like unburnished gold, very lissom and soft, had the characteristic blotches in the form of rosettes, which distinguish the panther from every other feline species.

This tranquil and formidable hostess snored in an attitude as graceful as that of a cat lying on a cushion. Her blood-stained paws, nervous and well-armed, were stretched out before her face, which rested upon them and from which radiated her straight, slender whiskers, like threads of silver.

If she had been like that in a cage, the Provençal would doubtless have admired the grace of the animal, and the vigorous contrasts of vivid color which gave her robe an imperial splendor; but just then his sight was troubled by her sinister appearance.

The presence of the panther, even asleep, could not fail to produce the effect which the magnetic eyes of the serpent are said to have on the nightingale.

For a moment the courage of the soldier began to fail before this danger, though no doubt it would have risen at the mouth of a cannon charged with shell. Nevertheless, a bold thought brought daylight to his soul and sealed up the source of the cold sweat which sprang forth on his brow. Like men driven to bay who defy death and offer their body to the smiter, so he, seeing in this merely a tragic episode, resolved to play his part with honor to the last.

"The day before yesterday the Arabs would have killed me perhaps," he said; so considering himself as good as dead already, he waited bravely, with excited curiosity, his enemy's awakening.

When the sun appeared, the panther suddenly opened her eyes; then she put out her paws with energy, as if to stretch them and get rid of cramp. At last she yawned, showing the formidable apparatus of her teeth and pointed tongue, rough as a file.

"A regular *petite maitresse*," thought the Frenchman, seeing her roll herself about so softly and coquettishly. She licked off the blood which stained her paws and muzzle, and scratched her head with reiterated gestures full of prettiness. "All right, make a little toilet," the Frenchman said to himself, beginning to recover his gaiety with his courage; "we'll say good morning to each other presently," and he seized the small, short dagger which he had taken from the Mangrabins. At this moment the panther turned her head toward the man and looked at him fixedly without moving.

The rigidity of her metallic eyes and their insupportable luster made him shudder, especially when the animal walked toward him. But he looked at her caressingly, staring into her eyes in order to magnetize her, and let her come quite close to him; then with a movement both gentle and amorous, as though he were caressing the most beautiful of women, he passed his hand over her whole body, from the head to the tail, scratching the flexible vertebrae which divided the panther's yellow back. The animal waved her tail voluptuously, and her eyes grew gentle; and when for the third time the Frenchman accomplished this interesting flattery, she gave forth one of those purrings by which our cats express their pleasure; but this murmur issued from a throat so powerful and so deep, that it resounded through the cave like the last vibrations of an organ in a church. The man, understanding the importance of his caresses, redoubled them in such a way as to surprise and stupefy his imperious courtesan. When he felt sure of having extinguished the ferocity of his capricious companion, whose hunger had so fortunately been satisfied the day before, he got up to go out of the cave; the panther let him go out, but when he had reached the summit of the hill she sprang with the lightness of a sparrow hopping from twig to twig, and rubbed herself against his legs, putting up her back after the manner of all the race of cats. Then regarding her guest with eyes whose glare had softened a little, she gave vent to that wild cry which naturalists compare to the grating of a saw.

"She is exacting," said the Frenchman, smilingly.

He was bold enough to play with her ears; he caressed her belly and scratched her head as hard as he could.

When he saw that he was successful, he tickled her skull with the point of his dagger, watching for the right moment to kill her, but the hardness of her bones made him tremble for his success.

The sultana of the desert showed herself gracious to her slave; she lifted her head, stretched out her neck, and manifested her delight by the tranquillity of her attitude. It suddenly occurred to the soldier that to kill this savage princess with one blow he must poignard her in the throat.

He raised the blade, when the panther, satisfied no doubt, laid herself gracefully at his feet, and cast up at him glances in which, in spite of their natural fierceness, was mingled confusedly a kind of good-will. The poor Provençal ate his dates, leaning against one of the palm trees, and casting his eyes alternately on the desert in quest of some liberator and on his terrible companion to watch her uncertain clemency.

The panther looked at the place where the date stones fell, and every time that he threw one down her eyes expressed an incredible mistrust.

She examined the man with an almost commercial prudence. However, this examination was favorable to him, for when he had finished his meager meal she licked his boots with her powerful rough tongue, brushing off with marvellous skill the dust gathered in the creases.

"Ah, but when she's really hungry!" thought the Frenchman. In spite of the shudder this thought caused him, the soldier began to measure curiously the proportions of the panther, certainly one of the most splendid specimens of its race. She was three feet high and four feet long without counting her tail; this powerful weapon, rounded like a cudgel, was nearly three feet long. The head, large as that of a lioness, was distinguished by a rare expression of refinement. The cold cruelty of a tiger was dominant, it was true but there was also a vague resemblance to the face of a sensual woman. Indeed, the face of this solitary queen had something of the gaiety of a drunken Nero: she had satiated herself with blood, and she wanted to play.

The soldier tried if he might walk up and down, and the panther left him free, contenting herself with following him with her eyes, less like a faithful dog than a big Angora cat, observing everything and every movement of her master.

When he looked around, he saw, by the spring, the remains of his horse; the panther had dragged the carcass all that way; about two-thirds of it had been devoured already. The sight reassured him.

It was easy to explain the panther's absence, and the respect she had had for him while he slept. The first piece of good luck emboldened him to tempt the future, and he conceived the wild hope of continuing on good terms with the panther during the entire day, neglecting no means of taming her, and remaining in her good graces.

He returned to her, and had the unspeakable joy of seeing her wag her tail with an almost imperceptible movement at his approach. He sat down then, without fear, by her side, and they began to play together; he took her paws and muzzle, pulled her ears, rolled her over on her back, stroked her warm, delicate flanks. She let him do whatever he liked, and when he began to stroke the hair on her feet she drew her claws in carefully.

The man, keeping the dagger in one hand, thought to plunge it into the belly of the too-confiding panther, but he was afraid that he would be immediately strangled in her last conclusive struggle; besides, he felt in his heart a sort of remorse which bid him respect a creature that had done him no harm. He seemed to have found a friend, in a boundless desert; half unconsciously he thought of his first sweetheart, whom he had nicknamed "Mignonne" by way of contrast, because she was so atrociously jealous that all the time of their love he was in fear of the knife with which she had always threatened him.

This memory of his early days suggested to him the idea of making the young panther answer to this name, now that he began to admire with less terror her swiftness, suppleness, and softness. Toward the end of the day he had familiarized himself with his perilous position; he now almost liked the painfulness of it. At last his companion had got into the habit of looking up at him whenever he cried in a falsetto voice, "Mignonne."

At the setting of the sun Mignonne gave, several times running, a profound melancholy cry. "She's been well brought up," said the lighthearted soldier; "she says her prayers." But this mental joke only occurred to him when he noticed what a pacific attitude his companion remained in. "Come, *ma petite blonde*, I'll let you go to bed first," he said to her, counting on the activity of his own legs to run away as quickly as possible, directly she was asleep, and seek another shelter for the night.

The soldier waited with impatience the hour of his flight, and when it had arrived he walked vigorously in the direction of the Nile; but hardly had he made a quarter of a league in the sand when he heard the panther bounding after him, crying with that saw-like cry more dreadful even than the sound of her leaping.

"Ah!" he said, "then she's taken a fancy to me; she has never met any one before, and it is really quite flattering to have her first love." That instant the man fell into one of those movable quicksands so terrible to travellers and from which it is impossible to save oneself. Feeling himself caught, he gave a shriek of alarm; the panther seized him with her teeth by the collar, and, springing vigorously backward, drew him as if by magic out of the whirling sand.

"Ah, Mignonne!" cried the soldier, caressing her enthusiastically; "we're bound together for life and death—but no jokes, mind!" and he retraced his steps.

From that time the desert seemed inhabited. It contained a being to whom the man could talk, and whose ferocity was rendered gentle by him, though he could not explain to himself the reason for their strange friendship. Great as was the soldier's desire to stay upon guard, he slept.

On awakening he could not find Mignonne; he mounted the hill, and in the distance saw her springing toward him after the habit of these animals, who cannot run on account of the extreme flexibility of the vertebral column. Mignonne arrived, her jaws covered with blood; she received the wonted caress of her companion, showing with much purring how happy it made her. Her eyes, full of languor, turned still more gently than the day before toward the Provençal who talked to her as one would to a tame animal.

"Ah! Mademoiselle, you are a nice girl, aren't you? Just look at that! so we like to be made much of, don't we? Aren't you ashamed of yourself? So you have been eating some Arab or other, have you? that doesn't matter. They're animals just the same as you are; but don't you take to eating Frenchmen, or I shan't like you any longer."

She played like a dog with its master, letting herself be rolled over, knocked about, and stroked, alternately; sometimes she herself would provoke the soldier, putting up her paw with a soliciting gesture.

Some days passed in this manner. This companionship permitted the Provençal to appreciate the sublime beauty of the desert; now that he had a living thing to think about, alternations of fear and quiet, and plenty to eat, his mind became filled with contrast and his life began to be diversified.

Solitude revealed to him all her secrets, and enveloped him in her delights. He discovered in the rising and setting of the sun sights unknown to the world. He knew what it was to tremble when he heard over his head the hiss of a bird's wing, so rarely did they pass, or when he saw the clouds, changing and many-colored travellers, melt one into another. He studied in the night time the effect of the moon upon the ocean of sand, where the simoom made waves swift of movement and rapid in their change. He lived the life of the Eastern day, marvelling at its wonderful pomp; then, after having revelled in the sight of a hurricane over the plain where the whirling sands made red, dry mists and death-bearing clouds, he would welcome the night with joy, for then fell the healthful freshness of the stars, and he listened to imaginary music in the skies. Then solitude taught him to unroll the treasures of dreams. He passed whole hours in remembering mere nothings, and comparing his present life with his past.

At last he grew passionately fond of the panther; for some sort of affection was a necessity.

Whether it was that his will powerfully projected had modified the character of his companion, or whether, because she found abundant food in her predatory excursions in the desert, she respected the man's life, he began to fear for it no longer, seeing her so well tamed.

He devoted the greater part of his time to sleep, but he was obliged to watch like a spider in its web that the moment of his deliverance might not escape him, if any one should pass the line marked by the horizon. He had sacrificed his shirt to make a flag with, which he hung at the top of a palm tree, whose foliage he had torn off. Taught by necessity, he found the means of keeping it spread out, by fastening it with little sticks; for the wind might not be blowing at the moment when the passing traveller was looking through the desert.

It was during the long hours, when he had abandoned hope, that he amused himself with the panther. He had come to learn the different inflections of her voice, the expressions of her eyes; he had studied the capricious patterns of all the rosettes which marked the gold of her robe. Mignonne was not even angry when he took hold of the tuft at the end of her tail to count her rings, those graceful ornaments which glittered in the sun like jewelry. It gave him pleasure to contemplate the supple, fine outlines of her form, the whiteness of her belly, the graceful pose of her head. But it was especially when she was playing that he felt most pleasure in looking at her; the agility and youthful lightness of her movements were a continual surprise to him; he wondered at the supple way in which she jumped and climbed, washed herself and arranged her fur, crouched down and prepared to spring. However rapid her spring might be, however slippery the stone she was on, she would always stop short at the word "Mignonne."

One day, in a bright mid-day sun, an enormous bird coursed through the air. The man left his panther to look at this new guest; but after waiting a moment the deserted sultana growled deeply.

"My goodness! I do believe she's jealous," he cried, seeing her eyes become hard again; "the soul of Virginie has passed into her body; that's certain."

The eagle disappeared into the air, while the soldier admired the curved contour of the panther.

But there was such youth and grace in her form! she was beautiful as a woman! the blond fur of her robe mingled well with the delicate tints of faint white which marked her flanks.

The profuse light cast down by the sun made this living gold, these russet markings, to burn in a way to give them an indefinable attraction.

The man and the panther looked at one another with a look full of meaning; the coquette quivered when she felt her friend stroke her head; her eyes flashed like lightning—then she shut them tightly.

"She has a soul," he said, looking at the stillness of this queen of the sands, golden like them, white like them, solitary and burning like them.

"Well," she said, "I have read your plea in favor of beasts; but how did two so well adapted to understand each other end?"

"Ah, well! you see, they ended as all great passions do end—by a misunderstanding. For some reason *one* suspects the other of treason; they don't come to an explanation through pride, and quarrel and part from sheer obstinacy."

"Yet sometimes at the best moments a single word or a look is enough—but anyhow go on with your story."

"It's horribly difficult, but you will understand, after what the old villain told me over his champagne.

"He said—'I don't know if I hurt her, but she turned round, as if enraged, and with her sharp teeth caught hold of my leg—gently, I daresay; but I, thinking she would devour me, plunged my dagger into her throat. She rolled over, giving a cry that froze my heart; and I saw her dying, still looking at me without anger. I would have given all the world—my cross even, which I had not got then—to have brought her to life again. It was as though I had murdered a real person; and the soldiers who had seen my flag, and were come to my assistance, found me in tears.'

" 'Well sir,' he said, after a moment of silence, 'since then I have been in war in Germany, in Spain, in Russia, in France; I've certainly carried my carcass about a good deal, but never have I seen anything like the desert. Ah! yes, it is very beautiful!'

" 'What did you feel there?' I asked him.

" 'Oh! that can't be described, young man. Besides, I am not always regretting my palm trees and my panther. I should have to be very melancholy for that. In the desert, you see, there is everything, and nothing.'

" 'Yes, but explain—'

" 'Well,' he said, with an impatient gesture, 'it is God without mankind.' "

BALZAC: *A Passion in the Desert*

1. *On the literal level, "A Passion in the Desert" suggests an adventure story, but some study will show that Balzac's ambition is not limited to an account of mere adventure. Where do you find clues that*

this is more than an adventure story? What is the real purpose of the author?

2. In connection with the above questions, what part does the desert play in conveying the author's meaning? Is it more or less pervasive in its importance than Camus' Algerian landscape, Joyce's Dublin, Lawrence's three islands, or Beckett's hospital?

3. Can you explain Balzac's description of the desert as "God without mankind"? Is this vision fully explicable? Why not? How does Balzac attempt to communicate it? Does his vision have any relation to the vision in Hesse's "Within and Without"?

4. What is meant by this line: "The silence was awful in its wild and terrible majesty."?

5. What possibilities does the relationship between the Frenchman and the panther suggest? Why does Balzac describe the relationship in terms of a love affair when evidently he means much more than that?

6. Must the beast be a panther? Would a goat or a camel or a dog serve as well? Why?

7. Both Balzac's Frenchman and Sartre's Ibbieta face destruction, yet the reaction of one is vastly different from that of the other. What does this difference tell you about the authors, and particularly about their points of view, one from the early nineteenth century, the other from the twentieth? Which one do you find truer to human experience?

Nathaniel Hawthorne

MY KINSMAN, MAJOR MOLINEUX

> *Nathaniel Hawthorne was born in Salem, Massachusetts, in 1804. After winning notice with his short stories (collected in* Twice-Told Tales*), he entered the Brook Farm Institute, a famous literary and economic community of a Utopian nature. There he came to know Emerson, Thoreau, Margaret Fuller, and other transcendentalists who were shaping New England's intellectual life. Beginning in 1850, with* The Scarlet Letter, *Hawthorne published the somber novels on which his reputation rests:* The House of the Seven Gables *(1851);* The Blithedale Romance *(1852), which gives a picture of the Brook Farm experiment; and* The Marble Faun *(1860). More than a century after his death in 1864, Hawthorne is regarded as one of the greatest American literary figures of the nineteenth century and a powerful influence upon the supernatural themes of Henry James. The following story is characteristic of Hawthorne in its blend of realism and melodrama, and in its preoccupation with darkness, Gothic imagery, and the mysteries of human behavior.*

AFTER the kings of Great Britain had assumed the right of appointing the colonial governors, the measures of the latter seldom met with the ready and generous approbation which had been paid to those of their predecessors, under the original charters. The people looked with most jealous scrutiny to the exercise of power which did not emanate from themselves, and they usually rewarded their rulers with slender gratitude for the compliances by which, in softening their instructions from beyond the sea, they had incurred the reprehension of those who gave them. The annals of Massachusetts Bay will inform us, that of six governors in the space of about forty years from the surrender of the old charter, under James II, two were imprisoned by a popular insurrection; a third, as Hutchinson inclines to believe, was driven from the province by the whizzing of a musket-ball; a fourth, in the opinion of the same historian, was hastened to his grave by continual bickerings with the House of Representatives, and the remaining two, as well as their successors, till the Revolution, were favored with few and brief intervals of peaceful sway. The inferior members of the court party, in times of high political excitement, led scarcely a more desirable life. These remarks may serve as a preface to the following adventures, which chanced upon a summer night, not far from a hundred years ago. The reader, in order to avoid a long and dry detail of colonial affairs, is requested to dispense with an account of the train of circumstances that had caused much temporary inflammation of the popular mind.

It was near nine o'clock of a moonlight evening, when a boat crossed the ferry with a single passenger, who had obtained his conveyance at that unusual hour by the promise of an extra fare. While he stood on the landing-place, searching in either pocket for the means of fulfilling his agreement, the ferryman lifted a lantern, by the aid of which, and the newly risen moon, he took a very accurate survey of the stranger's figure. He was a youth of barely eighteen years, evidently country-bred, and now, as it should seem, upon his first visit to town. He was clad in a coarse gray coat, well worn, but in excellent repair; his under garments were durably constructed of leather, and fitted tight to a pair of serviceable and well-shaped limbs; his stockings of blue yarn were the incontrovertible work of a mother or a sister; and on his head was a three-cornered hat, which in its better days had perhaps sheltered the graver brow of the lad's father. Under the left arm was a heavy cudgel formed of an oak sapling, and retaining a part of the hardened root; and his equipment was completed by a wallet, not so abundantly stocked as to incommode the vigorous shoulders on which it hung. Brown, curly hair, well-shaped features, and bright, cheerful eyes were nature's gifts, and worth all that art could have done for his adornment.

The youth, one of whose names was Robin, finally drew from his pocket the half of a little province bill of five shillings which, in the depreciation in that sort of currency, did but satisfy the ferryman's demand, with the surplus of a sexangular piece of parchment, valued at three pence. He then walked forward into the town, with as light a step as if his day's journey had not already exceeded thirty miles, and with as eager an eye as if he were entering London city, instead of the little metropolis of a New England colony. Before Robin had proceeded far, however, it occurred to him that he knew not whither to direct his steps; so he paused, and looked up and down the narrow street, scrutinizing the small and mean wooden buildings that were scattered on either side.

"This low hovel cannot be my kinsman's dwelling," thought he, "nor yonder old house, where the moonlight enters at the broken casement; and truly I see none hereabouts that might be worthy of him. It would have been wise to inquire my way of the ferryman, and doubtless he would have gone with me, and earned a shilling from the Major for his pains. But the next man I meet will do as well."

He resumed his walk, and was glad to perceive that the street now became wider and the houses more respectable in their appearance. He soon discerned a figure moving on moderately in advance, and hastened his steps to overtake it. As Robin drew nigh, he saw that the passenger was a man in years, with a full periwig of gray hair, a wide-skirted coat of dark cloth, and silk stockings rolled above his knees. He carried a long and polished cane, which he struck down perpendicularly before him at every step; and at regular intervals he uttered two successive hems, of a peculiarly solemn and sepulchral intonation. Having made these observations, Robin laid hold of the skirt of the old man's coat, just when the light from the open door and windows of a barber's shop fell upon both their figures.

"Good evening to you, honored sir," said he, making a low bow, and still retaining his hold of the skirt. "I pray you tell me whereabouts is the dwelling of my kinsman, Major Molineux."

The youth's question was uttered very loudly; and one of the barbers, whose razor was descending on a well-soaped chin, and another who was dressing a Ramillies wig, left their occupations, and came to the door. The citizen, in the meantime, turned a long-favored countenance upon Robin, and answered him in a tone of excessive anger and annoyance. His two sepulchral hems, however, broke into the very center of his rebuke, with most singular effect, like a thought of the cold grave obtruding among wrathful passions.

"Let go my garment, fellow! I tell you, I know not the man you speak of. What! I have authority, I have—hem, hem—authority; and if this be the respect you show for your betters, your feet shall be brought acquainted with the stocks by daylight, tomorrow morning!"

Robin released the old man's skirt, and hastened away, pursued by an ill-mannered roar of laughter from the barber's shop. He was at first considerably surprised by the result of the question, but, being a shrewd youth, soon thought himself able to account for the mystery.

"This is some country representative," was his conclusion, "who has never seen the inside of my kinsman's door, and lacks the breeding to answer a stranger civilly. The man is old, or verily—I might be tempted to turn back and smite him on the nose. Ah, Robin, Robin! even the barber's boys laugh at you for choosing such a guide! You will be wiser in time, friend Robin."

He now became entangled in a succession of crooked and narrow streets, which crossed each other, and meandered at no great distance from the water-side. The smell of tar was obvious to his nostrils, the masts of vessels pierced the moonlight above the tops of the buildings, and the numerous signs, which Robin paused to read, informed him that he was near the center of business. But the streets were empty, the shops were closed, and lights were visible only in the second stories of a few dwelling-houses. At length, on the corner of a narrow lane, through which he was passing, he beheld the broad countenance of a British hero swinging before the door of an inn, whence proceeded the voices of many guests. The casement of one of the lower windows was thrown back, and a very thin curtain permitted Robin to distinguish a party at supper, round a well-furnished table. The fragrance of the good cheer steamed forth into the outer air, and the youth could not fail to recollect that the last remnant of his travelling stock of provision had yielded to his morning appetite and that noon had found and left him dinnerless.

"Oh, that a parchment three-penny might give me a right to sit down at yonder table!" said Robin, with a sigh. "But the Major will make me welcome to the best of his victuals so I will even step boldly in, and inquire my way to his dwelling."

He entered the tavern, and was guided by the murmur of voices and the fumes of tobacco to the public-room. It was a long and low apartment, with oaken walls, grown dark in the continual smoke, and a floor which was thickly sanded, but of no immaculate purity. A number of persons—the larger part of whom appeared to be mariners, or in some way connected with the sea—occupied the wooden benches, or leather-bottomed chairs, conversing on various matters, and occasionally lending their attention to some topic of general interest. Three or four little groups were draining as many bowls of punch, which the West India trade had long since made a familiar drink in the colony. Others, who had the appearance of men who lived by regular and laborious handicraft, preferred the insulated bliss of an unshared potation, and became more taciturn under its influence. Nearly all, in short, evinced a predilection for the Good Creature in some of its various shapes, for this is a vice to which, as Fast Day sermons of a hundred years ago will testify, we have a long hereditary claim. The only guests to whom Robin's sympathies inclined him were two or three sheepish countrymen, who were using the inn somewhat after the fashion of a Turkish caravansary; they had gotten themselves into the darkest corner of the room, and heedless of the Nicotian atmosphere, were supping on the bread of their own ovens, and the bacon cured in their own chimney-smoke. But though Robin felt a sort of brotherhood with these strangers, his eyes were attracted from them to a person who stood near the door, holding whispered conversation with a group of ill-dressed associates. His features were separately striking almost to grotesqueness, and the whole face left a deep impression on the memory. The forehead bulged out into a double prominence, with a vale between; the nose came boldly forth in an irregular curve, and its bridge was of more than a finger's breadth; the eyebrows were deep and shaggy, and the eyes glowed beneath them like fire in a cave.

While Robin deliberated of whom to inquire respecting his kinsman's dwelling, he was accosted by the innkeeper, a little man in a stained white apron, who had come to pay his professional welcome to the stranger. Being in the second generation from a French Protestant, he seemed to have inherited the courtesy of his parent nation; but no variety of circumstances was ever known to change his voice from the one shrill note in which he now addressed Robin.

"From the country, I presume, sir?" said he, with a profound bow. "Beg leave to congratulate you on your arrival, and trust you intend a long stay with us. Fine town here, sir, beautiful buildings, and much that may interest a stranger. May I hope for the honor of your commands in respect to supper?"

"The man sees a family likeness! the rogue has guessed that I am related to the Major!" thought Robin, who had hitherto experienced little superfluous civility.

All eyes were now turned on the country lad, standing at the door, in his worn three-cornered hat, gray coat, leather breeches, and blue yarn stockings, leaning on an oaken cudgel, and bearing a wallet on his back.

Robin replied to the courteous innkeeper, with such an assumption of confidence as befitted the Major's relative. "My honest friend," he said, "I shall make it a point to patronize your house on some occasion, when"—here he could not help lowering his voice—"when I may have more than a parchment three-pence in my pocket. My present business," continued he, speaking with lofty confidence, "is merely to inquire my way to the dwelling of my kinsman, Major Molineux."

There was a sudden and general movement in the room, which Robin interpreted as expressing the eagerness of each individual to become his guide. But the innkeeper turned his eyes to a written paper on the wall, which he read, or seemed to read, with occasional recurrences to the young man's figure.

"What have we here?" said he, breaking his speech into little dry fragments. " 'Left the house of the subscriber, bounden servant, Hezekiah Mudge,—had on, when he went away, gray coat, leather breeches, master's third-best hat. One pound currency reward to whosoever shall lodge him in any jail of the providence.' Better trudge, boy; better trudge!''

Robin had begun to draw his hand towards the lighter end of the oak cudgel, but a strange hostility in every countenance induced him to relinquish his purpose of breaking the courteous innkeeper's head. As he turned to leave the room, he encountered a sneering glance from the bold-featured personage whom he had before noticed; and no sooner was he beyond the door, than he heard a general laugh, in which the innkeeper's voice might be distinguished, like the dropping of small stones into a kettle.

"Now, is it not strange," thought Robin, with his usual shrewdness,—"is it not strange that the confession of an empty pocket should outweigh the name of my kinsman, Major Molineux? Oh, if I had one of those grinning rascals in the woods, where I and my oak sapling grew together, I would teach him that my arm is heavy though my purse be light!"

On turning the corner of the narrow lane, Robin found himself in a spacious street, with an unbroken line of lofty houses on each side, and a steepled building at the upper end, whence the ringing of a bell announced the hour of nine. The light of the moon, and the lamps from the numerous shop-windows, discovered people promenading on the pavement, and amongst them Robin had hoped to recognize his hitherto inscrutable relative. The result of his former inquiries made him unwilling to hazard another, in a scene of such publicity, and he determined to walk slowly and silently up the street, thrusting his face close to that of every elderly gentleman, in search of the Major's lineaments. In his progress, Robin encountered many gay and gallant figures. Embroidered garments of showy colors, enormous periwigs, gold-laced hats, and silver-hilted swords glided past him and dazzled his optics. Travelled youths, imitators of the European fine gentlemen of the period, trod jauntily along, half dancing to the fashionable tunes which they hummed, and making poor Robin ashamed of his quiet and natural gait. At length, after many pauses to examine the gorgeous display of goods in the shop-windows, and after suffering some rebukes for the impertinence of his scrutiny into people's faces, the Major's kinsman found himself near the steepled building, still unsuccessful in his search. As yet, however, he had seen only one side of the thronged street; so Robin crossed, and continued the same sort of inquisition down the opposite pavement, with stronger hopes than the philosopher seeking an honest man, but with no better fortune. He had arrived about midway towards the lower end, from which his course began, when he overheard the approach of some one who struck down a cane on the flag-stones at every step, uttering at regular intervals, two sepulchral hems.

"Mercy on us!" quoth Robin, recognizing the sound.

Turning a corner, which chanced to be close at his right hand, he hastened to pursue his researches in some other part of the town. His patience now was wearing low, and he seemed to feel more fatigue from his rambles since he crossed the ferry, than from his journey of several days on the other side. Hunger also pleaded loudly within him, and Robin began to balance the propriety of demanding, violently, and with lifted cudgel, the necessary guidance from the first solitary passenger whom he should meet. While a resolution to this effect was gaining strength, he entered a street of mean appearance, on either side of which a row of ill-built houses was straggling towards the harbor. The moonlight fell upon no passenger along the whole extent, but in the third domicile which Robin passed there was a half-open door, and his keen glance detected a woman's garment within.

"My luck may be better here," said he to himself.

Accordingly, he approached the door, and beheld it shut closer as he did so; yet an open space remained, sufficing for the fair occupant to observe the stranger, without a corresponding displaying on her part. All that Robin could discern was a strip of scarlet petticoat, and the occasional sparkle of an eye, as if the moonbeams were trembling on some bright thing.

"Pretty mistress," for I may call her so with a good conscience, thought the shrewd youth, since I know nothing to the contrary,—"my sweet pretty mistress, will you be kind enough to tell me whereabouts I must seek the dwelling of my kinsman, Major Molineux?"

Robin's voice was plaintive and winning, and the female, seeing nothing to be shunned in the handsome country youth, thrust open the door, and came forth into the moonlight. She was a dainty little figure, with a white neck, round arms, and a tender waist, at the extremity of which her scarlet petticoat jutted out over a hoop, as if she were standing in a balloon. Moreover, her face was oval and pretty, her hair dark beneath the little cap, and her bright eyes possessed a sly freedom, which triumphed over those of Robin.

"Major Molineux dwells here," said this fair woman.

Now, her voice was the sweetest Robin had heard that night, yet he could not help doubting whether that sweet voice spoke Gospel truth. He looked up and down the mean street, and then surveyed the house before which they stood. It was a small dark edifice of two stories, the second of which projected over the lower floor, and the front apartment had the aspect of a shop for petty commodities.

"Now, truly, I am in luck," replied Robin cunningly, "and so indeed is my kinsman, the Major, in having so pretty a housekeeper. But I prithee trouble him to step to the door; I will deliver him a message from his friends in the country, and then go back to my lodgings at the inn."

"Nay, the Major has been abed this hour or more," said the lady of the scarlet petticoat; "and it would be to little purpose to disturb him tonight, seeing his evening draught was of the strongest. But he is a kindhearted man, and it would be as much as my life's worth to let a kinsman of his turn away from the door. You are the good old gentleman's very picture, and I could swear that was his rainy-weather hat. Also he has garments very much resembling those leather smallclothes. But come in, I pray, for I bid you hearty welcome in his name."

So saying, the fair and hospitable dame took our hero by the hand; and the touch was light, and the force was gentleness, and though Robin read in her eyes what he did not hear in her words, yet the slender-waisted woman in the scarlet petticoat proved stronger than the athletic country youth. She had drawn his half-willing footsteps nearly to the threshold, when the opening of a door in the neighborhood startled the Major's housekeeper, and, leaving the Major's kinsman, she vanished speedily into her own domicile. A heavy yawn preceded the appearance of a man, who, like the Moonshine of Pyramus and Thisbe, carried a lantern, needlessly aiding his sister luminary in the heavens. As he walked sleepily up the street, he turned his broad, dull face on Robin, and displayed a long staff, spiked at the end.

"Home, vagabond, home!" said the watchman, in accents that seemed to fall asleep as soon as they were uttered. "Home, or we'll set you in the stocks by peep of day!"

"This is the second hint of the kind," thought Robin. "I wish they would end my difficulties by setting me there to-night."

Nevertheless, the youth felt an instinctive antipathy towards the guardian of midnight order, which at first prevented him from asking his usual question. But just when the man was about to vanish behind the corner, Robin resolved not to lose the opportunity, and shouted lustily after him,—

"I say, friend! will you guide me to the house of my kinsman, Major Molineux?"

The watchman made no reply, but turned the corner and was gone; yet Robin seemed to hear the sound of drowsy laughter stealing along the solitary street. At that moment, also, a pleasant titter saluted him from the open window above his head; he looked up, and caught the sparkle of a saucy eye, a round arm beckoned to him, and next he heard light footsteps descending the staircase within. But Robin, being of the household of a New England clergyman, was a good youth, as well as a shrewd one; so he resisted temptation, and fled away.

He now roamed desperately, and at random, through the town, almost ready to believe that a spell was on him, like that by which a wizard of his country had once kept three pursuers wandering, a whole winter night, within twenty paces of the cottage which they sought. The streets lay before him, strange and desolate, and the lights were extinguished in almost every house. Twice, however, little parties of men, among whom Robin distinguished individuals in outlandish attire, came hurrying along; but though on both occasions, they paused to address him, such intercourse did not at all enlighten his perplexity. They did but utter a few words in some language of which Robin knew nothing, and perceiving his inability to answer, bestowed a curse upon him in plain English and hastened away. Finally, the lad determined to knock at the door of every mansion that might appear worthy to be occupied by his kinsman, trusting that perseverance would overcome the fatality that had hitherto thwarted him. Firm in this resolve, he was passing beneath the walls of a church, which formed the corner of two streets, when, as he turned into the shade of its steeple, he encountered a bulky stranger, muffled in a cloak. The man was proceeding with the speed of earnest business, but Robin planted himself full before him, holding the oak cudgel with both hands across his body as a bar to further passage.

"Halt, honest man, and answer me a question," said he, very resolutely. "Tell me, this instant, whereabouts is the dwelling of my kinsman, Major Molineux!"

"Keep your tongue between your teeth, fool, and let me pass!" said a deep, gruff voice, which Robin partly remembered. "Let me pass, or I'll strike you to the earth!"

"No, no, neighbor!" cried Robin, flourishing his cudgel, and then thrusting its large end close to the man's muffled face. "No, no, I'm not the fool you take me for, nor do you pass till I have an answer to my question. Whereabouts is the dwelling of my kinsman, Major Molineux?"

The stranger, instead of attempting to force his passage, stepped back into the moonlight, unmuffled his face, and stared full into that of Robin.

"Watch here an hour, and Major Molineux will pass by," said he.

Robin gazed with dismay and astonishment on the unprecedented physiognomy of the speaker. The forehead with its double prominence, the broad hooked nose, the shaggy eyebrows, and fiery eyes were those which he had noticed at the inn, but the man's complexion had undergone a singular, or, more properly, a two-fold change. One side of the face blazed in intense red, while the other was black as midnight, the division line being the broad bridge of the nose; and a mouth which seemed to extend from ear to ear was black or red, in contrast to the color of the cheek. The effect was as if two individual devils, a fiend of fire and a fiend of darkness, had united themselves to form this infernal visage. The stranger grinned in Robin's face, muffled his partly-colored features, and was out of sight in a moment.

"Strange things we travellers see!" ejaculated Robin.

He seated himself, however, upon the steps of the church-door, resolving to wait the appointed time for his kinsman. A few moments were consumed in philosophical speculations upon the species of man who had just left him; but having settled this point shrewdly, rationally, and satisfactorily, he was compelled to look elsewhere for his amusement. And first he threw his eyes along the street. It was of more respectable appearance than most of those into which he had wandered; and the moon, creating, like the imaginative power, a beautiful strangeness in familiar objects, gave something of romance to a scene that might not have possessed it in the light of day. The irregular and often quaint architecture of the houses, some of whose roofs were broken into numerous little peaks, while others ascended, steep and narrow, into a single point, and others again were square; the pure snow-white of some of their complexions, the aged darkness of others, and the thousand sparklings, reflected from bright substances in the walls of many; these matters engaged Robin's attention for a while, and then began to grow wearisome. Next he endeavored to define the forms of distant objects, starting away, with almost ghostly indistinctness, just as his eye appeared to grasp them; and finally he took a minute survey of an edifice which stood on the opposite side of the street, directly in front of the church-door, where he was stationed. It was a large, square mansion, distinguished from its neighbors by a balcony which rested on tall pillars, and by an elaborate Gothic window, communicating therewith.

"Perhaps this is the very house I have been seeking," thought Robin.

Then he strove to speed away the time by listening to a murmur which swept continually along the street, yet was scarcely audible, except to an unaccustomed ear like his; it was a low, dull, dreamy sound, compounded of many noises, each of which was at too great a distance to be separately heard. Robin marvelled at this snore of a sleeping town, and marvelled more whenever its continuity was broken by now and then a distant shout, apparently loud where it originated. But altogether it was a sleep-inspiring sound, and, to shake off its drowsy influence, Robin arose, and climbed a window-frame, that he might view the interior of the church. There the moonbeams came trembling in, and fell down upon the deserted pews, and extended along the quiet aisles. A fainter yet more awful radiance was hovering around the pulpit, and the solitary ray had dared to rest upon the open page of the great Bible. Had nature, in that deep hour, become a worshipper in the house which man had builded? Or was that heavenly light the visible sanctity of the place,—visible because no earthly and impure feet were within the walls? The scene made Robin's heart shiver with a sensation of loneliness stronger than he had ever felt in the remotest depths of his native woods; so he turned away and sat down again before the door. There were graves around the church, and now an uneasy thought obtruded into Robin's breast. What if the object of his search, which had been so often and so strangely thwarted, were all the time mouldering in his shroud? What if his kinsman should glide through yonder gate, and nod and smile to him in dimly passing by?

"Oh, that any breathing thing were here with me!" said Robin.

Recalling his thoughts from this uncomfortable track, he sent them over forest, hill, and stream, and attempted to imagine how that evening of ambiguity and weariness had been spent by his father's household. He pictured them assembled at the door, beneath the tree, the great old tree, which had been spared for its huge twisted trunk and venerable shade, when a thousand leafy brethren fell. There, at the going down of the summer sun, it was his father's custom to perform domestic worship, that the neighbors might come and join with him like brothers of the family, and that the wayfaring man might pause to drink at that fountain, and keep his heart pure by freshening the memory of home. Robin distinguished the seat of every individual of the little audience; he saw the good man in the midst, holding the Scriptures in the golden light that fell from the western clouds; he beheld him close the book and all rise up to pray. He heard the old thanksgivings for daily mercies, the old supplications for their continuance, to which he had so often listened in weariness, but which were now among his dear remembrances. He perceived the slight inequality of his father's voice when he came to speak of the absent one; he noted how his mother turned her face to the broad and knotted trunk; how his elder brother scorned, because the beard was rough upon his upper lip, to permit his features to be moved; how the younger sister drew down a low hanging branch before her eyes; and how the little one of all, whose sports had hitherto broken the decorum of the scene, understood the prayer for her playmate, and burst into clamorous grief. Then he saw them go in at the door; and when Robin would have entered also, the latch tinkled into its place, and he was excluded from his home.

"Am I here, or there?" cried Robin, starting; for all at once, when his thoughts had become visible and audible in a dream, the long, wide, solitary street shone out before him.

He aroused himself, and endeavored to fix his attention steadily upon the large edifice which he had surveyed before. But still his mind kept vibrating between fancy and reality; by turns, the pillars of the balcony lengthened into the tall, bare stems of pines, dwindled down to human figures, settled again into their true shape and size, and then commenced a new succession of changes. For a single moment, when he deemed himself awake, he could have sworn that a visage—one which he seemed to remember, yet could not absolutely name as his kinsman's—was looking toward him from the Gothic window. A deeper sleep wrestled with and nearly overcame him, but fled at the sound of footsteps along the opposite pavement. Robin rubbed his eyes, discerned a man passing at the foot of the balcony, and addressed him in a loud, peevish, and lamentable cry.

"Hallo, friend! must I wait here all night for my kinsman, Major Molineux?"

The sleeping echoes awoke, and answered the voice; and the passenger, barely able to discern a figure sitting in the oblique shade of the steeple, traversed the street to obtain a nearer view. He was himself a gentleman in his prime, of open, intelligent, cheerful and altogether prepossessing countenance. Perceiving a country youth, apparently homeless and without friends, he accosted him in a tone of real kindness, which had become strange to Robin's ears.

"Well, my good lad, why are you sitting here?" inquired he. "Can I be of service to you in any way?"

"I am afraid not, sir," replied Robin, despondingly; "yet I shall take it kindly, if you'll answer me a single question. I've been searching, half the night, for one Major Molineux; now, sir, is there really such a person in these parts, or am I dreaming?"

"Major Molineux! The name is not altogether strange to me," said the gentleman, smiling. "Have you any objection to telling me the nature of your business with him?"

Then Robin briefly related that his father was a clergyman, settled on a small salary, at a long distance back in the country, and that he and Major Molineux were brothers' children. The Major, having inherited riches, and acquired civil and military rank, had visited his cousin, in great pomp, a year or two before; had manifested much interest in Robin and an elder brother, and, being childless himself, had thrown out hints respecting the future establishment of one of them in life. The elder brother was destined to succeed to the farm which his father cultivated in the interval of sacred duties; it was therefore determined that Robin should profit by his kinsman's generous intentions, especially as he seemed to be rather the favorite, and was thought to possess other necessary endowments.

"For I have the name of being a shrewd youth," observed Robin, in this part of his story.

"I doubt not you deserve it," replied his new friend, good-naturedly; "but pray proceed."

"Well, sir, being nearly eighteen years old, and well grown, as you see," continued Robin, drawing himself up to his full height, "I thought it high time to begin in the world. So my mother and sister put me in handsome trim, and my father gave me half the remnant of his last year's salary, and five days ago I started for this place, to pay the Major a visit. But, would you believe it, sir! I crossed the ferry a little after dark, and have yet found nobody that would show me the way to his dwelling; only, an hour or two since, I was told to wait here, and Major Molineux would pass by."

"Can you describe the man who told you this?" inquired the gentleman.

"Oh, he was a very ill-favored fellow, sir," replied Robin, "with two great bumps on his forehead, a hook nose, fiery eyes; and what struck me as the strangest, his face was of two different colors. Do you happen to know such a man, sir?"

"Not intimately," answered the stranger, "but I chanced to meet him a little previous to your stopping me. I believe you may trust his word, and that the Major will very shortly pass through this street in the mean time, as I have a singular curiosity to witness your meeting, I will sit down here upon the steps and bear you company."

He seated himself accordingly, and soon engaged his companion in animated discourse. It was but of brief continuance, however, for a noise of shouting, which had long been remotely audible, drew so much nearer that Robin inquired its cause.

"What may be the meaning of this uproar?" asked he. "Truly, if your town be always as noisy, I shall find little sleep while I am an inhabitant."

"Why, indeed, friend Robin, there do appear to be three or four riotous fellows abroad to-night," replied the gentleman. "You must not expect all the stillness of your native woods here in our streets. But the watch will shortly be at the heels of these lads and—"

"Ay, and set them in the stocks by peep of day," interrupted Robin, recollecting his own encounter with the drowsy lantern-bearer. "But, dear sir, if I may trust my ears, an army of watchmen would never make head against such a multitude of rioters. There were at least a thousand voices went up to make that one shout."

"May not a man have several voices, Robin, as well as two complexions?" said his friend.

"Perhaps a man may; but Heaven forbid that a woman should!" responded the shrewd youth, thinking of the seductive tones of the Major's housekeeper.

The sounds of a trumpet in some neighboring street now became so evident and continual, that Robin's curiosity was strongly excited. In addition to the shouts, he heard frequent bursts from many instruments of discord, and a wild and confused laughter filled up the intervals. Robin rose from the steps, and looked wistfully towards a point whither people seemed to be hastening.

"Surely some prodigious merry-making is going on," exclaimed he. "I have laughed very little since I left home, sir, and should be sorry to lose an opportunity. Shall we step round the corner by that darkish house, and take our share of the fun?"

"Sit down again, sit down, good Robin," replied the gentleman, laying his hand on the skirt of the gray coat. "You forget that we must wait here for your kinsman; and there is reason to believe that he will pass by, in the course of a very few moments."

The near approach of the uproar had now disturbed the neighborhood; windows flew open on all sides; and many heads, in the attire of the pillow, and confused by sleep suddenly broken, were protruded to the gaze of whoever had leisure to observe them. Eager voices hailed each other from house to house, all demanding the explanation, which not a soul could give. Half-dressed men hurried towards the unknown commotion, stumbling as they went over the stone steps that thrust themselves into the narrow footwalk. The shouts, the laughter, and the tuneless bray, the antipodes of music, came onwards with increasing din, till scattered individuals, and then denser bodies began to appear round a corner at the distance of a hundred yards.

"Will you recognize your kinsman, if he passes in this crowd?" inquired the gentleman.

"Indeed, I can't warrant it, sir; but I'll take my stand here, and keep a bright look-out," answered Robin, descending to the outer edge of the pavement.

A mighty stream of people now emptied into the street and came rolling slowly towards the church. A single horseman wheeled the corner in the midst of them, and close behind him came a band of fearful wind-instruments, sending forth a fresher discord now that no intervening buildings kept it from the ear. Then a redder light disturbed the moonbeams, and a dense multitude of torches shone along the street concealing, by their glare, whatever object they illuminated. The single horseman, clad in a military dress, and bearing a drawn sword, rode onward as the leader, and, by his fierce and variegated countenance, appeared like war personified; the red of one cheek was an emblem of fire and sword; the blackness of the other betokened the mourning that attends them. In his train were wild figures in the Indian dress, and many fantastic shapes without a model, giving the whole march a visionary air, as if a dream had broken forth from some feverish brain and were sweeping visibly through the midnight streets. A mass of people, inactive, except as applauding spectators, hemmed the procession in; and several women ran along the sidewalk, piercing the confusion of heavier sounds with their shrill voices of mirth or terror.

"The double-faced fellow has his eye upon me," muttered Robin, with an indefinite but an uncomfortable idea that he was himself to bear a part in the pageantry.

The leader turned himself in the saddle and fixed his glance full upon the country youth, as the steed went slowly by. When Robin had freed his eyes from those fiery ones, the musicians were passing before him, and the torches were close at hand; but the unsteady brightness of the latter formed a veil which he could not penetrate. The rattling of wheels over the stones sometimes found its way to his ear, and confused traces of a human form appeared at intervals, and then melted into the vivid light. A moment more, and the leader thundered a command to halt: the trumpets vomited a horrid breath, and then held their peace; the shouts and laughter of the people died away, and there remained only a universal hum, allied to silence. Right before Robin's eyes was an uncovered cart. There the torches blazed the brightest, there the moon shone out like day, and there, in tar-and-feathery dignity, sat his kinsman, Major Molineux.

He was an elderly man, of large and majestic person, and strong, square features, betokening a steady soul; but steady as it was, his enemies had found means to shake it. His face was pale as death, and far more ghastly; the broad forehead was contracted in his agony, so that his eyebrows formed one grizzled line; his eyes were red and wild, and the foam hung white upon his quivering lip. His whole frame was agitated by a quick and continual tremor, which his pride strove to quell, even in those circumstances of overwhelming humiliation. But perhaps the bitterest pang of all was when his eyes met those of Robin; for he evidently knew him on the instant, as the youth stood witnessing the foul disgrace of a head grown gray in honor. They stared at each other in silence, and Robin's knees shook, and his hair bristled, with a mixture of pity and terror. Soon, however, a bewildering excitement began to seize upon his mind; the preceding adventures of the night, the unexpected appearance of the crowd, the torches, the confused din and the hush that followed, the spectre of his kinsman reviled by that great multitude,—all this, and, more than all, a perception of tremendous ridicule in the whole scene, affected him with a sort of mental inebriety. At that moment a voice of sluggish merriment saluted Robin's ears; he turned instinctively, and just behind the corner of the church stood the lantern-bearer, rubbing his eyes, and drowsily enjoying the lad's amazement. Then he heard a peal of laughter like the ringing of silvery bells; a woman twitched his arm, a saucy eye met his, and he saw the lady of the scarlet petticoat. A sharp, dry cachinnation appealed to his memory, and standing on tiptoe in the crowd, with his white apron over his head, he beheld the courteous little innkeeper. And lastly, there sailed over the heads of the multitude a great, broad laugh, broken in the midst by two sepulchral hems; thus, "Haw, haw, haw,—hem, hem,—haw, haw, haw, haw!"

The sound proceeded from the balcony of the opposite edifice, and thither Robin turned his eyes. In front of the Gothic window stood the old citizen, wrapped in a wide gown, his gray periwig exchanged for a nightcap, which was thrust back from his forehead, and his silk stockings hanging about his legs. He supported himself on his polished cane in a fit of convulsive merriment, which manifested itself on his solemn old features like a funny inscription on a tombstone. Then Robin seemed to hear the voices of the barbers, of the guests of the inn, and of all who had made sport of him that night. The contagion was spreading among the multitude, when all at once, it seized upon Robin, and he sent forth a shout of laughter that echoed through the street—every man shook his sides, every man emptied his lungs, but Robin's shout was the loudest there. The cloud-spirits peeped from their silvery islands, as the congregated mirth went roaring up the sky. The Man in the Moon heard the far bellow. "Oho," quoth he, "the old earth is frolicsome tonight!"

When there was a momentary calm in that tempestuous sea of sound, the leader gave the sign, the procession resumed its march. On they went, like fiends that throng in mockery around some dead potentate, mighty no more, but majestic still in his agony. On they went, in counterfeit pomp, in senseless uproar, in frenzied merriment, trampling all on an old man's heart. On swept the tumult, and left a silent street behind.

"Well, Robin, are you dreaming?" inquired the gentleman, laying his hand on the youth's shoulder.

Robin started, and withdrew his arm from the stone post to which he had instinctively clung, as the living stream rolled by him. His cheek was somewhat pale, and his eye not quite as lively as in the earlier part of the evening.

"Will you be kind enough to show me the way to the ferry?" said he, after a moment's pause.

"You have, then, adopted a new subject of inquiry?" observed his companion, with a smile.

"Why, yes, sir," replied Robin, rather dryly. "Thanks to you, and to my other friends, I have at last met my kinsman, and he will scarce desire to see my face again. I begin to grow weary of a town life, sir. Will you show me the way to the ferry?"

"No, my good friend Robin,—not tonight, at least," said the gentleman. "Some few days hence, if you wish it, I will speed you on your journey. Or, if you prefer to remain with us, perhaps, as you are a shrewd youth, you may rise in the world without the help of your kinsman, Major Molineux."

HAWTHORNE: *My Kinsman, Major Molineux*

1. *Q. D. Leavis calls this story a "prophetic forecast of . . . the rejection of England that was to occur in fact much later." Does this summary seem farfetched to you? How else would you account for the introductory material? Does the ending support this view?*

2. *This story is filled with Gothic trappings of hallucinations and grotesqueness. What do they contribute to the story?*

3. *Who is the "Major's housekeeper" actually? What article of apparel gives away her identity?*

4. *What is the significance of the contagious laugh that spreads through the crowd, even to Robin? Why is his laugh the loudest? Why does he join the laughter at all?*

5. *What is the nature of Robin's quest? What does he find out about the world? about himself? Malcolm Cowley believes Robin is "searching for a spiritual father and finds that the object of his search is an impostor." Is there evidence in the story for either part of this proposition?*

6. *How does Hawthorne maintain the suspense of the narrative?*

7. *Robert Lowell has adapted this story to the stage, under the title of* The Old Glory. *Compare the story to the play. How does Lowell "modernize" the story?*

Ivan Turgenev

THE DISTRICT DOCTOR

Among the Russian masters of realism, Ivan Turgenev contributed the most to shaping the raw material of life into the well-made story: a single subject, embodied in a dramatic situation worked out with economy of means, emphasizing character rather than plot. Born in 1818, the son of wealthy landowners in Orel, Turgenev attended the universities in Moscow and Berlin before making his mark with A Sportsman's Sketches *(1847-52), a collection of short stories highly praised by both Tolstoy and Dostoyevsky. In 1856, he took up residence in Paris, thereafter retaining his Russian roots (revealed in such novels as* Fathers and Sons *[1862];* Smoke *[1867]; and* Virgin Soil *[1876]) through periodic visits to his country estate, through contact with Russian emigrés like the young Tolstoy, and through a powerful memory capable of exact evocation. A regular visitor of his last years was Henry James, who admired and imitated Turgenev's art and brought it to the attention of the American public before his death in 1883.*

ONE day in autumn on my way back from a remote part of the country I caught cold and fell ill. Fortunately the fever attacked me in the district town at the inn; I sent for the doctor. In half-an-hour the district doctor appeared, a thin, dark-haired man of middle height. He prescribed me the usual sudorific, ordered a mustard plaster to be put on, very deftly slid a five-ruble note up his sleeve, coughing drily and looking away as he did so, and then was getting up to go home, but somehow fell into talk and remained. I was exhausted with feverishness; I foresaw a sleepless night, and was glad of a little chat with a pleasant companion. Tea was served. My doctor began to converse freely. He was a sensible fellow, and expressed himself with vigour and some humour. Queer things happen in the world: you may live a long while with some people, and be on friendly terms with them, and never once speak openly with them from your soul; with others you scarcely have time to get acquainted, and all at once you are pouring out to him or he

46]

to you—all your secrets, as though you were at confession. I don't know how I gained the confidence of my new friend—anyway, with nothing to lead up to it, he told me a rather curious incident; and here I will report his tale for the information of the indulgent reader. I will try to tell it in the doctor's own words.

"You don't happen to know," he began in a weak and quavering voice (the common result of the use of unmixed Berezov snuff); "you don't happen to know the judge here, Mylov, Pavel Lukich? . . . You don't know him? . . . Well, it's all the same." (He cleared his throat and rubbed his eyes.) "Well, you see, the thing happened, to tell you exactly without mistake, in Lent, at the very time of the thaws. I was sitting at his house—our judge's, you know—playing preference. Our judge is a good fellow, and fond of playing preference. Suddenly" (the doctor made frequent use of this word, suddenly) "they tell me, 'There's a servant asking for you.' I say 'What does he want?' They say 'He has brought a note—it must be from a patient.' 'Give me the note,' I say. So it is from a patient—well and good—you understand—it's our bread and butter. . . . But this is how it was: a lady, a widow, writes to me; she says, 'My daughter is dying. Come, for God's sake!' she says, 'and the horses have been sent for you!' . . . Well, that's all right. But she was twenty miles from town, and it was midnight out of doors, and the roads in such a state, my word! And as she was poor herself, one could not expect more than two silver rubles, and even that problematic; and perhaps it might only be a matter of a roll of linen and a sack of oatmeal in payment. However, duty, you know, before everything: a fellow-creature may be dying. I hand over my cards at once to Kalliopin, the member of the provincial commission, and return home. I look; a wretched little trap was standing at the steps, with peasant's horses, fat—too fat—and their coat as shaggy as felt; and the coachman sitting with his cap off out of respect. Well, I think to myself, 'It's clear, my friend, these patients aren't rolling in riches.' . . . You smile; but I tell you, a poor man like me has to take everything into consideration. . . . If the coachman sits like a prince, and doesn't touch his cap, and even sneers at you behind his beard, and flicks his whip—then you may bet on six rubles. But this case, I saw, had a very different air. However, I think there's no help for it; duty before everything. I snatch up the most necessary drugs, and set off. Will you believe it? I only just managed to get there at all. The road was infernal: streams, snow, watercourses, and the dyke had suddenly burst there—that was the worst of it! However, I arrived at last. It was a little thatched house. There was a light in the windows; that meant they expected me. I was met by an old lady, very venerable, in a cap. 'Save her!' she says; 'she is dying.' I say, 'Pray don't distress yourself— Where is the invalid?' 'Come this way.' I see a clean little room, a lamp in the corner; on the bed a girl of twenty, unconscious. She was in a burning heat, and breathing heavily—it was fever. There were two other girls, her sisters, scared and in tears. 'Yesterday,' they tell me, 'she was perfectly well and had a good appetite; this morning she complained of her head, and this evening, suddenly, you see, like this.' I say again: 'Pray don't be uneasy.' It's a doctor's duty, you know—and I went up to her and bled her, told them to put on a mustard plaster, and prescribed a mixture. Meantime I looked at her, you know—there, by God! I had never seen such a face!—she was a beauty, in a word! I felt quite shaken by pity. Such lovely features; such eyes! . . . But, thank God! she became easier; she fell into a perspiration, seemed to come to her senses, looked round, smiled, and passed her hand over her face. . . . Her sisters bent over her. They ask, 'How are you?' 'All right,' she says, and turns away. I looked at her; she had fallen asleep. 'Well,' I say, 'now the patient should be left alone.' So we all went out on tiptoe; only a maid remained, in case she was wanted. In the parlour there was a samovar standing on the table, and a bottle of rum; in our profession one can't get on without it. They gave me tea; asked me to stop the night. . . . I consented: where could I go, indeed, at that time of night? The old lady kept groaning. 'What is it?' I say; 'she will live; don't worry yourself; you had better take a little rest yourself; it is about two o'clock.' 'But will you send to wake me if anything happens?' 'Yes, yes.' The old lady went away, and the girls too went to their own room; they made up a bed for me in the parlour. Well, I went to bed—but I could not get to sleep, for a wonder! for in reality I was very tired. I could not get my patient out of my head. At last I could not put up with it any longer; I got up suddenly; I think to myself, 'I will go and see how the patient is getting on.' Her bedroom was next to the parlour. Well, I got up, and gently opened the door—how my heart beat! I looked in: the servant was asleep, her mouth wide open, and even snoring, the wretch! but the patient lay with her face towards me, and her arms flung wide apart, poor girl! I went up to her . . . when suddenly she opened her eyes and stared at me! 'Who is it? who is it?' I was in confusion. 'Don't be alarmed, madam,' I say; 'I am the doctor; I have come to see how you feel.' 'You the doctor?' 'Yes, the doctor; your mother sent for me from the town; we have bled you, madam; now pray go to sleep, and in a day or two, please God! we will set you on your feet again.' 'Ah, yes, yes, doctor, don't let me die . . . please, please.' 'Why do you talk like that? God bless you!' She is in a fever again, I think to myself; I felt her pulse; yes, she was feverish. She looked at me, and then took me by the hand. 'I will tell you why I don't want to die; I will tell you. . . . Now we are alone; and only, please don't you . . . not to anyone . . . Listen . . . !' I bent down; she moved her lips quite to my ear; she touched my cheek with her hair—I confess my head went round—and began to whisper. . . . I could make out nothing of it. . . . Ah, she was delirious! . . . She whispered and whispered, but so quickly, and as if it were not in Russian; at last she finished, and shivering dropped her head on the pillow, and threatened me with her finger: 'Remember, doctor, no one.' I calmed her somehow, gave her something to drink, waked the servant, and went away."

At this point the doctor again took snuff with exasperated energy, and for a moment seemed stupefied by its effects.

"However," he continued, "the next day, contrary to my expectations, the patient was no better. I thought and thought, and suddenly decided to remain there, even though my other patients were expecting me. . . . And you know one can't afford to disregard that; one's practice suffers if one does. But, in the first place, the patient was really in danger; and secondly to tell the truth, I felt strongly drawn to her. Besides, I liked the whole family. Though they were really badly off, they were singularly, I may say, cultivated people. . . . Their father had been a learned man, an author; he died, of course, in poverty, but he had managed before he died to give his children an excellent education; he left a lot of books too. Either because I looked after the invalid very carefully, or for some other reason; anyway, I can venture to say all the household loved me as one of the family. . . . Meantime the roads were in a worse state than ever; all communications, so to say, were cut off completely; even medicine could with difficulty be got from the town. . . . The sick girl was not getting better. . . . Day after day, and day after day . . . but . . . here. . . ." (The doctor made a brief pause.) "I declare I don't know how to tell you." . . . (He again took snuff, coughed, and swallowed a little tea.) "I will tell you without beating about the bush. My patient . . . how should I say? . . . Well she had fallen in love with me . . . or, no, it was not that she was in love . . . however . . . really, how should one say?" (The doctor looked down and grew red.) "No," he went on quickly, "in love, indeed! A man should not over-estimate himself. She was an educated girl, clever and well-read, and I had even forgotten my Latin, one may say, completely. As to appearance" (the doctor looked himself over with a smile) "I am nothing to boast of there either. But God Almighty did not make me a fool; I don't take black for white; I know a thing or two; I could see very clearly, for instance, that

Aleksandra Andreyevna—that was her name—did not feel love for me, but had a friendly, so to say, inclination—a respect or something for me. Though she herself perhaps mistook this sentiment, anyway this was her attitude; you may form your own judgment of it. But," added the doctor, who had brought out all these disconnected sentences without taking breath, and with obvious embarrassment, "I seem to be wandering rather—you won't understand anything like this. . . . There with your leave, I will relate it all in order."

He drank a glass of tea, and began in a calmer voice.

"Well, then. My patient kept getting worse and worse. You are not a doctor, my good sir; you cannot understand what passes in a poor fellow's heart, especially at first, when he begins to suspect that the disease is getting the upper hand of him. What becomes of his belief in himself? You suddenly grow so timid; it's indescribable. You fancy then that you have forgotten everything you knew, and that the patient has no faith in you, and that other people begin to notice how distracted you are, and tell you the symptoms with reluctance; that they are looking at you suspiciously, whispering. . . . Ah! it's horrid! There must be a remedy, you think, for this disease, if one could find it. Isn't this it? You try—no, that's not it! You don't allow the medicine the necessary time to do good. . . . You clutch at one thing, then at another. Sometimes you take up a book of medical prescriptions—here it is, you think! Sometimes, by Jove, you pick one out by chance, thinking to leave it to fate. . . . But meantime a fellow creature's dying, and another doctor would have saved him. 'We must have a consultation,' you say; 'I will not take the responsibility on myself.' And what a fool you look at such times! Well, in time you learn to bear it; it's nothing to you. A man has died—but it's not your fault; you treated him by the rules. But what's still more torture to you is to see blind faith in you, and to feel yourself that you are not able to be of use. Well, it was just this blind faith that the whole of Aleksandra Andreyevna's family had in me; they had forgotten to think that their daughter was in danger. I, too, on my side assure them that it is nothing, but meantime my heart sinks into my boots. To add to our troubles, the roads were in such a state that the coachman was gone for whole days together to get medicine. And I never left the patient's room; I could not tear myself away; I tell her amusing stories, you know, and play cards with her. I watch by her side at night. The old mother thanks me with tears in her eyes; but I think to myself, 'I don't deserve your gratitude.' I frankly confess to you—there is no object in concealing it now—I was in love with my patient. And Aleksandra Andreyevna had grown fond of me; she would not sometimes let any one be in her room but me. She began to talk to me, to ask me questions; where I had studied, how I lived, who are my people, whom I go to see. I feel that she ought not to talk; but to forbid her to—to forbid her resolutely, you know—I could not. Sometimes I held my head in my hands, and asked myself, 'What are you doing, villain?' ... And she would take my hand and hold it, give me a long, long look, and turn away, sigh, and say, 'How good you are!' Her hands were so feverish, her eyes so large and languid. . . . 'Yes,' she says, 'you are a good, kind man; you are not like our neighbours. . . . No, you are not like that. . . . Why did I not know you till now!' 'Aleksandra Andreyevna, calm yourself,' I say. . . . 'I feel, believe me, I don't know how I have gained . . . but there, calm yourself. . . . All will be right; you will be well again.' And meanwhile I must tell you," continued the doctor, bending forward and raising his eyebrows, "that they associated very little with the neighbours, because the smaller people were not on their level, and pride hindered them from being friendly with the rich. I tell you, they were an exceptionally cultivated family, so you know it was gratifying for me. She would only take her medicine from my hands . . . she would lift herself up, poor girl, with my aid, take it, and gaze at me. . . . My heart felt as if it were bursting. And meanwhile she was growing worse and worse, worse and worse, all the time; she will die, I think to myself; she must die. Believe me, I would sooner have gone to the grave myself; and here were her mother and sisters watching me, looking into my eyes . . . and their faith in me was wearing away. 'Well, how is she?' 'Oh, all right, all right.' All right, indeed! My mind was failing me. Well, I was sitting one night alone again by my patient. The maid was sitting there too, and snoring away in full swing; I can't find fault with the poor girl, though! she was worn out too. Aleksandra Andreyevna had felt very unwell all the evening; she was very feverish. Until midnight she kept tossing about; at last she seemed to fall asleep; at least, she lay still without stirring. The lamp was burning in the corner before the holy image. I sat here, you know, with my head bent; I even dozed a little. Suddenly it seemed as though someone touched me in the side; I turned round. . . . Good God! Aleksandra Andreyevna was gazing with intent eyes at me . . . her lips parted, her cheeks seemed burning. 'What is it?' 'Doctor, shall I die?' 'Merciful Heavens!' 'No, doctor, no; please don't tell me I shall live . . . don't say so. . . . If you knew. . . . Listen! For God's sake don't conceal my real position,' and her breath came so fast. 'If I can know for certain that I must die . . . then I will tell you all—all!' 'Aleksandra Andreyevna, I beg!' 'Listen; I have not been asleep at all . . . I have been looking at you a long while. . . . For God's sake! . . . I believe in you; you are a good man, an honest man; I entreat you by all that is sacred in the world—tell me the truth! If you knew how important it is for me. . . . Doctor, for God's sake tell me. . . . Am I in danger?' 'What can I tell you, Aleksandra Andreyevna pray?' 'For God's sake, I beseech you!' 'I can't conceal from you,' I say, 'Aleksandra Andreyevna; you are certainly in danger; but God is merciful.' 'I shall die, I shall die.' And it seemed as though she were pleased; her face grew so bright; I was alarmed. 'Don't be afraid, don't be afraid! I am not frightened by death at all.' She suddenly sat up and leaned on her elbow. 'Now . . . yes, now I can tell you that I thank you with my whole heart . . . that you are kind and good—that I love you!' I stared at her, like one possessed; it was terrible for me, you know. 'Do you hear, I love you!' 'Aleksandra Andreyevna, how have I deserved—' 'No, no, you don't—you don't understand me.' . . . And suddenly she stretched out her arms, and taking my head in her hands, she kissed it. . . . Believe me, I almost screamed aloud. . . . I threw myself on my knees, and buried my head in the pillow. She did not speak; her fingers trembled in my hair; I listen; she is weeping. I began to soothe her, to assure her. . . . I really don't know what I did say to her. 'You will wake up the girl,' I say to her; 'Aleksandra Andreyevna, I thank you . . . believe me . . . calm yourself.' 'Enough, enough!' she persisted, 'never mind all of them; let them wake, then; let them come in—it does not matter; I am dying, you see. . . . And what do you fear? Why are you afraid? Lift up your head. . . . Or, perhaps you don't love me; perhaps I am wrong. . . . In that case, forgive me.' 'Aleksandra Andreyevna, what are you saying! . . . I love you, Aleksandra Andreyevna.' She looked straight into my eyes, and opened her arms wide. 'Then take me in your arms.' I tell you frankly, I don't know how it was I did not go mad that night. I feel that my patient is killing herself; I see that she is not fully herself; I understand, too, that if she did not consider herself on the point of death she would never have thought of me; and, indeed, say what you will, it's hard to die at twenty without having known love; this was what was torturing her; this was why, in despair, she caught at me—do you understand now? But she held me in her arms, and would not let me go. 'Have pity on me, Aleksandra Andreyevna, and have pity on yourself,' I say. 'Why,' she says, 'what is there to think of? You know I must die.' . . . This she repeated incessantly. . . . 'If I knew that I should return to life, and be a proper young lady again, I should be ashamed . . . of course, ashamed . . . but why now?' 'But who has said you will die?' 'Oh, no, leave off! you will not deceive me; you don't know how to lie—look at your face.' . . . 'You shall live, Aleksandra Andreyevna; I will cure you;

we will ask your mother's blessing . . . we will be united—we will be happy.' 'No, no, I have your word; I must die. . . . you have promised me . . . you have told me.' . . . It was cruel for me—cruel for many reasons. And see what trifling things can do sometimes; it seems nothing at all, but it's painful. It occurred to her to ask me, what is my name; not my surname, but my first name. I must needs be so unlucky as to be called Trifon. Yes, indeed; Trifon Ivanich. Every one in the house called me doctor. However, there's no help for it. I say, 'Trifon, madam.' She frowned, shook her head, and muttered something in French—ah, something unpleasant, of course!—and then she laughed—disagreeably too. Well, I spent the whole night with her in this way. Before morning I went away, feeling as though I were mad. When I went again into her room it was daytime, after morning tea. Good God! I could scarcely recognise her; people are laid in their grave looking better than that. I swear to you, on my honour, I don't understand—I absolutely don't understand—now, how I lived through that experience. Three days and nights my patient still lingered on. And what nights! What things she said to me! And on the last night—only imagine to yourself—I was sitting near her, and kept praying to God for one thing only: 'Take her,' I said, 'quickly, and me with her.' Suddenly the old mother comes unexpectedly into the room. I had already the evening before told her—the mother—there was little hope, and it would be well to send for a priest. When the sick girl saw her mother she said: 'It's very well you have come; look at us, we love one another—we have given each other our word.' 'What does she say, doctor? what does she say?' I turned livid. 'She is wandering,' I say; 'the fever.' But she: 'Hush, hush; you told me something quite different just now, and have taken my ring. Why do you pretend? My mother is good—she will forgive—she will understand—and I am dying. . . . I have no need to tell lies; give me your hand.' I jumped up and ran out of the room. The old lady, of course, guessed how it was.

"I will not, however, weary you any longer, and to me, too, of course, it's painful to recall all this. My patient passed away the next day. God rest her soul!" the doctor added, speaking quickly and with a sigh. "Before her death she asked her family to go out and leave me alone with her.

" 'Forgive me,' she said; 'I am perhaps to blame towards you . . . my illness . . . but believe me, I have loved no one more than you . . . do not forget me . . . keep my ring.' "

The doctor turned away; I took his hand.

"Ah!" he said, "let us talk of something else, or would you care to play preference for a small stake? It is not for people like me to give way to exalted emotions. There's only one thing for me to think of; how to keep the children from crying and the wife from scolding. Since then, you know, I have had time to enter into lawful wedlock, as they say. . . . Oh . . . I took a merchant's daughter—seven thousand for her dowry. Her name's Akulina; it goes well with Trifon. She is an ill-tempered woman, I must tell you, but luckily she's asleep all day. . . . Well, shall it be preference?"

We sat down to preference for halfpenny points. Trifon Ivanich won two rubles and a half from me, and went home late, well pleased with his success.

TURGENEV: *The District Doctor*

1. *What prompts the doctor to tell his story? Why is it told in retrospect and not reported directly by the author himself?*

2. *What kind of person is the doctor in the story he tells? What kind outside the story, particularly at the end? What is Turgenev's point in this subtle shift of character?*

3. *Avrahm Yarmolinsky, Turgenev's biographer, writes of* A Sportsman's Sketches, *in which this story appeared: "There is little overt drama . . . the author stands outside looking in, a position which allows him perspective but makes for a somewhat chilling detachment." Do you feel this opinion accurately describes "The District Doctor," or do you find the author is involved in a moving narrative? What details would you cite to support your answer?*

4. *The influence of Turgenev on Henry James has been fully studied. Do you find evidence of it in "Europe"? Where, specifically?*

5. *Virginia Woolf writes: "Turgenev did not see his books as a succession of events; he saw them as a succession of emotions radiating from some character at the centre . . . the connection is not that of events, but of emotions. . . . Turgenev's ear for emotions was so fine that even if he uses an abrupt contrast, or passes from his people to the sky or to the forest, all is held together by the truth of his insight." Does this statement apply to this story? Does it apply equally well to other stories in this collection? Which in particular? What is the danger of this device?*

Gustave Flaubert

A SIMPLE HEART

In many ways, Gustave Flaubert has been the father of a whole literary movement which tried to raise prose fiction to the highest reaches of art. In this respect, he was the progenitor of purists and formalists such as Turgenev, Maupassant, James, Conrad, Joyce, and many others. Born in 1821, in Rouen, France, a member of the provincial bourgeoisie, Flaubert spent most of his literary life mocking and satirizing this same bourgeoisie from which he came. Starting out as a law student, he suffered a serious illness at twenty-two, then diagnosed as epilepsy, and subsequently devoted himself exclusively to literature. While his greatest and most influential work is generally considered to be Madame Bovary *(1857), his other literary accomplishments are equally elegant and polished in their search for* "le mot juste," *the right word to fit the meaning:* Salammbô *(1862),* L'Education sentimentale *(1869),* The Temptation of Saint Anthony *(1874),* Three Tales *(1877), from which "A Simple Heart" comes, and* Bouvard et Pécuchet *(1881), his great satire on the bourgeois which remained unfinished at his death in 1880.*

I

Madame Aubain's servant Félicité was the envy of the ladies of Pont-l'Évêque for half a century.

She received four pounds a year. For that she was cook and general servant, and did the sewing, washing, and ironing; she could bridle a horse, fatten poultry, and churn butter—and she remained faithful to her mistress, unamiable as the latter was.

Mme. Aubain had married a gay bachelor without money who died at the beginning of 1809, leaving her with two small children and a quantity of debts. She then sold all her property except the farms of Toucques and Geffosses, which brought in two hundred pounds a year at most, and left her house in Saint-Melaine for a less expensive one that had belonged to her family and was situated behind the market.

This house had a slate roof and stood between an alley and a lane that went down to the river. There was an unevenness in the levels of

[55

the rooms which made you stumble. A narrow hall divided the kitchen from the "parlour" where Mme. Aubain spent her day, sitting in a wicker easy chair by the window. Against the panels, which were painted white, was a row of eight mahogany chairs. On an old piano under the barometer a heap of wooden and cardboard boxes rose like a pyramid. A stuffed armchair stood on either side of the Louis-Quinze chimney-piece, which was in yellow marble with a clock in the middle of it modelled like a temple of Vesta. The whole room was a little musty, as the floor was lower than the garden.

The first floor began with "Madame's" room: very large, with a pale-flowered wallpaper and a portrait of "Monsieur" as a dandy of the period. It led to a smaller room, where there were two children's cots without mattresses. Next came the drawing-room, which was always shut up and full of furniture covered with sheets. Then there was a corridor leading to a study. The shelves of a large bookcase were respectably lined with books and papers, and its three wings surrounded a broad writing-table in darkwood. The two panels at the end of the room were covered with pen-drawings, water-colour landscapes, and engravings by Audran, all relics of better days and vanished splendour. Félicité's room on the top floor got its light from a dormer-window, which looked over the meadows.

She rose at daybreak to be in time for Mass, and worked till evening without stopping. Then, when dinner was over, the plates and dishes in order, and the door shut fast, she thrust the log under the ashes and went to sleep in front of the hearth with her rosary in her hand. Félicité was the stubbornest of all bargainers; and as for cleanness, the polish on her saucepans was the despair of other servants. Thrifty in all things, she ate slowly, gathering off the table in her fingers the crumbs of her loaf—a twelve-pound loaf expressly baked for her, which lasted for three weeks.

At all times of year she wore a print handkerchief fastened with a pin behind, a bonnet that covered her hair, grey stockings, a red skirt, and a bibbed apron—such as hospital nurses wear—over her jacket.

Her face was thin and her voice sharp. At twenty-five she looked like forty. From fifty onwards she seemed of no particular age; and with her silence, straight figure, and precise movements she was like a woman made of wood, and going by clockwork.

II

She had had her love-story like another.

Her father, a mason, had been killed by falling off some scaffolding. Then her mother died, her sisters scattered, and a farmer took her in and employed her, while she was still quite little, to herd the cows at pasture. She shivered in rags and would lie flat on the ground to drink water from the ponds; she was beaten for nothing, and finally turned out for the theft of a shilling which she did not steal. She went to another farm, where she became dairy-maid; and as she was liked by her employers her companions were jealous of her.

One evening in August (she was then eighteen) they took her to the assembly at Colleville. She was dazed and stupefied in an instant by the noise of the fiddlers, the lights in the trees, the gay medley of dresses, the lace, the gold crosses, and the throng of people jigging all together. While she kept shyly apart a young man with a well-to-do air, who was leaning on the shaft of a cart and smoking his pipe, came up to ask her to dance. He treated her to cider, coffee, and cake, and bought her a silk handkerchief; and then, imagining she had guessed his meaning, offered to see her home. At the edge of a field of oats he pushed her roughly down. She was frightened and began to cry out; and he went off.

One evening later she was on the Beaumont road. A big hay-wagon was moving slowly along; she wanted to get in front of it, and as she brushed past the wheels she recognized Theodore. He greeted her quite calmly, saying she must excuse it all because it was "the fault of the drink." She could not think of any answer and wanted to run away.

He began at once to talk about the harvest and the worthies of the commune, for his father had left Colleville for the farm at Les Ecots, so that now he and she were neighbours. "Ah!" she said. He added that they thought of settling him in life. Well, he was in no hurry; he was waiting for a wife to his fancy. She dropped her head; and then he asked her if she thought of marrying. She answered with a smile that it was mean to make fun of her.

"But I am not, I swear!"—and he passed his left hand round her waist. She walked in the support of his embrace; their steps grew slower. The wind was soft, the stars glittered, the huge wagon-load of hay swayed in front of them, and dust rose from the dragging steps of the four horses. Then, without a word of command, they turned to the right. He clasped her once more in his arms, and she disappeared into the shadow.

The week after Theodore secured some assignations with her.

They met at the end of farmyards, behind a wall, or under a solitary tree. She was not innocent as young ladies are—she had learned knowledge from the animals—but her reason and the instinct of her honour would not let her fall. Her resistance exasperated Theodore's passion; so much so that to satisfy it—or perhaps quite artlessly—he made her an offer of marriage. She was in doubt whether to trust him, but he swore great oaths of fidelity.

Soon he confessed to something troublesome; the year before his parents had bought him a substitute for the army, but any day he might be taken again, and the idea of serving was a terror to him. Félicité took this cowardice of his as a sign of affection, and it redoubled hers. She stole away at night to see him, and when she reached their meeting-place Theodore racked her with his anxieties and urgings.

At last he declared that he would go himself to the prefecture for information, and would tell her the result on the following Sunday, between eleven and midnight.

When the moment came she sped towards her lover. Instead of him she found one of his friends.

He told her that she would not see Theodore any more. To ensure himself against conscription he had married an old woman, Madame Lehoussais, of Toucques, who was very rich.

There was an uncontrollable burst of grief. She threw herself on the ground, screamed, called to the God of mercy, and moaned by herself in the fields till daylight came. Then she came back to the farm and announced that she was going to leave; and at the end of the month she received her wages, tied all her small belongings with a handkerchief, and went to Pont-l'Évêque.

In front of the inn there she made inquiries of a woman in a widow's cap, who, as it happened, was just looking for a cook. The girl did not know much, but her willingness seemed so great and her demands so small that Mme. Aubain ended by saying:

"Very well, then, I will take you."

A quarter of an hour afterwards Félicité was installed in her house.

She lived there at first in a tremble, as it were, at "the style of the house" and the memory of "Monsieur" floating over it all. Paul and Virginie, the first aged seven and the other hardly four, seemed to her beings of a precious substance; she carried them on her back like a horse; it was a sorrow to her that Mme. Aubain would not let her kiss them every minute. And yet she was happy there. Her grief had melted in the pleasantness of things all round.

Every Thursday regular visitors came in for a game of boston, and Félicité got the cards and foot-warmers ready beforehand. They arrived punctually at eight and left before the stroke of eleven.

On Monday mornings the dealer who lodged in the covered passage spread out all his old iron on the ground. Then a hum of voices began to fill the town, mingled with the neighing of horses, bleating of lambs, grunting of pigs, and the sharp rattle of carts along the street. About noon, when the market was at its height, you might see a tall, hook-nosed old countryman with his cap pushed back making his appearance at the door. It was Robelin, the farmer of Geffosses. A little later came Liébard, the farmer from Toucques—short, red, and corpulent—in a grey jacket and gaiters shod with spurs.

Both had poultry or cheese to offer their landlord. Félicité was invariably a match for their cunning, and they went away filled with respect for her.

At vague intervals Mme. Aubain had a visit from the Marquis de Gremanville, one of her uncles, who had ruined himself by debauchery and now lived at Falaise on his last remaining morsel of land. He invariably came at the luncheon hour, with a dreadful poodle whose paws left all the furniture in a mess. In spite of efforts to show his breeding, which he carried to the point of raising his hat every time he mentioned "my late father," habit was too strong for him; he poured himself out glass after glass and fired off improper remarks. Félicité edged him politely out of the house—"You have had enough, Monsieur de Gremanville! Another time!"—and she shut the door on him.

She opened it with pleasure to M. Bourais, who had been a lawyer. His baldness, his white stock, frilled shirt, and roomy brown coat, his way of rounding the arm as he took snuff—his whole person, in fact, created that disturbance of mind which overtakes us at the sight of extraordinary men.

As he looked after the property of "Madame" he remained shut up with her for hours in "Monsieur's" study, though all the time he was afraid of compromising himself. He respected the magistracy immensely, and had some pretensions to Latin.

To combine instruction and amusement he gave the children a geography book made up of a series of prints. They represented scenes in different parts of the world: cannibals with feathers on their heads, a monkey carrying off a young lady, Bedouins in the desert, the harpooning of a whale, and so on. Paul explained these engravings to Félicité; and that, in fact, was the whole of her literary education. The children's education was undertaken by Guyot, a poor creature employed at the town hall, who was famous for his beautiful hand and sharpened his penknife on his boots.

When the weather was bright the household set off early for a day at Geffosses Farm.

Its courtyard is on a slope, with the farmhouse in the middle, and the sea looks like a grey streak in the distance.

Félicité brought slices of cold meat out of her basket, and they breakfasted in a room adjoining the dairy. It was the only surviving fragment of a country house which was now no more. The wallpaper hung in tatters, and quivered in the draughts. Mme. Aubain sat with bowed head, overcome by her memories; the children became afraid to speak. "Why don't you play, then?" she would say, and off they went.

Paul climbed into the barn, caught birds, played at ducks and drakes over the pond, or hammered with his stick on the big casks which boomed like drums. Virginie fed the rabbits or dashed off to pick cornflowers, her quick legs showing their embroidered little drawers.

One autumn evening they went home by the fields. The moon was in its first quarter, lighting part of the sky; and mist floated like a scarf over the windings of the Toucques. Cattle, lying out in the middle of the grass, looked quietly at the four people as they passed. In the third meadow some of them got up and made a half-circle in front of the walkers. "There's nothing to be afraid of," said Félicité, as she stroked the nearest on the back with a kind of crooning song; he wheeled round and the others did the same. But when they crossed the next pasture there was a formidable bellow. It was a bull, hidden by the mist. Mme. Aubain was about to run. "No! no! don't go so fast!" They mended their pace, however, and heard a loud breathing behind them which came nearer. His hoofs thudded on the meadow grass like hammers; why, he was galloping now! Félicité turned round, and tore up clods of earth with both hands and threw them in his eyes. He lowered his muzzle, waved his horns, and quivered with fury, bellowing terribly. Mme. Aubain, now at the end of the pasture with her two little ones, was looking wildly for a place to get over the high bank. Félicité was retreating, still with her face to the bull, keeping up a shower of clods which blinded him, and crying all the time, "Be quick! be quick!"

Mme. Aubain went down into the ditch, pushed Virginie first and then Paul, fell several times as she tried to climb the bank, and managed it at last by dint of courage.

The bull had driven Félicité to bay against a rail-fence; his slaver was streaming into her face; another second, and he would have gored her. She had just time to slip between two of the rails, and the big animal stopped short in amazement.

This adventure was talked of at Pont-l'Evêque for many a year. Félicité did not pride herself on it in the least, not having the barest suspicion that she had done anything heroic.

Virginie was the sole object of her thoughts, for the child developed a nervous complaint as a result of her fright, and M. Poupart, the doctor, advised sea-bathing at Trouville. It was not a frequented place then. Mme. Aubain collected information, consulted Bourais, and made preparations as though for a long journey.

Her luggage started a day in advance, in Liébard's cart. The next day he brought round two horses, one of which had a lady's saddle with a velvet back to it, while a cloak was rolled up to make a kind of seat on the crupper of the other. Mme. Aubain rode on that, behind the farmer. Félicité took charge of Virginie, and Paul mounted M. Lechaptois' donkey, lent on condition that great care was taken of it.

The road was so bad that its five miles took two hours. The horses sank in the mud up to their pasterns, and their haunches jerked abruptly in the effort to get out; or else they stumbled in the ruts, and at other moments had to jump. In some places Liébard's mare came suddenly to a halt. He waited patiently until she went on again, talking about the people who had properties along the road, and adding moral reflections to their history. So it was that as they were in the middle of Toucques, and passed under some windows bowered with nasturtiums, he shrugged his shoulders and said: "There's a Mme. Lehoussais lives there; instead of taking a young man she . . ." Félicité did not hear the rest; the horses were trotting and the donkey galloping. They all turned down a bypath; a gate swung open and two boys appeared; and the party dismounted in front of a manure-heap at the very threshold of the farmhouse door.

When Mme. Liébard saw her mistress she gave lavish signs of joy. She served her a luncheon with a sirloin of beef, tripe, black-pudding, a fricassee of chicken, sparkling cider, a fruit tart, and brandied plums; seasoning it all with compliments to Madame, who seemed in better health; Mademoiselle, who was "splendid" now; and Monsieur Paul, who had "filled out" wonderfully. Nor did she forget their deceased grandparents, whom the Liébards had known, as they had been in the service of the family for several generations. The farm, like them, had the stamp of antiquity. The beams on the ceiling were worm-eaten, the walls blackened with smoke, and the window-panes grey with dust. There was an oak dresser laden with every sort of useful article—jugs, plates, pewter bowls, wolf-traps, and sheep-shears; and a huge syringe made the children laugh. There was not a tree in the three courtyards without mushrooms growing at the bottom of it or a tuft of mistletoe on its boughs. Several of them had been thrown down by the wind. They had taken root again at the middle; and all were bending under their wealth of apples. The thatched roofs, like brown velvet and of varying thickness, withstood the heaviest squalls. The cart-shed, however, was falling into ruin. Mme. Aubain said she would see about it, and ordered the animals to be saddled again.

It was another half-hour before they reached Trouville. The little caravan dismounted to pass Écores—it was an overhanging cliff with boats below it—and three minutes later they were at the end of the quay and entered the courtyard of the Golden Lamb, kept by good Mme. David.

From the first days of their stay Virginie began to feel less weak, thanks to the change of air and the effect of the sea-baths. These, for want of a bathing-dress, she took in her chemise; and her nurse dressed her afterwards in a coastguard's cabin which was used by the bathers.

In the afternoons they took the donkey and went off beyond the Black Rocks, in the direction of Hennequeville. The path climbed at first through ground with dells in it like the green sward of a park, and then reached a plateau where grass fields and arable lay side by side. Hollies rose stiffly out of the briary tangle at the edge of the road; and here and there a great withered tree made zigzags in the blue air with its branches.

They nearly always rested in a meadow, with Deauville on their left, Havre on their right, and the open sea in front. It glittered in the sunshine, smooth as a mirror and so quiet that its murmur was scarcely to be heard; sparrows chirped in hiding and the immense sky arched over it all. Mme. Aubain sat doing her needlework; Virginie plaited rushes by her side; Félicité pulled up lavender, and Paul was bored and anxious to start home.

Other days they crossed the Toucques in a boat and looked for shells. When the tide went out sea-urchins, starfish, and jelly-fish were left exposed; and the children ran in pursuit of the foam-flakes which scudded in the wind. The sleepy waves broke on the sand and unrolled all along the beach; it stretched away out of sight, bounded on the land-side by the dunes which parted it from the Marsh, a wide meadow shaped like an arena. As they came home that way, Trouville, on the hill-slope in the background, grew bigger at every step, and its miscellaneous throng of houses seemed to break into a gay disorder.

On days when it was too hot they did not leave their room. From the dazzling brilliance outside light fell in streaks between the laths of the blinds. There were no sounds in the village; and on the pavement below not a soul. This silence round them deepened the quietness of things. In the distance, where men were caulking, there was a tap of hammers as they plugged the hulls, and a sluggish breeze wafted up the smell of tar.

The chief amusement was the return of the fishing-boats. They began to tack as soon as they had passed the buoys. The sails came down on two of the three masts; and they drew on with the foresail swelling like a balloon, glided through the splash of the waves, and when they had reached the middle of the harbour suddenly dropped anchor. Then the boats drew up against the quay. The sailors threw quivering fish over the side; a row of carts was waiting, and women in cotton bonnets darted out to take the baskets and give their men a kiss.

One of them came up to Félicité one day, and she entered the lodgings a little later in a state of delight. She had found a sister again—and then Nastasie Barette, "wife of Leroux," appeared, holding an infant at her breast and another child with her right hand, while on her left was a little cabin boy with his hands on his hips and a cap over his ear.

After a quarter of an hour Mme. Aubain sent them off; but they were always to be found hanging about the kitchen, or encountered in the course of a walk. The husband never appeared.

Félicité was seized with affection for them. She bought them a blanket, some shirts, and a stove; it was clear that they were making a good thing out of her. Mme. Aubain was annoyed by this weakness of hers, and she did not like the liberties taken by the nephew, who said "thee" and "thou" to Paul. So as Virginie was coughing and the fine weather gone, she returned to Pont-l'Évêque.

There M. Bourais enlightened her on the choice of a boys' school. The one at Caen was reputed to be the best, and Paul was sent to it. He said his good-byes bravely, content enough at going to live in a house where he would have companions.

Mme. Aubain resigned herself to her son's absence as a thing that had to be. Virginie thought about it less and less. Félicité missed the noise he made. But she found an occupation to distract her; from Christmas onward she took the little girl to catechism every day.

III

After making a genuflexion at the door she walked up between the double row of chairs under the lofty nave, opened Mme. Aubain's pew, sat down, and began to look about her. The choir stalls were filled with the boys on the right and the girls on the left, and the curé stood by the lectern. On a painted window in the apse the Holy Ghost looked down upon the Virgin. Another window showed her on her knees before the child Jesus, and a group carved in wood behind the altar-shrine represented St. Michael overthrowing the dragon.

The priest began with a sketch of sacred history. The Garden, the Flood, the Tower of Babel, cities in flames, dying nations, and overturned idols passed like a dream before her eyes; and the dizzying vision left her with reverence for the Most High and fear of his wrath. Then she wept at the story of the Passion. Why had they crucified Him, when He loved the children, fed the multitudes, healed the blind, and had willed, in His meekness, to be born among the poor, on the dungheap of a stable? The sowings, harvests, wine-presses, all the familiar things the Gospel speaks of, were a part of her life. They had been made holy by God's passing; and she loved the lambs more tenderly for her love of the Lamb, and the doves because of the Holy Ghost.

She found it hard to imagine Him in person, for He was not merely a bird, but a flame as well, and a breath at other times. It may be His light, she thought, which flits at night about the edge of the marshes, His breathing which drives on the clouds, His voice which gives harmony to the bells; and she would sit rapt in adoration, enjoying the cool walls and the quiet of the church.

Of doctrines she understood nothing—did not even try to understand. The curé discoursed, the children repeated their lesson, and finally she went to sleep, waking up with a start when their wooden shoes clattered on the flagstones as they went away.

It was thus that Félicité, whose religious education had been neglected in her youth, learned the catechism by dint of hearing it; and from that time she copied all Virginie's observances, fasting as she did and confessing with her. On Corpus Christi Day they made a festal altar together.

The first communion loomed distractingly ahead. She fussed over the shoes, the rosary, the book and gloves; and how she trembled as she helped Virginie's mother to dress her!

All through the mass she was racked with anxiety. She could not see one side of the choir because of M. Bourais; but straight in front of her was the flock of maidens, with white crowns above their hanging veils, making the impression of a field of snow; and she knew her dear child at a distance by her dainty neck and thoughtful air. The bell tinkled. The heads bowed, and there was silence. As the organ pealed, singers and congregation took up the "Agnus Dei"; then the procession of the boys began, and after them the girls rose. Step by step, with their hands joined in prayer, they went towards the lighted altar, knelt on the first step, received the sacrament in turn, and came back in the same order to their places. When Virginie's turn came Félicité leaned forward to see her; and with the imaginativeness of deep and tender feeling it seemed to her that she actually was the child; Virginie's face became hers, she was dressed in her clothes, it was her heart beating in her breast. As the moment came to open her mouth she closed her eyes and nearly fainted.

She appeared early in the sacristy next morning for Monsieur the curé to give her the communion. She took it with devotion, but it did not give her the same exquisite delight.

Mme. Aubain wanted to make her daughter into an accomplished person; and as Guyot could not teach her music or English she decided to place her in the Ursuline Convent at Honfleur as a boarder. The child made no objection. Félicité sighed and thought that Madame lacked feeling. Then she reflected that her mistress might be right; matters of this kind were beyond her.

So one day an old spring-van drew up at the door, and out of it stepped a nun to fetch the young lady. Félicité hoisted the luggage on to the top, admonished the driver, and put six pots of preserves, a dozen pears, and a bunch of violets under the seat.

At the last moment Virginie broke into a fit of sobbing; she threw her arms round her mother, who kissed her on the forehead, saying over and over "Come, be brave! be brave!" The step was raised, and the carriage drove off.

Then Mme. Aubain's strength gave way; and in the evening all her friends—the Lormeau family, Mme. Lechaptois, the Rochefeuille ladies, M. de Houppeville, and Bourais—came in to console her.

To be without her daughter was very painful for her at first. But she heard from Virginie three times a week, wrote to her on the other days, walked in the garden, and so filled up the empty hours.

From sheer habit Félicité went into Virginie's room in the mornings and gazed at the walls. It was boredom to her not to have to comb the child's hair now, lace up her boots, tuck her into bed—and not to see her charming face perpetually and hold her hand when they went out together. In this idle condition she tried making lace. But her fingers were too heavy and broke the threads; she could not attend to anything, she had lost her sleep, and was, in her own words, "destroyed."

To "divert herself" she asked leave to have visits from her nephew Victor.

He arrived on Sundays after mass, rosy-cheeked, bare-chested, with the scent of the country he had walked through still about him. She laid her table promptly and they had lunch, sitting opposite each other. She ate as little as possible herself to save expense, but stuffed him with food so generously that at last he went to sleep. At the first stroke of vespers she woke him up, brushed his trousers, fastened his tie, and went to church, leaning on his arm with maternal pride.

Victor was always instructed by his parents to get something out of her—a packet of moist sugar, it might be, a cake of soap, spirits, or even money at times. He brought his things for her to mend and she took over the task, only too glad to have a reason for making him come back.

In August his father took him off on a coasting voyage. It was holiday time, and she was consoled by the arrival of the children. Paul, however, was getting selfish, and Virginie was too old to be called "thou" any longer; this put a constraint and barrier between them.

Victor went to Morlaix, Dunkirk, and Brighton in succession and made Félicité a present on his return from each voyage. It was a box made of shells the first time, a coffee cup the next, and on the third occasion a large gingerbread man. Victor was growing handsome. He was well made, had a hint of a moustache, good honest eyes, and a small leather hat pushed backwards like a pilot's. He entertained her by telling stories embroidered with nautical terms.

On a Monday, July 14, 1819 (she never forgot the date), he told her that he had signed on for the big voyage and next night but one he would take the Honfleur boat and join his schooner, which was to weigh anchor from Havre before long. Perhaps he would be gone two years.

The prospect of this long absence threw Félicité into deep distress; one more good-bye she must have, and on the Wednesday evening, when Madame's dinner was finished, she put on her clogs and made short work of the twelve miles between Pont-l'Évêque and Honfleur.

When she arrived in front of the Calvary she took the turn to the right instead of the left, got lost in the timber-yards, and retraced her steps; some people to whom she spoke advised her to be quick. She went all round the harbour basin, full of ships, and knocked against hawsers;

then the ground fell away, lights flashed across each other, and she thought her wits had left her, for she saw horses up in the sky.

Others were neighing by the quay-side, frightened at the sea. They were lifted by a tackle and deposited in a boat, where passengers jostled each other among cider casks, cheese baskets, and sacks of grain; fowls could be heard clucking, the captain swore; and a cabin-boy stood leaning over the bows, indifferent to it all. Félicité, who had not recognized him, called "Victor!" and he raised his head; all at once, as she was darting forwards, the gangway was drawn back.

The Honfleur packet, women singing as they hauled it, passed out of harbour. Its framework creaked and the heavy waves whipped its bows. The canvas had swung round, no one could be seen on board now; and on the moon-silvered sea the boat made a black speck which paled gradually, dipped, and vanished.

As Félicité passed by the Calvary she had a wish to commend to God what she cherished most, and she stood there praying a long time with her face bathed in tears and her eyes towards the clouds. The town was asleep, coastguards were walking to and fro; and water poured without cessation through the holes in the sluice, with the noise of a torrent. The clocks struck two.

The convent parlour would not be open before day. If Félicité were late Madame would most certainly be annoyed; and in spite of her desire to kiss the other child she turned home. The maids at the inn were waking up as she came in to Pont-l'Evêque.

So the poor slip of a boy was going to toss for months and months at sea! She had not been frightened by his previous voyages. From England or Brittany you came back safe enough; but America, the colonies, the islands—these were lost in a dim region at the other end of the world.

Félicité's thoughts from that moment ran entirely on her nephew. On sunny days she was harassed by the idea of thirst; when there was a storm she was afraid of the lightning on his account. As she listened to the wind growling in the chimney or carrying off the slates she pictured him lashed by that same tempest, at the top of a shattered mast, with his body thrown backwards under a sheet of foam; or else (with a reminiscence of the illustrated geography) he was being eaten by savages, captured in a wood by monkeys, or dying on a desert shore. And never did she mention her anxieties.

Mme. Aubain had anxieties of her own, about her daughter. The good sisters found her an affectionate but delicate child. The slightest emotion unnerved her. She had to give up the piano.

Her mother stipulated for regular letters from the convent. She lost patience one morning when the postman did not come, and walked to and fro in the parlour from her armchair to the window. It was really amazing; not a word for four days!

To console Mme. Aubain by her own example Félicité remarked:

"As for me, Madame, it's six months since I heard . . ."

"From whom, pray?"

"Why . . . from my nephew," the servant answered gently.

"Oh! your nephew!" And Mme. Aubain resumed her walk with a shrug of the shoulders, as much as to say: "I was not thinking of him! And what is more, it's absurd! A scamp of a cabin-boy—what does he matter? . . . whereas my daughter . . . why, just think!"

Félicité, though she had been brought up on harshness, felt indignant with Madame—and then forgot. It seemed the simplest thing in the world to her to lose one's head over the little girl. For her the two children were equally important; a bond in her heart made them one, and their destinies must be the same.

She heard from the druggist that Victor's ship had arrived at Havana. He had read this piece of news in a gazette.

Cigars—they made her imagine Havana as a place where no one does anything but smoke, and there was Victor moving among the negroes in a cloud of tobacco. Could you, she wondered, "in case you needed," return by land? What was the distance from Pont-l'Evêque? She questioned M. Bourais to find out.

He reached for his atlas and began explaining the longitudes; Félicité's consternation provoked a fine pedantic smile. Finally he marked with his pencil a black, imperceptible point in the indentations of an oval spot, and said as he did so, "Here it is." She bent over the map; the maze of coloured lines wearied her eyes without conveying anything; and on an invitation from Bourais to tell him her difficulty she begged him to show her the house where Victor was living. Bourais threw up his arms, sneezed, and laughed immensely: a simplicity like hers was a positive joy. And Félicité did not understand the reason; how could she when she expected, very likely, to see the actual image of her nephew—so stunted was her mind!

A fortnight afterwards Liébard came into the kitchen at market-time as usual and handed her a letter from her brother-in-law. As neither of them could read she took it to her mistress.

Mme. Aubain, who was counting the stitches in her knitting, put the work down by her side, broke the seal of the letter, started, and said in a low voice, with a look of meaning:

"It is bad news . . . that they have to tell you. Your nephew . . ."

He was dead. The letter said no more.

Félicité fell on to a chair, leaning her head against the wainscot; and she closed her eyelids, which suddenly flushed pink. Then with bent forehead, hands hanging, and fixed eyes, she said at intervals:

"Poor little lad! poor little lad!"

Liébard watched her and heaved sighs. Mme. Aubain trembled a little.

She suggested that Félicité should go to see her sister at Trouville. Félicité answered by a gesture that she had no need.

There was a silence. The worthy Liébard thought it was time for them to withdraw.

Then Félicité said:

"They don't care, not they!"

Her head dropped again; and she took up mechanically, from time to time, the long needles on her work-table.

Women passed in the yard with a barrow of dripping linen.

As she saw them through the window-panes she remembered her washing; she had put it to soak the day before, to-day she must wring it out; and she left the room.

Her plank and tub were at the edge of the Toucques. She threw a pile of linen on the bank, rolled up her sleeves, and taking her wooden beater dealt lusty blows whose sound carried to the neighbouring gardens. The meadows were empty, the river stirred in the wind; and down below long grasses wavered, like the hair of corpses floating in the water. She kept her grief down and was very brave until the evening; but once in her room she surrendered to it utterly, lying stretched on the mattress with her face in the pillow and her hands clenched against her temples.

Much later she heard, from the captain himself, the circumstances of Victor's end. They had bled him too much at the hospital for yellow fever. Four doctors held him at once. He had died instantly, and the chief had said:

"Bah! there goes another!"

His parents had always been brutal to him. She preferred not to see them again; and they made no advances, either because they forgot her or from the callousness of the wretchedly poor.

Virginie began to grow weaker.

Tightness in her chest, coughing, continual fever, and veinings on her cheek-bones betrayed some deep-seated complaint. M. Poupart had advised a stay in Provence. Mme. Aubain determined on it, and would have brought her daughter home at once but for the climate of Pont-l'Évêque.

She made an arrangement with a job-master, and he drove her to the convent every Tuesday. There is a terrace in the garden, with a view over the Seine. Virginie took walks there over the fallen vine-leaves, on her mother's arm. A shaft of sunlight through the clouds made her blink sometimes, as she gazed at the sails in the distance and the whole horizon from the castle of Tancarville to the lighthouses at Havre. Afterwards they rested in the arbour. Her mother had secured a little cask of excellent Malaga; and Virginie, laughing at the idea of getting tipsy, drank a thimble-full of it, no more.

Her strength came back visibly. The autumn glided gently away. Félicité reassured Mme. Aubain. But one evening, when she had been out on a commission in the neighbourhood, she found M. Poupart's gig at the door. He was in the hall, and Mme. Aubain was tying her bonnet.

"Give me my foot-warmer, purse, gloves! Quicker, come!"

Virginie had inflammation of the lungs; perhaps it was hopeless.

"Not yet!" said the doctor, and they both got into the carriage under whirling flakes of snow. Night was coming on and it was very cold.

Félicité rushed into the church to light a taper. Then she ran after the gig, came up with it in an hour, and jumped lightly in behind. As she hung on by the fringes a thought came into her mind: "The courtyard has not been shut up; supposing burglars got in!" And she jumped down.

At dawn next day she presented herself at the doctor's. He had come in and started for the country again. Then she waited in the inn, thinking that a letter would come by some hand or other. Finally, when it was twilight, she took the Lisieux coach.

The convent was at the end of a steep lane. When she was about halfway up it she heard strange sounds—a death-bell tolling. "It is for someone else," thought Félicité, and she pulled the knocker violently.

After some minutes there was a sound of trailing slippers, the door opened ajar, and a nun appeared.

The good sister, with an air of compunction, said that "she had just passed away." On the instant the bell of St. Leonard's tolled twice as fast.

Félicité went up to the second floor.

From the doorway she saw Virginie stretched on her back, with her hands joined, her mouth open, and head thrown back under a black crucifix that leaned towards her, between curtains that hung stiffly, less pale than was her face. Mme. Aubain, at the foot of the bed which she clasped with her arms, was choking with sobs of agony. The mother superior stood on the right. Three candlesticks on the chest of drawers made spots of red, and the mist came whitely through the windows. Nuns came and took Mme. Aubain away.

For two nights Félicité never left the dead child. She repeated the same prayers, sprinkled holy water over the sheets, came and sat down again, and watched her. At the end of the first vigil she noticed that the face had grown yellow, the lips turned blue, the nose was sharper, and the eyes sunk in. She kissed them several times, and would not have been immensely surprised if Virginie had opened them again; to minds like hers the supernatural is quite simple. She made the girl's toilette, wrapped her in her shroud, lifted her down into her bier, put a garland on her head, and spread out her hair. It was fair, and extraordinarily long for her age. Félicité cut off a big lock and slipped half of it into her bosom, determined that she should never part with it.

The body was brought back to Pont-l'Évêque, as Mme. Aubain intended; she followed the hearse in a closed carriage.

It took another three-quarters of an hour after the mass to reach the cemetery. Paul walked in front, sobbing. M. Bourais was behind, and then came the chief residents, the women shrouded in black mantles, and Félicité. She thought of her nephew; and because she had not been able to pay these honours to him her grief was doubled, as though the one were being buried with the other.

Mme. Aubain's despair was boundless. It was against God that she first rebelled, thinking it unjust of Him to have taken her daughter from her—she had never done evil and her conscience was so clear! Ah, no!—she ought to have taken Virginie off to the south. Other doctors would have saved her. She accused herself now, wanted to join her child, and broke into cries of distress in the middle of her dreams. One dream haunted her above all. Her husband, dressed as a sailor, was returning from a long voyage, and shedding tears he told her that he had been ordered to take Virginie away. Then they consulted how to hide her somewhere.

She came in once from the garden quite upset. A moment ago—and she pointed out the place—the father and daughter had appeared to her, standing side by side, and they did nothing, but they looked at her.

For several months after this she stayed inertly in her room. Félicité lectured her gently; she must live for her son's sake, and for the other, in remembrance of "her."

"Her?" answered Mme. Aubain, as though she were just waking up. "Ah, yes! . . . yes! . . . You do not forget her!" This was an allusion to the cemetery, where she was strictly forbidden to go.

Félicité went there every day.

Precisely at four she skirted the houses, climbed the hill, opened the gate, and came to Virginie's grave. It was a little column of pink marble with a stone underneath and a garden plot enclosed by chains. The beds were hidden under a coverlet of flowers. She watered their leaves, freshened the gravel, and knelt down to break up the earth better. When Mme. Aubain was able to come there she felt a relief and a sort of consolation.

Then years slipped away, one like another, and their only episodes were the great festivals as they recurred—Easter, the Assumption, All Saints' Day. Household occurrences marked dates that were referred to afterwards. In 1825, for instance, two glaziers whitewashed the hall; in 1827 a piece of the roof fell into the courtyard and nearly killed a man. In the summer of 1828 it was Madame's turn to offer the consecrated bread; Bourais, about this time, mysteriously absented himself; and one by one the old acquaintances passed away: Guyot, Liébard, Mme. Lechaptois, Robelin, and Uncle Gremanville, who had been paralysed for a long time.

One night the driver of the mail-coach announced the Revolution of July in Pont-l'Évêque. A new sub-prefect was appointed a few days later—Baron de Larsonnière, who had been consul in America, and brought with him, besides his wife, a sister-in-law and three young ladies, already growing up. They were to be seen about on their lawn, in loose blouses, and they had a negro and a parrot. They paid a call on Mme. Aubain which she did not fail to return. The moment they were seen in the distance Félicité ran to let her mistress know. But only one thing could really move her feelings—the letters from her son.

He was swallowed up in a tavern life and could follow no career. She paid his debts, he made new ones; and the sighs that Mme. Aubain uttered as she sat knitting by the window reached Félicité at her spinning-wheel in the kitchen.

They took walks together along the espaliered wall, always talking of Virginie and wondering if such and such a thing would have pleased her and what, on some occasion, she would have been likely to say.

All her small belongings filled a cupboard in the two-bedded room. Mme. Aubain inspected them as seldom as she could. One summer day she made up her mind to it—and some moths flew out of the wardrobe.

Virginie's dresses were in a row underneath a shelf, on which there were three dolls, some hoops, a set of toy pots and pans, and the basin that she used. They took out her petticoats as well, and the stockings and handkerchiefs, and laid them out on the two beds before folding them up again. The sunshine lit up these poor things, bringing out their stains and the creases made by the body's movements. The air was warm and blue, a blackbird warbled, life seemed bathed in a deep sweetness. They found a little plush hat with thick, chestnut-coloured pile; but it was eaten all over by moth. Félicité begged it for her own. Their eyes met fixedly and filled with tears; at last the mistress opened her arms, the servant threw herself into them, and they embraced each other, satisfying their grief in a kiss that made them equal.

It was the first time in their lives, Mme. Aubain's nature not being expansive. Félicité was as grateful as though she had received a favour, and cherished her mistress from that moment with the devotion of an animal and a religious worship.

The kindness of her heart unfolded.

When she heard the drums of a marching regiment in the street she posted herself at the door with a pitcher of cider and asked the soldiers to drink. She nursed cholera patients and protected the Polish refugees; one of these even declared that he wished to marry her. They quarrelled, however; for when she came back from the Angelus one morning she found that he had got into her kitchen and made himself a vinegar salad which he was quietly eating.

After the Poles came father Colmiche, an old man who was supposed to have committed atrocities in '93. He lived by the side of the river in the ruins of a pigsty. The little boys watched him through the cracks in the wall, and threw pebbles at him which fell on the pallet where he lay constantly shaken by a catarrh; his hair was very long, his eyes inflamed, and there was a tumour on his arm bigger than his head. She got him some linen and tried to clean up his miserable hole; her dream was to establish him in the bakehouse, without letting him annoy Madame. When the tumour burst she dressed it every day; sometimes she brought him cake, and would put him in the sunshine on a truss of straw. The poor old man, slobbering and trembling, thanked her in his worn-out voice, was terrified that he might lose her, and stretched out his hands when he saw her go away. He died; and she had a mass said for the repose of his soul.

That very day a great happiness befell her; just at dinner-time appeared Mme. de Larsonnière's negro, carrying the parrot in its cage, with perch, chain, and padlock. A note from the baroness informed

Mme. Aubain that her husband had been raised to a prefecture and they were starting that evening; she begged her to accept the bird as a memento and mark of her regard.

For a long time he had absorbed Félicité's imagination, because he came from America; and that name reminded her of Victor, so much so that she made inquiries of the negro. She had once gone so far as to say "How Madame would enjoy having him!"

The negro repeated the remark to his mistress; and as she could not take the bird away with her she chose this way of getting rid of him.

IV

His name was Loulou. His body was green and the tips of his wings rose-pink; his forehead was blue and his throat golden.

But he had the tiresome habits of biting his perch, tearing out his feathers, sprinkling his dirt about, and spattering the water of his tub. He annoyed Mme. Aubain, and she gave him to Félicité for good.

She endeavoured to train him; soon he could repeat "Nice boy! Your servant, sir! Good morning, Marie!" He was placed by the side of the door, and astonished several people by not answering to the name Jacquot, for all parrots are called Jacquot. People compared him to a turkey and a log of wood, and stabbed Félicité to the heart each time. Strange obstinacy on Loulou's part!—directly you looked at him he refused to speak.

None the less he was eager for society; for on Sundays, while the Rochefeuille ladies, M. de Houppeville, and new familiars—Onfroy the apothecary, Monsieur Varin, and Captain Mathieu—were playing their game of cards, he beat the windows with his wings and threw himself about so frantically that they could not hear each other speak.

Bourais' face, undoubtedly, struck him as extremely droll. Directly he saw it he began to laugh—and laugh with all his might. His peals rang through the courtyard and were repeated by the echo; the neighbours came to their windows and laughed too; while M. Bourais, gliding along under the wall to escape the parrot's eye, and hiding his profile with his hat, got to the river and then entered by the garden gate. There was a lack of tenderness in the looks which he darted at the bird.

Loulou had been slapped by the butcher-boy for making so free as to plunge his head into his basket; and since then he was always trying to nip him through his shirt. Fabu threatened to wring his neck, although he was not cruel, for all his tattooed arms and large whiskers. Far from it; he really rather liked the parrot, and in a jovial humour even wanted to teach him to swear. Félicité, who was alarmed by such proceedings, put the bird in the kitchen. His little chain was taken off and he roamed about the house.

His way of going downstairs was to lean on each step with the curve of his beak, raise the right foot, and then the left; and Félicité was afraid that these gymnastics brought on fits of giddiness. He fell ill and could not talk or eat any longer. There was a growth under his tongue, such as fowls have sometimes. She cured him by tearing the pellicle off with her finger-nails. Mr. Paul was thoughtless enough one day to blow some cigar smoke into his nostrils, and another time when Mme. Lormeau was teasing him with the end of her umbrella he snapped at the ferrule. Finally he got lost.

Félicité had put him on the grass to refresh him, and gone away for a minute, and when she came back—no sign of the parrot! She began by looking for him in the shrubs, by the waterside, and over the roofs, without listening to her mistress's cries of "Take care, do! You are out of your wits!" Then she investigated all the gardens in Pont-l'Evêque, and stopped the passers-by. "You don't ever happen to have seen my parrot, by any chance, do you?" And she gave a description of the parrot to those who did not know him. Suddenly, behind the mills at the foot of the hill she thought she could make out something green that fluttered. But on the top of the hill there was nothing. A hawker assured her that he had come across the parrot just before, at Saint-Melaine, in Mère Simon's shop. She rushed there; they had no idea of what she meant. At last she came home exhausted, with her slippers in shreds and despair in her soul; and as she was sitting in the middle of the garden-seat at Madame's side, telling the whole story of her efforts, a light weight dropped on to her shoulder—it was Loulou! What on earth had he been doing? Taking a walk in the neighbourhood, perhaps!

She had some trouble in recovering from this, or rather never did recover. As the result of a chill she had an attack of quinsy, and soon afterwards an earache. Three years later she was deaf; and she spoke very loud, even in church. Though Félicité's sins might have been published in every corner of the diocese without dishonour to her or scandal to anybody, his Reverence the priest thought it right now to hear her confession in the sacristy only.

Imaginary noises in the head completed her upset. Her mistress often said to her, "Heavens! how stupid you are!" "Yes, Madame," she replied, and looked about for something.

Her little circle of ideas grew still narrower; the peal of church-bells and the lowing of cattle ceased to exist for her. All living beings moved as silently as ghosts. One sound only reached her ears now—the parrot's voice.

Loulou, as though to amuse her, reproduced the click-clack of the turn-spit, the shrill call of a man selling fish, and the noise of the saw in the joiner's house opposite; when the bell rang he imitated Mme. Aubain's "Félicité! the door! the door!"

They carried on conversations, he endlessly reciting the three phrases in his repertory, to which she replied with words that were just as disconnected but uttered what was in her heart. Loulou was almost a son and a lover to her in her isolated state. He climbed up her fingers, nibbled at her lips, and clung to her kerchief; and when she bent her forehead and shook her head gently to and fro, as nurses do, the great wings of her bonnet and the bird's wings quivered together.

When the clouds massed and the thunder rumbled Loulou broke into cries, perhaps remembering the downpours in his native forests. The streaming rain made him absolutely mad; he fluttered wildly about, dashed up to the ceiling, upset everything, and went out through the window to dabble in the garden; but he was back quickly to perch on one of the fire-dogs and hopped about to dry himself, exhibiting his tail and his beak in turn.

One morning in the terrible winter of 1837 she had put him in front of the fireplace because of the cold. She found him dead, in the middle of his cage: head downwards, with his claws in the wires. He had died from congestion, no doubt. But Félicité thought he had been poisoned with parsley, and though there was no proof of any kind her suspicions inclined to Fabu.

She wept so piteously that her mistress said to her, "Well, then, have him stuffed!"

She asked advice from the druggist, who had always been kind to the parrot. He wrote to Havre, and a person called Fellacher undertook the business. But as parcels sometimes got lost in the coach she decided to take the parrot as far as Honfleur herself.

Along the sides of the road were leafless apple-trees, one after the other. Ice covered the ditches. Dogs barked about the farms; and Félicité, with her hands under her cloak, her little black sabots and her basket, walked briskly in the middle of the road.

She crossed the forest, passed High Oak, and reached St. Gatien.

A cloud of dust rose behind her, and in it a mail-coach, carried away by the steep hill, rushed down at full gallop like a hurricane. Seeing this woman who would not get out of the way, the driver stood up in front and the postilion shouted too. He could not hold in his four horses, which increased their pace, and the two leaders were grazing her when he threw them to one side with a jerk of the reins. But he was wild with rage, and lifting his arm as he passed at full speed, gave her such a lash from waist to neck with his big whip that she fell on her back.

Her first act, when she recovered consciousness, was to open her basket. Loulou was happily none the worse. She felt a burn in her right cheek, and when she put her hands against it they were red; the blood was flowing.

She sat down on a heap of stones and bound up her face with her handkerchief. Then she ate a crust of bread which she had put in the basket as a precaution, and found a consolation for her wound in gazing at the bird.

When she reached the crest of Ecquemauville she saw the Honfleur lights sparkling in the night sky like a company of stars; beyond, the sea stretched dimly. Then a faintness overtook her and she stopped; her wretched childhood, the disillusion of her first love, her nephew's going away, and Virginie's death all came back to her at once like the waves of an oncoming tide, rose to her throat, and choked her.

Afterwards, at the boat, she made a point of speaking to the captain, begging him to take care of the parcel, though she did not tell him what was in it.

Fellacher kept the parrot a long time. He was always promising it for the following week. After six months he announced that a packing-case had started, and then nothing more was heard of it. It really seemed as though Loulou was never coming back. "Ah, they have stolen him!" she thought.

He arrived at last, and looked superb. There he was, erect upon a branch which screwed into a mahogany socket, with a foot in the air and his head on one side, biting a nut which the bird-stuffer—with a taste for impressiveness—had gilded.

Félicité shut him up in her room. It was a place to which few people were admitted, and held so many religious objects and miscellaneous things that it looked like a chapel and bazaar in one.

A big cupboard impeded you as you opened the door. Opposite the window commanding the garden a little round one looked into the court; there was a table by the folding-bed with a water-jug, two combs, and a cube of blue soap in a chipped plate. On the walls hung rosaries, medals, several benign Virgins, and a holy water vessel made out of cocoa-nut; on the chest of drawers, which was covered with a cloth like an altar, was the shell box that Victor had given her, and after that a watering-can, a toy-balloon, exercise-books, the illustrated geography, and a pair of young lady's boots, and, fastened by its ribbons to the nail of the looking-glass, hung the little plush hat! Félicité carried observances of this kind so far as to keep one of Monsieur's frock-coats. All the old rubbish which Mme. Aubain did not want any longer she laid hands on for her room. That was why there were artificial flowers along the edge of the chest of drawers and a portrait of the Comte d'Artois in the little window recess.

With the aid of a bracket Loulou was established over the chimney, which jutted into the room. Every morning when she woke up she saw him there in the dawning light, and recalled old days and the smallest details of insignificant acts in a deep quietness which knew no pain.

Holding, as she did, no communication with anyone, Félicité lived as insensibly as if she were walking in her sleep. The Corpus Christi processions roused her to life again. Then she went round begging mats and candlesticks from the neighbours to decorate the altar they put up in the street.

In church she was always gazing at the Holy Ghost in the window, and observed that there was something of the parrot in him. The likeness was still clearer, she thought, on a crude colour-print representing the baptism of Our Lord. With his purple wings and emerald body he was the very image of Loulou.

She bought him, and hung him up instead of the Comte d'Artois, so that she could see them both together in one glance. They were linked in her thoughts; and the parrot was consecrated by his association with the Holy Ghost, which became more vivid to her eye and more intelligible. The Father could not have chosen to express Himself through a dove, for such creatures cannot speak; it must have been one of Loulou's ancestors, surely. And though Félicité looked at the picture while she said her prayers she swerved a little from time to time towards the parrot.

She wanted to join the Ladies of the Virgin, but Mme. Aubain dissuaded her.

And then a great event loomed up before them—Paul's marriage.

He had been a solicitor's clerk to begin with, and then tried business, the Customs, the Inland Revenue, and made efforts, even, to get into the Rivers and Forests. By an inspiration from heaven he had suddenly, at thirty-six, discovered his real line—the Registrar's Office. And there he showed such marked capacity that an inspector had offered him his daughter's hand and promised him his influence.

So Paul, grown serious, brought the lady to see his mother.

She sniffed at the ways of Pont-l'Évêque, gave herself great airs, and wounded Félicité's feelings. Mme. Aubain was relieved at her departure.

The week after came news of M. Bourais' death in an inn in Lower Brittany. The rumour of suicide was confirmed, and doubts arose as to his honesty. Mme. Aubain studied his accounts, and soon found out the whole tale of his misdoings—embezzled arrears, secret sales of wood, forged receipts, etc. Besides that he had an illegitimate child, and "relations with a person at Dozulé."

These shameful facts distressed her greatly. In March 1853 she was seized with a pain in the chest; her tongue seemed to be covered with film, and leeches did not ease the difficult breathing. On the ninth evening of her illness she died, just at seventy-two.

She passed as being younger, owing to the bands of brown hair which framed her pale, pock-marked face. There were few friends to regret her, for she had a stiffness of manner which kept people at a distance.

But Félicité mourned for her as one seldom mourns for a master. It upset her ideas and seemed contrary to the order of things, impossible and monstrous, that Madame should die before her.

Ten days afterwards, which was the time it took to hurry there from Besançon, the heirs arrived. The daughter-in-law ransacked the drawers, chose some furniture, and sold the rest; and then they went back to their registering.

Madame's armchair, her small round table, her foot-warmer, and the eight chairs were gone! Yellow patches in the middle of the panels showed where the engravings had hung. They had carried off the two little beds and the mattresses, and all Virginie's belongings had disappeared from the cupboard. Félicité went from floor to floor dazed with sorrow.

The next day there was a notice on the door, and the apothecary shouted in her ear that the house was for sale.

She tottered, and was obliged to sit down. What distressed her most of all was to give up her room, so suitable as it was for poor Loulou. She enveloped him with a look of anguish when she was imploring the Holy Ghost, and formed the idolatrous habit of kneeling in front of the parrot to say her prayers. Sometimes the sun shone in at the attic window and caught his glass eye, and a great luminous ray shot out of it and put her in an ecstasy.

She had a pension of fifteen pounds a year which her mistress had left her. The garden gave her a supply of vegetables. As for clothes, she had enough to last her to the end of her days, and she economized in candles by going to bed at dusk.

She hardly ever went out, as she did not like passing the dealer's shop, where some of the old furniture was exposed for sale. Since her fit of giddiness she dragged one leg; and as her strength was failing Mère Simon, whose grocery business had collapsed, came every morning to split the wood and pump water for her.

Her eyes grew feeble. The shutters ceased to be thrown open. Years and years passed, and the house was neither let nor sold.

Félicité never asked for repairs because she was afraid of being sent away. The boards on the roof rotted; her bolster was wet for a whole winter. After Easter she spat blood.

Then Mère Simon called in a doctor. Félicité wanted to know what was the matter with her. But she was too deaf to hear, and the only word which reached her was "pneumonia." It was a word she knew, and she answered softly "Ah! like Madame," thinking it natural that she should follow her mistress.

The time for the festal shrines was coming near. The first one was always at the bottom of the hill, the second in front of the postoffice, and the third towards the middle of the street. There was some rivalry in the matter of this one, and the women of the parish ended by choosing Mme. Aubain's courtyard.

The hard breathing and fever increased. Félicité was vexed at doing nothing for the altar. If only she could at least have put something there! Then she thought of the parrot. The neighbours objected that it would not be decent. But the priest gave her permission, which so intensely delighted her that she begged him to accept Loulou, her sole possession, when she died.

From Tuesday to Saturday, the eve of the festival, she coughed more often. By the evening her face had shrivelled, her lips stuck to her gums, and she had vomitings; and at twilight next morning, feeling herself very low, she sent for a priest.

Three kindly women were round her during the extreme unction. Then she announced that she must speak to Fabu. He arrived in his Sunday clothes, by no means at his ease in the funereal atmosphere.

"Forgive me," she said, with an effort to stretch out her arm; "I thought it was you who had killed him."

What did she mean by such stories? She suspected him of murder—a man like him! He waxed indignant, and was on the point of making a row.

"There," said the women, "she is no longer in her senses, you can see it well enough!"

Félicité spoke to shadows of her own from time to time. The

women went away, and Mère Simon had breakfast. A little later she took Loulou and brought him close to Félicité with the words:

"Come, now, say good-bye to him!"

Loulou was not a corpse, but the worms devoured him; one of his wings was broken, and the tow was coming out of his stomach. But she was blind now; she kissed him on the forehead and kept him close against her cheek. Mère Simon took him back from her to put him on the altar.

V

Summer scents came up from the meadows; flies buzzed; the sun made the river glitter and heated the slates. Mère Simon came back into the room and fell softly asleep.

She woke at the noise of bells; the people were coming out from vespers. Félicité's delirium subsided. She thought of the procession and saw it as if she had been there.

All the school children, the church-singers, and the firemen walked on the pavement, while in the middle of the road the verger armed with his hallebard and the beadle with a large cross advanced in front. Then came the schoolmaster, with an eye on the boys, and the sister, anxious about her little girls; three of the daintiest, with angelic curls, scattered rose-petals in the air; the deacon controlled the band with outstretched arms; and two censer-bearers turned back at every step towards the Holy Sacrament, which was borne by Monsieur the curé, wearing his beautiful chasuble, under a canopy of dark-red velvet held up by four churchwardens. A crowd of people pressed behind, between the white cloths covering the house walls, and they reached the bottom of the hill.

A cold sweat moistened Félicité's temples. Mère Simon sponged her with a piece of linen, saying to herself that one day she would have to go that way.

The hum of the crowd increased, was very loud for an instant, and then went further away.

A fusillade shook the window-panes. It was the postilions saluting the monstrance. Félicité rolled her eyes and said as audibly as she could: "Does he look well?" The parrot was weighing on her mind.

Her agony began. A death-rattle that grew more and more convulsed made her sides heave. Bubbles of froth came at the corners of her mouth and her whole body trembled.

Soon the booming of the ophicleides, the high voices of the children, and the deep voices of the men were distinguishable. At intervals all was silent, and the tread of feet, deadened by the flowers they walked on, sounded like a flock pattering on grass.

The clergy appeared in the courtyard. Mère Simon clambered on to a chair to reach the attic window, and so looked down straight upon the shrine. Green garlands hung over the altar, which was decked with a flounce of English lace. In the middle was a small frame with relics in it; there were two orange-trees at the corners, and all along stood silver candlesticks and china vases, with sunflowers, lilies, peonies, foxgloves, and tufts of hortensia. This heap of blazing colour slanted from the level of the altar to the carpet which went on over the pavement; and some rare objects caught the eye. There was a silver-gilt sugar-basin with a crown of violets; pendants of Alençon stone glittered on the moss, and two Chinese screens displayed their landscapes. Loulou was hidden under roses, and showed nothing but his blue forehead, like a plaque of lapis lazuli.

The churchwardens, singers, and children took their places round the three sides of the court. The priest went slowly up the steps, and placed his great, radiant golden sun upon the lace. Everyone knelt down. There was a deep silence; and the censers glided to and fro on the full swing of their chains.

An azure vapour rose up into Félicité's room. Her nostrils met it; she inhaled it sensuously, mystically; and then closed her eyes. Her lips smiled. The beats of her heart lessened one by one, vaguer each time and softer, as a fountain sinks, an echo disappears; and when she sighed her last breath she thought she saw an opening in the heavens, and a gigantic parrot hovering above her head.

Translated by Arthur McDowall

FLAUBERT: *A Simple Heart*

1. *What is the pace of the story? Does it fit the subject matter? Contrast it with the pace of Hemingway's "The Battler." With James' "Europe."*

2. *How does Flaubert achieve his distance from his material while not being cold or indifferent to his characters? Does he see his characters as if they were under a microscope, or is he less clinical?*

3. *Is Félicité (meaning: happiness) rightly named, or is her name ironic, even satiric?*

4. *What is the quality of Félicité's life? How does the author view*

her? Does she have a real existence in your eyes? Or does she fade in with the landscape and her daily tasks?

5. What is the purpose of the parrot? What is its relationship to its owner? What points does Flaubert appear to be making?

6. The Holy Ghost of Christian belief is represented by a dove. How does Flaubert use this Christian symbol to add pathos to the story of Félicité?

7. The story is as much a study of French provincial life as it is of a "simple heart." What does one learn of this life? How does it function? Does it have any connection to Faulkner's small-town life in "Dry September"? To Joyce's Dublin in "Counterparts"?

Feodor Dostoyevsky
THE GRAND INQUISITOR

Feodor Dostoyevsky was born in Moscow in 1821, son of a stern and authoritarian doctor. Educated in military engineering, he left this occupation in order to write. His first story, Poor Folk *(1846), struck a new chord in Russian literature by its deep psychological study of poor, unhappy people, who—along with the insulted and the injured, the strange and abnormal sufferers who defy society—were to be the actors in his tremendously dramatic and intensely individual works. In 1849, he was arrested for alleged conspiracy against the government and sentenced to Siberia (see* The House of the Dead, *1861-62). After four more years there as a soldier, he returned to St. Petersburg to resume his career. Despite the bitter poverty and personal tragedies of the next years, he established his name through* Notes from Underground *(1864) and* Crime and Punishment *(1866), and found himself ranked with Tolstoy and Turgenev after* The Idiot *(1869),* The Possessed *(1871) and* The Brothers Karamazov *(1880). He died in 1881, practically revered as a Slavic saint.*

Dostoyevsky's sweeping genius did not accommodate itself to the short story, and the self-contained selection that best represents his work comes from The Brothers Karamazov. *Dostoyevsky himself regarded this chapter as the culmination of the book, and V. Rozanov, a critic and philosopher who wrote a remarkable book on the legend of the Grand Inquisitor, affirmed that without it Dostoyevsky would never have written his masterpiece.*

The scene is laid in a screened-off corner of a shabby tavern, where, amid "shouts for the waiters, the sound of popping corks, the click of billiard balls," Ivan Karamazov opens his heart to his younger brother, the saintly Alyosha. Ivan tells him that it is a marvel that "the idea of the necessity of God could enter the head of such a savage, vicious beast as man." For his own part, he is prepared to admit the actual existence of God, and even grant that all creation moves toward an ultimate harmony, but he cannot accept the ways of a Deity who includes in his scheme the suffering of the innocent. Therefore he rejects the world created by Him, and even though "the humiliating absurdity of human contradictions" may someday vanish, he prefers to stay outside, intransigent, unreconciled, unforgiving of a small-minded God. Is there a being in the entire world, he asks, who has the right to forgive torturers of the innocent, who can justify suffering? Alyosha points to Christ. Thereupon Ivan recites the following story.

"Do you know, Alyosha—don't laugh! I made a poem about a year ago. If you can waste another ten minutes on me, I'll tell it to you."

"You wrote a poem?"

"Oh, no, I didn't write it," laughed Ivan, "and I've never written two lines of poetry in my life. But I made up this poem in prose and I remembered it. I was carried away when I made it up. You will be my first reader—that is, listener. Why should an author forego even one listener?" smiled Ivan. "Shall I tell it to you?"

"I am all attention," said Alyosha.

"My poem is called 'The Grand Inquisitor'; it's a ridiculous thing, but I want to tell it to you.

"Even this must have a preface—that is, a literary preface," laughed Ivan, "and I am a poor hand at making one. You see, my action takes place in the sixteenth century, and at that time, as you probably learnt at school, it was customary in poetry to bring down heavenly powers on earth. Not to speak of Dante, in France, clerks, as well as the monks in the monasteries, used to give regular performances in which the Madonna, the saints, the angels, Christ, and God Himself were brought on the stage. In those days it was done in all simplicity. In Victor Hugo's 'Notre Dame de Paris' an edifying and gratuitous spectacle was provided for the people in the Hotel de Ville of Paris in the reign of Louis XI in honour of the birth of the dauphin. It was called *Le bon jugement de la très sainte et gracieuse Vierge Marie*, and she appears herself on the stage and pronounces her *bon jugement*. Similar plays, chiefly from the Old Testament, were occasionally performed in Moscow too, up to the times of Peter the Great. But besides plays there were all sorts of legends and ballads scattered about the world, in which the saints and angels and all the powers of Heaven took part when required. In our monasteries the monks busied themselves in translating, copying, and even composing such poems—and even under the Tatars. There is, for instance, one such poem (of course, from the Greek), 'The Wanderings of Our Lady through Hell,' with descriptions as bold as Dante's. Our Lady visits Hell, and the Archangel Michael leads her through the torments. She sees the sinners and their punishment. There she sees among others one noteworthy set of sinners in a burning lake; some of them sink to the bottom of the lake so that they can't swim out, and 'these God forgets'—an expression of extraordinary depth and force. And so Our Lady, shocked and weeping, falls before the throne of God and begs for mercy for all in Hell—for all she has seen there, indiscriminately. Her conversation with God is immensely interesting. She beseeches Him, she will not desist, and when God points to the hands and feet of her Son, nailed to the Cross, and asks, 'How can I forgive His tormentors?' she bids all the saints, all the martyrs, all the angels and archangels to fall down with her and pray for mercy on all without distinction. It ends by her winning from God a respite of suffering every year from Good Friday till Trinity day, and the sinners at once raise a cry of thankfulness from Hell, chanting, 'Thou art just, O Lord, in this judgment.' Well, my poem would have been of that kind if it had appeared at that time. He comes on the scene in my poem, but He says nothing, only appears and passes on. Fifteen centuries have passed since He promised to come in His glory, fifteen centuries since His prophet wrote, 'Behold, I come quickly'; 'Of that day and that hour knoweth no man, neither the Son, but the Father,' as He Himself predicted on earth. But humanity awaits him with the same faith and with the same love. Oh, with greater faith, for it is fifteen centuries since man has ceased to see signs from Heaven.

> *No signs from Heaven come to-day*
> *To add to what the heart doth say.*

There was nothing left but faith in what the heart doth say. It is true there were many miracles in those days. There were saints who performed miraculous cures; some holy people, according to their biographies, were visited by the Queen of Heaven herself. But the devil did not slumber, and doubts were already arising among men of the truth of these miracles. And just then there appeared in the north of Germany a terrible new heresy. 'A huge star like to a torch' (that is, to a church) 'fell on the sources of the waters and they became bitter.' These heretics began, blasphemously denying miracles. But those who remained faithful were all the more ardent in their faith. The tears of humanity rose up to Him as before, awaited His coming, loved Him, hoped for Him, yearned to suffer and die for Him as before. And so many ages mankind had prayed with faith and fervour, 'O Lord our God, hasten Thy coming,' so many ages called upon Him, that in His infinite mercy He deigned to come down to His servants. Before that day He had come down, He had visited some holy men, martyrs and hermits, as is written in their 'Lives.' Among us, Tyutchev, with absolute faith in the truth of his words, bore witness that

> *Bearing the Cross, in slavish dress,*
> *Weary and worn, the Heavenly King*
> *Our mother, Russian, came to bless,*
> *And through our land went wandering.*

And that certainly was so, I assure you.

"And behold, He deigned to appear for a moment to the people, to the tortured, suffering people, sunk in iniquity, but loving Him like children. My story is laid in Spain, in Seville, in the most terrible time of the Inquisition, when fires were lighted every day to the glory of God, and 'in the splendid *auto da fé* the wicked heretics were burnt.' Oh, of course, this was not the coming in which He will appear according to His promise at the end of time in all His heavenly glory, and which will be sudden 'as lightning flashing from east to west.' No, He visited His children only for a moment, and there where the flames were crackling round the heretics. In His infinite mercy He came once more among men in that human shape in which He walked among men for three years fifteen centuries ago. He came down to the 'hot pavement' of the southern town in which on the day before almost a hundred heretics had, *ad majorem gloriam Dei*, been burnt by the cardinal, the Grand Inquisitor, in a magnificent *auto da fé* in the presence of the king, the court, the knights, the cardinals, the most charming ladies of the court, and the whole population of Seville.

"He came softly, unobserved, and yet, strange to say, every one recognised Him. That might be one of the best passages in the poem. I mean, why they recognised Him. The people are irresistibly drawn to Him, they surround Him, they flock about Him, follow Him. He moves silently in their midst with a gentle smile of infinite compassion. The sun of love burns in His heart, light and power shine from His eyes, and their radiance, shed on the people, stirs their hearts with responsive love. He holds out His hands to them, blesses them, and a healing virtue comes from contact with Him, even with His garments. An old man in the crowd, blind from childhood, cries out, 'O Lord, heal me and I shall see Thee!' and, as it were, scales fall from his eyes and the blind man sees Him. The crowd weeps and kisses the earth under His feet. Children throw flowers before Him, sing, and cry hosannah. 'It is He—it is He!'

all repeat. 'It must be He, it can be no one but Him!' He stops at the steps of the Seville cathedral at the moment when the weeping mourners are bringing in a little open white coffin. In it lies a child of seven, the only daughter of a prominent citizen. The dead child lies hidden in flowers. 'He will raise your child,' the crowd shouts to the weeping mother. The priest, coming to meet the coffin, looks perplexed, and frowns, but the mother of the dead child throws herself at His feet with a wail. 'If it is Thou, raise my child!' she cries, holding out her hands to Him. The procession halts, the coffin is laid on the steps at His feet. He looks with compassion, and His lips once more softly pronounce, 'Maiden, arise!' and the maiden arises. The little girl sits up in the coffin and looks round, smiling with wide-open wondering eyes, holding a bunch of white roses they had put in her hand.

"There are cries, sobs, confusion among the people, and at that moment the cardinal himself, the Grand Inquisitor, passes by the cathedral. He is an old man, almost ninety, tall and erect, with a withered face and sunken eyes, in which there is still a gleam of light. He is not dressed in his gorgeous cardinal's robes, as he was the day before, when he was burning the enemies of the Roman Church—at that moment he was wearing his coarse, old, monk's cassock. At a distance behind him come his gloomy assistants and slaves and the 'holy guard.' He stops at the sight of the crowd and watches it from a distance. He sees everything; he sees them set the coffin down at His feet, sees the child rise up, and his face darkens. He knits his thick grey brows and his eyes gleam with a sinister fire. He holds out his finger and bids the guards take Him. And such is his power, so completely are the people cowed into submission and trembling obedience to him, that the crowd immediately make way for the guards, and in the midst of deathlike silence they lay hands on Him and lead Him away. The crowd instantly bows down to the earth, like one man, before the old inquisitor. He blesses the people in silence and passes on. The guards lead their prisoner to the close, gloomy vaulted prison in the ancient palace of the Holy Inquisition and shut Him in it. The day passes and is followed by the dark, burning 'breathless' night of Seville. The air is 'fragrant with laurel and lemon.' In the pitch darkness the iron door of the prison is suddenly opened and the Grand Inquisitor himself comes in with a light in his hand. He is alone; the door is closed at once behind him. He stands in the doorway and for a minute or two gazes into His face. At last he goes up slowly, sets the light on the table and speaks.

" 'Is it Thou? Thou?' but receiving no answer, he adds at once, 'Don't answer, be silent. What canst Thou say, indeed? I know too well what

Thou wouldst say. And Thou hast no right to add anything to what Thou hadst said of old. Why, then, art Thou come to hinder us? For Thou hast come to hinder us, and Thou knowest that. But dost Thou know what will be to-morrow? I know not who Thou art and care not to know whether it is Thou or only a semblance of Him, but to-morrow I shall condemn Thee and burn Thee at the stake as the worst of heretics. And the very people who have to-day kissed Thy feet, to-morrow at the faintest sign from me will rush to heap up the embers of Thy fire. Knowest Thou that? Yes, maybe Thou knowest it,' he added with thoughtful penetration, never for a moment taking his eyes off the Prisoner.''

"I don't quite understand, Ivan. What does it mean?" Alyosha, who had been listening in silence, said with a smile, "Is it simply a wild fantasy, or a mistake on the part of the old man—some impossible *quidproquo?*"

"Take it as the last," said Ivan, laughing, "if you are so corrupted by modern realism and can't stand anything fantastic. If you like it to be a case of mistaken identity, let it be so. It is true," he went on, laughing, "the old man was ninety, and he might well be crazy over his set idea. He might have been struck by the appearance of the Prisoner. It might, in fact, be simply his ravings, the delusion of an old man of ninety, over-excited by the *auto da fé* of a hundred heretics the day before. But does it matter to us after all whether it was a mistake of identity or a wild fantasy? All that matters is that the old man should speak out, should speak openly of what he has thought in silence for ninety years."

"And the Prisoner too is silent? Does He look at him and not say a word?"

"That's inevitable in any case," Ivan laughed again. "The old man has told Him He hasn't the right to add anything to what He has said of old. One may say it is the most fundamental feature of Roman Catholicism, in my opinion at least. 'All has been given by Thee to the Pope,' they say, 'and all, therefore, is still in the Pope's hands, and there is no need for Thee to come now at all. Thou must not meddle for the time, at least.' That's how they speak and write too—the Jesuits, at any rate. I have read it myself in the works of their theologians. 'Hast Thou the right to reveal to us one of the mysteries of that world from which Thou hast come?' my old man asks Him, and answers the question for Him. 'No, Thou hast not;

that Thou mayest not add to what has been said of old, and mayest not take from men the freedom which Thou didst exalt when Thou wast on earth. Whatsoever Thou revealest anew will encroach on men's freedom of faith; for it will be manifest as a miracle, and the freedom of their faith was dearer to Thee than anything in those days fifteen hundred years ago. Didst Thou not often say then, "I will make you free"? But now Thou hast seen these "free" men,' the old man adds suddenly, with a pensive smile. 'Yes, we've paid dearly for it,' he goes on, looking sternly at Him, 'but at last we have completed that work in Thy name. For fifteen centuries we have been wrestling with Thy freedom, but now it is ended and over for good. Dost Thou not believe that it's over for good? Thou lookest meekly at me and deignest not even to be wroth with me. But let me tell Thee that now, to-day, people are more persuaded than ever that they have perfect freedom, yet they have brought their freedom to us and laid it humbly at our feet. But that has been our doing. Was this what Thou didst? Was this Thy freedom?' "

"I don't understand again," Alyosha broke in. "Is he ironical, is he jesting?"

"Not a bit of it! He claims it as a merit for himself and his Church that at last they have vanquished freedom and have done so to make men happy. 'For now' (he is speaking of the Inquisition, of course) 'for the first time it has become possible to think of the happiness of men. Man was created a rebel; and how can rebels be happy? Thou wast warned,' he says to Him. 'Thou hast had no lack of admonitions and warnings, but Thou didst not listen to those warnings; Thou didst reject the only way by which men might be made happy. But, fortunately, departing Thou didst hand on the work to us. Thou hast promised, Thou hast established by Thy word, Thou hast given to us the right to bind and to unbind, and now, of course, Thou canst not think of taking it away. Why, then, hast Thou come to hinder us?' "

"And what's the meaning of 'no lack of admonitions and warnings'?" asked Alyosha.

"Why, that's the chief part of what the old man must say."

" 'The wise and dread spirit, the spirit of self-destruction and non-existence,' the old man goes on, 'the great spirit talked with Thee in the wilderness, and we are told in the books that he "tempted" Thee. Is that so? And could anything truer be said than what he revealed to Thee in three questions and what Thou didst reject, and what in the books is called "the temptation"? And yet if there has ever been on earth a real stupendous miracle, it took place on that day, on the day of the three temptations. The statement of those three questions was itself the miracle. If it were possible to imagine simply for the sake of argument that those three questions of the dread spirit had perished utterly from the books, and that we had to restore them and to invent them anew, and to do so had gathered together all the wise men of the earth—rulers, chief priests, learned men, philosophers, poets—and had set them the task to invent three questions, such as would not only fit the occasion, but express in three words, three human phrases, the whole future history of the world and of humanity—dost Thou believe that all the wisdom of the earth united could have invented anything in depth and force equal to the three questions which were actually put to Thee then by the wise and mighty spirit in the wilderness? From those questions alone, from the miracle of their statement, we can see that we have here to do not with the fleeting human intelligence, but with the absolute and eternal. For in those three questions the whole subsequent history of mankind is, as it were, brought together into one whole, and foretold, and in them are united all the unsolved historical contradictions of human nature. At the time it could not be so clear, since the future was unknown; but now that fifteen hundred years have passed, we see that everything in those three questions was so justly divined and foretold, and has been so truly fulfilled, that nothing can be added to them or taken from them.

" 'Judge Thyself who was right—Thou or he who questioned Thee then? Remember the first question; its meaning, in other words, was this: "Thou wouldst go into the world, and art going with empty hands, with some promise of freedom which men in their simplicity and their natural unruliness cannot even understand, which they fear and dread—for nothing has ever been more insupportable for a man and a human society than freedom. But seest Thou these stones in this parched and barren wilderness? Turn them into bread, and mankind will run after Thee like a flock of sheep, grateful and obedient, though for ever trembling, lest Thou withdraw Thy hand and deny them Thy bread." But Thou wouldst not deprive man of freedom and didst reject the offer, thinking, what is that freedom worth, if obedience is bought with bread? Thou didst reply that man lives not by bread alone. But dost Thou know that for the sake of that earthly bread the spirit of the earth will rise up against Thee and will strive with Thee and overcome Thee, and all will follow him, crying, "Who can compare with this beast? He has given us fire from heaven!" Dost Thou know that the ages will pass, and humanity will proclaim by the lips of their sages that there is no crime, and therefore no sin; there is only hunger? "Feed men, and then ask of them virtue!" that's what they'll write on the banner, which they will raise against Thee, and with which they will destroy Thy temple. Where Thy temple stood will rise a new building; the terrible tower of Babel will be built again, and though, like the one of old, it will not be finished, yet Thou mightest have prevented that new tower and have cut short the sufferings of men for a thousand years; for they will come back to us after a thousand years of agony with their tower. They will seek us again, hidden underground in the catacombs, for we shall be again persecuted and tortured. They will find us and cry to us, "Feed us, for those who have promised us fire from heaven haven't given it!" And then we shall finish building their tower, for he finishes the building who feeds them. And we alone shall feed them in Thy name, declaring falsely that it is in Thy name. Oh, never, never can they feed themselves without us! no science will give them bread so long as they remain free. In the end they will lay their freedom at our feet, and say to us, "Make us your slaves, but feed us." They will understand themselves, at last, that freedom and bread enough for all are inconceivable together, for never, never will they be able to share between them! They will be convinced, too, that they can never be free, for they are weak, vicious, worthless and rebellious. Thou didst promise them the bread of Heaven, but, I repeat again, can it compare with earthly bread in the eyes of the weak, ever sinful and ignoble race of man? And if for the sake of the bread of Heaven thousands and tens of thousands shall follow Thee, what is to become of the millions and tens of thousands of millions of creatures who will not have the strength to forego the earthly bread for the sake of the heavenly? Or dost Thou care only for the tens of thousands of the great and strong, while the millions, numerous as the sands of the sea, who are weak but love Thee, must exist only for the sake of the great and strong? No, we care for the weak too. They are sinful and rebellious, but in the end they too will become obedient. They will marvel at us and look on us as gods, because we are ready to endure the freedom which they have found so dreadful and to rule over them—so awful it will seem to them to be free. But we shall tell them that we are Thy servants and rule them in Thy name. We shall deceive them again, for we will not let Thee come to us again. That deception will be our suffering, for we shall be forced to lie.

" 'This is the significance of the first question in the wilderness, and this is what Thou hast rejected for the sake of that freedom which Thou hast exalted above everything. Yet in this question lies hid the great secret of this world. Choosing "bread," Thou wouldst have satisfied the universal and everlasting craving of humanity—to find some one to worship. So long as man remains free he strives for nothing so incessantly and so painfully as to find some one to worship. But man seeks to worship what is established beyond dispute, so that all men would agree at once to worship it. For these pitiful creatures are concerned not only to find what one or the other can worship, but to find something that all would believe in and worship; what is essential is that all may be *together* in it. This craving for *community* of worship is the chief misery of every man individually and of all humanity from the beginning of time. For the sake of common worship they've slain each other with the sword. They have set up gods and challenged one another, "Put away your gods and come and worship ours, or we will kill you and your gods!" And so it will be to the end of the world, even when gods disappear from the earth; they will fall down before idols just the same. Thou didst know, Thou couldst not but have known, this fundamental secret of human nature, but Thou didst reject the one infallible banner which was offered Thee to make all men bow down to Thee alone—the banner of earthly bread; and Thou hast rejected it for the sake of freedom and the bread of Heaven. Behold what Thou didst further. And all again in the name of freedom! I tell Thee that man is tormented by no greater anxiety than to find some one quickly to whom he can hand over that gift of freedom with which the ill-fated creature is born. But only one who can appease their conscience can take over their freedom. In bread there was offered Thee an invincible banner; give bread, and man will worship Thee, for nothing is more certain than bread. But if some one else gains possession of his conscience —oh! then he will cast away Thy bread and follow after him who has ensnared his conscience. In that Thou wast right. For the secret of man's being is not only to live but to have something to live for. Without a stable conception of the object of life, man would not consent to go on living, and would rather destroy himself than remain on earth, though he had bread in abundance. That is true. But what happened? Instead of taking men's freedom from them,

Thou didst make it greater than ever! Didst Thou forget that man prefers peace, and even death, to freedom of choice in the knowledge of good and evil? Nothing is more seductive for man than his freedom of conscience, but nothing is a greater cause of suffering. And behold, instead of giving a firm foundation for setting the conscience of man at rest for ever, Thou didst choose all that is exceptional, vague and enigmatic; Thou didst choose what was utterly beyond the strength of men, acting as though Thou didst not love them at all—Thou who didst come to give Thy life for them! Instead of taking possession of men's freedom, Thou didst increase it, and burdened the spiritual kingdom of mankind with its sufferings for ever. Thou didst desire man's free love, that he should follow Thee freely, enticed and taken captive by Thee. In place of the rigid ancient law, man must hereafter with free heart decide for himself what is good and what is evil, having only Thy image before him as his guide. But didst Thou not know he would at last reject even Thy image and Thy truth, if he is weighed down with the fearful burden of free choice? They will cry aloud at last that the truth is not in Thee, for they could not have been left in greater confusion and suffering than Thou hast caused, laying upon them so many cares and unanswerable problems.

" 'So that, in truth, Thou didst Thyself lay the foundation for the destruction of Thy kingdom, and no one is more to blame for it. Yet what was offered Thee? There are three powers, three powers alone, able to conquer and to hold captive for ever the conscience of these impotent rebels for their happiness—those forces are miracle, mystery and authority. Thou hast rejected all three and hast set the example for doing so. When the wise and dread spirit set Thee on the pinnacle of the temple and said to Thee, "If Thou wouldst know whether Thou art the Son of God then cast Thyself down, for it is written: the angels shall hold him up lest he fall and bruise himself, and Thou shalt know then whether Thou art the Son of God and shalt prove then how great is Thy faith in Thy Father." But Thou didst refuse and wouldst not cast Thyself down. Oh! of course, Thou didst proudly and well, like God; but the weak, unruly race of men, are they gods? Oh, Thou didst know then that in taking one step, in making one movement to cast Thyself down, Thou wouldst be tempting God and have lost all Thy faith in Him, and wouldst have been dashed to pieces against that earth which Thou didst come to save. And the wise spirit that tempted Thee would have rejoiced. But I ask again, are there many like Thee? And couldst Thou believe for one moment that men, too, could face such a temptation? Is the nature of men such, that they can reject miracle, and at the great moments of their life, the moments of their deepest, most agonising spiritual difficulties, cling only to the free verdict of the heart? Oh, Thou didst know that Thy deed would be recorded in books, would be handed down to remote times and the utmost ends of the earth, and Thou didst hope that man, following Thee, would cling to God and not ask for a miracle. But Thou didst not know that when man rejects miracle he rejects God too; for man seeks not so much God as the miraculous. And as man cannot bear to be without the miraculous, he will create new miracles of his own for himself, and will worship deeds of sorcery and witchcraft, though he might be a hundred times over a rebel, heretic and infidel. Thou didst not come down from the Cross when they shouted to Thee, mocking and reviling Thee, 'Come down from the cross and we will believe that Thou art He.' Thou didst not come down, for again Thou wouldst not enslave man by a miracle, and didst crave faith given freely, not based on miracle. Thous didst crave for free love and not the base raptures of the slave before the might that has overawed him for ever. But Thou didst think too highly of men therein, for they are slaves, of course, though rebellious by nature. Look round and judge; fifteen centuries have passed, look upon them. Whom hast Thou raised up to Thyself? I swear, man is weaker and baser by nature than Thou hast believed him! Can he, can he do what Thou didst? By showing him so much respect, Thou didst, as it were, cease to feel for him, for Thou didst ask far too much from him—Thou who hast loved him more than Thyself! Respecting him less, Thou wouldst have asked less of him. That would have been more like love, for his burden would have been lighter. He is weak and vile. What though he is everywhere now rebelling against our power, and proud of his rebellion? It is the pride of a child and a schoolboy. They are little children rioting and barring out the teacher at school. But their childish delight will end; it will cost them dear. They will cast down temples and drench the earth with blood. But they will see at last, the foolish children, that, though they are rebels, they are impotent rebels, unable to keep up their own rebellion. Bathed in their foolish tears, they will recognise at last that He who created them rebels must have meant to mock at them. They will say this in despair, and their utterance will be a blasphemy which will make them more unhappy still, for man's nature cannot bear blasphemy, and in the end always avenges it on itself. And so unrest, confusion and unhappiness—that is the present lot of man after Thou didst bear so much for their freedom! Thy great prophet tells in vision and in image, that he saw all those who took part in the first resurrection and that there were of each tribe twelve thousand. But if there were so many of them, they must have been not men but gods. They had borne Thy cross, they had endured scores of years in the barren, hungry wilderness, living upon locusts and roots—and Thou mayest indeed point with pride at those children of freedom, of free love, of free and splendid sacrifice for Thy name. But remember that they were only some thousands; and what of the rest? And how are the other weak ones to blame, because they could not endure what the strong have endured? How is the weak soul to blame that it is unable to receive such terrible gifts? Canst Thou have simply come to the elect and for the elect? But if so, it is a mystery and we cannot understand it. And if it is a mystery, we too have a right to preach a mystery, and to teach them that it's not the free judgment of their hearts, not love that matters, but a mystery which they must follow blindly, even against their conscience. So we have done. We have corrected Thy work and have founded it upon *miracle, mystery* and *authority*. And men rejoiced that they were again led like sheep, and that the terrible gift that had brought them such suffering, was, at last, lifted from their hearts. Were we right teaching them this? Speak! Did we not love mankind, so meekly acknowledging their feebleness, lovingly lightening their burden, and permitting their weak nature even sin with our sanction? Why hast Thou come now to hinder us? And why dost Thou look silently and searchingly at me with Thy mild eyes? Be angry. I don't want Thy love, for I love Thee not. And what use is it for me to hide anything from Thee? Don't I know to Whom I am speaking? All that I can say is known to Thee already. And is it for me to conceal from Thee our mystery? Perhaps it is Thy will to hear it from my lips. Listen, then. We are not working with Thee, but with *him*—that is our mystery. It's long—eight centuries—since we have been on *his* side and not on Thine. Just eight centuries ago, we took from him what Thou didst reject with scorn, that last gift he offered Thee, showing Thee all the kingdoms of the earth. We took from him Rome and the sword of Caesar, and proclaimed ourselves sole rulers of the earth, though hitherto we have not been able to complete our work. But whose fault is that? Oh, the work is only beginning, but it has begun. It has long to await completion and the earth has yet much to suffer, but we shall triumph and shall be Caesars, and then we shall plan the universal happiness of man. But Thou mightest have taken even then the sword of Caesar. Why didst Thou reject that last gift? Hadst Thou accepted that last counsel of the mighty spirit, Thou wouldst have accomplished all that man seeks on earth—that is, some one to worship, some one to keep his conscience, and some means of uniting all in one unanimous and harmonious ant-heap, for the craving for universal unity is the third and last anguish of men. Mankind as a whole has always striven to organize a universal state. There have been many great nations with great histories, but the more highly they were developed the more unhappy they were, for they felt more acutely than other people the craving for worldwide union. The great conquerors, Timours and Ghenghis-Khans, whirled like hurricanes over the face of the earth striving to subdue its people, and they too were but the unconscious expression of the same craving for universal unity. Hadst Thou taken the world and Caesar's purple, Thou wouldst have founded the universal state and have given universal peace. For who can rule men if not he who holds their conscience and their bread in his hands? We have taken the sword of Caesar, and in taking it, of course, have rejected Thee and followed *him*. Oh, ages are yet to come of the confusion of free thought, of their science and cannibalism. For having begun to build their tower of Babel without us, they will end, of course, with cannibalism. But then the beast will crawl to us and lick our feet and spatter them with tears of blood. And we shall sit upon the beast and raise the cup, and on it will be written, "Mystery." But then, and only then, the reign of peace and happiness will come for men. Thou art proud of Thine elect, but Thou hast only the elect, while we give rest to all. And besides, how many of those elect, those mighty ones who could become elect, have grown weary waiting for Thee, and have transferred and will transfer the powers of their spirit and the warmth of their heart to the other camp, and end by raising their *free* banner against Thee. Thou didst Thyself lift up that banner. But with us all will be happy and will no more rebel nor destroy one another as under Thy freedom. Oh, we shall persuade them that they will only become free when they renounce their freedom to us and submit to us. And shall we be right or shall we be lying? They will be convinced that we are right, for they will remember the horrors of slavery and confusion to which Thy freedom brought them. Freedom, free thought and science, will lead them into such straits and will bring them face to face with such marvels and insoluble mysteries, that some of them, the fierce and rebellious, will destroy themselves, others, rebellious but weak, will destroy one another, while the rest, weak and unhappy, will crawl fawning to our feet and whine to us: "Yes, you were right, you alone possess His mystery, and we come back to you, save us from ourselves!"

" 'Receiving bread from us, they will see clearly that we take the bread made by their hands from them, to give it to them, without any miracle. They will see that we do not change the stones to bread, but in truth they will be more thankful for taking it from our hands than for the bread itself! For they will remember only too well that in old days, without our help, even the bread they made turned to stones in their hands, while since they have come back to us, the very stones have turned to bread in their hands. Too, too well they know the value of complete submission! And until men know that, they will be unhappy. Who is most to blame for their not knowing it, speak? Who scattered the flock and sent it astray on unknown paths? But the flock will come together again and will submit once more, and then it will be once for all. Then we shall give them the quiet humble happiness of weak creatures such as they are by nature. Oh, we shall persuade them at last not to be proud, for Thou didst lift them up and thereby taught them to be proud. We shall show them that they are weak, that they are only pitiful children, but that childlike happiness is the sweetest of all. They will become timid and will look to us and huddle close to us in fear, as chicks to the hen. They will marvel at us and will be awestricken before us, and will be proud at our being so powerful and clever, that we have been able to subdue such a turbulent flock of thousands of millions. They will tremble impotently before our wrath, their minds will grow fearful, they will be quick to shed tears like women and children, but they will be just as ready at a sign from us to pass to laughter and rejoicing, to happy mirth and childish song. Yes, we shall set them to work, but in their leisure hours we shall make their life like a child's game, with children's songs and innocent dance. Oh, we shall allow them even sin, they are weak and helpless, and they will love us like children because we allow them to sin. We shall tell them that every sin will be expiated, if it is done with our permission, that we allow them to sin because we love them, and the punishment for these sins we take upon ourselves. And we shall take it upon ourselves, and they will adore us as their saviours who have taken on themselves their sins before God. And they will have no secrets from us. We shall allow or forbid them to live with their wives and mistresses, to have or not to have children—according to whether they have been obedient or disobedient—and they will submit to us gladly and cheerfully. The most painful secrets of their conscience, all, all they will bring to us, and we shall have an answer for all. And they will be glad to believe our answer, for it will save them from the great anxiety and terrible agony they endure at present in making a free decision for themselves. And all will be happy, all the millions of creatures except the hundred thousand who rule over them. For only we, we who guard the mystery, shall be unhappy. There will be thousands of millions of happy babes, and a hundred thousand sufferers who have taken upon themselves the curse of the knowledge of good and evil. Peacefully they will die, peacefully they will expire in Thy name, and beyond the grave they will find nothing but death. But we shall keep the secret, and for their happiness we shall allure them with the reward of heaven and eternity. Though if there were anything in the other world, it certainly would not be for such as they. It is prophesied that Thou wilt come again in victory, Thou wilt come with Thy chosen, the proud and strong, but we will say that they have only saved themselves, but we have saved all. We are told that the harlot who sits upon the beast, and holds in her hands the *mystery*, shall be put to shame, that the weak will rise up again, and will rend her royal purple and will strip naked her loathsome body. But then I will stand up and point out to Thee the thousand millions of happy children who have known no sin. And we who have taken their sins upon us for their happiness will stand up before Thee and say: "Judge us if Thou canst and darest." Know that I fear Thee not. Know that I too have been in the wilderness, I too have lived on roots and locusts, I too prized the freedom with which Thou hast blessed men, and I too was striving to stand among Thy elect, among the strong and powerful, thirsting "to make up the number." But I awakened and would not serve madness. I turned back and joined the ranks of those *who have corrected Thy work*. I left the proud and went back to the humble, for the happiness of the humble. What I say to Thee will come to pass, and our dominion will be built up. I repeat, tomorrow Thou shalt see that obedient flock who at a sign from me will hasten to heap up the hot cinders about the pile on which I shall burn Thee for coming to hinder us. For if any one has ever deserved our fires, it is Thou. To-morrow I shall burn Thee. Dixi.'

". . . When the Inquisitor ceased speaking, he waited some time for his Prisoner to answer him. His silence weighed down upon him. He saw that the prisoner had listened intently all the time, looking gently in his face and evidently not wishing to reply. The old man longed for Him to say something, however bitter and terrible. But he suddenly approached the old man in silence and softly kissed him on his bloodless aged lips. That was all his answer. The old man shuddered. His lips moved. He went to the door, opened it, and said to Him: 'Go, and come no more . . . come not at all, never, never!' And he let Him out into the dark alleys of the town. The Prisoner went away."

"And the old man?"

"The kiss glows in his heart, but the old man adheres to his idea."

"And you with him, you too?" cried Alyosha, mournfully.

Ivan laughed.

"Why, it's all nonsense, Alyosha. It's only the senseless poem of a senseless student, who could never write two lines of verse. Why do you take it so seriously? . . ."

Translated by Constance Garnett

DOSTOYEVSKY: *The Grand Inquisitor*

1. *Why does Ivan call this piece a poem in prose? Do you accept his further evaluation of it as "only the senseless poem of a senseless student"?*

2. *Why does the Inquisitor wish to contain Jesus' notion of freedom? What dangers does he discern in it?*

3. *What is the significance of the first temptation in the wilderness—to give man bread?*

4. *What does the Inquisitor mean by: "In bread there was offered Thee an invincible banner; give bread, and man will worship Thee, for nothing is more certain than bread"?*

5. *What is the Inquisitor's argument about man's free choice? What is his view of man?*

6. *Why will the church burn Jesus if necessary? What is His*

reaction to the threat? What does Ivan hope to convey by having Jesus react this way?

7. What are the political and social overtones of Ivan's fantasy? Do you think his fantasy has validity today?

8. Turgenev once described Dostoyevsky as "the most vicious Christian" he had ever known. Does this selection bear out that accusation?

9. For many years, Tolstoy dismissed Dostoyevsky as a "morbid mediocrity," but toward the end of his life, The Brothers Karamazov *became Tolstoy's bedside book, the one he read and reread endlessly. William Barrett says that despite the tremendous differences in the literary and human atmospheres they create, both bring the same revelation to the philosophic mind. From the two stories representing these writers, can you say what that revelation is?*

10. Many readers of this chapter have seen in it a foreshadowing of twentieth-century existentialist thought. Do you see any connections.?

Leo Tolstoy

ALESHA THE POT

Honored as one of the world's greatest novelists, Leo Tolstoy was born on the family estate in the province of Tula, Russia, in 1828. In his early twenties when his attempt to establish a school for the peasants on his large estate failed, he turned to the carefree life available to a wealthy young nobleman in Moscow and St. Petersburg. While serving as an artillery officer in the Crimea, he began to write sketches and stories based upon his travels and military experiences. Encouraged by Ivan Turgenev, he settled down on his estate after his marriage and wrote the novels that gained him his fame, War and Peace *(1866) and* Anna Karenina *(1877). After 1876, he underwent a period of spiritual turmoil that lasted until his death in 1910.* The Death of Ivan Ilyich *(1886),* Master and Man *(1895), and stories like "Memoirs of a Lunatic" reflect his disenchantment with bourgeois, materialistic values and his discovery of a Christian way of life in the simple existence of the peasant. In the following story, a peasant boy who is everyone's drudge, is apotheosized as "the holy fool." D. S. Mirsky, the great Russian scholar, calls this story "one of the very few that make one forget the bedrock Luciferism and pride of the author."*

ALESHA was a younger brother. They called him "the Pot" because once, when his mother sent him to bring a pot of milk to the deacon, he stumbled and smashed the pot. His mother beat him, and the children began calling him "the Pot" to tease him. Alesha the Pot—that became his nickname.

Alesha was a thin lop-eared boy (his ears stuck out like wings), and his nose was large. The children used to tease him: "Alesha has a nose like a pointing dog." There was a school in the village, but Alesha was not taught reading and writing, as he had no time to study. His older brother lived with a merchant in town, and from infancy on, Alesha helped his father. When he was six years old he was already watching the cow and the sheep in the pasture with his sister, and he was not full grown when he began watching over the horses day and night. From the age of twelve on, he was plowing and carting. He had no strength, but had a certain knack. He was always gay. When children laughed at him, he was silent or laughed. When his father cursed him, he was silent and listened. And as soon as the cursing stopped, he would smile and set about the task before him.

Alesha was nineteen when his brother was drafted into the army. And his father put Alesha in his brother's place with the merchant as an errand boy. Alesha was given his brother's old boots, his father's cap and coat, and was taken to the city. Alesha could not have been more delighted with his clothes, but the merchant remained dissatisfied with Alesha's appearance.

"I thought you were putting a real man in Semon's place," said the merchant, glancing at Alesha. "But you've brought me this runt instead. What's he good for?"

"He can do everything—harness the horses, go anywhere, and work ferociously. He just looks like a sapling. But he's wiry."

"Well, all right, I'll see."

"And most of all—he's dutiful. Eager to work."

"What can one do with you? Leave him."

So Alesha began living at the merchant's.

The merchant's family was not large: the master, his old mother, his elder married son, of elementary schooling, who was in business with his father; and another son, who was educated, having completed secondary school and attended a university from which he had been expelled and had returned to live at home; and there was also an unmarried daughter in secondary school.

At first Alesha was not much liked—he was still very peasant-like and badly dressed, he had no manners and addressed everyone familiarly, but they soon became accustomed to him. He was even more useful than his brother. He was truly dutiful; he was sent on every sort of errand, and he did everything willingly and quickly, going from one task to the next without a break. And at the merchant's just as at home, all the work was heaped on Alesha. The more he did, the more tasks were heaped on him. The master and the master's mother and the master's daughter and the master's son and the overseer and the cook—all constantly sent him here and there, and assigned him first this and then that to do. All you could hear was: "Run, lad" or: "Alesha, fix this." "Alesha, you forgot this, didn't you?" "Watch out, don't forget, Alesha." And Alesha ran, fixed, and watched out, and did not forget, and always managed everything and was always smiling.

He soon wore out his brother's boots, and the master scolded him thoroughly for walking in tattered boots with his bare toes showing, and ordered him to buy new boots at the bazaar. The boots were new, and Alesha was delighted with them, but his feet were worn out and by evening they ached from running about, and he became angry with them. Alesha was afraid that when his father came to get the money he would be annoyed that the merchant had deducted the boots from his wages.

Alesha got up before dawn in winter, chopped firewood, swept out the house, and fed the cow and the horses and watered them. Then he lit the stove, cleaned the master's boots and clothes, put out the samovars and cleaned them; then the overseer would call him to fetch some goods, or the cook would order him to knead the dough, or to clean the pots. Then they sent him to town, either with a note, or to fetch the master's daughter at school, or for oil for the old woman. "Where've you been loitering, you wretch," first one, then the other said to him. "Why go yourself—Alesha will run over. Alesha! Oh Alesha!" And Alesha ran.

He had breakfast on the run, and rarely had time for dinner with the others. The cook cursed him for not being with the rest, but she was sorry for him all the same, and left him a hot dish for dinner and for supper. There was a particularly large amount of work before and during holidays. And Alesha was specially delighted with holidays because he was given a tip, although a small one, sixty kopecks in all; but, still, his own money, which he could spend as he wanted. He never set eyes on his salary. His father used to come, take it from the merchant, and give Alesha only reproaches for wearing out his boots so quickly. When Alesha had collected two rubles in tips, he purchased, on the advice of the cook, a red knitted jacket; and when he put it on, he was unable to keep his mouth closed, he was so contented.

Alesha said little, and when he said something, it was always disconnected and abrupt. When he was ordered to do something or asked whether he could do such and such, he always said, without the slightest hesitation: "Can do"—and immediately rushed out to do it, and did it.

He knew no prayers; he had forgotten those his mother had

taught him; but he still prayed in the morning and at night—he prayed with his hands, crossing himself.

Thus Alesha lived for a year and a half; then, in the second half of the second year, a most unusual event happened in his life. This event consisted of his realizing, to his own amazement, that outside of those relationships between people which stem from their need for each other, there were other completely special relationships; that a person did not always clean boots, or fetch a parcel, or harness a horse because it was necessary to someone else, but that a person could, without there being any need of any kind on the part of the other, do things for him out of an urge to serve him, to be kind to him, and that he, Alesha, was the object of such an urge. It was the cook, Ustinya, who made him realize this. Ustinya was an orphan, young, and a hard worker, just like Alesha. She began feeling sorry for Alesha, and Alesha felt, for the first time, that he was not her servant, but was himself appreciated by another. When his mother used to feel sorry for him, he had paid no attention, and it had seemed to him just as when he felt sorry for himself. But suddenly he noticed that with Ustinya it was completely different: he saw how she took pity on him, and left *kasha* with butter for him in the pot; and how, when he ate, she leaned with her hand tucked under her chin and watched him. And he would glance at her, and she would laugh, and he would laugh.

This was so new and strange that at first it frightened Alesha. He felt it would prevent him from serving as well as he had before. But he was glad just the same, and when he looked at his trousers, patched by Ustinya, he nodded his head and smiled. Often after work or while on the run he would think of Ustinya and say: "Ah, yes, Ustinya!" She helped him whenever she could, and he helped her. She often told him the story of her life, how she was orphaned, how her aunt took her in, how she was sent away to town, how a cook's son had tried to seduce her, and how she cut him short. She loved to talk and he found it pleasant to listen to her. He heard that in towns peasants hired as laborers often married cooks. Once she asked him whether he would get married soon. He said he did not know, and that he was unwilling to take anyone in his village.

"What then, have you found someone?" she asked.

"Yes, you. You will, won't you?"

"Oh, my Pot, my Pot, how cleverly you put it," she said, slapping him on the back with her hand. "Why wouldn't I?"

At Shrovetide Alesha's father came to town for the money. The merchant's wife knew Alesha planned to marry Ustinya, and she did not like it. "She'll become pregnant, and what good will she be with a child?" she had told her husband.

The master gave Alesha's father the money.

"Well, is the boy behaving?" said the peasant. "I told you he was dutiful."

"He's dutiful all right, but he's planning something stupid. He's thought up marrying the cook. And I won't keep a married couple. It's not convenient for us."

"The fool, the fool, what a thing to think of," said the father. "Don't give it a thought. I'll order him to drop it."

The father went into the kitchen, sat down, and waited for his son on the bench. Alesha was running errands and returned, huffing and puffing.

"I thought you were lost. Now, what's this you're planning?" said the father.

"But nothing."

"What do you mean, nothing? You decided to get married. I'll marry you when the time comes, and to the wife you need, and not a city trollop."

The father spoke at length. Alesha stood and sighed. When his father had finished, Alesha smiled.

"Well, then, it can be put aside."

"All right."

When his father went away and he was left alone with Ustinya (who had been standing behind the door listening), he told her: "Our plans didn't work out; didn't work. You heard? He's furious; won't have it."

She cried silently in her apron.

Alesha clicked his tongue.

"How can I not obey? Naturally, we must drop it."

In the evening when the merchant's wife called him to close the shutters, she said to him:

"Well then, you've obeyed your father, dropped your foolishness?"

"Naturally I dropped it," Alesha said, then laughed, and immediately burst into tears.

From that time on Alesha never spoke of marriage to Ustinya again, and he lived as before.

During Lent, the overseer sent him to clean the snow off the roof. He climbed out on the roof, cleared everything away, and had begun tearing off the snow frozen on the gutters, when his feet slid and he fell, shovel and all. Unfortunately he fell, not onto the snow, but onto the iron roof over the porch. Ustinya ran up to him and so did the master's daughter.

"Did you hurt yourself, Alesha?"

"It looks like I did. It doesn't matter."

He tried to stand up, but could not, and started to smile. They took him to his room. A doctor came. He examined him and asked where it hurt.

"It hurts everywhere, but it doesn't matter. Except the master will be annoyed. Send word to papa."

Alesha lay in bed two days; on the third, the priest was sent for.

"What, you're not going to die, are you?" asked Ustinya.

"But, what of it? As if we lived forever? We have to die some time," Alesha said, speaking as rapidly as ever. "Thank you, Ustinya, for pitying me. You see, it's better he called off the marriage, it would have been for nothing. Now everything's fine."

He prayed with the priest only with his hands and his heart. And in his heart he believed that if you are good here, if you obey and don't give offense, then it will be good there, too.

He said little. Just asked for water and kept smiling at something.

Then he looked surprised at something, stretched himself, and died.

Translated by Arthur Mendel
and Barbara Makanowitzky

TOLSTOY: *Alesha the Pot*

1. *D. S. Mirsky calls this story "a masterpiece of rare perfection . . . concentrated into . . . six pages." Do you agree or disagree with this judgment? Since the story covers almost the entire career of Alesha, should it have been much longer?*

2. *What social and spiritual values does Tolstoy dramatize in*

this story? Are they valid today? Or are they unworkable in a society much more complex than Tolstoy imagined at the end of the nineteenth century?

3. Alesha obeys his father, remains celibate, and suffers from his fall for three days (in the spring). Do you think these details are deliberately suggestive? In what sense might this story be regarded as a parable?

4. Do you find Alesha's unquestioning submission admirable or contemptible? Is it necessary to the true religious spirit?

5. In what ways does this story remind you of "The Simple Heart"? Which story do you prefer? Why?

6. In many of the stories in this volume, the protagonist is a conscious, rational, restless soul who is seeking greater consciousness. In your estimation, would the purity of conscience and perfect peace that Alesha achieves be possible for such people? Is it this state of mind that they seek? Is there something wrong in the way they seek it, and does Tolstoy, in your judgment, have the key to the quest?

Henry James
EUROPE

Born in 1843, Henry James spent most of his adult life attempting to make the novel into an art work, a devotion that extended until the year of his death, 1916. As a novelist and as a critic of the novel, he has exerted great influence on the entire course of twentieth-century American and English fiction, although he received little more than sporadic critical acclaim during his lifetime. His most famous novels include The American *(1876),* The Europeans *(1878),* Daisy Miller *(1878),* The Portrait of a Lady *(1880),* The Princess Casamassima *(1885),* The Wings of the Dove *(1902),* The Ambassadors *(1903), and* The Golden Bowl *(1904). Written on the eve of his great novelistic period, "Europe" is saturated with the typical Jamesian dialectic: America vs. Europe, the moral vs. the aesthetic life, innocence and youth vs. experience and age, Puritan constrictions vs. worldly expansion.*

I

"OUR feeling is, you know, that Becky should go." The earnest little remark comes back to me, even after long years, as the first note of something that began, for my observation, the day I went with my sister-in-law to take leave of her good friends. It's a memory of the American time, which revives so at present—under some touch that doesn't signify—that it rounds itself off as an anecdote. That walk to say good-bye was the beginning; and the end, so far as I enjoyed a view of it, was not till long after; yet even the end also appears to me now as of the old days. I went, in those days, on occasion, to see my sister-in-law, in whose affairs, on my brother's death, I had had to take a helpful hand. I continued to go indeed after these little matters were straightened out, for the pleasure, periodically, of the impression—the change to the almost pastoral sweetness of the good Boston suburb from the loud longitudinal New York. It was another world, with other manners, a different tone, a different taste; a savour nowhere so mild, yet so distinct, as in the square white house—with the pair of elms, like

[109

gigantic wheat-sheaves, in front, the rustic orchard not far behind, the old-fashioned door-lights, the big blue-and-white jars in the porch, the straight bricked walk from the high gate—that enshrined the extraordinary merit of Mrs. Rimmle and her three daughters.

These ladies were so much of the place and the place so much of themselves that from the first of their being revealed to me I felt that nothing else at Brookbridge much mattered. They were what, for me, at any rate, Brookbridge had most to give: I mean in the way of what it was naturally strongest in, the thing we called in New York the New England expression, the air of Puritanism reclaimed and refined. The Rimmles had brought this down to a wonderful delicacy. They struck me even then—all four almost equally—as very ancient and very earnest, and I think theirs must have been the house in all the world in which "culture" first came to the aid of morning calls. The head of the family was the widow of a great public character—as public characters were understood at Brookbridge—whose speeches on anniversaries formed a part of the body of national eloquence spouted in the New England schools by little boys covetous of the most marked, though perhaps the easiest, distinction. He was reported to have been celebrated, and in such fine declamatory connexions that he seemed to gesticulate even from the tomb. He was understood to have made, in his wife's company, the tour of Europe at a date not immensely removed from that of the battle of Waterloo. What was the age then of the bland firm antique Mrs. Rimmle at the period of her being first revealed to me? That's a point I'm not in a position to determine—I remember mainly that I was young enough to regard her as having reached the limit. And yet the limit for Mrs. Rimmle must have been prodigiously extended; the scale of its extension is in fact the very moral of this reminiscence. She was old, and her daughters were old, but I was destined to know them all as older. It was only by comparison and habit that—however much I recede—Rebecca, Maria and Jane were the "young ladies."

I think it was felt that, though their mother's life, after thirty years of widowhood, had had a grand backward stretch, her blandness and firmness—and this in spite of her extreme physical frailty—would be proof against any surrender not overwhelmingly justified by time. It had appeared, years before, at a crisis of which the waves had not even yet quite subsided, a surrender not justified by anything nameable that she should go to Europe with her daughters and for her health. Her health was supposed to require constant support; but when it had at that period tried conclusions with the idea of Europe it was not the idea of

Europe that had been insidious enough to prevail. She hadn't gone, and Becky, Maria and Jane hadn't gone, and this was long ago. They still merely floated in the air of the visit achieved, with such introductions and such acclamations, in the early part of the century; they still, with fond glances at the sunny parlour-walls, only referred, in conversation, to divers pictorial and other reminders of it. The Misses Rimmles had quite been brought up on it, but Becky, as the most literary, had most mastered the subject. There were framed letters—tributes to their eminent father—suspended among the mementoes, and of two or three of these, the most foreign and complimentary, Becky had executed translations that figured beside the text. She knew already, through this and other illumination, so much about Europe that it was hard to believe for her in that limit of adventure which consisted only of her having been twice to Philadelphia. The others hadn't been to Philadelphia, but there was a legend that Jane had been to Saratoga. Becky was a short stout fair person with round serious eyes, a high forehead, the sweetest neatest enunciation, and a miniature of her father—"done in Rome"—worn as a breastpin. She had written the life, she had edited the speeches, of the original of this ornament, and now at last, beyond the seas, she was really to tread in his footsteps.

Fine old Mrs. Rimmle, in the sunny parlour and with a certain austerity of cap and chair—though with a gay new "front" that looked like rusty brown plush—had had so unusually good a winter that the question of her sparing two members of her family for an absence had been threshed as fine, I could feel, as even under that Puritan roof any case of conscience had ever been threshed. They were to make their dash while the coast, as it were, was clear, and each of the daughters had tried—heroically, angelically and for the sake of each of her sisters—not to be one of the two. What I encountered that first time was an opportunity to concur with enthusiasm in the general idea that Becky's wonderful preparation would be wasted if she were the one to stay with their mother. Their talk of Becky's preparation (they had a sly old-maidish humour that was as mild as milk) might have been of some mixture, for application somewhere, that she kept in a precious bottle. It had been settled at all events that, armed with this concoction and borne aloft by their introductions, she and Jane were to start. They were wonderful on their introductions, which proceeded naturally from their mother and were addressed to the charming families that in vague generations had so admired vague Mr. Rimmle. Jane, I found at Brookbridge, had to be described, for want of other description, as the pretty one, but it wouldn't have served to identify her unless you had seen the others. *Her* preparation was only this figment of her prettiness—only, that is, unless one took into account something that, on the spot, I silently divined: the lifelong secret passionate ache of her little rebellious desire. They were all growing old in the yearning to go, but Jane's yearning was the sharpest. She struggled with it as people at Brookbridge mostly struggled with what they liked, but fate, by threatening to prevent what she *dis*liked and what was therefore duty—which was to stay at home instead of Maria—had bewildered her, I judged, not a little. It was she who, in the words I have quoted, mentioned to me Becky's case and Becky's affinity as the clearest of all. Her mother moreover had on the general subject still more to say.

"I positively desire, I really quite insist that they shall go," the old lady explained to us from her stiff chair. "We've talked about it so often, and they've had from me so clear an account—I've amused them again and again with it—of what's to be seen and enjoyed. If they've had hitherto too many duties to leave, the time seems to have come to recognise that there are also many duties to *seek*. Wherever we go we find them—I always remind the girls of that. There's a duty that calls them to those wonderful countries, just as it called, at the right time, their father and myself—if it be only that of laying-up for the years to come the same store of remarkable impressions, the same wealth of knowledge and food for conversation as, since my return, I've found myself so happy to possess." Mrs. Rimmle spoke of her return as of something of the year before last, but the future of her daughters was somehow, by a different law, to be on the scale of great vistas, of endless aftertastes. I think that, without my being quite ready to say it, even this first impression of her was somewhat upsetting; there was a large placid perversity, a grim secrecy of intention, in her estimate of the ages.

"Well, I'm so glad you don't delay it longer," I said to Miss Becky before we withdrew. "And whoever should go," I continued in the spirit of the sympathy with which the good sisters had already inspired me, "I quite feel, with your family, you know, that *you* should. But of course I hold that everyone should." I suppose I wished to attentuate my solemnity; there was, however, something in it I couldn't help. It must have been a faint foreknowledge.

"Have you been a great deal yourself?" Miss Jane, I remembered, enquired.

"Not so much but that I hope to go a good deal more. So perhaps we shall meet," I encouragingly suggested.

I recall something—something in the nature of susceptibility to encouragement—that this brought into the more expressive brown eyes to which Miss Jane mainly owed it that she was the pretty one. "Where, do you think?"

I tried to think. "Well, on the Italian lakes—Como, Bellaggio, Lugano." I liked to say the names to them.

" 'Sublime, but neither bleak nor bare—nor misty are the mountains there!' " Miss Jane softly breathed, while her sister looked at her as if her acquaintance with the poetry of the subject made her the most interesting feature of the scene she evoked.

But Miss Becky presently turned to me. "Do you know everything—?"

"Everything?"

"In Europe."

"Oh yes," I laughed, "and one or two things even in America."

The sisters seemed to me furtively to look at each other. "Well, you'll have to be quick—to meet *us*," Miss Jane resumed.

"But surely when you're once there you'll stay on."

"Stay on?"—they murmured it simultaneously and with the oddest vibration of dread as well as of desire. It was as if they had been in presence of a danger and yet wished me, who "knew everything," to torment them with still more of it.

Well, I did my best. "I mean it will never do to cut it short."

"No, that's just what I keep saying," said brilliant Jane. "It would be better in that case not to go."

"Oh, don't talk about not going—at this time!" It was none of my business, but I felt shocked and impatient.

"No, not at *this* time!" broke in Miss Maria, who, very red in the face, had joined us. Poor Miss Maria was known as the flushed one; but she was not flushed—she only had an unfortunate surface. The third day after this was to see them embark.

Miss Becky, however, desired as little as any one to be in any way extravagant. "It's only the thought of our mother," she explained.

I looked a moment at the old lady, with whom my sister-in-law was engaged. "Well—your mother's magnificent."

"*Isn't* she magnificent?"—they eagerly took it up.

She *was*—I could reiterate it with sincerity, though I perhaps mentally drew the line when Miss Maria again risked, as a fresh ejaculation: "I think she's better than Europe!"

"Maria!" they both, at this, exclaimed with a strange emphasis: it was as if they feared she had suddenly turned cynical over the deep domestic drama of their casting of lots. The innocent laugh with which she answered them gave the measure of her cynicism.

We separated at last, and my eyes met Mrs. Rimmle's as I held for an instant her aged hand. It was doubtless only my fancy that her calm cold look quietly accused me of something. Of what *could* it accuse me? Only, I thought, of thinking.

II

I left Brookbridge the next day, and for some time after that had no occasion to hear from my kinswoman; but when she finally wrote there was a passage in her letter that affected me more than all the rest. "Do you know the poor Rimmles never, after all, 'went'? The old lady, at the eleventh hour, broke down; everything broke down, and all of *them* on top of it, so that the dear things are with us still. Mrs. Rimmle, the night after our call, had, in the most unexpected manner, a turn for the worse —something in the nature (though they're rather mysterious about it) of a seizure; Becky and Jane felt it—dear devoted stupid angels that they are—heartless to leave her at such a moment, and Europe's indefinitely postponed. However, they think they're still going—or *think* they think it—when she's better. They also think—or think they think—that she *will* be better. I certainly pray she may." So did I— quite fervently. I was conscious of a real pang—I didn't know how much they had made me care.

Late that winter my sister-in-law spent a week in New York; when almost my first enquiry on meeting her was about the health of Mrs. Rimmle.

"Oh she's rather bad—she really is, you know. It's not surprising that at her age she should be infirm."

"Then what the deuce *is* her age?"

"I can't tell you to a year—but she's immensely old."

"That of course I saw," I replied—"unless you literally mean so old that the records have been lost."

My sister-in-law thought. "Well, I believe she wasn't positively young when she married. She lost three or four children before these women were born."

We surveyed together a little, on this, the "dark backward." "And they were born, I gather, *after* the famous tour? Well then, as the famous tour was in a manner to celebrate—wasn't it?—the restoration of the Bourbons—" I considered, I gasped. "My dear child, what on earth do you make her out?"

My relative, with her Brookbridge habit, transferred her share of the question to the moral plane—turned it forth to wander, by implication at least, in the sandy desert of responsibility. "Well, you know, we all immensely admire her."

"You can't admire her more than I do. She's awful."

My converser looked at me with a certain fear. "She's *really* ill."

"Too ill to get better?"

"Oh no—we hope not. Because then they'll be able to go."

"And *will* they go if she should?"

"Oh the moment they should be quite satisfied. I mean *really*," she added.

I'm afraid I laughed at her—the Brookbridge "really" was a thing so by itself. "But if she shouldn't get better?" I went on.

"Oh don't speak of it! They want so to go."

"It's a pity they're so infernally good," I mused.

"No—don't say that. It's what keeps them up."

"Yes, but isn't it what keeps *her* up too?"

My visitor looked grave. "Would you like them to kill her?"

I don't know that I was then prepared to say I should—though I believe I came very near it. But later on I burst all bounds, for the subject grew and grew. I went again before the good sisters ever did—I mean I went to Europe. I think I went twice, with a brief interval, before my fate again brought round for me a couple of days at Brookbridge. I had been there repeatedly, in the previous time, without making the acquaintance of the Rimmles; but now that I had had the revelation I couldn't have it too much, and the first request I preferred was to be taken again to see them. I remember well indeed the scruple I felt— the real delicacy—about betraying that *I* had, in the pride of my power, since our other meeting, stood as their phrase went, among romantic scenes; but they were themselves the first to speak of it, and what moreover came home to me was that the coming and going of their friends in general—Brookbridge itself having even at that period one foot in Europe—was such as to place constantly before them the pleasure that was only postponed. They were thrown back after all on what the situation, under a final analysis, had most to give—the sense that, as every one kindly said to them and they kindly said to every one, Europe would keep. Every one felt for them so deeply that their own kindness in alleviating every one's feeling was really what came out most.

Mrs. Rimmle was still in her stiff chair and in the sunny parlour, but if *she* made no scruple of introducing the Italia lakes my heart sank to observe that she dealt with them, as a topic, not in the least in the leave-taking manner in which Falstaff babbled of green fields.

I'm not sure that after this my pretexts for a day or two with my sister-in-law weren't apt to be a mere cover for another glimpse of these particulars: I at any rate never went to Brookbridge without an irrepressible eagerness for our customary call. A long time seems to me thus to have passed, with glimpses and lapses, considerable impatience and still more pity. Our visits indeed grew shorter, for, as my companion said, they were more and more of a strain. It finally struck me that the good sisters even shrank from me a little as from one who penetrated their consciousness in spite of himself. It was as if they knew where I thought they ought to be, and were moved to deprecate at last, by a systematic silence on the subject of that hemisphere, the criminality I fain would fix on them. They were full instead—as with the instinct of throwing dust in my eyes—of little pathetic hypocrisies about Brookbridge interests and delights. I dare say that as time went on my deeper sense of their situation came practically to rest on my companion's report of it. I certainly think I recollect every word we ever exchanged about them, even if I've lost the thread of the special occasions. The impression they made on me after each interval always broke out with extravagance as I walked away with her.

"*She* may be as old as she likes—I don't care. It's the fearful age the 'girls' are reaching that constitutes the scandal. One shouldn't pry into such matters, I know; but the years and the chances are really going. They're all growing old together—it will presently be too late; and their mother meanwhile perches over them like a vulture—what shall I call it?—calculating. Is she waiting for them successively to drop off? She'll survive them each and all. There's something too remorseless in it."

"Yes, but what do you want her to do? If the poor thing *can't* die she can't. Do you want her to take poison or to open a bloodvessel? I dare say she'd prefer to go."

"I beg your pardon," I must have replied; "you daren't say anything of the sort. If she'd prefer to go she *would* go. She'd feel the propriety, the decency, the necessity of going. She just prefers *not* to go. She prefers to stay and keep up the tension, and her calling them 'girls' and talking of the good time they'll still have is the mere conscious mischief of a subtle old witch. They won't have *any* time—there isn't any time to have! I mean there's, on her own part, no real loss of measure or of perspective in it. She *knows* she's a hundred and ten, and she takes a cruel pride in it."

My sister-in-law differed with me about this; she held that the old woman's attitude was an honest one and that her magnificent vitality, so great in spite of her infirmities, made it inevitable she should attribute youth to persons who had come into the world so much later. "Then suppose she should die?"—so my fellow student of the case always put it to me.

"Do you mean while her daughters are away? There's not the least fear of that—not even if at the very moment of their departure she should be *in extremis*. They'd find her all right on their return."

"But think how they'd feel not to have been with her!"

"That's only, I repeat, on the unsound assumption. If they'd only go tomorrow—literally make a good rush for it—they'll be with her when they come back. That will give them plenty of time." I'm afraid I even heartlessly added that if she *should*, against every probability, pass away in their absence they wouldn't have to come back at all—which would be just the compensation proper to their long privation. And then Maria would come out to join the two others, and they would be—though but for the too scanty remnant of their career—as merry as the day is long.

I remained ready, somehow, pending the fulfilment of that vision, to sacrifice Maria; it was only over the urgency of the case for the others respectively that I found myself balancing. Sometimes it was for Becky I thought the tragedy deepest—sometimes, and in quite a different manner, I thought it most dire for Jane. It was Jane after all who had most sense of life. I seemed in fact dimly to descry in Jane a sense—as yet undescried by herself or by any one—of all sorts of queer things. Why didn't *she* go? I used desperately to ask; why didn't she make a bold personal dash for it, strike up a partnership with some one or other of the travelling spinsters in whom Brookbridge more and more abounded? Well, there came a flash for me at a particular point of the grey middle desert: my correspondent was able to let me know that poor Jane at last *had* sailed. She had gone of a sudden—I liked my sister-in-law's view of suddenness—with the kind Hathaways, who had made an irresistible grab at her and lifted her off her feet. They were going for the summer and for Mr. Hathaway's health, so that the opportunity was perfect and it was impossible not to be glad that something very like physical force had finally prevailed. This was the general feeling at Brookbridge, and I might imagine what Brookbridge had been brought to from the fact that, at the very moment she was hustled off, the doctor, called to her mother at the peep of dawn, had considered that *he* at least must stay. There had been real alarm—greater than ever before; it actually did seem as if this time the end had come. But it was Becky, strange to say, who, though fully recognising the nature of the crisis, had kept the situation in hand and insisted upon action. This, I remember, brought back to me a discomfort with which I had been familiar from the first. One of the two had sailed, and I was sorry it wasn't the other. But if it had been the other I should have been equally sorry.

I saw with my eyes that very autumn what a fool Jane would have been if she had again backed out. Her mother had of course survived the peril of which I had heard, profiting by it indeed as she had profited by every other; she was sufficiently better again to have come downstairs. It was there that, as usual, I found her, but with a difference of effect produced somehow by the absence of one of the girls. It was as if, for the others, though they hadn't gone to Europe, Europe had come to them: Jane's letters had been so frequent and so beyond even what could have been hoped. It was the first time, however, that I perceived on the old woman's part a certain failure of lucidity. Jane's flight was clearly the great fact with her, but she spoke of it as if the fruit had now been plucked and the parenthesis closed. I don't know what sinking sense of still further physical duration I gathered, as a menace, from this first hint of her confusion of mind.

"My daughter has been; my daughter has been—" She kept saying it, but didn't say where; that seemed unnecessary, and she only repeated the words to her visitors with a face that was all puckers and yet now, save in so far as it expressed an ineffaceable complacency, all blankness. I think she rather wanted us to know how little she had stood in the way. It added to something—I scarce knew what—that I found myself desiring to extract privately from Becky. As our visit was to be of the shortest my opportunity—for one of the young ladies always came to the door with us—was at hand. Mrs. Rimmle, as we took leave, again sounded her phrase, but she added this time: "I'm so glad she's going to have always—"

I knew so well what she meant that, as she again dropped, looking at me queerly and becoming momentarily dim, I could help her out. "Going to have what *you* have?"

"Yes, yes—my privilege. Wonderful experience," she mumbled. She bowed to me a little as if I would understand. "She has things to tell."

I turned, slightly at a loss, to Becky. "She has then already arrived?"

Becky was at that moment looking a little strangely at her mother, who answered my question. "She reached New York this morning—she comes on today."

"Oh then—!" But I let the matter pass as I met Becky's eye—I saw there was a hitch somewhere. It was not she but Maria who came out with us; on which I cleared up the question of their sister's reappearance.

"Oh no, not tonight," Maria smiled; "that's only the way mother puts it. We shall see her about the end of November—the Hathaways are so indulgent. They kindly extended their tour."

"For *her* sake? How sweet of them!" my sister-in-law exclaimed.

I can see our friend's plain mild old face take on a deeper mildness, even though a higher colour, in the light of the open door. "Yes, it's for Jane they prolong it. And do you know what they write?" She gave us time, but it was too great a responsibility to guess. "Why that it has brought her out."

"Oh, I knew it *would!*" my companion sympathetically sighed.

Maria put it more strongly still. "They say we wouldn't know her."

This sounded a little awful, but it was after all what I had expected.

III

My correspondent in Brookbridge came to me that Christmas, with my niece, to spend a week; and the arrangement had of course been prefaced by an exchange of letters, the first of which from my sister-in-law scarce took space for acceptance of my invitation before going on to say: "The Hathaways are back—but without Miss Jane!" She presented in a few words the situation thus created at Brookbridge, but was not yet, I gathered, fully in possession of the other one—the situation created in "Europe" by the presence there of that lady. The two together, however that might be, demanded, I quickly felt, all my attention, and perhaps my impatience to receive my relative was a little sharpened by my desire for the whole story. I had it at last, by the Christmas fire, and I may say without reserve that it gave me all I could have hoped for. I listened eagerly, after which I produced the comment: "Then she simply refused—"

"To budge from Florence? Simply. She had it out there with the poor Hathaways, who felt responsible for her safety, pledged to restore her to her mother's, to her sisters' hands, and showed herself in a light, they mention under their breath, that made their dear old hair stand on end. Do you know what, when they first got back, they said of her—at least it was *his* phrase—to two or three people?"

I thought a moment. "That she had 'tasted blood'?"

My visitor fairly admired me. "How clever of you to guess! It's exactly what he did say. She appeared—she continues to appear, it seems—in a new character."

I wondered a little. "But that's exactly—don't you remember?—what Miss Maria reported to us from them; that we 'wouldn't know her.'"

My sister-in-law perfectly remembered. "Oh yes—she broke out from the first. But when they left her she was worse."

"Worse?"

"Well, different—different from anything she ever *had* been or—for that matter—had had a chance to be." My reporter hung fire a moment, but presently faced me. "Rather strange and free and obstreperous."

"Obstreperous?" I wondered again.

"Peculiarly so, I inferred, on the question of not coming away. She wouldn't hear of it and, when they spoke of her mother, said she had given her mother up. She had thought she should like Europe, but didn't know she should like it so much. They had been fools to bring her if they expected to take her away. She was going to see what she could—she hadn't yet seen half. The end of it at any rate was that they had to leave her alone."

I seemed to see it all—to see even the scared Hathaways. "So she *is* alone?"

"She told them, poor thing, it appears, and in a tone they'll never forget, that she was in any case quite old enough to be. She cried—she quite went on—over not having come sooner. That's why the only way for her," my companion mused, "*is*, I suppose, to stay. They wanted to put her with some people or other—to find some American family. But she says she's on her own feet."

"And she's still in Florence?"

"No—I believe she was to travel. She's bent on the East."

I burst out laughing. "Magnificent Jane! It's most interesting. Only I feel that I distinctly *should* 'know' her. To my sense, always, I must tell you, she had it in her."

My relative was silent a little. "So it now appears Becky always felt."

"And yet pushed her off? Magnificent Becky!"

My companion met my eyes a moment. "You don't know the queerest part. I mean the way it has *most* brought her out."

I turned it over; I felt I should like to know—to that degree indeed that, oddly enough, I jocosely disguised my eagerness. "You don't mean she has taken to drink?"

My visitor had a dignity—and yet had to have a freedom. "She has taken to flirting."

I expressed disappointment. "Oh she took to *that* long ago. Yes," I declared at my kinswoman's stare, "she positively flirted—with *me!*"

The stare perhaps sharpened. "Then you flirted with *her?*"

"How else could I have been as sure as I wanted to be? But has she means?"

"Means to flirt?"—my friend looked an instant as if she spoke literally. "I don't understand about the means—though of course they have something. But I have my impression," she went on. "I think that Becky—" It seemed almost too grave to say.

But *I* had no doubts. "That Becky's backing her?"

She brought it out. "Financing her."

"Stupendous Becky! So that morally then—"

"Becky's quite in sympathy. But isn't it too odd?" my sister-in-law asked.

"Not in the least. Didn't we know, as regards Jane, that Europe was to bring her out? Well, it has also brought out Rebecca."

"It has indeed!" my companion indulgently sighed. "So what would it do if she were there?"

"I should like immensely to see. And we *shall* see."

"Do you believe then she'll still go?"

"Certainly. She *must.*"

But my friend shook it off. "She won't."

"She shall!" I retorted with a laugh. But the next moment I said: "And what does the old woman say?"

"To Jane's behaviour? Not a word—never speaks of it. She talks now much less than she used—only seems to wait. But it's my belief she thinks."

"And—do you mean—knows?"

"Yes, knows she's abandoned. In her silence there she takes it in."

"It's her way of making Jane pay?" At this, somehow, I felt more serious. "Oh dear, dear—she'll disinherit her!"

When in the following June I went on to return my sister-in-law's visit the first object that met my eyes in her little white parlour was a figure that, to my stupefaction, presented itself for the moment as that of Mrs. Rimmle. I had gone to my room after arriving and had come down when dressed; the apparition I speak of had arisen in the interval. Its ambiguous character lasted, however, but a second or two—I had taken Becky for her mother because I knew no one but her mother of that extreme age. Becky's age was quite startling; it had made a great stride, though, strangely enough, irrecoverably seated as she now was in it, she had a wizened brightness that I had scarcely yet seen in her. I remember indulging on this occasion in two silent observations: one on the article of my not having hitherto been conscious of her full resemblance to the old lady, and the other to the effect that, as I had said to my sister-in-law at Christmas, "Europe," even as reaching her only through Jane's sensibilities, had really at last brought her out. She was in fact "out" in a manner of which this encounter offered to my eyes a unique example: it was the single hour, often as I had been at Brookbridge, of my meeting her elsewhere than in her mother's drawing-room. I surmise that, besides being adjusted to her more marked time of life, the garments she wore abroad, and in particular her little plain bonnet, presented points of resemblance to the close sable sheath and the quaint old headgear that, in the white house behind the elms, I had from far back associated with the eternal image in the stiff chair. Of course I immediately spoke of Jane, showing an interest and asking for news; on which she answered me with a smile, but not at all as I had expected.

"*Those* are not really the things you want to know—where she is, whom she's with, how she manages and where she's going next—oh no!" And the admirable woman gave a laugh that was somehow both light and sad—sad, in particular, with a strange long weariness. "What you do want to know is when she's coming back."

I shook my head very kindly, but out of a wealth of experience that, I flattered myself, was equal to Miss Becky's. "I do know it. Never."

Miss Becky exchanged with me at this a long deep look. "Never."

We had, in silence, a little luminous talk about it, at the end of which she seemed to have told me the most interesting things. "And how's your mother?" I then enquired.

She hesitated, but finally spoke with the same serenity. "My mother's all right. You see she's not alive."

"Oh Becky!" my sister-in-law pleadingly interjected.

But Becky only addressed herself to me. "Come and see if she is. *I* think she isn't—but Maria perhaps isn't so clear. Come at all events and judge and tell me."

It was a new note, and I was a little bewildered. "Ah but I'm not a doctor!"

"No, thank God—you're not. That's why I ask you." And now she said good-bye.

I kept her hand a moment. "*You're* more alive than ever!"

"I'm very tired." She took it with the same smile, but for Becky it was much to say.

IV

"Not alive," the next day, was certainly what Mrs. Rimmle looked when, arriving in pursuit of my promise, I found her, with Miss Maria, in her usual place. Though wasted and shrunken she still occupied her high-backed chair with a visible theory of erectness, and her intensely aged face—combined with something dauntless that belonged to her very presence and that was effective even in this extremity—might have been that of some immemorial sovereign, of indistinguishable sex, brought forth to be shown to the people in disproof of the rumour of extinction. Mummified and open-eyed she looked at me, but I had no impression that she made me out. I had come this time without my sister-in-law, who had frankly pleaded to me—which also, for a daughter of Brookbridge, was saying much—that the house had grown too painful. Poor Miss Maria excused Miss Becky on the score of her not being well—and that, it struck me, was saying most of all. The absence of the others gave the occasion a different note; but I talked with Miss Maria for five minutes and recognised that—save for her saying, of her own movement, anything about Jane—she now spoke as if her mother had lost hearing or sense, in fact both, alluding freely and distinctly, though indeed favourably, to her condition. "She has expected your visit and much enjoys it," my entertainer said, while the old woman, soundless and motionless, simply fixed me without expression. Of course there was little to keep me; but I became aware as I rose to go that there was more than I had supposed.

On my approaching her to take leave Mrs. Rimmle gave signs of consciousness. "Have you heard about Jane?"

I hesitated, feeling a responsibility, and appealed for direction to Maria's face. But Maria's face was troubled, was turned altogether to her mother's. "About her life in Europe?" I then rather helplessly asked.

The old lady fronted me on this in a manner that made me feel silly. "Her life?"—and her voice, with this second effort, came out stronger. "Her death, if you please."

"Her death?" I echoed, before I could stop myself, with the accent of deprecation.

Miss Maria uttered a vague sound of pain, and I felt her turn away, but the marvel of her mother's little unquenched spark still held me.

"Jane's dead. We've heard," said Mrs. Rimmle. "We've heard from—where is it we've heard from?" She had quite revived—she appealed to her daughter.

Ths poor old girl, crimson, rallied to her duty. "From Europe."

Mrs. Rimmle made at us both a little grim inclination of the head. "From Europe," I responded, in silence, by a deflexion from every rigour, and, still holding me, she went on: "And now Rebecca's going."

She had gathered by this time such emphasis to say it that again, before I could help myself, I vibrated in reply. "To Europe—now?" It was as if for an instant she had made me believe it.

She only stared at me, however, from her wizened mask; then her eyes followed my companion. "Has she gone?"

"Not yet, mother." Maria tried to treat it as a joke, but her smile was embarrassed and dim.

"Then where is she?"

"She's lying down."

The old woman kept up her hard queer gaze, but directing it after a minute to me. "She's going."

"Oh some day!" I foolishly laughed; and on this I got to the door, where I separated from my younger hostess, who came no further.

Only, as I held the door open, she said to me under cover of it and very quietly: "It's poor mother's idea."

I saw—it was her idea. Mine was—for some time after this, even after I had returned to New York and to my usual occupations—that I should never again see Becky. I had seen her for the last time, I believed, under my sister-in-law's roof, and in the autumn it was given to me to hear from that fellow admirer that she had succumbed at last to the situation. The day of the call I have just described had been a date in the process of her slow shrinkage—it was literally the first time she had, as they said at Brookbridge, given up. She had been ill for years, but the other state of health in the contemplation of which she had spent so much of her life had left her till too late no margin for heeding it. The power of attention came at last simply in the form of the discovery that it *was* too late; on which, naturally, she had given up more and more. I had heard indeed, for weeks before, by letter, how Brookbridge had watched her do so; in consequence of which the end found me in a manner prepared. Yet in spite of my preparation there remained with me a soreness, and when I was next—it was some months later—on the scene of her martyrdom I fear I replied with an almost rabid negative to the question put to me in due course by my kinswoman. "Call on them? Never again!"

I went none the less the very next day. Everything was the same in the sunny parlour—everything that most mattered, I mean: the centenarian mummy in the high chair and the tributes, in the little frames on the walls, to the celebrity of its late husband. Only Maria Rimmle was different: if Becky, on my last seeing her, had looked as old as her mother, Maria—save that she moved about—looked older. I remember she moved about, but I scarce remember what she said; and indeed what was there to say? When I risked a question, however, she found a reply.

"But *now* at least—?" I tried to put it to her suggestively.

At first she was vague. " 'Now'?"

"Won't Miss Jane come back?"

Oh the headshake she gave me! "Never." It positively pictured to me, for the instant, a well-preserved woman, a rich ripe *seconde jeunesse* by the Arno.

"Then that's only to make more sure of your finally joining her."

Maria Rimmle repeated her headshake. "Never."

We stood so a moment bleakly face to face; I could think of no attenuation that would be particularly happy. But while I heard a hoarse gasp that fortunately relieved me—a signal strange and at first formless from the occupant of the high-backed chair. "Mother wants to speak to you," Maria then said.

So it appeared from the drop of the old woman's jaw, the expression of her mouth opened as if for the emission of sound. It was somehow difficult to me to seem to sympathise without hypocrisy, but, so far as a step nearer could do that, I invited communication. "Have you heard where Becky's gone?" the wonderful witch's white lips then extraordinarily asked.

It drew from Maria, as on my previous visit, an uncontrollable groan, and this in turn made me take time to consider.

As I considered, however, I had an inspiration. "To Europe?"

I must have adorned it with a strange grimace, but my inspiration had been right. "To Europe," said Mrs. Rimmle.

HENRY JAMES: *Europe*

1. *How would you characterize the style? Oblique, circuitous, straightforward, elegant? Does it seem appropriate to the character of the narrator?*

2. *Europe evidently means different things to the different characters in the story. What does Europe represent to Mrs. Rimmle? To her daughters? To the narrator of the story?*

3. Why does Mrs. Rimmle break down on the eve of her daughters' departure, although she has herself experienced Europe? What point is James trying to establish?

4. What is the attitude of the narrator toward Mrs. Rimmle? Do you find James witty in this area? Can you see the entire piece as witty? To what extent is he witty about pathetic people? Is there any conflict between wit and pathos in the story?

5. Why does Jane bolt to Europe? Does her action involve factors that go beyond her personal need to "get away"?

6. Why is Jane's stay abroad sifted through narrators, as a form of witty gossip?

7. To what extent is a Puritan ethic delineated in this story? On what does it depend, and to what is it contrasted?

8. Why does James stress matters of age, the aged, aging itself, appearances, etc.?

9. Near the end, the story undergoes several reversals. To understand them, you should try to answer these questions. Why does Mrs. Rimmle consider Jane dead, although she is alive in Europe? Then why does she consider Rebecca in Europe when she is, in fact, dead? What personal attitudes must Mrs. Rimmle protect? Why did Rebecca die? What is Maria's fate?

10. How does James transform personal experience into cultural ideas, and cultural ideas into personal experiences?

11. James was a great admirer of Flaubert and Turgenev. Can you discern their influence on this story?

Guy de Maupassant

LITTLE LOUISE ROQUE

> *Born in Normandy in 1850, Maupassant was fortunate in having for a neighbor the novelist Flaubert, who introduced him to many of his literary friends. Under Flaubert's tutelage, Maupassant learned to write the kind of short story which became his stock in trade: the controlled precise work that drives to an inevitable climax and conclusion. By the time of his death in 1893, Maupassant had written sixteen volumes of stories whose quality remained high despite his prodigious output. Although less known than some of his other stories, "Little Louise Roque" is typical of Maupassant's mature work, with its sensuality, its sense of human tragedy, its recognition of forces which man cannot control.*

MEDERIC ROMPEL, the postman, familiarly called by the country people "Mederi," started at his usual hour from the posthouse at Rouy-le-Tors. Having passed through the little town, striding like an old trooper, he cut across the meadows of Villaumes in order to reach the bank of the Brindelle, which led him along the water's edge to the village of Carvelin, where his distribution commenced. He traveled quickly, following the course of the narrow river, which frothed, murmured, and boiled along its bed of grass under the arching willow trees. The big stones, impeding the flow of water, created around them a sort of aqueous necktie ending in a knot of foam. In some places, there were cascades a foot wide, often invisible, which made under the leaves, under the tendrils, under a roof of verdure, a noise at once angry and gentle. Further on, the banks widened out, and you saw a small, placid lake where trout were swimming in the midst of all that green vegetation which keeps undulating in the depths of tranquil streams.

Mederic went on without a halt, seeing nothing and with only one thought in his mind: "My first letter is for the Poivron family; then I have one for M. Renardet; so I must cross the wood."

[127

His blue blouse, fastened round his waist by a black leathern belt, moved in quick, regular fashion above the green hedge of willow-trees; and his stick of stout holly kept time with the steady march of his feet.

He crossed the Brindelle over a bridge formed of a single tree thrown lengthwise, with a rope attached to two stakes driven into the river banks as its only balustrade.

The wood, which belonged to M. Renardet, the mayor of Carvelin, and the largest landowner in the district, consisted of a number of huge old trees, straight as pillars, and extended for about half a league along the left bank of the stream which served as a boundary for this immense arch of foliage. Alongside the water there were large shrubs warmed by the sun: but under the trees you found nothing but moss, thick, soft, plastic moss, which exhaled into the stagnant air a light odor of loam and withered branches.

Mederic slackened his pace, took off his black cap trimmed with red lace, and wiped his forehead, for it was by this time hot in the meadows, though not yet eight o'clock in the morning.

He had just recovered from the effects of the heat, and had accelerated his pace when he noticed at the foot of a tree a knife, a child's small knife. As he picked it up, he discovered a thimble, and then a needlecase, not far away.

Having found these objects, he thought: "I'll intrust them to the mayor," and resumed his journey. But now he kept his eyes open, expecting to find something else.

All of a sudden, he drew up stiffly as if he had run up against a wooden bar. Ten paces in front of him on the moss, lay stretched on her back a little girl, quite naked. She was about twelve years old. Her arms were hanging down, her legs parted, and her face covered with a handkerchief. There were little spots of blood on her thighs.

Mederic now advanced on tiptoe, as if afraid to make a noise; he apprehended some danger, and glanced toward the spot uneasily.

What was this? No doubt, she was asleep. Then, he reflected that a person does not go to sleep thus, naked, at half past seven in the morning under cool trees. Then she must be dead; and he must be face to face with a crime. At this thought, a cold shiver ran through his frame, although he was an old soldier. And then a murder was such a rare thing in the country—and above all the murder of a child—that he could not believe his eyes. But she had no wound—nothing save these blood drops on her legs. How, then, had she been killed?

He stopped when quite near her and stared at her, while leaning on his stick. Certainly, he knew her, as he knew all the inhabitants of the district; but, not being able to get a look at her face, he could not guess her name. He stooped forward in order to take off the handkerchief which covered her face; then paused with outstretched hand, restrained by an idea that occurred to him.

Had he the right to disarrange anything in the condition of the corpse before the magisterial investigation? He pictured justice to himself as a general whom nothing escapes, who attaches as much importance to a lost button as to a stab of a knife in the stomach. Perhaps under this handkerchief evidence to support a capital charge could be found; in fact if there were sufficient proof there to secure a conviction, it might lose its value if touched by an awkward hand.

Then he straightened up with the intention of hastening toward the mayor's residence, but again another thought held him back. If the little girl was still alive, by any chance—he could not leave her lying there in this way. He sank on his knees very gently, a yard away from her, through precaution, and stretched his hand toward her feet. The flesh was icy cold, with that terrible coldness which makes dead flesh frightful, and leaves us no longer in doubt. The letter-carrier, as he touched her, felt his heart leap to his mouth, as he said himself afterward, and his lips were parched with dry saliva. Rising up abruptly he rushed off through the trees to M. Renardet's house.

He hurried on in double-quick time, with his stick under his arm, his hands clenched, and his head thrust forward, and his leathern bag, filled with letters and newspapers, flapping regularly at his side.

The mayor's residence was at the end of the wood, which he used as a park, and one side of it was washed by a little lagoon formed at this spot by the Brindelle.

It was a big, square house of gray stone, very old. It had stood many a siege in former days, and at the end of it was a huge tower, twenty meters high, built in the water. From the top of this fortress the entire country around could be seen in olden times. It was called the Fox's Tower, without anyone knowing exactly why; and from the appellation, no doubt, had come the name Renardet, borne by the owners of this fief, which had remained in the same family, it was said, for more than two hundred years. For the Renardets formed part of that upper middle class which is all but noble and was met with so often in the provinces before the Revolution.

The postman dashed into the kitchen where the servants were taking breakfast, and exclaimed:

"Is the mayor up? I want to speak to him at once."

Mederic was recognized as a man of weight and authority, and it was soon understood that something serious had happened.

As soon as word was brought to M. Renardet, he ordered the postman to be sent up to him. Pale and out of breath, with his cap in his hand, Mederic found the mayor seated in front of a long table covered with scattered papers.

He was a big, tall man, heavy and red-faced, strong as an ox, and greatly liked in the district, though of an excessively violent disposition. Very nearly forty years old, and a widower for the past six months, he lived on his estate like a country gentleman. His choleric temperament had often brought him into trouble, from which the magistrates of Rouy-le-Tors, like indulgent and prudent friends, had extricated him. Had he not one day thrown the conductor of the diligence from the top of his seat because the latter had nearly crushed his retriever, Micmac? Had he not broken the ribs of a gamekeeper, who had abused him for having passed through a neighbor's property with a gun in his hand? Had he not even caught by the collar the sub-prefect, who stopped in the village in the course of an administrative round described by M. Renardet as an electioneering tour; for he was against the government, according to his family tradition?

The mayor asked:

"What's the matter now, Mederic?"

"I have found a little girl dead in your wood."

Renardet rose up, with his face the color of brick.

"A little girl, do you say?"

"Yes, M'sieu', a little girl, quite naked, on her back, with blood on her, dead—quite dead!"

The mayor gave vent to an oath:

"By God, I'd make a bet 'tis little Louise Roque! *I* have just learned that she did not go home to her mother last night. Where did you find her?"

The postman pointed out where the place was, gave full details, and offered to conduct the mayor to the spot.

But Renardet became brusque:

"No. I don't need you. Send the steward, the mayor's secretary, and the doctor immediately to me, and resume your rounds. Quick, go quick, and tell them to meet me in the wood."

The letter-carrier, a man used to discipline, obeyed and withdrew, angry and grieved at not being able to be present at the investigation.

The mayor, in his turn, prepared to go out. He took his hat, a big soft hat, and paused for a few seconds on the threshold of his abode. In front of him stretched a wide lawn in which three large patches were conspicuous—three large beds of flowers in full bloom, one facing the house and the others at either side of it. Further on, rose skyward the principal trees in the wood, while at the left, above the spot where the Brindelle widened into a pool, could be seen long meadows, an entirely flat green sweep of country, cut by dykes and monster-like willows, twisted dwarf-trees, always cut short, having on their thick squat trunks a quivering tuft of branches.

To the right, behind the stables, the outhouses, and the buildings connected with the property, might be seen the village, which was prosperous, being mainly inhabited by raisers of oxen.

Renardet slowly descended the steps in front of his house, and, turning to the left, gained the water's edge, which he followed at a slow pace, his hands behind his back. He went on, with bent head, and from time to time he glanced round in search of the persons for whom he had sent.

When he stood beneath the trees, he stopped, took off his hat, and wiped his forehead as Mederic had done; for the burning sun was shedding its fiery rain upon the ground. Then the mayor resumed his journey, stopped once more, and retraced his steps. Suddenly stooping down, he steeped his handkerchief in the stream that glided at his feet and stretched it round his head, under his hat. Drops of water flowed along his temples, over his purple ears, over his strong red neck, and trickled one after the other, under his white shirt-collar.

As yet nobody had appeared; he began tapping with his foot, then he called out: "Hallo! Hallo!"

A voice at his right answered: "Hallo! Hallo!" and the doctor appeared under the trees. He was a thin little man, an ex-military surgeon, who passed in the neighborhood for a very skillful practitioner. He limped, having been wounded while in the service, and had to use a stick to assist him in walking.

Next came the steward and the mayor's secretary, who, having been sent for at the same time, arrived together. They seemed scared, as they hurried forward, out of breath, walking and trotting in turn in order to hasten, and moving their arms up and down so vigorously that they seemed to do more work with them than with their legs.

Renardet said to the doctor:

"You know what the trouble is about?"

"Yes, a child found dead in the wood by Mederic."

"That's quite correct. Come on."

They walked on side by side, followed by the two men.

Their steps made no noise on the moss, their eyes were gazing downward right in front of them.

The doctor hastened his steps, interested by the discovery. As soon as they were near the corpse, he bent down to examine it without touching it. He had put on a pair of glasses, as you do when you are looking at some curious object; then he turned round very quietly and said, without rising up:

"Violated and murdered, as we shall prove presently. The little girl, moreover, is almost a woman—look at her throat."

Her two breasts, already nearly full-developed, fell over her chest, relaxed by death. The doctor lightly drew away the handkerchief which covered her face. It was almost black, frightful to look at, the tongue protruding, the eyes bloodshot. He went on:

"Faith, she was strangled the moment the deed was done."

He felt her neck:

"Strangled with the hands without leaving any special trace, neither the mark of the nails nor the imprint of the fingers. Quite right. It is little Louise Roque, sure enough!"

He delicately replaced the handkerchief:

"There's nothing for me to do. She's been dead for the last hour at least. We must give notice of the matter to the authorities."

Renardet, standing up, with his hands behind his back, kept staring with a stony look at the little body exposed to view on the grass. He murmured:

"What a wretch! We must find the clothes."

The doctor felt the hands, the arms, the legs. He said:

"She must have been bathing, no doubt. They ought to be at the water's edge."

The mayor thereupon gave directions:

"Princèpe [this was his secretary], go and look for those clothes for me along the river. Maxime [this was the steward], hurry on towards Rouy-le-Tors, and bring on here to me the examining magistrate with the gendarmes. They must be here within an hour. You understand."

The two men quickly departed, and Renardet said to the doctor:

"What miscreant has been able to do such a deed in this part of the country?"

The doctor murmured:

"Who knows? Everyone is capable of that! Everyone in particular and nobody in general. However, it must be some prowler, some workman out of employment. As we live under a Republic, we must expect to meet this sort of miscreant along the roads."

Both of them were Bonapartists. The mayor went on:

"Yes, it could only be a stranger, a passer-by, a vagabond without heart or home."

The doctor added with the shadow of a smile on his face:

"And without a wife. Having neither a good supper nor a good bed, he procured the rest for himself. You can't tell how many men there may be in the world capable of a crime at a given moment. Did you know that this little girl had disappeared?"

And with the end of his stick he touched one after the other the stiffened fingers of the corpse, resting on them as on the keys of a piano.

"Yes, the mother came last night to look for me about nine o'clock, the child not having come home for supper up to seven. We went to try and find her along the roads up to midnight, but we did not think of the wood. However, we needed daylight to carry out a search with a practical result."

"Will you have a cigar?" said the doctor.

"Thanks, I don't care to smoke. It gives me a turn to look at this."

They remained standing in front of the young girl's body, pale and still, on the dark background of moss. A big fly was walking along one of the thighs, it stopped at the blood-stains, went on again, always rising higher, ran along the side with his lively, jerky movements, climbed up one of the breasts, then came back again to explore the other. The two men silently watched this wandering black speck. The doctor said:

"How tantalizing it is, a fly on the skin! The ladies of the last century had good reason to paste them on their faces. Why has the fashion gone out?"

But the mayor seemed not to hear, plunged as he was in deep thought.

All of a sudden he turned around, surprised by a shrill noise. A woman in a cap and a blue apron rushed up through the trees. It was the mother, La Roque. As soon as she saw Renardet she began to shriek:

"My little girl, where's my little girl?" in such a distracted manner that she did not glance down at the ground. Suddenly, she saw the corpse, stopped short, clasped her hands, and raised both her arms while she uttered a sharp, heartrending cry—the cry of a mutilated animal. Then, she rushed toward the body, fell on her knees, and snatched the handkerchief that covered the face. When she saw that frightful countenance, black and convulsed, she recoiled with a shudder, then pressed her face against the ground, giving vent to terrible and continuous choking screams, her mouth close to the thick moss.

Her tall, thin frame, to which her clothes clung tightly, was palpitating, shaken with convulsions. They could see her bony ankles and withered limbs covered with thick blue stockings, shivering horribly. Unconsciously she dug at the soil with her crooked fingers as if to make a grave in which to hide herself.

The doctor pityingly said in a low tone:

"Poor old woman!"

Renardet felt a strange rumbling in his stomach; then he gave vent to a sort of loud sneeze that issued at the same time through nose and mouth; and, drawing his handkerchief from his pocket, began to weep copiously, coughing, sobbing noisily, wiping his face, and stammering:

"Damn—damn—damned pig to do this! I would like to see him guillotined!"

But Princèpe reappeared, with his hands empty. He murmured:

"I have found nothing, M'sieu' le Maire, nothing at all anywhere."

The mayor, scared, replied in a thick voice, drowned in tears:

"What is it you could not find?"

"The little girl's clothes."

"Well—well—look again, and find them—or you'll have to answer to me."

The man, knowing that the mayor would not brook opposition, set forth again with hesitating steps, casting on the corpse horrified and timid glances.

Distant voices arose under the trees, confused sound, the noise of an approaching crowd; for Mederic had, in the course of his rounds, carried the news from door to door. The people of the neighborhood, stupefied at first, had gone gossiping from their own firesides into the street, and from one threshold to another. Then they gathered together. They talked over, discussed, and commented on the event for some minutes, and they had now come to see it for themselves.

They arrived in groups, a little faltering and uneasy through fear of the first impression of such a scene on their minds. When they saw the body they stopped, not daring to advance, and speaking low. Then they grew bold, went on a few steps, stopped again, advanced once more, and soon formed around the dead girl, her mother, the doctor, and Renardet, a thick circle, agitated and noisy, which swayed forward under the sudden pushes of the last comers. And now they touched the corpse. Some of them even bent down to feel it with their fingers. The doctor kept them back. But the mayor, waking abruptly out of his torpor, broke into a rage, and, seizing Dr. Labarbe's stick, flung himself on his townspeople, stammering:

"Clear out—clear out—you pack of brutes—clear out!"

And in a second the crowd of sightseers had fallen back two hundred metres.

La Roque was lifted up, turned round, and placed in a sitting posture; she remained weeping with her hands clasped over her face.

The occurrence was discussed among the crowd; and young lads, with eager eyes, curiously scrutinized the nude body of the girl. Renardet perceived this, and, abruptly taking off his vest, flung it over the little girl, who was entirely lost to view under the wide garment.

The spectators drew quietly nearer. The wood was filled with people, and a continuous hum of voices rose up under the tangled foliage of the tall trees.

The mayor, in his shirt-sleeves, remained standing, with his stick in his hands, in a fighting attitude. He seemed exasperated by this curiosity on the part of the people, and kept repeating:

"If one of you comes nearer, I'll break his head just as I would a dog's."

The peasants were greatly afraid of him. They held back. Dr. Labarbe, who was smoking, sat down beside La Roque, and spoke to her in order to distract her attention. The old woman soon removed her hands from her face, and replied with a flood of tearful words, pouring forth her grief in rapid sentences. She told the whole story of her life, her marriage, the death of her man—a bull-sticker, who had been gored to death—the infancy of her daughter, her wretched existence as a widow without resources and with a child to support. She had only this one, her little Louise, and the child had been killed—killed in this wood. All of a sudden, she felt anxious to see it again, and dragging herself on her knees toward the corpse, she raised up one corner of the garment that covered it; then she let it fall again, and began wailing once more. The crowd remained silent, eagerly watching the mother's gestures.

But all of a sudden there was a swaying of the crowd, and a cry of "The gendarmes! The gendarmes!"

Two gendarmes appeared in the distance, coming on at a rapid trot, escorting their captain and a little gentleman with red whiskers, who was bobbing up and down like a monkey on a big white mare.

The steward had found M. Putoin, the examining magistrate, just at the moment when he was mounting to take his daily ride, for he posed as a good horseman, to the great amusement of the officers.

He dismounted along with the captain, and pressed the hands of the mayor and the doctor, casting a ferret-like glance on the linen vest which swelled above the body lying underneath.

When he was thoroughly acquainted with the facts, he first gave orders to get rid of the public, whom the gendarmes drove out of the wood, but who soon reappeared in the meadow, and formed a line, a long line of excited and moving heads all along the Brindelle, on the other side of the stream.

The doctor in his turn gave explanations of which Renardet took a note in his memorandum book. All the evidence was given, taken down, and commented on without leading to any discovery. Maxime, too, came back without having found any trace of the clothes.

This surprised everybody; no one could explain it on the theory of theft, since these rags were not worth twenty sous; so this theory was inadmissible.

The examining magistrate, the mayor, the captain, and the doctor set to work by searching in pairs, putting aside the smallest branches along the water.

Renardet said to the judge:

"How does it happen that this wretch should conceal or carry away the clothes, and should then leave the body exposed in the open air and visible to everyone?"

The other, sly and knowing, answered:

"Perhaps a dodge. This crime has been committed either by a brute or by a crafty blackguard. In any case, we'll easily succeed in finding him."

The rolling of a vehicle made them turn their heads. It was the deputy magistrate, another doctor, and the registrar of the court who had arrived in their turn. They resumed their searches, all chatting in an animated fashion.

Renardet said suddenly:

"Do you know that I am expecting you to lunch with me?"

Everyone smilingly accepted the invitation, and the examining magistrate, finding that the case of little Louise Roque was quite enough to bother about for one day, turned toward the mayor:

"I can have the body brought to your house, can I not? You have a room in which you can keep it for me till this evening."

The other got confused, and stammered:

"Yes—no—no. To tell the truth, I prefer that it should not come into my house on account of—on account of my servants who are already talking about ghosts in—in my tower, in the Fox's Tower. You know—I could no longer keep a single one. No—I prefer not to have it in my house."

The magistrate began to smile:

"Good! I am going to get it carried off at once to Rouy, for the legal examination."

Turning toward the doctor:

"I can make use of your trap, can I not?"

"Yes, certainly."

Everybody came back to the place where the corpse lay. La Roque, now seated beside her daughter, had caught hold of her hand, and was staring right before her, with a wandering listless eye.

The two doctors endeavored to lead her away, so that she might not witness the dead girl's removal; but she understood at once what they wanted to do, and, flinging herself on the body, she seized it in both arms. Lying on top of the corpse, she exclaimed:

"You shall not have it—'tis mine—'tis mine now. They have killed her for me, and I want to keep her—you shall not have her——!"

All the men, affected and not knowing how to act, remained standing around her. Renardet fell on his knees, and said to her:

"Listen, La Roque, it is necessary—in order to find out who killed her. Without this it could not be found out. We must make a search for him in order to punish him. When we have found him, we'll give her up to you. I promise you this."

This explanation shook the woman's mind, and a feeling of hatred manifested in her distracted glance.

"So then they'll take him?"

"Yes, I promise you that."

She rose up, deciding to let them do as they liked; but when the captain remarked: " 'Tis surprising that her clothes cannot be found," a new idea, which she had not previously thought of, abruptly found an entrance into her brain, and she asked:

"Where are her clothes? They're mine. I want them. Where have they been put?"

They explained to her that they had not been found, then she called out for them with desperate obstinacy and with repeated moans:

"They're mine—I want them. Where are they? I want them!"

The more they tried to calm her, the more she sobbed, and persisted in her demands. She no longer wanted the body, she insisted on having the clothes, as much perhaps through the unconscious cupidity of a wretched being to whom a piece of silver represents a fortune, as through maternal tenderness.

And when the little body, rolled up in blankets which had been brought out from Renardet's house, had disappeared in the vehicle, the old woman, standing under the trees, held up by the mayor and the captain, exclaimed:

"I have nothing, nothing, nothing in the world, not even her little cap—her little cap."

The curé had just arrived, a young priest already growing stout. He took it on himself to carry off La Roque, and they went away together toward the village. The mother's grief was modified under the sugary words of the clergyman who promised her a thousand compensations. But she incessantly kept repeating: "If I had only her little cap."

This idea now dominated every other.

Before they were out of hearing Renardet exclaimed:

"You will lunch with us, Monsieur l'Abbé—in an hour's time?"

The priest turned his head round, and replied:

"With pleasure, Monsieur le Maire. I'll be with you at twelve."

And they all directed their steps toward the house, whose gray front and large tower, built on the edge of the Brindelle, could be seen through the branches.

The meal lasted a long time. They talked about the crime and everybody was of the same opinion. It had been committed by some tramp passing there by chance while the little girl was bathing.

Then the magistrates returned to Rouy, announcing that they would return next day at an early hour. The doctor and the curé went to their respective homes, while Renardet, after a long walk through the meadows, returned to the wood, where he remained walking till nightfall with slow steps, his hands behind his back.

He went to bed early, and was still asleep next morning when the examining magistrate entered his room. He rubbed his hands together with a self-satisfied air. He said:

"Ha! ha! Still sleeping? Well, my dear fellow, we have news this morning."

The mayor sat up on his bed.

"What pray?"

"Oh! Something strange. You remember well how the mother yesterday clamored for some memento of her daughter, especially her little cap? Well, on opening her door this morning, she found on the threshold her child's two little wooden shoes. This proves that the crime was perpetrated by some one from the district, some one who felt pity for her. Besides, the postman Mederic found and brought me the thimble, the scissors, and the needlecase of the dead girl. So then the man in carrying off the clothes in order to hide them, must have let fall the articles which were in the pocket. As for me, I attach special importance to the wooden shoes, as they indicate a certain moral culture and a faculty for tenderness on the part of the murderer. We will therefore, if you have no objection, pass in review together the principal inhabitants of your district."

The mayor got up. He rang for hot water to shave with, and said:

"With pleasure, but it will take rather a long time, so let us begin at once."

M. Putoin sat astride on a chair, thus pursuing even in a room, his mania for horsemanship. Renardet now covered his chin with a white lather while he looked at himself in the glass; then he sharpened his razor on the strop and went on:

"The principal inhabitant of Carvelin bears the name of Joseph Renardet, mayor, a rich landowner, a rough man who beats guards and coachmen—"

The examining magistrate burst out laughing:

"That's enough; let us pass on to the next."

"The second in importance is ill. Pelledent, his deputy, a rearer of oxen, an equally rich landowner, a crafty peasant, very sly, very close-fisted on every question of money, but incapable in my opinion of having perpetrated such a crime."

M. Putoin said:

"Let us pass on."

Then, while continuing to shave and wash himself, Renardet went on with the moral inspection of all the inhabitants of Carvelin. After two hours' discussion, their suspicions were fixed on three individuals who had hitherto borne a shady reputation—a poacher named Cavalle, a fisher for club and cray-fish named Paquet, and a bull-sticker named Clovis.

2

The search for the perpetrator of the crime lasted all the summer, but he was not discovered. Those who were suspected and those who were arrested easily proved their innocence, and the authorities were compelled to abandon the attempt to capture the criminal.

But the murder seemed to have moved the entire country in a singular fashion. It left a disquietude, a vague fear, a sensation of mysterious terror, springing not merely from the impossibility of discovering any trace of the assassin, but above all from that strange finding of the wooden shoes in front of La Roque's door on the day after the crime. The certainty that the murderer had assisted at the investigation and that he was doubtless still living in the village, left a gloomy impression on every mind, and hung over the neighborhood like a constant menace.

The wood, besides, had become a dreaded spot, a place to be avoided, and supposed to be haunted.

Formerly, the inhabitants used to come and lounge there every Sunday afternoon. They used to sit down on the moss at the foot of the huge trees, or walk along the water's edge watching the trout gliding under the green undergrowth. The boys used to play bowls, hide-and-seek, and other games in certain places where they had up-turned, smoothed out, and leveled the soil, and the girls, in rows of four or five, used to trip along holding one another by the arms, and screaming out with their shrill voices ballads which grated on the ear, disturbed the tranquil air with discord and set the teeth on edge like vinegar. Now nobody ventured into and under the towering trees, as if afraid of finding there some corpse lying on the ground.

Autumn arrived; the leaves began to fall. They fell day and night from the tall trees, whirling round and round to the ground; and the sky could be seen through the bare branches. Sometimes when a gust of wind swept over the tree-tops, the slow, continuous rain suddenly grew heavier, and became a hoarsely growling storm, which drenched the moss with thick yellow water that made the ground swampy and yielding. And the almost imperceptible murmur, the floating, ceaseless whisper, gentle and sad, of this rainfall seemed like a low wail, and the continually falling leaves, like tears, big tears shed by the tall mournful trees, which were weeping, as it were, day and night over the close of the year, over the ending of warm dawns and soft twilights, over the ending of hot breezes and bright suns, and also perhaps over the crime which they had seen committed under the shade of their branches, over the girl violated and killed at their feet. They wept in the silence of the desolate empty wood, the abandoned, dreaded wood, where the soul, the childish soul of the dead little girl must have been wandering all alone.

The Brindelle, swollen by the storms, rushed on more quickly, yellow and angry, between its dry banks, lined with thin, bare willow-hedges.

Renardet suddenly resumed his walks under the trees. Every day, at sunset, he came out of his house, descended the front steps slowly, and entered the wood, in a dreamy fashion with his hands in his pockets. For a long time he would pace over the damp, soft moss, while a legion of rooks, rushing to the spot from all the neighboring haunts in order to rest in the tall summits, spread themselves through space, like an immense mourning veil floating in the wind, uttering violent and sinister screams. Sometimes they would perch on the tangled branches dotting with black spots the red sky, the sky crimsoned with autumn twilight. Then, all of a sudden, they would set off again, croaking frightfully and trailing once more above the wood the long darkness of their flight. Then they would swoop down, at last, on the highest tree-tops, and gradually their cawings would die away, while advancing night merged their black plumes into the blackness of space.

Renardet was still strolling slowly under the trees; then, when the darkness prevented him from walking any longer, he went back to the house, sank all of a heap into his armchair in front of the glowing hearth and dried his feet at the fire.

Now, one morning, an important bit of news was circulated around the district: the mayor was getting his wood cut down.

Twenty woodcutters were already at work. They had commenced at the corner nearest to the house, and they worked rapidly in the master's presence.

At first the loppers climbed up the trunk. Tied to it by a rope collar, they clung round it in the beginning with both arms, then, lifting one leg, struck the tree hard with the edge of a steel instrument attached to each foot. The edge penetrated the wood and remained stuck in it; and the man rose up as if on a step in order to strike with the steel attached to the other foot, and then once more supported himself till he could lift his first foot again.

With every upward movement was slipped higher the rope collar which fastened him to the tree. Over his loins hung and glittered the steel hatchet. He kept continually climbing in easy fashion like some parasite attacking a giant, mounting slowly up the immense trunk, embracing it and spurring it in order to decapitate it.

As soon as he reached the lowest branches, he stopped, detached from his side the sharp ax, and struck. Slowly, methodically, he chopped at the limb close to the trunk. Suddenly the branch cracked, gave way, bent, tore itself off, and fell, grazing the neighboring trees in its fall. Then it crashed down on the ground with a great sound of broken wood, and its lighter branches quivered for a long time.

The soil was covered with fragments which other men cut in their turn, bound in bundles, and piled in heaps, while the trees which were still left standing looked like enormous posts, gigantic forms amputated and shorn by the keen steel axes of the cutters.

When the lopper had finished his task, he left at the top of the straight slender shaft of the tree the rope collar which he had brought up with him, descending again with spur-like prods along the discrowned trunk, which the woodcutters below attacked at the base, striking it with heavy blows which resounded through all the rest of the wood.

When the base of the tree seemed pierced deeply enough, some men commenced dragging, to the accompaniment of a signal cry in which all joined harmoniously, at the rope attached to the top. All of a sudden, the immense column cracked and tumbled to the earth with the dull sound and shock of a distant cannon-shot. Each day the wood grew thinner, losing its trees one by one as an army loses its soldiers.

Renardet no longer walked up and down. He remained from morning till night, contemplating, motionless, with his hands behind his back, the slow death of his wood. When a tree fell, he placed his foot on it as if it were a corpse. Then he raised his eyes to the next with a kind of secret, calm impatience, as if he expected or hoped for something at the end of this massacre.

Meanwhile, they were approaching the place where little Louise Roque had been found. At length, they came to it—one evening, at the hour of twilight.

As it was dark, the sky being overcast, the woodcutters wanted to stop their work, putting off till next day the fall of an enormous beech-tree. But Renardet objected to this, insisting that even at this late hour they should lop and cut down this giant, which had overshadowed and seen the crime.

When the lopper had laid it bare, had finished its toilet for the guillotine, and the woodcutters had sapped its base, five men commenced hauling at the rope attached to the top.

The tree resisted; its powerful trunk, although cut half-way through, was as rigid as iron. The workmen, altogether, with a sort of regular jump, strained at the rope, stooping down to the ground, and they gave vent to a cry with lungs out of breath, so as to indicate and direct their efforts.

Two woodcutters stood close to the giant, with axes in their grip, like two executioners ready to strike once more, and Renardet, motionless, with his hand on the bark, awaited the fall with an uneasy, nervous feeling.

One of the men said to him:

"You're too near, Monsieur le Maire. When it falls, it may hurt you."

He did not reply and did not recoil. He seemed ready to catch the beech-tree in his open arms in order to cast it on the ground like a wrestler.

All at once, at the foot of the tall column of wood there was a shudder which seemed to run to the top, like a painful shiver; it bent slightly, ready to fall, but still resisted. The men, in a state of excitement, stiffened their arms, renewed their efforts with greater vigor, and, just as the tree, breaking, came crashing down, Renardet suddenly made a forward step, then stopped, his shoulders raised to receive the irresistible shock, the mortal blow which would crush him to the earth.

But the beech-tree, having deviated a little, only grazed against his loins, throwing him on his face five metres away.

The workmen rushed forward to lift him up. He had already risen to his knees, stupefied, with wandering eyes, and passing his hand across his forehead, as if he were awaking out of an attack of madness.

When he had got to his feet once more, the men, astonished, questioned him, not being able to understand what he had done. He replied, in faltering tones, that he had had for a moment a fit of abstraction, or rather a return to the days of his childhood, that he imagined he had to pass under that tree, just as street-boys rush in front of vehicles driving rapidly past, that he had played at danger, that, for the past eight days, he felt this desire growing stronger within him, asking himself whether, every time a tree was cracking, was on the point of falling, he could pass beneath it without being touched. It was a piece of stupidity, he confessed; but everyone has these moments of insanity, these temptations to boyish folly.

He made this explanation in a slow tone, searching for his words and speaking in a stupefied fashion.

Then he went off saying:

"Till to-morrow, my friends—till to-morrow."

As soon as he had reached his study, he sat down before his table, which his lamp, covered with a shade, lighted up brightly, and, clasping his hands over his forehead, began to cry.

He remained crying for a long time, then wiped his eyes, raised his head, and looked at the clock. It was not yet six o'clock.

"I have time before dinner."

And he went to the door and locked it. He then came back, and sat down before his table. He pulled out a drawer in the middle of it, and taking from it a revolver, laid it down over his papers, under the glare of the lamp. The barrel of the firearm glittered, and cast reflections which resembled flames.

Renardet gazed at it for some time with the uneasy glance of a drunken man; then he rose and began to pace up and down the room.

He walked from one end of the apartment to the other, stopped from time to time and started to pace up and down again a moment afterward. Suddenly, he opened the door of his dressing-room, steeped a towel in the water-jug and moistened his forehead, as he had done on the morning of the crime.

Then he began to walk up and down once more. Each time he passed the table the gleaming revolver attracted his glance, and tempted his hand; but he kept watching the clock, thinking:

"I still have time."

It struck half past six. Then he took up the revolver, opened his mouth wide with a frightful grimace, and stuck the barrel into it, as if he wanted to swallow it. He remained in this position for some seconds without moving, his finger on the lock; then, suddenly, seized with a shudder of horror, he dropped the pistol on the carpet, and fell back on his armchair, sobbing:

"I can't. I dare not! My God! My God! My God! How can I have the courage to kill myself?"

There was a knock at the door. He rose up in a stupefied condition. A servant said:

"Monsieur's dinner is ready."

He replied: "All right. I'm going down."

He picked up the revolver, locked it up again in the drawer, then looked at himself in the glass over the mantelpiece to see whether his face did not look too much troubled. It was as red as usual, a little redder perhaps. That was all. He went down, and seated himself before the table.

He ate slowly, like a man who wants to drag on the meal, who does not want to be alone with himself.

Then he smoked several pipes in the dining-room while the plates were being removed. After that, he went back to his room.

As soon as he was alone, he looked under his bed, opened all his cupboards, explored every corner, rummaged through all the furniture. Then he lighted the tapers over the mantelpiece, and, turning round several times, ran his eye all over the apartment in an anguish of terror that made his face lose its color, for he knew well that he was going to see her, as he did every night—little Louise Roque, the little girl he had violated and afterward strangled.

Every night the odious vision came back again. First, it sounded in his ears like the snorting that is made by a thrashing machine or the distant passage of a train over a bridge. Then he commenced to pant, to feel suffocated, and had to unbutton his shirt-collar and loosen his belt. He moved about to make his blood circulate, he tried to read, he attempted to sing. It was in vain. His thoughts, in spite of himself, went back to the day of the murder, made him go through it again in all its most secret details, with all the violent emotions he had experienced from first to last.

He had felt on rising up that morning, the morning of the horrible day, a little vertigo and dizziness which he attributed to the heat, so that he remained in his room till the time came for lunch.

After the meal he had taken a siesta, then, toward the close of the afternoon, he had gone out to breathe the fresh, soothing breeze under the trees in the wood.

But, as soon as he was outside, the heavy scorching air of the plain oppressed him more. The sun, still high in the heavens, poured out on the parched, dry, and thirsty soil, floods of ardent light. Not a breath of wind stirred the leaves. Beasts and birds, even the grasshoppers, were silent. Renardet reached the tall trees, and began to walk over the moss where the Brindelle sent forth a slight, cool vapor under the immense roof of trees. But he felt ill at ease. It seemed to him that an unknown, invisible hand was squeezing his neck, and he could scarcely think rationally, having usually few ideas in his head. For the last three months, only one thought haunted him, the thought of marrying again. He suffered from living alone, suffered from it morally and physically. Accustomed for ten years past to feeling a woman near him, habituated to her presence every moment, to her embrace each successive day, he had need, an imperious and perplexing need, of incessant contact with her and the regular touch of her lips. Since Madame Renardet's death, he had suffered continually without knowing why, had suffered from not feeling her dress brush against his legs every day, and, above all, from no longer being able to grow calm and languid in her arms. He had been scarcely six months a widower, and he had already been looking out through the district for some young girl or some widow he might marry when his period of mourning was at an end.

He had a chaste soul, but it was lodged in a vigorous Herculean body, and carnal images began to disturb his sleep and his vigils. He drove them away; they came back again; and he murmured from time to time, smiling at himself:

"Here I am, like St. Antony."

Having had this morning several besetting visions, the desire suddenly came into his breast to bathe in the Brindelle in order to refresh himself and reduce his feverishness.

He knew, a little further on, of a large deep spot where the people of the neighborhood came sometimes to take a dip in the summer. He went there.

Thick willow-trees hid this clear pool of water where the current rested and went to sleep for a little while before starting on its way again. Renardet, as he appeared, thought he heard a light sound, a faint plash which was not that of the stream or the banks. He softly put aside the leaves and looked. A little girl, quite naked in the transparent water, was beating the waves with both hands, dancing about in them a little, and dipping herself with pretty movements. She was not a child nor was she yet a woman. She was plump and well formed, yet had an air of youthful precocity, as of one who had grown rapidly, and who was now almost ripe. He no longer moved, overcome with surprise, with a pang of desire, holding his breath with a strange, poignant emotion. He remained there, his heart beating as if one of his sensual dreams had just been realized; as if an impure fairy had conjured up before him this young creature, this little rustic Venus born of the river foam, who was making his heart beat faster.

Suddenly the little girl came out of the water, and without seeing him came over to where he stood, looking for her clothes in order to dress herself. While she was gradually approaching him with little hesitating steps, through fear of the sharp pointed stones, he felt himself pushed toward her by an irresistible force, by a bestial transport of passion, which stirred up all his carnality, stupefied his soul, and made him tremble from head to foot.

She remained standing some seconds behind the willow-tree which concealed him from view. Then, losing his reason entirely, he opened the branches, rushed on her, and seized her in his arms. She fell, too scared to offer any resistance, too much terror-stricken to cry out, and he possessed her without understanding what he was doing.

He woke up from his crime, as one wakes out of a nightmare. The child burst out weeping.

He said:

"Hold your tongue! Hold your tongue! I'll give you money."

But she did not hear him, she went on sobbing.

He went on:

"Come now, hold your tongue! Do hold your tongue. Keep quiet."

She still kept shrieking, writhing in the effort to get away from him. He suddenly realized that he was ruined, and he caught her by the neck to stop her from uttering these heartrending, dreadful screams. As she continued to struggle with the desperate strength of a being who is flying from death, he pressed his enormous hands on that little throat swollen with cries. In a few seconds he had strangled her, so furiously did he grip her, yet not intending to kill but only to silence her.

Then he rose up overwhelmed with horror.

She lay before him with her face bleeding and blackened. He was going to rush away when there sprang up in his agitated soul the mysterious and undefined instinct that guides all beings in the hour of danger.

It was necessary to throw the body into the water; but he did not; another impulse drove him toward the clothes, of which he made a thin parcel. Then, as he had a piece of twine, he tied it up and hid it in a deep portion of the stream, under the trunk of a tree, the foot of which was immersed in the Brindelle.

Then he went off at a rapid pace, reached the meadows, took a wide turn in order to show himself to peasants who dwelt some distance away on the opposite side of the district, and came back to dine at the usual hour, telling his servants all that was supposed to have happened during his walk.

He slept, however, that night—slept with a heavy, brutish sleep, such as the sleep of persons condemned to death must occasionally be. He opened his eyes at the first glimmer of dawn, and waited, tortured by the fear of having his crime discovered, for his usual waking hour.

Then he would have to be present at all the stages of the inquiry as to the cause of death. He did so after the fashion of a somnambulist, in a hallucination which showed him things and human beings in a sort of dream, in a cloud of intoxication, with that dubious sense of unreality which perplexes the mind at times of the greatest catastrophes.

The only thing that pierced his heart was La Roque's cry of anguish. At that moment he felt inclined to cast himself at the old woman's feet, and to exclaim: "It is I."

But he restrained himself. He went back, however, during the night, to fish up the dead girl's wooden shoes, in order to carry them to her mother's threshold.

As long as the inquiry lasted, so long as it was necessary to guide and aid justice, he was calm, master of himself, sly and smiling. He discussed quietly with the magistrates all the suppositions that passed through their minds, combated their opinions, and demolished their arguments. He even took a keen and mournful pleasure in disturbing their investigations, in confuting their ideas, in showing the innocence of those whom they suspected.

But from the day when the investigation came to a close, he became gradually nervous, more excitable than he had been before, although he mastered his irritability. Sudden noises made him jump up with fear; he shuddered at the slightest thing, trembled sometimes from head to foot when a fly alighted on his forehead. Then he was seized with an imperious desire for motion, which compelled him to keep continually on foot, and made him remain up whole nights walking to and fro in his own room.

It was not that he was goaded by remorse. His brutal mind did not lend itself to any shade of sentiment or of moral terror. A man of energy and even of violence, born to make war, to ravage conquered countries, and to massacre the vanquished, full of the savage instincts of the hunter and the fighter, he scarcely took count of human life. Though he respected the Church through policy, he believed neither in God nor in the devil, expecting consequently in another life neither chastisement nor recompense for his acts. As his sole creed, he retained a vague philosophy composed of all the ideas of the encyclopedists of the last century. He regarded religion as a moral sanction of the law, both one and the other having been invented by men to regulate social relations.

To kill anyone in a duel, or in a battle, or in a quarrel, or by accident, or for the sake of revenge, or even through bravado, would have seemed to him an amusing and clever thing, and would not have left more impression on his mind than a shot fired at a hare; but he had experienced a profound emotion at the murder of this child. He had, in the first place, perpetrated it in the distraction of an irresistible gust of passion, in a sort of sensual tempest that had overpowered his reason. And he had cherished in his heart, cherished in his flesh, cherished on his lips, cherished even to the very tips of his murderous fingers, a kind of bestial love, as well as a feeling of horror and grief, toward this little girl he had surprised and basely killed. Every moment his thoughts returned to that horrible scene, and, though he endeavored to drive away the picture from his mind, though he put it aside with terror, with disgust, he felt it surging through his soul, moving about in him, waiting incessantly for the moment to reappear.

Then, in the night, he was afraid, afraid of the shadows falling around him. He did not yet know why the darkness seemed frightful to him; but he instinctively feared it, felt that it was peopled with terrors. The bright daylight did not lend itself to fears. Things and beings were seen there; there only natural things and beings which could exhibit themselves in the light of day could be met. But the night, the impenetrable night, thicker than walls, and empty, the infinite night, so black, so vast, in which one might brush against frightful things, the night when one feels that mysterious terror is wandering, prowling about, appeared to him to conceal an unknown danger, close and menacing.

What was it?

He knew it before long. As he sat in his armchair, rather late, one evening when he could not sleep, he thought he saw the curtain of his window move. He waited, in an uneasy state of mind, with beating heart. The drapery did not stir, then, all of a sudden it moved once more. He did not venture to rise up; he no longer ventured to breathe, and yet he was brave. He had often fought, and he would have liked to catch thieves in his house.

Was it true that this curtain did move? he asked himself, fearing that his eyes had deceived him. It was, moreover, such a slight thing, a gentle flutter of lace, a kind of trembling in its folds, less than such an undulation as is caused by the wind.

Renardet sat still, with staring eyes, and outstretched neck. Then he sprang to his feet abruptly, ashamed of his fear, took four steps, seized the drapery with both hands, and pulled it wide apart. At first, he saw nothing but darkened glass, resembling plates of glittering ink. The night, the vast, impenetrable night stretched out before him as far as the invisible horizon. He remained standing in front of the illimitable shadow, and suddenly perceived a light, a moving light, which seemed some distance away.

Then he put his face close to the windowpane, thinking that a person looking for crayfish might be poaching in the Brindelle, for it was past midnight. The light rose up at the edge of the stream, under the trees. As he was not yet able to see clearly, Renardet placed his hands over his eyes. Suddenly this light became an illumination, and he beheld little Louise Roque naked and bleeding on the moss. He recoiled frozen with horror, sank into his chair and fell backward. He remained there some minutes, his soul in distress; then he sat up and began to reflect. He had had a hallucination—that was all: a hallucination due to the fact that a marauder of the night was walking with a lantern in his hand near the water's edge. What was there astonishing, besides, in the circumstance that the recollection of his crime should sometimes bring before him the vision of the dead girl?

He rose up, swallowed a glass of wine and sat down again. He thought:

"What am I to do if this came back?"

And it did come back; he felt it; he was sure of it. Already his glance was drawn toward the window; it called him; it attracted him. In order to avoid looking at it, he turned aside his chair. Then, he took a book and tried to read; but it seemed to him that he presently heard something stirring behind him, and he swung round his armchair on one foot.

The curtain still moved—unquestionably, it did move this time; he could no longer have any doubt about it.

He rushed forward and seized it in his grasp so violently that he knocked it down with its fastener. Then, he eagerly pressed his face against the glass. He saw nothing. All was black without; and he breathed with the delight of a man whose life has just been saved.

Then he went back to his chair, and sat down again; but almost immediately he felt a longing to look out through the window once more. Since the curtain had fallen, the space in front of him made a sort of dark patch, fascinating and terrible, on the obscure landscape. In order not to yield to this dangerous temptation, he took off his clothes, extinguished the lamp, and lay down, shutting his eyes.

Lying on his back motionless, his skin hot and moist, he awaited sleep. Suddenly a great gleam of light flashed across his eyelids. He opened them believing that his dwelling was on fire. All was black as before, and he leaned on his elbow in order to try to distinguish his window, which had still for him an unconquerable attraction. By dint of straining his eyes, he could perceive some stars, and he arose, groped his way across the room, discovered the panes with his outstretched hands, and placed his forehead close to them. There below, under the trees, the body of the little girl glittered like phosphorus, lighting up the surrounding darkness.

Renardet uttered a cry and rushed toward his bed, where he lay till morning, his head hidden under the pillow.

From that moment, his life became intolerable. He passed his days in apprehension of each succeeding night; and each night the vision came back again. As soon as he had locked himself up in his room, he strove to struggle; but in vain. An irresistible force lifted him up and pushed him against the glass, as if to call the phantom, and before long he saw it lying in the spot where the crime was committed, lying with arms and legs outspread, just in the way the body had been found.

Then the dead girl rose up and came toward him with little steps just as the child had done when she came out of the river. She advanced quietly, passing straight across the grass, and over the border of withered flowers. Then she rose up into the air toward Renardet's window. She came toward him, as she had come on the day of the crime. And the man recoiled before the apparition—he retreated to his bed, and sank down upon it, knowing well that the little one had entered the room, and that she now was standing behind the curtain, which presently moved. And until daybreak, he kept staring at this curtain, with a fixed glance, ever waiting to see his victim depart.

But she did not show herself any more; she remained there behind the curtain which quivered tremulously now and then.

And Renardet, his fingers clinging to the bedclothes, squeezed them as he had squeezed the throat of little Louise Roque.

He heard the clock striking the hours; and in the stillness the pendulum kept time with the loud beating of his heart. And he suffered, the wretched man, more than any man had ever suffered before.

Then, as soon as a white streak of light on the ceiling announced the approaching day, he felt himself free, alone at last, alone in his room; and then he went to sleep. He slept some hours—a restless, feverish sleep in which he retraced in dreams the horrible vision of the night just past.

When, later on, he went down to breakfast, he felt exhausted as if after prodigious fatigue; and he scarcely ate anything, haunted as he was by the fear of what he had seen the night before.

He knew, however, that it was not an apparition—that the dead do not come back, and that his sick soul, possessed by one thought alone, by an indelible remembrance, was the only cause of his punishment, was the only evoker of that awful image, brought back by it to life, called up by it and raised by it before his eyes, in which the ineffaceable resemblance remained imprinted. But he knew, too, that he could not cure it, that he could never escape from the savage persecution of his memory; and he resolved to die, rather than endure these tortures any longer.

Then, he pondered how he would kill himself. He wished for some simple and natural death which would preclude the idea of suicide. For he clung to his reputation, to the name bequeathed to him by his ancestors; and if there was any suspicion as to the cause of his death, people's thoughts might be perhaps directed toward the mysterious crime, toward the murderer who could not be found, and they would not hesitate to accuse him.

A strange idea came into his head, that of letting himself be crushed by the tree at the foot of which he had murdered little Louise Roque. So he determined to have the wood cut down and to simulate an accident. But the beech-tree refused to smash his ribs.

Returning to his house, a prey to utter despair, he had snatched up his revolver, and then he did not dare to fire it.

The dinner bell summoned him. He could eat nothing, and went upstairs again. But he did not know what he was going to do. Now that he had escaped the first time, he felt himself a coward. Presently, he would be ready, fortified, decided, master of his courage and of his resolution; just now, he was weak, and feared death as much as he did the dead girl.

He faltered out to himself:

"I will not venture it again—I will not venture it."

Then he glanced with terror, first at the revolver on the table, and next at the curtain which hid his window. It seemed to him, moreover, that something horrible would occur as soon as his life was ended. Something? What? A meeting with her, perhaps! She was watching for him; she was waiting for him; she was calling him; and her object was to seize him in her turn, to exhibit herself to him every night so that she might draw him toward the doom that would avenge her, and lead him to death.

He began to cry like a child, repeating:

"I will not venture it again—I will not venture it."

Then he fell on his knees, and murmured: "My God! my God!" without believing, nevertheless, in God. He no longer dared, in fact, to look out through his window where he knew the apparition was visible, nor at the table where his revolver gleamed.

When he had risen up, he said:

"This cannot last; there must be an end of it."

The sound of his voice in the silent room made a shiver of fear pass through his limbs, but, as he could not come to a decision, as he felt certain that his finger would always refuse to pull the trigger of his revolver, he turned round to hide his head under the bedclothes, and to plunge into reflection.

He would have to find some way in which he could force himself to die, to invent some device against himself, which would not permit of any hesitation on his part, any delay, any possible regrets. He began to envy condemned criminals who are led to the scaffold surrounded by soldiers. Oh! if he could only beg of some one to shoot him; if he could, confessing the state of his soul, confessing his crime to a sure friend who would never divulge it, obtain from him death.

But from whom could he ask this terrible service? From whom? He cast about for one among his friends whom he knew intimately. The doctor? No, he would talk about it afterward, most certainly. And suddenly a fantastic idea entered his mind. He would write to the examining magistrate, who was on terms of close friendship with him and would denounce himself as the perpetrator of the crime. He would in this letter confess everything, revealing how his soul had been tortured, how he had resolved to die, how he had hesitated about carrying out his resolution, and what means he had employed to strengthen his failing courage. And in the name of their old friendship he would implore of the other to destroy the letter as soon as he had ascertained that the culprit had inflicted justice on himself. Renardet could rely on this magistrate; he knew him to be sure, discreet, incapable of even an idle word. He was one of those men who have an inflexible conscience, governed, directed, regulated by their reason alone.

Scarcely had he formed this project when a strange feeling of joy took possession of his heart. He was calm now. He would write his letter slowly, then at daybreak he would deposit it in the box nailed to the wall in his office, then he would ascend his tower to watch for the postman's arrival, and when the man in the blue blouse came in sight, he would cast himself headlong on to the rocks on which the foundations rested. First he would take care to be seen by the workmen who were cutting down his wood. He would then climb to the parapet some distance up which bore the flagstaff displayed on *fête* days. He would smash this pole with a shake and precipitate it along with him.

Who would suspect that it was not an accident? And he would be dashed to pieces, having regard to his weight and the height of the tower.

Presently he got out of bed, went over to the table, and began to write. He omitted nothing, not a single detail of the crime, not a single detail of the torments of his heart, and he ended by announcing that he had passed sentence on himself—that he was going to execute the criminal—and begged of his friend, his old friend, to be careful that there should never be any stain on his memory.

When he had finished his letter, he saw that the day had dawned.

He closed it, sealed it, and wrote the address; then he descended with light steps, hurried toward the little white box fastened to the wall in the corner of the farmhouse, and when he had thrown into it the fatal paper which made his hand tremble, he came back quickly, shot the bolts of the great door, and climbed up to his tower to wait for the passing of the postman, who would convey his death sentence.

He felt self-possessed, now. Liberated! Saved!

A cold dry wind, an icy wind, passed across his face. He inhaled it eagerly, with open mouth, drinking in its chilling kiss. The sky was red, with a burning red, the red of winter, and all the plain whitened with frost glistened under the first rays of the sun, as if it had been powdered with bruised glass.

Renardet, standing up, with his head bare, gazed at the vast tract of country before him, the meadow to the left, and to the right the village whose chimneys were beginning to smoke with the preparations for the morning meal. At his feet he saw the Brindelle flowing toward the rocks, where he would soon be crushed to death. He felt himself reborn on that beautiful frosty morning, full of strength, full of life. The light bathed him and penetrated him like a newborn hope. A thousand recollections assailed him, recollections of similar mornings, of rapid walks, the hard earth which rang under his footsteps, of happy chases on the edges of pools where wild ducks sleep. At the good things that he loved, the good things of existence rushed into memory, penetrated him with fresh desires, awakened all the vigorous appetites of his active, powerful body.

And he was about to die? Why? He was going to kill himself stupidly, because he was afraid of a shadow—afraid of nothing. He was still rich and in the prime of life! What folly! All he wanted was distraction, absence, a voyage in order to forget.

This night even he had not seen the little girl because his mind was preoccupied, and so had wandered toward some other subject. Perhaps he would not see her any more? And even if she still haunted him in his house, certainly she would not follow him elsewhere! The earth was wide, the future was long.

Why die?

His glance traveled across the meadows, and he perceived a blue spot in the path which wound along-side of the Brindelle. It was Mederic coming to bring letters from the town and to carry away those of the village.

Renardet got a start, a sensation of pain shot through his breast, and he rushed toward the winding staircase to get back his letter, to demand it back from the postman. Little did it matter to him now whether he was seen. He hurried across the grass moistened by the light frost of the previous night, and he arrived in front of the box in the corner of the farmhouse exactly at the same time as the letter-carrier.

The latter had opened the little wooden door, and drew forth the papers deposited there by the inhabitants of the locality.

Renardet said to him:

"Good morrow, Mederic."

"Good morrow, M'sieu' le Maire."

"I say, Mederic, I threw a letter into the box that I want back again. I came to ask you to give it back to me."

"That's all right, M'sieu' le Maire—you'll get it."

And the postman raised his eyes. He stood petrified at the sight of Renardet's face. The mayor's cheeks were purple, his eyes were glaring with black circles round them as if they were sunk in his head, his hair was all tangled, his beard untrimmed, his necktie unfastened. It was evident that he had not gone to bed.

The postman asked:

"Are you ill, M'sieu' le Maire?"

The other suddenly comprehending that his appearance must be unusual, lost countenance and faltered:

"Oh! no—oh! no. Only I jumped out of bed to ask you for this letter. I was asleep. You understand?"

Said Mederic: "What letter?"

"The one you are going to give back to me."

Mederic now began to hesitate. The mayor's attitude did not strike him as natural. There was perhaps a secret in that letter, a political secret. He knew Renardet was not a Republican and he knew all the tricks and chicaneries employed at elections.

He asked:

"To whom is it addressed, this letter of yours?"

"To M. Putoin, the examining magistrate—you know my friend, M. Putoin, well!"

The postman searched through the papers, and found the one asked for. Then he began looking at it, turning it round and round between his fingers, much perplexed, much troubled by the fear of committing a grave offense or of making an enemy for himself of the mayor.

Seeing his hesitation, Renardet made a movement for the purpose of seizing the letter and snatching it away from him. This abrupt action convinced Mederic that some important secret was at stake and made him resolve to do his duty, cost what it might.

So he flung the letter into his bag and fastened it up, with the reply:

"No, I can't, M'sieu' le Maire. From the moment it is addressed and sent to the magistrate, I can't."

A dreadful pang wrung Renardet's heart, and he murmured:

"Why, you know me well. You are even able to recognize my handwriting. I tell you I want that paper."

"I can't."

"Look here, Mederic, you know that I'm incapable of deceiving you—I tell you I want it."

"No, I can't."

A tremor of rage passed through Renardet's soul.

"Damn it all, take care! You know that I don't go in for chaffing, and that I could get you out of your job, my good fellow, and without much delay either. And then, I am the mayor of the district after all; and I now order you to give me back that paper."

The postman answered firmly:

"No, I can't, M'sieu' le Maire."

Thereupon Renardet, losing his head, caught hold of the postman's arms in order to take away his bag; but, freeing himself by a strong effort, and springing backward, the letter-carrier raised his holly stick. Without losing his temper, he said emphatically:

"Don't touch me, M'sieu' le Maire, or I'll strike. Take care, I'm only doing my duty!"

Feeling that he was lost, Renardet suddenly became humble, gentle, appealing to him like a crying child:

"Look here, look here, my friend, give me back that letter, and I'll give you money. Stop! Stop! I'll give you a hundred francs, you understand—a hundred francs!"

The postman turned on his heel and started on his journey.

Renardet followed him, out of breath, faltering:

"Mederic, Mederic, listen! I'll give you a thousand francs, you understand—a thousand francs."

The postman still went on without giving any answer.

Renardet went on:

"I'll make your fortune, you understand—whatever you wish—fifty thousand francs—fifty thousand francs—fifty thousand francs for that letter! What does it matter to you? You won't? Well, a hundred thousand—I say—a hundred thousand francs—a hundred thousand francs."

The postman turned back, his face hard, his eyes severe:

"Enough of this, or else I'll repeat to the magistrate everything you have just said to me."

Renardet stopped abruptly. It was all over. He turned back and rushed toward his house, running like a hunted animal.

Then, in his turn, Mederic stopped, and watched this flight with stupefaction. He saw the mayor re-entering his own house and he waited still as if something astonishing was about to happen.

Presently the tall form of Renardet appeared on the summit of the Fox's Tower. He ran round the platform like a madman. Then he seized the flagstaff and shook it furiously without succeeding in breaking it; then, all of a sudden, like a swimmer taking a plunge, he dived into the air with his two hands in front of him.

Mederic rushed forward to give succor. As he crossed the park, he saw the woodcutters going to work. He called out to them, telling them an accident had occurred, and at the foot of the walls they found a bleeding body the head of which was crushed on a rock. The Brindelle surrounded this rock, and over its clear, calm waters, swollen at this point, could be seen a long, thin, red stream of mingled brains and blood.

MAUPASSANT: *Little Louise Roque*

1. *At what specific point in the story did you suspect the mayor of the crime? Why, at an early point, does the author reveal the identity of the slayer?*

2. *Why is the character of the postman, who seems to be little more than the counterpart of the messenger in the Greek plays, developed in some detail at the beginning of the story?*

3. *What is the significance of the river Brindelle in the story?*

4. *What is the purpose of the tree-cutting episode? What is the significance of the images that Maupassant creates? Do they work? Why does the mayor place himself before a falling tree? If you have read D. H. Lawrence's "The Fox," compare the two incidents.*

5. *Why does the murder of the child so upset the mayor when killing itself is not repugnant to him?*

6. *Has Maupassant succeeded in transforming a grisly episode into a moving tale? If you think he succeeds, how does he do it? Where does the story fail? Can any subject be suitable for fiction if it is sensitively and effectively handled?*

7. *Is Maupassant suggesting that respectability may cloak the worst of criminals? That many criminals escape notice because of their social position? Or that the ordinary person may have moments of criminal passion without having a criminal temperament? In Unamuno's story, Dr. Montarco makes a simple distinction between the sane and the insane. Does it have any relevance to this story?*

Joseph Conrad

IL CONDE

> *Joseph Conrad was born in Berdiczew, Poland, on December 3, 1857, and died in England on August 3, 1924. Trained as a seaman, he turned to fiction under the encouragement of Edward Garnett, then a publisher's reader. Once he gave up thoughts of returning to the sea, Conrad rapidly published a large number of novels and stories which brought him critical acclaim, although popular success was not to come until later with the publication of* Chance *(1914) and* Victory *(1915). The turning point in his career came with the writing of* The Nigger of the "Narcissus" *(1897), which indicated a marked development in his fiction. In the next ten or so years, he wrote most of his major works: "Heart of Darkness" (1899),* Lord Jim *(1900),* Nostromo *(1904),* The Secret Agent *(1907) and* Under Western Eyes *(1911). Conceived and written during this period, "Il Conde" contains in miniature several of his most important themes.*

"Vedi Napoli e poi mori."

THE first time we got into conversation was in the National Museum in Naples, in the rooms on the ground floor containing the famous collection of bronzes from Herculaneum and Pompeii: that marvelous legacy of antique art whose delicate perfection has been preserved for us by the catastrophic fury of a volcano.

He addressed me first, over the celebrated Resting Hermes which we had been looking at side by side. He said the right things about that wholly admirable piece. Nothing profound. His taste was natural rather than cultivated. He had obviously seen many fine things in his life and appreciated them; but he had no jargon of a dilettante or the connoisseur. A hateful tribe. He spoke like a fairly intelligent man of the world, a perfectly unaffected gentleman.

We had known each other by sight for some few days past. Staying in the same hotel—good, but not extravagantly up to date—I had noticed him in the vestibule going in and out. I judged he was an old and valued client. The bow of the hotelkeeper was cordial in its deference, and he acknowledged it with familiar courtesy. For the servants he was *Il Conde*. There was some squabble over a man's parasol—yellow silk with white lining sort of thing—the waiter had discovered abandoned outside the dining-room door. Our gold-laced doorkeeper recognized it and I heard him directing one of the lift boys to run after *Il Conde* with it. Perhaps he was the only count staying in the hotel, or perhaps he had the distinction of being *the* Count *par excellence*, conferred upon him because of his tried fidelity to the house.

Having conversed at the Museo—(and by the by he had expressed his dislike of the busts and statues of Roman emperors in the gallery of marbles: their faces were too vigorous, too pronounced for him)—having conversed already in the morning I did not think I was intruding when in the evening, finding the dining room very full, I proposed to share his little table. Judging by the quiet urbanity of his consent he did not think so either. His smile was very attractive.

He dined in an evening waistcoat and a "smoking" (he called it so) with a black tie. All this of very good cut, not new—just as these things should be. He was, morning or evening, very correct in his dress. I have no doubt that his whole existence had been correct, well ordered and conventional, undisturbed by startling events. His white hair brushed upwards off a lofty forehead gave him the air of an idealist, of an imaginative man. His white mustache, heavy but carefully trimmed and arranged, was not unpleasantly tinted a golden yellow in the middle. The faint scent of some very good perfume, and of good cigars (that last an odor quite remarkable to come upon in Italy) reached me across the table. It was in his eyes that his age showed most. They were a little weary with creased eyelids. He must have been sixty or a couple of years more. And he was communicative. I would not go so far as to call it garrulous—but distinctly communicative.

He had tried various climates, of Abbazia, of the Riviera, of other places, too, he told me, but the only one which suited him was the climate of the Gulf of Naples. The ancient Romans, who, he pointed out to me were men expert in the art of living, knew very well what they were doing when they built their villas on these shores, in Baiae, in Vico, in Capri. They came down to this seaside in search of health, bringing with them their trains of mimes and flute-players to amuse their leisure. He thought it extremely probable that the Romans of the higher classes were specially predisposed to painful rheumatic affections.

This was the only personal opinion I heard him express. It was based on no special erudition. He knew no more of the Romans than an average informed man of the world is expected to know. He argued from personal experience. He had suffered himself from a painful and dangerous rheumatic affection till he found relief in this particular spot of Southern Europe.

This was three years ago, and ever since he had taken up his quarters on the shores of the gulf, either in one of the hotels in Sorrento or hiring a small villa in Capri. He had a piano, a few books; picked up transient acquaintances of a day, week, or month in the stream of travelers from all Europe. One can imagine him going out for his walks in the streets and lanes, becoming known to beggars, shopkeepers, children, country people; talking amiably over the walls to the *contadini*—and coming back to his rooms or his villa to sit before the piano, with his white hair brushed up and his thick orderly mustache, "to make a little music for myself." And, of course, for a change there was Naples near by—life, movement, animation, opera. A little amusement, as he said, is necessary for health. Mimes and flute-players, in fact. Only unlike the magnates of ancient Rome, he had no affairs of the city to call him away from these moderate delights. He had no affairs at all. Probably he had never had any grave affairs to attend to in his life. It was a kindly existence, with its joys and sorrows regulated by the course of Nature—marriages, births, deaths—ruled by the prescribed usages of good society and protected by the State.

He was a widower; but in the months of July and August he ventured to cross the Alps for six weeks on a visit to his married daughter. He told me her name. It was that of a very aristocratic family. She had a castle—in Bohemia, I think. This is as near as I ever came to ascertaining his nationality. His own name, strangely enough, he never mentioned. Perhaps he thought I had seen in to the published list. Truth to say, I never looked. At any rate, he was a good European—he spoke four languages to my certain knowledge—and a man of fortune. Not of great fortune evidently and appropriately. I imagine that to be extremely rich would have appeared to him improper, *outré*—too blatant altogether. And obviously, too, the fortune was not of his making. The making of a fortune cannot be achieved without some roughness. It is a matter of temperament. His nature was too kindly for strife. In the course of conversation he mentioned his estate quite by the way, in reference to that painful and alarming rheumatic affection. One year, staying incautiously beyond the Alps as late as the middle of September, he had been laid up for three months in that lonely country house with no one but his valet and the caretaking couple to attend to him. Because, as he expressed it, he "kept no establishment there." He had only gone for a couple of days to confer with his land agent. He promised himself never to be so imprudent in the future. The first weeks of September would find him on the shores of his beloved gulf.

Sometimes in traveling one comes upon such lonely men, whose only business is to wait for the unavoidable. Deaths and marriages have made a solitude round them, and one really cannot blame their endeavors to make the waiting as easy as possible. As he remarked to me, "At my time of life freedom from physical pain is a very important matter."

It must not be imagined that he was a wearisome hypochondriac. He was really much too well bred to be a nuisance. He had an eye for the small weaknesses of humanity. But it was a good-natured eye. He made a restful, easy, pleasant companion for the hours between dinner and bedtime. We spent three evenings together, and then I had to leave Naples in a hurry to look after a friend who had fallen seriously ill in Taormina. Having nothing to do, *Il Conde* came to see me off at the station. I was somewhat upset, and his idleness was always ready to take a kindly form. He was by no means an indolent man.

He went along the train peering into the carriages for a good seat for me, and then remained talking cheerily from below. He declared he would miss me that evening very much and announced his intention of going after dinner to listen to the band in the public garden, the Villa Nazionale. He would amuse himself by hearing excellent music and looking at the best society. There would be a lot of people, as usual.

I seem to see him yet—his raised face with a friendly smile under the thick mustaches, and his kind, fatigued eyes. As the train began to move, he addressed me in two languages: first in French, saying, *"Bon voyage"*; then in his very good, somewhat emphatic English, encouragingly, because he could see my concern: "All will—be—well—yet!"

My friend's illness having taken a decidedly favorable turn, I returned to Naples on the tenth day. I cannot say I had given much thought to *Il Conde* during my absence, but entering the dining room I looked for him in his habitual place. I had an idea he might have gone back to Sorrento to his piano and his books and his fishing. He was great friends with all the boatmen, and fished a good deal with lines from a boat. But I made out his white head in the crowd of heads, and even from a distance noticed something unusual in his attitude. Instead of sitting erect, gazing all round with alert urbanity, he drooped over his plate. I stood opposite him for some time before he looked up, a little wildly, if such a strong word can be used in connection with his correct appearance.

"Ah, my dear sir! Is it you?" he greeted me. "I hope all is well."

He was very nice about my friend. Indeed, he was always nice, with the niceness of people whose hearts are genuinely humane. But this time it cost him an effort. His attempts at general conversation broke down into dullness. It occurred to me he might have been indisposed. But before I could frame the inquiry he muttered:

"You find me here very sad."

"I am sorry for that," I said. "You haven't had bad news, I hope?"

It was very kind of me to take an interest. No. It was not that. No bad news, thank God. And he became very still as if holding his breath. Then, leaning forward a little, and in an odd tone of awed embarrassment, he took me into his confidence.

"The truth is that I have had a very—a very—how shall I say?—abominable adventure happen to me."

The energy of the epithet was sufficiently startling in that man of moderate feelings and toned-down vocabulary. The word unpleasant I should have thought would have fitted amply the worst experience likely to befall a man of his stamp. And an adventure, too. Incredible! But it is in human nature to believe the worst; and I confess I eyed him stealthily, wondering what he had been up to. In a moment, however, my unworthy suspicions vanished. There was a fundamental refinement of nature about the man which made me dismiss all idea of some more or less disreputable scrape.

"It is very serious. Very serious." He went on, nervously. "I will tell you after dinner, if you will allow me."

I expressed my perfect acquiescence by a little bow, nothing more. I wished him to understand that I was not likely to hold him to that offer, if he thought better of it later on. We talked of indif-

Il Conde [165

ferent things, but with a sense of difficulty quite unlike our former easy, gossipy intercourse. The hand raising a piece of bread to his lips, I noticed, trembled slightly. This symptom, in regard to my reading of the man, was no less than startling.

In the smoking room he did not hang back at all. Directly we had taken our usual seats he leaned sideways over the arm of his chair and looked straight into my eyes earnestly.

"You remember," he began, "that day you went away? I told you then I would go to the Villa Nazionale to hear some music in the evening."

I remembered. His handsome old face, so fresh for his age, unmarked by any trying experience, appeared haggard for an instant. It was like the passing of a shadow. Returning his steadfast gaze, I took a sip of my black coffee. He was systematically minute in his narrative, simply in order, I think, not to let his excitement get the better of him.

After leaving the railway station, he had an ice, and read the paper in a café. Then he went back to the hotel, dressed for dinner, and dined with a good appetite. After dinner he lingered in the hall (there were chairs and tables there) smoking his cigar; talked to the little girl of the Primo Tenore of the San Carlo Theater, and exchanged a few words with that "amiable lady," the wife of the Primo Tenore. There was no performance that evening, and these people were going to the Villa also. They went out of the hotel. Very well.

At the moment of following their example—it was half-past nine already—he remembered he had a rather large sum of money in his pocketbook. He entered, therefore, the office and deposited the greater part of it with the bookkeeper of the hotel. This done, he took a *carozella* and drove to the seashore. He got out of the cab and entered the Villa on foot from the Largo di Vittoria end.

He stared at me very hard. And I understood then how really impressionable he was. Every small fact and event of that evening stood out in his memory as if endowed with mystic significance. If he did not mention to me the color of the pony which drew the *carozella*, and the aspect of the man who drove, it was a mere oversight arising from his agitation, which he repressed manfully.

He had then entered the Villa Nazionale from the Largo di Vittoria end. The Villa Nazionale is a public pleasure-ground laid out in grass plots, bushes, and flowerbeds between the houses of the Riviera di Chiaja and the waters of the bay. Alleys of trees, more or less parallel, stretch its whole length—which is considerable. On the Riviera di Chiaja side the electric tramcars run close to the railings. Between the garden and the sea is the fashionable drive, a broad road bordered by a low wall, beyond which the Mediterranean splashes with gentle murmurs when the weather is fine.

As life goes on late at night in Naples, the broad drive was all astir with a brilliant swarm of carriage lamps moving in pairs, some creeping slowly, others running rapidly under the thin, motionless line of electric lamps defining the shore. And a brilliant swarm of stars hung above the land humming with voices, piled up with houses, glittering with lights—and over the silent flat shadows of the sea.

The gardens themselves are not very well lit. Our friend went forward in the warm gloom, his eyes fixed upon a distant luminous region extending nearly across the whole width of the Villa, as if the air had glowed there with its own cold, bluish, and dazzling light. This magic spot, behind the black trunks of trees and masses of inky foliage, breathed out sweet sounds mingled with bursts of brassy roar, sudden clashes of metal, and grave, vibrating thuds.

As he walked on, all these noises combined together into a piece of elaborate music whose harmonious phrases came persuasively through a great disorderly murmur of voices and shuffling of feet on the gravel of that open space. An enormous crowd immersed in the electric light, as if in a bath of some radiant and tenuous fluid shed upon their heads by luminous globes, drifted in hundreds round the band. Hundreds more sat on chairs in more or less concentric circles, receiving unflinchingly the great waves of sonority that ebbed out into the darkness. The Count penetrated the throng, drifted with it in tranquil enjoyment, listening and looking at the faces. All people of good society: mothers with their daughters, parents and children, young men and young women all talking, smiling, nodding to each other. Very many pretty faces, and very many pretty toilettes. There was, of course, a quantity of diverse types: showy old fellows with white mustaches, fat men, thin men, officers in uniform; but what predominated, he told me, was the South Italian type of young man, with a colorless, clear complexion, red lips, jet-black little mustache and liquid black eyes so wonderfully effective in leering or scowling.

Withdrawing from the throng, the Count shared a little table in front of the café with a young man of just such a type. Our friend had some lemonade. The young man was sitting moodily before an empty glass. He looked up once, and then looked down again. He also tilted his hat forward. Like this—

The Count made the gesture of a man pulling his hat down over his brow, and went on:

"I think to myself: he is sad; something is wrong with him; young men have their troubles. I take no notice of him, of course. I pay for my lemonade, and go away."

Strolling about in the neighborhood of the band, the Count thinks he saw twice that young man wandering alone in the crowd. Once their eyes met. It must have been the same young man, but there were so many there of that type that he could not be certain. Moreover, he was not very much concerned except in so far that he had been struck by the marked, peevish discontent of that face.

Presently, tired of the feeling of confinement one experiences in a crowd, the Count edged away from the band. An alley, very somber by contrast, presented itself invitingly with its promise of solitude and coolness. He entered it, walking slowly on till the sound of the orchestra became distinctly deadened. Then he walked back and turned about once more. He did this several times before he noticed that there was somebody occupying one of the benches.

The spot being midway between two lampposts the light was faint.

The man lolled back in the corner of the seat, his legs stretched out, his arms folded and his head drooping on his breast. He never stirred, as though he had fallen asleep there, but when the Count passed by next time he had changed his attitude. He sat leaning forward. His elbows were propped on his knees, and his hands were rolling a cigarette. He never looked up from that occupation.

The Count continued his stroll away from the band. He returned slowly, he said. I can imagine him enjoying to the full, but with his usual tranquility, the balminess of this southern night and the sounds of music softened delightfully by the distance.

Presently, he approached for the third time the man on the garden seat, still leaning forward with his elbows on his knees. It was a dejected pose. In the semiobscurity of the alley his high shirt collar and his cuffs made small patches of vivid whiteness. The Count said that he had noticed him getting up brusquely as if to walk away, but almost before he was aware of it the man stood before him asking in a low, gentle tone whether the signore would have the kindness to oblige him with a light.

The Count answered this request by a polite "Certainly," and dropped his hands with the intention of exploring both pockets of his trousers for the matches.

"I dropped my hands," he said, "but I never put them in my pockets. I felt a pressure there—"

He put the tip of his finger on a spot close under his breastbone, the very spot of the human body where a Japanese gentleman begins the operations of the hara-kiri, which is a form of suicide following upon dishonor, upon an intolerable outrage to the delicacy of one's feelings.

"I glance down," the Count continued in an awe-struck voice, "and what do I see? A knife! A long knife—"

"You don't mean to say," I exclaimed, amazed, "that you have been held up like this in the Villa at half-past ten o'clock, within a stone's throw of a thousand people!"

He nodded several times, staring at me with all his might.

"The clarinet," he declared, solemnly, "was finishing its solo, and I assure you I could hear every note. Then the band crashed *fortissimo*, and that creature rolled its eyes and gnashed its teeth hissing at me with the greatest ferocity, 'Be silent! No noise or—' "

I could not get over my astonishment.

"What sort of knife was it?" I asked, stupidly.

"A long blade. A stiletto—perhaps a kitchen knife. A long narrow blade. It gleamed. And his eyes gleamed. His white teeth, too. I could see them. He was very ferocious. I thought to myself: 'If I hit him he will kill me.' How could I fight with him? He had the knife and I had nothing. I am nearly seventy, you know, and that was a young man. I seemed even to recognize him. The moody young man of the café. The young man I met in the crowd. But I could not tell. There are so many like him in this country."

The distress of that moment was reflected in his face. I should think that physically he must have been paralyzed by surprise. His thoughts, however, remained extremely active. They ranged over every alarming possibility. The idea of setting up a vigorous shouting for help occurred to him, too. But he did nothing of the kind, and the reason why he refrained gave me a good opinion of his mental self-possession. He saw in a flash that nothing prevented the other from shouting, too.

"That young man might in an instant have thrown away his knife and pretended I was the aggressor. Why not? He might have said I attacked him. Why not? It was one incredible story against another! He might have said anything—bring some dishonoring charge against me—what do I know? By his dress he was no common robber. He seemed to belong to the better classes. What could I say? He was an Italian—I am a foreigner. Of course, I have my passport, and there is our consul—but to be arrested, dragged at night to the police office like a criminal!"

He shuddered. It was in his character to shrink from scandal much more than from mere death. And certainly for many people this would have always remained—considering certain peculiarities of Neapolitan manners—a deucedly queer story. The Count was no fool. His belief in the respectable placidity of life having received this rude shock, he thought that now anything might happen. But also a notion came into his head that this young man was perhaps merely an infuriated lunatic.

This was for me the first hint of his attitude towards this adventure. In his exaggerated delicacy of sentiment he felt that nobody's self-esteem need be affected by what a madman may choose to do to one. It became apparent, however, that the Count was to be denied that consolation. He enlarged upon the abominably savage way in which that young man rolled his glistening eyes and gnashed his white teeth. The band was going now through a slow movement of solemn braying by all the trombones, with deliberately repeated bangs of the big drum.

"But what did you do?" I asked, greatly excited.

"Nothing," answered the Cònt. "I let my hands hang down very still. I told him quietly I did not intend making a noise. He snarled like a dog, then said in an ordinary voice:

" *'Vostro portofolio.'* "

"So I naturally," continued the Count—and from this point acted the whole thing in pantomime. Holding me with his eyes, he went through all the motions of reaching into his inside breast pocket, taking out a pocketbook, and handing it over. But that young man, still bearing steadily on the knife, refused to touch it.

He directed the Count to take the money out himself, received it into his left hand, motioned the pocketbook to be returned to the pocket, all this being done to the sweet trilling of flutes and clarinets sustained by the emotional drone of the hautboys. And the "young man," as the Count called him, said: "This seems very little."

"It was, indeed, only 340 or 360 lire," the Count pursued. "I had left my money in the hotel, as you know. I told him this was all I had on me. He shook his head impatiently and said:

" *'Vostro orologio.'* "

The Count gave me the dumb show of pulling out his watch, detaching it. But, as it happened, the valuable gold half-chronometer he possessed had been left at a watchmaker's for cleaning. He wore that evening (on a leather guard) the Waterbury fifty-franc thing he used to take with him on his fishing expeditions. Perceiving the nature of this booty, the well-dressed robber made a contemptuous clicking sound with his tongue like this, "Tse-Ah!" and waved it away hastily. Then, as the Count was returning the disdained object to his pocket, he demanded with a threateningly increased pressure of the knife on the epigastrium, by way of reminder:

"Vostri anelli."

"One of the rings," went on the Count, "was given me many years ago by my wife; the other is the signet ring of my father. I said, 'No. *That* you shall not have!' "

Here the Count reproduced the gesture corresponding to that declaration by clapping one hand upon the other, and pressing both thus against his chest. It was touching in its resignation. "That you shall not have," he repeated, firmly, and closed his eyes, fully expecting—I don't know whether I am right in recording that such an unpleasant word had passed his lips—fully expecting to feel himself being—I really hesitate to say—being disemboweled by the push of the long, sharp blade resting murderously against the pit of his stomach—the very seat, in all human beings, of anguishing sensations.

Great waves of harmony went on flowing from the band.

Suddenly the Count felt the nightmarish pressure removed from the sensitive spot. He opened his eyes. He was alone. He had heard nothing. It is probable that "the young man" had departed, with light steps, some time before, but the sense of the horrid pressure had lingered even after the knife had gone. A feeling of weakness came over him. He had just time to stagger to the garden seat. He felt as though he had held his breath for a long time. He sat all in a heap, panting with the shock of the reaction.

The band was executing, with immense bravura, the complicated finale. It ended with a tremendous crash. He heard it, unreal and remote, as if his ears had been stopped, and then the hard clapping of a thousand, more or less, pairs of hands, like a sudden hail shower passing away. The profound silence which succeeded recalled him to himself.

A tramcar resembling a long glass box wherein people sat with their heads strongly lighted, ran along swiftly within sixty yards of the spot where he had been robbed. Then another rustled by, and yet another going the other way. The audience about the band had broken up, and were entering the alley in small conversing groups. The Count sat up straight and tried to think calmly of what had happened to him. The vileness of it took his breath away again. As far as I can make it out he was disgusted with himself. I do not mean to say with his behavior. Indeed, if his pantomimic rendering of it for my information was to be trusted, it was simply perfect. No, it was not that. He was not ashamed. He was shocked at being the elected victim, not of robbery so much as of contempt. His tranquillity had been wantonly desecrated. His lifelong, kindly nicety of outlook had been defaced.

Nevertheless, at that stage, before the iron had time to sink deep, he was able to argue himself into comparative equanimity. As his agitation calmed down somewhat, he became aware that he was frightfully hungry. Yes, hungry. The sheer emotion had made him simply ravenous. He left the seat and, after walking for some time, found himself outside the gardens and before an arrested tramcar, without knowing very well how he came there. He got in as if in a dream, by a sort of instinct. Fortunately he found in his trouser pocket a copper to satisfy the conductor. Then the car stopped, and as everybody was getting out he got out, too. He recognized the Piazza San Ferdinando, but apparently it did not occur to him to take a cab and drive to the hotel. He remained in distress on the Piazza like a lost dog, thinking vaguely of the best way of getting something to eat at once.

Suddenly he remembered his twenty-franc piece. He explained to me that he had that piece of French gold for something like three years. He used to carry it about with him as a sort of reserve in case of accident. Anybody is liable to have his pocket picked—a quite different thing from a brazen and insulting robbery.

The monumental arch of the Galleria Umberto faced him at the top of a noble flight of stairs. He climbed these without loss of time, and directed his steps towards the Café Umberto. All the tables outside were occupied by a lot of people who were drinking. But as he wanted something to eat, he went inside into the café, which is divided into aisles by square pillars set all round with long looking glasses. The Count sat down on a red plush bench against one of these pillars, waiting for his *risotto*. And his mind reverted to his abominable adventure.

He thought of the moody, well-dressed young man, with whom he had exchanged glances in the crowd around the bandstand, and who, he felt confident, was the robber. Would he recognize him again? Doubtless. But he did not want ever to see him again. The best thing was to forget this humiliating episode.

The Count looked round anxiously for the coming of his *risotto*, and, behold! to the left against the wall—there sat the young man. He was alone at a table, with a bottle of some sort of wine or syrup and a carafe of iced water before him. The smooth olive cheeks, the red lips, the little jet-black mustache turned up gallantly, the fine black eyes a little heavy and shaded by long eyelashes, that peculiar expression of cruel discontent to be seen only in the busts of some Roman emperors—it was he, no doubt at all. But that was a type. The Count looked away hastily. The young officer over there reading a paper was like that, too. Same type. Two young men farther away playing checkers also resembled—

The Count lowered his head with the fear in his heart of being everlastingly haunted by the vision of that young man. He began to eat his *risotto*. Presently he heard the young man on his left call the waiter in a bad-tempered tone.

At the call, not only his own waiter, but two other idle waiters belonging to a quite different row of tables, rushed towards him with obsequious alacrity, which is not the general characteristic of the waiters in the Café Umberto. The young man muttered something and one of the waiters walking rapidly to the nearest door called out into the Galleria: "Pasquale! O! Pasquale!"

Everybody knows Pasquale, the shabby old fellow who, shuffling between the tables, offers for sale cigars, cigarettes, picture postcards, and matches to the clients of the café. He is in many respects an engaging scoundrel. The Count saw the gray-haired, unshaven ruffian enter the café, the glass case hanging from his neck by a leather strap, and, at a word from the waiter, make his shuffling way with a sudden spurt to the young man's table. The young man was in need of a cigar with which Pasquale served him fawningly. The old peddler was going out, when the Count, cn a sudden impulse, beckoned to him.

Pasquale approached, the smile of deferential recognition combining oddly with the cynical searching expression of his eyes. Leaning his case on the table, he lifted the glass lid without a word. The Count took a box of cigarettes and urged by a fearful curiosity, asked as casually as he could—

"Tell me, Pasquale, who is that young signore sitting over there?"

The other bent over his box confidentially.

"That, *Signor Conde*," he said, beginning to rearrange his wares busily and without looking up, "that is a young *Cavaliere* of a very good family from Bari. He studies in the University here, and is the chief, *capo*, of an association of young men—of very nice young men."

He paused, and then, with mingled discretion and pride of knowledge, murmured the explanatory word *"Camorra"* and shut down the lid. "A very powerful *Camorra*," he breathed out. "The professors themselves respect it greatly . . . *una lira e cinquanti centesimi, Signor Conde.*"

Our friend paid with the gold piece. While Pasquale was making up the change, he observed that the young man, of whom he had heard so much in a few words, was watching the transaction covertly. After the old vagabond had withdrawn with a bow, the Count settled with the waiter and sat still. A numbness, he told me, had come over him.

The young man paid, too, got up, and crossed over, apparently for the purpose of looking at himself in the mirror set in the pillar nearest to the Count's seat. He was dressed all in black with a dark green bow tie. The count looked round, and was startled by meeting a vicious glance out of the corners of the other's eyes. The young *Cavaliere* from Bari (according to Pasquale; but Pasquale is, of course, an accomplished liar) went on arranging his tie, settling his hat before the glass, and meantime he spoke just loud enough to be heard by the Count. He spoke through his teeth with the most insulting venom of contempt and gazing straight into the mirror.

"Ah! So you had some gold on you—you old liar—you old *birba*—you *furfante!* But you are not done with me yet."

The fiendishness of his expression vanished like lightning, and he lounged out of the café with a moody impassive face.

The poor Count, after telling me this last episode fell back trembling in his chair. His forehead broke into perspiration. There was a wanton insolence in the spirit of this outrage which appalled even me. What it was to the Count's delicacy I won't attempt to guess. I am sure that if he had been not too refined to do such a blatantly vulgar thing as dying from apoplexy in a café, he would have had a fatal stroke there and then. All irony apart, my difficulty was to keep him from seeing the full extent of my commiseration. He shrank from every excessive sentiment, and my commiseration was practically unbounded. It did not surprise me to hear that he had been in bed a week. He had got up to make his arrangements for leaving Southern Italy for good and all.

And the man was convinced that he could not live through a whole year in any other climate!

No argument of mine had any effect. It was not timidity, though he did say to me once: "You do not know what a *Camorra* is, my dear sir. I am a marked man." He was not afraid of what could be done to him. His delicate conception of his dignity was defiled by a degrading experience. He couldn't stand that. No Japanese gentleman, outraged in his exaggerated sense of honor, could have gone about his preparations for hara-kiri with greater resolution. To go home really amounted to suicide for the poor Count.

There is a saying of Neapolitan patriotism, intended for the information of foreigners, I presume: "See Naples and then die." *Vedi Napoli e poi mori*. It is a saying of excessive vanity, and everything excessive was abhorrent to the nice moderation of the poor Count. Yet, as I was seeing him off at the railway station, I thought he was behaving with singular fidelity to its conceited spirit. *Vedi Napoli!* . . . He had seen it! He had seen it with startling thoroughness—and now he was going to his grave. He was going to it by the *train de luxe* of the International Sleeping Car Company, via Trieste and Vienna. As the four long, somber coaches pulled out of the station I raised my hat with the solemn feeling of paying the last tribute of respect to a funeral cortège. *Il Conde*'s profile, much aged already, glided away from me in stony immobility, behind the lighted pane of glass—*Vedi Napoli e poi mori!*

CONRAD: *Il Conde*

1. *What is the significance of the first paragraph, with its description of the collection of bronzes in the National Museum in Naples?*
2. *What does the old Count represent?*

Il Conde   [175

3. *What does the young man with the knife represent? Why does Conrad make him well-born?*

4. *Why does Conrad have the confrontation take place in gardens, against the backdrop of a beautiful Italian night?*

5. *What is the importance of the concert in this scene? Compare Conrad's use of music in the background with Mann's in "Little Lizzie."*

6. *Why does the experience in the garden so upset the Count, beyond the usual fear that such a meeting would cause?*

7. *What relevance does the epigraph, "See Naples and then die," have to the story?*

8. *Can you see any political and social significance to the events in the story?*

9. *Does the pace of this story seem too slow? What justification is there for such a leisurely pace? Does Conrad extract the full drama from the situation? Would the Hemingway style be more effective for this episode?*

10. *Conrad claimed in his now-famous preface to* The Nigger of the Narcissus *that the writer's job is "to make you hear, to make you feel—it is, before all, to make you see." Does Conrad succeed in doing so? Indicate some of the ways in which he makes you hear, feel, see—that is, how he creates a tangible and lifelike sense of reality.*

Sholom Aleichem

TIT FOR TAT

Sholom Aleichem (b. Solomon Rabinowitz) was born in Pereyaslav, Russia, in 1859. Educated in traditional Hebrew lore, he was supporting himself at seventeen by tutoring the children of the wealthy. He served as a government rabbi in the town of Yuben for several years, gained and lost a family fortune by 1900, and retired from business to devote himself to writing. The pogrom of 1905 forced him to flee Russia with his family, and he lived quietly in western Europe until the outbreak of World War I, when he came to this country. He died in New York in 1916. He is generally regarded as the greatest of the modern Yiddish writers for his tragicomic presentation of Jewish life, and his novels such as Tevia der Milchiger *and* Der Blutiger Shpass *have been translated into many languages. "Tit for Tat" is a typical Aleichem story, with its undertones of humor, its realistic representation of his people, and its great warmth and feeling for erring human beings.*

ONCE I was a rabbiner. A rabbiner, not a rabbi. That is, I was called rabbi—but a rabbi of the crown.

To old-country Jews I don't have to explain what a rabbi of the crown is. They know the breed. What are his great responsibilities? He fills out birth certificates, officiates at circumcisions, performs marriages, grants divorces. He gets his share from the living and the dead. In the synagogue he has a place of honor, and when the congregation rises, he is the first to stand. On legal holidays he appears in a stovepipe hat and holds forth in his best Russian: *"Gospoda Prihozhane!"* To take it for granted that among our people a rabbiner is well loved—let's not say any more. Say rather that we put up with him, as we do a government inspector or a deputy sheriff. And yet he is chosen from among the people, that is, every three years a proclamation is sent us: *"Na Osnavania Predpisania . . ."* Or, as we would say: "Your Lord, the Governor, orders you to come together in the synagogue, poor little Jews, and pick out a rabbiner for yourselves . . ."

Then the campaign begins. Candidates, hot discussions, brandy, and maybe even a bribe or two. After which come charges and countercharges, the elections are annulled, and we are ordered to hold new elections. Again the proclamations: *"Na Osnavania Predpisania . . ."* Again candidates, discussions, party organizations, brandy, a bribe or two . . . That was the life!

Well, there I was—a rabbiner in a small town in the province of Poltava. But I was anxious to be a modern one. I wanted to serve the public. So I dropped the formalities of my position and began to mingle with the people—as we say: to stick my head into the community pot. I got busy with the *Talmud Torah*, the charity fund; interpreted a law, settled disputes or just gave plain advice.

The love of settling disputes, helping people out, or advising them, I inherited from my father and my uncles. They—may they rest in peace—also enjoyed being bothered all the time with other people's business. There are two kinds of people in the world: those that you can't bother at all, and others whom you can bother all the time. You can climb right on their heads—naturally not in one jump, but gradually. First you climb into their laps, then onto their shoulders, then their heads—and after that you can jump up and down on their heads and stamp on their hearts with your heavy boots—as long as you want to.

I was that kind, and without boasting I can tell you that I had plenty of ardent followers and plain hangers-on who weren't ashamed to come every day and fill my head with their clamoring and sit around till late at night. They never refused a glass of tea, or cigarettes. Newspapers and books they took without asking. In short, I was a regular fellow.

Well, there came a day . . . The door opened, and in walked the very foremost men of the town, the sparkling best, the very cream of the city. Four householders—men of affairs—you could almost say: real men of substance. And who were these men? Three of them were the *Troika*—that was what we called them in our town because they were together all the time—partners in whatever business any one of them was in. They always fought, they were always suspicious of each other, and watched everything the others did, and still they never separated—working always in this principle: if the business is a good one and there is profit to be made, why shouldn't I have a lick at the bone too? And on the other hand, if it should end in disaster—you'll be buried along with me, and lie with me deep in the earth. And what does God do? He brings together the three partners with a fourth one. They operate together a little less than a year and end up in a brawl. That is why they're here.

What had happened? "Since God created thieves, swindlers and crooks, you never saw a thief, swindler or crook like this one." That is the way the three old partners described the fourth one to me. And he, the fourth, said the same about them. Exactly the same, word for word. And who was this fourth one? He was a quiet little man, a little innocent-looking fellow, with thick, dark eyebrows under which a pair of shrewd, ironic, little eyes watched everything you did. Everyone called him Nachman Lekach.

His real name was Nachman Noss'n, but everybody called him Nachman Lekach, because as you know, *Noss'n* is the Hebrew for "he gave," and *Lekach* means "he took," and in all the time we knew him, no one had ever seen him give anything to anyone—while at taking no one was better.

Where were we? Oh, yes . . . So they came to the rabbiner with the complaints, to see if he could find a way of straightening out their tangled accounts. "Whatever you decide, Rabbi, and whatever you decree, and whatever you say, will be final."

That is how the three old partners said it, and the fourth, Reb Nachman, nodded with that innocent look on his face to indicate that he too left it all up to me: "For the reason," his eyes said, "that I know that I have done no wrong." And he sat down in a corner, folded his arms across his chest like an old woman, fixed his shrewd, ironic, little eyes on me, and waited to see what his partners would have to say. And when they had all laid out their complaints and charges, presented all their evidence, said all they had to say, he got up, patted down his thick eyebrows, and not looking at the others at all, only at me, with those deep, deep, shrewd little eyes of his, he proceeded to demolish their claims and charges—so completely, that it looked as if they were the thieves, swindlers and crooks—the three partners of his—and he, Nachman Lekach, was a man of virtue and piety, the little chicken that is slaughtered before *Yom Kippur* to atone for our sins—a sacrificial lamb. "And every word that you heard them say is a complete lie, it never was and never could be. It's simply out of the question." And he proved with evidence, arguments and supporting data that everything he said was true and holy, as if Moses himself had said it.

All the time he was talking, the others, the *Troika*, could hardly sit in their chairs. Every moment one or another of them jumped up, clutched his head—or his heart: "Of all things! How can a man talk like that! Such lies and falsehoods!" It was almost impossible to calm them down, to keep them from tearing at the fourth one's beard. As for me—the rabbiner—it was hard, very hard to crawl out from this horrible tangle, because by now it was clear that I had a fine band to deal with, all four of them swindlers, thieves and crooks, and informers to boot, and all four of them deserving a severe punishment. But what? At last this idea occurred to me, and I said to them:

"Are you ready, my friends? I am prepared to hand down my decision. My mind is made up. But I won't disclose what I have to say until each of you has deposited twenty-five *rubles*—to prove that you will act upon the decision I am about to hand down."

"With the greatest of pleasure," the three spoke out at once, and Nachman Lekach nodded his head, and all four reached into their pockets, and each one counted out his twenty-five on the table. I gathered up the money, locked it up in a drawer, and then I gave them my decision in these words:

"Having heard the complaints and the arguments of both parties, and having examined your accounts and studied your evidence, I find according to my understanding and deep conviction, that all four of you are in the wrong, and not only in the wrong, but that it is a shame and a scandal for Jewish people to conduct themselves in such a manner—to falsify accounts, perjure yourselves and even act as informers. Therefore I have decided that since we have a *Talmud Torah* in our town with many children who have neither clothes nor shoes, and whose parents have nothing with which to pay their tuition, and since there has been no help at all from you gentlemen (to get a few pennies from you one has to reach down into your very gizzards) therefore it is my decision that this hundred *rubles* of yours shall go to the *Talmud Torah*, and as for you, gentlemen, you can go home, in good health, and thanks for your contribution. The poor children will now have some shoes and socks and shirts and pants, and I'm sure they'll pray to God for you and your children. Amen."

Having heard the sentence, the three old partners—the

Troika—looked from one to the other—flushed, unable to speak. A decision like this they had not anticipated. The only one who could say a word was Reb Nachman Lekach. He got up, patted down his thick eyebrows, held out a hand, and looking at me with his ironic little eyes, said this:

"I thank you, Rabbi Rabbiner, in behalf of all four of us, for the wise decision which you have just made known. Such a judgment could have been made by no one since King Solomon himself. There is only one thing that you forgot to say, Rabbi Rabbiner, and that is: what is your fee for this wise and just decision?"

"I beg your pardon," I tell him. "You've come to the wrong address. I am not one of those rabbiners who tax the living and the dead." That is the way I answered him, like a real gentleman. And this was his reply:

"If that's the case, then you are not only a sage and a rabbi among men, you're an honest man besides. So, if you would care to listen, I'd like to tell you a story. Say that we will pay you for your pains at least with a story."

"Good enough. Even with two stories."

"In that case, sit down, Rabbi Rabbiner, and let us have your cigarette case. I'll tell you an interesting story, a true one, too, something that happened to me. What happened to others I don't like to talk about."

And we lit our cigarettes, sat down around the table, and Reb Nachman spread out his thick eyebrows, and looking at me with his shrewd, smiling, little eyes, he slowly began to tell his true story of what had once happened to him himself.

All this happened to me a long time ago. I was still a young man and I was living not far from here, in a village near the railroad. I traded in this and that, I had a small tavern, made a living. A Rothschild I didn't become, but bread we had, and in time there were about ten Jewish families living close by—because, as you know, if one of us makes a living, others come around. They think you're shoveling up gold . . . But that isn't the point. What I was getting at was that right in the midst of the busy season one year, when things were moving and traffic was heavy, my wife had to go and have a baby—our boy—our first son. What do you say to that? "Congratulations! Congratulations everybody!" But that isn't all. You have to have a *bris*, the circumcision. I dropped everything, went into town, bought all the good things I could find, and came back with the *Mohel* with all his instruments, and for good measure I also brought the *shammes* of the synagogue. I thought that with these two holy men and myself and the neighbors we'd have the ten men that we needed, with one to spare. But what does God do? He has one of my neighbors get sick—he is sick in bed and can't come to the *bris*, you can't carry him. And another has to pack up and go off to the city. He can't wait another day! And here I am without the ten men. Go do something. Here it is—Friday! Of all days, my wife has to pick Friday to have the *bris*—the day before the Sabbath. The *Mohel* is frantic—he has to go back right away. The *shammes* is actually in tears. "What did you ever drag us off here for?" they both want to know. And what can I do?

All I can think of is to run off to the railroad station. Who knows—so many people come through every day—maybe God will send some one. And that's just what happened. I come running up to the station—the agent has just called out that a train is about to leave. I look around—a little roly-poly man carrying a huge traveling bag comes flying by, all sweating and out of breath, straight toward the lunch counter. He looks over the dishes—what is there a good Jew can take in a country railroad station? A piece of herring—an egg. Poor fellow—you could see his mouth was watering. I grab him by the sleeve. "Uncle, are you looking for something to eat?" I ask him, and the look he gives me says: "How did you know that?" I keep on talking: "May you live to be a hundred—God himself must have sent you." He still doesn't understand, so I proceed: "Do you want to earn the blessings of eternity—and at the same time eat a beef roast that will melt in your mouth, with a fresh, white loaf right out of the oven?" He still looks at me as if I'm crazy. "Who are you? What do you want?"

So I tell him the whole story—what a misfortune had overtaken us: here we are, all ready for the *bris*, the *Mohel* is waiting, the food is ready—and such food!—and we need a tenth man! "What's that got to do with me?" he asks, and I tell him: "What's that got to do with you? Why—everything depends on you—you're the tenth man! I beg you—come with me. You will earn all the rewards of heaven—and have a delicious dinner in the bargain!" "Are you crazy," he asks me, "or are you just out of your head? My train is leaving in a few minutes, and it's Friday afternoon—almost sundown. Do you know what that means? In a few more hours the Sabbath will catch up with me, and I'll be stranded." "So what!" I tell him. "So you'll take the next train. And in the meantime you'll earn eternal life—and taste a soup, with fresh dumplings, that only my wife can make . . ."

Well, why make the story long? I had my way. The roast and the hot soup with fresh dumplings did their work. You could see my customer licking his lips. So I grab the traveling bag and I lead him home, and we go through the *bris*. It was a real pleasure! You could smell the roast all over the house, it had so much garlic in it. A roast like that, with fresh warm twist, is a delicacy from heaven. And when you consider that we had some fresh dill pickles, and a bottle of beer, and some cognac before the meal and cherry cider after the meal—you can imagine the state our guest was in! His cheeks shone and his forehead glistened. But what then? Before we knew it the afternoon was gone. My guest jumps up, he looks around, sees what time it is, and almost has a stroke! He reaches for his traveling bag: "Where is it?" I say to him, "What's your hurry? In the first place, do you think we'll let you run off like that—before the Sabbath? And in the second place—who are you to leave on a journey an hour or two before the Sabbath? And if you're going to get caught out in the country somewhere, you might just as well stay here with us."

He groans and he sighs. How could I do a thing like that to him—keep him so late? What did I have against him? Why hadn't I reminded him earlier? He doesn't stop bothering me. So I say to him: "In the first place, did I have to tell you that it was Friday afternoon? Didn't you know it yourself? And in the second place, how do you know—maybe it's the way God wanted it? Maybe He wanted you to stay here for the Sabbath so you could taste some of my wife's fish? I can guarantee you, that as long as you've eaten fish, you haven't eaten fish like my wife's fish—not even in a dream!" Well, that ended the argument. We said our evening prayers, had a glass of wine, and my wife brings the fish to the table. My guest's nostrils swell out, a new light shines in his eyes and he goes after that fish as if he hadn't eaten a thing all day. He can't get over it. He praises it to the skies. He fills a glass with brandy and drinks a toast to the fish. And then comes the soup, a specially rich Sabbath soup with noodles. And he likes that, too, and the *tzimmes* also, and the meat that goes with the *tzimmes*, a nice, fat piece of brisket. I'm telling you, he just sat there licking his fingers! When we're finishing the last course he turns to me: "Do you know what I'll tell you? Now that it's all over, I'm really glad that I stayed over for *Shabbes*. It's been a long time since I've enjoyed a Sabbath as I've enjoyed this one." "If that's how you feel, I'm happy," I tell him. "But wait. This is only a sample. Wait till tomorrow. Then you'll see what my wife can do."

And so it was. The next day, after services, we sit down at the table. Well, you should have seen the spread. First the appetizers: crisp wafers and chopped herring, and onions and chicken fat, with radishes and chopped liver and eggs and *gribbenes*. And after that the cold fish and the meat from yesterday's *tzimmes*, and then the jellied neat's foot, or *fisnoga* as you call it, with thin slices of garlic, and after that the potato *cholent* with the *kugel* that had been in the oven all night—and you know what that smells like when you take it out of the oven and take the cover off the pot. And what it tastes like. Our visitor could not find words to praise it. So I tell him: "This is still nothing. Wait until you have tasted our borsht tonight, then you'll know what good food is." At that he laughs out loud—a friendly laugh, it is true—and says to me: "Yes, but how far do you think I'll be from here by the time your borsht is ready?" So I laugh even louder than he does, and say: "You can forget that right now! Do you think you'll be going off tonight?"

And so it was. As soon as the lights were lit and we had a glass of wine to start off the new week, my friend begins to pack his things again. So I call out to him: "Are you crazy? Do you think we'll let you go off, the Lord knows where, at night? And besides, where's your train?" "What?" he yells at me. "No train? Why, you're murdering me! You know I have to leave!" But I say, "May this be the greatest misfortune in your life. Your train will come, if all is well, around dawn tomorrow. In the meantime I hope your appetite and digestion are good, because I can smell the borsht already! All I ask," I say, "is just tell me the truth. Tell me if you've ever touched a borsht like this before. But I want the absolute truth!" What's the use of talking—he had to admit it: never before in all his life had he tasted a borsht like this. Never. He even started to ask how you made the borsht, what you put into it, and how long you cooked it. Everything. And I say: "Don't worry about that! Here, taste this wine and tell me what you think of *it*. After all, you're an expert. But the truth! Remember—nothing but the truth! Because if there is anything I hate, it's flattery . . ."

So we took a glass, and then another glass, and we went to bed. And what do you think happened? My traveler overslept, and missed the early morning train. When he wakes up he boils over! He jumps on me like a murderer. Wasn't it up to me, out of fairness and decency, to wake him up in time? Because of me he's going to have to take a loss, a heavy loss—he doesn't even know himself how heavy. It was all my fault. I ruined him. I! . . . So I let him talk. I listen, quietly, and when he's all through, I say: "Tell me yourself, aren't you a queer sort of person? In the first place, what's your hurry? What are you rushing for? How long is a person's life altogether? Does he have to spoil that little with rushing and hurrying? And in the second place, have you forgotten that today is the third day since the *bris?* Doesn't that mean a thing to you? Where we come from, on the third day we're in the habit of putting on a feast better than the one at the *bris* itself. The third day—it's something to celebrate! You're not going to spoil the celebration, are you?"

What can he do? He can't control himself any more, and he starts laughing—a hysterical laugh. "What good does it do to talk?" he says. "You're a real leech!" "Just as you say," I tell him, "but after all, you're a visitor, aren't you?"

At the dinner table, after we've had a drink or two, I call out to him: "Look," I say, "it may not be proper—after all, we're Jews—to talk about milk and such things while we're eating meat, but I'd like to know your honest opinion: what do you think of *kreplach* with cheese?" He looks at me with distrust. "How did we get around to that?" he asks. "Just like this," I explain to him. "I'd like to have you try the cheese *kreplach* that my wife makes—because tonight, you see, we're going to have a dairy supper . . ." This is too much for him, and he comes right back at me with, "Not this time! You're trying to keep me here another day, I can see that. But you can't do it. It isn't right! It isn't right!" And from the way he fusses and fumes it's easy to see that I won't have to coax him too long, or fight with him either, because what is he but a man with an appetite, who has only one philosophy, which he practices at the table? So I say this to him: "I give you my word of honor, and if that isn't enough, I'll give you my hand as well—here, shake—that tomorrow I'll wake you up in time for the earliest train. I promise it, even if the world turns upside down. If I don't, may I—you know what!" At this he softens and says to me: "Remember, we're shaking hands on that!" And I: "A promise is a promise." And my wife makes a dairy supper—how can I describe it to you? With such *kreplach* that my traveler has to admit that it was all true: he has a wife too, and she makes *kreplach* too, but how can you compare hers with these? It's like night to day!

And I kept my word, because a promise is a promise. I woke him when it was still dark, and started the samovar. He finished packing and began to say goodbye to me and the rest of the household in a very handsome, friendly style. You could see he was a gentleman. But I interrupt him: "We'll say goodbye a little later. First, we have to settle up." "What do you mean—settle up?" "Settle up," I say, "means to add up the figures. That's what I'm going to do now. I'll add them up, let you know what it comes to, and you will be so kind as to pay me."

His face flames red. "Pay you?" he shouts. "Pay you for what?" "For what?" I repeat. "You want to know for what? For everything. The food, the drink, the lodging." This time he becomes white—not red—and he says to me: "I don't understand you at all. You came and invited me to the *bris*. You stopped me at the train. You took my bag away from me. You promised me eternal life." "That's right," I interrupt him. "That's right. But what's one thing got to do with the other? When you came to the *bris* you earned your reward in heaven. But food and drink and lodging—do I have to give you these things for nothing? After all, you're a businessman, aren't you? You should understand that fish costs money, and that the wine you drank was the very best, and the beer, too, and the cherry cider. And you remember how you praised the *tzimmes* and the puddings and the borsht. You remember how you licked your fingers. And the cheese *kreplach* smelled pretty good to you, too. Now, I'm glad you enjoyed these things; I don't begrudge you that in the least. But certainly you wouldn't expect that just because you earned a reward in heaven, and enjoyed yourself in the bargain, that *I* should pay for it?" My traveling friend was really sweating; he looked as if he'd have a stroke. He began to throw himself around, yell, scream, call for help. "This is Sodom!" he cried. "Worse than Sodom! It's the worst outrage the world has ever heard of! How much do you want?" Calmly I took a piece of paper and a pencil and began to add it up. I itemized everything, I gave him an inventory of everything he ate, of every hour he spent in my place. All in all it added up to something like thirty-odd *rubles* and some *kopeks*—I don't remember it exactly.

When he saw the total, my good man went green and yellow, his hands shook, and his eyes almost popped out, and again he let out a yell, louder than before. "What did I fall into—a nest of thieves? Isn't there a single human being here? Is there a God anywhere?" So I say to him, "Look, sir, do you know what? Do you know what you're yelling about? Do you have to eat your heart out? Here is my suggestion: let's ride into town together—it's not far from here—and we'll find some people—there's a *rabbiner* there—let's ask the rabbi. And we'll abide by what he says." When he heard me talk like that, he quieted down a little. And—don't worry—we hired a horse and wagon, climbed in, and rode off to town, the two of us, and went straight to the rabbi.

When we got to the rabbi's house, we found him just finishing his morning prayers. He folded up his prayer shawl and put his philacteries away. "Good morning," we said to him, and he: "What's the news today?" The news? My friend tears loose and lets him have the whole story—everything from A to Z. He doesn't leave a word out. He tells how he stopped at the station, and so on and so on, and when he's through he whips out the bill I had given him and hands it to the rabbi. And when the rabbi had heard everything, he says: "Having heard one side I should now like to hear the other." And turning to me, he asks, "What do you have to say to all that?" I answer: "Everything he says is true. There's not a word I can add. Only one thing I'd like to have him tell you—on his word of honor: did he eat the fish, and did he drink the beer and cognac and the cider, and did he smack his lips over the borsht that my wife made?" At this the man becomes almost frantic, he jumps and he thrashes about like an apoplectic. The rabbi begs him not to boil like that, not to be so angry, because anger is a grave sin. And he asks him again about the fish and the borsht and the *kreplach*, and if it was true that he had drunk not only the wine, but beer and cognac and cider as well. Then the rabbi puts on his spectacles, looks the bill over from top to bottom, checks every line, and finds it correct! Thirty-odd *rubles* and some *kopeks*, and he makes his judgment brief: he tells the man to pay the whole thing, and for the wagon back and forth, and a judgment fee for the rabbi himself . . .

The man stumbles out of the rabbi's house looking as if he'd been in a steam bath too long, takes out his purse, pulls out two twenty-fives and snaps at me: "Give me the change." "What change?" I ask, and he says: "For the thirty you charged me—for that bill you gave me." "Bill? What bill? What thirty are you talking about? What do you think I am, a highwayman? Do you expect me to take money from you? I see a man at the railroad station, a total stranger; I take his bag away from him, and drag him off almost by force to our own *bris*, and spend a wonderful *Shabbes* with him. So am I going to charge him for the favor he did me, and for the pleasure I had?" Now he looks at me as if I really am crazy, and says: "Then why did you carry on like this? Why did you drag me to the rabbi?" "Why this? Why that?" I say to him. "You're a queer sort of person, you are! I wanted to show you what kind of man our rabbi was, that's all . . ."

When he finished the story, my litigant, Reb Nachman Lekach, got up with a flourish, and the other three partners followed him. They buttoned their coats and prepared to leave. But I held them off. I passed the cigarettes around again, and said to the storyteller:

"So you told me a story about a rabbi. Now maybe you'll be so kind as to let me tell you a story—also about a rabbi, but a much shorter story than the one you told."

And without waiting for a yes or no, I started right in, and made it brief:

This happened, I began, not so long ago, and in a large city, on *Yom Kippur* eve. A stranger falls into the town—a business, a traveler, who goes here and there, everywhere, sells merchandise, collects money . . . On this day he comes into the city, walks up and down in front of the synagogue, holding his sides with both hands, asks everybody he sees where he can find the rabbi. "What do you want the rabbi for?" people ask. "What business is that of yours?" he wants to know. So they don't tell him. And he asks one man, he asks another: "Can you tell where the rabbi lives?" "What do you want the rabbi for?" "What do you care?" This one and that one, till finally he gets the answer, finds the rabbi's house, goes in, still holding his sides with both hands. He calls the rabbi aside, shuts the door, and says, "Rabbi, this is my story. I am a traveling man, and I have money with me, quite a pile. It's not my money. It belongs to my clients—first to God and then to my clients. It's *Yom Kippur* eve. I can't carry money with me on *Yom Kippur*, and I'm afraid to leave it at my lodgings. A sum like that! So do me a favor—take it, put it away in your strong box till tomorrow night, after *Yom Kippur*."

And without waiting, the man unbuttons his vest and draws out one pack after another, crisp and clean, the real red, crackling, hundred *ruble* notes!

Seeing how much there was, the rabbi said to him: "I beg your pardon. You don't know me, you don't know who I am." "What do you mean, I don't know who you are? You're a rabbi, aren't you?"

"Yes, I'm a rabbi. But I don't know *you*—who you are or what you are." They bargain back and forth. The traveler: "You're a rabbi." The rabbi: "I don't know who you are." And time does not stand still. It's almost *Yom Kippur!* Finally the rabbi agrees to take the money. The only thing is, who should be the witnesses? You can't trust just anyone in a matter like that.

So the rabbi sends for the leading townspeople, the very cream, rich and respectable citizens, and says to them: "This is what I called you for. This man has money with him, a tidy sum, not his own, but first God's and then his clients'. He wants me to keep it for him till after *Yom Kippur*. Therefore I want you to be witnesses, to see how much he leaves with me, so that later—you understand?" And the rabbi took the trouble to count it all over three times before the eyes of the townspeople, wrapped the notes in a kerchief, sealed the kerchief with wax, and stamped his initials on the seal. He passed this from one man to the other, saying, "Now look. Here is my signature, and remember, you're the witnesses." The kerchief with the money in it he handed over to his wife, had her lock it in a chest, and hide the keys where no one could find them. And he himself, the rabbi, went to *shul*, and prayed and fasted as it was ordained, lived through *Yom Kippur*, came home, had a bite to eat, looked up, and there was the traveler. "Good evening, Rabbi." "Good evening. Sit down. What can I do for you?" "Nothing. I came for my package." "What package?" "The money." "What money?" "The money I left with you to keep for me." "You gave *me* money to keep for you? When was that?"

The traveler laughs out loud. He thinks the rabbi is joking with him. The rabbi asks: "What are you laughing at?" And the man says: "It's the first time I met a rabbi who liked to play tricks." At this the rabbi is insulted. No one, he pointed out, had ever called him a trickster before. "Tell me, my good man, what do you want here?"

When he heard these words, the stranger felt his heart stop. "Why, Rabbi, in the name of all that's holy, do you want to kill me? Didn't I give you all my money? That is, not mine, but first God's and then my clients'? I'll remind you, you wrapped it in a kerchief, sealed it with wax, locked it in your wife's chest, hid the key where no one could find it. And here is better proof: there were witnesses, the leading citizens of the city!" And he goes ahead and calls them all off by name. In the midst of it a cold sweat breaks out on his forehead, he feels faint, and asks for a glass of water.

The rabbi sends the *shammes* off to the men the traveler had named—the leading citizens, the flower of the community. They come running from all directions. "What's the matter? What's happened?" "A misfortune. A plot! A millstone around our necks! He insists that he brought a pile of money to me yesterday, to keep over *Yom Kippur*, and that you were witnesses to the act."

The householders look at each other, as if to say: "Here is where we get a nice bone to lick!" And they fall on the traveler: how could he do a thing like that? He ought to be ashamed of himself! Thinking up an ugly plot like that against their rabbi!

When he saw what was happening, his arms and legs went limp, he just about fainted. But the rabbi got up, went to the chest, took out the kerchief and handed it to him.

"What's the matter with you! Here! Here is your money! Take it and count it, see if it's right, here in front of your witnesses. The seal, as you see, is untouched. The wax is whole, just as it ought to be."

The traveler felt as if a new soul had been installed in his body. His hands trembled and tears stood in his eyes.

"Why did you have to do it, Rabbi? Why did you have to play this trick on me? A trick like this."

"I just wanted to show you—the kind—of—leading citizens—we have in our town."

*Translated by Julius
and Frances Butwin*

ALEICHEM: *Tit for Tat*

1. *How does Sholom Aleichem achieve his humorous effects? How does his technique differ from that of Henry James in "Europe" or Samuel Beckett in "Yellow"?*
2. *What is the point of Reb Nachman Lekach's story?*
3. *What is the point of the rabbiner's story?*
4. *Is the rabbiner's decision to "tax" Troika and Lekach a wise one? Or is it mainly an act of vengeance? Why does Lekach, who is victimized, compare the rabbiner to Solomon?*
5. *Is there much difference between this story and the ordinary*

humorous anecdote or "shaggy dog" story? What are the essential differences? In answering this question, you will come to a clearer understanding of the writer's purpose in a short story.

6. *The anecdotes are told in the first person, but that first person is not the narrator of the story. Why does Sholom Aleichem use a double narrator? How does this technique of narration give the story its special quality?*

7. *What sense of life do you obtain from the rabbiner's community? Compare Aleichem's "feeling for life" with that of two other Jewish writers represented in this volume, Franz Kafka and Isaac Babel.*

Anton Chekhov

THE BET

Born in Taganrog, Russia, in 1860, Anton Chekhov first took up writing to support himself while studying to be a doctor. From these beginnings—Chekhov was the son of a shopkeeper and the grandson of a serf—there developed the greatest of Russian short-story writers and one of the greatest of playwrights. His principal dramas, most of which were written during the last six years of his life, include The Sea Gull *(1896),* Uncle Vanya *(1899),* The Three Sisters *(1901), and* The Cherry Orchard *(1904), while before his death in 1904 he had written hundreds of short stories and novellas. His influence on future generations of short-story writers both in Europe and in the United States has been immense. In "The Bet," Chekhov begins typically with a light scene only to proceed into a tragic situation in which life is itself too much for his characters.*

It was a dark autumn night. The old banker was pacing from corner to corner of his study, recalling to his mind the party he gave in the autumn fifteen years before. There were many clever people at the party and much interesting conversation. They talked among other things of capital punishment. The guests, among them not a few scholars and journalists, for the most part disapproved of capital punishment, found it obsolete as a means of punishment, unfitted to a Christian State, and immoral. Some of them thought that capital punishment should be replaced universally by life-imprisonment.

"I don't agree with you," said the host. "I myself have experienced neither capital punishment nor life-imprisonment, but if one may judge *a priori*, then in my opinion capital punishment is more moral and more humane than imprisonment. Execution kills instantly, life-imprisonment kills by degrees. Who is the more humane executioner, one who kills you in a few seconds or one who draws the life out of you incessantly, for years?"

[191

"They're both equally immoral," remarked one of the guests, "because their purpose is the same, to take away life. The State is not God. It has no right to take away that which it cannot give back, if it should so desire."

Among the company was a lawyer, a young man about twenty-five. On being asked his opinion, he said:

"Capital punishment and life-imprisonment are equally immoral; but if I were offered the choice between them, I would certainly choose the second. It's better to live somehow than not to live at all."

There ensued a lively discussion. The banker who was then younger and more nervous suddenly lost his temper, banged his fist on the table, and turning to the young lawyer, cried out:

"It's a lie. I bet you two millions you wouldn't stick in a cell even for five years."

"If you mean it seriously," replied the lawyer, "then I bet I'll stay not five but fifteen."

"Fifteen! Done!" cried the banker. "Gentlemen, I stake two millions."

"Agreed. You stake two millions, I my freedom," said the lawyer.

So this wild, ridiculous bet came to pass. The banker, who at that time had too many millions to count, spoiled and capricious, was beside himself with rapture. During supper he said to the lawyer jokingly:

"Come to your senses, young man, before it's too late. Two millions are nothing to me, but you stand to lose three or four of the best years of your life. I say three or four, because you'll never stick it out any longer. Don't forget either, you unhappy man, that voluntary is much heavier than enforced imprisonment. The idea that you have the right to free yourself at any moment will poison the whole of your life in the cell. I pity you."

And now the banker, pacing from corner to corner, recalled all this and asked himself:

"Why did I make this bet? What's the good? The lawyer loses fifteen years of his life and I throw away two millions. Will it convince people that capital punishment is worse or better than imprisonment for life? No, no! all stuff and rubbish. On my part, it was the caprice of a well-fed man; on the lawyer's, pure greed of gold."

He recollected further what happened after the evening party. It was decided that the lawyer must undergo his imprisonment under the strictest observation, in a garden wing of the banker's house. It was agreed that during the period he would be deprived of the right to cross the threshold, to see living people, to hear human voices, and to receive letters and newspapers. He was permitted to have a musical instrument, to read books, to write letters, to drink wine and smoke tobacco. By the agreement he could communicate, but only in silence, with the outside world through a little window specially constructed for this purpose. Everything necessary, books, music, wine, he would receive in any quantity by sending a note through the window. The agreement provided for all the minutest details, which made the confinement strictly solitary, and it obliged the lawyer to remain exactly fifteen years from twelve o'clock of November 14th, 1870, to twelve o'clock of November 14th, 1885. The least attempt on his part to violate the conditions, to escape if only for two minutes before the time, freed the banker from the obligation to pay him the two millions.

During the first year of imprisonment, the lawyer, as far as it was possible to judge from his short notes, suffered terribly from loneliness and boredom. From his wing day and night came the sound of the piano. He rejected wine and tobacco. "Wine," he wrote, "excites desires, and desires are the chief foes of a prisoner; besides, nothing is more boring than to drink good wine alone," and tobacco spoiled the air in his room. During the first year the lawyer was sent books of a light character; novels with a complicated love interest, stories of crime and fantasy, comedies, and so on.

In the second year the piano was heard no longer and the lawyer asked only for classics. In the fifth year, music was heard again, and the prisoner asked for wine. Those who watched him said that during the whole of that year he was only eating, drinking, and lying on his bed. He yawned often and talked angrily to himself. Books he did not read. Sometimes at night he would sit down to write. He would write for a long time and tear it all up in the morning. More than once he was heard to weep.

In the second half of the sixth year, the prisoner began zealously to study languages, philosophy, and history. He fell on these subjects so hungrily that the banker hardly had time to get books enough for him. In the space of four years about six hundred volumes were bought at his request. It was while that passion lasted that the banker received the following letter from the prisoner:

"My dear jailer, I am writing these lines in six languages. Show them to experts. Let them read them. If they do not find one single mistake, I beg you to give orders to have a gun fired off in the garden. By the noise I shall know that my efforts have not been in vain. The geniuses of all ages and countries speak in different languages; but in them all burns the same flame. Oh, if you knew my heavenly happiness now that I can understand them!" The prisoner's desire was fulfilled. Two shots were fired in the garden by the banker's order.

Later on, after the tenth year, the lawyer sat immovable before his table and read only the New Testament. The banker found it strange that a man who in four years had mastered six hundred erudite volumes, should have spent nearly a year in reading one book, easy to understand and by no means thick. The New Testament was then replaced by the history of religions and theology.

During the last two years of his confinement the prisoner read an extraordinary amount, quite haphazard. Now he would apply himself to the natural sciences, then he would read Byron or Shakespeare. Notes used to come from him in which he asked to be sent at the same time a book on chemistry, a text-book of medicine, a novel, and some treatise on philosophy or theology. He read as though he were swimming in the sea among broken pieces of wreckage, and in his desire to save his life was eagerly grasping one piece after another.

The banker recalled all this, and thought:

"To-morrow at twelve o'clock he receives his freedom. Under the agreement, I shall have to pay him two millions. If I pay, it's all over with me. I am ruined forever . . ."

Fifteen years before he had too many millions to count, but now he was afraid to ask himself which he had more of, money or debts. Gambling on the Stock-Exchange, risky speculation, and the recklessness of which he could not rid himself even in old age, had gradually brought his business to decay; and the fearless, self-confident, proud man of business had become an ordinary banker, trembling at every rise and fall in the market.

"That cursed bet," murmured the old man clutching his head in despair. . . . "Why didn't the man die? He's only forty years old. He will take away my last farthing, marry, enjoy life, gamble on the Exchange, and I will look on like an envious beggar and hear the same words from him every day: 'I'm obliged to you for the happiness of my life. Let me help you.' No, it's too much! The only escape from bankruptcy and disgrace—is that the man should die."

The clock had just struck three. The banker was listening. In the house every one was asleep, and one could hear only the frozen trees whining outside the windows. Trying to make no sound, he took out of his safe the key of the door which had not been opened for fifteen years, put on his overcoat, and went out of the house. The garden was dark and cold. It was raining. A damp, penetrating wind howled in the garden and gave the trees no rest. Though he strained his eyes, the banker could see neither the ground, nor the white statues, nor the garden wing, nor the trees. Approaching the garden wing, he called the watchman twice. There was no answer. Evidently the watchman had taken shelter from the bad weather and was now asleep somewhere in the kitchen or the greenhouse.

"If I have the courage to fulfil my intention," thought the old man, "the suspicion will fall on the watchman first of all."

In the darkness he groped for the steps and the door and entered the hall of the garden-wing, then poked his way into a narrow passage and struck a match. Not a soul was there. Some one's bed, with no bedclothes on it, stood there, and an iron stove loomed dark in the corner. The seals on the door that led into the prisoner's room were unbroken.

When the match went out, the old man, trembling from agitation peeped into the little window.

In the prisoner's room a candle was burning dimly. The prisoner himself sat by the table. Only his back, the hair on his head and his hand were visible. Open books were strewn about on the table, the two chairs and on the carpet near the table.

Five minutes passed and the prisoner never once stirred. Fifteen years' confinement had taught him to sit motionless. The banker tapped on the window with his finger, but the prisoner made no movement in reply. Then the banker cautiously tore the seals from the door and put the key into the lock. The rusty lock gave a hoarse groan and the door creaked. The banker expected instantly to hear a cry of surprise and the sound of steps. Three minutes passed and it was as quiet inside as it had been before. He made up his mind to enter.

Before the table sat a man, unlike an ordinary human being. It was a skeleton, with tight-drawn skin, with long curly hair like a woman's, and a shaggy beard. The color of his face was yellow, of an earthy shade; the cheeks were sunken, the back long and narrow, and the hand upon which he leaned his hairy head was so lean and skinny that it was painful to look upon. His hair was already silvering with gray, and no one who glanced at the senile emaciation of the face would have believed that he was only forty years old. On the table, before his bended head, lay a sheet of paper on which something was written in a tiny hand.

"Poor devil," thought the banker, "he's asleep and probably seeing millions in his dreams. I have only to take and throw this half-dead thing on the bed, smother him a moment with the pillow, and the most careful examination will find no trace of unnatural death. But, first, let us read what he has written here."

The banker took the sheet from the table and read:

"Tomorrow at twelve o'clock midnight, I shall obtain my freedom and the right to mix with people. But before I leave this room and see the sun I think it necessary to say a few words to you. On my own clear conscience and before God who sees me I declare to you that I despise freedom, life, health, and all that your books call the blessings of the world.

"For fifteen years I have diligently studied earthly life. True, I saw neither the earth nor the people, but in your books I drank fragrant wine, sang songs, hunted deer and wild boar in the forests, loved women. . . . And beautiful women, like clouds ethereal, created by the magic of your poets' genius, visited me by night and whispered to me wonderful tales, which made my head drunken. In your books I climbed the summits of Elbruz and Mont Blanc and saw from there how the sun rose in the morning, and in the evening suffused the sky, the ocean and the mountain ridges with a purple gold. I saw from there how above the lightnings glimmered, cleaving the clouds; I saw green forests, fields, rivers, lakes, cities; I heard sirens singing, and the playing of the pipes of Pan; I touched the wings of beautiful devils who came flying to me to speak of God. . . In your books I cast myself into bottomless abysses, worked miracles, burned cities to the ground, preached new religions, conquered whole countries. . . .

"Your books gave me wisdom. All that unwearying human thought created in the centuries is compressed to a little lump in my skull. I know that I am cleverer than you all.

"And I despise your books, despise all worldly blessings and wisdom. Everything is void, frail, visionary and delusive as a mirage. Though you be proud and wise and beautiful, yet will death wipe you from the face of the earth like the mice underground; and your posterity, your history, and the immortality of your men of genius will be as frozen slag, burnt down together with the terrestrial globe.

"You are mad, and gone the wrong way. You take falsehood for truth and ugliness for beauty. You would marvel if suddenly apple and orange trees should bear frogs and lizards instead of fruit, and if roses should begin to breathe the odor of a sweating horse. So do I marvel at you, who have bartered heaven for earth. I do not want to understand you.

"That I may show you in deed my contempt for that by which you live, I waive the two millions of which I once dreamed as of paradise, and which I now despise. That I may deprive myself of my right to them, I shall come out from here five minutes before the stipulated term, and thus shall violate the agreement."

When he had read, the banker put the sheet on the table, kissed the head of the strange man, and began to weep. He went out of the wing. Never at any other time, not even after his terrible losses on the Exchange, had he felt such contempt for himself as now. Coming home, he lay down on his bed, but agitation and tears kept him a long time from sleeping. . . .

The next morning the poor watchman came running to him and told him that they had seen the man who lived in the wing climb through the window into the garden. He had gone to the gate and disappeared. The banker instantly went with his servants to the wing and established the escape of his prisoner. To avoid unnecessary rumors he took the paper with the renunciation from the table and, on his return, locked it in his safe.

CHEKHOV: *The Bet*

1. *Does the title suggest a view of life? What is at stake here?*
2. *Why does Chekhov rush right into the bet without much preparation?*
3. *Does the bet prove that life imprisonment is preferable to capital punishment? What does it prove? Is it better to live somehow than not to live at all? Compare Sartre's view in "The Wall."*
4. *Why is knowledge by itself insufficient for the prisoner's satisfaction?*

5. *Fifteen years of contemplation might lead to saintliness, but here what does it lead to?*

6. *Can you understand why the prisoner would willfully wish to break the pact for which he suffered so greatly? What is involved here in terms of attitudes toward life? If the prisoner had honored the pact up to the end, what would he have gained?*

7. *Has the prisoner been ennobled or degraded? Has the imprisoner been ennobled or degraded? What point is Chekhov making?*

8. *Does Chekhov seem closer to his fellow countrymen like Tolstoy and Dostoyevsky or to later authors like Moravia, Sartre, Lagerkvist?*

9. *Can you find any scenic elements in the story, qualities that would indicate that the author was also a great playwright?*

10. *Chekhov himself provided an alternative ending to this story. Can you devise one that would be more satisfactory to you, or do you find the present conclusion right?*

11. *Do you think Chekhov is making a subtle argument against the entire penal institution that modern society has developed?*

Miguel de Unamuno y Jugo
THE MADNESS OF DR. MONTARCO

A figure of dissent in his homeland, Miguel de Unamuno y Jugo spent his life attempting to resolve the tragic conflicts that split man into fragments. Born in the Basque seaport of Bilbao in 1864, Unamuno earned a doctorate at the University of Madrid and at 27 received a chair in Greek at the University of Salamanca. His growing reputation as a writer and scholar was enhanced by the publication of The Life of Don Quixote *(1905) and* The Tragic Sense of Life *(1912). In his short novel* Abel Sanchez *(1917), he created in the opposing selves of Abel Sanchez, the calm man of the world, and Joaquin Monegro, the obsessed man who would be God, the same dualism that appears in "The Madness of Dr. Montarco." As Unamuno saw his characters, so he saw himself; as he saw Spain, so he saw the world, torn by its quixotic nature, unable to reconcile its desire for mortality with its longing for immortality. In 1936, Unamuno died, true to his quixotic nature, having first supported Franco's rebels in the Spanish Civil War and then later denouncing them.*

I FIRST met Dr. Montarco just after his arrival in the city. A secret attraction drew me to him. His appearance was obviously in his favor, and his face had an open and guileless look about it. He was tall, blond, robust, yet quick in movement. He immediately made a friend of everyone he knew, because if he was not to make a person his friend, he restrained from making him his acquaintance. It was difficult to know which of his gestures were natural and which were studied, so subtly had he combined naturalness and art. From this proceeded the fact that while there were some who criticized him for affectation and found his simplicity studied, others of us thought that whatever he did was natural and spontaneous. He himself told me later: "There are gestures which, natural enough to begin with, later become artificial after they have been repeatedly praised. And then there are other gestures which, though we have acquired them after hard work and even against our very nature, end by becoming completely natural and seemingly native to us."

This observation should be enough to show that Dr. Montarco was not, while he was still of sound mind, the extravagant personality which many claimed. Far from it. He was, on the contrary, a man who in conversation expressed discreet and judicious opinions. Only on rare occasions, and even then only with persons completely in his confidence (as I came to be), did he unbridle his feelings and let himself go; it was then he would indulge in vehement invective against the people who surrounded him and from whom he had to gain his livelihood. And thus was prefigured the abyss into which his spirit was finally to fall.

He was one of the most orderly and simple men I have ever known. He was not a "connoisseur" or collector of anything, not even of books, nor did I ever detect in him any monomania whatever. His practice, his home, and his literary work: these were his only preoccupations. He had a wife and two daughters, aged eight and ten, when he arrived in the city. He was preceded by a very good reputation as a doctor; nevertheless, it was no secret that he had been forced by his peculiar conduct to leave his native town. His greatest peculiarity, in the eyes of his medical colleagues, lay in the fact that although he was an excellent practitioner and very well versed in medical science and biology, and that although he was a voluminous writer, it never seemed to occur to him to write about medicine. As he told me once, in his characteristically violent manner: "Why must these idiots insist that I write of professional matters? I studied medicine simply to cure sick people and earn my living doing so. Do I cure them? I do; and therefore let them leave me in peace and spare me their nonsense, and let them keep out of my business. I earn my living as conscientiously as I can, and, once my living is made, I do with my life what I want, and not what these louts want me to do. You can't imagine what profound misery of a moral sort there is in the attempt, which so many people make, to confine everybody to a specialty. For my part, I find a tremendous advantage in living *from* one activity and *for* another. . . . You probably don't need to be reminded of Schopenhauer's justified denunciation of professional philosophers and busybodies."

A little while after arriving in the city, and after he had built up a better than average practice and had acquired the reputation of a serious, careful, painstaking and well-endowed doctor, a local journal published his first story, a story half-way between fantasy and humor, without descriptive writing and without a moral. Two days later I found him very upset; when I asked the reason, he burst forth: "Do you think I'm going to be able to resist the overwhelming pressure of the idiocy prevailing here? Tell me, do you think so? It's the same thing all over again, exactly the same as in my town, the very same! And just as happened there, I'll end by becoming known as a madman. I, who am a marvel of calm. And my patients will gradually drop away, and I'll lose my practice. Then the dismal days will come again, days filled with despair, disgust, and bad temper, and I will have to leave here just as I had to leave my own town."

"But what has happened?" I was finally able to ask.

"What has happened? Simply that five people have already approached me to ask what I meant by writing the piece of fiction I just published, what I intended to say, and what bearing did it have. Idiots, idiots, and thrice idiots! They're worse than children who break dolls to find out what's inside. This town has no hope of salvation, my friend; it's simply condemned to seriousness and silliness, two blood sisters. People here have the souls of school teachers. They believe no one could write except to prove something, or defend or attack some proposition, or from an ulterior motive. One of these blockheads asked me the meaning of my story and by way of reply I asked *him:* 'Did it amuse you?' And he answered: 'As far as that goes, it certainly did; as a matter of fact, I found it quite amusing; but . . .' I left the last word in his mouth, because as soon as he reached this point in the conversation, I turned my back on him and walked away. That a piece of writing is amusing wasn't enough for this monster. They have the souls of school teachers, the souls of school teachers!"

"But, now . . ." I ventured to take up the argument.

"Listen," he interrupted, "don't you come at me with any more 'buts.' Don't bother. The infectious disease, the itch of our Spanish literature is the urge to preach. Everywhere a sermon, and a bad sermon at that. Every little Christ sets himself up to dispense advice, and does it with a poker-face. I remember picking up the *Moral Epistle to Fabian* and being unable to get beyond the first three verses; I simply couldn't stomach it. This breed of men is totally devoid of imagination, and so all their madness is merely silly. An oyster-like breed—there's no use of your denying it—; oysters, that's what they are, nothing but oysters. Everything here savors of oyster beds, or ground-muck. I feel like I'm living among human tubers. And they don't even break through the ground, or lift their heads up, like regular tubers."

In any case, Dr. Montarco did not take heed, and he went and published another story, more satirical and fantastic than the first. I recall Servando Fernández Gómez, a patient of Dr. Montarco, discussing it with me.

"Well sir," said the good Fernández Gómez, "I really don't know what to do now that my doctor has published his stories."

"How is that?" I asked him with some surprise.

"Frankly, it seems rather risky, putting oneself in the hands of a man who writes things like that."

"Come, now, he gives you good care as a doctor, doesn't he?"

"There's no question of that. I've no complaint on that score. Ever since putting myself in his hands, consulting with him and following his regimen, I'm much better and every day I notice a further improvement. Still, those pieces of his . . . he must not be well himself. He sounds as if he had a head full of crickets."

"Don't be alarmed, Don Servando. I have many dealings with him, as you know, and I've observed nothing at all wrong with him. He is a very sensible man."

"When one talks to him he answers appropriately enough and what he says is very sensible, but . . ."

"Listen, I'd rather have a man operate on me who had a steady hand and eye even if he did speak wildly (though Montarco doesn't do that either), than a man who was exquisitely proper, full of sententious wisdom and every kind of platitude and then went ahead and threw my whole body out of joint."

"That may be. Still . . ."

The next day I asked Dr. Montarco about Fernández Gómez, and he responded dryly: "A constitutional fool!"

"What's that?"

"A fool by physiological constitution, *a nativitate*, congenital, irremediable."

"Sounds like the absolute and eternal fool."

"No doubt . . . for, in this area an Absolute fool and a Constitutional one are the same thing; it's not as in politics, where the Absolutists and the Constitutionalists are at opposite poles."

"He says your head must be full of crickets. . . ."

"And his head, and those of his kind, are full of cockroaches. And cockroaches are merely mute crickets. At least mine can sing, or chirrup, or creak out something."

A short time later the doctor published his third tale; and this time the narrative was more pointed, full of ironies, mockery and ill-concealed invective.

"I don't know whether you're doing the wisest thing by publishing these stories," I told him.

"By heaven, I have to. I simply have to express myself and work off my feelings. If I didn't write out these atrocities I'd end by committing them. I know well enough what I'm doing."

"There are some people who say that all this doesn't suit a man of your age, position, and profession. . . ." I said by way of drawing him out.

At this, he jumped to his feet and exclaimed:

"Just as I told you, exactly what I've said a thousand times: I'll have to go away from here, or I shall die of hunger, or they'll drive me crazy, or all of these things together. Yes, that's it, all three at once: I shall have to leave, a madman, to die of hunger. And they talk about my position, do they? What do those blockheads mean by position? Listen, believe me, we shall never emerge from barbarism in Spain, never be more than fancy Moroccans, fancy and false, for we'd be better off being our simple African selves, until we stop insisting that our chief of state be illiterate, that he write not a word, not even a volume of epigrams, or some children's tales, or a farce, while he is in office. He risks his prestige by literacy, they say. Meanwhile, we risk our history and our evolution with the opposite. How stupid and heavy-handed we are!"

Thus impelled by a fatal insight did Dr. Montarco set himself to combat the public sentiment of the city in which he lived and worked. At the same time he strove to be more and more conscientious and meticulous in his professional duties and in his civic and domestic obligations. He took extreme care to attend to his patients in every way, and to study their ills. He greeted everyone with extreme affability; he was rude to no one. In speaking to a person he would choose the topic he thought most likely to interest them, seeking thus to please them. In his private life he continued to be the ideal, the exemplary, husband and father. Still, his tales continued to grow more fanciful and extravagant: such was the opinion of the multitude, who also thought he was straying further and further from the "normal", the "usual". And his patients were beginning to abandon him, creating a void around him. Whereupon his ill-concealed animosity became evident once more.

And this was not the worst of it, for a malicious rumor began to take form and to spread: he was said to be arrogant. Without foundation of any sort, it began to be whispered that the doctor was a haughty spirit, a man concerned only with himself, who gave himself airs and considered himself a genius, while he thought other people poor devils incapable of understanding him. I told him about this consensus and this time, instead of breaking out into one of his customary diatribes, as I had expected, he answered me calmly:

"Haughty and proud am I? No! Only ignorant people, fools, are ever really haughty; and frankly, I don't consider myself a fool; my type of foolishness doesn't qualify me. If we actually could peer into the depths of each other's conscience like that! I know they think I am disdainful of others, but they are wrong. The truth is merely that I don't have the same opinion of them that they have of themselves. And besides—I might as well tell you what I'm really thinking—what is all this talk about pride and striving for superiority worth anyway? For the truth is, my friend, that when a man tries to get ahead of others he is simply trying to save himself. When a man tries to drown out the names of other men he is merely trying to insure that his own be preserved in the memory of living men, because he knows that posterity is a closemeshed sieve which allows few names to get through to other ages. For instance, have you ever noticed the way a fly-trap works?"

"What do you mean? What kind of a . . . ?"

"One of those bottles filled with water, which in the country are set around to catch flies. The poor flies try to save themselves and, since there is no way out but to climb on the backs of others, and thus navigate on cadavers in those enclosed waters of death, a ferocious struggle takes place to see which one can win out. They do not in the least mean to drown each other; all they are trying to do is to stay afloat. Just so in the struggle for fame, which is a thousand times more terrible than the struggle for bread."

"And the struggle for life," I added, "is the same, too. Darwin . . ."

"Darwin?" he cut me off. "Do you know the book *Biological Problems* by William Henry Rolph?"

"No."

"Well, read it. Read it and you will see that it is not the growth and multiplication of a species which necessitates more food and which leads to such struggle, but rather that it is a tendency toward needing more and more food, an impulse to go beyond the purely necessary, to exceed it, which causes a species to grow and multiply. It is not an instinct toward self-preservation which impels us to action, but rather an instinct toward expansion, toward invasion and encroachment. We don't strive to maintain ourselves only, but to be more than we are already, to be everything. In the strong words of Father Alonso Rodriguez, that great man, we are driven by an 'appetite for the divine.' Yes, an appetite for the divine. 'You will be as gods!': thus it was the Devil tempted our first parents, they say. Whoever doesn't aspire to be more than he is, will not be anything. All or nothing! There is profound meaning in that. Whatever Reason may tell us—that great liar who has invented, for the consolation of failures, the doctrine of the golden mean, the *aurea mediocritas*, the 'neither envied nor envying' and other such nonsense—whatever Reason may tell us—and she is not only a liar but a great whore—in our innermost soul, which we now call the Unconscious, with a capital U, in the depths of our spirit, we know that in order to avoid becoming, sooner or later, nothing, the best course to follow is to attempt to become all.

"The struggle for life, for the more-than-life, rather, is an offensive and not a defensive struggle. . . . In this Rolph is quite right. And I, my friend, do not defend myself; I am never on the defensive, instead I believe in the attack. I don't want a shield, which would only weigh me down and hinder me. I don't want anything but a sword. I would rather deliver fifty blows, and receive ten back, than deliver only ten and not receive any. Attack, attack, and no defense. Let them say what they want about me; I won't hear them, I'll take no notice, I will stop my ears, and if in spite of my precautions, word of what they say reaches me, I will not answer them. If we had centuries of time to spare, I would sooner be able to convince them that they are fools—and you may imagine the difficulty in doing that—than they would convince me I am mad or over-proud."

"But this purely offensive system of yours, Montarco, my friend . . ." I began.

"Yes, yes," he interrupted me again, "it has its flaws. And even one great danger, and that is that on the day my arm weakens or my sword is blunted they will trample me under their feet, drag me about, and make dust of me. But before that happens they will have already accomplished their purpose: they will have driven me mad."

And so it was to be. I began to suspect it when I heard him talk repeatedly about the character of madness, and to inveigh against reason. In the end, they would succeed in driving him mad.

He persisted in issuing his stories, fictions totally different from anything current at this time and place; and he persisted, simultaneously, in not departing one whit from the reasonable sort of life he outwardly led. His patients continued to leave him. Eventually, dire want made itself felt in his household. Finally, as a culmination to his troubles, he could no longer find a journal or paper to print his contributions, nor did his name make any headway or gain any ground in the republic of letters. It all came to an end when a few of us who were his friends took over responsibility for his wife and daughters, and arranged for him to go into an asylum. His verbal aggression had been growing steadily more pronounced.

I remember as if it were yesterday the first day I visited him in the asylum where he was confined. The director, Dr. Atienza, had been a fellow student of Dr. Montarco and manifested an affection and sympathy for him.

"Well, he is quieter these days, more tranquil than at the beginning," the director told me. "He reads a little, very little; I think it would be unwise to deprive him of reading matter absolutely. Mostly, he reads the *Quixote*, and, if you were to pick up his copy of the book and open it at random, it would almost certainly open to Chapter 32, of the Second Part, where is to be found the reply made by Don Quixote to his critic, the ponderous ecclesiastic who at the table of the duke and duchess severely reprimanded the knight-errant for his mad fancies. If you want, we will go and see him now."

And we did so.

"I am very glad that you've come to call," he exclaimed as soon as he saw me, raising his eyes from the *Quixote*, "I'm glad. I was just thinking and wondering if, despite what Christ tells us in the twenty-second verse of the fifth chapter of St. Matthew, we are ever permitted to make use of the forbidden weapon."

"And what is the forbidden weapon?" I asked him.

" 'Whoever shall call his brother "Fool!" shall be liable to the fires of Gehenna.' You see what a terrible sentence that is. It doesn't say whoever calls him assassin, or thief, or bandit, or swindler, or coward, or whoreson, or cuckold, or liberal; no, it says, whosoever shall call him a 'fool.' That, then, is the forbidden weapon. Everything can be questioned except the intelligence, wit and judgment of other people. When a man takes it into his head to have aspirations, to presume to some special knowledge or talent, it's even more complicated. There have been popes who, because they considered themselves great Latinists, would rather have been condemned as heretics than as poor Latinists guilty of solecisms. And there are weighty cardinals who take greater pride in the purity of their literary style than in being good Christians, and for them orthodoxy is no more than a consequence of literary purity. The forbidden weapon! Just consider the comedy of politics: the participants accuse one another of the ugliest crimes, they charge each other covertly

The Madness of Dr. Montarco

with grave offenses, but they are always careful to call each other eloquent, clever, well-intentioned, talented. . . . For, 'Whosoever shall call his brother a fool, shall be liable to the fires of Gehenna.' Nevertheless, do you know why we make no real progress?"

"Perhaps because we must carry tradition on our backs," I ventured to say.

"No, no. It's simply because it is impossible to convince the fools that they *are* fools. On the day on which fools, that is to say, mankind, become truly convinced that they are just that, fools, on that day progress will have reached its goal. Man is born foolish. . . . And yet whosoever calls his brother a fool shall expose himself to the fires of Gehenna. And expose himself to hellfire he did, that grave clergyman, 'one of those who presume tc govern great men's houses, and who, not being nobly born themselves, don't know how to instruct those that are, but would have the liberality of the great measured by the narrowness of their own souls, making those whom they govern stingy, when they pretend to teach them frugality . . .' "

"Do you see," Dr. Atienza whispered to me, "he knows chapters 31 and 32 of the second part of our book by heart."

"He exposed himself to hellfire, I say," the poor madman went on, "this grave ecclesiastic who came out with the duke and duchess to receive Don Quixote, and who sat down at table with him, face to face while they ate. For, a little while later, furious, stupidly envious, and animated by low passions decked out as high wisdom, this boor charged the duke with responsibility before Our Lord for the actions of this 'good man'. . . . *This good man*, the ridiculous and pompous cleric called Don Quixote, and then went on to call him Mister Fool. Mister Fool!, and he the greatest madman of all time! But he condemned himself to hellfire for calling him that. And in hell he lies."

"Perhaps he is only in purgatory, for the mercy of God is infinite," I dared to say.

"But the guilt of the grave ecclesiastic—who clearly stands for our country in the book, and nothing else—is an enormous one, really enormous," he continued, ignoring my qualifying suggestion. "That ponderous idiot, a genuine incarnation and representative, if there ever was one, of that section of our population which considers itself cultured, that insufferable pedant, after rising peevishly from table and questioning the good sense of his lord, who was feeding him—though it is doubtful if he did anything to earn his keep,—said: 'Well may fools be mad, when wise men celebrate their madness. Your Grace may remain with this pair, if you please, but for my part, as long as they are in this house, I shall keep to my quarters, and thus save myself the labor of reprehending what I can't mend.' And with that, 'leaving the rest of his dinner behind him, away he flung.' He went away; but not entirely, for he and his like still prowl about, classifying people as sane or mad, and deciding which persons are which. . . . It's scandalous and hypocritical, but these great judges call Don Quixote 'the sublime madman' in public—and another packet of phrases they have heard somewhere—and in private, alone with themselves, they call him Mister Fool. Don Quixote, who, in order to go off in pursuit of an empire, the empire of fame, left Sancho Panza the government of an Island! And what office did Mister Fool keep for himself? Not even a ministry! And after all, why did God create the world? For His greater glory, they say, to make it manifest. And should we do less? . . . Pride! Pride! Diabolic pride! That's the cry of the weak and impotent. Bring them here, all those grave and ponderous gentlemen infected with common sense. . . .''

"Let's leave," Dr. Atienza whispered, "he is getting excited."

We cut short the visit with some excuse or other, and I took leave of my poor friend.

"He has been driven mad," Dr. Atienza said as soon as we were alone. "One of the wisest and sanest men I ever knew, and he has been driven mad."

"Why do you say that?" I asked, "Why 'driven'?"

"The greatest difference between the sane and the insane," he answered me, "is that the sane, even though they may occasionally have mad thoughts, neither express them nor carry them out, while the insane—unless they are hopeless, in which case they do not think mad thoughts at all—have no power of inhibition, no ability to contain themselves. Who has not thought of carrying out some piece of madness—unless he is a person whose lack of imagination borders on imbecility? But he has known how to control himself. And if he doesn't know, he evolves into a madman or a genius, to a greater or lesser extent of one or the other depending on his form of madness. It is very convenient to speak of 'delusions' in this connection, but any delusion which proves itself to be practical, or which impels us to maintain, advance or intensify life, is just as real an emotion and makes as valid an impression as any which can be registered, in a more precise manner, by the scientific instruments so far invented for the purpose. That necessary store of madness—to give it its plainest name—which is indispensable for any progress, the lack of balance which propels the world of the spirit and without which there would be absolute repose—that is, death—this madness, this imbalance, must be made use of in some way or other. Dr. Montarco used it to create his fantastic narratives, and in doing so he freed himself from it and was able to carry on the very orderly and sensible life which he led. And really, those stories. . . ."

"Ah!" I interrupted, "they are profoundly suggestive, they are rich in surprising points of view. I can read and re-read them because of their freshness, for I find nothing more tedious than to be told something in writing which I have already ruminated. I can always read stories like these, without a moral and without description. I have been thinking of writing a critical study of his work, and I entertain the hope that once the public is put on the right track they will finally see in them what they don't today. The public isn't as slow-witted or disdainful as we sometimes think; their limitation is that they want everything given them already masticated, predigested, and made up into capsules ready to be swallowed. Everyone has enough to do simply making a living and can't take the time to chew on a cud which tastes bitter when it is first put in the mouth. But a worthwhile commentary can bring out the virtues of a writer like Dr. Montarco, in whose work only the letter and not the spirit has so far been apperceived."

"Well, his stories certainly fell on rocky ground," Dr. Atienza resumed. "His very strangeness, which in another country would have attracted readers, scared people away here. At every step of the way and confronted with the simplest things, people surfeited with the most didactic and pedantic junk asked insistently: 'Now what does he mean here, what is this man trying to say in this passage?' And then, you know how his patients all deserted him, despite the fact that he gave them perfect care. People began to call him mad, despite his exemplary life. He was accused of passions which, in spite of appearances, did not really dominate him. His writings were all rejected. And then, when he and his family found themselves in actual need, he gave way to mad talk and acts; and it was this madness which he had previously vented in his writings."

"Madness?" I interrupted.

"No, you're right. It wasn't madness. But, now they have succeeded in making it turn into madness. I have been reading his work since he has been here and I realize now that one of their mistakes was to take him for a man of ideas, a writer of ideas, when fundamentally he is no such thing. His ideas were a point of departure, mere raw material, and had as much importance in his writing as earth used by Velásquez in making the pigments had to do with his painting, or as the type of stone

Michelangelo used had to do with his *Moses*. And what would we say of a man who, equipped with a microscope and reagent, went to make an analysis of the marble by way of arriving at a judgment of the *Venus de Milo?* At best, ideas are no more than raw material, as I've already said, for works of art, or philosophy, or for polemics."

"I have always thought so," I said, "but I have found this to be one of the doctrines which meets with the most resistance on the part of the public. I remember that once, in the course of watching a game of chess, I witnessed the most intense drama of which I have ever been spectator. It was a truly terrible spectacle. The players did no more than move the chessmen, and they were limited by the canons of the game and by the chessboard; nevertheless, you can not imagine what intensity of passion there was, what tension of a truly spiritual nature, what flow of vital energy! Those who only followed the progress of the game thought they were attending an everyday match, for the two players certainly played without great skill. For my part I was watching the way they picked out the chessmen and played them; I was attentive to the solemn silence, the frowns on the players' brows. There was one move, one of the most ordinary and undistinguished no doubt, a check which did not eventuate in a checkmate, which was nevertheless most extraordinary. You should have seen how the one player grasped his knight with his whole hand and placed him on the board with a rap, and how he exclaimed 'Check!' And those two passed for two commonplace players! Commonplace? I'm certain that Morphy or Philidor were more so. . . . Poor Montarco!"

"Yes, poor Montarco! And today you have heard him speak more or less reasonably. . . . Rarely, only rarely, does he talk complete extravagance. When he does, he imagines he is a grotesque character whom he calls the Privy Counsellor Herr Schmarotzender; he puts on a wig which he has found somewhere, gets up on a chair, and makes a wild speech,—full of spirit, however, and in words which somehow echo all the longing and eternal seeking of humanity. At the end, he gets down and asks me: 'Don't you think, Atienza, my friend, that there is a good deal of truth, basically, in the ravings of the poor Privy Counsellor Herr Schmarotzender?' And, in fact, it often strikes me that the feeling of veneration accorded madmen in certain countries is quite justified."

"You know, it seems to me that you should give up the management of this place."

"Don't concern yourself, my friend. It's not that I believe that the veil of a superior world, a world hidden from us, is lifted for these unfortunates; it's simply that I think they say things we all think but don't dare express because of timidity or shame. Reason, which we have acquired in the struggle for life and which is a conservative force, tolerates only what serves to conserve or affirm this life. We don't understand anything but what we must understand in order to live. But who can say that the inextinguishable longing to survive, the thirst for immortality, is not the proof, the revelation of another world, a world which envelops, and also makes possible, our world? And who can say that when reason and its chains have been broken, such dreams and delirium, such frenzied outbursts as Dr. Montarco's, are not desperate leaps by the spirit to reach this other world?"

"It seems to me, and you will forgive my bluntness in saying so, that instead of your treating Dr. Montarco, Dr. Montarco is treating you. The speeches of the Privy Counsellor are beginning to affect you adversely."

"It may be. The only thing I am sure of is that every day I immure myself deeper in this asylum; for I would rather watch over madmen, than have to put up with fools. The only trouble, really, is that there are many madmen who are also fools. But now I have Dr. Montarco to devote myself to. Poor Montarco!"

"Poor Spain!" I said. I extended my hand and we parted.

Dr. Montarco did not last long in the asylum. He was gradually overcome by a profound melancholy, a crushing depression, and finally sank into an obstinate state of muteness. He emerged from his silence only to murmur: "All or nothing. . . . All or nothing. . . . All or nothing. . . ." His illness deepened and ended in death.

After his death, the drawer to his desk yielded a bulky manuscript whose title page read:

ALL OR NOTHING
I request that on my death this manuscript be burned without being read.

I don't know whether Dr. Atienza resisted the temptation to read it; or whether, in compliance with the madman's last wish, he burned it.

Poor Dr. Montarco! May he rest in peace, for he deserved both peace and final rest.

Translated by Anthony Kerrigan

UNAMUNO: *The Madness of Dr. Montarco*

1. Are the townspeople justified in suspecting Dr. Montarco's motives for writing stories?
2. Why does he persist in publishing in the face of public sentiment?
3. What does the image of the "fly-trap" signify? Do you agree with Dr. Montarco's point?
4. Dr. Montarco explains his philosophy thus: "I would rather deliver fifty blows, and receive ten back, than deliver only ten and not receive any." What does he mean? Does the metaphor mask nothing more than a belligerent nature which, when frustrated, takes an extreme course?
5. Did you think Dr. Montarco is right in attacking the statement of Jesus Christ: "Whoever shall call his brother 'Fool!' shall be liable to the fires of Gehenna [Hell]"?
6. What is the relevance of Don Quixote to this story? One critic calls Unamuno a descendant of Don Quixote rather than of Cervantes. Do you agree?
7. What does the narrator mean by "Poor Spain" after Dr. Atienza comments "Poor Montarco!"?
8. Is Dr. Montarco, after all, a madman?
9. Sartre and Unamuno set their stories in Spain. How does the setting enter into each of these stories?
10. Is there any similarity between the stories of Unamuno and Borges? What are the chief differences in style and structure?
11. Arturo Barea writes of Unamuno: "With passionate, self-centered energy Unamuno pursued a few basic problems through everything he wrote, through repetition, interpretation, exaggeration and contradiction. . . . Those problems were his own, but he conceived them also as the problems of other Spaniards, of his country as a whole, and of humanity." Does this statement apply to "The Madness of Dr. Montarco"? How?

Luigi Pirandello

THE SOFT TOUCH OF GRASS

Luigi Pirandello was born (in 1867) and raised in Sicily, whose bitter landscape dominates the spirit of his early work. After taking a doctorate at Bonn, he began to teach literature at a Roman school, writing poetry and short stories as an avocation before he turned to the theater. Though his fiction develops out of the naturalistic style of his friend Giovanni Verga, it is distinguished by an attitude of benevolent pity and irony toward people pinioned uncomfortably, sometimes grotesquely or terrifyingly, to an alien time or place. Often his compassionate bitterness worked to best advantage in his plays, in, for example, Six Characters in Search of an Author *(1921),* Henry IV *(1922), and* As You Desire Me *(1931). After 1918, Pirandello devoted himself fully to his last love, the theater, and achieved an international reputation through his satirical and symbolic dramas. He died in Rome in 1936, two years after receiving the Nobel Prize.*

THEY went into the next room, where he was sleeping in a big chair, to ask if he wanted to look at her for the last time before the lid was put on the coffin.

"It's dark. What time is it?" he asked.

It was nine-thirty in the morning, but the day was overcast and the light dim. The funeral had been set for ten o'clock.

Signor Pardi stared up at them with dull eyes. It hardly seemed possible that he could have slept so long and well all night. He was still numb with sleep and the sorrow of these last days. He would have liked to cover his face with his hands to shut out the faces of his neighbors grouped about his chair in the thin light; but sleep had weighted his body like lead, and although there was a tingling in his toes urging him to rise, it quickly went away. Should he still give way to his grief? He happened to say aloud, "Always . . ." but he said it like someone settling himself under the covers to go back to sleep. They all looked at him questioningly. Always what?

Always dark, even in the daytime, he had wanted to say, but it made

[213

no sense. The day after her death, the day of her funeral, he would always remember this wan light and his deep sleep, too, with her lying dead in the next room. Perhaps the windows . . .

"The windows?"

Yes, they were still closed. They had not been opened during the night, and the warm glow of those big dripping candles lingered. The bed had been taken away and she was there in her padded casket, rigid and ashen against the creamy satin.

No. Enough. He had seen her.

He closed his eyes, for they burned from all the crying he had done these past few days. Enough. He had slept and everything had been washed away with that sleep. Now he was relaxed, with a sense of sorrowful emptiness. Let the casket be closed and carried away with all it held of his past life.

But since she was still there . . .

He jumped to his feet and tottered. They caught him and, with eyes still closed, he allowed himself to be led to the open casket. When he opened his eyes and saw her, he called her by name, her name that lived for him alone, the name in which he saw her and knew her in all the fullness of the life they had shared together. He glared resentfully at the others daring to stare at her lying still in death. What did they know about her? They could not even imagine what it meant to him to be deprived of her. He felt like screaming, and it must have been apparent, for his son hurried over to take him away. He was quick to see the meaning of this and felt a chill as though he were stripped bare. For shame—those foolish ideas up to the very last, even after his night-long sleep. Now they must hurry so as not to keep the friends waiting who had come to follow the coffin to the church.

"Come on, Papa. Be reasonable."

With angry, piteous eyes, the bereaved man turned back to his big chair.

Reasonable, yes; it was useless to cry out the anguish that welled within him and that could never be expressed by words or deeds. For a husband who is left a widower at a certain age, a man still yearning for his wife, can the loss be the same as that of a son for whom—at a certain point—it is almost timely to be left an orphan? Timely, since he was on the point of getting married and would, as soon as the three months' mourning were passed, now that he had the added excuse that it was better for both of them to have a woman to look after the house.

"Pardi! Pardi!" they shouted from the entrance hall.

His chill became more intense when he understood clearly for the first time that they were not calling him but his son. From now on their surname would belong more to his son than to him. And he, like a fool, had gone in there to cry out the living name of his mate, like a profanation. For shame! Yes, useless, foolish ideas, he now realized, after that long sleep which had washed him clean of everything.

Now the one vital thing to keep him going was his curiosity as to how their new home would be arranged. Where, for example, were they going to have him sleep? The big double bed had been removed. Would he have a small bed? he wondered. Yes, probably his son's single bed. Now he would have the small bed. And his son would soon be lying in a big bed, his wife beside him within arm's reach. He, alone, in his little bed, would stretch out his arms into thin air.

He felt torpid, perplexed, with a sensation of emptiness inside and all around him. His body was numb from sitting so long. If he tried now to get up he felt sure that he would rise light as a feather in all that emptiness, now that his life was reduced to nothing. There was hardly any difference between himself and the big chair. Yet that chair appeared secure on its four legs, whereas he no longer knew where his feet and legs belonged nor what to do with his hands. What did he care about his life? He did not care particularly about the lives of others, either. Yet as he was still alive he must go on. Begin again—some sort of life which he could not yet conceive and which he certainly would never have contemplated if things had not changed in his own world. Now, deposed like this all of a sudden, not old and yet no longer young . . .

He smiled and shrugged his shoulders. For his son, all at once, he had become a child. But after all, as everyone knows, fathers are children to their grown sons who are full of worldly ambition and have successfully outdistanced them in positions of importance. They keep their fathers in idleness to repay all they have received when they themselves were small, and their fathers in turn become young again.

The single bed . . .

But they did not even give him the little room where his son had slept. Instead, they said, he would feel more independent in another, almost hidden on the courtyard; he would feel free there to do as he liked. They refurnished it with all the best pieces, so it would not occur to anyone that it had once been a servant's room. After the marriage, all the front rooms were pretentiously decorated and newly furnished, even to the luxury of carpets. Not a trace remained of the way the old house had looked. Even with his own furniture relegated to that little dark room, out of the mainstream of the young people's existence, he did not feel at home. Yet, oddly enough, he did not resent the disregard he seemed to have reaped along with the old furniture, because he admired the new rooms and was satisfied with his son's success.

But there was another deeper reason, not too clear as yet, a promise of another life, all shining and colorful, which was erasing the memory of the old one. He even drew a secret hope from it that a new life might begin for him too. Unconsciously, he sensed the luminous opening of a door at his back whence he might escape at the right moment, easy enough now that no one bothered about him, leaving him as if on holiday in the sanctuary of his little room "to do as he pleased." He felt lighter than air. His eyes had a gleam in them that colored everything, leading him from marvel to marvel, as though he really were a child again. He had the eyes of a child—lively and open wide on a world which was still new.

He took the habit of going out early in the morning to begin his holiday which was to last as long as his life lasted. Relieved of all responsibilities, he agreed to pay his son so much every month out of his pension for his maintenance. It was very little. Though he needed nothing, his son thought he should keep some money for himself to satisfy any need he might have. But need for what? He was satisfied now just to look on at life.

Having shaken off the weight of experience, he no longer knew how to get along with oldsters. He avoided them. And the younger people considered him too old, so he went to the park where the children played.

That was how he started his new life—in the meadow among the children in the grass. What an exhilarating scent the grass had, and so fresh where it grew thick and high. The children played hide-and-seek there. The constant trickle of some hidden stream outpurled the rustle of the leaves. Forgetting their game, the children pulled off their shoes and stockings. What a delicious feeling to sink into all that freshness of soft new grass with bare feet!

He took off one shoe and was stealthily removing the other when a young girl appeared before him, her face flaming. "You pig!" she cried, her eyes flashing.

Her dress was caught up in front on a bush, and she quickly pulled it down over her legs, because he was looking up at her from where he sat on the ground.

He was stunned. What had she imagined? Already she had disappeared. He had wanted to enjoy the children's innocent fun. Bending down, he put his two hands over his hard, bare feet. What had she seen wrong? Was he too old to share a child's delight in going barefoot in the grass? Must one immediately think evil because he was old? Ah, he knew that he could change in a flash from being a child to becoming a man again, if he must. He was still a man, after all, but he didn't want to think about it. He refused to think about it. It was really as a child that he had taken off his shoes. How wrong it was of that wretched girl to insult him like that! He threw himself face down on the grass. All his grief, his loss, his daily loneliness had brought about this gesture, interpreted now in the light of vulgar malice. His gorge rose in disgust and bitterness. Stupid girl! If he had wanted that—even his son admitted he might have "some desires"—he had plenty of money in his pocket for such needs.

Indignant, he pulled himself upright. Shamefacedly, with trembling hands, he put on his shoes again. All the blood had gone to his head and the pulse now beat hot behind his eyes. Yes, he knew where to go for that. He knew.

Calmer now, he got up and went back to the house. In the welter of furniture which seemed to have been placed there on purpose to drive him mad, he threw himself on the bed and turned his face to the wall.

Translated by Lily Duplaix

PIRANDELLO: *The Soft Touch of Grass*

1. *On one level, both this story and Kafka's are concerned with the relationship between parents and their children. Compare and contrast the situations.*

2. *On another level, this story, like Turgenev's and Balzac's, dramatizes a man's reaction to the death of a dear being. Again, compare and contrast the handling of this theme in each story. Does Hawthorne approach this theme in "My Kinsman"? In which of the four stories is* irony *used consistently? What is the effect of it?*

3. *Why are we never told the name of the deceased?*

4. *Why does Pirandello juxtapose Pardi and the chair? His single bed and the coffin?*

5. *Why does Pardi turn to the children of the park for solace? Why not to his own child?*

6. *What does the rejection in the park mean to him?*

7. *Though he denies it, does Pardi unconsciously nurse a motive similar to that of the mayor in "Little Louise Roque"? Or is the child's*

accusation entirely unjust? Are you reminded of Akutagawa's view of a shifting reality?

8. *Discuss the final paragraph of the story. Does Pirandello reach a level of tragedy? If you have the chance, read Katherine Mansfield's "Miss Brill" and compare it to this story.*

Marcel Proust

THE MELANCHOLY SUMMER

OF MADAME DE BREYVES

> Marcel Proust's name is of course best known for his long series of interconnected novels which brilliantly bring to life a generation of French society, Remembrance of Things Past. *Born in a Paris suburb in 1871, Proust suffered from ill-health for nearly his entire life, virtually isolating himself except for late-evening forays into high society. "The Melancholy Summer of Madame de Breyves" was written long before Proust began his great work in 1906, but like so many other works of short fiction by major writers, it sets out in small what was later to be developed at length. Until his death in 1922, Proust worked on* Remembrance, *what has since become a monument in twentieth-century fiction.*

"Adriadne, O my Sister, by what a love wounded
Have you died, on those same shores abandoned!"

1

FRANÇOISE DE BREYVES that evening could not make up her mind whether to go to the reception of the Princess Elizabeth A—, to the opera, or to see the Livrays' plays.

At the house where she had dined they had left the table more than an hour ago. She really must decide.

Her friend Genevieve, who was to leave with her, wanted to go to the reception, while Madame de Breyves would have preferred either of the other alternatives, or even a third, going home to bed. The carriage was announced. She was still undecided.

"Really," said Genevieve, "you're being horrid—Reszke is probably going to sing and that would amuse me. One would think something dreadful was going to happen to you if you went to Elizabeth's. Besides, you know, you haven't been to one of her big affairs this season, and, being such a close friend, it's really not nice of you."

Françoise, since the death of her husband, who had left her a widow at twenty—that was four years ago—rarely went anywhere without Genevieve and always tried to please her. She could resist no longer, and after taking leave of her hosts and of the guests, disappointed at the departure of one of the most popular women of Paris, said to the footman, "To the Princess A—'s."

2

The evening at the Princess A—'s was very boring. Once Madame de Breyves asked Genevieve, "Who is the young man who escorted you to the buffet?"

"He is a Monsieur de Laléande whom I never heard of. Would you like me to introduce him? In fact, he asked me to, but I was evasive because he is so insignificant and boring, and as he thinks you very pretty you'd never get rid of him."

"Then decidedly no!" said Françoise. "Besides, he's rather ugly and vulgar-looking in spite of his beautiful eyes."

"You are right," said Genevieve. "And as you would be meeting him often it might be embarrassing if you knew him."

Then she added, laughing, "Unless, of course, you'd like a more intimate acquaintance—in that case you're missing a fine opportunity."

"Yes, a fine opportunity," said Françoise, already thinking of something else.

"But after all," Genevieve added, probably seized with remorse at having been such an unfaithful emissary, gratuitously depriving the young man of a pleasure, "this is one of the last affairs of the season, so it wouldn't really matter and might be more civil."

"So be it, if he comes over this way."

He was on the other side of the drawing room facing them, and did not come over.

"We should be going," Genevieve said a moment later.

"Oh, just a second," said Françoise.

And out of caprice, above all impelled by an urge to flirt with a young man who must indeed find her pretty, she began to look at him a little lingeringly, quickly dropping her eyes and then staring at him again. She made her expression as caressing as possible, she hardly knew why, for no reason, for the pleasure of it, the pleasure of being charitable, the pleasure of vanity, too, and of futility, the pleasure of those who write their names on trees for a passer-by they will never see, of those who throw bottles into the ocean. It was getting late. Monsieur de Laléande was going toward the door. As it remained open after he had left, Madame de Breyves could see him at the other end of the entrance-hall, holding out his number to the cloakroom attendant.

"You're right. We really must be going," she said to Genevieve.

They both rose. But by chance Genevieve being detained by one of her friends for a moment, Françoise was left alone near the cloakroom. There was no one there at the moment but Monsieur de Laléande, who could not find his cane. To amuse herself, Françoise gave him one last lingering look. He passed close to her, lightly rubbing his elbow against hers, and while still touching her, his eyes very bright, and still pretending to be looking for his cane, said, "Come to my place, 5 Rue Royale."

This was something she had so little anticipated, and Monsieur de Laléande was so seriously searching for his cane again, that she was never able to decide later whether it was only an hallucination or not. Above all she was horribly frightened and, Prince A— passing just then, she called to him and began talking volubly, arranging for an outing the next day. During this conversation Monsieur de Laléande had left. In another moment Genevieve arrived and the two women took their departure. Madame de Breyves said nothing. She was still shocked and flattered and, at bottom, indifferent. Two days later, recalling the incident by chance, she began to wonder if Monsieur de Laléande had really spoken those words. Trying in vain to remember, she decided she must have heard them as in a dream, and that the movement of his elbow had been involuntary. Then she thought no more of Monsieur de Laléande and when by chance she heard his name mentioned, she vaguely recalled his face but had entirely forgotten what must have been an hallucination outside the cloakroom.

She saw him again at the last reception of the season (June was nearly over), dared not ask to have him presented and yet, in spite of the fact that she thought him almost ugly, knew he was not intelligent, felt a desire to meet him. She went up to Genevieve and said, "After all, you might introduce Monsieur de Laléande. I don't like to be impolite. But don't say I suggested it, for I don't want to get myself involved."

"All right, later if we see him. He isn't around just now."

"But can't you look for him?"

"He may have left."

"Oh, no," Françoise said quickly, "he couldn't have left, it's too early. Oh, twelve o'clock already! Darling, please, it isn't so difficult. The other evening you were keen on it. It has a special interest for me."

Genevieve looked at her, a little surprised, and went in search of Monsieur de Laléande. He had left.

"You see, I was right," said Genevieve, coming back to Françoise.

"I'm too bored for words," said Françoise, "and I have a headache. Let's go home. Do you mind?"

3

Françoise never missed an evening at the opera now and, with vague hope, accepted all the dinner invitations she received. Two weeks went by without her seeing Monsieur de Laléande again, and she would wake up in the night trying to devise some scheme for meeting him. While all the time repeating to herself that he was boring and not even handsome, she thought of him more than of all the witty and charming men she knew. The season being over, there would be no chance of seeing him again, and she decided to create an opportunity, thought of nothing else.

One evening she said to Genevieve, "Didn't you tell me that you knew a Monsieur de Laléande?"

"Jacques de Laléande? Yes and no; he was introduced to me, but he never left cards and I don't see him."

"Well, you know, I have a certain interest, a considerable interest, I might say—oh, nothing to do with me, and I can't say anything about it for a month" (before then she would have devised with him some plausible story, and the thought of a secret shared with him alone gave her a delicious thrill) "in seeing and talking to him. Do try to manage it, because now that the season is over there won't be any more parties where I might meet him."

The practice of close friendship, so purifying when it is sincere, saved Genevieve, as well as Françoise, from that curiosity which is the shameful amusement of most people in society. So it was that Genevieve with all her heart and without for an instant entertaining the intention or the desire or even an idea of questioning her friend, began her search for Monsieur de Laléande, distressed only because she was unable to find him.

"It is unfortunate that Elizabeth A— has left. Of course there is Monsieur de Grumello, but that doesn't help us very much, for what are we to say to him? Oh! I have an idea. Monsieur de Laléande plays the cello—badly, but that doesn't matter. Monsieur de Grumello admires him and is so stupid and besides, he would be overjoyed to please you. The only thing is—you've always avoided him and, as you hate dropping people after making use of them, you would be obliged to invite him next season."

But Françoise was already flushed with joy. "That doesn't matter, I don't care; I'd invite all the upstarts and adventurers of Paris if necessary. Oh! Please, darling, don't waste a second!"

And Genevieve wrote:

The Melancholy Summer of Madame de Breyves

Monsieur,

You know that I would do anything in the world to please my friend, Madame de Breyves, whom you must have met. I have heard her say several times, when the cello was mentioned, how much she regretted never having heard your good friend Monsieur de Laléande play. I wonder if you could get him to play for her and for me. Now that we all have more time, perhaps this will not inconvenience you too much, and it would be very good of you. With kindest regards,

Alériouvre Buivres

"Take this letter to Monsieur de Grumello," Françoise said to a servant. "Do not wait for an answer, but make sure that he receives it at once."

The next day Genevieve had Monsieur de Grumello's reply taken by hand to Madame de Breyves:

Madame,

I should have been more delighted than you can imagine to have been able to satisfy your desire and that of Madame de Breyves, whom I know slightly but for whom I feel the most respectful and the keenest sympathy. And I am utterly disconsolate that by a most unhappy chance Monsieur de Laléande left for Biarritz two days ago, where, alas! he will remain for several months.

Please accept, madame, etc.
Grumello

Françoise, as white as a sheet, rushed to her room to lock herself in. She had hardly time to reach it before she was shaken by sobs, and tears were flowing. Until then, preoccupied as she had been in imagining all sorts of romantic ways of meeting and knowing him, believing that she could realize them when she wished, she had been, perhaps unconsciously, living on this desire and this hope. Deeply implanted in her, they had sent down a thousand little imperceptible roots and started a new mysterious sap coursing through her. And now, all at once, they were uprooted and thrown into the discard. She suffered the agonizing laceration of that hidden self suddenly torn up by the roots. Now she saw clearly through all the lies that hope and desire had held out to her and, at last, from the depths of her grief came suddenly face to face with the reality of her love.

4

Every day Françoise seemed to grow more and more indifferent to all her habitual pleasures. Even from her most intense and intimate joys, those shared with her mother and with Genevieve, even from the hours she gave to music, from her reading, from her walks, her heart was absent, devoured by a jealous sorrow that never left her. And she felt that there was no end to this pain, since it was impossible for her to go to Biarritz and, even had that been possible, she was determined not to compromise by any desperate action the prestige she might enjoy in the eyes of Monsieur de Laléande. Poor little victim, tortured without knowing why, she was terrified to think that this suffering might last for months without relief, drive away sleep, trouble her dreams. She worried, too, thinking that, without her knowing it, he might pass through Paris again. And her fear of letting happiness so near at hand once more escape her gave her the courage to send a servant to make inquiries of Monsieur de Laléande's concierge. He knew nothing. Then, realizing that there was now no hope of a sail appearing on the horizon of this sea of sorrow which spread out infinitely and beyond which it seemed there was nothing, and that earth had ended, she felt she was being driven to some folly, what, she did not know—writing to him, perhaps—and to calm herself a little, becoming her own doctor, she decided on a scheme for letting him know that she had deliberately tried to see him. To that end she wrote to Monsieur de Grumello:

Monsieur,
Madame de Buivres has told me of your kind thought. How touched I was, how grateful to you! But there is something that worries me. Did Monsieur de Laléande think me indiscreet? In case you do not know, would you ask him, and when you have found out let me know and promise to tell me the exact truth. I am curious, and you would be doing me a kindness. Again thank you, monsieur, etc.
                                                Voragines Breyves

One hour later a servant brought this letter:

You have no cause to worry, madame, Monsieur de Laléande does not know of your request to hear him play. I wrote asking him what days he would be free to play at my house without mentioning for whom. He replied from Biarritz that he would not be in

Paris again till January. You must not thank me. My greatest joy would be to add the merest trifle to yours, etc.

Grumello

There was nothing more she could do. She gave up trying and grew sadder and sadder, saddening her mother, ashamed of her sadness. She went to spend a few days in the country, then left for Trouville. She heard people discussing Monsieur de Laléande's social ambitions, and when a prince, trying his best to be agreeable to her, said: "What can I do that would please you most?" she felt almost like laughing when she thought of his surprise if she were to answer truthfully, and felt all the concentrated and bitter irony of the contrast between the great and difficult things always being done for her and the one little thing, so easy and so impossible, that would have brought back peace, health, and happiness to her, and the happiness of those dearest to her. She only knew a little relief when she was alone with the servants who waited on her, sensing her sadness. Their respectful and grieved silence spoke to her of Monsieur de Laléande. It gave her a voluptuous pleasure, and she would make them serve her luncheon slowly, lingering over it, to put off the moment when she would have to see her friends and to dissimulate her sorrow. She wanted to relish the sweet and bitter taste of the sadness that, because of him, surrounded her. She would have liked to see more people dominated by him, to feel that what took up so much room in her heart was also occupying a little of the space around her. She would have liked to possess healthy, lively animals who, gradually stricken with her ill, would go into a decline. Desperate at moments, she wanted to write to him, have someone write, demean herself. "Nothing matters any longer." But she was restrained by the thought that even in the interest of her love she must keep her position in society, since it might give her greater power over him one day, if that day ever came. And if a short intimacy with him should break the spell he had cast over her (she did not wish to believe, could not believe, or even imagine it, for an instant, but her mind, more discerning than her blind heart, foresaw the cruel eventuality), she would be left without a single support in the world. And if some other love should come to her she would lack all the resources of this power which on her return to Paris would facilitate her intimacy with Monsieur de Laléande. Trying to separate her feelings from herself and to examine them as an object, she would say to herself: "I know that he is mediocre and have always known it. That was my first opinion of him. It has not changed. Since then emotion has intervened but without, for all that, altering my opinion. He is nothing at all and it is for this nonentity I live. I live for Jacques de Laléande." But as soon as she had said his name, by an involuntary association, this time unanalyzed, she could see him again, and felt such contentment and such pain that she knew that it did not matter what a nonentity he really was, since he gave her the sensation of joys and sorrows compared to which others were as nothing. And although she realized that when she came to know him better all this would disappear, this mirage still constituted all the reality of her pain and voluptuous pleasure. A phrase from *Die Meistersinger* she had heard that evening at the Princess A—'s had the power of bringing him vividly back to her *(Dem Vogel der heut sang dem war der Schnabel hold gewachsen)*. Unconsciously it had become for her the leitmotiv of Monsieur de Laléande, and, hearing it one day at a concert in Trouville, she had burst into tears. From time to time, not too often, for fear of mitigating the effect, she would lock herself in her room and, sitting at the piano (she had had it brought for no other purpose), would begin to play, closing her eyes to see him the more clearly. It was her sole intoxicating joy that ended in disillusionment, the opium she craved. Sometimes stopping to listen to the flow of her sorrow, as one leans over a spring to hear the sweet and ceaseless lamentation of the water, and thinking of the atrocious alternatives before her: either future shame and the despair of those dear to her or (if she did not yield) her own eternal sorrow—she would revile herself for having so artfully measured the doses of pleasure and pain of her love, which she had been powerless to reject at once as an invidious poison, or later to cure. Above all she reviled her eyes, or perhaps even before them her sense of curiosity and of coquetry which had made them open like flowers to tempt the young man, and had then exposed her to Monsieur de Laléande's own glances as sure as arrows and more invincibly sweet than shots of morphine. She reviled her imagination too. So tenderly had she nurtured it that she sometimes wondered if it alone had not given birth to this love which now tyrannized over its mother and tortured her. She reviled her ingenuity which had so cleverly, so well, and so ill, contrived so many romances for their meeting that their hopeless impossibility had perhaps bound her even more irrevocably to their hero; reviled the uprightness and the delicacy of her heart which would, if she should give herself, poison with remorse and shame all the joys of her guilty love; reviled her will, so impetuous, so headstrong, so bold in leaping over obstacles when her desires drove her toward an impossible goal, so weak, so soft, so broken, not only when they had to be denied, but when some other emotion seized and carried her away. Finally she reviled her mind in its divinest form, that supreme gift she had received and which is given every imaginable name without the true one ever being found—poet's intuition, ecstasy of the believer, profound sense of nature and of music—which had set up before her love infinite heights and horizons, had let it bathe in the supernatural light of her love's own charm and had, in return, lent to her love something of itself, had interested in this love, associated and confounded with it all its deepest and most secret inner life, had consecrated to it, like the treasures of the church to the Madonna, all the most precious gems of her imagination and her heart, which, in the evening or on the water, she would hear lamenting, whose melancholy and her own, at never seeing him now, were sisters; she reviled that inexpressible feeling of the mystery of things, when our spirit loses itself in the radiance of beauty like that of the sun when it sinks into the sea, for having deepened her love, for having immaterialized, broadened, infinitized it without, for all that, making it less agonizing, for as Baudelaire says (speaking of the end of autumn days), "there are certain delicious sensations which are no less intense for being vague; and there is no sharper point than that of infinity."

5

... and was consumed from the rising of the Sun on the seaweed by the shore, keeping in the depths of his heart like an arrow in the liver, the burning wound of the great Kypris.

THEOCRITUS: *The Cyclops*

I have just come across Madame de Breyves again here at Trouville. I have known her in happier hours. Nothing can cure her. If only she loved Monsieur de Laléande because he was handsome or because he was witty, one could hope to find a handsomer and a wittier young man to distract her. If it were his kindness or his love for her that had attracted her, someone else might try loving her with greater fidelity. But Monsieur de Laléande is neither handsome nor intelligent, has had no opportunity of proving whether he is tender or brutal, fickle or faithful. It is then really himself she loves, not his merits nor his charms, which can be found to as high a degree in others; it is really himself she loves in spite of his imperfections, in spite of his mediocrity; therefore, in spite of everything, she is doomed to love him. *Himself*, does she know what that is, except that it is something that has caused her such shudders of desolation or felicity that the rest of her life has counted for nothing, nothing else has mattered? The most beautiful physiognomy, the most original intelligence would not have that particular and mysterious essence, so unique that no human being will ever find his exact double in all the infinitude of worlds, in the whole eternity of time. If it hadn't been for Genevieve de Buivres, who innocently insisted on her going to Madame A——'s, all this would not have happened. Caught by circumstances and imprisoned, she is the victim of an ill for which there is no remedy, because it is without a reason. Certainly Monsieur de Laléande, who is probably leading a very banal life on the beach at Biarritz, indulging in harmless dreams, would be very much astonished if he knew of this other existence of his, so miraculously intense that it subordinates everything to itself, annihilates everything that is not itself, if he knew that in Madame de Breyves' soul he enjoyed an existence as continuous as his own personal existence, manifested just as effectively in actions, differing only in its heightened consciousness, less intermittent, more abundant. How surprised he would be if he knew that he, ordinarily so little sought after in his fleshly guise, is an object of interest wherever Madame de Breyves goes, among the most highly gifted people, in the most exclusive drawing rooms, amid scenery quite sufficient in itself, and that this woman, so popular everywhere, has not a thought, not a feeling, not an attention for anything but the recollection of this intruder before whom everything else fades, as though he alone were a real person and the persons present as vain as memories or shadows.

Whether Madame de Breyves takes a walk with a poet or lunches with an archduchess, whether she is alone and reading or talking with a cherished friend, whether she rides horseback or sleeps, the name, the image of Monsieur de Laléande is always over her, deliciously, cruelly, inevitably as the sky is over our heads. She has even reached the point, she who always detested Biarritz, where she finds in everything connected with that city a touching and painful charm. She is preoccupied with the people who are there, or those who are about to go and who will see him, perhaps, without knowing it, who will live with him without joy. She bears them no grudge and, without daring to give them any messages, questions them ceaselessly, wondering sometimes how, hearing her talk continually about all the things surrounding her secret, no one has guessed it. A huge photograph of Biarritz is one of the only ornaments in her room. She imagines that one of the strollers in it looks like Monsieur de Laléande. If she knew the cheap music he liked, those despised songs would without a doubt soon take the place, on her piano and in her heart, of the symphonies of Beethoven and the operas of Wagner, both because they have lowered her standards and because of the charm that he, from whom all charm and all sorrow now come,

The Melancholy Summer of Madame de Breyves

casts over them. Sometimes the image of this man whom she has seen twice only, and then only for an instant, who occupies such a tiny place in the exterior events of her life but in her heart and in her mind one so exorbitant that it absorbs them altogether, grows blurred before the tired eyes of her memory. She no longer sees him, cannot remember his features, his form, has almost forgotten even his eyes. Yet this image is all she has of him. She is beside herself at the thought that she might lose it, that her desire—which it is true tortures her but which is now her whole self, in which she has taken refuge after fleeing all the rest, to which she clings as one clings to one's own conservation, one's life, good or bad—might vanish and that he would leave her with nothing but the uneasiness and desolation of a dream, no longer knowing the object that has caused them, would no longer see him even in her mind in which she could no longer cherish him. Then suddenly, after the momentary blurring of her inner vision, his image returns. Her sorrow can begin again, and it is now almost a joy.

How will Madame de Breyves endure her return to Paris from which, until January, he will still be absent? What will she do from now until then? What will she do—what will he do—afterwards?

A dozen times I have been on the point of going to Biarritz to bring back Monsieur de Laléande. The consequences might well be terrible, but speculation is futile, since she will not hear of it. But I am desolate, seeing her little temples beaten from within, seeing her shattered by the blows without surcease of this inexplicable passion. Her whole life follows its rhythm in an anguished mode. Often she imagines that he will come to Trouville, come up to her, tell her that he loves her. She sees him; his eyes shine. He speaks to her in that colorless voice of dream which prevents our believing, while all the time forcing us to listen. It is he. He speaks the words that intoxicate even though we hear them only in dreams, when we see, radiant and touching, the divine and confident smile of two destinies uniting. And then almost at once she is awakened by the feeling that the two worlds, the world of reality and the world of her desire, are parallel, that it is as impossible for them ever to meet as a shadow the body that projected it. Then, remembering that moment by the cloakroom when her elbow rubbed his elbow, when he offered her that body which, if she had wished, if she had known, she might now be clasping to her own and which is now far away, perhaps forever, she feels cries of despair and revolt rising in her from all sides, like those one hears on sinking ships. If, sometimes, walking along the beach or in the woods, she lets the pleasure of contemplation or of reverie, or even a sweet odor, or a song brought from a distance and muffled by the breeze, gently take possession of her, make her for an instant forget her pain, all at once she feels a terrible blow and a wound in her heart—and above the waves, higher than the leaves, in the misty horizon of woods or sea, she catches sight of the vague image of her invisible and ever-present conqueror, his eyes shining through the clouds, as on the day when he offered himself to her, and sees him vanish with the quiver from which he has taken and let fly another arrow.

Translated by Louise Varese

PROUST: *The Melancholy Summer of Madame de Breyves*

1. *What are some of the unconventional elements of this love story?*
2. *What impels Madame de Breyves to flirt with a man she regards as ugly and vulgar-looking?*
3. *Is Madame de Breyves wrong not to pursue her loved one further? Would it be possible for her to do so? Does she really wish to do so any longer? Why?*
4. *According to Proust, does love convey pleasure or pain? (The story is taken from a volume called* Pleasures and Days.*) Can the situation in this story be regarded as a symbol of Proust's view of the entire world? Does this view have anything in common with that expressed in Mann's "Little Lizzy"?*
5. *In his great novel sequence,* Remembrance of Things Past, *Proust is profoundly interested in memory association. We recapture and preserve the precious past, he suggests, not by any conscious mental effort, but through the accidental stimulus of an odor, a musical phrase, a movement of the body, a flavor upon the tongue. In this early story, do you see any evidence of this belief taking form?*
6. *Joseph Wood Krutch says of Proust: "His life was a retirement, step by step, from life; a penetration, step by step, into that particular world of art which was his." In what way does Madame de Breyves' existence foreshadow Proust's?*
7. *At the beginning of Part 5, a first-person narrator suddenly appears. What significance do you draw from the shift from third person to first? Who has been telling the story for the first four parts? Compare Proust's technique of narration with James's. (Proust's great novel* Remembrance *is narrated entirely in the first person, but the "I" of the narrative is a man of many selves: he is the fictionalized Marcel; in part Swann, the man of fashion; Bergotte, the man of letters; Bloch, the Jew; and others.)*

Thomas Mann
LITTLE LIZZY

Perhaps the foremost German writer of his generation, Thomas Mann was born in Lübeck, Germany, in 1875, and died in Zurich on August 12, 1955. He gained early recognition with the publication of Buddenbrooks *in 1900, when he was only twenty-five, and then for the next fifty-five years, he remained a prolific author of stories and long philosophical novels. The most famous stories are "Tonio Kröger," "Death in Venice," and "Mario and the Magician."* The Magic Mountain, *which helped him win the Nobel Prize for Literature in 1929, gave him an international reputation after its appearance in 1924. In the decade from 1933 to 1943, Mann wrote a tetralogy based on the Biblical story of Joseph. In 1948, there appeared* Dr. Faustus, *a deeply ambitious novel which repeats in symbolic form many of Mann's major themes. "Little Lizzy," while early in Mann's career—it predates* Buddenbrooks—*nevertheless contains the dominant note of sadism and grotesqueness which are never far from his most significant work.*

THERE are marriages which the imagination, even the most practiced literary one, cannot conceive. You must just accept them, as you do in the theater when you see the ancient and doddering married to the beautiful and gay, as the given premises on which the farce is mechanically built up.

Yes, the wife of Jacoby the lawyer was lovely and young, a woman of unusual charm. Some years—shall we say thirty years?—ago, she had been christened with the names of Anna, Margarete, Rosa, Amalie; but the name she went by was always Amra, composed of the initials of her four real ones; it suited to perfection her somewhat exotic personality. Her soft, heavy hair, which she wore parted on one side and brushed straight back above her ears from the narrow temples, had only the darkness of the glossy chestnut; but her skin displayed the dull, dark sallowness of the south and clothed a form which southern suns must have ripened. Her slow, voluptuous indolent presence suggested the harem; each sensuous, lazy movement of her body strengthened the im-

[231

pression that with her the head was entirely subordinate to the heart. She needed only to have looked at you once, with her artless brown eyes, lifting her brows in the pathetically narrow forehead, horizontally, in a quaint way she had, for you to be certain of that. But she herself was not so simple as not to know it too. Quite simply, she avoided exposing herself, she spoke seldom and little—and what is there to say against a woman who is both beautiful and silent? Yes, the word "simple" is probably the last which should be applied to her. Her glance was artless; but also it had a kind of luxurious cunning—you could see that she was not dull, also that she might be a mischief-maker. In profile her nose was rather too thick; but her full, large mouth was utterly lovely, if also lacking in any expression save sensuality.

This disturbing phenomenon was the wife of Jacoby the lawyer, a man of forty. Whoever looked at him was bound to be amazed at the fact. He was stout, Jacoby the lawyer; but stout is not the word, he was a perfect colossus of a man! His legs, in their columnar clumsiness and the slate-gray trousers he always wore, reminded one of an elephant's. His round, fat-upholstered back was that of a bear; and over the vast round of his belly his funny little gray jacket was held by a single button strained so tight that when it was unbuttoned the jacket came wide open with a pop. Scarcely anything which could be called a neck united this huge torso with the little head atop. The head had narrow watery eyes, a squabby nose, and a wee mouth between cheeks drooping with fullness. The upper lip and the round head were covered with harsh, scanty, light-colored bristles that showed the naked skin, as on an overfed dog. There was no doubt that Jacoby's fatness was not of a healthy kind. His gigantic body, tall as well as stout, was not muscular, but flabby. The blood would sometimes rush to his puffy face, then ebb away leaving it of a yellowish pallor; the mouth would be drawn and sour.

Jacoby's practice was a limited one; but he was well-to-do, partly from his wife's side; and the childless pair lived in a comfortable apartment in the Kaiserstrasse and entertained a good deal. This must have been Frau Amra's taste, for it is unthinkable that the lawyer could have cared for it; he participated with an enthusiasm of a peculiarly painful kind. This fat man's character was the oddest in the world. No human being could have been politer, more accommodating, more complaisant than he. But you unconsciously knew that this over-obligingness was somehow forced, that its true source was an inward insecurity and cowardice—the impression it gave was not very pleasant. A man who despises himself is a very ugly sight; worse still when vanity combines with his cowardice to make him wish to please. This was the case, I should say, with Jacoby: his obsequiousness was almost crawling, it went beyond the bounds of personal decency. He was quite capable of saying to a lady as he escorted her to table: "My dear lady, I am a disgusting creature, but will you do me the honor?" No humor would be mingled with the remark; it was simply cloying, bitter, self-tortured—in a word, disgusting, as he said.

The following once actually happened: the lawyer was taking a walk, and a clumsy porter with a hand-cart ran over his foot. Too late the man stopped his cart and turned round—whereupon Jacoby, quite pale and dazed, his cheeks shaking up and down, took off his hat and stuttered: "I b-beg your pardon." A thing like that is infuriating. But this extraordinary colossus seemed perpetually to suffer from a plague of conscience. When he took a walk with his wife on the Lerchenberg, the Corso of the little city, he would roll his eyes round at Amra, walking with her wonderful elastic gait at his side, and bow so anxiously, diligently, and zealously in all directions that he seemed to be begging pardon of all the lieutenants they met for being in unworthy possession of such a beautiful wife. His mouth had a pathetically ingratiating expression, as though he wanted to disarm their scorn.

I have already hinted that the reason why Amra married Jacoby is unfathomable. As for him, he was in love with her; ardently, as people of his physical make-up seldom are, and with such anxious humility as fitted the rest of his character. Sometimes, late in the evening, he would enter their large sleeping-chamber with its high windows and flowered hangings—softly, so softly that there was no sound, only the slow shaking of floor and furniture. He would come up to Amra's massive bed, where she already lay, kneel down, and with infinite caution take her hand. She would lift her brows in a level line, in the quaint way she had, and look at her husband, abject before her in the dim light, with a look of malice and sensuality combined. With his puffy, trembling hands he would softly stroke back the sleeve and press his tragic fat face into the soft brown flesh of her wrist, where little blue veins stood out. And he would speak to her, in a shaking, half-smothered voice, as a sensible man in everyday life never speaks:

"Amra, my dear Amra! I am not disturbing you? You were not asleep yet? Dear God! I have been thinking all day how beautiful you are and how much I love you. I beg you to listen, for it is so very hard to express what I feel: I love you so much that sometimes my heart contracts and I do not know where to turn. I love you beyond my strength. You do not understand that, I know; but you believe it, and you must say, just one single time, that you are a little grateful to me. For, you see, such a love as mine to you is precious, it has its value in this life of ours. And that you will never betray or deceive me, even if you cannot love me, just out of gratitude for this love. I have come to you to beg you, as seriously, as fervently as I can . . ." here the lawyer's speech would be dissolved in sobs, in low, bitter weeping, as he knelt. Amra would feel moved; she would stroke her husband's bristles and say over and over, in the soothing, contemptuous singsong one uses to a dog who comes to lick one's feet: "Yes, yes, good doggy, good doggy!"

And this behavior of Amra's was certainly not that of a moral woman. For to relieve my mind of the truth which I have so far withheld, she did already deceive her husband; she betrayed him for the embraces of a gentleman named Alfred Läutner, a gifted young musician, who at twenty-seven had made himself a small reputation with amusing little compositions. He was a slim young chap with a provocative face, a flowing blond mane, and a sunny smile in his eyes, of which he was quite aware. He belonged to the present-day race of small artists, who do not demand the utmost of themselves, whose first requirement is to be jolly and happy, who employ their pleasing little talents to heighten their personal charms. It pleases them to play in society the rôle of the naïve genius. Consciously childlike, entirely unmoral and unscrupulous, merry and self-satisfied as they are, and healthy enough to enjoy even their disorders, they are agreeable even in their vanity, so long as that has not been wounded. But woe to these wretched little poseurs when serious misfortune befalls them, with which there is no coquetting, and when they can no longer be pleasant in their own eyes. They will not know how to be wretched decently and in order, they do not know how to attack the problem of suffering. They will be destroyed. All that is a story in itself. But Herr Alfred Läutner wrote pretty things, mostly waltzes and mazurkas. They would have been rather too gay and popular to be considered music as I understand it, if each of them had not contained a passage of some originality, a modulation, a harmonic phrasing, some sort of bold effect that betrayed wit and invention, which was evidently the point of the whole and which made it interesting to genuine musicians. Often these two single measures would have a strange plaintive, melancholy tone which would come out abruptly in the midst of a piece of dance-music and as suddenly be gone.

Amra Jacoby was on fire with guilty passion for this young man, and as for him he had not enough moral fibre to resist her seductions. They met here, they met there, and for some years an immoral relation had subsisted between them, known to the whole town, who laughed at it behind the lawyer's back. But what did he think? Amra was not sensitive enough to betray herself on account of a guilty conscience, so we must take it as certain that, however the lawyer's heart, he could cherish no definite suspicions.

Spring had come, rejoicing all hearts; and Amra conceived the most charming idea.

"Christian," said she—Jacoby's name was Christian—"let us give a party, a beer party to celebrate the new beer—of course quite simple, but let's have a lot of people."

"Certainly," said the lawyer, "but could we not have it a little later?"

To which Amra made no reply, having passed on to the consideration of details.

"It will be so large that we cannot have it here, we must hire a place, some sort of outdoor restaurant where there is plenty of room and fresh air. You see that, of course. The place I am thinking of is Wendelin's big hall at the foot of the Lerchenberg. The hall is independent of the restaurant and brewery, connected by a passage only. We can decorate it for the occasion and set up long tables, drink our bocks, and dance—we must have music and even perhaps some sort of entertainment. There is a little stage, as I happen to know, that makes it very suitable. It will be a very original party and no end to fun."

The lawyer's face had gone a pale yellow as she spoke, and the corners of his mouth went down. He said:

"My dear Amra! How delightful it will be! I can leave it all to you, you are so clever. Make any arrangements you like."

And Amra made her arrangements. She took counsel of various ladies and gentlemen, she went in person to hire the hall, she even formed a committee of people who were invited or who volunteered to cooperate in the entertainment. These were exclusively men, except for the wife of Herr Hildebrandt, an actor at the Hoftheater, who was herself a singer. Then there was Herr Hildebrandt, an Assessor Witznagel, a young painter, Alfred Läutner the musician, and some students brought in by Herr Witznagel, who were to do Negro dances.

A week after Amra had made her plan, this committee met in Amra's drawing-room in the Kaiserstrasse—a small crowded, overheated room, with a heavy carpet, a sofa with quantities of cushions, a fan table, English leather chairs, and a splay-legged mahogany table with a velvet cover, upon which rested several large illustrated morocco-bound volumes. There was a fireplace too, with a small fire still burning, and on the marble chimney-top were plates of dainty sandwiches, glasses, and two decanters of sherry. Amra reclined in one corner of the sofa under the fan palm, with her legs crossed. She had the beauty of a warm summer night. A thin blouse of light-colored silk covered her bosom, but her skirt was of heavy dark stuff embroidered with large flowers. Sometimes she put up one hand to brush back the chestnut hair from her narrow forehead. Frau Hildebrandt sat beside her on the sofa; she had red hair and wore riding clothes. Opposite the two all the gentlemen formed a semicircle—among them Jacoby himself, in the lowest chair he could find. He looked unutterably wretched, kept drawing a long breath and swallowing as though struggling against increasing nausea. Herr Alfred Läutner was in tennis clothes—he would not take a chair, but leaned decoratively against the chimney-piece, saying merrily that he could not sit still so long.

Herr Hildebrandt talked sonorously about English songs. He was a most respectable gentleman, in a black suit, with a Roman head and an assured manner—in short a proper actor for a court theater, cultured, knowledgeable, and with enlightened tastes. He liked to hold forth in condemnation of Ibsen, Zola, and Tolstoi, all of whom had the same objectionable aims. But today he was benignly interested in the small affair under discussion.

"Do you know that priceless song 'That's Maria!'?" he asked. "Perhaps it is a little racy—but very effective. And then" so-and-so—he suggested other songs, upon which they came to an agreement and Frau Hildebrandt said that she would sing them. The young painter, who had sloping shoulders and a very blond beard, was to give a burlesque conjuring turn. Herr Hildebrandt offered to impersonate various famous characters. In short, everything was developing nicely, the programme was apparently arranged, when Assessor Witznagel, who had command of fluent gesture and a good many duelling scars, suddenly took the word.

"All very well, ladies and gentlemen, it looks like being most amusing. But if I may say so, it still lacks something; it wants some kind of high spot, a climax as it were, something a bit startling, perhaps, to round the thing off. I leave it to you, I have nothing particular in mind, I only think . . ."

"That is true enough!" Alfred Läutner's tenor voice came from the chimney-piece where he leaned. "Witznagel is right. We need a climax. Let us put our heads together!" He settled his red belt and looked engagingly about him.

"Well, if we do not consider the famous characters as the high spot," said Herr Hildebrandt. Everybody agreed with the Assessor. Something piquant was wanted for the principal number. Even Jacoby nodded, and murmured: "Yes, yes, something jolly and striking. . . ." They all reflected.

At the end of a minute's pause, which was broken only by stifled exclamations, an extraordinary thing happened. Amra was sitting reclined among the cushions, gnawing as busily as a mouse at the pointed nail of her little finger. She had a very odd look on her face: a vacant, almost an irresponsible smile, which betrayed a sensuality both tormented and cruel. Her eyes, very bright and wide, turned slowly to the chimney-piece, where for a second they met the musician's. Then suddenly she jerked her whole body to one side as she sat, in the direction of her husband. With both hands in her lap she stared into his face with an avid and clinging gaze, her own growing visibly paler, and said in her rich, slow voice:

"Christian, suppose you come on at the end as a *chanteuse*, in a red satin baby frock, and do a dance."

The effect of these few words was tremendous. The young painter essayed to laugh good-humoredly; Herr Hildebrandt, stony-faced, brushed a crumb from his sleeve; his wife colored up, a rare thing for her; the students coughed and used their handkerchiefs loudly; and Herr Assessor Witznagel simply left the field and got himself a sandwich. The lawyer sat huddled on his little chair, yellow in the face, with a terrified smile. He looked all around the circle, and stammered:

"But, by God . . . I—I—I am not up to—not that I—I beg pardon, but . . ."

Alfred Läutner had lost his insouciant expression; he even seemed to have reddened a little, and he thrust out his neck to peer searchingly into Amra's face. He looked puzzled and upset.

But she, Amra, holding the same persuasive pose, went on with the same impressiveness:

"And you must sing, too, Christian, a song which Herr Läutner shall compose, and he can accompany you on the piano. We could not have a better or more effective climax."

There was a pause, an oppressive pause. Then this extraordinary thing happened, that Herr Läutner, as it were seized upon and carried away by his excitement, took a step forward and his voice fairly trembled with enthusiasm as he said:

"Herr Jacoby, that is a priceless idea, and I am more than ready to compose something. You must have a dance and song, anything else is unthinkable as a wind-up to our affair. You will see, it will be the best thing I have ever written or ever shall write. In a red satin baby frock. Oh, your wife is an artist, only an artist could have hit upon the idea! Do say yes, I beg of you. I will do my part, you will see, it will be an achievement."

Here the circle broke up and the meeting became lively. Out of politeness, or out of malice, the company began to storm the lawyer with entreaties—Frau Hildebrandt went so far as to say, quite loudly, in her Brünnhilde voice:

"Herr Jacoby, after all, you are such a jolly and entertaining man!"

But the lawyer had pulled himself together and spoke, a little yellow, but with a strong effort at resolution:

"But listen to me, ladies and gentlemen—what can I say to you? It isn't my line, believe me. I have no comic gift, and besides . . . in short, no, it is quite impossible, alas!"

He stuck obstinately to his refusal, and Amra no longer insisted, but sat still with her absent look. Herr Läutner was silent too, staring in deep abstraction at a pattern in the rug. Herr Hildebrandt changed the subject, and presently the committee meeting broke up without coming to a final decision about the "climax."

On the evening of the same day Amra had gone to bed and was lying there with her eyes wide open; her husband came lumbering into the bedroom, drew a chair up beside the bed, dropped into it, and said, in a low, hesitating voice:

"Listen, Amra; to be quite frank, I am feeling very disturbed. I refused them today—I did not mean to be offensive—goodness knows I did not mean that. Or do you seriously feel that—I beg you to tell me."

Amra was silent for a moment, while her brows rose slowly. Then she shrugged her shoulders and said:

"I do not know, my dear friend, how to answer you. You behaved in a way I should not have expected from you. You were unfriendly, you refused to support our enterprise in a way which they flatteringly considered to be indispensable to it. To put it mildly, you disappointed everybody and upset the whole company with your rude lack of compliance. Whereas it was your duty as host—"

The lawyer hung his head and sighed heavily. He said:

"Believe me, Amra, I had no intention to be disobliging. I do not like to offend anybody; if I have behaved badly I am ready to make amends. It is only a joke, after all, an innocent little dressing-up—why not? I will not upset the whole affair, I am ready to . . ."

The following afternoon Amra went out again to "make preparations." She drove to Number 78 Holzstrasse and went up to the second storey, where she had an appointment. And when she lay relaxed by the expression of her love she pressed her lover's head passionately to her breast and whispered:

"Write it for four hands. We will accompany him together while he sings and dances. I will see to the costume myself."

And an extraordinary shiver, a suppressed and spasmodic burst of laughter went through the limbs of both.

For anyone who wants to give a large party out of doors Herr Wendelin's place on the slope of the Lerchenberg is to be recommended. You enter it from the pretty suburban street through a tall trellised gateway and pass into the parklike garden, in the center of which stands a large hall, connected only by a narrow passage with restaurant, kitchen, and brewery. It is a large, brightly painted wooden hall, in an amusing mixture of Chinese and Renaissance styles. It has folding doors which stand open in good weather to admit the woodland air, and it will hold a great many people.

On this evening as the carriages rolled up they were greeted from afar by the gleam of colored lights. The whole gateway, the trees, and the hall itself were set thick with lanterns, while the interior made an entrancing sight. Heavy garlands were draped across the ceiling and studded with paper lanterns. Hosts of electric lights hung among the decorations of the walls, which consisted of pine boughs, flags, and artificial flowers; the whole hall was brilliantly lighted. The stage had foliage plants grouped on either side, and a red curtain with a painted design of a presiding genius hovering in the air. A long row of decorated tables ran almost the whole length of the hall. And at these tables the guests of Attorney Jacoby were doing themselves well on cold roast veal and bock beer. There were certainly more than a hundred and fifty people: officers, lawyers, business men, artists, upper officials, with their wives and daughters. They were quite simply dressed, in black coats and light spring toilettes, for this was a jolly, informal occasion. The gentlemen carried their mugs in person to the big casks against one of the walls; the spacious, festive, brightly lighted room was filled with a heavy sweetish atmosphere of evergreen boughs, flowers, beer, food, and human beings; and there was a clatter and buzz of laughter and talk—the loud, simple talk and the high, good-natured, unrestrained, carefree laughter of the sort of people there assembled.

The attorney sat shapeless and helpless at one end of the table, near the stage. He drank little and now and then addressed a labored remark to his neighbor, Frau Regierungsrat Havermann. He breathed offensively, the corners of his mouth hung down, he stared fixedly with his bulging watery eyes into the lively scene, with a sort of melancholy remoteness, as though there resided in all this noisy merriment something inexpressively painful and perplexing.

Large fruit tarts were now being handed round for the company to cut from; they drank sweet wine with these, and the time for the speeches arrived. Herr Hildebrandt celebrated the new brew in a speech almost entirely composed of classical quotations, even Greek. Herr Witznagel, with florid gestures and ingenious turns of phrase, toasted the ladies, taking a handful of flowers from the nearest vase and comparing each flower to some feminine charm. Amra Jacoby, who sat opposite him in a pale-yellow silk frock, he called "a lovelier sister of the Maréchal Niel."

Then she nodded meaningfully to her husband, brushing back her hair from her forehead; whereupon the fat man arose and almost ruined the whole atmosphere by stammering a few words with painful effort, smiling a repulsive smile. Some half-hearted bravos rewarded him, then there was an oppressive pause, after which jollity resumed its sway. All smoking, all a little elevated by drink, they rose from table and with their own hands and a great deal of noise removed the tables from the hall to make way for the dancing.

It was after eleven and high spirits reigned supreme. Some of the guests streamed out into the brightly lighted garden to get the fresh air; others stood about the hall in groups, smoking, chatting, drawing beer from the kegs, and drinking it standing. Then a loud trumpet call sounded from the stage, summoning everybody to the entertainment. The band arrived and took its place before the curtains; rows of chairs were put in place and red programmes distributed on them; the gentlemen ranged themselves along the walls. There was an expectant hush.

The band played a noisy overture, and the curtains parted to reveal a row of Negroes horrifying to behold in their barbaric costumes and their blood-red lips, gnashing their teeth and emitting savage yells.

Certainly the entertainment was the crowning success of Amra's party. As it went on, the applause grew more and more enthusiastic. Frau Hildebrandt came on in a powdered wig, pounded with a shepherdess' crook on the floor and sang—in too large a voice—"That's Maria!" A conjuror in a dress coat covered with orders performed the most amazing feats; Herr Hildebrandt impersonated Goethe, Bismarck, and Napoleon in an amazingly lifelike manner; and a newspaper editor, Dr.

Wiesensprung, improvised a humorous lecture which had as its theme bock beer and its social significance. And now the suspense reached its height, for it was time for the last, the mysterious number which appeared on the programme framed in a laurel wreath and was entitled: "*Little Lizzy*. Song and Dance. Music by Alfred Läutner."

A movement swept through the hall, and people's eyes met as the band sat down at their instruments and Alfred Läutner came from the doorway where he had been lounging with a cigarette between his pouting lips to take his place beside Amra Jacoby at the piano, which stood in the center of the stage in front of the curtains. Herr Läutner's face was flushed and he turned over his manuscript score nervously; Amra for her part was rather pale. She leaned one arm on the back of her chair and looked loweringly at the audience. The bell rang, the pianist played a few bars of an insignificant accompaniment, the curtains parted, little Lizzy appeared.

The whole audience stiffened with amazement as that tragic and bedizened bulk shambled with a sort of bear-dance into view. It was Jacoby. A wide, shapeless garment of crimson satin, without folds, fell to his feet; it was cut out above to make a repulsive display of the fat neck, stippled with white powder. The sleeves consisted merely of a shoulder puff, but the flabby arms were covered by long lemon-colored gloves; on the head perched a high blond wig with a swaying green feather. And under the wig was a face, a puffy, pasty, unhappy, and desperately mirthful face, with cheeks that shook pathetically up and down and little red-rimmed eyes that strained in anguish towards the floor and saw nothing else at all. The fat man hoisted himself with effort from one leg to the other, while with his hands he either held up his skirts or else weakly raised his index fingers—these two gestures he had and knew no others. In a choked and gasping voice he sang, to the accompaniment of the piano.

The lamentable figure exhaled more than ever a cold breath of anguish. It killed every light-hearted enjoyment and lay like an oppressive weight upon the assembled audience. Horror was in the depths of all these spellbound eyes, gazing at this pair at the piano and at that husband there. The monstrous, unspeakable scandal lasted five long minutes.

Then came a moment which none of those present will forget as long as they live. Let us picture to ourselves what happened in that frightful and frightfully involved little instant of time.

You know of course the absurd little jingle called "Lizzy." And you remember the lines:

> *I can polka until I am dizzy,*
> *I can waltz with the best and beyond,*
> *I'm the popular pet, little Lizzy,*
> *Who makes all the menfolks so fond—*

which form the trivial and unlovely refrain to three longish stanzas. Alfred Läutner had composed a new setting to the verses I have quoted, and it was, as he had said it would be, his masterpiece. He had, that is, brought to its highest pitch his little artifice of introducing into a fairly vulgar and humorous piece of hackwork a sudden phrase of genuine creative art. The melody, in C-sharp major, had been in the first bars rather pretty and perfectly banal. At the beginning of the refrain the rhythm became livelier and dissonances occurred, which by means of the constant accentuation of a B-natural made one expect a transition into F-sharp major. These dissonances went on developing until the word "beyond"; and after the "I'm the" a culmination into F-sharp major should have followed. Instead of which the most surprising thing happened. That is, through a harsh turn, by means of an inspiration which was almost a stroke of genius, the key changed to F-major, and this little interlude which followed, with the use of both pedals on the long-drawn-out first syllable of the word "Lizzy," was indescribably, almost gruesomely effective. It was a complete surprise, an abrupt assault on the nerves, it shivered down the back, it was a miracle, a revelation, it was like a curtain suddenly torn away to reveal something nude.

And on the F-major chord Attorney Jacoby stopped dancing. He stood still, he stood as though rooted to the stage with his two forefingers lifted, one a little lower than the other. The word "Lizzy" stuck in his throat, he was dumb; almost at the same time the accompaniment broke sharp off, and the incredible, absurd, and ghastly figure stood there frozen, with his head thrust forward like a steer's, staring with inflamed eyes straight before him. He stared into the brightly lighted, decorated, crowded hall, in which, like an exhalation from all these people, the scandal hung and thickened into visibility. He stared at all these upturned faces, foreshortened and distorted by the lighting, into these hundreds of pairs of eyes all directed with the same knowing expression upon himself and the two at the piano. In a frightful stillness, unbroken by the smallest sound, his gaze traveled slowly and uneasily from the pair to the audience, from the audience to the pair, while his eyes widened more and more. Then knowledge seemed to flash across his face, like a sudden rush of blood, making it red as the frock he wore, only to give way to a waxen yellow pallor—and the fat man collapsed, making the platform creak beneath his weight.

For another moment the stillness reigned. Then there came shrieks, hubbub ensued, a few gentlemen took heart to spring upon the platform, among them a young doctor—and the curtains were drawn together.

Amra Jacoby and Alfred Läutner still sat at the piano. They had turned a little away from each other, and he, with his head bent, seemed to be listening to the echo of his F-major chord, while she, with her birdlike brain, had not yet grasped the situation, but gazed round her with vacant face.

The young doctor came back presently. He was a little Jewish gentleman with a serious face and a small pointed beard. Some people surrounded him at the door with questions—to which he replied with a shrug of the shoulders and the words:

"All over."

Translated by H. T. Lowe-Porter

MANN: *Little Lizzy*

1. *What is the theme of the story? How does Mann initially suggest it?*
2. *What is the "personality" of each of the three main characters? How is "personality" related to physique? What is the reason for this connection?*
3. *What is the real reason that Amra wants her husband to perform?*
4. *Why does Jacoby go through with the performance? Does he have any choice? What causes his death?*
5. *Why is Läutner nervous during Jacoby's performance? Why does he add the F-major chord? (See question 2.)*
6. *Will the relationship between Amra and Läutner continue? What clues are there in the story?*
7. *Mann's experimentation with musical counterpoint in his fiction is reflected in this story. How does he use music to underline his point? (See question 1.) Compare it to Conrad's.*
8. *This story also reflects Mann's interest in pathetic, frustrated, and often freakish persons who lack the ability to cope with life—in other words, with forms of human sickness. Is Jacoby sick? Amra?—Läutner? How? Is sickness a valid subject for literature? Compare this story to Kafka's "The Judgment." How are the two alike? Is the attitude of the author the same toward the protagonist in each story?*

Hermann Hesse

WITHIN AND WITHOUT

Though Thomas Mann had eulogized his craft and T. S. Eliot had acknowledged his inspiration (in The Waste Land*), Hermann Hesse was practically a stranger in America before he received the Nobel Prize in 1946. Born in Calw, Württemberg, in 1877, Hesse drifted through a succession of occupations until two novels,* Peter Camenzind *(1904) and* Unser Rad *(1905), established him as a rival to Mann and Musil. Like the author himself, whose quest for peace took him to India in 1911, the characters of his subsequent fiction (especially in his masterpiece,* Steppenwolf *[1927]), are sensitive and lonely men searching for harmony in the jungle of the world, fascinated yet perplexed by the dualism of the material and the spiritual in man. It was not until his last great novel,* Magister Ludi *(1943), that the conflict was resolved. Hesse died in 1962.*

THERE was once a man by the name of Frederick; he devoted himself to intellectual pursuits and had a wide range of knowledge. But not all knowledge was the same to him, nor was any thought as good as any other: he loved a certain type of thinking, and disdained and abominated the others. What he loved and revered was logic—that so admirable method—and, in general, what he called "science."

"Twice two is four," he used to say. "This I believe; and man must do his thinking on the basis of this truth."

He was not unaware, to be sure, that there were other sorts of thinking and knowledge; but they were not "science," and he held a low opinion of them. Although a freethinker, he was not intolerant of religion. Religion was founded on a tacit agreement among scientists. For several centuries their science had embraced nearly everything that existed on earth and was worth knowing, with the exception of one single province: the human soul. It had become a sort of custom, as time went on, to leave this to religion, and to tolerate its speculations on the soul, though without taking them seriously. Thus Frederick too was tolerant toward religion; but everything he recognized as superstition was profoundly odious and repugnant to him. Alien, uncultured, and retarded peoples might occupy themselves with it; in remote antiquity there might have been mystical or magical thinking; but since the birth of science and logic there was no longer any sense in making use of these outmoded and dubious tools.

So he said and so he thought; and when traces of superstition came to his attention he became angry and felt as if he had been touched by something hostile.

It angered him most of all, however, if he found such traces among his own sort, among educated men who were conversant with the principles of scientific thinking. And nothing was more painful and intolerable to him than that scandalous notion which lately he had sometimes heard expressed and discussed even by men of great culture—that absurd idea that "scientific thinking" was possibly not a supreme, timeless, eternal, foreordained, and unassailable mode of thought, but merely one of many, a transient way of thinking, not impervious to change and downfall. This irreverent, destructive, poisonous notion was abroad—even Frederick could not deny it; it had cropped up here and there as a result of the distress throughout the world brought about by war, revolution, and hunger, like a warning, like a white hand's ghostly writing on a white wall.

The more Frederick suffered from the fact that this idea existed and could so deeply distress him, the more passionately he assailed it and those whom he suspected of secretly believing in it. So far only a very few from among the truly educated had openly and frankly professed their belief in this new doctrine, a doctrine that seemed destined, should it gain in circulation and power, to destroy all spiritual values on earth and call forth chaos. Well, matters had not reached that point yet, and the scattered individuals who openly embraced the idea were still so few in number that they could be considered oddities and crotchety, peculiar fellows. But a drop of the poison, an emanation of that idea, could be perceived first on this side, then on that. Among the people and the half-educated no end of new doctrines could be found anyway, esoteric doctrines, sects, and discipleships; the world was full of them; everywhere one could scent out superstition, mysticism, spiritualistic cults, and other mysterious forces, which it was really necessary to combat, but to which science, as if from a private feeling of weakness, had for the present given free rein.

One day Frederick went to the house of one of his friends, with whom he had often studied. It so happened that he had not seen this friend for some time. While he was climbing the stairs of the house he tried to recall when and where it was that he had last been in his friend's company; but much as he could pride himself on his good memory for other things he could not remember. Because of this he fell imperceptibly into a certain vexation and ill humor, from which, as he stood before his friend's door, he was obliged forcibly to free himself.

Hardly had he greeted Erwin, his friend, when he noticed on his genial countenance a certain, as it were forbearing, smile, which it seemed to him he had never seen there before. And hardly had he seen this smile, which despite its friendliness he at once felt to be somehow mocking or hostile, when he immediately remembered what he had just been searching his memory for in vain—his last previous meeting with Erwin. He remembered that they had parted then without having quarreled, to be sure, but yet with a sense of inner discord and dissatisfaction, because Erwin, as it had seemed to him, had given far too little support to his attacks at that time on the realm of superstition.

It was strange. How could he have forgotten that entirely? And now he also knew that this was his only reason for not having sought out his friend for so long, merely this dissatisfaction, and that he had known this all the time, although he had invented for himself a host of other excuses for his repeated postponement of this visit.

Now they confronted one another; and it seemed to Frederick as if the little rift of that day had meantime tremendously widened. He felt that in this moment something was lacking between him and Erwin that had always been there before, an aura of solidarity, of spontaneous understanding—indeed, even of affection. Instead of these there was a vacuum. They greeted each other; spoke of the weather, their acquaintances, their health; and—God knows why! with every word Frederick had the disquieting sensation that he was not quite understanding his friend, that his friend did not really know him, that his words were missing their mark, that they could find no common ground for a real conversation. Moreover Erwin still had that friendly smile on his face, which Frederick was beginning almost to hate.

During a pause in the laborious conversation Frederick looked about the studio he knew so well and saw, pinned loosely on the wall, a sheet of paper. This sight moved him strangely and awakened ancient memories; for he recalled that, long ago in their student years, this had been a habit of Erwin's, a way he sometimes chose of keeping a thinker's saying or a poet's verse fresh in his mind. He stood up and went to the wall to read the paper.

There, in Erwin's beautiful script, he read the words: "Nothing is without, nothing is within; for what is without is within."

Blanching, he stood motionless for a moment. There it was! There he stood face to face with what he feared! At another time he would have let this leaf of paper pass, would have tolerated it charitably as a whim, as a harmless foible to which anyone was entitled, perhaps as a trifling sentimentality calling for indulgence. But now it was different. He felt that these words had not been set down for the sake of a fleeting poetic mood; it was not a vagary that Erwin had returned after so many years to a practice of his youth. What stood written here, as an avowal of his friend's concern at the moment, was mysticism! Erwin was unfaithful!

Slowly he turned to face him, whose smile was again radiant.

"Explain this to me!" he demanded.

Erwin nodded, brimming with friendliness.

"Haven't you ever read this saying?"

"Certainly!" Frederick cried. "Of course I know it. It's mysticism, it's Gnosticism. It may be poetic, but—well, anyway, explain the saying to me, and why it's hanging on your wall!"

"Gladly," Erwin said. "The saying is a first introduction to an epistemology that I've been going into lately, and which has already brought me much happiness."

Frederick restrained his temper. He asked, "A new epistemology? Is there such a thing? And what is it called?"

"Oh," Erwin answered, "it's only new to me. It's already very old and venerable. It's called magic."

The word had been uttered. Profoundly astonished and startled by so candid a confession, Frederick, with a shudder, felt that he was confronted eye to eye with the arch-enemy, in the person of his friend. He did not know whether he was nearer rage or tears; the bitter feeling of irreparable loss possessed him. For a long time he remained silent.

Then, with a pretended decision in his voice, he began, "So now you want to become a magician?"

"Yes," Erwin replied unhesitatingly.

"A sort of sorcerer's apprentice, eh?"

"Certainly."

A clock could be heard ticking in the adjoining room, it was so quiet.

Then Frederick said, "This means, you know, that you are abandoning all fellowship with serious science, and hence all fellowship with me."

"I hope that is not so," Erwin answered. "But if that's the way it has to be, what else can I do?"

"What else can you do?" Frederick burst out. "Why, break, break once and for all with this childishness, this wretched and contemptible belief in magic! That's what else you can do, if you want to keep my respect."

Erwin smiled a little, although he too no longer seemed cheerful.

"You speak as if," he said, so gently that through his quiet words Frederick's angry voice still seemed to be echoing about the room, "you speak as if that lay within my will, as if I had a choice, Frederick. That is not the case. I have no choice. It was not I that chose magic: magic chose me."

Frederick sighed deeply. "Then goodby," he said wearily, and stood up, without offering to shake hands.

"Not like that!" Erwin cried out. "No, you must not go from me like that. Pretend that one of us is lying on his deathbed—and that is so!—and that we must say farewell."

"But which of us, Erwin, is dying?"

"Today it is probably I, my friend. Whoever wishes to be born anew must be prepared to die."

Once more Frederick went up to the sheet of paper and read the saying about within and without.

"Very well," he said finally. "You are right, it won't do any good to part in anger. I'll do what you wish; I'll pretend that one of us is dying. Before I go I want to make a last request of you."

"I'm glad," Erwin said. "Tell me, what kindness can I show you on our leavetaking?"

"I repeat my first question, and this is also my request: explain this saying to me, as well as you can."

Erwin reflected a moment and then spoke:

"Nothing is without, nothing is within. You know the religious meaning of this: God is everywhere. He is in the spirit, and also in nature. All is divine, because God is all. Formerly this was called pantheism. Then the philosophic meaning: we are used to divorcing the within from the without in our thinking, but this is not necessary. Our spirit is capable of withdrawing behind the limits we have set for it, into the beyond. Beyond the pair of antitheses of which our world consists a new and different knowledge begins. . . . But, my dear friend, I must confess to you—since my thinking has changed there are no longer any unambiguous words and sayings for me: every word has tens and hundreds of meanings. And here what you fear begins—magic."

Frederick wrinkled his brow and was about to interrupt, but Erwin looked at him disarmingly and continued, speaking more distinctly, "Let me give you an example. Take something of mine along with you, any object, and examine it a little from time to time. Soon the principle of the within and the without will reveal one of its many means to you."

He glanced about the room, took a small clay figurine from a wall shelf, and gave it to Frederick, saying:

"Take this with you as my parting gift. When this thing that I am now placing in your hands ceases to be outside you and is within you, come to me again! But if it remains outside you, the way it is now, forever, then this parting of yours from me shall also be forever!"

Frederick wanted to say a great deal more; but Erwin took his hand, pressed it, and bade him farewell with an expression that permitted no further conversation.

Frederick left; descended the stairs (how prodigiously long ago he had climbed them!); went through the streets to his home, the little earthen figure in his hand, perplexed and sick of heart. In front of his house he stopped, shook the fist fiercely for a moment in which he was clutching the figurine, and felt a great urge to smash the ridiculous thing to the ground. He did not do so; he bit his lip and entered the house. Never before had he been so agitated, so tormented by conflicting emotions.

He looked for a place for his friend's gift, and put the figure on top of a bookcase. For the time being it stayed there.

Occasionally, as the days went by, he looked at it, brooding on it and on its origins, and pondering the meaning that this foolish thing was to have for him. It was a small figure of a man or a god or an idol, with two faces, like the Roman god Janus, modeled rather crudely of clay and covered with a burnt and somewhat cracked glaze. The little image looked coarse and insignificant; certainly it was not Roman or Greek workmanship; more likely it was the work of some backward, primitive race in Africa or the South Seas. The two faces, which were exactly alike, bore an apathetic, indolent faintly grinning smile—it was downright ugly the way the little gnome squandered his stupid smile.

Frederick could not get used to the figure. It was totally unpleasant and offensive to him, it got in his way, it disturbed him. The very next day he took it down and put it on the stove, and a few days later moved it to a cupboard. Again and again it got in the path of his vision, as if it were forcing itself upon him; it laughed at him coldy and dull-wittedly, put on airs, demanded attention. After a few weeks he put it in the anteroom, between the photographs of Italy and the trivial little souvenirs which no one ever looked at. Now at least he saw the idol only when he was entering or leaving, and then he passed it quickly, without examining it more closely. But here too the thing still bothered him, though he did not admit this to himself.

With this shard, this two-faced monstrosity, vexation and torment had entered his life.

One day, months later, he returned from a short trip—he undertook such excursions now from time to time, as if something were driving him restlessly about; he entered his house, went through the anteroom, was greeted by the maid, and read the letters waiting for him. But he was ill at ease, as if he had forgotten something important; no book tempted him, no chair was comfortable. He began to rack his mind—what was the cause of this? Had he neglected something important? eaten something unsettling? In reflecting it occurred to him that this disturbing feeling had come over him as he had entered the apartment. He returned to the anteroom and involuntarily his first glance sought the clay figure.

A strange fright went through him when he did not see the idol. It had disappeared. It was missing. Had it walked away on its little crockery legs? Flown away? By magic?

Frederick pulled himself together, and smiled at his nervousness. Then he began quietly to search the whole room. When he found nothing he called the maid. She came, was embarrassed, and admitted at once that she had dropped the thing while cleaning up.

"Where is it?"

It was not there any more. It had seemed so solid, that little thing; she had often had it in her hands; and yet it had shattered to a hundred little pieces and splinters, and could not be fixed. She had taken the fragments to a glazier, who had simply laughed at her; and then she had thrown them away.

Frederick dismissed the maid. He smiled. That was perfectly all right with him. He did not feel bad about the idol, God knows. The abomination was gone; now he would have peace. If only he had knocked the thing to pieces that very first day! What he had suffered in all this time! How sluggishly, strangely, craftily, evilly, satanically that idol had smiled at him! Well, now that it was gone he could admit it to himself: he had feared it, truly and sincerely feared it, this earthen god. Was it not the emblem and symbol of everything that was repugnant and intolerable to him, everything that he had recognized all along as pernicious, inimical, and worthy of suppression—an emblem of all superstitions, all darkness, all coercion of conscience and spirit? Did it not represent that ghastly power that one sometimes felt raging in the bowels of the earth, that distant earthquake, that approaching extinction of culture, that looming chaos? Had not this contemptible figure robbed him of his best friend—nay, not merely robbed, but made of the friend an enemy? Well, now the thing was gone. Vanished. Smashed to pieces. Done for. It was good so; it was much better than if he had destroyed it himself.

So he thought, or said. And he went about his affairs as before.

But it was like a curse. Now, just when he had got more or less used to that ridiculous figure, just when the sight of it in its usual place on the anteroom table had gradually become a bit familiar and unimportant to him, now its absence began to torment him! Yes, he missed it everytime he went through that room; all he could see there was the empty spot where it had formerly stood, and emptiness emanated from the spot and filled the room with strangeness.

Bad days and worse nights began for Frederick. He could no longer go through the anteroom without thinking of the idol with the two faces, missing it, and feeling that his thoughts were tethered to it. This became an agonizing compulsion for him. And it was not by any means simply on the occasions when he went through that room that he was gripped by this compulsion—ah, no. Just as emptiness and desolation radiated from the now empty spot on the anteroom table, so this compulsive idea radiated within him, gradually crowded all else aside, rankling and filling him with emptiness and strangeness.

Again and again he pictured the figure with utmost distinctness, just to make it clear to himself how preposterous it was to grieve its loss. He could see it in all its stupid ugliness and barbarity, with its vacuous yet crafty smile, with its two faces—indeed, as if under duress, full of hatred and with his mouth drawn awry, he found himself attempting to reproduce that smile. The question pestered him whether the two faces were really exactly alike. Had not one of them, perhaps only because of a little roughness or a crack in the glaze, had a somewhat different expression? Something quizzical? Something sphinxlike? And how peculiar the color of that glaze had been! Green, and blue, and gray, but also red, were in it—a glaze that he now kept finding often in other objects, in a window's reflection of the sun or in the mirrorings of a wet pavement.

He brooded a great deal on this glaze, at night too. It also struck him what a strange, foreign, ill-sounding, unfamiliar, almost malignant word "glaze" was. He analyzed the word, and once he even reversed the order of its letters. Then it read "ezalg." Now where the devil did this word get its sound from? He knew this word "ezalg," certainly he knew it; moreover, it was an unfriendly and bad word, a word with ugly and disturbing connotations. For a long while he tormented himself with this question. Finally he hit upon it: "ezalg" reminded him of a book that he had bought and read many years ago on a trip, and that had dismayed, plagued, and yet secretly fascinated him; it had been entitled *Princess Ezalka*. It was like a curse: everything connected with the figurine—the glaze, the blue, the green, the smile—signified hostility, tormenting and poisoning him. And how very peculiarly *he*, Erwin, his erstwhile friend, had smiled as he had given the idol into his hand! How very peculiarly, how very significantly, how very hostilely.

Frederick resisted manfully—and on many days not without success—the compulsive trend of his thoughts. He sensed the danger clearly: he did not want to go insane! No, it were better to die. Reason was necessary, life was not. And it occurred to him that perhaps *this* was magic, that Erwin, with the aid of that figure, had in some way enchanted him, and that he should fall as a sacrifice, as the defender of reason and science against these dismal powers. But if this were so, if he could even conceive of that as possible, then there *was* such a thing as magic, then there *was* sorcery. No, it were better to die!

A doctor recommended walks and baths; and sometimes, in search of amusement, he spent an evening at an inn. But it helped very little. He cursed Erwin; he cursed himself.

One night, as he often did now, he retired early and lay restlessly awake in bed, unable to sleep. He felt unwell and uneasy. He wanted to meditate; he wanted to find solace, wanted to speak sentences of some sort to himself, good sentences, comforting, reassuring ones, something with the straightforward serenity and lucidity of the sentence, "Twice two is four." Nothing came to mind; but, in a state almost of lightheadedness, he mumbled sounds and syllables to himself. Gradually words formed on his lips, and several times, without being sensible of its meaning, he said the same short sentence to himself, which had somehow taken form in him. He muttered it to himself, as if it might stupefy him, as if he might grope his way along it, as along a parapet, to the sleep that eluded him on the narrow, narrow path that skirted the abyss.

But suddenly, when he spoke somewhat louder, the words he was mumbling penetrated his consciousness. He knew them: they were, "Yes, now you are within me!" And instantly he knew. He knew what they meant—that they referred to the clay idol and that now, in this gray night hour, he had accurately and exactly fulfilled the prophecy Erwin had made on that unearthly day, that now the figure, which he had held contemptuously in his fingers then, was no longer outside him but within him! "For what is without is within."

Bounding up in a leap, he felt as if transfused with ice and fire. The world reeled about him, the planets stared at him insanely. He threw on some clothes, put on the light, left his house and ran in the middle of the night to Erwin's. There he saw a light burning in the studio window he knew so well; the door to the house was unlocked: everything seemed to be awaiting him. He rushed up the stairs. He walked unsteadily into Erwin's study, supported himself with trembling hands on the table. Erwin sat by the lamp, in its gentle light, contemplative, smiling.

Graciously Erwin arose. "You have come. That is good."

"Have you been expecting me?" Frederick whispered.

"I have been expecting you, as you know, from the moment you left here, taking my little gift with you. Has what I said then happened?"

"It has happened," Frederick said. "The idol is within me. I can't bear it any longer."

"Can I help you?" Erwin asked.

"I don't know. Do as you will. Tell me more of your magic! Tell me how the idol can get out of me again."

Erwin placed his hand on his friend's shoulder. He led him to an armchair and pressed him down in it. Then he spoke cordially to Frederick, smiling in an almost brotherly tone of voice:

"The idol will come out of you again. Have trust in me. Have trust in yourself. You have learned to believe in it. Now learn to love it! It is within you, but it is still dead, it is still a phantom to you. Awaken it, speak to it, question it! For it is you yourself! Do not hate it any longer, do not fear it, do not torment it—how you have tormented this poor idol, who was yet you yourself! How you have tormented yourself!"

"Is this the way of magic?" Frederick asked. He sat deep in the chair, as if he had grown older, and his voice was low.

"This is the way," Erwin replied, "and perhaps you have already taken the most difficult step. You have found by experience: the without can become the within. You have been beyond the pair of antitheses. It seemed hell to you; learn, my friend, it is heaven! For it is heaven that awaits you. Behold, this is magic: to interchange the without and the within, not by compulsion, not in anguish, as you have done it, but freely, voluntarily. Summon up the past, summon up the future: both are in you! Until today you have been the slave of the within. Learn to be its master. That is magic."

Translated by T. K. Brown, III

HESSE: *Within and Without*

1. What is Hesse attacking in the scientific mind? Is it a valid attack? Compare Hesse's attack here with Lawrence's in "The Man Who Loved Islands."
2. Is Frederick right to be incredulous of his friend Erwin's interest in magic? How does Hesse make us share Frederick's disbelief? Is it necessary that we should?
3. Discuss the symbolism of the figurine. Why two faces? Why like Janus? Why does Frederick even accept it?
4. Why does the figurine—even after it is smashed to fragments—continue to obsess Frederick?
5. What happens to Frederick? What experience does he undergo? Can it be precisely explained? How does Hesse consciously avoid precision?
6. Does the acceptance of the figurine mean that Frederick must reject the world? What does Hesse mean by the merging of within and without? Is such a merging possible within our daily lives? Is it at all possible within Western society, or practicable only within a society that encourages asceticism and withdrawal?
7. Does Hesse's view have any parallels in orthodox religious terms? Why is the figurine clearly not a Christian symbol?
8. Compare this story with Dostoyevsky's "The Grand Inquisitor." Can you see the deep influence that Dostoyevsky had on Hesse? In what areas? Would the Frederick of the early part of the story share the attitudes of Dostoyevsky's Inquisitor?
9. Why does the story begin as though it were a fairy tale ("Once upon a time there lived . . .")?

Robert Musil

A MAN WITHOUT CHARACTER

Born in 1880 in Klagenfurt, Austria, Robert Musil was educated at a military academy and then studied engineering and logic. In 1906, his short novel Young Torless *brought him critical acclaim, and he gave up his academic career for writing, later serving as an officer in the Austrian army in the First World War. In 1933, to escape the Nazis, he fled to Vienna and then to Switzerland, where he died in 1942. His most famous fiction is the unfinished* The Man Without Qualities, *which many continental critics have called the greatest European novel of this century. In "A Man Without Character," Musil joins with his contemporaries Thomas Mann and Franz Kafka in treating ironically the always fascinating theme of man's identity in a world whose values are ever-changing.*

TO FIND people with character nowadays means searching for them with a torch, yet going about with a burning light by day might lay us open to ridicule. I am therefore going to tell the story of a man who always had difficulty with his character, yes, in plain words, someone who never really had a character. Only it troubles me that I may merely have failed to grasp his significance in time, or that he may in the last analysis have represented a kind of pioneer or precursor of a new type.

We were neighbors as children. Whenever he perpetrated one of those little pranks which are so clever that one is loath to recount them, his mother would sigh, for the thrashing she would give him would prove a physical strain. "Boy," she'd lament, "you have no trace of character in you; God knows what's to become of you!" But in more difficult cases it was Father who would be consulted, and then the thrashing would be marked by a certain solemnity and grave dignity—somewhat as on ceremonial occasions at school. Before accounts were settled, my friend would himself have to hand the Auditor-in-Chief a cane, the primary function of which was to beat the dust out of clothes, for which it was kept in the cook's custody, while, when it was all over, the son was expected to bestow on the paternal hand a kiss with an expression of gratitude for the reprimand and an apology to the dear parents for the worries he had caused them. My friend would reverse the order. He would whine and beg pardon in advance, and continue to do so from one stroke to the next, but when it was all finished be unable to utter another word, his face turning purple as he swallowed his saliva and tears and by means of vigorous rubbing sought to erase the imprint of what he could still feel. "I don't know," his father would say, "what's to become of this boy; the fellow's completely without character!"

Thus character in our youth was something for which, even though one was without it, one would receive a thrashing. There seemed to be a certain injustice attached to this. My friend's parents, when demanding character of him and for once resorting to explanations, would explain that character was the ideological opposite of poor grades, school hours lost through truancy, tin-cups tied to dogtails, chatting and secret tomfoolery in class, obstinate subterfuges, scatterbrains, or a slingshot wantonly aimed at some innocent bird. But the natural opposite of all this was after all the terror of punishment, the fear of being found out, and the pangs of conscience which torture the soul with that sense of remorse which one would be able to feel if things should turn out to have gone awry. This was all-absorbing; to accommodate character there was neither room nor activity to spare; it was something totally superfluous. Yet it was demanded of us.

Perhaps the words spoken from time to time to my friend by way of explanation in the course of these punishments should have provided a clue, such as: "Haven't you got any pride, boy?" Or: "How can anyone be such a base liar!" But I must say I find it hard to imagine to this day how anyone can be expected to show pride when receiving a box on the ear or while under a rain of blows across someone's knees. I can imagine rage, but that was precisely what we were not supposed to feel! And it was the same with lying: what sort of liar could one be expected to be if not a base one? An unskilled one perhaps? As I think about it I imagine that what one would have liked us most to be would have been honest liars. That would have meant being charged twice over as it were: one, you shall not lie; two, if you do lie, make sure you don't lie mendaciously. Perhaps this is something adult criminals are able to distinguish, since what is always reckoned against them as especially infamous in court is a crime committed in cold blood, with precautions, or with premeditation; but to expect such a distinction from boys would decidedly be asking too much. I'm afraid the only reason why I did not show such striking faults of character as my friend was the fact that I hadn't been so carefully brought up as he.

Of all the parental pronouncements concerning character the most illuminating were those which coupled its regrettable lack with the warning that we would be sorely in need of it as men. "And such a boy wants to become a man!" or words to that effect. Even disregarding the fact that the question of one's wanting to wasn't altogether clear, the rest still proved that character was something one would have need of only in the future; why then all those overhasty preparations now? This was exactly what we were thinking, too.

Although my friend did not possess a character at that time, he did not miss it either. This only happened later, when we were between sixteen and seventeen. It was the time when we began going to the theatre and to read novels. My friend's imagination, more receptive to the deceptive allurements of art than mine, was captured by the villain on the local stage, by the affectionate father, the heroic lover, the figure of fun, yes, even by the diabolic parlor snake, and the ravishing lady of innocence. His speech, now all fake, suddenly ran the whole gamut of what the German stage had to offer in the way of character. When he promised something, one could never be sure whether his word of honor was that of a hero or a stage villain. He might start out on a note of malice and end up being sincere; he might receive us, his friends, full of bluster, and, all at once, with the sophisticated smile of a *bon vivant*, offer us cookies and sweets or, while embracing us with a paternal hug, filch the cigarettes from our pockets.

But this was harmless and candid compared with the effect the reading of novels had on him. Novels contain descriptions of the most wonderful directions for conduct in any number of situations in life. The great drawback is that the situations in which one finds oneself in real life never quite correspond to those for which in fiction there is a provision as to how to act and what to say. World literature is an enormous magazine where millions of souls are clothed with generosity, rage, pride, love, scorn, jealousy, nobility, and meanness. When a woman we adore tramples on our feelings we know we must glance at her with a punitively soulful look; when a scoundrel maltreats an orphan we know we must fell him to the ground with one blow. But what are we to do if the adored woman, having just trampled on our feelings, slams the door of her room shut so that our soulful look can no longer reach her? Or if a table set with priceless glasses stands between us and the scoundrel maltreating the orphan? Are we to smash in the door in order to cast a soft glance through the opening; and are we carefully to clear away the expensive glasses before raising our arm for the blow? Literature invariably leaves us in the lurch in really important cases such as these.

Perhaps with a greater wealth of descriptions things will have improved in a few hundred years.

Meanwhile the consequences for the well-read reader finding himself in a so-called situation of real life are especially awkward. Fully a dozen unfinished sentences, half-raised eyebrows or clenched fists, turned backs, and throbbing chests—none of them quite suited to the occasion, yet not unsuited either—are simmering in him; the corners of his mouth are simultaneously drawn up and down, his forehead frowns in gloom and is lit up by gleams of light, a vengeful look darts from his eyes even as they are retracting in shame: and this is very awkward, for what it amounts to is, so to speak, a mutual infliction of pain on the self. The result is often the familiar gulping and twitching that affect lips, eyes, hands, and throat, yes, at times to such an extent the entire body that it keeps turning like a screw to which the nut has been lost.

It was at that time that my friend discovered how much more convenient it would be to have a single character of one's own, and he began to look for it.

But he landed in new adventures. I met him again years later after he had turned to practicing law. He was wearing spectacles, had shaved off his beard, and spoke in a soft voice. "You're staring at me?" he remarked. I couldn't deny it; there was something about his appearance that made me seek for an answer. "Do I look like a lawyer?" he asked. I didn't mean to dispute it. He explained to me: "Lawyers have a very definite way of looking through their pince-nez, which is different, say, from the way doctors have. Another thing one can say about them is that all their movements and phrases are more sharply pointed or jagged than the rounded and gnarled ones of theologians. They are as different from them as a *feuilleton* is from a sermon, in other words, just as fish don't fly from tree to tree, so lawyers are immersed in an element from which they never emerge."

"Character of a career man," I said. My friend was satisfied with me. "It wasn't any too easy," he said. "When I started out I was growing a Christ's beard, but my chief forbade it, because it didn't go with the character of a lawyer. Whereupon I began walking around, looking like a painter, and when that wasn't allowed, like a seaman on leave." "For God's sake, why?" I asked. "Because of course I wanted to guard against taking on the character of a man with a career," he replied. "The trouble is there's no evading it. Of course there are lawyers who look like poets, just as there are poets who look like greengrocers, and greengrocers who have the heads of intellectuals. But they all have something of a glass-eye or false beard or poorly healed wound about them. I don't understand why, but isn't it so?" He smiled after his fashion, adding humbly: "As you know, I don't even have a personal character. . . ."

I reminded him of the numerous stage characters. "Days of our youth!" he commented with a sigh. "In becoming a man one acquires a sexual, cultural, national, class, and geographic character. Then there's the character associated with one's handwriting, the lines in one's palm, the shape of one's skull, and maybe the constellation of the stars at the moment of birth. That's too much for me. I never know which of my characters I'm to side with." Again that unobtrusive smile of his appeared. "Fortunately, my fiancée is of the opinion that I don't possess a character at all, because I haven't yet made good on my promise to marry her. That's precisely the reason I'm going to marry her; her sober judgment is indispensable to me." "Who is your fiancée?"

"According to which character? Mind you," he interrupted himself, "she knows all the same what she wants. She was originally a charmingly helpless little girl—I've known her for a long time—, but she's learned a lot from me. She thinks it's dreadful when I lie, and when I'm late getting to the office in the morning she swears I'll never be able to support a family, and when I fail to stick by something I promised I'd do, she knows only a scoundrel would behave like that."

My friend smiled once more. He was a charming person in those days, and people would look down on him with a friendly smile. Nobody seriously thought he would ever accomplish anything. What struck one even about his appearance was the fact that as soon as he began to speak every limb of his body would shift its position, his eyes would focus evasively sideways, shoulders, hands, and arms would move in directions opposite to each other, and at least one of his legs would quiver with the up-and-down swing of a letter scale in the joint of the knee. To repeat, he was an amiable person, modest, shy, respectful; and sometimes he was the opposite of all this, but one always remained fond of him if only out of curiosity.

When I saw him again he had a car and said woman for a wife now his shadow, as well as a responsible and influential position in his job. How he managed to achieve this, I don't know, but my hunch is that the whole secret was due to the fact that he was getting fat. His timid, mobile face had disappeared. Looking critically one could see it was still there, but it lay concealed under a thick layer of fat. His eyes, which in the past when he had committed some mischief could be as touching as a sad little monkey's, had not actually lost the lustre with which they shone from within, but his padded cheeks now made it difficult for them to focus sideways, hence they would stare straight ahead with a haughty expression of annoyance. The inner movements of his limbs were as jerky as ever, but their flexing was cushioned from the outside by the fatty shock absorbers at the joints, and the resulting gesturing resembled the bluntness of resolute speech. And the whole man had become like this. His will-o'-the-wisp mind had become encased in rigid walls, and was filled with heavy convictions. There would still be an occasional flash, but it no longer radiated any light in the man; rather, it was a shot fired to impress, or to fulfil a particular purpose. He had really lost a good deal compared with the past. He now talked nineteen to the dozen, though the dozen was made up of good, solid material. And he treated his past as one recalls some youthful piece of foolishness.

On one occasion I succeeded in bringing him back to our old topic of conversation—character. "I'm convinced the development of character is connected with the method of waging war," he expounded, gasping for air, "so that today one comes across it only in near-savages. Those who fight with knives and spears can't afford to do without it if they're not to get the worst of the bargain. But what character, however determined, can stand up to tanks, flamethrowers, and clouds of poison gas? Therefore, what we need today is not character, but discipline!"

I did not contradict him. But the curious thing was—and that's why I have taken the liberty of committing this reminiscence to paper—that as he stood there talking and I kept looking at him, I constantly had the feeling that he still carried his old self within him. It resided in him, enclosed in the enlarged bodily replica of the original person. The look in his eyes reflected the look in the eyes of the other, his words those of the other. It was almost uncanny. I have seen him several times since, and each time found this impression confirmed. It was evident he would have liked, if I may say so, to step up close to the window-pane, but something always prevented him.

Translated by E. M. Valk

MUSIL: *A Man Without Character*

1. *Musil's extraordinary novel,* Young Torless, *is generally regarded as a microcosmic prefiguration of the Nazi world. In "A Man Without Character," what kind of world to come does the narrator's friend foreshadow (" '. . . he may in the last analysis have represented a kind of pioneer or precursor of a new type.' ")?*

2. Musil is saying something about a man's identity and how he acquires it. Does this slight piece bear the burden of so profound a theme?

3. What does the narrator's friend mean by " '. . . what we need today is not character, but discipline.' "? To what part of the story is this statement relevant?

4. Why does Musil make the narrator's friend a lawyer? Why is he lacking even a name? (Cf. the story by Pirandello.)

5. Is Musil being straightforward or ironic in this tale? How do you know what he is really suggesting? Does the narrator speak for Musil, or is he, as in the Henry James story, merely a mask?

6. Mann, Hesse, Musil, and Kafka were roughly contemporaries who wrote their stories in German. Does the original language seem in any way to influence the style of their stories?

James Joyce
COUNTERPARTS

James Joyce was born in 1882 in Dublin, the city that was to occupy his thoughts until his death in 1941 although he spent most of his adult years as a voluntary exile from his homeland. Dublin is interwoven into the fabric of his short stories, Dubliners *(1914); into his first novel,* A Portrait of the Artist as a Young Man *(1916); and into the two long works which became the keystones of his career,* Ulysses *(1922) and* Finnegans Wake *(1939). In the twenty or so years since his death, Joyce has continued to tower over the twentieth-century English novel, a literary force whose original techniques and genius with language have as yet found no equal. Although representative of Joyce's early work, "Counterparts" nevertheless suggests a view of Dublin—one composed of attachment and dismay—that was to predominate in all of his fiction.*

THE BELL rang furiously and, when Miss Parker went to the tube, a furious voice called out in a piercing North of Ireland accent:

"Send Farrington here!"

Miss Parker returned to her machine, saying to a man who was writing at a desk:

"Mr. Alleyne wants you upstairs."

The man muttered "*Blast* him!" under his breath and pushed back his chair to stand up. When he stood up he was tall and of great bulk. He had a hanging face, dark wine-coloured, with fair eyebrows and moustache: his eyes bulged forward slightly and the whites of them were dirty. He lifted up the counter and, passing by the clients, went out of the office with a heavy step.

He went heavily upstairs until he came to the second landing, where a door bore a brass plate with the inscription *Mr. Alleyne*. Here he halted, puffing with labour and vexation, and knocked. The shrill voice cried:

"Come in!"

The man entered Mr. Alleyne's room. Simultaneously Mr. Alleyne, a little man wearing gold-rimmed glasses on a clean-shaven face, shot his head up over a pile of documents. The head itself was so pink and hairless it seemed like a large egg reposing on the papers. Mr. Alleyne did not lose a moment:

"Farrington? What is the meaning of this? Why have I always to complain of you? May I ask you why you haven't made a copy of that contract between Bodley and Kirwan? I told you it must be ready by four o'clock."

"But Mr. Shelley said, sir——"

"*Mr. Shelley said, sir.* . . . Kindly attend to what I say and not to what *Mr. Shelley says, sir.* You have always some excuse or another for shirking work. Let me tell you that if the contract is not copied before this evening I'll lay the matter before Mr. Crosbie. . . . Do you hear me now?"

"Yes, sir."

"Do you hear me now? . . . Ay and another little matter! I might as well be talking to the wall as talking to you. Understand once for all that you get a half an hour for your lunch and not an hour and a half. How many courses do you want, I'd like to know. . . . Do you mind me now?"

"Yes, sir."

Mr. Alleyne bent his head again upon his pile of papers. The man stared fixedly at the polished skull which directed the affairs of Crosbie and Alleyne, gauging its fragility. A spasm of rage gripped his throat for a few moments and then passed, leaving after it a sharp sensation of thirst. The man recognised the sensation and felt that he must have a good night's drinking. The middle of the month was passed and, if he could get the copy done in time, Mr. Alleyne might give him an order on the cashier. He stood still, gazing fixedly at the head upon the pile of papers. Suddenly Mr. Alleyne began to upset all the papers, searching for something. Then, as if he had been unaware of the man's presence till that moment, he shot up his head again, saying:

"Eh? Are you going to stand there all day? Upon my word, Farrington, you take things easy!"

"I was waiting to see . . ."

"Very good, you needn't wait to see. Go downstairs and do your work."

The man walked heavily towards the door and, as he went out of the room, he heard Mr. Alleyne cry after him that if the contract was not copied by evening Mr. Crosbie would hear of the matter.

He returned to his desk in the lower office and counted the sheets which remained to be copied. He took up his pen and dipped it in the ink but he continued to stare stupidly at the last words he had written: *In no case shall the said Bernard Bodley be* . . . The evening was falling and in a few minutes they would be lighting the gas: then he could write. He felt that he must slake the thirst in his throat. He stood up from his desk and, lifting the counter as before, passed out of the office. As he was passing out the chief clerk looked at him inquiringly.

"It's all right, Mr. Shelley," said the man, pointing with his finger to indicate the objective of his journey.

The chief clerk glanced at the hat-rack, but, seeing the row complete, offered no remark. As soon as he was on the landing the man pulled a shepherd's plaid cap out of his pocket, put it on his head and ran quickly down the rickety stairs. From the street door he walked on furtively on the inner side of the path towards the corner and all at once dived into a doorway. He was now safe in the dark snug of O'Neill's shop, and, filling up the little window that looked into the bar with his inflamed face, the colour of dark wine or dark meat, he called out:

"Here, Pat, give us a g.p., like a good fellow."

The curate brought him a glass of plain porter. The man drank it at a gulp and asked for a caraway seed. He put his penny on the counter and, leaving the curate to grope for it in the gloom, retreated out of the snug as furtively as he had entered it.

Darkness, accompanied by a thick fog, was gaining upon the dusk of February and the lamps in Eustace Street had been lit. The man went up by the houses until he reached the door of the office, wondering whether he could finish his copy in time. On the stairs a moist pungent odour of perfumes saluted his nose: evidently Miss Delacour had come while he was out in O'Neill's. He crammed his cap back again into his pocket and re-entered the office, assuming an air of absent-mindedness.

"Mr. Alleyne has been calling for you," said the chief clerk severely. "Where were you?"

The man glanced at the two clients who were standing at the counter as if to intimate that their presence prevented him from answering. As the clients were both male the chief clerk allowed himself a laugh.

"I know that game," he said. "Five times in one day is a little bit. . . . Well, you better look sharp and get a copy of our correspondence in the Delacour case for Mr. Alleyne."

This address in the presence of the public, his run upstairs and the porter he had gulped down so hastily confused the man and, as he sat down at his desk to get what was required, he realised how hopeless was the task of finishing his copy of the contract before half past five. The dark damp night was coming and he longed to spend it in the bars, drinking with his friends amid the glare of gas and the clatter of glasses. He got out the Delacour correspondence and passed out of the office. He hoped Mr. Alleyne would not discover that the last two letters were missing.

The moist pungent perfume lay all the way up to Mr. Alleyne's room. Miss Delacour was a middle-aged woman of Jewish appearance. Mr. Alleyne was said to be sweet on her or on her money. She came to the office often and stayed a long time when she came. She was sitting beside his desk now in an aroma of perfumes, smoothing the handle of her umbrella and nodding the great black feather in her hat. Mr. Alleyne had swivelled his chair round to face her and thrown his right foot jauntily upon his left knee. The man put the correspondence on the desk and bowed respectfully but neither Mr. Alleyne nor Miss Delacour took any notice of his bow. Mr. Alleyne tapped a finger on the correspondence and then flicked it towards him as if to say: *"That's all right: you can go."*

The man returned to the lower office and sat down again at his desk. He stared intently at the incomplete phrase: *In no case shall the said Bernard Bodley be* . . . and thought how strange it was that the last three words began with the same letter. The chief clerk began to hurry Miss Parker, saying she would never have the letters typed in time for post. The man listened to the clicking of the machine for a few minutes and then set to work to finish his copy. But his head was not clear and his mind wandered away to the glare and rattle of the public-house. It was a night for hot punches. He struggled on with his copy, but when the clock struck five he had still fourteen pages to write. Blast it! He couldn't finish it in time. He longed to execrate aloud, to bring his fist down on something violently. He was so enraged that he wrote *Bernard Bernard* instead of *Bernard Bodley* and had to begin again on a clean sheet.

He felt strong enough to clear out the whole office single-handed. His body ached to do something, to rush out and revel in violence. All the indignities of his life enraged him. . . . Could he ask the cashier privately for an advance? No, the cashier was no good, no damn good: he wouldn't give an advance. . . . He knew where he would meet the boys: Leonard and O'Halloran and Nosey Flynn. The barometer of his emotional nature was set for a spell of riot.

His imagination had so abstracted him that his name was called twice before he answered. Mr. Alleyne and Miss Delacour were standing outside the counter and all the clerks had turned round in anticipation of something. The man got up from his desk. Mr. Alleyne began a tirade of abuse, saying that two letters were missing. The man answered that he knew nothing about them, that he had made a faithful copy. The tirade continued: it was so bitter and violent that the man could hardly restrain his fist from descending upon the head of the manikin before him:

"I know nothing about any other two letters," he said stupidly.

"*You—know—nothing.* Of course you know nothing," said Mr. Alleyne. "Tell me," he added, glancing first for approval to the lady beside him, "do you take me for a fool? Do you think me an utter fool?"

The man glanced from the lady's face to the little egg-shaped head and back again; and, almost before he was aware of it, his tongue had found a felicitous moment:

"I don't think, sir," he said, "that that's a fair question to put to me."

There was a pause in the very breathing of the clerks. Everyone was astounded (the author of the witticism no less than his neighbours) and Miss Delacour, who was a stout amiable person, began to smile broadly. Mr. Alleyne flushed to the hue of a wild rose and his mouth twitched with a dwarf's passion. He shook his fist in the man's face till it seemed to vibrate like the knob of some electric machine:

"You impertinent ruffian! You impertinent ruffian! I'll make short work of you. Wait till you see! You'll apologise to me for your impertinence or you'll quit the office instanter! You'll quit this, I'm telling you, or you'll apologise to me!"

He stood in a doorway opposite the office watching to see if the cashier would come out alone. All the clerks passed out and finally the cashier came out with the chief clerk. It was no use trying to say a word to him when he was with the chief clerk. The man felt that his position was bad enough. He had been obliged to offer an abject apology to Mr. Alleyne for his impertinence but he knew what a hornet's nest the office would be for him. He could remember the way in which Mr. Alleyne had hounded little Peake out of the office in order to make room for his own nephew. He felt savage and thirsty and revengeful, annoyed with himself and with everyone else. Mr. Alleyne would never give him an hour's rest; his life would be a hell to him. He had made a proper fool of himself this time. Could he not keep his tongue in his cheek? But they had never pulled together from the first, he and Mr. Alleyne, ever since the day Mr. Alleyne had overheard him mimicking his North of Ireland accent to amuse Higgins and Miss Parker; that had been the beginning of it. He might have tried Higgins for the money, but sure Higgins never had anything for himself. A man with two establishments to keep up, of course he couldn't. . . .

He felt his great body again aching for the comfort of the public-house. The fog had begun to chill him and he wondered could he touch Pat in O'Neill's. He could not touch him for more than a bob—and a bob was no use. Yet he must get money somewhere or other: he had spent his last penny for the g.p. and soon it would be too late for getting money anywhere. Suddenly, as he was fingering his watch-chain, he thought of Terry Kelly's pawn-office in Fleet Street. That was the dart! Why didn't he think of it sooner?

He went through the narrow alley of Temple Bar quickly, muttering to himself that they could all go to hell because he was going to have a good night of it. The clerk in Terry Kelly's said *A crown!* but the consignor held out for six shillings; and in the end the six shillings was allowed him literally. He came out of the pawn-office joyfully, making a little cylinder of the coins between his thumb and fingers. In Westmoreland Street the footpaths were crowded with young men and women returning from business and ragged urchins ran here and there yelling out the names of the evening editions. The man passed through the crowd, looking on the spectacle generally with proud satisfaction and staring masterfully at the office-girls. His head was full of the noises of tram-gongs and swishing trolleys and his nose already sniffed the curling fumes of punch. As he walked on he preconsidered the terms in which he would narrate the incident to the boys:

"So, I just looked at him—coolly, you know, and looked at her. Then I looked back at him again—taking my time, you know. 'I don't think that's a fair question to put to me,' says I."

Nosey Flynn was sitting up in his usual corner of Davy Byrne's and, when he heard the story, he stood Farrington a half-one, saying it was as smart a thing as ever he heard. Farrington stood a drink in his turn. After a while O'Halloran and Paddy Leonard came in and the story was repeated to them. O'Halloran stood tailors of malt hot all round and told the story of the retort he had made to the chief clerk when he was in Callan's of Fownes's Street; but, as the retort was after the manner of the liberal shepherds in the eclogues, he had to admit that it was not as clever as Farrington's retort. At this Farrington told the boys to polish off that and have another.

Just as they were naming their poisons who should come in but Higgins! Of course he had to join in with the others. The men asked him to give his version of it, and he did so with great vivacity for the sight of five small hot whiskies was very exhilarating. Everyone roared laughing when he showed the way in which Mr. Alleyne shook his fist in Farrington's face. Then he imitated Farrington, saying, *"And here was my nabs, as cool as you please,"* while Farrington looked at the company out of his heavy dirty eyes, smiling and at times drawing forth stray drops of liquor from his moustache with the aid of his lower lip.

When that round was over there was a pause. O'Halloran had money but neither of the other two seemed to have any; so the whole party left the shop somewhat regretfully. At the corner of Duke Street Higgins and Nosey Flynn bevelled off to the left while the other three turned back towards the city. Rain was drizzling down on the cold streets and, when they reached the Ballast Office, Farrington suggested the Scotch House. The bar was full of men and loud with the noise of tongues and glasses. The three men pushed past the whining match-sellers at the door and formed a little party at the corner of the counter. They began to exchange stories. Leonard introduced them to a young fellow named Weathers who was performing at the Tivoli as an acrobat and knockabout *artiste*. Farrington stood a drink all round. Weathers said he would take a small Irish and Apollinaris. Farrington, who had definite notions of what was what, asked the boys would they have an Apollinaris too; but the boys told Tim to make theirs hot. The talk became theatrical. O'Halloran stood a round and then Farrington stood another round, Weathers protesting that the hospitality was too Irish. He promised to get them in behind the scenes and introduce them to some nice girls. O'Halloran said that he and Leonard would go, but that Farrington wouldn't go because he was a married man; and Farrington's heavy dirty eyes leered at the company in token that he understood he was being chaffed. Weathers made them all have just one little tincture at his expense and promised to meet them later on at Mulligan's in Poolbeg Street.

When the Scotch House closed they went round to Mulligan's. They went into the parlour at the back and O'Halloran ordered small hot specials all around. They were all beginning to feel mellow. Farrington was just standing another round when Weathers came back. Much to Farrington's relief he drank a glass of bitter this time. Funds were getting low but they had enough to keep them going. Presently two young women with big hats and a young man in a check suit came in and sat at a table close by. Weathers saluted them and told the company that they were out of the Tivoli. Farrington's eyes wandered at every moment in the direction of one of the young women. There was something striking in her appearance. An immense scarf of peacock-blue muslin was wound round her hat and knotted in a great bow under her chin; and she wore bright yellow gloves, reaching to the elbow. Farrington gazed admiringly at the plump arm which she moved very often and with much grace; and when, after a little time, she answered his gaze he admired still more her large dark brown eyes. The oblique staring expression in them fascinated him. She glanced at him once or twice and, when the party was leaving the room, she brushed against his chair and said *"O, pardon!"* in a London accent. He watched her leave the room in the hope that she would look back at him, but he was disappointed. He cursed his want of money and cursed all the rounds he had stood, particularly all the whiskies and Apollinaris which he had stood to Weathers. If there was one thing that he hated it was a sponge. He was so angry that he lost count of the conversation of his friends.

When Paddy Leonard called him he found that they were talking about feats of strength. Weathers was showing his biceps muscle to the company and boasting so much that the other two had called on Farrington to uphold the national honour. Farrington pulled up his sleeve accordingly and showed his biceps muscle to the company. The two arms were examined and compared and finally it was agreed to have a trial of strength. The table was cleared and the two men rested their elbows on it, clasping hands. When Paddy Leonard said *"Go!"* each was to try to bring down the other's hand on to the table. Farrington looked very serious and determined.

The trial began. After about thirty seconds Weathers brought his opponent's hand slowly down on to the table. Farrington's dark wine-coloured face flushed darker still with anger and humiliation at having been defeated by such a stripling.

"You're not to put the weight of your body behind it. Play fair," he said.

"Who's not playing fair?" said the other.

"Come on again. The two best out of three."

The trial began again. The veins stood out on Farrington's forehead, and the pallor of Weathers' complexion changed to peony. Their hands and arms trembled under the stress. After a long struggle Weathers again brought his opponent's hand slowly on to the table. There was a murmur of applause from the spectators. The curate, who was standing beside the table, nodded his red head towards the victor and said with stupid familiarity:

"Ah! that's the knack!"

"What the hell do you know about it?" said Farrington fiercely, turning on the man. "What do you put in your gab for?"

"Sh, sh!" said O'Halloran, observing the violent expression of Farrington's face. "Pony up, boys. We'll have just one little smahan more and then we'll be off."

A very sullen-faced man stood at the corner of O'Connell Bridge waiting for the little Sandymount tram to take him home. He was full of smouldering anger and revengefulness. He felt humiliated and discontented; he did not even feel drunk; and he had only two-pence in his pocket. He cursed everything. He had done for himself in the office, pawned his watch, spent all his money; and he had not even got drunk. He began to feel thirsty again and he longed to be back again in the hot reeking public-house. He had lost his reputation as a strong man, having been defeated twice by a mere boy. His heart swelled with fury and, when he thought of the woman in the big hat who had brushed against him and said *Pardon!* his fury nearly choked him.

His tram let him down at Shelbourne Road and he steered his great body along in the shadow of the wall of the barracks. He loathed returning to his home. When he went in by the side-door he found the kitchen empty and the kitchen fire nearly out. He bawled upstairs:

"Ada! Ada!"

His wife was a little sharp-faced woman who bullied her husband when he was sober and was bullied by him when he was drunk. They had five children. A little boy came running down the stairs.

"Who is that?" said the man, peering through the darkness.

"Me, pa."

"Who are you? Charlie?"

"No, pa. Tom."

"Where's your mother?"

"She's out at the chapel."

"That's right.... Did she think of leaving any dinner for me?"

"Yes, pa. I——"

"Light the lamp. What do you mean by having the place in darkness? Are the other children in bed?"

The man sat down heavily on one of the chairs while the little boy lit the lamp. He began to mimic his son's flat accent, saying half to himself: *"At the chapel. At the chapel, if you please!"* When the lamp was lit he banged his fist on the table and shouted:

"What's for my dinner?"

"I'm going... to cook it, pa," said the little boy.

The man jumped up furiously and pointed to the fire.

"On that fire! You let the fire out! By God, I'll teach you to do that again!"

He took a step to the door and seized the walking-stick which was standing behind it.

"I'll teach you to let the fire out!" he said, rolling up his sleeve in order to give his arm free play.

The little boy cried *"O, pa!"* and ran whimpering round the table, but the man followed him and caught him by the coat. The little boy looked about him wildly but, seeing no way of escape, fell upon his knees.

"Now, you'll let the fire out the next time!" said the man, striking at him vigorously with the stick. "Take that, you little whelp!"

The boy uttered a squeal of pain as the stick cut his thigh. He clasped his hands together in the air and his voice shook with fright.

"O, pa!" he cried. "Don't beat me, pa! And I'll . . . I'll say a *Hail Mary* for you. . . . I'll say a *Hail Mary* for you, pa, if you don't beat me. . . . I'll say a *Hail Mary*. . . ."

JOYCE: *Counterparts*

1. *The title refers to several pairings in the story. What are they?*
2. *"Counterparts" comes from Joyce's collection of short stories,* Dubliners. *The people and places Joyce writes about in this volume make it an excellent entry to his masterpiece,* Ulysses, *but the predominant mood is somewhat different: it is one of entrapment. Who is trapped in the story? Is Farrington? Can he help himself, or is he trapped by life, by a tedious job, without any chance of escape? If so, what is Joyce getting at? In what way is the story reminiscent of Moravia's? Is Mr. Alleyne trapped? Farrington's wife? Son?*
3. *The story begins: "The bell rang furiously. . . ." How does this foreshadow the ending and tie the story together? How is fury related to entrapment?*
4. *What are some of the things which contribute to Farrington's retort? Why does Farrington write* Bernard Bernard *instead of* Bernard Bodley? *What does this contribute to the falling-out?*
5. *How does Farrington's rage naturally lead him to the pub, the scene of his second defeat?*
6. *Why is most of the conversation at the bar reported indirectly? What does the plain and conversational style add to the effect of the story? What is the point of the feat of strength?*
7. *Is there anything of what we usually call a story line here (cf. "Little Louise Roque")? How is the story constructed? (Cf. Turgenev.)*
8. *How do you explain the cruel ending? Is it a third defeat?*
9. *What is the function of the three women in the story?*

Franz Kafka

THE JUDGMENT

Franz Kafka was born in Prague in 1883, a Jew in Austrian-Czech surroundings and the son of a domineering father. He studied law, then worked in the office of the workmen's compensation division of the Austrian government. He had just become engaged when tuberculosis felled him, and he died, at forty-one, in 1924. His novels—The Trial (1925), The Castle (1926), Amerika (1927)—were not yet in print. Since his death, his reputation has grown into major dimension, with many critics regarding him as second to no other German prose writer. In "The Judgment," as in most of his fiction, he combined realistic detail with symbolic, dreamlike situations and scenes that reveal the anxieties and isolation of modern man.

IT WAS a Sunday morning in the very height of spring. Georg Bendemann, a young merchant, was sitting in his own room on the first floor of one of a long row of small, ramshackle houses stretching beside the river which were scarcely distinguishable from each other except in height and coloring. He had just finished a letter to an old friend of his who was now living abroad, had put it into its envelope in a slow and dreamy fashion, and with his elbows propped on the writing table was gazing out of the window at the river, the bridge and the hills on the farther bank with their tender green.

He was thinking about his friend, who had actually run away to Russia some years before, being dissatisifed with his prospects at home. Now he was carrying on a business in St. Petersburg, which had flourished to begin with but had long been going downhill, as he always complained on his increasingly rare visits. So he was wearing himself out to no purpose in a foreign country; the unfamiliar full beard he wore did not quite conceal the face Georg had known so well since childhood, and his skin was growing so yellow as to indicate some latent disease. By his own account he had no regular connection with the colony of his fellow countrymen out there and almost no social intercourse with Russian families, so that he was resigning himself to becoming a permanent bachelor.

What could one write to such a man, who had obviously run off the rails, a man one could be sorry for but could not help? Should one advise him to come home, to transplant himself and take up his old friendships again—there was nothing to hinder him—and in general to rely on the help of his friends? But that was as good as telling him, and the more kindly the more offensively, that all his efforts hitherto had miscarried, that he should finally give up, come back home, and be gaped at by everyone as a returned prodigal, that only his friends knew what was what and that he himself was just a big child who should do what his successful and home-keeping friends prescribed. And was it certain, besides, that all the pain one would have to inflict on him would achieve its object? Perhaps it would not even be possible to get him to come home at all—he said himself that he was now out of touch with commerce in his native country—and then he would still be left an alien in a foreign land embittered by his friends' advice and more than ever estranged from them. But if he did follow their advice and then didn't fit in a home—not out of malice, of course, but through force of circumstances—couldn't get on with his friends or without them, felt humiliated, couldn't be said to have either friends or a country of his own any longer, wouldn't it have been better for him to stay abroad just as he was? Taking all this into account, how could one be sure that he would make a success of life at home?

For such reasons, supposing one wanted to keep up correspondence with him, one could not send him any real news such as could frankly be told to the most distant acquaintance. It was more than three years since his last visit, and for this he offered the lame excuse that the political situation in Russia was too uncertain, which apparently would not permit even the briefest absence of a small business man while it allowed hundreds of thousands of Russians to travel peacefully abroad. But during these three years Georg's own position in life had changed a lot. Two years ago his mother had died, since when he and his father had shared the household together, and his friend had of course been informed of that and had expressed his sympathy in a letter phrased so dryly that the grief caused by such an event, one had to conclude, could not be realized in a distant country. Since that time, however, Georg had applied himself with greater determination to the business as well as to everything else.

Perhaps during his mother's lifetime his father's insistence on having everything his own way in the business had hindered him from developing any real activity of his own, perhaps since her death his father had become less aggressive, although he was still active in the business, perhaps it was mostly due to an accidental run of good fortune—which was very probable indeed—but at any rate during those two years the business had developed in a most unexpected way, the staff had had to be doubled, the turnover was five times as great, no doubt about it, further progress lay just ahead.

But Georg's friend had no inkling of this improvement. In earlier years, perhaps for the last time in that letter of condolence, he had tried to persuade Georg to emigrate to Russia and had enlarged upon the prospects of success for precisely Georg's branch of trade. The figures quoted were microscopic by comparison with the range of Georg's present operations. Yet he shrank from letting his friend know about his business success, and if he were to do it now retrospectively that certainly would look peculiar.

So Georg confined himself to giving his friend unimportant items of gossip such as rise at random in the memory when one is idly thinking things over on a quiet Sunday. All he desired was to leave undisturbed the idea of the home town which his friend must have built up to his own content during the long interval. And so it happened to Georg that three times in three fairly widely separated letters he had told his friend about the engagement of an unimportant man to an equally unimportant girl, until indeed, quite contrary to his intentions, his friend began to show some interest in this notable event.

Yet Georg preferred to write about things like these rather than to confess that he himself had got engaged a month ago to a Fräulein Frieda Brandenfeld, a girl from a well-to-do family. He often discussed this friend of his with his fiancée and the peculiar relationship that had developed between them in their correspondence. "So he won't be coming to our wedding," said she, "and yet I have a right to get to know all your friends." "I don't want to trouble him," answered Georg. "Don't misunderstand me, he would probably come, at least I think so, but he would feel that his hand had been forced and he would be hurt, perhaps he would envy me and certainly he'd be discontented and without being able to do anything about his discontent he'd have to go away again alone. Alone—do you know what that means?" "Yes, but may he not hear about our wedding in some other fashion?" "I can't prevent that, of course, but it's unlikely, considering the way he lives." "Since your friends are like that, Georg, you shouldn't ever have got engaged at all." "Well, we're both to blame for that; but I wouldn't have it any other way now." And when, breathing quickly under his kisses, she still brought out: "All the same, I do feel upset," he thought it could not really involve him in trouble were he to send the news to his friend. "That's the kind of man I am and he'll just have to take me as I am," he said to himself, "I can't cut myself to another pattern that might make a more suitable friend for him."

And in fact he did inform his friend, in the long letter he had been writing that Sunday morning, about his engagement, with these words: "I have saved my best news to the end. I have got engaged to a Fräulein Frieda Brandenfeld, a girl from a well-to-do family, who only came to live here a long time after you went away, so that you're hardly likely to know her. There will be time to tell you more about her later, for today let me just say that I am very happy and as between you and me the only difference in our relationship is that instead of a quite ordinary kind of friend you will now have in me a happy friend. Besides that, you will acquire in my fiancée, who sends her warm greetings and will soon write you herself, a genuine friend of the opposite sex, which is not without importance to a bachelor. I know that there are many reasons why you can't come to see us, but would not my wedding be precisely the right occasion for giving all obstacles the go-by? Still, however that may be, do just as seems good to you without regarding any interests but your own."

With this letter in his hand Georg had been sitting a long time at the writing table, his face turned towards the window. He had barely acknowledged, with an absent smile, a greeting waved to him from the street by a passing acquaintance.

At last he put the letter in his pocket and went out of his room across a small lobby into his father's room, which he had not entered for months. There was in fact no need for him to enter it, since he saw his father daily at business and they took their midday meal together at an eating house; in the evening, it was true, each did as he pleased, yet even then, unless Georg—as mostly happened—went out with friends or, more recently, visited his fiancée, they always sat for a while, each with his newspaper, in their common sitting room.

It surprised Georg how dark his father's room was even on this sunny morning. So it was overshadowed as much as that by the high wall on the other side of the narrow courtyard. His father was sitting by the window in a corner hung with various mementoes of Georg's dead mother, reading a newspaper which he held to one side before his eyes in an attempt to overcome a defect of vision. On the table stood the remains of his breakfast, not much of which seemed to have been eaten.

"Ah, Georg," said his father, rising at once to meet him. His heavy dressing gown swung open as he walked and the skirts of it fluttered round him.—"My father is still a giant of a man," said Georg to himself.

"It's unbearably dark here," he said aloud.

"Yes, it's dark enough," answered his father.

"And you've shut the window, too?"

"I prefer it like that."

"Well, it's quite warm outside," said Georg, as if continuing his previous remark, and sat down.

His father cleared away the breakfast dishes and set them on a chest.

"I really only wanted to tell you," went on Georg, who had been vacantly following the old man's movements, "that I am now sending the news of my engagement to St. Petersburg." He drew the letter a little way from his pocket and let it drop back again.

"To St. Petersburg?" asked his father.

"To my friend there," said Georg, trying to meet his father's eye.—In business hours he's quite different, he was thinking. How solidly he sits here with his arms crossed.

"Oh, yes. To your friend," said his father, with peculiar emphasis.

"Well, you know, Father, that I wanted not to tell him about my engagement at first. Out of consideration for him, that was the only reason. You know yourself he's a difficult man. I said to myself that someone else might tell him about my engagement, although he's such a solitary creature that that was hardly likely—I couldn't prevent that—but I wasn't ever going to tell him myself."

"And now you've changed your mind?" asked his father, laying his enormous newspaper on the window sill and on top of it his spectacles, which he covered with one hand.

"Yes, I've been thinking it over. If he's a good friend of mine, I said to myself, my being happily engaged should make him happy too. And so I wouldn't put off telling him any longer. But before I posted the letter I wanted to let you know."

"Georg," said his father, lengthening his toothless mouth, "listen to me! You've come to me about this business, to talk it over with me. No doubt that does you honor. But it's nothing, it's worse than nothing, if you don't tell me the whole truth. I don't want to stir up matters that shouldn't be mentioned here. Since the death of our dear mother certain things have been done that aren't right. Maybe the time will come for mentioning them, and maybe sooner than we think. There's many a thing in the business I'm not aware of, maybe it's not done behind my back—I'm not going to say that it's done behind my back—I'm not equal to things any longer, my memory's failing, I haven't an eye for so many things any longer. That's the course of nature in the first place, and in the second place the death of our dear mother hit me harder than it did you.—But since we're talking about it, about this letter, I beg you, Georg, don't deceive me. It's a trivial affair, it's hardly worth mentioning, so don't deceive me. Do you really have this friend in St. Petersburg?''

Georg rose in embarrassment. "Never mind my friends. A thousand friends wouldn't make up to me for my father. Do you know what I think? You're not taking enough care of yourself. But old age must be taken care of. I can't do without you in the business, you know that very well, but if the business is going to undermine your health, I'm ready to close it down tomorrow forever. And that won't do. We'll have to make a change in your way of living. But a radical change. You sit here in the dark, and in the sitting room you would have plenty of light. You just take a bite of breakfast instead of properly keeping up your strength. You sit by a closed window, and the air would be so good for you. No, Father! I'll get the doctor to come, and we'll follow his orders. We'll change your room, you can move into the front room and I'll move in here. You won't notice the change, all your things will be moved with you. But there's time for all that later. I'll put you to bed now for a little; I'm sure you need to rest. Come, I'll help you to take off your things, you'll see I can do it. Or if you would rather go into the front room at once, you can lie down in my bed for the present. That would be the most sensible thing."

Georg stood close beside his father, who had let his head with its unkempt white hair sink on his chest.

"Georg," said his father in a low voice, without moving.

Georg knelt down at once beside his father. In the old man's weary face he saw the pupils, over-large, fixedly looking at him from the corners of the eyes.

"You have a friend in St. Petersburg. You've always been a leg-puller and you haven't even shrunk from pulling my leg. How could you have a friend out there! I can't believe it."

"Just think back a bit, Father," said Georg, lifting his father from the chair and slipping off his dressing gown as he stood feebly enough, "it'll soon be three years since my friend came to see us last. I remember that you used not to like him very much. At least twice I kept you from seeing him, although he was actually sitting with me in my room. I could quite well understand your dislike of him, my friend has his peculiarities. But then, later, you got on with him very well. I was proud because you listened to him and nodded and asked him questions. If you think back you're bound to remember. He used to tell us the most incredible stories of the Russian Revolution. For instance, when he was on a business trip to Kiev and ran into a riot, and saw a priest on a balcony who cut a broad cross in blood on the palm of his hand and held the hand up and appealed to the mob. You've told that story yourself once or twice since."

Meanwhile Georg had succeeded in lowering his father down again and carefully taking off the woollen drawers he wore over his linen underpants and his socks. The not particularly clean appearance of this underwear made him reproach himself for having been neglectful. It should have certainly been his duty to see that his father had clean changes of underwear. He had not yet explicitly discussed with his bride-to-be what arrangements should be made for his father in the future, for they had both of them silently taken it for granted that the old man would go on living alone in the old house. But now he made a quick, firm decision to take him into his own future establishment. It almost looked, on closer inspection, as if the care he meant to lavish on his father might come too late.

He carried his father to bed in his arms. It gave him a dreadful feeling to notice that while he took the few steps towards the bed the old man on his breast was playing with his watch chain. He could not lay him down on the bed for a moment, so firmly did he hang on to the watch chain.

But as soon as he was laid in bed, all seemed well. He covered himself up and even drew the blankets farther than usual over his shoulders. He looked up at Georg with a not unfriendly eye.

"You begin to remember my friend, don't you?" asked Georg, giving him an encouraging nod.

"Am I well covered up now?" asked his father, as if he were not able to see whether his feet were properly tucked in or not.

"So you find it snug in bed already," said Georg, and tucked the blankets more closely around him.

"Am I well covered up?" asked the father once more, seeming to be strangely intent upon the answer.

"Don't worry, you're well covered up."

"No!" cried his father, cutting short the answer, threw the blankets off with a strength that sent them all flying in a moment and sprang erect in bed. Only one hand lightly touched the ceiling to steady him.

"You wanted to cover me up, I know, my young sprig, but I'm far from being covered up yet. And even if this is the last strength I have, it's enough for you, too much for you. Of course I know your friend. He would have been a son after my own heart. That's why you've been playing him false all these years. Why else? Do you think I haven't been sorry for him? And that's why you had to lock yourself up in your office—the Chief is busy, mustn't be disturbed—just so that you could write your lying little letters to Russia. But thank goodness a father doesn't need to be taught how to see through his son. And now that you thought you'd got him down, so far down that you could set your bottom on him and sit on him and he wouldn't move, then my fine son makes up his mind to get married!''

Georg stared at the bogey conjured up by his father. His friend in St. Petersburg, whom his father suddenly knew too well, touched his imagination as never before. Lost in the vastness of Russia he saw him. At the door of an empty, plundered warehouse he saw him. Among the wreckage of his showcases, the slashed remnants of his wares, the falling gas brackets, he was just standing up. Why did he have to go so far away!

"But attend to me!" cried his father, and Georg almost distracted, ran towards the bed to take everything in, yet came to a stop halfway.

"Because she lifted up her skirts," his father began to flute, "because she lifted her skirts like this, the nasty creature," and mimicking her he lifted his shirt so high that one could see the scar on his thigh from his war wound, "because she lifted her skirts like this and this you made up to her, and in order to make free with her undisturbed you have disgraced your mother's memory, betrayed your friend and stuck your father into bed so that he can't move. But he can move, or can't he?''

And he stood up quite unsupported and kicked his legs out. His insight made him radiant.

Georg shrank into a corner, as far away from his father as possible. A long time ago he had firmly made up his mind to watch closely every least movement so that he should not be surprised by any indirect attack, a pounce from behind or above. At this moment he recalled this long-forgotten resolve and forgot it again, like a man drawing a short thread through the eye of a needle.

"But your friend hasn't been betrayed after all!" cried his father, emphasizing the point with stabs of his forefinger. "I've been representing him here on the spot.''

"You comedian!" Georg could not resist the retort, realized at once the harm done and, his eyes starting in his head, bit his tongue back, only too late, till the pain made his knees give.

"Yes, of course I've been playing a comedy! A comedy! That's a good expression! What other comfort was left to a poor old widower? Tell me—and while you're answering me be you still my living son—what else was left to me, in my back room, plagued by a disloyal staff, old to the marrow of my bones? And my son strutting through the world, finishing off deals that I had prepared for him, bursting with triumphant glee and stalking away from his father with the closed face of a respectable business man! Do you think I didn't love you, I, from whom you are sprung?"

Now he'll lean forward, thought Georg. What if he topples and smashes himself! These words went hissing through his mind.

His father leaned forward but did not topple. Since Georg did not come any nearer, as he had expected, he straightened himself again.

"Stay where you are, I don't need you! You think you have strength enough to come over here and that you're only hanging back of your own accord. Don't be too sure! I am still much the stronger of us two. All by myself I might have had to give way, but your mother has given me so much of her strength that I've established a fine connection with your friend and I have your customers here in my pocket!"

"He has pockets even in his shirt!" said Georg to himself, and believed that with this remark he could make him an impossible figure for all the world. Only for a moment did he think so, since he kept on forgetting everything.

"Just take your bride on your arm and try getting in my way! I'll sweep her from your very side, you don't know how!"

Georg made a grimace of disbelief. His father only nodded, confirming the truth of his words, towards Georg's corner.

"How you amused me today, coming to ask me if you should tell your friend about your engagement. He knows it already, you stupid boy, he knows it all! I've been writing to him, for you forgot to take my writing things away from me. That's why he hasn't been here for years, he knows everything a hundred times better than you do yourself, in his left hand he crumples your letters unopened while in his right hand he holds up my letters to read through!"

In his enthusiasm he waved his arm over his head. "He knows everything a thousand times better!" he cried.

"Ten thousand times!" said Georg, to make fun of his father, but in his very mouth the words turned into deadly earnest.

"For years I've been waiting for you to come with some such question! Do you think I concern myself with anything else? Do you think I read my newspapers? Look!" and he threw Georg a newspaper sheet, which he had somehow taken to bed with him. An old newspaper, with a name entirely unknown to Georg.

"How long a time you've taken to grow up! Your mother had to die, she couldn't see the happy day, your friend is going to pieces in Russia, even three years ago he was yellow enough to be thrown away, and as for me, you see what condition I'm in. You have eyes in your head for that!"

"So you've been lying in wait for me!" cried Georg.

His father said pityingly, in an offhand manner: "I suppose you wanted to say that sooner. But now it doesn't matter." And in a louder voice: "So now you know what else there was in the world besides yourself, till now you've known only about yourself! An innocent child, yes, that you were, truly, but still more truly have you been a devilish human being!—And therefore take note: I sentence you now to death by drowning!"

Georg felt himself urged from the room. The crash with which his father fell on the bed behind him was still in his ears as he fled. On the staircase, which he rushed down as if its steps were an inclined plane, he ran into his charwoman on her way up to do the morning cleaning of the room. "Jesus!" she cried, and covered her face with her apron, but he was already gone. Out of the front door he rushed, across the roadway, driven towards the water. Already he was grasping at the railings as a starving man clutches food. He swung himself over, like the distinguished gymnast he had once been in his youth, to his parents' pride. With weakening grip he was still holding on when he spied between the railings a motor-bus coming which would easily cover the noise of his fall, called in a low voice: "Dear parents, I have always loved you, all the same," and let himself drop.

At this moment an unending stream of traffic was just going over the bridge.

Translated by Willa and Edwin Muir

KAFKA: *The Judgment*

1. *What is the relationship between Georg and his father? Through this relationship, what is Kafka trying to indicate?*
2. *Why does Kafka stress the role of Georg's friend? What relevance does the friend have to Georg? To his father?*

3. *Why does Georg shrink from telling his friend the truth about himself? Do you accept his explanation: "Perhaps he would envy me."?*

4. *What is the relationship between Georg and his fiancée? Between his fiancée and his father? What role do these relationships have in the dénouement?*

5. *Why does Mr. Bendemann desire his son's death? Why by drowning?*

6. *Why does Georg carry out the sentence?*

7. *How does Kafka convey the tone of morbidity? Mention some details. Is there also an element of comedy ("I've been playing a comedy")? Mention some details. Do they clash with the dominant tone of the story?*

8. *A critic once remarked that in Dostoyevsky there is crime with punishment, in Kafka punishment without crime. Do you agree?*

9. *Is Kafka describing a disordered personality, a disordered society, or a disordered cosmos? Why does he do it in such orderly fashion?*

10. *Though dream and reality fuse in a way that obscures any neat meaning in Kafka, his language is always clear and concrete. What effect does this contrast produce?*

D. H. Lawrence
THE MAN WHO LOVED ISLANDS

Like Conrad, Lawrence started out in a profession which ultimately he was to forsake, here school teaching. Born in Eastwood, Notts, on September 11, 1885, Lawrence re-created the atmosphere and some of the facts of his early home life in his third novel, Sons and Lovers *(1913). Lawrence, however, was dissatisfied with this novel, and subsequently turned to a more poetic vision of life with* The Rainbow *(1915) and* Women in Love *(1920), two of the novels on which his serious reputation rests. These two long works seemed to indicate his general direction, for in the next ten years there appeared* Aaron's Rod *(1911),* St.Mawr *(1925),* The Plumed Serpent *(1926),* Lady Chatterley's Lover *(1928), and* The Man Who Died *(1929), which he wrote shortly before his death. "The Man Who Loved Islands" fits loosely into his later work, concerned as it is with a man who destroys himself because of his inability to "connect" with other people. On March 2, 1930, Lawrence died of tuberculosis at Vence, in the south of France.*

THE FIRST ISLAND

THERE was a man who loved islands. He was born on one, but it didn't suit him, as there were too many other people on it, besides himself. He wanted an island all of his own; not necessarily to be alone on it, but to make it a world of his own.

An island, if it is big enough, is no better than a continent. It has to be really quite small, before it *feels like* an island; and this story will show how tiny it has to be, before you can presume to fill it with your own personality.

Now circumstances so worked out, that this lover of islands, by the time he was thirty-five, actually acquired an island of his own. He didn't own it as freehold property, but he had a ninety-nine years' lease of it, which, as far as a man and an island are concerned, is as good as everlasting. Since, if you are like Abraham, and want your offspring to be numberless as the sands of the sea-shore, you don't choose an island

[283

to start breeding on. Too soon there would be overpopulation, overcrowding, and slum conditions. Which is a horrid thought, for one who loves an island for its insulation. No, an island is a nest which holds one egg, and one only. This egg is the islander himself.

The island acquired by our potential islander was not in the remote oceans. It was quite near at home, no palm-trees nor boom of surf on the reef, nor any of that kind of thing; but a good solid dwelling-house, rather gloomy, above the landing-place, and beyond, a small farmhouse with sheds, and a few outlying fields. Down on the little landing bay were three cottages in a row, like coastguards' cottages, all neat and whitewashed.

What could be more cozy and home-like? It was four miles if you walked all round your island, through the gorse and the blackthorn bushes, above the steep rocks of the sea and down in the little glades where the primroses grew. If you walked straight over the two humps of hills, the length of it, through the rocky fields where the cows lay chewing, and through the rather sparse oats, on into the gorse again, and so to the low cliff's edge, it took you only twenty minutes. And when you came to the edge, you could see another, bigger island lying beyond. But the sea was between you and it. And as you returned over the turf where the short, downland cowslips nodded you saw to the east still another island, a tiny one this time, like the calf of the cow. This tiny island also belonged to the islander.

Thus it seems that even islands like to keep each other company.

Our islander loved his island very much. In early spring, the little ways and glades were a snow of blackthorn, a vivid white among the celtic stillness of close green and grey rock, blackbirds calling out in the whiteness their first long, triumphant calls. After the blackthorn and the nestling primroses came the blue apparition of hyacinths, like elfin lakes and slipping sheets of blue, among the bushes and under the glade of trees. And many birds with nests you could peep into, on the island all your own. Wonderful what a great world it was!

Followed summer, and the cowslips gone, the wild roses faintly fragrant through the haze. There was a field of hay, the foxgloves stood looking down. In a little cove, the sun was on the pale granite where you bathed, and the shadow was in the rocks. Before the mist came stealing, and you went home through the ripening oats, the glare of the sea fading from the high air as the foghorn started to moo on the other island. And then the sea-fog went, it was autumn, and oat-sheaves lying prone; the great moon, another island, rose golden out of the sea, and, rising higher, the world of the sea was white.

So autumn ended with rain, and winter came, dark skies and dampness and rain, but rarely frost. The island, your island, cowered dark, holding away from you. You could feel down in the wet, sombre hollows, the resentful spirit coiled upon itself, like a wet dog coiled in gloom, or a snake that is neither asleep nor awake. Then in the night, when the wind left off blowing in great gusts and volleys, as at sea, you felt that your island was a universe, infinite and old as the darkness; not an island at all, but an infinite dark world where all the souls from all the other bygone nights lived on, and the infinite distance was near.

Strangely, from your little island in space, you were gone forth into the dark, great realms of time, where all the souls that never die veer and swoop on their vast, strange errands. The little earthly island has dwindled, like a jumping-off place, into nothingness, for you have jumped off, you know not how, into the dark wide mystery of time, where the past is vastly alive, and the future is not separated off.

This is the danger of becoming an islander. When, in the city, you wear your white spats and dodge the traffic with the fear of death down your spine, then you are quite safe from the terrors of infinite time. The moment is your little islet in time, it is the spatial universe that careers round you.

But once isolate yourself on a little island in the sea of space, and the moment begins to heave and expand in great circles, the solid earth is gone, and your slippery, naked dark soul finds herself out in the timeless world, where the chariots of the so-called dead dash down the old streets of centuries, and souls crowd on the footways that we, in the moment, call bygone years. The souls of all the dead are alive again, and pulsating actively around you. You are out in the other infinity.

Something of this happened to our islander. Mysterious "feelings" came upon him, that he wasn't used to; strange awarenesses of old, far-gone men, and other influences; men of Gaul, with big moustaches, who had been on his island, and had vanished from the face of it, but not out of the air of night. They were there still, hurtling their big, violent, unseen bodies through the night. And there were priests, with golden knives and mistletoe; then other priests, with a crucifix; then pirates with murder on the sea.

Our islander was uneasy. He didn't believe, in the daytime, in any of this nonsense. But at night it just was so. He had reduced himself to a single point in space, and, a point being that which has neither length nor breadth, he had to step off it into somewhere else. Just as you must step into the sea, if the waters wash your foothold away, so he had, at night, to step off into the other world of undying time.

He was uncannily aware, as he lay in the dark, that the blackthorn grove that seemed a bit uncanny even in the realm of space and day, at night was crying with old men of an invisible race, around the altar stone. What was a ruin under the hornbeam trees by day, was a moaning of bloodstained priests with crucifixes, on the ineffable night. What was a cave and a hidden beach between coarse rocks, became in the invisible dark the purple-lipped imprecation of pirates.

To escape any more of this sort of awareness, our islander daily concentrated upon his material island. Why should it not be the Happy Isle at last? Why not the last small isle of the Hesperides, the perfect place, all filled with his own gracious, blossom-like spirit? A minute world of pure perfection, made by man, himself.

He began, as we begin all our attempts to regain Paradise, by spending money. The old, semi-feudal dwelling-house he restored, let in more light, put clear lovely carpets on the floor, clear, flower-petal curtains at the sullen windows, and wines in the cellars of rock. He brought over a buxom housekeeper from the world, and a soft-spoken, much-experienced butler. These too were to be islanders.

In the farm-house he put a bailiff, with two farm-hands. There were Jersey cows, tinkling a slow bell, among the gorse. There was a call to meals at midday, and the peaceful smoking of chimneys at evening, when rest descended.

A jaunty sailing-boat with a motor accessory rode in the shelter in the bay, just below the row of three white cottages. There was also a little yawl, and two row-boats drawn up on the sand. A fishing net was drying on its supports, a boat-load of new white planks stood criss-cross, a woman was going to the well with a bucket.

In the end cottage lived the skipper of the yacht, and his wife and son. He was a man from the other, large island, at home on this sea. Every fine day he went out fishing, with his son, every fine day there was fresh fish on the island.

In the middle cottage lived an old man and wife, a very faithful couple. The old man was a carpenter, and man of many jobs. He was always working, always the sound of his plane or his saw: lost in his work, he was another kind of islander.

In the third cottage was the mason, a widower with a son and two daughters. With the help of his boy, this man dug ditches and built fences, raised buttresses and erected a new outbuilding, and hewed stone from the little quarry. His daughters worked at the big house.

It was a quiet, busy little world. When the islander brought you over as his guest, you met first the dark-bearded, thin, smiling skipper, Arnold, then his boy Charles. At the house, the smooth-lipped butler who had lived all over the world valeted you, and created that curious creamy-smooth, disarming sense of luxury around you which only a perfect and rather untrustworthy servant can create. He disarmed you and had you at his mercy. The buxom housekeeper smiled and treated you with the subtly respectful familiarity, that is only dealt out to the true gentry. And the rosy maid threw a glance at you, as if you were very wonderful, coming from the great outer world. Then you met the smiling but watchful bailiff, who came from Cornwall, and the shy farm-hand from Berkshire, with his clean wife and two little children, then the rather sulky farm-hand from Suffolk. The mason, a Kent man, would talk to you by the yard, if you let him. Only the old carpenter was gruff and elsewhere absorbed.

Well then, it was a little world to itself, and everybody feeling very safe, and being very nice to you, as if you were really something special. But it was the islander's world, not yours. He was the Master. The special smile, the special attention was to the Master. They all knew how well off they were. So the islander was no longer Mr. So-and-So. To everyone on the island, even to you yourself, he was "the Master."

Well, it was ideal. The Master was no tyrant. Ah no! He was a delicate, sensitive, handsome Master, who wanted everything perfect and everybody happy. Himself, of course, to be the fount of this happiness and perfection.

But in his way, he was a poet. He treated his guests royally, his servants liberally. Yet he was shrewd, and very wise. He never came the boss over his people. Yet he kept his eye on everything, like a shrewd, blue-eyed young Hermes. And it was amazing what a lot of knowledge he had at hand. Amazing what he knew about Jersey cows, and cheese-making, ditching and fencing, flowers and gardening, ships and the sailing of ships. He was a fount of knowledge about everything, and this knowledge he imparted to his people in an odd, half-ironical, half-portentous fashion, as if he really belonged to the quaint, half-real world of the gods.

They listened to him with their hats in their hands. He loved white clothes; or creamy white; and cloaks, and broad hats. So, in fine weather, the bailiff would see the elegant tall figure in creamy-white serge coming like some bird over the fallow, to look at the weeding of the turnips. Then there would be a doffing of hats, and a few minutes of whimsical, shrewd, wise talk, to which the bailiff answered admiringly, and the farm-hands listened in silent wonder, leaning on their hoes. The bailiff was almost tender, to the Master.

Or, on a windy morning, he would stand with his cloak blowing in the sticky sea-wind, on the edge of the ditch that was being dug to drain a little swamp, talking in the teeth of the wind to the man below, who looked up at him with steady and inscrutable eyes.

Or at evening in the rain he would be seen hurrying across the yard, the broad hat turned against the rain. And the farm-wife would hurriedly exclaim: "The Master! Get up, John, and clear him a place on the sofa." And then the door opened, and it was a cry of: "Why of all things, if it isn't the Master! Why have ye turned out then of a night like this, to come across to the like of we?" And the bailiff took his cloak, and the farm-wife his hat, the two farm-hands drew their chairs to the back, he sat on the sofa and took a child up near him. He was wonderful with children, talked to them simply wonderful, make you think of Our Saviour Himself, said the woman.

Always he was greeted with smiles, and the same peculiar deference, as if he were a higher, but also frailer being. They handled him almost tenderly, and almost with adulation. But when he left, or when they spoke of him, they had often a subtle, mocking smile on their faces. There was no need to be afraid of "the Master." Just let him have his own way. Only the old carpenter was sometimes sincerely rude to him; so he didn't care for the old man.

It is doubtful whether any of them really liked him, man to man, or even woman to man. But then it is doubtful if he really liked any of them, as man to man, or man to woman. He wanted them to be happy, and the little world to be perfect. But any one who wants the world to be perfect must be careful not to have real likes and dislikes. A general good-will is all you can afford.

The sad fact is, alas, that general good-will is always felt as something of an insult, by the mere object of it; and so it breeds a quite special brand of malice. Surely general good-will is a form of egoism, that it should have such a result!

Our islander, however, had his own resources. He spent long hours in his library, for he was compiling a book of reference to all the flowers mentioned in the Greek and Latin authors. He was not a great classical scholar: the usual public-school equipment. But there are such excellent translations nowadays. And it was so lovely, tracing flower after flower as it blossomed in the ancient world.

So the first year on the island passed by. A great deal had been done. Now the bills flooded in, and the Master, conscientious in all things, began to study them. The study left him pale and breathless. He was not a rich man. He knew he had been making a hole in his capital, to get the island into running order. When he came to look however, there was hardly anything left but hole. Thousands and thousands of pounds had the island swallowed into nothingness.

But surely the bulk of the spending was over! Surely the island would now begin to be self-supporting, even if it made no profit! Surely he was safe. He paid a good many of the bills, and took a little heart. But he had had a shock, and the next year, the coming year, there must be economy, frugality. He told his people so, in simple and touching language. And they said: "Why surely! Surely!"

So, while the wind blew and the rain lashed outside, he would sit in his library with the bailiff over a pipe and a pot of beer, discussing farm projects. He lifted his narrow handsome face, and his blue eye became dreamy. "*What* a wind!" It blew like cannon shots. He thought of his island, lashed with foam, and inaccessible, and he exulted. . . . No, he must not lose it. He turned back to the farm projects with the zest of genius, and his hands flicked white emphasis, while the bailiff intoned: "Yes, Sir! Yes, Sir! You're right, Master!"

But the man was hardly listening. He was looking at the Master's blue lawn shirt and curious pink tie with the fiery red stone, at the enamel sleeve-links, and at the ring with the peculiar scarab. The brown searching eyes of the man of the soil glanced repeatedly over the fine, immaculate figure of the Master, with a sort of slow, calculating wonder. But if he happened to catch the Master's bright, exalted glance, his own eye lit up with a careful cordiality and deference, as he bowed his head slightly.

Thus between them they decided what crops should be sown, what fertilizers should be used in different places, which breed of pigs should be imported, and which line of turkeys. That is to say, the bailiff, by continually cautiously agreeing with the Master, kept out of it, and let the young man have his own way.

The Master knew what he was talking about. He was brilliant at grasping the gist of a book, and knowing how to apply his knowledge. On the whole, his ideas were sound. The bailiff even knew it. But in the man of the soil there was no answering enthusiasm. The brown eyes smiled their cordial deference, but the thin lips never changed. The Master pursed his own flexible mouth in a boyish versatility, as he cleverly sketched in his ideas to the other man, and the bailiff made eyes of admiration, but in his heart he was not attending, he was only watching the Master as he would have watched a queer, alien animal, quite without sympathy, not implicated.

So, it was settled, and the Master rang for Elvery, the butler, to bring a sandwich. He, the Master, was pleased. The butler saw it, and came back with anchovy and ham sandwiches, and a newly opened bottle of vermouth. There was always a newly opened bottle of something.

It was the same with the mason. The Master and he discussed the drainage of a bit of land, and more pipes were ordered, more special bricks, more this, more that.

Fine weather came at last, there was a little lull in the hard work on the island. The Master went for a short cruise in his yacht. It was not really a yacht, just a neat little bit of a yawl. They sailed along the coast of the mainland, and put in at the ports. At every port some friend turned up, the butler made elegant little meals in the cabin. Then the Master was invited to villas and hotels, his people disembarked him as if he were a prince.

And oh, how expensive it turned out! He had to telegraph to the bank for money. And he went home again, to economize.

The marsh-marigolds were blazing in the little swamp where the ditches were being dug for drainage. He almost regretted, now, the work in hand. The yellow beauties would not blaze again.

Harvest came, and a bumper crop. There must be a harvest-home supper. The long barn was now completely restored and added to. The carpenter had made long tables. Lanterns hung from the beams of the high-pitched roof. All the people of the island were assembled. The bailiff presided. It was a gay scene.

Towards the end of the supper the Master, in a velvet jacket, appeared with his guests. Then the bailiff rose and proposed: "The Master! Long life and health to the Master!" All the people drank the health with great enthusiasm and cheering. The Master replied with a little speech: They were on an island in a little world of their own. It depended on them all to make this world a world of true happiness and content. Each must do his part. He hoped he himself did what he could, for his heart was in his island, and with the people of his island.

The butler responded: As long as the island had such a Master, it could not but be a little heaven for all the people on it.—This was seconded with virile warmth by the bailiff and the mason, the skipper was beside himself. Then there was dancing, the old carpenter was fiddler.

But under all this, things were not well. The very next morning came the farm-boy to say that a cow had fallen over the cliff. The Master went to look. He peered over the not very high declivity, and saw her lying dead, on a green ledge under a bit of late-flowering broom. A beautiful, expensive creature, already looking swollen. But what a fool, to fall so unnecessarily!

It was a question of getting several men to haul her up the bank: and then of skinning and burying her. No one would eat the meat. How repulsive it all was!

This was symbolic of the island. As sure as the spirits rose in the human breast, with a movement of joy, an invisible hand struck malevolently out of the silence. There must not be any joy, nor even any quiet peace. A man broke a leg, another was crippled with rheumatic fever. The pigs had some strange disease. A storm drove the yacht on a rock. The mason hated the butler, and refused to let his daughter serve at the house.

Out of the very air came a stony, heavy malevolence. The island itself seemed malicious. It would go on being hurtful and evil for weeks at a time. Then suddenly again one morning it would be fair, lovely as a morning in Paradise, everything beautiful and flowing. And everybody would begin to feel a great relief, and a hope for happiness.

Then as soon as the Master was opened out in spirit like an open flower, some ugly blow would fall. Somebody would send him an anonymous note, accusing some other person on the island. Somebody else would come hinting things against one of his servants.

"Some folks thinks they've got an easy job out here, with all the pickings they make!" the mason's daughter screamed at the suave butler, in the Master's hearing. He pretended not to hear.

"My man says this island is surely one of the lean kine of Egypt, it would swallow a sight of money, and you'd never get anything back out of it," confided the farm-hand's wife to one of the Master's visitors.

The people were not contented. They were not islanders. "We feel we're not doing right by the children," said those who had children. "We feel we're not doing right by ourselves," said those who had no children. And the various families fairly came to hate one another.

Yet the island was so lovely. When there was a scent of honeysuckle, and the moon brightly flickering down on the sea, then even the grumblers felt a strange nostalgia for it. It set you yearning, with a wild yearning; perhaps for the past, to be far back in the mysterious past of the island, when the blood had a different throb. Strange floods of passion came over you, strange violent lusts and imaginations of cruelty. The blood and the passion and the lust which the island had known. Uncanny dreams, half-dreams, half-evoked yearnings.

The Master himself began to be a little afraid of his island. He felt here strange violent feelings he had never felt before, and lustful desires that he had been quite free from. He knew quite well now that his people didn't love him at all. He knew that their spirits were secretly against him, malicious, jeering, envious, and lurking to down him. He became just as wary and secretive with regard to them.

But it was too much. At the end of the second year, several departures took place. The housekeeper went. The Master always blamed self-important women most. The mason said he wasn't going to be monkeyed about any more, so he took his departure, with his family. The rheumatic farm-hand left.

And then the year's bills came in, the Master made up his accounts. In spite of good crops, the assets were ridiculous, against the spending. The island had again lost, not hundreds but thousands of pounds. It was incredible. But you simply couldn't believe it! Where had it all gone?

The Master spent gloomy nights and days, going through accounts in the library. He was thorough. It became evident, now the housekeeper had gone, that she had swindled him. Probably everybody was swindling him. But he hated to think it, so he put the thought away.

He emerged, however, pale and hollow-eyed from his balancing of unbalanceable accounts, looking as if something had kicked him in the stomach. It was pitiable. But the money had gone, and there was an end of it. Another great hole in his capital. How could people be so heartless?

It couldn't go on, that was evident. He would soon be bankrupt. He had to give regretful notice to his butler. He was afraid to find out how much his butler had swindled him. Because the man was such a wonderful butler, after all. And the farm-bailiff had to go. The Master had no regrets in that quarter. The losses on the farm had almost embittered him.

The third year was spent in rigid cutting down of expenses. The island was still mysterious and fascinating. But it was also treacherous and cruel, secretly, fathomlessly malevolent. In spite of all its fair show of white blossom and bluebells, and the lovely dignity of foxgloves bending their rose-red bells, it was your implacable enemy.

With reduced staff, reduced wages, reduced splendour, the third year went by. But it was fighting against hope. The farm still lost a good deal. And once more, there was a hole in that remnant of capital. Another hole, in that which was already a mere remnant round the old holes. The island was mysterious in this also: it seemed to pick the very money out of your pocket, as if it were an octopus with invisible arms stealing from you in every direction.

Yet the Master still loved it. But with a touch of rancour now.

He spent, however, the second half of the fourth year intensely working on the mainland, to be rid of it. And it was amazing how difficult he found it to dispose of an island. He had thought that everybody was pining for such an island as his; but not at all. Nobody would pay any price for it. And he wanted now to get rid of it, as a man who wants a divorce at any cost.

It was not till the middle of the fifth year that he transferred it, at a considerable loss to himself, to an hotel company who were willing to speculate in it. They were to turn it into a handy honeymoon-and-golf island!

There, take that, island which didn't know when it was well off! Now be a honeymoon-and-golf island!

THE SECOND ISLAND

The islander had to move. But he was not going to the mainland. Oh, no! He moved to the smaller island, which still belonged to him. And he took with him the faithful old carpenter and wife, the couple he never really cared for; also a widow and daughter, who had kept house for him the last year; also an orphan lad, to help the old man.

The small island was very small; but, being a hump of rock in the sea, it was bigger than it looked. There was a little track among rocks and bushes, winding and scrambling up and down around the islet, so that it took you twenty minutes to do the circuit. It was more than you would have expected.

Still, it was an island. The islander moved himself, with all his books, into the commonplace six-roomed house up to which you had to scramble from the rocky landing-place. There were also two joined-together cottages. The old carpenter lived in one, with his wife and the lad, the widow and daughter lived in the other.

At last all was in order. The Master's books filled two rooms. It was already autumn, Orion lifting out of the sea. And in the dark nights, the Master could see the lights on his late island, where the hotel company were entertaining guests who would advertise the new resort for honeymoon-golfers.

On his hump of rock, however, the Master was still master. He explored the crannies, the odd handbreadths of grassy level, the steep little cliffs where the last harebells hung, and the seeds of summer were brown above the sea, lonely and untouched. He peered down the old well. He examined the stone pen where the pig had been kept. Himself, he had a goat.

Yes, it was an island. Always, always, underneath among the rocks the celtic sea sucked and washed and smote its feathery greyness. How many different noises of the sea! deep explosions, rumblings, strange long sighs and whistling noises; then voices, real voices of people clamouring as if they were in a market, under the waters; and again, the far-off ringing of a bell, surely an actual bell! then a tremulous trilling noise, very long and alarming, and an undertone of hoarse gasping.

On this island there were no human ghosts, no ghosts of any ancient race. The sea, and the spume and the wind and the weather, had washed them all out, washed them out, so there was only the sound of the sea itself, its own ghost, myriad-voiced, communing and plotting and shouting all winter long. And only the smell of the sea, with a few bristly bushes of gorse and coarse tufts of heather, among the grey, pellucid rocks, in the grey, more pellucid air. The coldness, the greyness, even the soft, creeping fog of the sea! and the islet of rock humped up in it all, like the last point in space.

Green star Sirius stood over the sea's rim. The island was a shadow. Out at sea a ship showed small lights. Below, in the rocky cove, the rowboat and the motor-boat were safe. A light shone in the carpenter's kitchen. That was all.

Save, of course, that the lamp was lit in the house, where the widow was preparing supper, her daughter helping. The islander went in to his meal. Here he was no longer the Master, he was an islander again and he had peace. The old carpenter, the widow and daughter were all faithfulness itself. The old man worked while ever there was light to see, because he had a passion for work. The widow and her quiet, rather delicate daughter of thirty-three worked for the Master, because they loved looking after him, and they were infinitely grateful for the haven he provided them. But they didn't call him "the Master." They gave him his name: "Mr. Cathcart, Sir!" softly, and reverently. And he spoke back to them also softly, gently, like people far from the world, afraid to make a noise.

The island was no longer a "world." It was a sort of refuge. The islander no longer struggled for anything. He had no need. It was as if he and his few dependents were a small flock of sea-birds alighted on this rock, as they travelled through space, and keeping together without a word. The silent mystery of travelling birds.

He spent most of his day in his study. His book was coming along. The widow's daughter could type out his manuscript for him, she was not uneducated. It was the one strange sound on the island, the typewriter. But soon even its spattering fitted in with the sea's noises, and the wind's.

The months went by. The islander worked away in his study, the people of the island went quietly about their concerns. The goat had a little black kid with yellow eyes. There were mackerel in the sea. The old man went fishing in the rowboat, with the lad. When the weather was calm enough, they went off in the motor-boat to the biggest island, for the post. And they brought supplies, never a penny wasted. And the days went by, and the nights, without desire, without *ennui*.

The strange stillness from all desire was a kind of wonder to the islander. He didn't want anything. His soul at last was still in him, his spirit was like a dim-lit cave under water, where strange sea-foliage expands upon the watery atmosphere, and scarcely sways, and a mute fish shadowly slips in and slips away again. All still and soft and uncrying, yet alive as rooted sea-weed is alive.

The islander said to himself: "Is this happiness?" He said to himself: "I am turned into a dream. I feel nothing, or I don't know what I feel. Yet it seems to me I am happy."

Only he had to have something upon which his mental activity could work. So he spent long, silent hours in his study, working not very fast, nor very importantly, letting the writing spin softly from him as if it were drowsy gossamer. He no longer fretted whether it were good or not, what he produced. He slowly, softly spun it like gossamer, and, if it were to melt away as gossamer in autumn melts, he would not mind. It was only the soft evanescence of gossamy things which now seemed to him permanent. The very mist of eternity was in them. Whereas stone buildings, cathedrals for example, seemed to him to howl with temporary resistance, knowing they must fall at last: the tension of their long endurance seemed to howl forth from them all the time.

Sometimes he went to the mainland and to the city. Then he went elegantly, dressed in the latest style, to his club. He sat in a stall at the theater, he shopped in Bond Street. He discussed terms for publishing his book. But over his face was that gossamery look of having dropped out of the race of progress, which made the vulgar city people feel they had won it over him, and made him glad to go back to his island.

He didn't mind if he never published his book. The years were blending into a soft mist, from which nothing obtruded. Spring came. There was never a primrose on his island, but he found a winter-aconite. There were two little sprayed bushes of blackthorn, and some windflowers. He began to make a list of the flowers on his islet, and that was absorbing. He noted a wild currant bush, and watched for the elder flowers on a stunted little tree, then for the first yellow rags of the broom, and wild roses. Bladder campion, orchids, stitchwort, celandine, he was prouder of them than if they had been people on his island. When he came across the golden saxifrage, so inconspicuous in a damp corner, he crouched over it in a trance, he knew not for how long, looking at it. Yet it was nothing to look at. As the widow's daughter found, when he showed it her.

He had said to her, in real triumph:

"I found the golden saxifrage this morning."

The name sounded splendid. She looked at him with fascinated brown eyes, in which was a hollow ache that frightened him a little.

"Did you, Sir? Is it a nice flower?"

He pursed his lips and tilted his brows.

"Well—not showy exactly. I'll show it you if you like."

"I should like to see it."

She was so quiet, so wistful. But he sensed in her a persistency which made him uneasy. She said she was so happy: really happy. She followed him quietly, like a shadow, on the rocky track where there was never room for two people to walk side by side. He went first, and could feel her there, immediately behind him, following so submissively, gloating on him from behind.

It was a kind of pity for her which made him become her lover: though he never realized the extent of the power she had gained over him, and how *she* willed it. But the moment he had fallen, a jangling feeling came upon him, that it was all wrong. He felt a nervous dislike of her. He had not wanted it. And it seemed to him, as far as her physical self went, she had not wanted it either. It was just her will. He went away, and climbed at the risk of his neck down to a ledge near the sea. There he sat for hours, gazing all jangled at the sea, and saying miserably to himself: "We didn't want it. We didn't really want it."

It was the automatism of sex that had caught him again. Not that he hated sex. He deemed it, as the Chinese do, one of the great life-mysteries. But it had become mechanical, automatic, and he wanted to escape that. Automatic sex shattered him, and filled him with a sort of death. He thought he had come through, to a new fresh delicacy of desire, an unentered frail communion of two people meeting on untrodden ground.

But be that as it might, this was not it. This was nothing new or fresh. It was automatic, and driven from the will. Even she, in her true self, hadn't wanted it. It was automatic in her.

When he came home, very late, and saw her face white with fear and apprehension of his feeling against her, he pitied her and spoke to her delicately, reassuringly. But he kept himself remote from her.

She gave no sign. She served him with the same silence, the same hidden hunger to serve him, to be near where he was. He felt her love following him with strange, awful persistency. She claimed nothing. Yet now, when he met her bright, brown, curiously vacant eyes, he saw in them the mute question. The question came direct at him, with a force and a power of will he never realized.

So he succumbed, and asked her again.

"Not," she said, "if it will make you hate me."

"Why should it?" he replied, nettled. "Of course not."

"You know I would do anything on earth for you."

It was only afterwards, in his exasperation, he remembered what she had said, and was more exasperated. Why should she pretend to do this *for him?* Why not for herself? But in his exasperation, he drove himself deeper in. In order to achieve some sort of satisfaction, which he never did achieve, he abandoned himself to her. Everybody on the island knew. But he did not care.

Then even what desire he had left him, and he felt only shattered. He felt that only with her will had she wanted him. Now he was shattered and full of self-contempt. His island was smirched and spoiled. He had lost his place in the rare desireless levels of Time to which he had at last arrived, and he had fallen right back. If only it had been true, delicate desire between them, and a delicate meeting on the third rare place where a man might meet a woman, when they were both true to the frail, sensitive, crocus flame of desire in them. But it had been no such thing: automatic, an act of will, not of true desire, it left him feeling humiliated.

He went away from the islet, in spite of her mute reproach. And he wandered about the continent, vainly seeking a place where he could stay. He was out of key; he did not fit in the world any more.

There came a letter from Flora—her name was Flora—to say she was afraid she was going to have a child. He sat down as if he were shot, and he remained sitting. But he replied to her: "Why be afraid? If it is so, it is so, and we should rather be pleased than afraid."

At this very moment, it happened there was an auction of islands. He got the maps, and studied them. And at the auction he bought, for very little money, another island. It was just a few acres of rock away in the north, on the outer fringe of the isles. It was low, it rose out of the great ocean. There was not a building, not even a tree on it. Only northern sea-turf, a pool of rain-water, a bit of sedge, rock, and sea-birds. Nothing else. Under the weeping wet western sky.

He made a trip to visit his new possession. For several days, owing to the seas, he could not approach it. Then, in a light sea-mist, he landed, and saw it hazy, low, stretching apparently a long way. But it was illusion. He walked over the wet, springy turf, and dark-grey sheep tossed away from him, spectral, bleating hoarsely. And he came to the dark pool, with the sedge. Then on in the dampness, to the grey sea sucking angrily among the rocks.

This was indeed an island.

So he went home to Flora. She looked at him with guilty fear, but also with a triumphant brightness in her uncanny eyes. And again he was gentle, he reassured her, even he wanted her again, with that curious desire that was almost like toothache. So he took her to the mainland, and they were married, since she was going to have his child.

They returned to the island. She still brought in his meals, her own along with them. She sat and ate with him. He would have it so. The widowed mother preferred to stay in the kitchen. And Flora slept in the guest-room of his house, mistress of his house.

His desire, whatever it was, died in him with nauseous finality. The child would still be months coming. His island was hateful to him, vulgar, a suburb. He himself had lost all his finer distinction. The weeks passed in a sort of prison, in humiliation. Yet he stuck it out, till the child was born. But he was meditating escape. Flora did not even know.

A nurse appeared, and ate at table with them. The doctor came sometimes, and, if the sea were rough, he too had to stay. He was cheery over his whisky.

They might have been a young couple in Golders Green.

The daughter was born at last. The father looked at the baby, and felt depressed, almost more than he could bear. The millstone was tied round his neck. But he tried not to show what he felt. And Flora did not know. She still smiled with a kind of half-witted triumph in her joy, as she got well again. Then she began again to look at him with those aching, suggestive, somehow impudent eyes. She adored him so.

This he could not stand. He told her that he had to go away for a time. She wept, but she thought she had got him. He told her he had settled the best part of his property on her, and wrote down for her what income it would produce. She hardly listened, only looked at him with those heavy, adoring, impudent eyes. He gave her a cheque-book, with the amount of her credit duly entered. This did arouse her interest. And he told her, if she got tired of the island, she could choose her home wherever she wished.

She followed him with those aching, persistent brown eyes, when he left, and he never even saw her weep.

He went straight north, to prepare his third island.

THE THIRD ISLAND

The third island was soon made habitable. With cement and the big pebbles from the shingle beach, two men built him a hut, and roofed it with corrugated iron. A boat brought over a bed and table, and three chairs, with a good cupboard, and a few books. He laid in a supply of coal and paraffin and food—he wanted so little.

The house stood near the flat shingle bay where he landed and where he pulled up his light boat. On a sunny day in August the men sailed away and left him. The sea was still and pale blue. On the horizon he saw the small mail-steamer slowly passing northwards, as if she were walking. She served the outer isles twice a week. He could row out to her if need be, in calm weather, and he could signal her from a flagstaff behind his cottage.

Half a dozen sheep still remained on the island, as company; and he had a cat to rub against his legs. While the sweet, sunny days of the northern autumn lasted, he would walk among the rocks, and over the springy turf of his small domain, always coming to the ceaseless, restless sea. He looked at every leaf that might be different from another, and he watched the endless expansion and contraction of the water-tossed sea-weed. He had never a tree, not even a bit of heather to guard. Only the turf, and tiny turf-plants, and the sedge by the pool, the sea-weed in the ocean. He was glad. He didn't want trees or bushes. They stood up like people, too assertive. His bare, low-pitched island in the pale blue sea was all he wanted.

He no longer worked at his book. The interest had gone. He liked to sit on the low elevation of his island, and see the sea; nothing but the pale, quiet sea. And to feel his mind turn soft and hazy, like the hazy ocean. Sometimes, like a mirage, he would see the shadow of land rise hovering to northwards. It was a big island beyond. But quite without substance.

He was soon almost startled when he perceived the steamer on the near horizon, and his heart contracted with fear, lest it were going to pause and molest him. Anxiously he watched it go, and not till it was out of sight did he feel truly relieved, himself again. The tension of waiting for human approach was cruel. He did not want to be approached. He did not want to hear voices. He was shocked by the sound of his own voice, if he inadvertently spoke to his cat. He rebuked himself for having broken the great silence. And he was irritated when his cat would look up at him and mew faintly, plaintively. He frowned at her. And she knew. She was becoming wild, lurking in the rocks, perhaps fishing.

But what he disliked most was when one of the lumps of sheep opened its mouth and baa-ed its hoarse, raucous baa. He watched it, and it looked to him hideous and gross. He came to dislike the sheep very much.

He wanted only to hear the whispering sound of the sea, and the sharp cries of the gulls, cries that came out of another world to him. And best of all, the great silence.

He decided to get rid of the sheep, when the boat came. They were accustomed to him now, and stood and stared at him with yellow or colourless eyes, in an insolence that was almost cold ridicule. There was a suggestion of cold indecency about them. He disliked them very much. And when they jumped with staccato jumps off the rocks, and their hoofs made the dry, sharp hit, and the fleece flopped on their square backs—he found them repulsive, degrading.

The fine weather passed, and it rained all day. He lay a great deal on his bed, listening to the water trickling from his roof into the zinc water-butt, looking through the open door at the rain, the dark rocks, the hidden sea. Many gulls were on the island now: many sea-birds of all sorts. It was another world of life. Many of the birds he had never seen before. His old impulse came over him, to send for a book, to know their names. In a flicker of the old passion, to know the name of everything he saw, he even decided to row out to the steamer. The names of these birds! he must know their names, otherwise he had not got them, they were not quite alive to him.

But the desire left him, and he merely watched the birds as they wheeled or walked around him, watched them vaguely, without discrimination. All interest had left him. Only there was one gull, a big handsome fellow, who would walk back and forth, back and forth in front of the open door of the cabin, as if he had some mission there. He was big, and pearl-grey, and his roundnesses were as smooth and lovely as a pearl. Only the folded wings had shut black pinions, and on the closed black feathers were three very distinct white dots, making a pattern. The islander wondered very much, why this bit of trimming on the bird out of the far, cold seas. And as the gull walked back and forth, back and forth in front of the cabin, strutting on pale-dusky gold feet, holding up his pale yellow beak, that was curved at the tip, with curious alien importance, the man wondered over him. He was portentous, he had a meaning.

Then the bird came no more. The island, which had been full of seabirds, the flash of wings, the sound and cut of wings and sharp eerie cries in the air, began to be deserted again. No longer they sat like living eggs on the rocks and turf, moving their heads, but scarcely rising into flight round his head. No longer they ran across the turf among the sheep, and lifted themselves upon low wings. The host had gone. But some remained, always.

The days shortened, and the world grew eerie. One day the boat came: as if suddenly, swooping down. The islander found it a violation. It was torture to talk to those two men, in their homely clumsy clothes. The air of familiarity around them was very repugnant to him. Himself, he was neatly dressed, his cabin was neat and tidy. He resented any intrusion, the clumsy homeliness, the heavy-footedness of the two fishermen was really repulsive to him.

The letters they had brought, he left lying unopened in a little box. In one of them was his money. But he could not bear to open even that one. Any kind of contact was repulsive to him. Even to read his name on an envelope. He hid the letters away.

And the hustle and horror of getting the sheep caught and tied and put in the ship made him loathe with profound repulsion the whole of the animal creation. What repulsive god invented animals, and evil-smelling men? To his nostrils, the fishermen and the sheep alike smelled foul; an uncleanness on the fresh earth.

He was still nerve-racked and tortured when the ship at last lifted sail and was drawing away, over the still sea. And sometimes days after he would start with repulsion, thinking he heard the munching of sheep.

The dark days of winter drew on. Sometimes there was no real day at all. He felt ill, as if he were dissolving, as if dissolution had already set in inside him. Everything was twilight, outside, and in his mind and soul. Once, when he went to the door, he saw black heads of men swimming in his bay. For some moments he swooned unconscious. It was the shock, the horror of unexpected human approach. The horror in the twilight! And not till the shock had undermined him and left him disembodied, did he realize that the black heads were the heads of seals swimming in. A sick relief came over him. But he was barely conscious, after the shock. Later on, he sat and wept with gratitude, because they were not men. But he never realized that he wept. He was too dim. Like some strange, ethereal animal, he no longer realized what he was doing.

Only he still derived his single satisfaction from being alone, absolutely alone, with the space soaking into him. The grey sea alone, and the footing of his sea-washed island. No other contact. Nothing human to bring its horror into contact with him. Only space, damp, twilit, sea-washed space! This was the bread of his soul.

For this reason, he was most glad when there was a storm, or when the sea was high. Then nothing could get at him. Nothing could come through to him from the outer world. True, the terrific violence of the wind made him suffer badly. At the same time, it swept the world utterly out of existence for him. He always liked the sea to be heavily rolling and tearing. Then no boat could get at him. It was like eternal ramparts round his island.

He kept no track of time, and no longer thought of opening a book. The print, the printed letters, so like the depravity of speech, looked obscene. He tore the brass label from his paraffin stove. He obliterated any bit of lettering in his cabin.

His cat had disappeared. He was rather glad. He shivered at her thin, obtrusive call. She had lived in the coal shed. And each morning he had put her a dish of porridge, the same as he ate. He washed her saucer with repulsion. He did not like her writhing about. But he fed her scrupulously. Then one day she did not come for her porridge: she always mewed for it. She did not come again.

He prowled about his island in the rain, in a big oil-skin coat, not knowing what he was looking at, nor what he went out to see. Time had ceased to pass. He stood for long spaces, gazing from a white, sharp face, with those keen, far-off blue eyes of his, gazing fiercely and almost cruelly at the dark sea under the dark sky. And if he saw the labouring sail of a fishing boat away on the cold waters, a strange malevolent anger passed over his features.

Sometimes he was ill. He knew he was ill, because he staggered as he walked, and easily fell down. Then he paused to think what it was. And he went to his stores and took out dried milk and malt, and ate that. Then he forgot again. He ceased to register his own feelings.

The days were beginning to lengthen. All winter the weather had been comparatively mild, but with much rain, much rain. He had forgotten the sun. Suddenly, however, the air was very cold, and he began to shiver. A fear came over him. The sky was level and grey, and never a star appeared at night. It was very cold. More birds began to arrive. The island was freezing. With trembling hands he made a fire in his grate. The cold frightened him.

And now it continued, day after day, a dull, deathly cold. Occasional crumblings of snow were in the air. The days were greyly longer, but no change in the cold. Frozen grey daylight. The birds passed away, flying away. Some he saw lying frozen. It was as if all life were drawing away, contracting away from the north, contracting southwards. "Soon," he said to himself, "it will all be gone, and in all these regions nothing will be alive." He felt a cruel satisfaction in the thought.

Then one night there seemed to be a relief: he slept better, did not tremble half awake, and writhe so much, half-conscious. He had become so used to the quaking and writhing of his body, he hardly noticed it. But when for once it slept deep, he noticed that.

He awoke in the morning to a curious whiteness. His window was muffled. It had snowed. He got up and opened his door, and shuddered. Ugh! how cold! All white, with a dark leaden sea, and black rocks curiously speckled with white. The foam was no longer pure. It seemed dirty. And the sea ate at the whiteness of the corpse-like land. Crumbles of snow were silting down the dead air.

On the ground the snow was a foot deep, white and smooth and soft, windless. He took a shovel to clear round his house and shed. The pallor of morning darkened. There was a strange rumbling of far-off thunder, in the frozen air, and through the newly-falling snow, a dim flash of lightning. Snow now fell steadily down, in the motionless obscurity.

He went out for a few minutes. But it was difficult. He stumbled and fell in the snow, which burned his face. Weak, faint, he toiled home. And when he recovered, he took the trouble to make hot milk.

It snowed all the time. In the afternoon again there was a muffled rumbling of thunder, and flashes of lightning blinking reddish through the falling snow. Uneasy, he went to bed and lay staring fixedly at nothing.

Morning seemed never to come. An eternity long he lay and waited for one alleviating pallor on the night. And at last it seemed the air was paler. His house was a cell faintly illuminated with white light. He realized the snow was walled outside his window. He got up, in the dead cold. When he opened his door, the motionless snow stopped him in a wall as high as his breast. Looking over the top of it, he felt the dead wind slowly driving, saw the snow-powder lift and travel like a funeral train. The blackish sea churned and champed, seeming to bite at the snow, impotent. The sky was grey, but luminous.

He began to work in a frenzy, to get at his boat. If he was to be shut in, it must be by his own choice, not by the mechanical power of the elements. He must get to the sea. He must be able to get at his boat.

But he was weak, and at times the snow overcame him. It fell on him, and he lay buried and lifeless. Yet every time, he struggled alive before it was too late, and fell upon the snow with the energy of fever. Exhausted, he would not give in. He crept indoors and made coffee and bacon. Long since he had cooked so much. Then he went at the snow once more. He must conquer the snow, this new, white brute force which had accumulated against him.

He worked in the awful, dead wind, pushing the snow aside, pressing it with his shovel. It was cold, freezing hard in the wind, even when the sun came out for a while, and showed him his white, lifeless surroundings, the black sea rolling sullen, flecked with dull spume, away to the horizons. Yet the sun had power on his face. It was March.

He reached the boat. He pushed the snow away, then sat down under the lee of the boat, looking at the sea, which nearly swirled to his feet, in the high tide. Curiously natural the pebbles looked, in a world gone all uncanny. The sun shone no more. Snow was falling in hard crumbs, that vanished as if by miracle as they touched the hard blackness of the sea. Hoarse waves rang in the shingle, rushing up at the snow. The wet rocks were brutally black. And all the time the myriad swooping crumbs of snow, demonish, touched the dark sea and disappeared.

During the night there was a great storm. It seemed to him he could hear the vast mass of the snow striking all the world with a ceaseless thud; and over it all, the wind roared in strange hollow volleys, in between which came a jump of blindfold lightning, then the low roll of thunder heavier than the wind. When at last the dawn faintly discoloured the dark, the storm had more or less subsided, but a steady wind drove on. The snow was up to the top of his door.

Sullenly, he worked to dig himself out. And he managed, through sheer persistency, to get out. He was in the tail of a great drift, many feet high. When he got through, the frozen snow was not more than two feet deep. But his island was gone. Its shape was all changed, great heaping white hills rose where no hills had been, inaccessible, and they fumed like volcanoes, but with snow powder. He was sickened and overcome.

His boat was in another, smaller drift. But he had not the strength to clear it. He looked at it helplessly. The shovel slipped from his hands, and he sank in the snow, to forget. In the snow itself, the sea resounded.

Something brought him to. He crept to his house. He was almost without feeling. Yet he managed to warm himself, just that part of him which leaned in snow-sleep over the coal fire. Then again, he made hot milk. After which, carefully, he built up the fire.

The wind dropped. Was it night again? In the silence, it seemed he could hear the panther-like dropping of infinite snow. Thunder rumbled nearer, crackled quick after the bleared reddened lightning. He lay in bed in a kind of stupor. The elements! The elements! His mind repeated the word dumbly. You can't win against the elements.

How long it went on, he never knew. Once, like a wraith, he got out, and climbed to the top of a white hill on his unrecognizable island. The sun was hot. "It is summer," he said to himself, "and the time of leaves." He looked stupidly over the whiteness of his foreign island, over the waste of the lifeless sea. He pretended to imagine he saw the wink of a sail. Because he knew too well there would never again be a sail on that stark sea.

As he looked, the sky mysteriously darkened and chilled. From far off came the mutter of the unsatisfied thunder, and he knew it was the signal of the snow rolling over the sea. He turned, and felt its breath on him.

LAWRENCE: *The Man Who Loved Islands*

1. *The story begins: "There was a man who loved islands." Hesse's "Within and Without" opens: "There was once a man named Frederick"; Aleichem's "Tit for Tat" starts: "Once I was a rabbiner." Do you attach any significance to this phrasing of the introduction?*

2. *What kind of man is Cathcart? What, according to Lawrence, does he stand for? Is he a saint or a devil?*

3. *Why is Lawrence antagonistic and ironic toward his protagonist?*

4. *Why does Cathcart go from one island to another? Why are there three islands and not two or four?*

5. *What is the significance of his experiences on each island? How are they related?*

6. *What does Cathcart reject? What does he attempt to embrace?*

7. *Why is there such a preponderance of the color white in the story? What symbolic meaning does the snow have? If you have the chance, read Joyce's "The Dead" and Conrad Aiken's "Silent Snow, Secret*

Snow" and compare the use of snow as a symbol in each story. Does snow have symbolic importance in "The District Doctor"? How can you tell?

8. Lawrence's imagery helps to carry the burden of his theme. How would you describe it?

9. A noted Lawrence critic, Mark Schorer, speaks of Lawrence's style as "symbolic." What do you think he means? Use this story to illustrate.

10. A persistent theme in Lawrence's earlier work is his hatred of vulgar humanity and his need to withdraw from it into isolation. For example, in a letter to Bertrand Russell, he talks about standing outside the mob and throwing bombs into it. Is this story an intensification of this doctrine or a denial of it?

Pär Lagerkvist

THE CHILDREN'S CAMPAIGN

> *Those who admire the haunted landscapes and dark allegories of Ingmar Bergman should be attracted to the work of Pär Lagerkvist, Swedish novelist, poet, and dramatist. Born in Växjö in 1891 and schooled at Uppsala, Lagerkvist left Sweden to educate himself in European letters; the influence of the Cubist and Expressionist experiments is discernible especially in the collection called* The Eternal Smile, *the source of the following story. In 1930, he returned to Sweden and, according to critics, created a trend in Swedish poetry comparable to T. S. Eliot's impact on English. His plays have also won high praise at home, but it is as a writer of novels with Swiftian undertones like* The Hangman *(1933),* The Dwarf *(1944), and* Barabbas *(1950) that he was awarded the Nobel Prize in 1951. Like his novels, "The Children's Campaign" is an ironic tale in which Lagerkvist indicts an entire age.*

EVEN the children at that time received military training, were assembled in army units and exercised just as though on active service, had their own headquarters and annual maneuvers when everything was conducted as in a real state of war. The grownups had nothing directly to do with this training; the children actually exercised themselves and all command was entrusted to them. The only use made of adult experience was to arrange officers' training courses for especially suitable boys, who were chosen with the greatest care and who were then put in charge of the military education of their comrades in the ranks.

These schools were of high standing and there was hardly a boy throughout the land who did not dream of going to them. But the entrance tests were particularly hard; not only a perfect physique was required but also a highly developed intelligence and character. The age of admission was six to seven years and the small cadets then received an excellent training, both purely military and in all other respects, chiefly the further molding of character. It was also greatly to one's credit in after life to have passed through one of these schools. It was

[307

really on the splendid foundation laid here that the quality, organization and efficiency of the child army rested.

Thereafter, as already mentioned, the grownups in no way interfered but everything was entrusted to the children themselves. No adult might meddle in the command, in organizational details or matters of promotion. Everything was managed and supervised by the children; all decisions, even the most vital, being reached by their own little general staff. No one over fourteen was allowed. The boys then passed automatically into the first age group of the regular troops with no mean military training already behind them.

The large child army, which was the object of the whole nation's love and admiration, amounted to three army corps of four divisions: infantry, light field artillery, medical and service corps. All physically fit boys were enrolled in it and a large number of girls belonged to it as nurses, all volunteers.

Now it so happened that a smaller, quite insignificant nation behaved in a high-handed and unseemly way toward its powerful neighbor, and the insult was all the greater since this nation was by no means an equal. Indignation was great and general and, since people's feelings were running high, it was necessary to rebuke the malapert and at the same time take the chance to subjugate the country in question. In this situation the child army came forward and through its high command asked to be charged with the crushing and subduing of the foe. The news of this caused a sensation and a wave of fervor throughout the country. The proposal was given serious consideration in supreme quarters and as a result the commission was given, with some hesitation, to the children. It was in fact a task well suited to this army, and the people's obvious wishes in the matter had also to be met, if possible.

The Foreign Office therefore sent the defiant country an unacceptable ultimatum and, pending the reply, the child army was mobilized within twenty-four hours. The reply was found to be unsatisfactory and war was declared immediately.

Unparalleled enthusiasm marked the departure for the front. The intrepid little youngsters had green sprigs in the barrels of their rifles and were pelted with flowers. As is so often the case, the campaign was begun in the spring, and this time the general opinion was that there was something symbolic in it. In the capital the little commander in chief and chief of general staff, in the presence of huge crowds, made a passionate speech to the troops in which he expressed the gravity of the hour and his conviction of their unswerving valor and willingness to offer their lives for their country.

The speech, made in a strong voice, aroused the greatest ecstasy. The boy—who had a brilliant career behind him and had reached his exalted position at the age of only twelve and a half—was acclaimed with wild rejoicing and from this moment was the avowed hero of the entire nation. There was not a dry eye and those of the many mothers especially shone with pride and happiness. For them it was the greatest day in their lives. The troops marched past below fluttering banners, each regiment with its music corps at the head. It was an unforgettable spectacle.

There were also many touching incidents, evincing a proud patriotism, as when a little four-year-old, who had been lifted upon his mother's arm so that he could see, howled with despair and shouted, "I want to go, too. I want to go, too!" while his mother tried to hush him, explaining that he was too small. "Small am I, eh?" he exclaimed, punching her face so that her nose bled. The evening papers were full of such episodes showing the mood of the people and of the troops who were so sure of victory. The big march past was broadcast and the c in c's speech, which had been recorded, was broadcast every evening during the days that followed at 7:15 P.M.

Military operations had already begun, however, and reports of victory began to come in at once from the front. The children had quickly taken the offensive and on one sector of the front had inflicted a heavy defeat on the enemy, seven hundred dead and wounded and over twelve hundred prisoners, while their own losses amounted to only a hundred or so fallen. The victory was celebrated at home with indescribable rejoicing and with thanksgiving services in the churches. The newspapers were filled with accounts of individual instances of valor and pictures several columns wide of the high command, of which the leading personalities, later so well-known, began to appear now for the first time. In their joy, mothers and aunts sent so much chocolate and other sweets to the army that headquarters had to issue a strict order that all such parcels were, for the time being at any rate, forbidden, since they had made whole regiments unfit for battle and these in their turn had nearly been surrounded by the enemy.

For the child army was already far inside enemy territory and still managed to keep the initiative. The advance sector did retreat slightly in order to establish contact with its wings but only improved its positions by so doing. A stalemate ensued in the theater of war for some time after this.

During July, however, troops were concentrated for a big attack along the whole line and huge reserves—the child army's, in comparison with those of its opponent, were almost inexhaustible—were mustered to the front. The new offensive, which lasted for several weeks, resulted, too, in an almost decisive victory for the whole army, even though casualties were high. The children defeated the enemy all along the line but did not manage to pursue him and thereby exploit their success to the full, because he was greatly favored by the fact that his legs were so much longer, an advantage of which he made good use. By dint of forced marches, however, the children finally succeeded in cutting the enemy's right flank to pieces. They were now in the very heart of the country and their outposts were only a few days' march from the capital.

It was a pitched battle on a big scale and the newspapers had enormous headlines every day which depicted the dramatic course of events. At set hours the radio broadcast the gunfire and a résumé of the position. The war correspondents described in rapturous words and vivid colors the state of affairs at the front—the children's incredible feats, their indomitable courage and self-sacrifice, the whole morale of the army. It was no exaggeration. The youngsters showed the greatest bravery; they really behaved like heroes. One only had to see their discipline and contempt of death during an attack, as though they had been grown-up men at least.

It was an unforgettable sight to see them storm ahead under murderous machine gun fire and the small medical orderlies dart nimbly forward and pick them up as they fell. Or the wounded and dying who were moved behind the front, those who had had a leg shot away or their bellies ripped open by a bayonet so that their entrails hung out—but without one sound of complaint crossing their small lips. The hand-to-hand fighting had been very fierce and a great number of children fell in this, while they were superior in the actual firing. Losses were estimated at 4,000 on the enemy side and 7,000 among the children, according to the secret reports. The victory had been hard won but all the more complete.

This battle became very famous and was also of far greater importance than any previously. It was now clear beyond all doubt that the children were incomparably superior in tactics, discipline and individual courage. At the same time, however, it was admitted by experts that the enemy's headlong retreat was very skillfully carried out, that his strength was evidently in defense and that he should not be underrated too much. Toward the end, also, he had unexpectedly made a stubborn resistance which had prevented any further penetration.

This observation was not without truth. In actual fact the enemy was anything but a warlike nation, and indeed his forces found it very difficult to hold their own. Nevertheless, they improved with practice during the fighting and became more efficient as time went on. This meant that they caused the children a good deal of trouble in each succeeding battle. They also had certain advantages on their side. As their opponents were so small, for instance, it was possible after a little practice to spit several of them on the bayonet at once, and often a kick was enough to fell them to the ground.

But against this, the children were so much more numerous and also braver. They were everywhere. They swarmed over one and in between one's legs and the unwarlike people were nearly demented by all these small monsters who fought like fiends. Little fiends was also what they were generally called—not without reason—and this name was even adopted in the children's homeland, but there it was a mark of honor and a pet name. The enemy troops had all their work cut out merely defending themselves. At last, however, they were able to check the others' advance and even venture on one or two counterattacks. Everything then came to a standstill for a while and there was a breathing space.

The children were now in possession of a large part of the country. But this was not always so easy. The population did not particularly like them and proved not to be very fond of children. It was alleged that snipers fired on the boys from houses and that they were ambushed when they moved in small detachments. Children had even been found impaled on stakes or with their eyes gouged out, so it was said. And in many cases these stories were no doubt true. The population had quite lost their heads, were obviously goaded into a frenzy, and as they were of little use as a warlike nation and their cruelty could therefore find no natural outlet, they tried to revenge themselves by atrocities. They felt overrun by all the foreign children as by troublesome vermin and, being at their wits' end, they simply killed whenever they had the chance. In order to put an end to these outrages the children burned one village after the other and shot hundreds of people daily, but this did not improve matters. The despicable deeds of these craven guerrillas caused them endless trouble.

At home, the accounts of all this naturally aroused the most bitter resentment. People's blood boiled to think that their small soldiers were treated in this way by those who had nothing to do with the war, by barbarous civilians who had no notion of established and judicial forms. Even greater indignation was caused, however, by an incident that occurred inside the occupied area some time after the big summer battle just mentioned.

A lieutenant who was out walking in the countryside came to a stream where a large, fat woman knelt washing clothes. He asked her the way to a village close by. The woman, who probably suspected him of evil intent, retorted, "What are you doing here? You ought to be at home with your mother." Whereupon the lieutenant drew his saber to kill her, but the woman grabbed hold of him and, putting him over her knee, thwacked him black and blue with her washboard so that he was unable to sit down for several days afterward. He was so taken aback that he did nothing, armed though he was to the teeth. Luckily no one saw the incident, but there were orders that all outrages on the part of the population were to be reported to headquarters. The lieutenant therefore duly reported what had happened to him. True, it gave him little satisfaction, but as he had to obey orders he had no choice. And so it all came out.

The incident aroused a storm of rage, particularly among those at home. The infamous deed was a humiliation for the country, an insult which nothing could wipe out. It implied a deliberate violation by this militarily ignorant people of the simplest rules of warfare. Everywhere, in the press, in propaganda speeches, in ordinary conversation, the deepest contempt and disgust for the deed was expressed. The lieutenant who had so flagrantly shamed the army had his officer's epaulettes ripped off in front of the assembled troops and was declared unworthy to serve any longer in the field. He was instantly sent home to his parents, who belonged to one of the most noted families but who now had to retire into obscurity in a remote part of the country.

The woman, on the other hand, became a heroic figure among her people and the object of their rapturous admiration. During the whole of the war she and her deed were a rallying national symbol which people looked up to and which spurred them on to further effort. She subsequently became a favorite motif in the profuse literature about their desperate struggle for freedom; a vastly popular figure, brought to life again and again as time passed, now in a rugged, everyday way which appealed to the man in the street, now in heroic female form on a grandiose scale, to become gradually more and more legendary, wreathed in saga and myth. In some versions she was shot by the enemy; in others she lived to a ripe old age, loved and revered by her people.

This incident, more than anything else, helped to increase the bad feelings between the two countries and to make them wage the war with ever greater ruthlessness. In the late summer, before the autumn rains began, both armies, ignorant of each other's plans, simultaneously launched a violent offensive, which devastated both sides. On large sectors of the front the troops completely annihilated each other so that there was not a single survivor left. Any peaceful inhabitants thereabouts who were still alive and ventured out of their cellars thought that the war was over, because all were slain.

But soon new detachments came up and began fighting again. Great confusion arose in other quarters from the fact that in the heat of attack men ran past each other and had to turn around in order to go on fighting; and that some parts of the line rushed ahead while others came behind, so that the troops were both in front of and behind where they should have been and time and again attacked each other in the rear. The battle raged in this way with extreme violence and shots were fired from all directions at once.

When at last the fighting ceased and stock was taken of the situation, it appeared that no one had won. On both sides there was an equal number of fallen, 12,924, and after all attacks and retreats the position of the armies was exactly the same as at the start of the battle. It was agreed that both should claim the victory. Thereafter the rain set in and the armies went to earth in trenches and put up barbed wire entanglements.

The children were the first to finish their trenches, since they had had more to do with that kind of thing, and settled down in them as best they could. They soon felt at home. Filthy and lousy, they lived there in the darkness as though they had never done anything else. With the adaptability of children they quickly got into the way of it. The enemy found this more difficult; he felt miserable and homesick for the life above ground to which he was accustomed. Not so the children. When one saw them in their small gray uniforms, which were caked thick with mud, and their small gas masks, one could easily think they had been born to this existence. They crept in and out of the holes down into the earth and scampered about the passages like mice. When their burrows were attacked they were instantly up on the parapet and snapped back in blind fury. As the months passed, this hopeless, harrowing life put endurance to an increasingly severe test. But they never lost courage or the will to fight.

For the enemy the strain was often too much; the glaring pointlessness of it all made many completely apathetic. But the little ones did not react like this. Children are really more fitted for war and take more pleasure in it, while grownups tire of it after a while and think it is boring. The boys continued to find the whole thing exciting and they wanted to go on living as they were now. They also had a more natural herd instinct; their unity and camaraderie helped them a great deal, made it easier to hold out.

But, of course, even they suffered great hardship. Especially when winter set in with its incessant rain, a cold sleet which made everything sodden and filled the trenches with mud. It was enough to unman anyone. But it would never have entered their heads to complain. However bad things were, nothing could have made them admit it. At home everyone was very proud of them. All the cinemas showed parades behind the front and the little c in c and his generals pinning medals for bravery on their soldiers' breasts. People thought of them a great deal out there, of their little fiends, realizing that they must be having a hard time.

At Christmas, in particular, thoughts went out to them, to the lighted Christmas trees and all the sparkling childish eyes out in the trenches; in every home people sat wondering how they were faring. But the children did not think of home. They were soldiers out and out, absorbed by their duty and their new life. They attacked in several places on the morning of Christmas Eve, inflicting fairly big losses on the enemy in killed and wounded, and did not stop until it was time to open their parcels. They had the real fighting spirit which might have been a lesson even to adults.

There was nothing sentimental about them. The war had hardened and developed them, made them men. It did happen that one poor little chap burst into tears when the Christmas tree was lighted, but he was made the laughing-stock of them all. "Are you homesick for your mummy, you bastard?" they said, and kept on jeering at him all evening. He was the object of their scorn all through Christmas; he behaved suspiciously and tried to keep to himself. Once he walked a hundred yards away from the post and, because he might well have been thinking of flight, he was seized and court-martialed. He could give no reason for having absented himself and since he had obviously intended to desert he was shot.

If those at home had been fully aware of the morale out there, they need not have worried. As it was, they wondered if the children could really hold their ground and half-regretted having entrusted them with the campaign, now that it was dragging on so long because of this nerve-racking stationary warfare. After the New Year help was even offered in secret, but it was rejected with proud indignation.

The morale of the enemy, on the other hand, was not so high. They did intend to fight to the last man, but the certainty of a complete victory was not so general as it should have been. They could not help thinking, either, how hopeless their fight really was; that in the long run they could not hold their own against these people who were armed to the very milk teeth, and this often dampened their courage.

Hardly had nature begun to come to life and seethe with the newly awakened forces of spring before the children started with incredible intensity to prepare for the decisive battle. Heavy mechanized artillery was brought up and placed in strong positions; huge troop movements went on night and day; all available fighting forces were concentrated in the very front lines. After murderous gunfire which lasted for six days, an attack was launched with great force and extreme skill. Individual bravery was, if possible, more dazzling than ever. The whole army was also a year older, and that means much at that age. But their opponents, too, were determined to do their utmost. They had assembled all their reserves, and their spirits, now that the rain had stopped and the weather was fine, were full of hope.

It was a terrible battle. The hospital trains immediately started going back from both sides packed with wounded and dying. Machine guns, tanks and gas played fearful havoc. For several days the outcome was impossible to foresee, since both armies appeared equally strong and the tide of battle constantly changed. The position gradually cleared, however. The enemy had expected the main attack in the center, but the child army turned out to be weakest there. Use was made of this, especially because they themselves were best prepared at this very point, and this part of the children's front was soon made to waver and was forced farther and farther back by repeated attack. Advantage was also taken of an ideal evening breeze from just the right quarter to gas the children in thousands. Encouraged by their victory, the troops pursued the offensive with all their might and with equal success.

The child army's retreat, however, turned out to be a stratagem, brilliantly conceived and carried out. Its center gave way more and more and the enemy, giving all his attention to this, forgot that at the same time he himself was wavering on both wings. In this way he ran his head into a noose. When the children considered that they had retreated far enough they halted, while the troops on the outermost wings, already far ahead, advanced swiftly until they met behind the enemy's back. The latter's entire army was thereby surrounded and in the grip of an iron hand. All the children's army had to do now was to draw the noose tighter. At last the gallant defenders had to surrender and let themselves be taken prisoner, which in fact they already were. It was the most disastrous defeat in history; not a single one escaped other than by death.

This victory became much more famous than any of the others and was eagerly studied at all military academies on account of its brilliantly executed, doubly effective encircling movement. The great general Sludelsnorp borrowed its tactics outright seventy years later at his victory over the Slivokvarks in the year 2048.

The war could not go on any longer now, because there was nothing left to fight, and the children marched to the capital with the imprisoned army between them to dictate the peace terms. These were handed over by the little commander in chief in the hall of mirrors in the stately old palace at a historic scene which was to be immortalized time and again in art and even now was reproduced everywhere in the weekly press. The film cameras whirred, the flashlights hissed and the radio broadcast the great moment to the world. The commander in chief, with austere and haughty mien and one foot slightly in front of the other, delivered the historic document with his right hand. The first and most important condition was the complete cession of the country, besides which the expenses of its capture were to be borne by the enemy, who thus had to pay the cost of the war on both sides, the last clause on account of the fact that he had been the challenging party and, according to his own admission, the cause of the war. The document was signed in dead silence, the only sound was the scratching of the fountain pen, which, according to the commentator's whisper, was solid gold and undoubtedly a future museum piece.

With this, everything was settled and the children's army returned to its own country, where it was received with indescribable rapture. Everywhere along the roads the troops were greeted with wild rejoicing; their homecoming was one long victory parade. The march into the capital and the dismissal there of the troops, which took place before vast crowds, were especially impressive. People waved and shouted in the streets as they passed, were beside themselves with enthusiasm, bands played, eyes were filled with tears of joy. Some of the loudest cheering was for the small invalids at the rear of the procession, blind and with limbs amputated, who had sacrificed themselves for their country. Many of them had already got small artificial arms and legs so that they looked just the same as before. The victory salute thundered, bayonets flashed in the sun. It was an unforgettable spectacle.

A strange, new leaf was written in the great book of history which would be read with admiration in time to come. The nation had seen many illustrious deeds performed, but never anything as proud as this. What these children had done in their devotion and fervent patriotism could never be forgotten.

Nor was it. Each spring, on the day of victory, school children marched out with flags in their hands to the cemeteries with all the small graves where the heroes rested under their small white crosses. The mounds were strewn with flowers and passionate speeches were made, reminding everyone of the glorious past, their imperishable honor and youthful, heroic spirit of self-sacrifice. The flags floated in the sun and the voices rang out clear as they sang their rousing songs, radiant childish eyes looking ahead to new deeds of glory.

Translated by Alan Blair

LAGERKVIST: *The Children's Campaign*

1. *What effect does Lagerkvist's cool, detached style create? Does the story read like a fable? Explain.*

2. *Are children really more fitted than adults for war, as Lagerkvist develops the story? What point is he making? Should he make it directly? What would he lose by direct statement of his position?*

3. *What is the point of the episode involving the child-lieutenant and the fat woman who spanks him? Why the episode with the Christmas tree?*

4. *How does Lagerkvist tip his hand about his position? Or is this really a good way to fight small wars? Why should children not fight wars if their elders do?*

5. *Compare this story with Swift's "A Modest Proposal." And, of course, with William Golding's* Lord of the Flies. *How does it recall each?*

6. *Is such training suitable for children, to build character and physique? Would you recommend it? Who would?*

7. *Does this story convey the horror that is intended? How? Or does it miss horror because we are accustomed to worse things?*

8. *Do you see any connection between Lagerkvist's point of view and that expressed in Musil's "A Man Without Character" or Lawrence's "The Man Who Loved Islands"? What do they have in common?*

Ryūnosuke Akutagawa

IN A GROVE

> *Ryūnosuke Akutagawa was born in 1892 and died a suicide in 1927. He lived in Tokyo, attended the University there, later taught, and then worked as a journalist. Among his first publications were translations of Western writers, particularly the poetry of William Butler Yeats and the prose of Anatole France. Characteristic of all his work—which includes about a hundred short stories and much incidental writing—is his precise, impersonal, restrained prose. "In a Grove," with its conflicting testimony, raises the question of what is fact and what is fiction, what is subjective and what objective, a dialectic that fits perfectly Akutagawa's own tortured personality and protean vision of reality. The tale is more commonly known to western readers as* Rashomon.

THE TESTIMONY OF A WOODCUTTER QUESTIONED BY A HIGH POLICE COMMISSIONER

YES, SIR. Certainly, it was I who found the body. This morning, as usual, I went to cut my daily quota of cedars, when I found the body in a grove in a hollow in the mountains. The exact location? About 150 meters off the Yamashina stage road. It's an out-of-the-way grove of bamboo and cedars.

The body was lying flat on its back dressed in a bluish silk kimono and a wrinkled head-dress of the Kyoto style. A single sword-stroke had pierced the breast. The fallen bamboo-blades around it were stained with bloody blossoms. No, the blood was no longer running. The wound had dried up, I believe. And also, a gadfly was stuck fast there, hardly noticing my footsteps.

You ask me if I saw a sword or any such thing?

No, nothing, sir. I found only a rope at the root of a cedar near by. And . . . well, in addition to a rope, I found a comb. That was all. Apparently he must have made a battle of it before he was murdered, because the grass and fallen bamboo-blades had been trampled down all around.

"A horse was near by?"

No, sir. It's hard enough for a man to enter, let alone a horse.

THE TESTIMONY OF A TRAVELING BUDDHIST PRIEST QUESTIONED BY A HIGH POLICE COMMISSIONER

The time? Certainly, it was about noon yesterday, sir. The unfortunate man was on the road from Sekiyama to Yamashina. He was walking toward Sekiyama with a woman accompanying him on horseback, who I have since learned was his wife. A scarf hanging from her head hid her face from view. All I saw was the color of her clothes, a lilac-colored suit. Her horse was a sorrel with a fine mane. The lady's height? Oh, about four feet five inches. Since I am a Buddhist priest, I took little notice about her details. Well, the man was armed with a sword as well as a bow and arrows. And I remember that he carried some twenty odd arrows in his quiver.

Little did I expect that he would meet such a fate. Truly human life is as evanescent as the morning dew or a flash of lightning. My words are inadequate to express my sympathy for him.

THE TESTIMONY OF A POLICEMAN QUESTIONED BY A HIGH POLICE COMMISSIONER

The man that I arrested? He is a notorious brigand called Tajomaru. When I arrested him, he had fallen off his horse. He was groaning on the bridge at Awataguchi. The time? It was in the early hours of last night. For the record, I might say that the other day I tried to arrest him, but unfortunately he escaped. He was wearing a dark blue silk kimono and a large plain sword. And, as you see, he got a bow and arrows somewhere. You say that this bow and these arrows look like the ones owned by the dead man? Then Tajomaru must be the murderer. The bow wound with leather strips, the black lacquered quiver, the seventeen arrows with hawk feathers—these were all in his possession I believe. Yes, sir, the horse is, as you say, a sorrel with a fine mane. A little beyond the stone bridge I found the horse grazing by the roadside, with his long rein dangling. Surely there is some providence in his having been thrown by the horse.

Of all the robbers prowling around Kyoto, this Tajomaru has given the most grief to the women in town. Last autumn a wife who came to the mountain back of the Pindora of the Toribe Temple, presumably to pay a visit, was murdered, along with a girl. It has been suspected that it was his doing. If this criminal murdered the man, you cannot tell what he may have done with the man's wife. May it please your honor to look into this problem as well.

THE TESTIMONY OF AN OLD WOMAN QUESTIONED BY A HIGH POLICE COMMISSIONER

Yes, sir, that corpse is the man who married my daughter. He does not come from Kyoto. He was a samurai in the town of Kokufu in the province of Wakasa. His name was Kanazawa no Takehiko and his age was twenty-six. He was of a gentle disposition, so I am sure he did nothing to provoke the anger of others.

My daughter? Her name is Masago, and her age is nineteen. She is a spirited, fun-loving girl, but I am sure she has never known any man except Takehiko. She has a small, oval, dark-complected face with a mole at the corner of her left eye.

Yesterday Takehiko left for Wakasa with my daughter. What bad luck it is that things should have come to such a sad end! What has become of my daughter? I am resigned to giving up my son-in-law as lost, but the fate of my daughter worries me sick. For heaven's sake leave no stone unturned to find her. I hate that robber Tajomaru, or whatever his name is. Not only my son-in-law, but my daughter . . . (Her later words were drowned in tears.)

TAJOMARU'S CONFESSION

I killed him, but not her. Where's she gone? I can't tell. Oh, wait a minute. No torture can make me confess what I don't know. Now things have come to such a head, I won't keep anything from you.

Yesterday a little past noon I met that couple. Just then a puff of wind blew, and raised her hanging scarf, so that I caught a glimpse of her face. Instantly it was again covered from my view. That may have been one reason; she looked like a Bodhisattva. At that moment I made up my mind to capture her even if I had to kill her man.

Why? To me killing isn't a matter of such great consequence as you might think. When a woman is captured, her man has to be killed anyway. In killing, I use the sword I wear at my side. Am I the only one who kills people? You, you don't use your swords. You kill people with your power, with your money. Sometimes you kill them on the pretext of working for their good. It's true they don't bleed. They are in the best of health, but all the same you've killed them. It's hard to say who is a greater sinner, you or me. (An ironical smile.)

But it would be good if I could capture a woman without killing her man. So, I made up my mind to capture her, and do my best not to kill him. But it's out of the question on the Yamashina stage road. So I managed to lure the couple into the mountains.

It was quite easy. I became their traveling companion, and I told them there was an old mound in the mountain over there, and that I had dug it open and found many mirrors and swords. I went on to tell them I'd buried the things in a grove behind the mountain, and that I'd like to sell them at a low price to anyone who would care to have them. Then . . . you see, isn't greed terrible? He was beginning to be moved by my talk before he knew it. In less than half an hour they were driving their horse toward the mountain with me.

When he came in front of the grove, I told them that the treasures were buried in it, and I asked them to come and see. The man had no objection—he was blinded by greed. The woman said she would wait on horseback. It was natural for her to say so, at the sight of a thick grove. To tell you the truth, my plan worked just as I wished, so I went into the grove with him, leaving her behind alone.

The grove is only bamboo for some distance. About fifty yards ahead there's a rather open clump of cedars. It was a convenient spot for my purpose. Pushing my way through the grove, I told him a plausible lie that the treasures were buried under the cedars. When I told him this, he pushed his laborious way toward the slender cedar visible through the grove. After a while the bamboo thinned out, and we came to where a number of cedars grew in a row. As soon as we got there, I seized him from behind. Because he was a trained, sword-bearing warrior, he was quite strong, but he was taken by surprise, so there was no help for him. I soon tied him up to the root of a cedar. Where did I get a rope? Thank heaven, being a robber, I had a rope with me, since I might have to scale a wall at any moment. Of course it was easy to stop him from calling out by gagging his mouth with fallen bamboo leaves.

When I disposed of him, I went to his woman and asked her to come and see him, because he seemed to have been suddenly taken sick. It's needless to say that this plan also worked well. The woman, her sedge hat off, came into the depths of the grove, where I led her by the hand. The instant she caught sight of her husband, she drew a small sword. I've never seen a woman of such violent temper. If I'd been off guard, I'd have got a thrust in my side. I dodged, but she kept on slashing at me. She might have wounded me deeply or killed me. But I'm Tajomaru. I managed to strike down her small sword without drawing my own. The most spirited woman is defenseless without a weapon. At least I could satisfy my desire for her without taking her husband's life.

Yes, . . . without taking his life. I had no wish to kill him. I was about to run away from the grove, leaving the woman behind in tears, when she frantically clung to my arm. In broken fragments of words, she asked that either her husband or I die. She said it was more trying than death to have her shame known to two men. She gasped out that she wanted to be the wife of whichever survived. Then a furious desire to kill him seized me. (Gloomy excitement.)

Telling you in this way, no doubt I seem a crueler man than you. But that's because you didn't see her face. Especially her burning eyes at that moment. As I saw her eye to eye, I wanted to make her my wife even if I were to be struck by lightning. I wanted to make her my wife . . . this single desire filled my mind. This was not only lust, as you might think. At that time if I'd had no other desire than lust, I'd surely not have minded knocking her down and running away. Then I wouldn't have stained my sword with his blood. But the moment I gazed at her face in the dark grove, I decided not to leave there without killing him.

But I didn't like to resort to unfair means to kill him. I untied him and told him to cross swords with me. (The rope that was found at the root of the cedar is the rope I dropped at the time.) Furious with anger, he drew his thick sword. And quick as thought, he sprang at me ferociously, without speaking a word. I needn't tell you how our fight turned out. The twenty-third stroke . . . please remember this. I'm impressed with this fact still. Nobody under the sun has ever clashed swords with me twenty strokes. (A cheerful smile.)

When he fell, I turned toward her, lowering my blood-stained sword. But to my great astonishment she was gone. I wondered to where she had run away. I looked for her in the clump of cedars. I listened, but heard only a groaning sound from the throat of the dying man.

As soon as we started to cross swords, she may have run away through the grove to call for help. When I thought of that, I decided it was a matter of life and death to me. So, robbing him of his sword, and bow and arrows, I ran out to the mountain road. There I found her horse still grazing quietly. It would be a mere waste of words to tell you the later details, but before I entered town I had already parted with the sword. That's all my confession. I know that my head will be hung in chains anyway, so put me down for the maximum penalty. (A defiant attitude.)

THE CONFESSION OF A WOMAN WHO HAS COME TO THE *SHIMIZU* TEMPLE

That man in the blue silk kimono, after forcing me to yield to him, laughed mockingly as he looked at my bound husband. How horrified my husband must have been! But no matter how hard he struggled in agony, the rope cut into him all the more tightly. In spite of myself I ran stumblingly toward his side. Or rather I tried to run toward him, but the man instantly knocked me down. Just at that moment I saw an indescribable light in my husband's eyes. Something beyond expression . . . his eyes make me shudder even now. That instantaneous look of my husband, who couldn't speak a word, told me all his heart. The flash in his eyes was neither anger nor sorrow . . . only a cold light, a look of loathing. More struck by the look in his eyes than by the blow of the thief, I called out in spite of myself and fell unconscious.

In the course of time I came to, and found that the man in blue silk was gone. I saw only my husband still bound to the root of the cedar. I raised myself from the bamboo-blades with difficulty, and looked into his face; but the expression in his eyes was just the same as before.

Beneath the cold contempt in his eyes, there was hatred. Shame, grief, and anger . . . I don't know how to express my heart at that time. Reeling to my feet, I went up to my husband.

"Takejiro," I said to him, "since things have come to this pass, I cannot live with you. I'm determined to die, . . . but you must die, too. You saw my shame. I can't leave you alive as you are."

This was all I could say. Still he went on gazing at me with loathing and contempt. My heart breaking, I looked for his sword. It must have been taken by the robber. Neither his sword nor his bow and arrows were to be seen in the grove. But fortunately my small sword was lying at my feet. Raising it over head, once more I said, "Now give me your life. I'll follow you right away."

When he heard these words, he moved his lips with difficulty. Since his mouth was stuffed with leaves, of course his voice could not be heard at all. But at a glance I understood his words. Despising me, his look said only, "Kill me." Neither conscious nor unconscious, I stabbed the small sword through the lilac-colored kimono into his breast.

Again at this time I must have fainted. By the time I managed to look up, he had already breathed his last—still in bonds. A streak of sinking sunlight streamed through the clump of cedars and bamboos, and shone on his pale face. Gulping down my sobs, I untied the rope from his dead body. And . . . and what has become of me since I have no more strength to tell you. Anyway I hadn't the strength to die. I stabbed my own throat with the small sword, I threw myself into a pond at the foot of the mountain, and I tried to kill myself in many ways. Unable to end my life, I am still living in dishonor. (A lonely smile.) Worthless as I am, I must have been forsaken even by the most merciful Kwannon. I killed my own husband. I was violated by the robber. Whatever can I do? Whatever can I . . . I . . . (Gradually, violent sobbing.)

THE STORY OF THE MURDERED MAN, AS TOLD THROUGH A MEDIUM

After violating my wife, the robber, sitting there, began to speak comforting words to her. Of course I couldn't speak. My whole body was tied fast to the root of a cedar. But meanwhile I winked at her many times, as much as to say "Don't believe the robber." I wanted to convey some such meaning to her. But my wife, sitting dejectedly on the bamboo leaves, was looking hard at her lap. To all appearances, she was listening to his words. I was agonized by jealousy. In the meantime the robber went on with his clever talk, from one subject to another. The robber finally made his bold, brazen proposal. "Once your virtue is stained, you won't get along well with your husband, so won't you be my wife instead? It's my love for you that made me be violent toward you."

While the criminal talked, my wife raised her face as if in a trance. She had never looked so beautiful as at that moment. What did my beautiful wife say in answer to him while I was sitting bound there? I am lost in space, but I have never thought of her answer without burning with anger and jealousy. Truly she said, . . . "Then take me away with you wherever you go."

This is not the whole of her sin. If that were all, I would not be tormented so much in the dark. When she was going out of the grove as if in a dream, her hand in the robber's, she suddenly turned pale, and pointed at me tied to the root of the cedar, and said, "Kill him! I cannot marry you as long as he lives." "Kill him!" she cried many times, as if she had gone crazy. Even now these words threaten to blow me headlong into the bottomless abyss of darkness. Has such a hateful thing come out of a human mouth ever before? Have such cursed words ever struck a human ear, even once? Even once such a . . . (A sudden cry of scorn.) At these words the robber himself turned pale. "Kill him," she cried, clinging to his arms. Looking hard at her, he answered neither yes nor no . . . but hardly had I thought about his answer before she had been knocked down into the bamboo leaves. (Again a cry of scorn.) Quietly folding his arms, he looked at me and said, "What will you do with her? Kill her or save her? You have only to nod. Kill her?" For these words alone I would like to pardon his crime.

While I hesitated, she shrieked and ran into the depths of the grove. The robber instantly snatched at her, but he failed even to grasp her sleeve.

After she ran away, he took up my sword, and my bow and arrows. With a single stroke he cut one of my bonds. I remember his mumbling, "My fate is next." Then he disappeared from the grove. All was silent after that. No, I heard someone crying. Untying the rest of my bonds, I listened carefully, and I noticed that it was my own crying. (Long silence.)

I raised my exhausted body from the root of the cedar. In front of me there was shining the small sword which my wife had dropped. I took it up and stabbed it into my breast. A bloody lump rose to my mouth, but I didn't feel any pain. When my breast grew cold, everything was as silent as the dead in their graves. What profound silence! Not a single bird-note was heard in the sky over this grave in the hollow of the mountains. Only a lonely light lingered on the cedars and mountains. By and by the light gradually grew fainter, till the cedars and bamboo were lost to view. Lying there, I was enveloped in deep silence.

Then someone crept up to me. I tried to see who it was. But darkness had already been gathering round me. Someone . . . that someone drew the small sword softly out of my breast in its invisible hand. At the same time once more blood flowed into my mouth. And once and for all I sank down into the darkness of space.

Translated by Takashi Kojima

AKUTAGAWA: *In a Grove (Rashomon)*

1. *What is Akutagawa attempting to do in this story told by multiple narrators? Would the effect be spoiled if he introduced at the end the omniscient author who "knows" the truth?*
2. *Why is this method of multiple narrators appropriate to the subject?*
3. *Why should Tajomaru, the robber, claim that he killed the husband?*
4. *Why should the wife claim that she killed her husband?*
5. *Why should the husband claim to have committed suicide?*

6. *Which version is the truth?*

7. *The ghost of the murdered man tells his story through a medium. Does the introduction of this supernatural device disturb the realistic surface of the story?*

8. *What elements in this Japanese story distinguish it from a Western narrative?*

9. *Osamu Shimizu writes of Akutagawa: "He hated moralists, but was himself a moralist of considerable sincerity." What if any is the "moral" of the story?*

10. *When one learns that this story was expanded into a two-hour motion picture and a three-hour play, he is reminded of Ernest Hemingway's statement: "The dignity of movement of an iceberg is due to only one-eighth of it being above water." If you were directing the motion picture, what subsurface elements would you dramatize or make more explicit? Would you be adding to or detracting from the effect of the original?*

Isaac Babel

MY FIRST GOOSE

> *Isaac Emmanuilovich Babel was born in Odessa, Russia, in 1894, a time when Russian oppression against the Jews was particularly severe. Nevertheless, Odessan Jews remained relatively free, and Babel was able to pick up much material there that he incorporated into* Tales of Odessa *(1924). By 1915, he was ready to attempt the life of a writer and went to St. Petersburg, where his fortunes remained poor until Maxim Gorki discovered him and published two of his stories. Under Gorki's counsel, Babel sought out a life of adventure, and toward this end joined the Czar's army; his service in Poland led to his most famous collection of stories,* Red Cavalry *(1926), from which "My First Goose" is taken. Until his death, reputedly in a Russian concentration camp, in 1939 or 1940, Babel went through the vicissitudes of most Russian writers in the thirties who tried to retain their individual voices. "My First Goose" is typical of Babel's Cossack tales in that it shows how he, an intellectual and a Jew, attempted to come to terms with the violence and primitivism of these fierce soldiers who honored only a man's ability to fight.*

SAVITSKY, Commander of the VI Division, rose when he saw me, and I wondered at the beauty of his giant's body. He rose, the purple of his riding breeches and the crimson of his little tilted cap and the decorations stuck on his chest cleaving the hut as a standard cleaves the sky. A smell of scent and the sickly sweet freshness of soap emanated from him. His long legs were like girls sheathed to the neck in shining riding boots.

He smiled at me, struck his riding whip on the table, and drew toward him an order that the Chief of Staff had just finished dictating. It was an order for Ivan Chesnokov to advance on Chugunov-Dobryvodka with the regiment entrusted to him, to make contact with the enemy and destroy the same.

"For which destruction," the Commander began to write, smearing the whole sheet, "I make this same Chesnokov entirely responsible, up to and including the supreme penalty, and will if necessary strike him down on the spot; which you, Chesnokov, who have been working with me at the front for some months now, cannot doubt."

[327

The Commander signed the order with a flourish, tossed it to his orderlies and turned upon me gray eyes that danced with merriment.

I handed him a paper with my appointment to the Staff of the Division.

"Put it down in the Order of the Day," said the Commander. "Put him down for every satisfaction save the front one. Can you read and write?"

"Yes, I can read and write," I replied, envying the flower and iron of that youthfulness. "I graduated in law from St. Petersburg University."

"Oh, are you one of those grinds?" he laughed. "Specs on your nose, too! What a nasty little object! They've sent you along without making any enquiries; and this is a hot place for specs. Think you'll get on with us?"

"I'll get on all right," I answered, and went off to the village with the quartermaster to find a billet for the night.

The quartermaster carried my trunk on his shoulder. Before us stretched the village street. The dying sun, round and yellow as a pumpkin was giving up its roseate ghost to the skies.

We went up to a hut painted over with garlands. The quartermaster stopped, and said suddenly, with a guilty smile:

"Nuisance with specs. Can't do anything to stop it, either. Not a life for the brainy type here. But you go and mess up a lady, and a good lady too, and you'll have the boys patting you on the back."

He hesitated, my little trunk on his shoulder; then he came quite close to me, only to dart away again despairingly and run to the nearest yard. Cossacks were sitting there, shaving one another.

"Here, you soldiers," said the quartermaster, setting my little trunk down on the ground. "Comrade Savitsky's orders are that you're to take this chap in your billets, so no nonsense about it, because the chap's been through a lot in the learning line."

The quartermaster, purple in the face, left us without looking back. I raised my hand to my cap and saluted the Cossacks. A lad with long straight flaxen hair and the handsome face of the Ryazan Cossacks went over to my little trunk and tossed it out at the gate. Then he turned his back on me and with remarkable skill emitted a series of shameful noises.

"To your guns—number double-zero!" an older Cossack shouted at him, and burst out laughing. "Running fire!"

His guileless art exhausted, the lad made off. Then, crawling over the ground, I began to gather together the manuscripts and tattered garments that had fallen out of the trunk. I gathered them up and carried them to the other end of the yard. Near the hut, on a brick stove, stood a cauldron in which pork was cooking. The steam that rose from it was like the far-off smoke of home in the village, and it mingled hunger with desperate loneliness in my head. Then I covered my little broken trunk with hay, turning it into a pillow, and lay down on the ground to read in *Pravda* Lenin's speech at the Second Congress of the Comintern. The sun fell upon me from behind the toothed hillocks, the Cossacks trod on my feet, the lad made fun of me untiringly, the beloved lines came toward me along a thorny path and could not reach me. Then I put aside the paper and went out to the landlady, who was spinning on the porch.

"Landlady," I said, "I've got to eat."

The old woman raised to me the diffused whites of her purblind eyes and lowered them again.

"Comrade," she said, after a pause, "what with all this going on, I want to go and hang myself."

"Christ!" I muttered, and pushed the old woman in the chest with my fist. "You don't suppose I'm going to go into explanations with you, do you?"

And turning around I saw somebody's sword lying within reach. A severe-looking goose was waddling about the yard, inoffensively preening its feathers. I overtook it and pressed it to the ground. Its head cracked beneath my boot, cracked and emptied itself. The white neck lay stretched out in the dung, the wings twitched.

"Christ!" I said, digging into the goose with my sword. "Go and cook it for me, landlady."

Her blind eyes and glasses glistening, the old woman picked up the slaughtered bird, wrapped it in her apron, and started to bear it off toward the kitchen.

"Comrade," she said to me, after a while, "I want to go and hang myself." And she closed the door behind her.

The Cossacks in the yard were already sitting around their cauldron. They sat motionless, stiff as heathen priests at a sacrifice, and had not looked at the goose.

"The lad's all right," one of them said, winking and scooping up the cabbage soup with his spoon.

The Cossacks commenced their supper with all the elegance and restraint of peasants who respect one another. And I wiped the sword with sand, went out at the gate, and came in again, depressed. Already the moon hung above the yard like a cheap earring.

"Hey, you," suddenly said Surovkov, an older Cossack. "Sit down and feed with us till your goose is done."

He produced a spare spoon from his boot and handed it to me. We supped up the cabbage soup they had made, and ate the pork.

"What's in the newspaper?" asked the flaxen-haired lad, making room for me.

"Lenin writes in the paper," I said, pulling out *Pravda*. "Lenin writes that there's a shortage of everything."

And loudly, like a triumphant man hard of hearing, I read Lenin's speech out to the Cossacks.

Evening wrapped about me the quickening moisture of its twilight sheets; evening laid a mother's hand upon my burning forehead. I read on and rejoiced, spying out exultingly the secret curve of Lenin's straight line.

"Truth tickles everyone's nostrils," said Surovkov, when I had come to the end. "The question is, how's it to be pulled from the heap. But he goes and strikes at it straight off like a hen pecking at a grain!"

This remark about Lenin was made by Surovkov, platoon commander of the Staff Squadron; after which we lay down to sleep in the hayloft. We slept, all six of us, beneath a wooden roof that let in the stars, warming one another, our legs intermingled. I dreamed: and in my dreams saw women. But my heart, stained with bloodshed, grated and brimmed over.

Translated by Walter Morison

BABEL: *My First Goose*

1. If we call this a story of initiation, what do we mean? Into what is the narrator initiated? What does he gain? What does he lose?

2. How does Babel indicate the differences between the narrator and the regular Cossacks with whom he is billeted?

3. What purpose is served by the lyrical description of Savitsky at the beginning of the story?

4. Why do the Cossacks accept the narrator only after he kills the goose?

5. Does Babel seem to argue that violence and brutality provide the sole possible way to exist?

6. What purpose does the old woman serve?

7. Compare the descriptions at the beginning and the end of the story: What point does Babel seem to be making about people?

8. Does the brutality of the story shock you? If it does not, how does Babel manage to blunt the sheer ferocity of the event?

William Faulkner

DRY SEPTEMBER

Born in 1897 in New Albany, Mississippi, about thirty-five miles from Oxford (the Yoknapatawpha County of many of his novels and stories), William Faulkner has been generally regarded as the leading exponent of the Southern school of writing, as well as, possibly, America's finest novelist of the twentieth century. Although he began as a poet, he early turned to fiction, with Soldiers' Pay *(1926),* Mosquitoes *(1927), and* Sartoris *(1929). But it was not until his "golden period," from* The Sound and the Fury *(in 1929) to* A Fable *(in 1954), that he found his proper subject matter; and his novels and stories of this twenty-five-year stretch are a roll call of major work:* As I Lay Dying *(1930);* Sanctuary *(1931);* Light in August *(1932);* Absalom, Absalom! *(1936);* The Wild Palms *(1938);* The Hamlet *(1940);* Go Down, Moses and Other Stories *(1942); as well as the numerous stories published in 1950 as* Collected Stories. *Faulkner's subject matter is a sensitive, anguished, tortured examination of a South forced to reevaluate itself as it and the world slowly change. His is a grand, almost panoramic theme because it encompasses decline and decay, the deterioration of an entire culture, even as another is growing to replace it; and it also involves the agony of racial relationships which Faulkner recognized as a festering wound in the Southern body politic. In 1950 Faulkner was awarded the Nobel Prize for Literature. He died, in Oxford, Mississippi, in 1962.*

I

THROUGH the bloody September twilight, aftermath of sixty-two rainless days, it had gone like a fire in dry grass—the rumor, the story, whatever it was. Something about Miss Minnie Cooper and a Negro. Attacked, insulted, frightened: none of them, gathered in the barber shop on that Saturday evening where the ceiling fan stirred, without freshening it, the vitiated air, sending back upon them, in recurrent surges of stale pomade and lotion, their own stale breath and odors, knew exactly what had happened.

[331

"Except it wasn't Will Mayes," a barber said. He was a man of middle age; a thin, sand-colored man with a mild face, who was shaving a client. "I know Will Mayes. He's a good nigger. And I know Miss Minnie Cooper, too."

"What do you know about her?" a second barber said.

"Who is she?" the client said. "A young girl?"

"No," the barber said. "She's about forty, I reckon. She aint married. That's why I dont believe—"

"Believe, hell!" a hulking youth in a sweat-stained silk shirt said. "Wont you take a white woman's word before a nigger's?"

"I dont believe Will Mayes did it," the barber said. "I know Will Mayes."

"Maybe you know who did it, then. Maybe you already got him out of town, you damn niggerlover."

"I dont believe anybody did anything. I dont believe anything happened. I leave it to you fellows if them ladies that get old without getting married dont have notions that a man cant—"

"Then you are a hell of a white man," the client said. He moved under the cloth. The youth had sprung to his feet.

"You dont?" he said. "Do you accuse a white woman of lying?"

The barber held the razor poised above the half-risen client. He did not look around.

"It's this durn weather," another said. "It's enough to make a man do anything. Even to her."

Nobody laughed. The barber said in his mild, stubborn tone: "I aint accusing nobody of nothing. I just know and you fellows know how a woman that never—"

"You damn niggerlover!" the youth said.

"Shut up, Butch," another said. "We'll get the facts in plenty of time to act."

"Who is? Who's getting them?" the youth said. "Facts, hell! I—"

"You're a fine white man," the client said. "Aint you?" In his frothy beard he looked like a desert rat in the moving pictures. "You tell them, Jack," he said to the youth. "If there aint any white men in this town, you can count on me, even if I aint only a drummer and a stranger."

"That's right, boys," the barber said. "Find out the truth first. I know Will Mayes."

"Well, by God!" the youth shouted. "To think that a white man in this town—"

"Shut up, Butch," the second speaker said. "We got plenty of time."

The client sat up. He looked at the speaker. "Do you claim that anything excuses a nigger attacking a white woman? Do you mean to tell me you are a white man and you'll stand for it? You better go back North where you came from. The South dont want your kind here."

"North what?" the second said. "I was born and raised in this town."

"Well, by God!" the youth said. He looked about with a strained, baffled gaze, as if he was trying to remember what it was he wanted to say or to do. He drew his sleeve across his sweating face. "Damn if I'm going to let a white woman—"

"You tell them, Jack," the drummer said. "By God, if they—"

The screen door crashed open. A man stood in the floor, his feet apart and his heavy-set body poised easily. His white shirt was open at the throat; he wore a felt hat. His hot, bold glance swept the group. His name was McLendon. He had commanded troops at the front in France and had been decorated for valor.

"Well," he said, "are you going to sit there and let a black son rape a white woman on the streets of Jefferson?"

Butch sprang up again. The silk of his shirt clung flat to his heavy shoulders. At each armpit was a dark halfmoon. "That's what I been telling them! That's what I—"

"Did it really happen?" a third said. "This aint the first man scare she ever had, like Hawkshaw says. Wasn't there something about a man on the kitchen roof, watching her undress, about a year ago?"

"What?" the client said. "What's that?" The barber had been slowly forcing him back into the chair; he arrested himself reclining, his head lifted, the barber still pressing him down.

McLendon whirled on the third speaker. "Happen? What the hell difference does it make? Are you going to let the black sons get away with it until one really does it?"

"That's what I'm telling them!" Butch shouted. He cursed, long and steady, pointless.

"Here, here," a fourth said. "Not so loud. Dont talk so loud."

"Sure," McLendon said; "No talking necessary at all. I've done my talking. Who's with me?" He poised on the balls of his feet, roving his gaze.

The barber held the drummer's face down, the razor poised. "Find out the facts first, boys. I know Willy Mayes. It wasn't him. Let's get the sheriff and do this thing right."

McLendon whirled upon him his furious, rigid face. The barber did not look away. They looked like men of different races. The other barbers had ceased also above their prone clients. "You mean to tell me," McLendon said, "that you'd take a nigger's word before a white woman's? Why, you damn niggerloving—"

The third speaker rose and grasped McLendon's arm; he too had been a soldier. "Now, now. Let's figure this thing out. Who knows anything about what really happened?"

"Figure out hell!" McLendon jerked his arm free. "All that're with me get up from there. The ones that aint—" He roved his gaze, dragging his sleeve across his face.

Three men rose. The drummer in the chair sat up. "Here," he said, jerking at the cloth about his neck; "get this rag off me. I'm with him. I dont live here, but by God, if our mothers and wives and sisters—" He smeared the cloth over his face and flung it to the floor. McLendon stood in the floor and cursed the others. Another rose and moved toward him. The remainder sat uncomfortable, not looking at one another, then one by one they rose and joined him.

The barber picked the cloth from the floor. He began to fold it neatly. "Boys, dont do that. Will Mayes never done it. I know."

"Come on," McLendon said. He whirled. From his hip pocket protruded the butt of a heavy automatic pistol. They went out. The screen door crashed behind them reverberant in the dead air.

The barber wiped the razor carefully and swiftly, and put it away, and ran to the rear, and took his hat from the wall. "I'll be back as soon as I can," he said to the other barbers. "I cant let—" He went out, running. The two other barbers followed him to the door and caught it on the rebound, leaning out and looking up the street after him. The air was flat and dead. It had a metallic taste at the base of the tongue.

"What can he do?" the first said. The second one was saying "Jees Christ, Jees Christ" under his breath. "I'd just as lief be Will Mayes as Hawk, if he gets McLendon riled."

"Jees Christ, Jees Christ," the second whispered.

"You reckon he really done it to her?" the first said.

II

She was thirty-eight or thirty-nine. She lived in a small frame house with her invalid mother and a thin, sallow, unflagging aunt, where each morning between ten and eleven she would appear on the porch in a lace-trimmed boudoir cap, to sit swinging in the porch swing until noon. After dinner she lay down for a while, until the afternoon began to cool.

Then, in one of the three or four new voile dresses which she had each summer, she would go downtown to spend the afternoon in the stores with the other ladies, where they would handle the goods and haggle over the prices in cold, immediate voices, without any intention of buying.

She was of comfortable people—not the best in Jefferson, but good people enough—and she was still on the slender side of ordinary looking, with a bright, faintly haggard manner and dress. When she was young she had had a slender, nervous body and a sort of hard vivacity which had enabled her for a time to ride upon the crest of the town's social life as exemplified by the high school party and church social period conscious.

She was the last to realize that she was losing ground; that those among whom she had been a little brighter and louder flame than any other were beginning to learn the pleasure of snobbery—male—and retaliation—female. That was when her face began to wear that bright, haggard look. She still carried it to parties on shadowy porticoes and summer lawns, like a mask or a flag, with that bafflement of furious repudiation of truth in her eyes. One evening at a party she heard a boy and two girls, all schoolmates, talking. She never accepted another invitation.

She watched the girls with whom she had grown up as they married and got homes and children, but no man ever called on her steadily until the children of the other girls had been calling her "aunty" for several years, the while their mothers told them in bright voices about how popular Aunt Minnie had been as a girl. Then the town began to see her driving on Sunday afternoons with the cashier in the bank. He was a widower of about forty—a high-colored man, smelling always faintly of the barber shop or of whisky. He owned the first automobile in town, a red runabout; Minnie had the first motoring bonnet and veil the town ever saw. Then the town began to say: "Poor Minnie." "But she is old enough to take care of herself," others said. That was when she began to ask her old schoolmates that their children call her "cousin" instead of "aunty."

It was twelve years now since she had been relegated into adultery by public opinion, and eight years since the cashier had gone to a Memphis bank, returning for one day each Christmas, which he spent at an annual bachelors' party at a hunting club on the river. From behind their curtains the neighbors would see the party pass, and during the over-the-way Christmas day visiting they would tell her about him, about how well he looked, and how they heard that he was prospering in the city, watching with bright, secret eyes her haggard, bright face. Usually by that hour there would be the scent of whisky on her breath. It was supplied her by a youth, a clerk at the soda fountain: "Sure; I buy it for the old gal. I reckon she's entitled to a little fun."

Her mother kept to her room altogether now; the gaunt aunt ran the house. Against that background Minnie's bright dresses, her idle and empty days, had a quality of furious unreality. She went out in the evenings only with women now, neighbors, to the moving pictures. Each afternoon she dressed in one of the new dresses and went downtown alone, where her young "cousins" were already strolling in the late afternoons with their delicate, silken heads and thin, awkward arms and conscious hips, clinging to one another or shrieking and giggling with paired boys in the soda fountain when she passed and went on along the serried store fronts, in the doors of which the sitting and lounging men did not even follow her with their eyes any more.

III

The barber went swiftly up the street where the sparse lights, insect-swirled, glared in rigid and violent suspension in the lifeless air. The day had died in a pall of dust; above the darkened square, shrouded by the spent dust, the sky was as clear as the inside of a brass bell. Below the east was a rumor of the twice-waxed moon.

When he overtook them McLendon and three others were getting into a car parked in an alley. McLendon stooped his thick head, peering out beneath the top. "Changed your mind, did you?" he said. "Damn good thing; by God, tomorrow when this town hears about how you talked tonight—"

"Now, now," the other ex-soldier said. "Hawkshaw's all right. Come on, Hawk; jump in."

"Will Mayes never done it, boys," the barber said. "If anybody done it. Why, you all know well as I do there aint any town where they got better niggers than us. And you know how a lady will kind of think things about men when there aint any reason to, and Miss Minnie anyway—"

"Sure, sure," the soldier said. "We're just going to talk to him a little; that's all."

"Talk hell!" Butch said. "When we're through with the—"

"Shut up, for God's sake!" the soldier said. "Do you want everybody in town—"

"Tell them, by God!" McLendon said. "Tell every one of the sons that'll let a white woman—"

"Let's go; let's go: here's the other car." The second car slid squealing out of a cloud of dust at the alley mouth. McLendon started his car and took the lead. Dust lay like fog in the street. The street lights hung nimbused as in water. They drove on out of town.

A rutted lane turned at right angles. Dust hung above it too, and above all the land. The dark bulk of the ice plant, where the Negro Mayes was night watchman, rose against the sky. "Better stop here, hadn't we?" the soldier said. McLendon did not reply. He hurled the car up and slammed to a stop, the headlights glaring on the blank wall.

"Listen here, boys," the barber said; "if he's here, dont that prove he never done it? Dont it? If it was him, he would run. Dont you see he would?" The second car came up and stopped. McLendon got down; Butch sprang down beside him. "Listen, boys," the barber said.

"Cut the lights off!" McLendon said. The breathless dark rushed down. There was no sound in it save their lungs as they sought air in the parched dust in which for two months they had lived; then the diminishing crunch of McLendon's and Butch's feet, and a moment later McLendon's voice:

"Will! . . . Will!"

Below the east the wan hemorrhage of the moon increased. It heaved above the ridge, silvering the air, the dust, so that they seemed to breathe, live, in a bowl of molten lead. There was no sound of nightbird nor insect, no sound save their breathing and a faint ticking of contracting metal about the cars. Where their bodies touched one another they seemed to sweat dryly, for no more moisture came. "Christ!" a voice said; "let's get out of here."

But they didn't move until vague noises began to grow out of the darkness ahead; then they got out and waited tensely in the breathless dark. There was another sound: a blow, a hissing expulsion of breath and McLendon cursing in undertone. They stood a moment longer, then they ran forward. They ran in a stumbling clump, as though they were fleeing something. "Kill him, kill the son," a voice whispered. McLendon flung them back.

"Not here," he said. "Get him into the car." "Kill him kill the black son!" the voice murmured. They dragged the Negro to the car. The barber had waited beside the car. He could feel himself sweating and he knew he was going to be sick at the stomach.

"What is it, captains?" the Negro said. "I aint done nothing. 'Fore God, Mr John." Someone produced handcuffs. They worked busily about the Negro as though he were a post, quiet, intent, getting in one another's way. He submitted to the handcuffs, looking swiftly and constantly from dim face to dim face. "Who's here, captains?" he said, leaning to peer into the faces until they could feel his breath and smell his sweaty reek. He spoke a name or two. "What you all say I done, Mr John?"

McLendon jerked the car door open. "Get in!" he said.

The Negro did not move. "What you all going to do with me, Mr John? I aint done nothing. White folks, captains, I aint done nothing: I swear 'fore God." He called another name.

"Get in!" McLendon said. He struck the Negro. The others expelled their breath in a dry hissing and struck him with random blows and he whirled and cursed them, and swept his manacled hands across their faces and slashed the barber upon the mouth, and the barber struck him also. "Get him in there," McLendon said. They pushed at him. He ceased struggling and got in and sat quietly as the others took their places. He sat between the barber and the soldier, drawing his limbs in so as not to touch them, his eyes going swiftly and constantly from face to face. Butch clung to the running board. The car moved on. The barber nursed his mouth with his handkerchief.

"What's the matter, Hawk?" the soldier said.

"Nothing," the barber said. They regained the highroad and turned away from town. The second car dropped back out of the dust. They went on, gaining speed; the final fringe of houses dropped behind.

"Goddamn, he stinks!" the soldier said.

"We'll fix that," the drummer in front beside McLendon said. On the running board Butch cursed into the hot rush of air. The barber leaned suddenly forward and touched McLendon's arm.

"Let me out, John," he said.

"Jump out, niggerlover," McLendon said without turning his head. He drove swiftly. Behind them the sourceless lights of the second car glared in the dust. Presently McLendon turned into a narrow road. It was rutted with disuse. It led back to an abandoned brick kiln—a series of reddish mounds and weed- and vine-choked vats without bottom. It had been used for pasture once, until one day the owner missed one of his mules. Although he prodded carefully in the vats with a long pole, he could not even find the bottom of them.

"John," the barber said.

"Jump out, then," McLendon said, hurling the car along the ruts. Beside the barber the Negro spoke:

"Mr Henry."

The barber sat forward. The narrow tunnel of the road rushed up and past. Their motion was like an extinct furnace blast: cooler, but utterly dead. The car bounded from rut to rut.

"Mr Henry," the Negro said.

The barber began to tug furiously at the door. "Look out, there!" the soldier said, but the barber had already kicked the door open and swung onto the running board. The soldier leaned across the Negro and grasped at him, but he had already jumped. The car went on without checking speed.

The impetus hurled him crashing through dust-sheathed weeds, into the ditch. Dust puffed about him, and in a thin, vicious crackling of sapless stems he lay choking and retching until the second car passed and died away. Then he rose and limped on until he reached the highroad and turned toward town, brushing at his clothes with his hands. The moon was higher, riding high and clear of the dust at last, and after a while the town began to glare beneath the dust. He went on, limping. Presently he heard cars and the glow of them grew in the dust behind him and he left the road and crouched again in the weeds until they passed. McLendon's car came last now. There were four people in it and Butch was not on the running board.

They went on; the dust swallowed them; the glare and the sound died away. The dust of them hung for a while, but soon the eternal dust absorbed it again. The barber climbed back onto the road and limped on toward town.

IV

As she dressed for supper on that Saturday evening, her own flesh felt like fever. Her hands trembled among the hooks and eyes, and her eyes had a feverish look, and her hair swirled crisp and crackling under the comb. While she was still dressing the friends called for her and sat while she donned her sheerest underthings and stockings and a new voile dress. "Do you feel strong enough to go out?" they said, their eyes bright too, with a dark glitter. "When you have had time to get over the shock, you must tell us what happened. What he said and did; everything."

In the leafed darkness, as they walked toward the square, she began to breathe deeply, something like a swimmer preparing to dive, until she ceased trembling, the four of them walking slowly because of the terrible heat and out of solicitude for her. But as they neared the square she began to tremble again, walking with her head up, her hands clenched at her sides, their voices about her murmurous, also with that feverish, glittering quality of their eyes.

They entered the square, she in the center of the group, fragile in her fresh dress. She was trembling worse. She walked slower and slower, as children eat ice cream, her head up and her eyes bright in the haggard banner of her face, passing the hotel and the coatless drummers in chairs along the curb looking around at her: "That's the one: see? The one in pink in the middle." "Is that her? What did they do with the nigger? Did they—?" "Sure. He's all right." "All right, is he?" "Sure. He went on a little trip." Then the drug store, where even the young men lounging in the doorway tipped their hats and followed with their eyes the motion of her hips and legs when she passed.

They went on, passing the lifted hats of the gentlemen, the suddenly ceased voices, deferent, protective. "Do you see?" the friends said. Their voices sounded like long, hovering sighs of hissing exultation. "There's not a Negro on the square. Not one."

They reached the picture show. It was like a miniature fairyland with its lighted lobby and colored lithographs of life caught in its terrible and beautiful mutations. Her lips began to tingle. In the dark, when the picture began, it would be all right; she could hold back the laughing so it would not waste away so fast and so soon. So she hurried on before the turning faces, the undertones of low astonishment, and they took their accustomed places where she could see the aisle against the silver glare and the young men and girls coming in two and two against it.

The lights flicked away; the screen glowed silver, and soon life began to unfold, beautiful and passionate and sad, while still the young men and girls entered, scented and sibilant in the half dark, their paired backs in silhouette delicate and sleek, their slim, quick bodies awkward, divinely young, while beyond them the silver dream accumulated, inevitably on and on. She began to laugh. In trying to suppress it, it made more noise than ever; heads began to turn. Still laughing, her friends raised her and led her out, and she stood at the curb, laughing on a high, sustained note, until the taxi came up and they helped her in.

They removed the pink voile and the sheer underthings and the stockings, and put her to bed, and cracked ice for her temples, and sent for the doctor. He was hard to locate, so they ministered to her with hushed ejaculations, renewing the ice and fanning her. While the ice was fresh and cold she stopped laughing and lay still for a time, moaning only a little. But soon the laughing welled again and her voice rose screaming.

"Shhhhhhhhhhh! Shhhhhhhhhhhhhh!" they said, freshening the icepack, smoothing her hair, examining it for gray; "poor girl!" Then to one another: "Do you suppose anything really happened?" their eyes darkly aglitter, secret and passionate. "Shhhhhhhhhh! Poor girl! Poor Minnie!"

V

It was midnight when McLendon drove up to his neat new house. It was trim and fresh as a birdcage and almost as small, with its clean, green-and-white paint. He locked the car and mounted the porch and entered. His wife rose from a chair beside the reading lamp. McLendon stopped in the floor and stared at her until she looked down.

"Look at that clock," he said, lifting his arm, pointing. She stood before him, her face lowered, a magazine in her hands. Her face was pale, strained, and weary-looking. "Haven't I told you about sitting up like this, waiting to see when I come in?"

"John," she said. She laid the magazine down. Poised on the balls of his feet, he glared at her with his hot eyes, his sweating face.

"Didn't I tell you?" He went toward her. She looked up then. He caught her shoulder. She stood passive, looking at him.

"Don't, John. I couldn't sleep . . . The heat; something. Please, John. You're hurting me."

"Didn't I tell you?" He released her and half struck, half flung her across the chair, and she lay there and watched him quietly as he left the room.

He went on through the house, ripping off his shirt, and on the dark, screened porch at the rear he stood and mopped his head and shoulders with the shirt and flung it away. He took the pistol from his hip and laid it on the table beside the bed, and sat on the bed and removed his shoes, and rose and slipped his trousers off. He was sweating again already, and he stooped and hunted furiously for the shirt. At last he found it and wiped his body again, and, with his body pressed against the dusty screen, he stood panting. There was no movement, no sound, not even an insect. The dark world seemed to lie stricken beneath the cold moon and the lidless stars.

FAULKNER: *Dry September*

1. Although the details of Faulkner's story appear to involve an earlier time in Southern white and black relationships, do you find any contemporary application? Does Faulkner view such relationships as stereotypes, or does he understand both the black and white characters?
2. Why is there such a stress on dryness? Or the weather?
3. Why is a barber shop used for the opening scene? What does this tell you about the locale? About the characters? About the quality of life?
4. Characterize the barber: the hangers-on at his shop; Minnie Cooper.
5. McLendon is a complicated individual. When you characterize him, what do you know of him personally (or psychologically), socially, politically? Why does he murder a black man who he knows is innocent of any crime?
6. Does Will Mayes take on qualities of his own, or is his role only to be a victim? Contrast Wright's black sailor in "Big Black Good Man"—is the difference in conception simply because Wright was himself black and Faulkner white? Or are there other assumptions at stake?
7. The story has, as it were, two endings: Part IV, with Minnie Cooper: Part V, with McLendon. Is her hysterical laugh somehow connected to his violence with his wife? Parts II and IV belong to Minnie Cooper. Why does Faulkner structure the story as he does?
8. How does the final paragraph make a political statement about the South? About all racial relationships?
9. A Faulkner novel is called *Light in August.* Does the *"September"* of the title seem to have special meaning?
10. Do you see anything in this story to justify James Baldwin's accusation that Faulkner was an unconscious racist?

Ernest Hemingway

THE BATTLER

> *Born in Illinois in 1899, Ernest Hemingway began his career as a journalist. His first novel,* The Sun Also Rises *(1926), as well as* A Farewell to Arms *(1929) and several dozen vigorous and terse short stories, quickly established him as a major author. His succinct prose style was soon found in the work of a hundred writers, but Hemingway's remained unique, inimitable. Although his later work, that of the 1940's and 1950's, rarely attained the clarity and power of his early novels and stories, his reputation has remained high. "The Battler" comes from a series of short fictions,* In Our Time, *published in 1925. These little masterpieces more or less set the standard for the American short story for the next two generations. Hemingway was awarded the Nobel Prize for Literature in 1954 and died in 1961, a suicide.*

NICK stood up. He was all right. He looked up the track at the lights of the caboose going out of sight around the curve. There was water on both sides of the track, then tamarack swamp.

He felt of his knee. The pants were torn and the skin was barked. His hands were scraped and there were sand and cinders driven up under his nails. He went over to the edge of the track down the little slope to the water and washed his hands. He washed them carefully in the cold water, getting the dirt out from the nails. He squatted down and bathed his knee.

That lousy crut of a brakeman. He would get him some day. He would know him again. That was a fine way to act.

"Come here, kid," he said. "I got something for you."

He had fallen for it. What a lousy kid thing to have done. They would never suck him in that way again.

"Come here, kid, I got something for you." Then *wham* and he lit on his hands and knees beside the track.

Nick rubbed his eye. There was a big bump coming up. He would have a black eye, all right. It ached already. That son of a crutting brakeman.

He touched the bump over his eye with his fingers. Oh, well, it was only a black eye. That was all he had gotten out of it. Cheap at the price. He wished he could see it. Could not see it looking into the water, though. It was dark and he was a long way off from anywhere. He wiped his hands on his trousers and stood up, then climbed the embankment to the rails.

He started up the track. It was well ballasted and made easy walking, sand and gravel packed between the ties, solid walking. The smooth roadbed like a causeway went on ahead through the swamp. Nick walked along. He must get to somewhere.

Nick had swung on to the freight train when it slowed down for the yards outside of Walton Junction. The train, with Nick on it, had passed through Kalkaska as it started to get dark. Now he must be nearly to Mancelona. Three or four miles of swamp. He stepped along the track, walking so he kept on the ballast between the ties, the swamp ghostly in the rising mist. His eye ached and he was hungry. He kept on hiking, putting the miles of track back of him. The swamp was all the same on both sides of the track.

Ahead there was a bridge. Nick crossed it, his boots ringing hollow on the iron. Down below the water showed black between the slits of ties. Nick kicked a loose spike and it dropped into the water. Beyond the bridge were hills. It was high and dark on both sides of the track. Up the track Nick saw a fire.

He came up the track toward the fire carefully. It was off to one side of the track, below the railway embankment. He had only seen the light from it. The track came out through a cut and where the fire was burning the country opened out and fell away into woods. Nick dropped carefully down the embankment and cut into the woods to come up to the fire through the trees. It was a beechwood forest and the fallen beechnut burrs were under his shoes as he walked between the trees. The fire was bright now, just at the edge of the trees. There was a man sitting by it. Nick waited behind the tree and watched. The man looked to be alone. He was sitting there with his head in his hands looking at the fire. Nick stepped out and walked into the firelight.

The man sat there looking into the fire. When Nick stopped quite close to him he did not move.

"Hello!" Nick said.

The man looked up.

"Where did you get the shiner?" he said.

"A brakeman busted me."

"Off the through freight?"

"Yes."

"I saw the bastard," the man said. "He went through here 'bout an hour and a half ago. He was walking along the top of the cars slapping his arms and singing."

"The bastard!"

"It must have made him feel good to bust you," the man said seriously.

"I'll bust him."

"Get him with a rock sometime when he's going through," the man advised.

"I'll get him."

"You're a tough one, aren't you?"

"No," Nick answered.

"All you kids are tough."

"You got to be tough," Nick said.

"That's what I said."

The man looked at Nick and smiled. In the firelight Nick saw that his face was misshapen. His nose was sunken, his eyes were slits, he had queer-shaped lips. Nick did not perceive all this at once, he only saw the man's face was queerly formed and mutilated. It was like putty in color. Dead looking in the firelight.

"Don't you like my pan?" the man asked.

Nick was embarrassed.

"Sure," he said.

"Look here!" the man took off his cap.

He had only one ear. It was thickened and tight against the side of his head. Where the other ear should have been there was a stump.

"Ever see one like that?"

"No," said Nick. It made him a little sick.

"I could take it," the man said. "Don't you think I could take it, kid?"

"You bet!"

"They all bust their hands on me," the little man said. "They couldn't hurt me."

He looked at Nick. "Sit down," he said. "Want to eat?"

"Don't bother," Nick said. "I'm going on to the town."

"Listen!" the man said. "Call me Ad."

"Sure!"

"Listen," the little man said. "I'm not quite right."

"What's the matter?"

"I'm crazy."

He put on his cap. Nick felt like laughing.

"You're all right," he said.

"No, I'm not. I'm crazy. Listen, you ever been crazy?"

"No," Nick said. "How does it get you?"

"I don't know," Ad said. "When you got it you don't know about it. You know me, don't you?"

"No."

"I'm Ad Francis."

"Honest to God?"

"Don't you believe it?"

"Yes."

Nick knew it must be true.

"You know how I beat them?"

"No," Nick said.

"My heart's slow. It only beats forty a minute. Feel it."

Nick hesitated.

"Come on," the man took hold of his hand. "Take hold of my wrist. Put your fingers there."

The little man's wrist was thick and the muscles bulged above the bone. Nick felt the slow pumping under his fingers.

"Got a watch?"

"No."

"Neither have I," Ad said. "It ain't any good if you haven't got a watch."

Nick dropped his wrist.

"Listen," Ad Francis said. "Take ahold again. You count and I'll count up to sixty."

Feeling the slow hard throb under his fingers Nick started to count. Heard the little man counting slowly, one, two, three, four, five, and on—aloud.

"Sixty," Ad finished. "That's a minute. What did you make it?"

"Forty," Nick said.

"That's right," Ad said happily. "She never speeds up."

A man dropped down the railroad embankment and came across the clearing to the fire.

"Hello, Bugs!" Ad said.

"Hello!" Bugs answered. It was a negro's voice. Nick knew from the way he walked that he was a negro. He stood with his back to them, bending over the fire. He straightened up.

"This is my pal Bugs," Ad said. "He's crazy, too."

"Glad to meet you," Bugs said. "Where you say you're from?"

"Chicago," Nick said.

"That's a fine town," the negro said. "I didn't catch your name."

"Adams. Nick Adams."

"He says he's never been crazy, Bugs," Ad said.

"He's got a lot coming to him," the negro said. He was unwrapping a package by the fire.

"When are we going to eat, Bugs?" the prizefighter asked.

"Right away."

"Are you hungry, Nick?"

"Hungry as hell."

"Hear that, Bugs?"

"I hear most of what goes on."

"That ain't what I asked you."

"Yes. I heard what the gentleman said."

Into a skillet he was laying slices of ham. As the skillet grew hot the grease sputtered and Bugs, crouching on long nigger legs over the fire, turned the ham and broke eggs into the skillet, tipping it from side to side to baste the eggs with the hot fat.

"Will you cut some bread out of that bag, Mister Adams?" Bugs turned from the fire.

"Sure."

Nick reached in the bag and brought out a loaf of bread. He cut six slices. Ad watched him and leaned forward.

"Let me take your knife, Nick," he said.

"No, you don't," the negro said. "Hang onto your knife, Mister Adams."

The prizefighter sat back.

"Will you bring me the bread, Mister Adams?" Bugs asked. Nick brought it over.

"Do you like to dip your bread in the ham fat?" the negro asked.

"You bet!"

"Perhaps we'd better wait until later. It's better at the finish of the meal. Here."

The negro picked up a slice of ham and laid it on one of the pieces of bread, then slid an egg on top of it.

"Just close that sandwich, will you, please, and give it to Mister Francis."

Ad took the sandwich and started eating.

"Watch out how that egg runs," the negro warned. "This is for you, Mister Adams. The remainder for myself."

Nick bit into the sandwich. The negro was sitting opposite him beside Ad. The hot fried ham and eggs tasted wonderful.

"Mister Adams is right hungry," the negro said. The little man whom Nick knew by name as a former champion fighter was silent. He had said nothing since the negro had spoken about the knife.

"May I offer you a slice of bread dipped right in the hot ham fat?" Bugs said.

"Thanks a lot."

The little white man looked at Nick.

"Will you have some, Mister Adolph Francis?" Bugs offered from the skillet.

Ad did not answer. He was looking at Nick.

"Mister Francis?" came the nigger's soft voice.

Ad did not answer. He was looking at Nick.

"I spoke to you, Mister Francis," the nigger said softly.

Ad kept on looking at Nick. He had his cap down over his eyes. Nick felt nervous.

"How the hell do you get that way?" came out from under the cap sharply at Nick.

"Who the hell do you think you are? You're a snotty bastard. You come in here where nobody asks you and eat a man's food and when he asks to borrow a knife you get snotty."

He glared at Nick, his face was white and his eyes almost out of sight under the cap.

"You're a hot sketch. Who the hell asked you to butt in here?"

"Nobody."

"You're damn right nobody did. Nobody asked you to stay either. You come in here and act snotty about my face and smoke my cigars and drink my liquor and then talk snotty. Where the hell do you think you get off?"

Nick said nothing. Ad stood up.

"I'll tell you, you yellow-livered Chicago bastard. You're going to get your can knocked off. Do you get that?"

Nick stepped back. The little man came toward him slowly, stepping flat-footed forward, his left foot stepping forward, his right dragging up to it.

"Hit me," he moved his head. "Try and hit me."

"I don't want to hit you."

"You won't get out of it that way. You're going to take a beating, see? Come on and lead at me."

"Cut it out," Nick said.

"All right, then, you bastard."

The little man looked down at Nick's feet. As he looked down the negro, who had followed behind him as he moved away from the fire, set himself and tapped him across the base of the skull. He fell forward and Bugs dropped the cloth-wrapped blackjack on the grass. The little man lay there, his face in the grass. The negro picked him up, his head hanging and carried him to the fire. His face looked bad, the eyes open. Bugs laid him down gently.

"Will you bring me the water in the bucket, Mister Adams," he said. "I'm afraid I hit him just a little hard."

The negro splashed water with his hand on the man's face and pulled his ears gently. The eyes closed.

Bugs stood up.

"He's all right," he said. "There's nothing to worry about. I'm sorry, Mister Adams."

"It's all right." Nick was looking down at the little man. He saw the blackjack on the grass and picked it up. It had a flexible handle and was limber in his hand. It was made of worn black leather with a handkerchief wrapped around the heavy end.

"That's a whalebone handle," the negro smiled. "They don't make them any more. I didn't know how well you could take care of yourself and, anyway, I didn't want you to hurt him or mark him up no more than he is."

The negro smiled again.

"You hurt him yourself."

"I know how to do it. He won't remember nothing of it. I have to do it to change him when he gets that way."

Nick was still looking down at the little man, lying, his eyes closed in the firelight. Bugs put some wood on the fire.

"Don't you worry about him none, Mister Adams. I seen him like this plenty of times before."

"What made him crazy?" Nick asked.

"Oh, a lot of things," the negro answered from the fire. "Would you like a cup of this coffee, Mister Adams?"

He handed Nick the cup and smoothed the coat he had placed under the unconscious man's head.

"He took too many beatings, for one thing," the negro sipped the coffee. "But that just made him sort of simple. Then his sister was his manager and they was always being written up in the papers all about brothers and sisters and how she loved her brother and how he loved his sister, and then they got married in New York and that made a lot of unpleasantness."

"I remember about it."

"Sure. Of course they wasn't brother and sister no more than a rabbit, but there was a lot of people didn't like it either way and they commenced to have disagreements, and one day she just went off and never come back."

He drank the coffee and wiped his lips with the pink palm of his hand.

"He just went crazy. Will you have some more coffee, Mister Adams?"

"Thanks."

"I seen her a couple of times," the negro went on. "She was an awful good-looking woman. Looked enough like him to be twins. He wouldn't be bad-looking without his face all busted."

He stopped. The story seemed to be over.

"Where did you meet him?" asked Nick.

"I met him in jail," the negro said. "He was busting people all the time after she went away and they put him in jail. I was in for cuttin' a man."

He smiled, and went on soft-voiced:

"Right away I liked him and when I got out I looked him up. He likes to think I'm crazy and I don't mind. I like to be with him and I like seeing the country and I don't have to commit no larceny to do it. I like living like a gentleman."

"What do you all do?" Nick asked.

"Oh, nothing. Just move around. He's got money."

"He must have made a lot of money."

"Sure. He spent all his money, though. Or they took it away from him. She sends him money."

He poked up the fire.

"She's a mighty fine woman," he said. "She looks enough like him to be his own twin."

The negro looked over at the little man, lying breathing heavily. His blond hair was down over his forehead. His mutilated face looked childish in repose.

"I can wake him up any time now, Mister Adams. If you don't mind I wish you'd sort of pull out. I don't like to not be hospitable, but it might disturb him back again to see you. I hate to have to thump him and it's the only thing to do when he gets started. I have to sort of keep him away from people. You don't mind, do you, Mister Adams? No, don't thank me, Mister Adams. I'd have warned you about him but he seemed to have taken such a liking to you and I thought things were going to be all right. You'll hit a town about two miles up the track. Mancelona they call it. Good-bye. I wish we could ask you to stay the night but it's just out of the question. Would you like to take some of that ham and some bread with you? No? You better take a sandwich," all this in a low, smooth, polite nigger voice.

"Good. Well, good-bye, Mister Adams. Good-bye and good luck!"

Nick walked away from the fire across the clearing to the railway tracks. Out of the range of the fire he listened. The low soft voice of the negro was talking. Nick could not hear the words. Then he heard the little man say, "I got an awful headache, Bugs."

"You'll feel better, Mister Francis," the negro's voice soothed. "Just you drink a cup of this hot coffee."

Nick climbed the embankment and started up the track. He found he had a ham sandwich in his hand and put it in his pocket. Looking back from the mounting grade before the track curved into the hills he could see the firelight in the clearing.

HEMINGWAY: *The Battler*

1. *How much can you tell about Nick himself from Hemingway's sketchy description? Does the author provide enough, or do you feel you need more to understand Nick and the story?*

2. *Hemingway's purpose is to make you see, to make details visual and tangible. What are some of the ways in which he accomplishes his purpose? Do you feel he only partially succeeds?*

3. *Ad Francis, the ex-boxer, is a typical Hemingway character, sometimes peripheral, but often the protagonist. How does the author make you see and understand him? Do you visualize him the way Nick does or differently?*

4. *Is Hemingway's presentation of the Negro racist? In what ways? Can the reader understand him and his role only racially? Or does race become irrelevant at some point?*

5. *What is the relationship between the Negro and the ex-boxer? Is it complicated, or as simple as Hemingway presents it?*

6. *What is the function of the Negro's explanation to Nick of what he did and why he did it? To what levels has Hemingway moved the story by its final page or two?*

7. *What does Nick "know" at the end of "The Battler"? Is it comparable to what Robin "knows" at the end of the Hawthorne story?*

8. *The railroad bum, like lynchings, belongs to our bitter past, but as in Faulkner's story, the encounter is relevant to our time. Can you see how?*

Jorge Luis Borges
THE SECRET MIRACLE

Jorge Luis Borges was born in 1899, in Buenos Aires, Argentina, and his personal background (Spanish, English, Portuguese Jewish) is almost as varied as the materials of his short fictions. Similar to those of both Kafka and Cervantes, his stories are fantastic and visionary. As Anthony Kerrigan has put it, Borges' work "is a species of international literary metaphor," whose borrowings from different literatures make his work a summation of Western humanism, at the same time that he questions all its hypotheses and conclusions. Borges is an ironist, a parodist, a ritualist, a man, like Lawrence, obsessed by words, colors, tones, shapes. His interest in words is further borne out by his numerous translations into Spanish of Faulkner, Woolf, Kafka, and Gide. His original works include the short fictions of Labyrinths, Ficciones, A Personal Anthology, The Book of Imaginary Beings, *and* The Aleph and Other Stories. *Awarded (with Samuel Beckett) the Formentor International Publishers Prize for 1961, Borges has often been mentioned as a leading candidate for the Nobel Prize for Literature.*

> And God had him die for a hundred years and then revived him and said:
> "How long have you been here?"
> "A day or a part of a day," he answered.
>
> Koran, II, 261

THE night of March 14, 1943, in an apartment in the Zeltnergasse of Prague, Jaromir Hladik, the author of the unfinished drama entitled *The Enemies*, of *Vindication of Eternity*, and of a study of the indirect Jewish sources of Jakob Böhme, had a dream of a long game of chess. The players were not two persons, but two illustrious families; the game had been going on for centuries. Nobody could remember what the stakes were, but it was rumored that they were enormous, perhaps infinite; the chessmen and the board were in a secret tower. Jaromir (in his dream) was the first-born of one of the contending families. The clock struck the hour for the game, which could not be postponed. The dreamer raced over the sands of a rainy desert, and was unable to recall either the pieces or the rules of chess. At that moment he awoke. The clangor of the rain and of the terrible clocks ceased. A rhythmic, unanimous noise, punctuated by shouts of command, arose from the Zeltnergasse. It was dawn, and the armored vanguard of the Third Reich was entering Prague.

On the nineteenth the authorities received a denunciation; that same nineteenth, toward evening, Jaromir Hladik was arrested. He was taken to an aseptic, white barracks on the opposite bank of the Moldau. He was unable to refute a single one of the Gestapo's charges; his mother's family name was Jaroslavski, he was of Jewish blood, his study on Böhme had a marked Jewish emphasis, his signature had been one more on the protest against the *Anschluss*. In 1928 he had translated the *Sepher Yezirah* for the publishing house of Hermann Barsdorf. The fulsome catalogue of the firm had exaggerated, for publicity purposes, the translator's reputation, and the catalogue had been examined by Julius Rothe, one of the officials who held Hladik's fate in his hands. There is not a person who, except in the field of his own specialization, is not credulous; two or three adjectives in Gothic type were enough to persuade Julius Rothe of Hladik's importance, and he ordered him sentenced to death *pour encourager les autres*. The execution was set for March 29th, at 9:00 A.M. This delay (whose importance the reader will grasp later) was owing to the desire on the authorities' part to proceed impersonally and slowly, after the manner of vegetables and plants.

Hladik's first reaction was mere terror. He felt he would not have shrunk from the gallows, the block, or the knife, but that death by a firing squad was unbearable. In vain he tried to convince himself that the plain, unvarnished fact of dying was the fearsome thing, not the attendant circumstances. He never wearied of conjuring up these circumstances, senselessly trying to exhaust all their possible variations. He infinitely anticipated the process of his dying, from the sleepless dawn to the mysterious volley. Before the day set by Julius Rothe he died hundreds of deaths in courtyards whose forms and angles strained geometrical probabilities, machine-gunned by variable soldiers in changing numbers, who at times killed him from a distance, at others from close by. He faced these imaginary executions with real terror (perhaps with real bravery); each simulacrum lasted a few seconds. When the circle was closed, Jaromir returned once more and interminably to the tremulous vespers of his death. Then he reflected that reality does not usually coincide with our anticipation of it; with a logic of his own he inferred that to foresee a circumstantial detail is to prevent its happening. Trusting in this weak magic, he invented, *so that they would not happen*, the most gruesome details. Finally, as was natural, he came to fear that they were prophetic. Miserable in the night, he endeavored to find some way to hold fast to the fleeting substance of time. He knew that it was rushing headlong toward the dawn of the twenty-ninth. He reasoned aloud: "I am now in the night of the twenty-second; while this night lasts (and for six nights more), I am invulnerable, immortal." The nights of sleep seemed to him deep, dark pools in which he could submerge himself. There were moments when he longed impatiently for the final burst of fire that would free him, for better or for worse, from the vain compulsion of his imaginings. On the twenty-eighth, as the last sunset was reverberating from the high barred windows, the thought of his drama, *The Enemies*, deflected him from these abject considerations.

Hladik had rounded forty. Aside from a few friendships and many habits, the problematic exercise of literature constituted his life. Like all writers, he measured the achievements of others by what they had accomplished, asking of them that they measure him by what he envisaged or planned. All the books he had published had left him with a complex feeling of repentance. His studies of the work of Böhme, of Ibn Ezra, and of Fludd had been characterized essentially by mere application; his translation of the *Sepher Yezirah*, by carelessness, fatigue, and conjecture. *Vindication of Eternity* perhaps had fewer shortcomings. The first volume gave a history of man's various concepts of eternity, from the immutable Being of Parmenides to the modifiable Past of Hinton. The second denied (with Francis Bradley) that all the events of the universe make up a temporal series, arguing that the number of man's possible experiences is not infinite, and that a single "repetition" suffices to prove that time is a fallacy . . . Unfortunately, the arguments that demonstrate this fallacy are equally fallacious. Hladik was in the habit of going over them with a kind of contemptuous perplexity. He had also composed a series of Expressionist poems; to the poet's chagrin they had been included in an anthology published in 1924, and no subsequent anthology but inherited them. From all this equivocal, uninspired past Hladik had hoped to redeem himself with his drama in verse, *The Enemies*. (Hladik felt the verse form to be essential because it makes it impossible for the spectators to lose sight of irreality, one of art's requisites.)

The drama observed the unities of time, place, and action. The scene was laid in Hradcany, in the library of Baron von Roemerstadt, on one of the last afternoons of the nineteenth century. In the first scene of the first act a strange man visits Roemerstadt. (A clock was striking seven, the vehemence of the setting sun's rays glorified the windows, a passionate, familiar Hungarian music floated in the air.) This visit is followed by others; Roemerstadt does not know the people who are importuning him, but he has the uncomfortable feeling that he has seen them somewhere, perhaps in a dream. They all fawn upon him, but it is apparent—first to the audience and then to the Baron—that they are secret enemies, in league to ruin him. Roemerstadt succeeds in checking or evading their involved schemings. In the dialogue mention is made of his sweetheart, Julia von Weidenau, and a certain Jaroslav Kubin, who at one time pressed his attentions on her. Kubin has now lost his mind, and believes himself to be Roemerstadt. The dangers increase; Roemerstadt, at the end of the second act, is forced to kill one of the conspirators. The third and final act opens. The incoherencies gradually increase; actors who had seemed out of the play reappear; the man Roemerstadt killed returns for a moment. Someone points out that evening has not fallen; the clock strikes seven, the high windows reverberate in the western sun, the air carries an impassioned Hungarian melody. The first actor comes on and repeats the lines he had spoken in the first scene of the first act. Roemerstadt speaks to him without surprise; the audience understands the Roemerstadt is the miserable Jaroslav Kubin. The drama has never taken place; it is the circular delirium that Kubin lives and relives endlessly.

Hladik had never asked himself whether this tragicomedy of errors was preposterous or admirable, well thought out or slipshod. He felt that the plot I have just sketched was best contrived to cover up his defects and point up his abilities and held the possibility of allowing him to redeem (symbolically) the meaning of his life. He had finished the first act and one or two scenes of the third; the metrical nature of the work made it possible for him to keep working it over, changing the hexameters, without the manuscript in front of him. He thought how he still had two acts to do, and that he was going to die very soon. He spoke with God in the darkness: "If in some fashion I exist, if I am not one of Your repetitions and mistakes, I exist as the author of *The Enemies*. To finish this drama, which can justify me and justify You, I need another year. Grant me these days, You to whom the centuries and time belong." This was the last night, the most dreadful of all, but ten minutes later sleep flooded over him like a dark water.

Toward dawn he dreamed that he had concealed himself in one of the naves of the Clementine Library. A librarian wearing dark glasses asked him: "What are you looking for?" Hladik answered: "I am looking for God." The librarian said to him: "God is in one of the letters on one of the pages of one of the four hundred thousand volumes of the Clementine. My fathers and the fathers of my fathers have searched for this letter; I have grown blind seeking it." He removed his glasses, and Hladik saw his eyes, which were dead. A reader came in to return an atlas. "This atlas is worthless," he said, and handed it to Hladik, who opened it at random. He saw a map of India as in a daze. Suddenly sure of himself, he touched one of the tiniest letters. A ubiquitous voice said to him: "The time of your labor has been granted." At this point Hladik awoke.

He remembered that men's dreams belong to God, and that Maimonides had written that the words heard in a dream are divine when they are distinct and clear and the person uttering them cannot be seen. He dressed: two soldiers came into the cell and ordered him to follow them.

From behind the door, Hladik had envisaged a labyrinth of passageways, stairs, and separate buildings. The reality was less spectacular: they descended to an inner court by a narrow iron stairway. Several soldiers—some with uniform unbuttoned—were examining a motorcycle and discussing it. The sergeant looked at the clock; it was 8:44. They had to wait until it struck nine. Hladik, more insignificant than pitiable, sat down on a pile of wood. He noticed that the soldiers' eyes avoided his. To ease his wait, the sergeant handed him a cigarette. Hladik did not smoke; he accepted it out of politeness or humility. As he lighted it, he noticed that his hands were shaking. The day was clouding over; the soldiers spoke in a low voice as though he were already dead. Vainly he tried to recall the woman of whom Julia von Weidenau was the symbol.

The squad formed and stood at attention. Hladik, standing against the barracks wall, waited for the volley. Someone pointed out that the wall was going to be stained with blood; the victim was ordered to step forward a few paces. Incongruously, this reminded Hladik of the fumbling preparations of photographers. A big drop of rain struck one of Hladik's temples and rolled slowly down his cheek; the sergeant shouted the final order.

The physical universe came to a halt.

The guns converged on Hladik, but the men who were to kill him stood motionless. The sergeant's arm eternized an unfinished gesture. On a paving stone of the courtyard a bee cast an unchanging shadow. The wind had ceased, as in a picture. Hladik attempted a cry, a word, a movement of the hand. He realized that he was paralyzed. Not a sound reached him from the halted world. He thought: "I am in hell, I am dead." He thought: "I am mad." He thought: "Time has stopped." Then he reflected that if that was the case, his mind would have stopped too. He wanted to test this; he repeated (without moving his lips) Vergil's mysterious fourth Eclogue. He imagined that the now remote soldiers must be sharing his anxiety; he longed to be able to communicate with them. It astonished him not to feel the least fatigue, not even the numbness of his protracted immobility. After an indeterminate time he fell asleep. When he awoke the world continued motionless and mute. The drop of water still clung to his cheek, the shadow of the bee to the stone. The smoke from the cigarette he had thrown away had not dispersed. Another "day" went by before Hladik understood.

He had asked God for a whole year to finish his work; His omnipotence had granted it. God had worked a secret miracle for him; German lead would kill him at the set hour, but in his mind a year would go by between the order and its execution. From perplexity he passed to stupor, from stupor to resignation, from resignation to sudden gratitude.

He had no document but his memory; the training he had acquired with each added hexameter gave him a discipline unsuspected by those who set down and forget temporary, incomplete paragraphs. He was not working for posterity or even for God, whose literary tastes were unknown to him. Meticulously, motionlessly, secretly, he wrought in time his lofty, invisible labyrinth. He worked the third act over twice. He eliminated certain symbols as over-obvious, such as the repeated striking of the clock, the music. Nothing hurried him. He omitted, he condensed, he amplified. In certain instances he came back to the original version. He came to feel an affection for the courtyard, the barracks; one of the faces before him modified his conception of Roemerstadt's character. He discovered that the wearying cacophonies that bothered Flaubert so much are mere visual superstitions, weakness and limitation of the written word, not the spoken . . . He concluded his drama. He had only the problem of a single phrase. He found it. The drop of water slid down his cheek. He opened his mouth in a maddened cry, moved his face, dropped under the quadruple blast.

Jaromir Hladik died on March 29, at 9:02 A.M.

Translated by Harriet de Onís

BORGES: *The Secret Miracle*

1. *According to André Maurois, certain metaphysical "fables" or ideas fascinated Borges: that of Endless Recurrence, or the circular repetition of all the history of the world; that of the dream within a dream; that of centuries that seem minutes and seconds that seem years; and that of the hallucinatory nature of the world. How many of these fables does Borges touch upon in this story? Is the story "burdened" by these ideas?*
2. *How does the epigraph, from the Koran, function in the story?*
3. *What is the significance of Hladik's dream in the first paragraph?*
4. *What does Hladik mean when he says he is "immortal" in the week before the execution?*
5. *How does Hladik's drama,* The Enemies, *relate to the "play" of his own life? Is his dream in the Clementine Library relevant to his predicament?*
6. *Why is the firing squad as a mode of execution so terrifying to Hladik? Of what significance is the map of India in connection with the stay of execution? Why at the end does Hladik open his mouth "in a maddened cry"?*
7. *Characterize Hladik's final moments—why the dreamlike sense? What happens to time? To the physical universe? What is Hladik's triumph? Is it convincing—that is, is it a triumph?*
8. *Borges has frequently been compared to Kafka. Does there seem to be any resemblance between this story and "The Judgment"? Sartre's "The Wall"?*

Ignazio Silone
THE TRAP

Throughout his life, Ignazio Silone has fought for humanitarian ideals, becoming in his way the conscience of his generation. Born in Italy in 1900, Silone (b. Secondo Tranquilli) early became an active Socialist. After Mussolini's march on Rome, Silone was exiled from Italy, but he returned in 1925 as a militant Communist and opposed the Fascists. In 1930, he left the party (see The God That Failed*) and settled in Switzerland. Engrossed with ethical and political problems to the same degree that the young Moravia was with social, he was particularly suited to voice the plight of the abused peasants of his native Abruzzi. This he did in* Fontamara *(1933);* Mr. Aristotle *(1935), and a collection of short stories;* Bread and Wine *(1937), his masterpiece;* A Handful of Blackberries *(1953) and* The Secret of Luca *(1956). His creativity turned almost exclusively to the field of active politics when, after the liberation, he returned to Italy. Lately,* The Fox and the Camellias *(1961) suggests that the craft of the novel has reclaimed him, even though he returns to the material of "The Trap" for his inspiration.*

DANIEL was still out at the pig-sty, looking after the sow who was having young ones, when someone called to him from the house thirty yards away. He had much to do yet, and had told them once that he did not care to be disturbed; so he did not answer. It was Daniel's wife, Filomena; she had called him two or three times.

"Daniel! Oh, Daniel! There's someone wants to talk to you." When she received no reply, she was silent.

Daniel had done all he could to see that the sow had an easy time of it; but that is the sort of thing you can never be sure about. The night before, he had put the animal on a strict diet and, by way of further precaution, had given her a strenuous castor-oil enema. What he feared more than anything else was that she would become constipated, which might result in a paralysis of the lower regions and the drying up of her milk. He had summoned to help him one Agostino, a native of Bergamo, who had lived at Ticino for a number of years. Agostino was a mason by trade, but in the off-season he was a man of all work.

[359

Things had started off well. Three pigs had already made their appearance, looking like three enormous rats emerging from a bloody flask. Agostino's chief concern was with finding a suitable name for each. The fourth one was slow in coming, and while Agostino held its snout, Daniel had to put his bare arm, smeared with oil, up the sow's vagina. In this fashion, he had drawn the young one out, leaving the way open for the others.

"We ought to call this one Benito," suggested Agostino.

"Nothing doing!" replied Daniel. "These pigs have already been sold to an Italian firm."

"You haven't the nerve!" said the man from Bergamo.

At this point, the voice of Daniel's younger daughter, Luisa, was heard.

"Daddy! There's someone wants to talk to you!"

Daniel meanwhile went on with the umbilical dressings of the young pigs, which was to avoid infection. Had he not already told them at the house that he did not want to be bothered by anything but his work? Again he made no reply. He put the young animals in a large wooden crate lined with straw and covered them over with a woolen blanket, while Agostino saw to the cleaning of the pig-sty and the removing of the evidences of the obstetrical operation. Silvia, Daniel's elder daughter, now called from the path which ran down to the pig-sty.

"Daddy! There's someone here who wants to speak to you!"

Silvia was accompanied by Caterina, the seamstress, an old lady from the province of Florence, who had been a dressmaker at Minusio for years, but who earned the better part of her living by going around from house to house and doing mending. When Daniel saw Caterina, he was annoyed.

"Is that why you've been yelling at me for the last hour?" he demanded. For Caterina was not exactly what you would call a person of few words.

"Caterina wants to talk to you," Silvia went on, taking no notice of her father's reproof. Agostino and Silvia went off toward the house, and Caterina was left alone with Daniel.

"You know very well," Caterina began, "that I have always attended strictly to my own business—"

"That's no business of mine," said Daniel; his tone was anything but encouraging.

"Well, you know, don't you, that all the years I've lived at Ticino I've never meddled with other people's affairs?"

"That doesn't concern me," said Daniel as he made for the house.

When she saw that he had no intention of listening to her, Caterina abandoned all preliminaries and got down to facts.

"An Italian gentleman has just been to see me," she said; "he made me a proposition; he wants me to play the spy!"

Daniel stopped short. Caterina caught her breath and then went on to tell about the call she had received from this gentleman, whom she had met once by chance in an office at Locarno.

" 'You've lived here at Ticino for a good many years,' he said to me, 'you ought to know everybody. Your business takes you everywhere, into any number of homes; you listen to any number of conversations. You're an old woman and alone in the world; no one is afraid to talk in front of you—' I told him that everybody certainly did respect me, because I've always minded my own business. He kept on talking that way, and then at last he said: 'If you've a mind to get certain information for me concerning the activities of some of the anti-Fascist Italians here in Ticino, between Ascona and Bellinzona, you can earn a little something that will make it easier for you in your old age—' "

Daniel had recovered from his surprise and was watching Caterina closely as, trembling and sighing, she went on with her story.

"Why did you come to me?" he wanted to know.

"Why did I come to you?" Caterina echoed.

"I am a native of Ticino," said Daniel, "and the affairs of these Italians don't interest me; that's the reason I'd like to know why you came to me. Who sent you?"

The old lady was taken aback.

"What do you mean?" she stammered. "You've known me for thirty years. You know that I've always been a hard worker and have always minded my own business!"

"What I want to know," Daniel broke in on her, raising his voice, "what I want to know is, who sent you here?"

"Nobody!" Caterina insisted. "I'm sorry to have bothered you; I'll be going."

Caterina took the foot-path which skirted Daniel's house and which came out on the Gordola-Minusio highway. Daniel followed her and, after a bit, resumed the discussion.

"If no one sent you, then why did you come?"

"I wanted some advice," said Caterina, and she kept on walking.

"What kind of advice?"

"Whether or not I should accept the gentleman's offer." The old lady came to a stop. "I don't know what to do. I never was in such a predicament in all my life. If I accept, I'll earn something substantial, but by doing harm to those who have never harmed me. If I refuse, they're sure to look on me as an anti-Fascist and persecute me every way they can. You've known me for thirty years. You know that I'm neither a Fascist nor an anti-Fascist. You know that I've always been a hard worker and minded my business."

Daniel was lost in thought for a moment. Caterina started to walk away again, sighing resignedly. Once more he followed her. At the end of the path, Agostino was waiting.

"I'll tell you what," Daniel suddenly said to her, "you needn't be afraid. So long as you're honest you have nothing to fear. Tell Agostino what you've just told me and do as he says."

He watched the pair as they went down the road in the direction of Gordola; then he turned back to the pig-sty, to look after the sow.

It was one morning while Daniel was at work with his daughter Silvia on the vines in the arbor that Agostino went past again for the first time. The vines were being eaten by an insect which had bored its way through the bark, and Daniel had wanted to take advantage of a free morning to get at them. He would run a metal scraper over the ailing stalks in such a manner as to remove the bark and lay bare the hidden chrysales, and Silvia would come after him to sprinkle the shoots with boiling water. It was at this time that Agostino went by upon a truck-load of brick and shouted to Daniel:

"Did you hear about it? That business is coming along!"

"What business?" Daniel answered him, although he understood well enough what Agostino meant.

"You know, that business we were talking about!" And Agostino gave a wave of his hand as the truck disappeared down the road. Daniel shook his head.

"Those Italians are all right," he remarked, turning to his daughter. "Big-hearted, impulsive, never think of danger—but they talk too much!"

"Listen, Daddy," said Silvia, plucking up courage at this point to voice a wish she had been cherishing for a long time, "I know that, though you don't say anything about it, you are doing a great deal to help free Italy, and I too would like so much to help!"

"Silvia," was her father's reply, "I wish you would pick up the pieces of bark which I have chipped off the vines, and which are lying around on the ground here, and burn them. That is all you have to do just now!"

His daughter obeyed. Daniel watched her as she went about the ar-

The Trap

bor, bending down at the foot of each vine and gathering up in her apron the tiny pieces of bark. Silvia had been twenty last November. And there was pride and trepidation in her father's glance as it rested on her. She was the dearest thing in his life, and the one over which hung the greatest threat.

Some days afterward Agostino came past a second time, one Sunday morning. Daniel and Filomena were talking with a woman who was telling them how, at Cadenazzo and at Robasacco, the night before, a number of hen-houses had been raided by foxes.

"They found fifty hens with their throats slit and their blood sucked!" The woman was precise regarding details.

"If that's the case," Daniel disagreed, "then it's not a fox but a polecat."

At this point, a chauffeur from Cadenazzo came past and they put the question up to him.

"It's a fox," declared the chauffeur, "and maybe more than one. In one hen-house, all they found left was a bunch of wing-feathers."

"We'll have to be looking after our hens," said Filomena to Daniel. "Last year they were sick, and this year, of course, it would have to be foxes!"

"The thing to do," suggested Daniel, "is to set a trap."

Agostino now arrived on the scene.

"It's coming to a head," he said to Daniel, calling him over to one side. "Caterina did what I told her to, and that fellow from the police has swallowed the hook. We'll have to be on the watch now!"

"What are you thinking about doing?" inquired Daniel.

"The thing to do is to set a trap," Agostino answered.

Daniel burst out laughing when he heard the word trap, and Filomena, who had caught nothing more than the word, now took a hand in the conversation.

"A trap's not always enough," she observed, turning to Agostino. "The fox is too wise for that. Almost always, before nibbling at the bait, he feels all around it, and he doesn't take it in his mouth right away but joggles it about and draws it over to him with his paw. It's all right to set a trap, but it's a good thing to put a little poisoned food around the hen-house at the same time."

Agostino did not get the drift at first.

"But you can't be sure of poison, even," said Daniel to his wife; "a fox has to be pretty hungry if, when he's near a hen-house, he wastes any time in picking up what's lying around on the ground. And even if he eats a piece of poisoned meat or a few chestnuts soaked in strychnine, you can't be sure then. No one has ever yet found just the right dose of strychnine to give a fox, when you don't know what kind of a fox it is. If he's big and strong, and there isn't much strychnine, all he gets is a little belly-ache, which doesn't keep him from eating the hens; but if it's a strong dose, he'll vomit it up right away, get it off his stomach, and have all the keener an appetite for chickens."

"It seems, then, there's no chance of catching a fox!" Agostino had finally realized what it was they had been talking about before he came.

"There is a chance," said Daniel, "but it's not easy. And anyway," he added, "no fox ever yet was caught by talking about it."

Filomena now went back into the house, for Luisa, the younger daughter, had called her; the two men went out into the garden back of the house to continue their conversation.

"Caterina," Agostino was saying, "after many qualms and no end of holding back, has finally taken the job of spying on the work that we are doing here in Locarno. That fellow from the Italian police came to see her again yesterday and left her an address in Pallanza to which she is to write in case she has any information to give him."

"He didn't tell Caterina who the persons are she is supposed to spy on?" asked Daniel.

"It seems not, for the present," said Agostino, "but he told her in a general way that she was to get the names of all those Italian migratory workers who are all the time crossing the border into Switzerland and who there are in touch with revolutionary circles. He told her also that she could make a nice little sum of money if she would help him track down those who are responsible for smuggling revolutionary books and publications into Italy."

"He didn't say who it was he suspected of doing that?"

"Apparently not," said Agostino, "from the story that Caterina gave me." And then he went on: "I had to promise Caterina that, in case of any trouble, we'd see to it that she got out all right; I told her we'd provide her with the means to go to Zurich and live. For the thirty years she's been here in Ticino, as you know, that's all she's dreamed of, to be able to live in Zurich."

"Does Caterina suspect that I have any connection with the Italian revolutionists?"

"You can put that out of your head," Agostino assured him. "Every time she's talked to me—you know Caterina, with a sigh after every other word—she's told me how she has always minded her own affairs and always means to, and how Mr. Daniel, fine man that he is, is one Ticinese who has never meddled in politics, she can swear to that—"

Silvia, from the window of her room, had caught sight of her father and Agostino at the far end of the garden.

"May I come down?" she called to her father.

"Of course!" the two men replied.

The girl left the house and came down the garden path. As she reached them, the pair changed the conversation and began talking about the weather.

Every night Daniel set a trap at the entrance to the hen-house and put some poisoned food about, but no fox came. And Agostino's fox seemingly was in no more of a hurry to set foot in the man from Bergamo's trap, for Daniel had heard no more about it.

"A farmer's life," he would say, "is one continual war with the weather and with animal parasites, but the hardest war of all is the one against the fox."

The work of scraping the vines had been finished, and he now began on the fruit trees. He would clean the trunks of their dried branches, dead bark, and moss, by way of uncovering the parasites' nests. Wherever there was a hole surrounded by a little streak of red, Silvia would then insert an iron wire to kill the wood-worm hidden at the bottom. When the cleaning was finished, Filomena came with a pail of lime, and each trunk was given a whitewashing to the height of a man's head.

"The trees," observed Daniel, "are now protected on the earth side, but who is going to protect them from the heavens?"

Agostino, exchanging pleasantries with Luisa, was waiting for Daniel at the door of the house.

"What's new?" was Daniel's question.

"The trap is ready!" the man from Bergamo replied.

"And the fox, what about him?"

"He'll be there tonight!"

"If only we could finish off all the foxes at once!" Daniel exclaimed.

Agostino then proceeded to inform Daniel of the way in which the provocateur was to be trapped.

"Caterina has written him that she has important information to give him, and she's made an appointment for nine o'clock tonight, at Rivapiana, down by the lake, opposite the old chapel of San Quirico. Caterina will be there, and I mean to be there too, with a couple of others."

"But don't you think," said Daniel, "that it might be well to notify the police?"

"That wouldn't be wise at all," said Agostino. "The consulate might get wind of it right away, and the fox wouldn't show up."

Daniel could not very well offer an objection to this, seeing that a number of subordinates among the police were suspected of being disloyal. The thing that worried him more than anything else was the possible trouble that might be caused the Italian emigrants.

"It ought to be done by Ticinesi!" said Daniel; but Agostino was not of this opinion.

"Too many people would be in on it then; and what's more, an Italian fox—an Italian trap!"

That evening Daniel took the train for Locarno; and along about ten o'clock he started strolling along the lake toward Saleggi, as he waited for Agostino, who was to let him know how the thing had turned out. About half-past ten, in place of Agostino, there appeared one Lucca, an Italian carpenter who lived at Minusio.

"Agostino," he told Daniel, "has been slightly wounded in one hand, and so he did not come, because he did not want to attract attention by going around with a bandaged hand."

"And what about the other man?"

"We left him lying on the ground! He came to keep the appointment with a couple of others, who went off and left him alone with Caterina, saying they would be back in an hour. We were in behind San Quirico, and we waited until they were a good distance away—they left in the direction of Navigia. In the meantime, Caterina, with her usual tears and sighs, was filling the informer with all sorts of foolishness, telling him over and over again how she had never in all her life meddled with anyone's business but her own and never would, but how all the same she had discovered, beyond any doubt, that revolutionary books and magazines to be taken into Italy were being deposited in the Franciscan Convent at Madonna del Sasso, up above Locarno."

Daniel had a good laugh at this.

"Agostino went up alone at first," Lucca went on, "leaving us there behind the church. It had been agreed that he was to make use of his revolver only in case the fellow tried to take him. He acted as if he just happened to be passing. As it was dark, he lighted a cigarette, and pretended to recognize the stranger by the glow of the match. 'Ha!' he called out, and then the rumpus began. We came out of our hiding place, while Caterina took to her heels."

"Did you have a hand in it, too?"

"Oh, there wasn't any need of that. All we did was keep a watch to see that nobody came. Agostino soon enough had the best of him. He threw him to the ground and held him with his knee and then started pounding his face as if he were crushing stone. We knew how strong Agostino was, but we never knew how much hate he had in him—"

"You mustn't forget," Daniel reminded Lucca, "that the Fascists killed Agostino's brother! You say he was wounded in the hand?"

"Yes, the spy bit him. He got Agostino's hand between his teeth and wouldn't let go. With his free hand Agostino was pounding the fellow on the jaw like a madman, but the spy held on with his teeth. Then Agostino took him by the throat and choked him just about to death."

"Did he finish him?" Daniel was alarmed.

"I think he did."

"Then Agostino in all probability will have to clear out of the country," Daniel said. "He may have to go to France—"

In view of the unforeseen turn which events had taken, Daniel made up his mind to spend the night at Locarno and to go to Bellinzona the following morning. In order that his family might not be worried about him, he went into a café and telephoned to Silvia.

"It's a lucky thing you called," his daughter said. "I've been trying for an hour to reach you, everywhere in Locarno where you're known—"

"Why, what's happened?" Daniel asked in some alarm.

"Nothing at our house," Silvia hastened to reassure him. "But not far away, on the Gordola road, there's been an automobile collision and one man was seriously injured. They got a doctor as quick as they could, and the doctor said his injuries were so serious that it would be dangerous to move him very far. They inquired in a number of houses whether they could take him in; but you know very well that, here in our neighborhood, there are nothing but hovels, like stables. And so the neighbors assured them that our house was the only possible one. Mother, to tell the truth, was rather put out about it; she said that, you being away from home, we couldn't very well take in a stranger, but I told her that I knew you would approve of it—"

"Certainly!" Daniel interrupted her. "Where did you put him?"

"In my room, on the second floor," said Silvia. "I'll sleep with Luisa; she'll be only too glad to have me."

"Is he in danger of death?"

"The doctor wouldn't say as to that. He said that he would send a nurse in this very night, although I told him that I could do everything that was necessary without any help."

"Where is he from? What's his name?" Daniel questioned her further.

"The poor fellow can't talk yet," his daughter explained. "He must come from a well-to-do family, though, for the doctor insisted that mother accept something as a deposit, to cover any expense that we might be put to."

"I'm really very sorry," said Daniel in conclusion, "that I can't come home tonight; but I'm staying over in Locarno, and tomorrow morning I'm going to Bellinzona, on some business that can't be put off. I leave everything to you; be a good girl and do whatever the doctor tells you to."

Daniel telephoned from Bellinzona the next day to find out if the injured man was still alive. It was Luisa who answered the phone, as Silvia had gone out to make a few purchases.

"He's a little better," said the young girl. "A nurse came in an automobile last night, but Silvia insisted on staying up anyway—and now the doctor's here again."

The doctor came to the telephone.

"Doctor, I want you to make yourself perfectly at home in my house," Daniel said to him. "I regret very much having to be so far from home at a time like this."

"I think the patient may be considered out of danger," the physician replied. "He's had rather a severe cerebral shake-up, but I don't look for any complications. So far as your family is concerned, I will take care of everything."

"Who is he?" inquired Daniel. "Where are his people?"

"He is Umberto Stella, an Italian engineer from Bologna. You may have heard the name. He came to Switzerland to make a study of certain hydroelectric plants."

"Whoever he may be," said Daniel, "I want you to feel that my house and my family are at your disposal."

At Bellinzona Daniel at once set about endeavoring to find out just what course the authorities might have taken in their investigation of the semi-homicidal affair at Rivapiana. He prudently refrained from bringing up the subject himself, leaving to others to speak of it first. With such an object in view, he called on his lawyer and went with him to the courthouse, by way of settling certain formalities which, as it happened, were not at all pressing. He stopped everyone he knew on the street. He bought a couple of morning newspapers but found in them not the slightest allusion to what had occurred the evening before. It was evident that nothing whatever was known of the affair at Bellinzona. Upon finding himself alone with his lawyer, he finally ventured a hint.

"I hear," he began, "that there was some kind of a political fracas among the Italians, not far from Locarno, last night—"

"Nobody's heard anything of it around here," replied the lawyer. "It must have been one that didn't get anywhere. If it had been anything serious, they would have known of it here at once. The tension between the two parties is very high in this town!"

This answer confirmed Daniel in a suspicion he already had, to the effect that Lucca's imagination had been working overtime and had dramatized a comparatively unimportant incident.

"Those Italians," said Daniel, by way of bringing the conversation to a close, "are fine fellows, big-hearted and impulsive, but they don't know when to stop talking."

"It's better the way it is," he thought to himself, "or otherwise, Agostino and Caterina would have had to leave Switzerland." Nevertheless, the fact that he had spent a night away from home and lost a day on account of such an affair annoyed him more than a little. On the train going back, he found himself in the company of a number of farmers who were talking of the fox and how it was massacring the chickens at Magadino.

"That fox is pretty clever," one of them was saying; "he's too clever for any trap!"

"But there's a new kind of trap," a second one put in, "an Italian invention—"

"It makes a lot of noise, but it doesn't catch anything!" was the first speaker's rejoinder.

"That's true enough," said Daniel, joining in the discussion, "it does make a lot of noise, and it doesn't catch a thing. All you have is a fracas that doesn't get anywhere."

Upon reaching home, Daniel went up at once to the second floor to see the patient. But on the threshold of the room Silvia barred his way, putting a finger to her lips for him to be silent.

"He has need of complete rest," the daughter whispered in her father's ear; "no visitors, no formalities, nothing that can disturb him mentally, the doctor says."

"Then there's nothing that I can do?" Daniel was a bit crestfallen.

"Before you go back downstairs, you can take your shoes off so as not to make so much noise," Silvia advised him in a hushed tone.

Daniel took off his shoes and went back down the stairs and out into the garden. He entered the toolshed and started sharpening stakes with a hedge-knife. He had no sooner begun than Silvia came running out in her slippered feet.

"Are you crazy?" she said. "Here we have a sick man in the house, and you're making all this noise."

Daniel put down the hedge-knife.

"I suppose I may at least eat?" he plaintively inquired.

Silvia nodded and ran back upstairs. Daniel took the spade and began digging up a corner of the garden. In a little while he saw Silvia leave the house with a market-basket. He then went back into the house, took off his shoes, and hastily crept up to the second floor. At the door he met the nurse, who told him that he might enter, "but only for a moment."

There in Silvia's little white bed, Daniel had a glimpse of an enormous head all bandaged in white. Although he was not naturally of a humorous turn of mind, he could not help thinking of the head of St. Nicholas of the Snows. In that huge expanse of white, there was a tiny hole for an eye, and another one a little larger which probably represented a mouth.

"There, that will do," the nurse said, ushering Daniel to the door. Going downstairs, shoes in hand, the latter met Silvia coming back.

"Where have *you* been?" Silvia demanded in a tone of reproof.

"Is that any way to speak to your father?" said Daniel, and he went back to digging in the garden. As he was digging away, Filomena came out to him.

"Silvia's lost her head!" Filomena complained to her husband. "Ever since yesterday, she hasn't shut an eye nor touched a morsel of food."

"Silvia has found her head!" Daniel answered; "she is one girl who has a heart."

"Too much of a one!" responded Silvia's mother.

"Too much of a one? You can never have too much heart," said Daniel. He was well satisfied with his daughter. His glance, always, as he gazed at her was one filled with pride and trepidation.

At the foot of the garden wall there were a few cowslips growing. Silvia came out and plucked them all, for the patient's room.

"But he can't see them! He has his eyes bandaged!" Filomena objected.

"Mother," said Silvia, "you know very well that you can see flowers with your eyes shut."

Daniel spent a good part of the following day in a vineyard which he had on the hillside. Upon coming home in the evening, he inquired after the patient's condition and learned from Silvia that their guest was improving rapidly. They had let the nurse go, and Silvia had taken the care of the patient upon herself. Daniel had a glimpse of the man only two or three times, and the impression he received was an altogether favorable one. He had, moreover, a good many other things on his mind, and so failed to notice the profound change that was taking place in the girl.

"You might give a little less thought to others and a little more to your own daughter!" his wife reproved him one evening.

"Silvia is not a child any longer, and she has a good head on her," was Daniel's curt response.

"She has a head all right, but no experience," replied his wife, who had resolved to unburden herself of what had been on her mind for a number of days past. Daniel reflected.

"You think I ought to speak to her?" he asked.

"I think you had better before it is too late!"

The next day Daniel had to go to bring a bag of seedling peas to a friend of his who lived at Comuna, in Val Verzasca, and Silvia went with him. At Comuna it did not take him long to get through with what little business he had, and he refused all invitations to go to the café.

"I prefer a little walk with my daughter," he explained to his acquaintances; "she's getting a trifle pale lately and needs the exercise."

Father and daughter then set out in silence along the road to Gordola. The wagon-road at this point ran at a considerable elevation above the stream, which could be heard tumbling down before them.

"Couldn't we walk along it?" Silvia asked.

"I don't believe so," said Daniel; but with the desire of giving in to any whim his daughter might have, he added: "We have plenty of time, though; we might go down to the river."

They found a small foot path, steep as a stair, and after many windings and turnings, they came to where the torrent was foaming against a wall of rock. The water was clear-running, and they could see every stone at the bottom. Up to this time father and daughter had exchanged only the briefest and most insignificant of words. This more than anything else gave Daniel a sense of the change which had taken place in their relations.

"Oh, look!" cried Silvia, pointing down at her feet to a strip of sand a dozen inches or so underwater, "how pretty!"

"That is spawn," her father informed her. "At the end of September the trout leave the lower part of the river and come up toward the source, and the females, full of eggs, start looking for a well-protected sandy spot. With the aid of their tails they displace the gravel and drop their eggs, which are mixed with the sand."

"And is that the way trout are born?"

"The fertilizing is done by the males, which come along after the females and sprinkle over the spot where the eggs have been deposited a thick white milky fluid. The eggs ought to be hatching about now."

Silvia looked in wonderment at the strip of sand where this mystery was accomplished.

"How beautiful," she said, "and how simple!"

"Trout, my dear girl, don't go to church!"

That was all that was said between them during this jaunt.

"Did you speak to her?" Daniel's wife asked him when they came home.

"Yes."

"What did you say?"

"Nothing."

The engineer had left his room for the first time one day and was lying stretched out on a reclining chair in the garden, when Caterina arrived from Gordola at the same time as Daniel.

"Miss Silvia!" the engineer was calling.

Caterina stopped instantly. Going up to the hedge which hid the garden from the street, she strove to see who it was that had called.

"Mr. Daniel," she said trembling all over, "that man whom you've taken in is the spy who came to Rivapiana that evening!"

"You're out of your senses!" Daniel exclaimed; and he went on to tell Caterina how it was, in his absence, the stranger had come to be brought there. Caterina went up to the hedge again and studied the convalescent intently, as he sat in the garden jesting with Silvia.

"That's the one!" she repeated; "I'm going away before he sees me."

"Very well," said Daniel, who had turned pale. "Tell Agostino to come here tomorrow at this same time; tell him, I'll make sure that no one sees him."

Sylvia came running up to meet her father.

"Now that our patient is better," she said, "I think it would be nice of you to have a little talk with him. You will see what a really fine person it is that chance has thrown our way."

"Yes, I should be very much interested in having a talk with him," said Daniel, who was doing his best to keep from showing how disturbed he was; "we can have lunch together today."

At the table, however, as he saw the man sitting there between Silvia and Luisa, the situation became unbearable to Daniel, and, pretending that he was feeling slightly ill, he excused himself and went outside. The others joined him in the garden.

"What's new in the papers?" the self-styled engineer inquired of Danniel. "It's been weeks since I've seen a newspaper."

"There's a fresh tragedy every day," replied Daniel. "Yesterday it was a big railroad wreck in France, with hundreds of dead."

"Every day a tragedy," said the alleged engineer, "but the most tragic thing of all is the way in which men go to meet their tragedies. Think of all those hundreds of persons killed in that railroad disaster. In the same train were farmers and merchants, doctors and lawyers, students, army officers, fashionable modistes, what not. They were all on the same train, and they were not on the same train. The farmer was thinking of the prices he would get from the merchant, the lawyer was thinking of the Cross of the Legion of Honor, the army officer was thinking of his wealthy fiancée, the doctor was engaged in a mental lawsuit with the mayor of his village, and the student, out of the corner of his eye, was admiring his new necktie. Each was thus traveling in his own train. And each of us has his own train in society, until, of a sudden, we all find that we are on the same train, the train of death. The student's necktie ends up under the countryman's clogs, the officer's sword is run through the traveling salesman's belly, and the modiste's latest model goes up in smoke. For all were on the same train, and they did not know it."

"But the railroad company soon enough saw to that," said Daniel; "they soon saw to it that the unity which had been reëstablished by death was broken, by putting the fur-coated corpses on one side and those in plain workmen's blouses on the other."

"Can it be," said Silvia, "that human beings are condemned to be set over against one another like that, even after death?"

"There is a vast gulf," replied the convalescent, "between man's nature, his destiny, and the thing that society makes of him. During these past days, when I was fighting off death, that subject became an obsession with me. Each of us is traveling on his own train, and we are all on the same train!"

"Present-day society," said Daniel, "is based upon keeping men divided and set against one another. The vast majority of them are separated from and set against the fruit of their own labor. For no sooner does it leave their hands than the product of men ceases to belong to those who have made it but becomes instead their enemy; the thing produced is set over against the human beings who produced it, the inanimate object becomes the fetish before which living man must bow."

"But must it always be like that?" persisted Silvia.

"When I was young," the invalid went on, "I too hoped for a society that would be different from the one we have."

Daniel rose and went back to his spading. Spring was coming on, and it was time that the work was getting under way. It was with an unwonted vigor that he sank the spade in the earth, throwing the entire weight of his body upon his right foot and tossing the clods into the air. Behind him came Filomena, breaking up the clods with a three-pronged rake. A pleasing odor of moist earth hung over the garden. The sweat was trickling down Daniel's face; internally, he was very much upset. The invalid remained in the garden, stretched out in the armchair, until the first evening stars appeared from behind Monte Ceneri.

"It's been so long," he said, half to himself, "it's been so many, many years since I've had a glimpse of the sky."

Silvia rose and returned shortly with a book.

"There is a similar case here," she told him, "in this first volume of Tolstoy's *War and Peace*. Prince Andrei, in November, 1805, had fallen wounded in the outskirts of Pratzen, in a battle between the Russian troops and those of Napoleon. Here is what Tolstoy has to say about it:

" 'Then he opened his eyes, to see what the outcome of the struggle between the two Frenchmen and the artilleryman had been, whether the red-haired artilleryman had been slain or not; he also wanted to know whether the cannon had been saved or captured. But all he could see was the high heavens up above him, no longer filled with light, but immeasurably far above, and covered over with tranquil-gliding gray clouds. "How calm and still and restful it all is," thinks Prince Andrei. "All that has no resemblance whatsoever to this running, shrieking and fighting of ours; the tranquil gliding of those clouds over the high unending heavens has nothing in common with this struggle of the Frenchmen and the artilleryman, as with grim, distorted faces they strive for the possession of a cannon swob. How does it happen that I have never seen these heavens before? How happy I am to have seen them at last. Yes, all is as naught, it is nothing, nothing beyond that. Yet even it does not exist; there is nothing but stillness and peace. And God be thanked for it!" ' "

The moon came up, flooding the Magadino plain with an eerie light.

"The moon," Luisa observed, "has eyes and a nose like us."

"Those things," Silvia explained to her younger sister, "are seas and mountains."

Their guest took it upon himself to round out the explanation.

"If the inhabitants of the moon," he said, "happen to be looking down at the earth at this moment, we probably look much the same to them as the moon does to us. Seen from up there, what are the great cities of the earth? Italy must look like a comma and Switzerland like a period."

"And how does Mussolini look from up there?" Luisa wanted to know.

"You'd better watch out," said Daniel, "or you'll be straining your eyes."

A general laugh went round at this.

The next day, when Daniel saw Agostino coming, he went out to meet him and brought him into the house from the side opposite the garden, where the engineer was seated out in the sun. The two men went up to Luisa's room, and there, from behind the Venetian shutters, Agostino was able to take a good look at the man without being seen.

"That is the one!" he said softly; and rubbing his hands, he added: "This time he's not going to get away from us!"

"What do you mean?" said Daniel with a frown.

"I mean just that, that he's not going to get away from us this time."

"You're joking." The tone of Daniel's voice took his friend from Bergamo by surprise.

"The fox is in the trap," said the latter; "do you mean to say, you're going to let him go? We've got in our hands at last, without his knowing it, one of those who in Italy have been massacring our people, in prison and on the deportation islands; and should we let him get away?" Agostino was wrought up about the matter.

"That man is a guest in my house," Daniel calmly announced.

"He's a spy!" said Agostino.

"He was a spy," answered Daniel, in the same calm voice, "but now he's a guest. He came to my house at the point of death and sought hospitality, and he has been cured in my house."

It was all Agostino could do to believe his ears.

"I can't understand such scruples as that," he said. "You know as well as I do the methods that the Fascists use against us; you know, don't you, there are no moral scruples where they are concerned?"

"I know it," was Daniel's response; "that's why I'm not a Fascist."

"And that's why we're always beaten!"

"That's why we'll win out in the end!" This was Daniel's last word. Agostino could only shake his head, in the face of such stubbornness as this.

"How long is he going to be here yet?"

"Another week, perhaps; he's not very strong yet."

"Then we'll have time to talk it over before he has a chance to get away."

Daniel decided to say nothing about it to the other members of the family, so as not to alarm them or arouse their guest's suspicions. It was at this time that one of Filomena's sisters who lived at Vira had a child and Daniel with his wife and Silvia went to pay her a visit, leaving Luisa at home with the invalid.

"You've been here all these weeks," said the little girl, "and you haven't yet seen our house."

"That's because I've been in bed all the time," said the engineer.

Luisa then proceeded to show him the storeroom, where they kept the potatoes, the onions, their fruit, and the garden tools. On the second floor she showed him her own room, which her sister Silvia shared with her for the time being. The guest's attention was attracted by a photograph fastened up on the wall with a tissue paper flower on either side.

"Who is that?" he asked.

"That's Matteotti," Luisa informed him.

The engineer dropped down on a chair.

"Who is Matteotti?" was his next question.

"He was the man who stuck up for the poor people, and for that reason he was killed by Mussolini."

"Are you an anti-Fascist?"

"I most certainly am!"

"And Silvia, what about her?"

"She's more of a one than I am."

"And your father?"

"More than any of us—not in what he says, but in what he does."

Luisa then showed the guest the third floor.

"This is my parents' room," she said.

"And what's this?" The engineer pointed to a small room adjoining.

"Oh, you mustn't go in there; Daddy doesn't allow it. He has a lot of papers in there, and he doesn't want us to muss them up."

Luisa and the guest went back to the garden. The invalid began striding up and down the path and kept it up for a good half hour. Then, as if he had made up his mind to something, he came up to Luisa.

"Would you mind running down with a telegram for me?" And when he had given the little girl the wording of the telegram and a few pennies, he added: "I'm tired; I am going to bed at once."

It was in vain that Silvia knocked at their guest's door the next morning, when she came to bring him his breakfast. Her repeated knocking brought not the slightest response. The door was locked. Feeling certain that something dreadful had happened, Silvia began calling at the top of her voice, and the whole family came running up. When Daniel had taken the door off its hinges, it was found that the guest was not in his room. The bed had not been slept in. His suitcases had disappeared.

"He's gone!" Silvia cried.

"He left without saying good-by!" wailed Luisa.

"He's been gone ever since yesterday," Filomena declared, pointing to the bed.

In a couple of bounds, Daniel was on the third floor, and a moment later, the other members of the family were terror-struck by his furious outcries:

"Thief! Crook! Traitor! He's taken all my papers with him! He's taken away all my papers!"

It was like a mortal blow to Daniel. When the women came up, their eyes fell on the disordered room; all the drawers had been overturned on the floor. At this point, Agostino came in. He did not know what had happened yet, but he was very pale and he seemed excited.

"Yesterday evening," Daniel explained to him, "the spy left the house while I was away and took all my papers with him, among others, those about the smuggling. Quick! There's not a minute to lose; we must let the ones concerned know."

"This morning," said Agostino, "at Luino, a score of seasonal laborers, who are in the habit of coming over to work in Switzerland during the daytime and going back into Italy at night, were arrested."

Silvia stood staring at her father and Agostino, as if all this were some kind of play which they were putting on for her benefit.

"No! no!" she moaned, "it's not true! It's all a joke! Agostino, for heaven's sake, tell me that it's not true!"

Daniel was on his feet.

"We've got to think of saving the others, before that spy gets his hands on them!"

And he and Agostino were off in a hurry.

It was late in the evening when Daniel came home. Filomena and Luisa were seated by the hearth, while Silvia sat on a chest, over in one corner of the dark kitchen.

"The smugglers," announced Daniel from the kitchen door, "were arrested early this morning. A consignment of books at Brissago was seized at noon today. The police have been to Caterina's house. I hear that Agostino has been arrested, and that he will probably be expelled from the country. Haven't they been here yet?"

"No," said Filomena.

Daniel dropped down on the doorsill. The night wore slowly on, with the slow procession of the stars. The cock crowed for the first time, but no one so much as thought of going to bed, no one thought of going up to the second floor where *that man* had lived until yesterday. The cock crowed a second time. Mother and daughter still sat by the hearth, the elder daughter on a chest over in a corner of the kitchen, and the father there on the doorsill. It was like a wake for the dead. The cock crowed a third time.

Then came an animal's shrill cry, like the yelp of a dog in pain, and the squawking of hens broke in upon the silence of the night. Daniel leaped to his feet and ran across the garden to the hen-house. In front of it he saw a fox with one paw in the trap; planting its remaining feet upon the ground and arching its back, the animal was doing its utmost to free the prisoned member. When it saw the man approaching, it began leaping furiously from side to side, tugging on the chain by which the trap was securely fastened.

"At last!" said Daniel in a ferocious tone of voice. And snatching up an ax which lay beside the hen-house, as if he were hewing at an oak, he began raining terrible blows upon the animal's head, its back, its belly, its legs—blow after blow, the blows of a madman, death-dealing blows continued to rain down, even after the little beast had been hacked to tiny bits and reduced to nothing more than a puddle of blood-soaked mush.

Translated by Samuel Putnam

SILONE: *The Trap*

1. *How does the title apply to the events? Is it simply a device or a view of life? Explain how Silone makes the trap into a vast symbol.*

2. *What does the fox signify in the story? the flowers? Why does Daniel want to call one pig "Benito"?*

3. *How does Silone make us aware of the time of the action?*

4. *What does the convalescent mean by " 'Each of us is travelling on his own train, and we are all in the same train' "? Can you see Silone's political views suggested by this statement?*

5. *Is Daniel right in permitting the convalescent to recover even though he is a Fascist opposed to everything Daniel believes in? Does one honor rules in a struggle of this sort? Do you admire Daniel for his action, or do you think him foolish?*

6. *Explain the ending in terms of the fox, of Fascism, of Daniel himself.*

7. What values does Silone seem to honor in this story? Compare his views with Camus' in "The Guest" and Moravia's in "The Ruin of Humanity." What does Silone share with Camus? How do they differ from Moravia?

8. Compare the ending of this story with that of Pirandello's "The Soft Touch of Grass." Is the frustration of one character comparable to the other's?

9. You may be reminded of D. H. Lawrence's "The Fox" after finishing this story. How does the fox symbolism differ in the two works?

Graham Greene

BROTHER

Graham Greene's early years outwardly showed little of the violence and furious bursts of belief and unbelief which mark his serious work, although his inner life, we learn from his essays, was tumultuous. Born in Hertfordshire, England, in 1904, the son of a headmaster, Greene attended Oxford University and then took up newspaper work. In the 1930's, he began to write what he called "entertainments" (This Gun for Hire, The Confidential Agent, The Ministry of Fear), *but his first major work,* Brighton Rock *(1938), was not to appear for nearly another ten years. Then followed a series of artistic successes:* The Power and the Glory *(1940),* The Heart of the Matter *(1948),* The End of the Affair *(1951), as well as several short stories and numerous essays and reviews. Two recent plays that brought his name to Broadway,* The Potting Shed *and* The Complaisant Lover, *and a novel that many critics have acclaimed as his masterpiece,* The Burnt-Out Case *(1961), remind us that Greene's creative energies showed few signs of flagging as he entered his sixties. In that decade, he wrote books as different in content and form as* The Comedians *and* Travels with Charley. *While "Brother" lacks his characteristic preoccupation with Catholic problems, it nevertheless does adumbrate his social and political views.*

THE Communists were the first to appear. They walked quickly, a group of about a dozen, up the boulevard which runs from Combat to Ménilmontant; a young man and a girl lagged a little way behind because the man's leg was hurt and the girl was helping him along. They looked impatient, harassed, hopeless, as if they were trying to catch a train which they knew already in their hearts they were too late to catch.

The proprietor of the café saw them coming when they were still a long way off; the lamps at that time were still alight (it was later that the bullets broke the bulbs and dropped darkness all over that quarter of Paris), and the group showed up plainly in the wide barren boulevard. Since sunset only one customer had entered the café, and very soon

380]

after sunset firing could be heard from the direction of Combat; the Métro station had closed hours ago. And yet something obstinate and undefeatable in the proprietor's character prevented him from putting up the shutters; it might have been avarice; he could not himself have told what it was as he pressed his broad yellow forehead against the glass and stared this way and that, up the boulevard and down the boulevard.

But when he saw the group and their air of hurry he began immediately to close his café. First he went and warned his only customer, who was practising billiard shots, walking round and round the table, frowning and stroking a thin moustache between shots, a little green in the face under the low diffused lights.

"The Reds are coming," the proprietor said, "you'd better be off. I'm putting up the shutters."

"Don't interrupt. They won't harm me," the customer said. "This is a tricky shot. Red's in baulk. Off the cushion. Screw on spot." He shot his ball straight into a pocket.

"I knew you couldn't do anything with that," the proprietor said, nodding his bald head. "You might just as well go home. Give me a hand with the shutters first. I've sent my wife away." The customer turned on him maliciously, rattling the cue between his fingers. "It was your talking that spoilt the shot. You've cause to be frightened, I dare say. But I'm a poor man. I'm safe. I'm not going to stir." He went across to his coat and took out a dry cigar. "Bring me a bock." He walked round the table on his toes and the balls clicked and the proprietor padded back into the bar, elderly and irritated. He did not fetch the beer but began to close the shutters; every move he made was slow and clumsy. Long before he had finished the group of Communists was outside.

He stopped what he was doing and watched them with furtive dislike. He was afraid that the rattle of the shutters would attract their attention. If I am very quiet and still, he thought, they may go on, and he remembered with malicious pleasure the police barricade across the Place de la République. That will finish them. In the meanwhile I must be very quiet, very still, and he felt a kind of warm satisfaction at the idea that worldly wisdom dictated the very attitude most suited to his nature. So he stared through the edge of a shutter, yellow, plump, cautious, hearing the billiard balls crackle in the other room, seeing the young man come limping up the pavement on the girl's arm, watching them stand and stare with dubious faces up the boulevard towards Combat.

But when they came into the café he was already behind the bar, smiling and bowing and missing nothing, noticing how they had divided forces, how six of them had begun to run back the way they had come.

The young man sat down in a dark corner above the cellar stairs and the others stood round the door waiting for something to happen. It gave the proprietor an odd feeling that they should stand there in his café not asking for a drink, knowing what to expect, when he, the owner, knew nothing, understood nothing. At last the girl said "Cognac," leaving the others and coming to the bar, but when he had poured it out for her, very careful to give a fair and not a generous measure, she simply took it to the man sitting in the dark and held it to his mouth.

"Three francs," the proprietor said. She took the glass and sipped a little and turned it so that the man's lips might touch the same spot. Then she knelt down and rested her forehead against the man's forehead and so they stayed.

"Three francs," the proprietor said, but he could not make his voice bold. The man was no longer visible in his corner, only the girl's back, thin and shabby in a black cotton frock, as she knelt, leaning forward to find the man's face. The proprietor was daunted by the four men at the door, by the knowledge that they were Reds who had no respect for private property, who would drink his wine and go away without paying, who would rape his women (but there was only his wife, and she was not there), who would rob his bank, who would murder him as soon as look at him. So with fear in his heart he gave up the three francs as lost rather than attract any more attention.

Then the worst that he contemplated happened.

One of the men at the door came up to the bar and told him to pour out four glasses of cognac. "Yes, yes," the proprietor said, fumbling with the cork, praying secretly to the Virgin to send an angel, to send the police, to send the Gardes Mobiles, now, immediately, before the cork came out, "that will be twelve francs."

"Oh, no," the man said, "we are all comrades here. Share and share alike. Listen," he said, with earnest mockery, leaning across the bar, "all we have is yours just as much as it's ours, comrade," and stepping back a pace he presented himself to the proprietor, so that he might take his choice of stringy tie, of threadbare trousers, of starved features. "And it follows from that, comrade, that all you have is ours. So four cognacs. Share and share alike."

"Of course," the proprietor said, "I was only joking." Then he stood with bottle poised, and the four glasses tingled upon the counter. "A machine-gun," he said, "up by Combat," and smiled to see how for the moment the men forgot their brandy as they fidgeted near the door. Very soon now, he thought, and I shall be quit of them.

"A machine-gun," the Red said incredulously, "they're using machine-guns?"

"Well," the proprietor said, encouraged by this sign that the Gardes Mobiles were not very far away, "you can't pretend that you aren't armed yourselves." He leant across the bar in a way that was almost paternal. "After all, you know, your ideas—they wouldn't do in France. Free love."

"Who's talking of free love?" the Red said.

The proprietor shrugged and smiled and nodded at the corner. The girl knelt with her head on the man's shoulder, her back to the room. They were quite silent and the glass of brandy stood on the floor beside them. The girl's beret was pushed back on her head and one stocking was laddered and darned from knee to ankle.

"What, those two? They aren't lovers."

"I," the proprietor said, "with my bourgeois notions would have thought . . ."

"He's her brother," the Red said.

The men came clustering round the bar and laughed at him, but softly as if a sleeper or a sick person were in the house. All the time they were listening for something. Between their shoulders the proprietor could look out across the boulevard; he could see the corner of the Faubourg du Temple.

"What are you waiting for?"

"For friends," the Red said. He made a gesture with open palm as if to say, You see, we share and share alike. We have no secrets.

Something moved at the corner of the Faubourg du Temple.

"Four more cognacs," the Red said.

"What about those two?" the proprietor asked.

"Leave them alone. They'll look after themselves. They're tired."

How tired they were. No walk up the boulevard from Ménilmontant could explain the tiredness. They seemed to have come farther and fared a great deal worse than their companions. They were more starved; they were infinitely more hopeless, sitting in their dark corner away from the friendly gossip, the amicable desperate voices which now confused the proprietor's brain, until for a moment he believed himself to be a host entertaining friends.

He laughed and made a broad joke directed at the two of them; but they made no sign of understanding. Perhaps they were to be pitied, cut off from the camaraderie round the counter; perhaps they were to be envied for their deeper comradeship. The proprietor thought for no reason at all of the bare grey trees of the Tuileries like a series of exclamation marks drawn against the winter sky. Puzzled, disintegrated, with all his bearings lost, he stared out through the door towards the Faubourg.

It was as if they had not seen each other for a long while and would soon again be saying good-bye. Hardly aware of what he was doing he filled the four glasses with brandy. They stretched out worn blunted fingers for them.

"Wait," he said. "I've got something better than this"; then paused, conscious of what was happening across the boulevard. The lamplight splashed down on blue steel helmets; the Gardes Mobiles were lining out across the entrance to the Faubourg, and a machine-gun pointed directly at the café windows.

So, the proprietor thought, my prayers are answered. Now I must do my part, not look, not warn them, save myself. Have they covered the side door? I will get the other bottle. Real Napoleon brandy. Share and share alike.

He felt a curious lack of triumph as he opened the trap of the bar and came out. He tried not to walk quickly back towards the billiard room. Nothing that he did must warn these men; he tried to spur himself with the thought that every slow casual step he took was a blow for France, for his café, for his savings. He had to step over the girl's feet to pass her; she was asleep. He noted the sharp shoulder blades thrusting through the cotton, and raised his eyes and met her brother's, filled with pain and despair.

He stopped. He found he could not pass without a word. It was as if he needed to explain something, as if he belonged to the wrong party. With false bonhomie he waved the corkscrew he carried in the other's face. "Another cognac, eh?"

"It's no good talking to them," the Red said. "They're German. They don't understand a word."

"German?"

"That's what's wrong with his leg. A concentration camp."

The proprietor told himself that he must be quick, that he must put a door between him and them, that the end was very close, but he was bewildered by the hopelessness in the man's gaze. "What's he doing here?" Nobody answered him. It was as if his question were too foolish to need a reply. With his head sunk upon his breast the proprietor went past, and the girl slept on. He was like a stranger leaving a room where all the rest are friends. A German. They don't understand a word; and up, up through the heavy darkness of his mind, through the avarice and the dubious triumph, a few German words remembered from very old days climbed like spies into the light: a line from the *Lorelei* learnt at school, *Kamerad* with its war-time suggestion of fear and surrender, and oddly from nowhere the phrase *mein Bruder*. He opened the door of the billiard room and closed it behind him and softly turned the key.

"Spot in baulk," the customer explained and leant across the great green table, but while he took aim, wrinkling his narrow peevish eyes, the firing started. It came in two bursts with a rip of glass between. The girl cried out something, but it was not one of the words he knew. Then feet ran across the floor, the trap of the bar slammed. The proprietor sat back against the table and listened and listened for any further sound; but silence came in under the door and silence through the keyhole.

"The cloth. My God, the cloth," the customer said, and the proprietor looked down at his own hand which was working the corkscrew into the table.

"Will this absurdity never end?" the customer said. "I shall go home."

"Wait," the proprietor said. "Wait." He was listening to voices and footsteps in the other room. These were voices he did not recognize. Then a car drove up and presently drove away again. Somebody rattled the handle of the door.

"Who is it?" the proprietor called.

"Who are you? Open that door."

"Ah," the customer said with relief, "the police. Where was I now? Spot in baulk." He began to chalk his cue. The proprietor opened the door. Yes, the Gardes Mobiles had arrived; he was safe again, though his windows were smashed. The Reds had vanished as if they had never been. He looked at the raised trap, at the smashed electric bulbs, at the broken bottle which dripped behind the bar. The café was full of men, and he remembered with odd relief that he had not had time to lock the side door.

"Are you the owner?" the officer asked. "A bock for each of these men and a cognac for myself. Be quick about it."

The proprietor calculated: "Nine francs fifty," and watched closely with bent head the coins rattle down upon the counter.

"You see," the officer said with significance, "we pay." He nodded towards the side door. "Those others: did they pay?"

No, the proprietor admitted, they had not paid, but as he counted the coins and slipped them into the till, he caught himself silently repeating the officer's order—"A bock for each of these men." Those others, he thought, one's got to say that for them, they weren't mean about the drink. It was four cognacs with them. But, of course, they did not pay. "And my windows," he complained aloud with sudden asperity, "what about my windows?"

"Never you mind," the officer said, "the government will pay. You have only to send in your bill. Hurry up now with my cognac. I have no time for gossip."

"You can see for yourself," the proprietor said, "how the bottles have been broken. Who will pay for that?"

"Everything will be paid for," the officer said.

"And now I must go to the cellar to fetch more."

He was angry at the reiteration of the word pay. They enter my café, he thought, they smash my windows, they order me about and think that all is well if they pay, pay, pay. It occurred to him that these men were intruders.

"Step to it," the officer said and turned and rebuked one of the men who had leant his rifle against the bar.

At the top of the cellar stairs the proprietor stopped. They were in darkness, but by the light from the bar he could just make out a body half-way down. He began to tremble violently and it was some seconds before he could strike a match. The young German lay head downwards, and the blood from his head had dropped on to the step below. His eyes were open and stared back at the proprietor with the old despairing expression of life. The proprietor would not believe that he was dead. "Kamerad," he said bending down, while the match singed his fingers and went out, trying to recall some phrase in German, but he could only remember, as he bent lower still, "mein Bruder." Then suddenly he turned and ran up the steps, waved the match-box in the officer's face, and called out in a low hysterical voice to him and his men and to the customer stooping under the low green shade, "Cochons. Cochons."

"What was that? What was that?" the officer exclaimed. "Did you say that he was your brother? It's impossible," and he frowned incredulously at the proprietor and rattled the coins in his pocket.

GREENE: *Brother*

1. *Why does Greene omit the background to the events of the story?*
2. *Greene says there was "something obstinate and undefeatable" in*

the proprietor. What does he mean? How is this quality related to the last two paragraphs?

3. What is the effect of the man practicing billiards in the background?

4. When does the proprietor begin to change his mind about his visitors? Why at that particular point? Do you agree with the proprietor's frame of mind at this moment? Why?

5. Why does the proprietor, who depends upon payment to survive, become sympathetic to the men who do not pay for their drinks and hostile to the men who do? Does the last line of the story seem relevant here?

6. Does the story have any significance beyond this small vignette? How does the word "Kamerad" fit into this scheme?

7. Should common humanity prevail over political differences? Or are the latter so great that people must put aside their humanity? What is Greene's position here?

8. Greene's novels are characterized by his sympathetic portrayals of outsiders and outlaws of every degree: the adulterer, the whisky priest, the pathological gunman, the punk hoodlum, the philandering policeman, the burnt-out case, and, in this story, the Communist refugee. Do you believe that an artist should present such outcasts, some of them vicious enemies of society, in so sympathetic and human a light? Does it mean that he approves of their habits and practices?

9. Is Catholic France a better setting for this story than, say, Protestant England or Scandinavia?

Jean-Paul Sartre

THE WALL

Born in 1905, Jean-Paul Sartre has been not only a prolific writer of fiction, but also an influential philosopher, social commentator, and playwright. Certainly one of the most brilliant men of letters alive, his is also the most important name among the Parisian Existentialists active in the 1940's and 1950's. His best-known fiction is Nausea *(1938),* "The Wall" *(1939), and the novels making up the incomplete tetralogy,* Roads to Freedom. *Such plays as* No Exit, Dirty Hands, *and* The Flies *have been performed often and have gained him distinction both for the cogency of their ideas and for their technical brilliance. His latest work for the theater,* The Condemned of Altona *(1960), is one of the masterpieces of modern times.* "The Wall" *illustrates a typical Existentialist situation, wherein men who face death must come to terms with what they are and how they have lived. Having rejected the Nobel Prize for Literature, Sartre, in the 1960's, turned increasingly to polemical writing and to his enormous biography of Flaubert, of which the published Part I numbers more than two thousand pages.*

THEY pushed us into a big white room and I began to blink because the light hurt my eyes. Then I saw a table and four men behind the table, civilians, looking over the papers. They had bunched another group of prisoners in the back and we had to cross the whole room to join them. There were several I knew and some others who must have been foreigners. The two in front of me were blond with round skulls; they looked alike. I supposed they were French. The smaller one kept hitching up his pants; nerves.

It lasted about three hours; I was dizzy and my head was empty; but the room was well heated and I found that pleasant enough: for the past 24 hours we hadn't stopped shivering. The guards brought the prisoners up to the table, one after the other. The four men asked each one his name and occupation. Most of the time they didn't go any further—or they would simply ask a question here and there: "Did you have anything to do with the sabotage of munitions?" Or "Where were you the morning of the 9th and what were you doing?" They didn't listen to the answers or at least didn't seem to. They were quiet for a moment and then looking straight in front of them began to write. They asked Tom if it were true he was in the International Brigade; Tom couldn't tell them otherwise because of the papers they found in his coat. They didn't ask Juan anything but they wrote for a long time after he told them his name.

"My brother José is the anarchist," Juan said, "you know he isn't here any more. I don't belong to any party, I never had anything to do with politics."

They didn't answer. Juan went on, "I haven't done anything. I don't want to pay for somebody else."

His lips trembled. A guard shut him up and took him away. It was my turn.

"Your name is Pablo Ibbieta?"

"Yes."

The man looked at the papers and asked me, "Where's Ramon Gris?"

"I don't know."

"You hid him in your house from the 6th to the 19th."

"No."

They wrote for a minute and then the guards took me out. In the corridor Tom and Juan were waiting between two guards. We started walking. Tom asked one of the guards, "So?"

"So what?" the guard said.

"Was that the cross-examination or the sentence?"

"Sentence," the guard said.

"What are they going to do with us?"

The guard answered dryly, "Sentence will be read in your cell."

As a matter of fact, our cell was one of the hospital cellars. It was terrifically cold there because of the drafts. We shivered all night and it wasn't much better during the day. I had spent the previous five days in a cell in a monastery, a sort of hole in the wall that must have dated from the middle ages: since there were a lot of prisoners and not much room, they locked us up anywhere. I didn't miss my cell; I hadn't suffered too much from the cold but I was alone; after a long time it gets irritating. In the cellar I had company. Juan hardly ever spoke: he was afraid and he was too young to have anything to say. But Tom was a good talker and he knew Spanish well.

There was a bench in the cellar and four mats. When they took us back we sat and waited in silence. After a long moment, Tom said, "We're screwed."

"I think so too," I said, "but I don't think they'll do anything to the kid."

"They don't have a thing against him," said Tom. "He's the brother of a militiaman and that's all."

I looked at Juan: he didn't seem to hear. Tom went on, "You know what they do in Saragossa? They lay the men down on the road and run over them with trucks. A Moroccan deserter told us that. They said it was to save ammunition."

"It doesn't save gas," I said.

I was annoyed at Tom: he shouldn't have said that.

"Then there's officers walking along the road," he went on, "supervising it all. They stick their hands in their pockets and smoke cigarettes. You think they finish off the guys? Hell no. They let them scream. Sometimes for an hour. The Moroccan said he damned near puked the first time."

"I don't believe they'll do that here," I said. "Unless they're really short on ammunition."

Day was coming in through four airholes and a round opening they had made in the ceiling on the left, and you could see the sky through it. Through this hole, usually closed by a trap, they unloaded coal into the cellar. Just below the hole there was a big pile of coal dust; it had been used to heat the hospital but since the beginning of the war the patients were evacuated and the coal stayed there, unused; sometimes it even got rained on because they had forgotten to close the trap.

Tom began to shiver. "Good Jesus Christ I'm cold," he said. "Here it goes again."

He got up and began to do exercises. At each movement his shirt opened on his chest, white and hairy. He lay on his back, raised his legs in the air and bicycled. I saw his great rump trembling. Tom was husky but he had too much fat. I thought how rifle bullets or the sharp points of bayonets would soon be sunk into this mass of tender flesh as in a lump of butter. It wouldn't have made me feel like that if he'd been thin.

I wasn't exactly cold, but I couldn't feel my arms and shoulders any more. Sometimes I had the impression I was missing something and began to look around for my coat and then suddenly remembered they hadn't given me a coat. It was rather uncomfortable. They took our clothes and gave them to their soldiers, leaving us only our shirts—and those canvas pants that hospital patients wear in the middle of summer. After a while Tom got up and sat next to me, breathing heavily.

"Warmer?"

"Good Christ, no. But I'm out of wind."

Around eight o'clock in the evening a major came in with two *falangistas*. He had a sheet of paper in his hand. He asked the guard, "What are the names of those three?"

"Steinbock, Ibbieta and Mirbal," the guard said.

The major put on his eyeglasses and scanned the list: "Steinbock . . . Steinbock . . . Oh yes . . . You are sentenced to death. You will be shot tomorrow morning." He went on looking. "The other two as well."

"That's not possible," Juan said. "Not me."

The major looked at him amazed. "What's your name?"

"Juan Mirbal," he said.

"Well, your name is there," said the major. "You're sentenced."

"I didn't do anything," Juan said

The major shrugged his shoulders and turned to Tom and me.

"You're Basque?"

"Nobody is Basque."

He looked annoyed. "They told me there were three Basques. I'm not going to waste my time running after them. Then naturally you don't want a priest?"

We didn't even answer.

He said, "A Belgian doctor is coming shortly. He is authorized to spend the night with you." He made a military salute and left.

"What did I tell you," Tom said. "We get it."

"Yes," I said, "it's a rotten deal for the kid."

I said that to be decent but I didn't like the kid. His face was too thin and fear and suffering had disfigured it, twisting all his features. Three days before he was a smart sort of kid, not too bad; but now he looked like an old fairy and I thought how he'd never be young again, even if they were to let him go. It wouldn't have been too hard to have a little pity for him but pity disgusts me, or rather it horrifies me. He hadn't said anything more but he had turned grey; his face and hands were both grey. He sat down again and looked at the ground with round eyes. Tom was good hearted, he wanted to take his arm, but the kid tore himself away violently and made a face.

"Let him alone," I said in a low voice, "you can see he's going to blubber."

Tom obeyed regretfully; he would have liked to comfort the kid, it would have passed his time and he wouldn't have been tempted to think about himself. But it annoyed me: I'd never thought about death because I never had any reason to, but now the reason was here and there was nothing to do but think about it.

Tom began to talk. "So you think you've knocked guys off, do you?"

he asked me. I didn't answer. He began explaining to me that he had knocked off six since the beginning of August; he didn't realize the situation and I could tell he didn't *want* to realize it. I hadn't quite realized it myself, I wondered if it hurt much, I thought of bullets, I imagined their burning hail through my body. All that was beside the real question; but I was calm: we had all night to understand. After a while Tom stopped talking and I watched him out of the corner of my eye; I saw he too had turned grey and he looked rotten; I told myself "Now it starts." It was almost dark, a dim glow filtered through the airholes and the pile of coal and made a big stain beneath the spot of sky; I could already see a star through the hole in the ceiling: the night would be pure and icy.

The door opened and two guards came in, followed by a blonde man in a tan uniform. He saluted us. "I am the doctor," he said. "I have authorization to help you in these trying hours."

He had an agreeable and distinguished voice. I said, "What do you want here?"

"I am at your disposal. I shall do all I can to make your last moments less difficult."

"What did you come here for? There are others, the hospital's full of them."

"I was sent here," he answered with a vague look. "Ah! Would you like to smoke?" he added hurriedly, "I have cigarettes and even cigars."

He offered us English cigarettes and *puros*, but we refused. I looked him in the eyes and he seemed irritated. I said to him, "You aren't here on an errand of mercy. Besides, I know you. I saw you with the fascists in the barracks yard the day I was arrested."

I was going to continue, but something surprising suddenly happened to me; the presence of this doctor no longer interested me. Generally when I'm on somebody I don't let go. But the desire to talk left me completely; I shrugged and turned my eyes away. A little later I raised my head; he was watching me curiously. The guards were sitting on a mat. Pedro, the tall thin one, was twiddling his thumbs, the other shook his head from time to time to keep from falling asleep.

"Do you want a light?" Pedro suddenly asked the doctor. The other nodded "Yes": I think he was about as smart as a log, but he surely wasn't bad. Looking in his cold blue eyes it seemed to me that his only sin was lack of imagination. Pedro went out and came back with an oil lamp which he set on the corner of the bench. It gave a bad light but it was better than nothing: they had left us in the dark the night before. For a long time I watched the circle of light the lamp made on the ceiling. I was fascinated. Then suddenly I woke up, the circle of light disappeared and I felt myself crushed under an enormous weight. It was not the thought of death or fear; it was nameless. My cheeks burned and my head ached.

I shook myself and looked at my two friends. Tom had hidden his face in his hands. I could only see the fat white nape of his neck. Little Juan was the worst; his mouth was open and his nostrils trembled. The doctor went to him and put his hand on his shoulder to comfort him, but his eyes stayed cold. Then I saw the Belgian's hand drop stealthily along Juan's arm, down to the wrist. Juan paid no attention. The Belgian took his wrist between three fingers, distractedly, the same time drawing back a little and turning his back to me. But I leaned backward and saw him take a watch from his pocket and look at it for a moment, never letting go of the wrist. After a minute he let the hand fall inert and went and leaned his back against the wall, then, as if he suddenly remembered something very important which had to be jotted down on the spot, he took a notebook from his pocket and wrote a few lines. "Bastard," I thought angrily, "let him come and take my pulse. I'll shove my fist in his rotten face."

He didn't come but I felt him watching me. I raised my head and returned his look. Impersonally, he said to me, "Doesn't it seem cold to you here?" He looked cold, he was blue.

"I'm not cold," I told him.

He never took his hard eyes off me. Suddenly I understood and my hands went to my face: I was drenched in sweat. In this cellar, in the midst of winter, in the midst of drafts, I was sweating. I ran my hands through my hair, gummed together with perspiration; at the same time I saw my shirt was damp and sticking to my skin: I had been dripping for an hour and hadn't felt it. But that swine of a Belgian hadn't missed a thing; he had seen the drops rolling down my cheeks and thought: this is the manifestation of an almost pathological state of terror; and he had felt normal and proud of being alive because he was cold. I wanted to stand up and smash his face but no sooner had I made the slightest gesture than my rage and shame were wiped out; I fell back on the bench with indifference.

I satisfied myself by rubbing my neck with my handkerchief because now I felt the sweat dropping from my hair onto my neck and it was unpleasant. I soon gave up rubbing, it was useless; my handkerchief was already soaked and I was still sweating. My buttocks were sweating too and my damp trousers were glued to the bench.

Suddenly Juan spoke. "You're a doctor?"

"Yes," the Belgian said.

"Does it hurt . . . very long?"

"Huh? When . . . ? Oh, no," the Belgian said paternally. "Not at all. It's over quickly." He acted as though he were calming a cash customer.

"But I . . . they told me . . . sometimes they have to fire twice."

"Sometimes," the Belgian said, nodding. "It may happen that the first volley reaches no vital organs."

"Then they have to reload their rifles and aim all over again?" He thought for a moment and then added hoarsely, "That takes time!"

He had a terrible fear of suffering, it was all he thought about: it was his age. I never thought much about it and it wasn't fear of suffering that made me sweat.

I got up and walked to the pile of coal dust. Tom jumped up and threw me a hateful look: I had annoyed him because my shoes squeaked. I wondered if my face looked as frightened as his: I saw he was sweating too. The sky was superb, no light filtered into the dark corner and I had only to raise my head to see the Big Dipper. But it wasn't like it had been: the night before I could see a great piece of sky from my monastery cell and each hour of the day brought me a different memory. Morning, when the sky was a hard, light blue, I thought of beaches on the Atlantic; at noon I saw the sun and I remembered a bar in Seville where I drank *manzanilla* and ate olives and anchovies; afternoons I was in the shade and I thought of the deep shadow which spreads over half a bull-ring leaving the other half shimmering in sunlight; it was really hard to see the whole world reflected in the sky like that. But now I could watch the sky as much as I pleased, it no longer evoked anything in me. I liked that better. I came back and sat near Tom. A long moment passed.

Tom began speaking in a low voice. He had to talk, without that he wouldn't have been able to recognize himself in his own mind. I thought he was talking to me but he wasn't looking at me. He was undoubtedly afraid to see me as I was, grey and sweating: we were alike and worse than mirrors of each other. He watched the Belgian, the living.

"Do you understand?" he said. "I don't understand."

I began to speak in a low voice too. I watched the Belgian.

"Why? What's the matter?"

"Something is going to happen to us that I can't understand."

There was a strange smell about Tom. It seemed to me I was more sensitive than usual to odors. I grinned. "You'll understand in a while."

"It isn't clear," he said obstinately. "I want to be brave but first I have to know . . . Listen, they're going to take us into the courtyard. Good. They're going to stand up in front of us. How many?"

"I don't know. Five or eight. Not more."

"All right. There'll be eight. Someone'll holler 'aim!' and I'll see eight rifles looking at me. I'll think how I'd like to get inside the wall, I'll push against it with my back . . . with every ounce of strength I have, but the wall will stay, like in a nightmare. I can imagine all that. If you only knew how well I can imagine it."

"All right, all right!" I said, "I can imagine it too."

"It must hurt like hell. You know, they aim at the eyes and the mouth to disfigure you," he added mechanically. "I can feel the wounds already; I've had pains in my head and in my neck for the past hour. Not real pains. Worse. This is what I'm going to feel tomorrow morning. And then what?"

I well understood what he meant but I didn't want to act as if I did. I had pains too, pains in my body like a crowd of tiny scars. I couldn't get used to it. But I was like him, I attached no importance to it. "After," I said, "you'll be pushing up daisies."

He began to talk to himself: he never stopped watching the Belgian. The Belgian didn't seem to be listening. I knew what he had come to do; he wasn't interested in what we thought; he came to watch our bodies, bodies dying in agony while yet alive.

"It's like a nightmare," Tom was saying. "You want to think of something, you always have the impression that it's all right, that you're going to understand and then it slips, it escapes you and fades away. I tell myself there will be nothing afterwards. But I don't understand what it means. Sometimes I almost can . . . and then it fades away and I start thinking about the pains again, bullets, explosions. I'm a materialist, I swear it to you; I'm not going crazy. But something's the matter. I see my corpse; that's not hard but *I'm* the one who sees it, with *my* eyes. I've got to think . . . think that I won't see anything anymore and the world will go on for the others. We aren't made to think that, Pablo. Believe me: I've already stayed up a whole night waiting for something. But this isn't the same: this will creep up behind us, Pablo, and we won't be able to prepare for it."

"Shut up," I said, "Do you want me to call a priest?"

He didn't answer. I had already noticed he had the tendency to act like a prophet and call me Pablo, speaking in a toneless voice. I didn't like that: but it seems all the Irish are that way. I had the vague impression he smelled of urine. Fundamentally, I hadn't much sympathy for Tom and I didn't see why, under the pretext of dying together, I should have any more. It would have been different with some others. With Ramon Gris, for example. But I felt alone between Tom and Juan. I liked that better, anyhow: with Ramon I might have been more deeply moved. But I was terribly hard just then and I wanted to stay hard.

He kept on chewing his words, with something like distraction. He certainly talked to keep himself from thinking. He smelled of urine like an old prostate case. Naturally, I agreed with him, I could have said everything he said: it isn't *natural* to die. And since I was going to die, nothing seemed natural to me, not this pile of coal dust, or the bench, or Pedro's ugly face. Only it didn't please me to think the same things as Tom. And I knew that, all through the night, every five minutes, we would keep on thinking things at the same time. I looked at him sideways and for the first time he seemed strange to me: he wore death on his face. My pride was wounded: for the past twenty-four hours I had lived next to Tom, I had listened to him, I had spoken to him and I knew we had nothing in common. And now we looked as much alike as twin brothers, simply because we were going to die together. Tom took my hand without looking at me.

"Pablo, I wonder . . . I wonder if it's really true that everything ends."

I took my hand away and said, "Look between your feet, you pig."

There was a big puddle between his feet and drops fell from his pants-leg.

"What is it?" he asked frightened.

"You're pissing in your pants," I told him.

"It isn't true," he said furiously. "I'm not pissing. I don't feel anything."

The Belgian approached us. He asked with false solicitude, "Do you feel ill?"

Tom did not answer. The Belgian looked at the puddle and said nothing.

"I don't know what it is," Tom said ferociously. "But I'm not afraid. I swear I'm not afraid."

The Belgian did not answer. Tom got up and went to piss in a corner. He came back buttoning his fly, and sat down without a word. The Belgian was taking notes.

All three of us watched him because he was alive. He had the motions of a living human being, the cares of a living human being; he shivered in the cellar the way the living are supposed to shiver; he had an obedient, well-fed body. The rest of us hardly felt ours—not in the same way anyhow. I wanted to feel my pants between my legs but I didn't dare; I watched the Belgian, balancing on his legs, master of his muscles, someone who could think about tomorrow. There we were, three bloodless shadows; we watched him and we sucked his life like vampires.

Finally he went over to little Juan. Did he want to feel his neck for some professional motive or was he obeying an impulse of charity? If he was acting by charity it was the only time during the whole night.

He caressed Juan's head and neck. The kid let himself be handled, his eyes never leaving him, then suddenly, he seized the hand and looked at it strangely. He held the Belgian's hand between his own two hands and there was nothing pleasant about them, two grey pincers gripping this fat and reddish hand. I suspected what was going to happen and Tom must have suspected it too: but the Belgian didn't see a thing, he smiled paternally. After a moment the kid brought the fat red hand to his mouth and tried to bite it. The Belgian pulled away quickly and stumbled back against the wall. For a second he looked at us with horror, he must have suddenly understood that we were not men like him. I began to laugh and one of the guards jumped up. The other was asleep, his wide open eyes were blank.

I felt relaxed and over-excited at the same time. I didn't want to think any more about what would happen at dawn, at death. It made no sense. I only found words or emptiness. But as soon as I tried to think of anything else I saw rifle barrels pointing at me. Perhaps I lived through my execution twenty times; once I even thought it was for good: I must have slept a minute. They were dragging me to the wall and I was struggling; I was asking for mercy. I woke up with a start and looked at the Belgian: I was afraid I might have cried out in my sleep. But he was stroking his moustache, he hadn't noticed anything. If I had wanted to, I think I could have slept a while; I had been awake for forty-eight hours. I was at the end of my rope. But I didn't want to lose two hours of life: they would come to wake me up at dawn, I would follow them, stupefied with sleep and I would have croaked without so much as an "Oof!"; I didn't want that, I didn't want to die like an animal, I wanted to understand. Then I was afraid of having nightmares. I got up, walked back and forth, and, to change my ideas, I began to think about my past life. A crowd of memories came back to me pell-mell. There were good and bad ones—or at least I called them that *before*. There were faces and incidents. I saw the face of a little *novillero* who was gored in Valencia during the *Feria*, the face of one of my uncles, the face of Ramon Gris. I remembered my whole life: how I was out of work for three months in 1926, how I almost starved to death. I remembered a night I spent on a bench in Grenada: I hadn't eaten for three days. I was angry, I didn't want to die. That made me smile. How madly I ran after happiness, after women, after liberty. Why? I wanted to free Spain, I admired Pi y Margall, I joined the anarchist movement, I spoke in public meetings: I took everything as seriously as if I were immortal.

At that moment I felt that I had my whole life in front of me, and I thought, "It's a damned lie." It was worth nothing because it was finished. I wondered how I'd been able to walk, to laugh with the girls: I wouldn't have moved so much as my little finger if I had only imagined I would die like this. My life was in front of me, shut, closed, like a bag and yet everything inside of it was unfinished. For an instant I tried to judge it. I wanted to tell myself, this is a beautiful life. But I couldn't pass judgment on it; it was only a sketch; I had spent my time counterfeiting eternity, I had understood nothing. I missed nothing: there were so many things I could have missed, the taste of *manzanilla* or the baths I took in summer in a little creek near Cadiz; but death had disenchanted everything.

The Belgian suddenly had a bright idea. "My friends," he told us, "I will undertake—if the military administration will allow it—to send a message for you, a souvenir to those who love you . . ."

Tom mumbled, "I don't have anybody."

I said nothing. Tom waited an instant then looked at me with curiosity. "You don't have anything to say to Concha?"

"No."

I hated this tender complicity: it was my own fault, I had talked about Concha the night before, I should have controlled myself. I was with her for a year. Last night I would have given an arm to see her again for five minutes. That was why I talked about her, it was stronger than I was. Now I had no more desire to see her, I had nothing more to say to her. I would not even have wanted to hold her in my arms: my body filled me with horror because it was grey and sweating—and I wasn't sure that her body didn't fill me with horror. Concha would cry when she found out I was dead, she would have no taste for life for months afterward. But I was still the one who was going to die. I thought of her soft, beautiful eyes. When she looked at me something passed from her to me. But I knew it was over: if she looked at me *now* the look would stay in her eyes, it wouldn't reach me. I was alone.

Tom was alone too but not in the same way. Sitting cross-legged, he had begun to stare at the bench with a sort of smile, he looked amazed. He put out his hand and touched the wood cautiously as if he were afraid of breaking something, then drew back his hand quickly and shuddered. If I had been Tom I wouldn't have amused myself by touching the bench; this was some more Irish nonsense, but I too found that objects had a funny look: they were more obliterated, less dense than usual. It was enough for me to look at the bench, the lamp, the pile of coal dust, to feel that I was going to die. Naturally I couldn't think clearly about my death but I saw it everywhere, on things, in the way things fell back and kept their distance, discreetly, as people who speak quietly at the bedside of a dying man. It was *his* death which Tom had just touched on the bench.

In the state I was in, if someone had come and told me I could go home quietly, that they would leave me my life whole, it would have left me cold: several hours or several years of waiting is all the same when you have lost the illusion of being eternal. I clung to nothing, in a way I was calm. But it was a horrible calm—because of my body; my body, I saw with its eyes, I heard with its ears, but it was no longer me; it sweated and trembled by itself and I didn't recognize it any more. I had to touch it and look at it to find out what was happening, as if it were the body of someone else. At times I could still feel it, I felt sinkings, and fallings, as when you're in a plane taking a nosedive, or I felt my heart beating. But that didn't reassure me. Everything that came from my body was all cock-eyed. Most of the time it was quiet and I felt no more than a sort of weight, a filthy presence against me; I had the impression of being tied to an enormous vermin. Once I felt my pants and I felt they were damp; I didn't know whether it was sweat or urine, but I went to piss on the coal pile as a precaution.

The Belgian took out his watch, looked at it. He said, "It's three-thirty."

Bastard! He must have done it on purpose. Tom jumped; we hadn't noticed time was running out; night surrounded us like a shapeless, somber mass, I couldn't even remember that it had begun.

Little Juan began to cry. He wrung his hands, pleaded, "I don't want to die. I don't want to die."

He ran across the whole cellar waving his arms in the air, then fell sobbing on one of the mats. Tom watched him with mournful eyes, without the slightest desire to console him. Because it wasn't worth the trouble: the kid made more noise than we did, but he was less touched: he was like a sick man who defends himself against his illness by fever. It's much more serious when there isn't any fever.

He wept: I could clearly see he was pitying himself; he wasn't thinking about death. For one second, one single second, I wanted to weep myself, to weep with pity for myself. But the opposite happened: I glanced at the kid, I saw his thin sobbing shoulders and I felt inhuman: I could pity neither the others nor myself. I said to myself, "I want to die cleanly."

Tom had gotten up, he placed himself just under the round opening and began to watch for daylight. I was determined to die cleanly and I only thought of that. But ever since the doctor told us the time, I felt time flying, flowing away drop by drop.

It was still dark when I heard Tom's voice: "Do you hear them?"

Men were marching in the courtyard.

"Yes."

"What the hell are they doing? They can't shoot in the dark."

After a while we heard no more. I said to Tom, "It's day."

Pedro got up, yawning, and came to blow out the lamp. He said to his buddy, "Cold as hell."

The cellar was all grey. We heard shots in the distance.

"It's starting," I told Tom. "They must do it in the court in the rear."

Tom asked the doctor for a cigarette. I didn't want one; I didn't want cigarettes or alcohol. From that moment on they didn't stop firing.

"Do you realize what's happening," Tom said.

He wanted to add something but kept quiet, watching the door. The door opened and a lieutenant came in with four soldiers. Tom dropped his cigarette.

"Steinbock?"

Tom didn't answer. Pedro pointed him out.

"Juan Mirbal?"

"On the mat."

"Get up," the lieutenant said.

Juan did not move. Two soldiers took him under the arms and set him on his feet. But he fell as soon as they released him.

The soldiers hesitated.

"He's not the first sick one," said the lieutenant. "You two carry him; they'll fix it up down there."

He turned to Tom. "Let's go."

Tom went out between two soldiers. Two others followed, carrying the kid by the armpits. He hadn't fainted; his eyes were wide open and tears ran down his cheeks. When I wanted to go out the lieutenant stopped me.

"You Ibbieta?"

"Yes."

"You wait here; they'll come for you later."

They left. The Belgian and the two jailers left too, I was alone. I did not understand what was happening to me but I would have liked it better if they had gotten it over with right away. I heard shots at almost regular intervals; I shook with each one of them. I wanted to scream and tear out my hair. But I gritted my teeth and pushed my hands in my pockets because I wanted to stay clean.

After an hour they came to get me and led me to the first floor, to a small room that smelt of cigars and where the heat was stifling. There were two officers sitting smoking in the armchairs, papers on their knees.

"You're Ibbieta?"

"Yes."

"Where is Ramon Gris?"

"I don't know."

The one questioning me was short and fat. His eyes were hard behind his glasses. He said to me, "Come here."

I went to him. He got up and took my arms, staring at me with a look that should have pushed me into the earth. At the same time he pinched my biceps with all his might. It wasn't to hurt me, it was only a game: he wanted to dominate me. He also thought he had to blow his stinking breath square in my face. We stayed for a moment like that, and I almost felt like laughing. It takes a lot to intimidate a man who is going to die; it didn't work. He pushed me back violently and sat down again. He said, "It's his life against yours. You can have yours if you tell us where he is."

These men dolled up with their riding crops and boots were still going to die. A little later than I, but not too much. They busied themselves looking for names in their crumpled papers, they ran after other men to imprison or suppress them; they had opinions on the future of Spain and on other subjects. Their little activities seemed shocking and burlesqued to me; I couldn't put myself in their place, I thought they were insane. The little man was still looking at me, whipping his boots with the riding crop. All his gestures were calculated to give him the look of a live and ferocious beast.

"So? You understand?"

"I don't know where Gris is," I answered. "I thought he was in Madrid."

The other officer raised his pale hand indolently. This indolence was also calculated. I saw through all their little schemes and I was stupefied to find there were men who amused themselves that way.

"You have a quarter of an hour to think it over," he said slowly. "Take him to the laundry, bring him back in fifteen minutes. If he still refuses he will be executed on the spot."

They knew what they were doing: I had passed the night in waiting; then they had made me wait an hour in the cellar while they shot Tom and Juan and now they were locking me up in the laundry; they must have prepared their game the night before. They told themselves that nerves eventually wear out and they hoped to get me that way.

They were badly mistaken. In the laundry I sat on a stool because I felt very weak and I began to think. But not about their proposition. Of course I knew where Gris was; he was hiding with his cousins, four kilometers from the city. I also knew that I would not reveal his hiding place unless they tortured me (but they didn't seem to be thinking about that). All that was perfectly regulated, definite and in no way interested me. Only I would have liked to understand the reasons for my conduct. I would rather die than give up Gris. Why? I didn't like Ramon Gris any more. My friendship for him had died a little while before dawn at the same time as my love for Concha, at the same time as my desire to live. Undoubtedly I thought highly of him: he was tough. But it was not for this reason that I consented to die in his place; his life had no more value than mine; no life had value. They were going to slap a man up against a wall and shoot at him until he died, whether it was I or Gris or somebody else made no difference. I knew he was more useful than I to the cause of Spain but I thought to hell with Spain and anarchy; nothing was important. Yet I was there, I could save my skin and give up Gris and I refused to do it. I found that somehow comic; it was obstinacy. I thought, "I must be stubborn!" And a droll sort of gaiety spread over me.

They came for me and brought me back to the two officers. A rat ran out from under my feet and that amused me. I turned to one of the *falangistas* and said, "Did you see the rat?"

He didn't answer. He was very sober, he took himself seriously. I wanted to laugh but I held myself back because I was afraid that once I got started I wouldn't be able to stop. The *falangista* had a moustache. I said to him again, "You ought to shave off your moustache, idiot." I thought it funny that he would let the hairs of his living being invade his face. He kicked me without great conviction and I kept quiet.

"Well," said the fat officer, "have you thought about it?"

I looked at them with curiosity, as insects of a very rare species. I told them, "I know where he is. He is hidden in the cemetery. In a vault or in the gravediggers' shack."

It was a farce. I wanted to see them stand up, buckle their belts and give orders busily.

They jumped to their feet. "Let's go. Molés, go get fifteen men from Lieutenant Lopez. You," the fat man said, "I'll let you off if you're telling the truth, but it'll cost you plenty if you're making monkeys out of us."

They left in a great clatter and I waited peacefully under the guard of *falangistas*. From time to time I smiled, thinking about the spectacle they would make. I felt stunned and malicious. I imagined them lifting up tombstones, opening the doors of the vaults one by one. I represented this situation to myself as if I had been someone else: this prisoner obstinately playing the hero, these grim *falangistas* with their moustaches and their men in uniform running among the graves; it was irresistibly funny. After half an hour the little fat man came back alone. I thought he had come to give the orders to execute me. The others must have stayed in the cemetery.

The officer looked at me. He didn't look at all sheepish. "Take him into the big courtyard with the others," he said. "After the military operations a regular court will decide what happens to him."

"Then they're not . . . not going to shoot me? . . ."

"Not now, anyway. What happens afterwards is none of my business."

I still didn't understand. I asked, "But why?"

He shrugged his shoulders without answering and the soldiers took me away. In the big courtyard there were about a hundred prisoners, women, children and a few old men. I began walking around the central grass-plot, I was stupefied. At noon they let us eat in the mess hall. Two or three people questioned me. I must have known them, but I didn't answer: I didn't even know where I was.

Around evening they pushed about ten new prisoners into the court. I recognized Garcia, the baker. He said, "What damned luck you have! I didn't think I'd see you alive."

"They sentenced me to death," I said, "and then they changed their minds. I don't know why."

"They arrested me at two o'clock," Garcia said.

"Why?" Garcia had nothing to do with politics.

"I don't know," he said. "They arrest everybody who doesn't think the way they do." He lowered his voice. "They got Gris."

I began to tremble. "When?"

"This morning. He messed it up. He left his cousin's on Tuesday because they had an argument. There were plenty of people to hide him but he didn't want to owe anything to anybody. He said, 'I'd go and hide in Ibbieta's place, but they got him, so I'll go hide in the cemetery.' "

"In the cemetery?"

"Yes. What a fool. Of course they went by there this morning, that was sure to happen. They found him in the gravediggers' shack. He shot at them and they got him."

"In the cemetery!"

Everything began to spin and I found myself sitting on the ground: I laughed so hard I cried.

Translated by Lloyd Alexander

SARTRE: *The Wall*

1. *Can you explain why Sartre puts the three men in a situation in which their doom is sealed?*
2. *Characterize the three men. Are they sufficiently differentiated?*
3. *Why does Sartre bring in the Belgian doctor? What psychological purpose does he serve? Why does Juan bite his hand?*
4. *Why does Ibbieta protect Ramon Gris when he feels little sympathy for Gris himself?*
5. *Does Ibbieta gain or lose stature by facing his death? What is Sartre's point? Do the challenge and his statement—"I want to die cleanly"—seem reminiscent of Hemingway? What else in the story reminds you of him?*
6. *What effect does imminent death have on Ibbieta's thoughts? on his physical reactions? Why does Sartre stress the physical reaction of all three men when he is evidently more concerned with the psychological?*
7. *Why does Ibbieta restrain himself from feeling pity for the suffering of the others and even for himself?*
8. *What is the point of the ending? Is it effective within the framework of the rest of the story? Is there any foreshadowing of this coincidence? Where?*
9. *Sartre has been accused of using his plays and novels to convey his own brand of Existentialist philosophy. Do you find this story suffers from over-philosophizing?*

Samuel Beckett

YELLOW

Like Joyce, Samuel Beckett was born in Dublin (in 1906) and then spent most of his adult life on the continent, basing himself principally in Paris. Again like Joyce, he retained a great love for words, an infatuation with the potentialities of language. More concerned than Joyce with seaminess and more morbid than any of his contemporaries, Beckett has explored the underworld and come up with his cast of isolated philosophers, tramps, bums, and madmen, the chief characters of Murphy *(1938),* Watt *(1953),* Molloy *(1951),* Malone Dies *(1952), and* The Unnamable *(1953). The Belacqua of "Yellow," which originally appeared in* More Pricks Than Kicks, *is a typical Beckett "hero"—indolent, marginal to society, aimless, yet curiously dignified and reminiscent in more than one way of the two derelicts in that classic of the modern theater,* Waiting for Godot. *Winner of the Nobel Prize for Literature, Beckett forced the Nobel Committee to reinterpret the rules of the award to encompass his wittily ironic portraits of mankind sinking into slime and anomie.*

THE night-nurse bounced in on the tick of five and turned on the light. Belacqua waked feeling greatly refreshed and eager to wrestle with this new day. He had underlined, as quite a callow boy, a phrase in Hardy's *Tess*, won by dint of cogging in the Synod: "When grief ceases to be speculative, sleep sees her opportunity." He had manipulated that sentence for many years now, amending its terms, as "joy" for "grief," to answer his occasions, even calling upon it to bear the strain of certain applications for which he feared it had not been intended, and still it held good through it all. He waked with it now in his mind, as though it had been there all the time he slept, holding that fragile place against dreams.

The nurse brought a pot of tea and a glass of strong salts on a tray.

"Pfui!" exclaimed Belacqua.

But the callous girl preferred to disregard this.

"When are they doing me?" he asked.

"You are down for twelve," she said.

[405

Down . . . !

She took herself off.

He drank the salts and two cups of tea, and be damned to the whole of them. Then of course he was wide awake, poor fellow. But what cared he, what cared saucy Belacqua? He switched off the lamp and lay on his back in this the darkest hour, smoking.

Carry it off as he might, he was in a dreadful situation. At twelve sharp he would be sliced open—zeep!—with a bistoury. This was the idea that his mind, for the moment, was in no fit state to entertain. If this Hunnish idea once got a foothold in his little psyche in its present unready condition, topsy-turvy after yesterday's debauch of anxiety and then the good night's sleep coming on top of that, it would be annihilated. The psyche, not the idea—which was precisely the reverse of what he wished. For himself, to do him justice, he did not care. His mind might cave in for all he cared, he was tired of the old bastardo. But the unfortunate part of it was that this would appear in his behavior, he would scream and kick and bite and scratch when they came for him, beg for execution to be stayed and perhaps even wet the bed, and what a reflection on his late family that would be! The grand old Huguenot family guts, he could not do the dirty on them like that (to say nothing of his natural anxiety to be put to rights with as little fuss as possible).

"My sufferings under the anesthetic," he reflected, "will be exquisite, but I shall not remember them."

He dashed out his cigarette and put on the lamp, this not so much for the company of the light as in order to postpone daybreak until he should feel a little more sure of himself. Daybreak, with its suggestion of a nasty birth, he could not bear. Downright and all as he was, he could not bear the sight of this punctilious and almost, he sometimes felt, superfluous delivery. This was mere folly and well he knew it. He tried hard to cure himself, to frighten or laugh himself out of this weakness, but to no avail. He would grow tired and say to himself: "I am what I am." That was the end of all his meditations and endeavours: "I am what I am." He had read the phrase somewhere and liked it and made it his own.

But God at least was good—as He usually is if we only know how to take Him—in this way: that six hours separated him, Belacqua, from the ordeal, six hours were allotted to him in which to make up his mind, as a pretty drab her face for an enemy. His getting the fleam* in the neck, his suffering the tortures of the damned while seeming to slumber as

---

* A kind of lancet, as for opening a vein.

peacefully as a little child, were of no consequence, as hope-saved they were not, so long as his mind was master of the thought of them. What he had to do, and had with typical slackness put off doing till the last moment, was to arrange a hot reception in his mind for the thought of all the little acts of kindness that he was to endure before the day was out. Then he would be able to put a good face on it. Otherwise not. Otherwise he would bite, scratch, etc., when they came for him. Now the good face was all that concerned him, the bold devil-may-care expression (except of course that he was also anxious to be made well with the least possible ado). He did not pause to consider himself in this matter, nor the light that the coming ordeal would shed on his irrevocable self, because he really was tired of that old bastardo. No, his whole concern was with other people, the lift-boy, nurses and sisters, the local doc coming to put him off, the eminent surgeon, the handy man at hand to clean up and put the bits into the incinerator, and all the friends of his late family, who would ferret out the whole truth. It did not matter about him, he was what he was. But these outsiders, the family guts, and so on and so forth, all these things had to be considered.

An asthmatic in the room overhead was coughing his heart up. "God bless you," thought Belacqua, "you make things easier for me." But when did the unfortunate sleep? During the day, the livelong day, through the stress of the day. At twelve sharp he would be sound, or, better again, just dozing off. Meantime he coughed, as Crusoe labored to bring his gear ashore, the snugger to be.

Belacqua made a long arm and switched off the lamp. It threw shadows. He would close his eyes, he would bilk the dawn in that way. What were the eyes anyway? The posterns of the mind. They were safer closed.

If only he were well-bred or, failing that, plucky. Blue blood or gamecock! Even if he lived in his mind as much as was his boast. Then he need not be at all this pains to make himself ready. Then it would only be a question of finding a comfortable position in the strange bed, trying to sleep or reading a book, waiting calmly for the Angelus. But he was an indolent bourgeois poltroon, very talented up to a point, but not fitted for private life in the best and brightest sense, in the sense to which he referred when he bragged of how he furnished his mind and lived there, because it was the last ditch when all was said and done. But he preferred not to wait till then, he fancied it might be wiser to settle down there straight away and not wait till he was kicked into it by the world, just at the moment maybe when he was beginning to feel at home in the world. He could no more go back into his heart in that way than he could keep out of it altogether. So now there was nothing for it but to lie on his back in the dark, and exercise his talent. Unless of course he chose to distress the friends of his late family (to say nothing of perhaps jeopardizing the cure for which the friends of his late family were paying). But he had too much of the grocer's sense of honor for that. Rather than have that happen he would persist with his psyche, he would ginger up his little psyche for the occasion.

Poor Belacqua, he seems to be having a very dull, irksome morning, preparing for the fray in this manner. But he will make up for it later on, there is a good time coming for him later on, when the doctors have given him a new lease of apathy.

What were his tactics in this crisis?

In a less tight corner he might have been content to barricade his mind against the idea. But this was at the best a slipshod method, since the idea, howsoever blatant an enemy and despite the strictest guard, was almost certain to sidle in sooner or later under the skirts of a friend, and then the game was up. Still, in the ordinary run of adversity, he would doubtless have bowed to his natural indolence and adopted such a course, he would have been content merely to think of other things and hope for the best. But this was no common or garden fix, he was properly up against it this time, there could be no question of half-measures on this melancholy occasion.

His plan therefore was not to refuse admission to the idea, but to keep it at bay until his mind was ready to receive it. Then let it in and pulverize it. Obliterate the bastard. He ground his teeth in the bed. Flitter the———, tear it into pieces like a priest. So far so good. But by what means? Belacqua ransacked his mind for a suitable engine of destruction.

At this crucial point the good God came to his assistance with a phrase from a paradox of Donne: "Now among our wise men, I doubt not but many would be found, who would laugh at Heraclitus weeping, none which would weep at Democritus laughing." This was a godsend and no error. Not the phrase as a judgment, but its terms, the extremes of wisdom that it tendered to Belacqua. It is true that he did not care for these black and white alternatives as a rule. Indeed he even went so far as to hazard a little paradox on his own account, to the effect that between contraries no alternation was possible. But was it the moment for a man to be nice? Belacqua snatched eagerly at the issue. Was it to be laughter or tears? It came to the same thing in the end, but which was it to be *now?* It was too late to arrange for the luxury of both. Now in a moment he would fill his mind with one or other of these two orders of rays, shall we say ultrared and ultraviolet, and prepare to perforate his adversary.

"Really," thought Belacqua, "I cannot remember having ever spent a more dreary morning; but needs must, that was a true saying, when the devil drives."

At this all-important juncture of his delirium Belacqua found himself blinking his eyes rapidly, a regular nictation, so that little flaws of dawn gushed into his mind. This had not been done with intent, but when he found that it seemed to be benefiting him in some curious way he kept it up, until gradually the inside of his skull began to feel sore. Then he desisted and went back to the dilemma.

Here, as indeed at every crux of the enterprise, he sacrificed his sense of what was personal and proper to himself to the desirability of making a certain impression on other people, an impression almost of gallantry. He must efface himself altogether and do the little soldier. It was this paramount consideration that made him decide in favor of Bim and Bom, Grock, Democritus, whatever you are pleased to call it, and postpone its dark converse to a less public occasion. This was an abnegation if you like, for Belacqua could not resist a lachrymose philosopher, and still less when, as was the case with Heraclitus, he was obscure at the same time. He was in his element in dingy tears, and luxuriously so when these were furnished by a pre-Socratic man of acknowledged distinction. How often had he not exclaimed, skies being grey: "Another minute of this and I consecrate the remnant of my life to Heraclitus of Ephesus, I shall be that Delian diver who, after the third or fourth submersion, returns no more to the surface!"

But weeping in this charnel house would be misconstrued. All the staff, from matron to lift-boy, would make the mistake of ascribing his tears, or, perhaps better, his tragic demeanor, not to the follies of humanity at large—which of course covered themselves—but rather to the tumor the size of a brick that he had on the back of his neck. This would be a very natural mistake and Belacqua was not blaming them. No blame attached to any living person in this matter. But the news would get round that Belacqua, so far from grinning and bearing, had piped his eye, or had been on the point of doing so. Then he would be disgraced and, by extension, his late family also.

So now his course was clear. He would arm his mind with laughter—laughter is not quite the word but it will have to serve—at every point, then he would admit the idea and blow it to pieces. Smears, as after a gorge of blackberries, of hilarity—which is not quite the word either—would be adhering to his lips as he stepped smartly, *ohne Hast aber ohne Rast*, into the torture-chamber. His fortitude would be generally commended.

How did he proceed to put this plan into execution?

He has forgotten, he has no use for it any more.

The night-nurse broke in upon him at seven with another pot of tea and two cuts of toast.

"That's all you'll get now," she said.

The impertinent slut! Belacqua very nearly told her to work it up. "Did the salts talk to you?" she said.

The sick man appraised her as she took his temperature and pulse. She was a tight, trim little bit.

"They whispered to me," he said.

When she was gone, he thought, What an all-but-flawless brunette, so spick and span too after having been on the go all night, at the beck and call of the first lousy old squaw who let fall her book or could not sleep for the roar of the traffic in Merrion Row. What the hell did anything matter anyway!

Pale wales in the east beyond the Land Commission. The day was going alone nicely.

The night-nurse came back for the tray. That made her third appearance, if he was not mistaken. She would very shortly be relieved, she would eat her supper and go to bed. But not to sleep. The place was too full of noise and light at that hour, her bed a refrigerator. She could not get used to this night duty, she really could not. She lost weight and her little face became cavernous. Also it was very difficult to arrange anything with her fiancé. What a life!

"See you later," she said.

There was no controverting this. Belacqua cast about wildly for a reply that would please her and do him justice at the same time. *"Au plaisir"* was of course the very thing, but the wrong language. Finally he settled on "I suppose so" and discharged it at her in a very halfhearted manner, when she was more than half out of the door. He would have been very much better advised to let it alone and say nothing.

While he was still wasting his valuable time cursing himself for a fool, the door burst open and the day-nurse came in with a mighty rushing sound of starched apron. She was to have charge of him by day. She just missed being beautiful, this Presbyterian from Aberdeen. Aberdeen!

After a little conversation *obiter*, Belacqua let fall casually, as though the idea had only just occurred to him, whereas in fact it had been tormenting him insidiously for some time:

"Oh nurse the W.C. perhaps it might be as well to know." Like that, all in a rush, without any punctuation.

When she had finished telling him, he knew roughly where the place was. But he stupidly elected to linger on in the bed with his uneasy load, codding himself that it would be more decent not to act incontinent on intelligence of so intimate a kind. In his anxiety to give color to this pause he asked Miranda when he was being done.

"Didn't the night-nurse tell you?" she said sharply. "At twelve."

So the night-nurse had split. The treacherous darling!

He got up and set out, leaving Miranda at work on the bed. When he got back she was gone. He got back into the made bed.

Now the sun, that creature of habit, shone in through the window.

A little Aschenputtel, gummy and pert, skipped in with sticks and coal for the fire.

"Morning," she said.

"Yes," said Belacqua. But he retrieved himself at once. "What a lovely room," he exclaimed. "All the morning sun."

No more was needed to give Aschenputtel his measure.

"Very lovely," she said bitterly, "right on me fire." She tore down the blind. "Putting out me good fire," she said.

That was certainly one way of looking at it.

"I had one old one in here," she said, "and he might be snoring but he wouldn't let the blind down."

Some old put had crossed her, that was patent.

"Not for God," she said, "so what did I do?" She screwed round on her knees from building the fire. Belacqua obliged her.

"What was that?" he said.

She turned back with a chuckle to her task. "I block it with a chair," she said, "and his shirt over the back."

"Ha," exclaimed Belacqua.

"Again he'd be up," she exulted, "don't you know." She laughed happily at the memory of this little deception. "I kep' it off all right," she said.

She talked and talked, and poor Belacqua, with his mind unfinished, had to keep his end up. Somehow he managed to create a very favorable impression.

"Well," she said at last, in an indescribable singsong, "g'bye now. See you later."

"That's right," said Belacqua.

Achenputtel was engaged to be married to handy Andy; she had been for years. Meantime she gave him a dog's life.

Soon the fire was roaring up the chimney and Belacqua could not resist the temptation to get up and sit before it, clad only in his thin blue 100,000 Chemises pajamas. The coughing aloft had greatly abated since he first heard it. The man was gradually settling down, it did not require a Sherlock Holmes to realize that. But on the grand old yaller wall, crowding in upon his left hand, a pillar of higher tone, representing the sun, was spinning out its placid deiseal. This dribble of time, thought Belacqua, like sanies into a bucket, the world wants a new washer. He would draw the blind, both blinds.

But he was foiled by the entry of the matron with the morning paper—this, save the mark, by way of taking his mind off it. It is impossible to describe the matron. She was all right. She made him nervous the way she flung herself about.

Belacqua turned on the flow:

"What a lovely morning," he gushed, "a lovely room, all the morning sun."

The matron simply disappeared, there is no other word for it. The woman was there one moment and gone the next. It was extraordinary.

The theater sister came in. What a number of women there seemed to be in this place! She was a great raw châteaubriant of a woman, like the one on the Wincarnis bottle. She took a quick look at his neck.

"Pah," she scoffed, "that's nothing."

"Not at all," said Belacqua.

"Is that the lot?"

Belacqua did not altogether care for her tone.

"And a toe," he said, "to come off, or rather, portion of a toe."

"Top," she guffawed, "and bottom."

There was no controverting this. But he had learned his lesson. He let it pass.

This woman was found to improve on acquaintance. She had a coarse manner, but she was exceedingly gentle. She taught all her more likely patients to wind bandages. To do this well with the crazy little hand-windlass that she provided was no easy matter. The roll would become fusiform. But when one got to know the humors of the apparatus, then it could be coaxed into yielding the hard slender spools, perfect cylinders, that delighted her. All these willing slaves that passed through her hands, she blandished each one in turn. "I never had such tight, straight bandages," she would say. Then, just as the friendship established on this basis seemed about to develop into something more—how shall I say?—substantial, the patient would all of a sudden be well enough to go home. Some malignant destiny pursued this splendid woman. Years later, when the rest of the staff was forgotten, she would drift into the mind. She marked down Belacqua for the bandages.

Miranda came back, this time with the dressing tray. That voluptuous undershot cast of mouth, the clenched lips, almost *bocca romanā*, how had he failed to notice it before? Was it the same woman?

"Now," she said.

She lashed into the part with picric and ether. It beat him to understand why she should be so severe on his little bump of amativeness. It was not septic to the best of his knowledge. Then why this severity? Merely on the off-chance of its coming in for the fag end of a dig? It was very strange. It had not even been shaved. It jutted out under the short hairs like a cuckoo's bill. He trusted it would come to no harm. Really he could not afford to have it curtailed. His little bump of amativeness.

When his entire nape was as a bride's adorned (bating the obscene stain of the picric) and so tightly bandaged that he felt his eyes bulging, she transferred her compassion to the toes. She scoured the whole phalanx, top and bottom. Suddenly she began to titter. Belacqua nearly kicked her in the eye, he got such a shock. How dared she trespass on his program! He refusing to be tickled in this petty local way, trying with his teeth to reach his under lip and gouging his palms, and she forgetting herself, there was no other word for it. There were limits, he felt, to Democritus.

"Such a lang tootsy," she giggled.

Heavenly Father, the creature was bilingual. A lang tootsy! Belacqua swallowed his choler.

"Soon to be syne," he said in a loud voice. What his repartee lacked in wit it made up for in style. But it was lost on this granite Medusa.

"A long foot," he said agreeably, "I know, or a long nose. But a long toe, what does that denote?"

No answer. Was the woman then altogether cretinous? Or did she not hear him? Belting away there with her urinous picric and cooling her porridge in advance. He would try her again.

"I say," he roared, "that that toe you like so much will soon be only a memory." He could not put it plainer than that.

"Yes,"—the word died away and was repeated—"yes, his troubles are nearly over."

Belacqua broke down completely, he could not help it. This distant voice, like a *cor anglais* coming through the evening, and then the "his," the "his" was the last straw. He buried his face in his hands, he did not care who saw him.

"I would like," he sobbed, "the cat to have it, if I might."

She would never have done with her bandage, it cannot have measured less than a furlong. But of course it would never do to leave anything to chance, Belacqua could appreciate that. Still, it seemed somehow disproportioned to the length of even his toe. At last she made all fast round his shin. Then she packed her tray and left. Some people go, others leave. Belacqua felt like the rejected of these two that night in a bed. He felt he had set Miranda somehow against him. Was this then the haporth of paint? Miranda on whom so much depended. *Merde!*

It was all Lister's fault. These damned happy Victorians.

His heart gave a great leap in its box with a fulminating sense that he was all wrong, that anger would stand by him better than the other thing, the laugh seemed so feeble, so like a whinge in the end. But on second thoughts, no; anger would turn aside when it came to the point, leaving him like a sheep. Anyhow it was too late to turn back. He tried cautiously what it felt like to have the idea in his mind. . . . Nothing happened, he felt no shock. So at least he had spiked the brute, that was something.

At this point he went downstairs and had a truly military evacuation, Army Service Corps. Coming back he did not doubt that all would yet be well. He whistled a snatch outside the duty-room. There was nothing left of his room when he got back but Miranda, Miranda more prognathous than ever, loading a syringe. Belacqua tried to make light of this.

"What now?" he said.

But she had the weapon into his bottom and discharged before he realized what was happening. Not a cry escaped him.

"Did you hear what I said?" he said. "I insist, it is my right, on knowing the meaning of this, the purpose of this injection, do you hear me?"

"It is what every patient gets," she said, "before going down to the theater."

Down to the theater! Was there a conspiracy in this place to destroy him, body and soul? His tongue clave to his palate. They had desiccated his secretions. First blood to the profession!

The theater-socks were the next little bit of excitement. Really, the theater seemed to take itself very seriously. To hell with your socks, he thought, it's your mind I want.

Now events began to move more rapidly. First of all an angel of the Lord came to his assistance with a funny story, really very funny indeed—it always made Belacqua laugh till he cried—about the parson who was invited to take a small part in an amateur production. All he had to do was to snatch at his heart when the revolver went off, cry "By God! I'm shot!" and drop dead. The parson said certainly, he would be most happy, if they would have no objection to his drawing the line at "By God!" on such a secular occasion. He would replace it, if they had no objection, by "Mercy!" or "Upon my word!" or something of that kind. "Oh my! I'm shot!", how would that be?

But the production was so amateur that the revolver went off indeed and the man of God was transfixed.

"Oh!" he cried, "Oh! . . . BY CHRIST! I *AM* SHOT!"

It was a mercy that Belacqua was a dirty, low-down Low Church

Protestant highbrow and able to laugh at this sottish jest. Laugh! How he did laugh, to be sure. Till he cried.

He got up and began to titivate himself. Now he could hear the asthmatic breathing if he listened hard. The day was out of danger, any fool could see that. A little sealed cardboard box lying on the mantelpiece caught his eye. He read the inscription: Fraisse's Ferruginous Ampoules for the Intensive Treatment of Anaemia by Intramuscular Squirtation. Registered Trademark—Mozart. The little Hexenmeister of Don Giovanni, now in his narrow cell forever mislaid, dragged into bloodlessness! How very amusing. Really, the world was in great form this morning.

Now two further women—there was no end to them—the one of a certain age, the other not, entered, ripping off their regulation cuffs as they advanced. They pounced on the bed. The precautionary oil sheet, the cradle . . . Belacqua padded up and down before the fire, the ends of his pajamas tucked like a cyclist's into the sinister socks. He would smoke one more cigarette, nor count the cost. It was astonishing, when he came to think of it, how the entire routine of this place, down to the meanest detail, was calculated to a cow's toe to promote a single end, the relief of suffering in the long run. Observe how he dots his i's now and crucifies his t's to the top of his bent. He was being put to his trumps.

Surreptitiously they searched his yellow face for signs of discomposure. In vain. It was a mask. But perhaps his voice would tremble. One, she whose life had changed, took it upon herself to say in a peevish tone:

"Sister Beamish won't bless you for soiling her good socks."

Sister Beamish would not bless him.

The voice of this person was in ruins, but she abused it further.

"Would you not stand on the mat?"

His mind was made up in a flash: he would stand on the mat. He would meet them in this matter. If he refused to stand on the mat he was lost in the eyes of these two women.

"Anything," he said, "to oblige Sister Beamish."

Miranda was having a busy morning. Now she appeared for the fourth or fifth time, he had lost count, complete with shadowy assistants. The room seemed full of grey women. It was like a dream.

"If you have any false teeth," she said, "you may remove them."

His hour was at hand, there was no blinking at the fact.

Going down in the lift with Miranda he felt his glasses under his hand. This was a blessed accident if you like, just when the silence was becoming awkward.

"Can I trust you with these?" he said.

She put them into her bosom. The divine creature! He would assault her in another minute.

"No smoking," she said, "in the operating theater."

The surgeon was washing his invaluable hands as Belacqua swaggered through the antechamber. He that hath clean hands shall be stronger. Belacqua cut the surgeon. But he flashed a dazzling smile at the Wincarnis. She would not forget that in a hurry.

He bounced up on to the table like a bridegroom. The local doc was in great form, he had just come from standing best man, he was all togged up under his vestments. He recited his exhortation and clapped on the nozzle.

"Are you right?" said Belacqua.

The mixture was too rich, there could be no question about that. His heart was running away, terrible yellow yerks in his skull. "One of the best," he heard those words that did not refer to him. The expression reassured him. The best man clawed at his tap.

By Christ! He did die!

They had clean forgotten to auscultate him!

BECKETT: *Yellow*

1. *What does the title tell you about the patient? What does it tell you about Beckett? Does it immediately indicate a point of view?*
2. *Does Beckett's wit seem appropriate in describing the emotions of a man about to undergo an operation? How does the wit function?*
3. *How does Belacqua decide to act before the operation? Why? What does his decision tell you about him? about Beckett?*
4. *What is his attitude toward the hospital personnel? Theirs toward him?*
5. *What relevance does the anecdote about the parson have to the story? Mention some of the other stories in this collection in which anecdotes are significant.*
6. *Explain the ending of the story. Why is it funny? Or is it tragic?*
7. *What view of life does Beckett suggest in this story? Is it one you agree with? What alternatives are there?*
8. *Contrast Beckett's attitudes with, say, Tolstoy's. Even though Beckett and Hesse seem vastly different in method and point of view, there are some surprising analogies. Can you see any in their stories?*

Alberto Moravia
THE RUIN OF HUMANITY

Born in 1907 to an upper middle-class family of Rome, Alberto Moravia (b. Alberto Pincherle) in the last ten years has emerged as the leading Italian novelist and short-story writer of his generation. Confined by an early illness, he educated himself through omniverous reading. From classical drama, he acquired the art of dialogue and tight structure; from Dostoyevsky and Joyce, he learned how to dramatize philosophy and psychology in fiction. These lessons he applied to depicting modern men and women against their social background, in such works as The Time of Indifference *(1929),* Two Adolescents *(1944, 1948),* The Woman of Rome *(1949),* The Conformist *(1951),* Two Women *(1958),* The Empty Canvas *(1961),* The Lie *(1965), and a book of nonfiction,* The Red Book and the Great Wall: An Impression of Mao's China *(1967). Nakedly sensual in his approach to his characters, he also catches their ennui, their sadness, their indifference, their loss of will, no less than their ability to survey what seems to overwhelm them. In its brief span, the following tale manages to embrace most of these themes, as well as to underscore the eternal war between the sexes.*

ABOUT the middle of February the north wind, which had made me feel so wretched during the winter, dropped, the sky filled with clouds, and a moist breeze, which seemed to be coming from the sea, started to blow. At the soft breath of this breeze I felt myself coming to life again, although in a melancholy sort of way, as if it were whispering in my ear: "Come along, cheer up, while there's life there's hope." But, just because I felt that winter was over and spring beginning, I knew that I could no longer bear to go and work in my uncle's workshop. I had gone into the workshop a year before, like a train going into a tunnel, and I had not come out yet and I could not even see daylight at the other end. Not that the work was unpleasant or repugnant to me personally: there are worse jobs. The workshop consisted of a large shed, situated at the far end of an enclosed piece of ground which served as a depôt for a brick factory, halfway along the Via della Magliana. Inside the shed the air was always full of white, flour-like sawdust, as in a mill; and in the midst of this cloud of dust, and of the continuous humming of saws and electric lathes, we workers and my uncle, looking like floury millers, moved about, busy from morning till night making furniture and fittings. My uncle, poor man, loved me like a son, the workmen were all good chaps and, as I have already said, the work was not repugnant: first a tree-trunk, of oak or maple or chestnut, long, twisted, leaning up against the wall of the workshop, with all its bark upon it and even, still remaining under the bark, the ants that had inhabited it when it was a tree; then, after the saw had dealt with it, so many clean, white planks; then, out of these planks, with the lathe or the plane or other tools, as occasion demanded, table-legs, parts of wardrobes, cornices; and finally, after the piece of furniture had been nailed and screwed and glued together, the painting and polishing. For anyone who takes pleasure in his work, this gradual progress from a tree-trunk to a piece of furniture may become a passion; it is always interesting, or, at the least, it is never boring. But evidently I am made in a different way to other people: after a few months, I could not bear the work any longer. It was not that I am not a good worker, but that I like, every little while, to pause in my work and look round me—just so as to see who I am and where I am and what point I've reached. My uncle, on the other hand, was exactly the opposite: he was always working, fiercely, passionately, never stopping to take breath or reflect; and thus, from a chair to a bracket, from a bracket to a wardrobe, from a wardrobe to a night-table, from a night-table to a chair, he had turned fifty—for that was his age—and you could see that he would go on in the same way until his death, which would be rather like the death of a lathe that falls to pieces or a saw that loses its teeth, the death, in fact, of a tool and not of a man. And on Sundays, indeed, when he put on his best suit and walked very slowly along the pavements of the Via Arenula in company with his wife and children, his eyes half closed, his mouth twisted, and two deep lines between his mouth and his eyes, he really looked like a discarded, useless, broken tool; and I could not help remembering that he had acquired that appearance by stooping over his lathe and his saw and screwing up his eyes in a perpetual cloud of sawdust; and I said to myself that life was not worth living unless you paused now and then and reflected that you *were* alive.

The bus that starts from the Trastevere station goes out into the country and back. Peasants, labourers and all sorts of poor people bring mud into it on their boots, and the smell of sweat from their working clothes, and perhaps a few insects as well. And so, at the starting-point, they spray some kind of stinking disinfectant on the floor and even on the seats, which catches you in the throat and, like an onion, makes you weep. On one of those soft February mornings, while I was waiting—my eyes full of tears because of the disinfectant—for the bus to start, the wind from the sea, coming in through the windows, gave me a great longing to go off on my own account, to pause for a little and reflect about myself. And so, when I got off the bus near the workshop, instead of going to the right, towards the shed, I went to the left, towards the meadows that lie between the main road and the Tiber. I walked off over the pallid grass, in the gentle, moist wind, facing a sky full of white clouds. The Tiber itself I could not see, because at that point it runs through a dip in the ground; away beyond it I could see abandoned factories, a big building with arches looking like a great dovecot, and a church with a dome and pillars that support nothing and look like the wooden pillars in a child's building game. Behind me was the industrial district of Rome—tall chimneys with long plumes of black smoke, factory sheds full of big windows, the low, broad cylinders of two or three gasometers and the high, narrow ones of silos. When I thought of the workmen toiling in those factories, my leisure seemed to me even more agreeable. I felt full of cunning and watchfulness, as though I were going out hunting. And hunting indeed I was—not for game, however, but for myself.

When I reached the river, at a point where the bank is not so very steep, I slithered down the slope to the edge and sat down amongst the bushes. Only one step from my feet ran the Tiber, and I could see it twisting through the countryside like a snake, the dazzling light from the cloudy sky reflected in its yellow, wrinkled surface. On the other side of the river were more pale green meadows and, scattered over them, sheep nibbling at the grass, sheep with puffed-out, dirty wool, and here and there a perfectly white lamb, whose wool had not yet had time to go grey. I sat clasping my knees and stared at the yellow water, which at this point formed a little whirlpool from which a black branch projected, shaggy and untidy and looking like the hair of a drowned woman. And then, in the silence, with the branch, black as ebony, quivering from the force of the current but not moving, I felt all at once as though inspired; and, not with thought but with a feeling more profound than thought, I seemed to have understood something of great importance. Or rather, to be able to understand it, if only I did my utmost to grasp it. This thing, in fact, was poised delicately; it was like having, as they say, a word on the tip of one's tongue. And, in order to hold on to it and prevent its falling back into the darkness, I said, suddenly, aloud: "My name is Gerardo Mucchietto."

Immediately a mocking voice from above said: "Commonly called Mucchio. . . . Well, well, are you talking to yourself?"

I turned round and right above me saw, standing on the edge of the bank, the daughter of the custodian of the brick-yard. Gioconda, in a black velvet skirt and a pink sweater, stockingless, her hair fluttering in the wind. Now, of all the people I knew in the whole world, Gioconda was the one I would least have wished to see at that moment. She had taken a fancy to me and she persecuted me, although I had made it plain to her in every possible way that I did not care for her. I had an immediate impulse to say something unpleasant to her, so that she should go away and leave me alone to return to the thing I had been on the point of grasping when she arrived. Without moving, I said to her: "Take care, you're showing too much leg."

But brazenly she slid down beside me. "D'you mind if I keep you company?" she asked.

"I don't know what to do with your company," I said, still without looking at her; "and besides, how can you sit on the ground here, in all this dust?"

But she lifted up her dress and sat down, well satisfied, saying: "I haven't much on underneath, anyhow." The thing I wanted to think about was still there, luckily, perched on the edge of my mind, like a bird on a window-sill. Gioconda, in the meantime, all sweet and sugary, was clinging on to my arm and saying: "Gerardo, why are you so faithless? . . . I *am* so fond of you."

"I'm not faithless, it's just that I don't like you, that's all."

"Why don't you like me?"

I said hastily, fearing that, as I spoke, the thing I wanted to think about might vanish: "I don't like you because you've got a big red face covered with pimples. . . . You look like a cabbage rose. . . ."

What would most women have done after a remark like that? Gone away at once. She, on the contrary, pressed herself close up against me and said coyly: "Gerardo dear, why can't you be nicer to me?"

"All right, I will be," I said desperately, "provided you go away."

"Why, were you expecting some other woman, Gerardo dear?"

"No, no one; I wanted to be alone."

"Why alone? No, let's stay together. . . . It's so lovely to be together."

This time I said nothing: the thing was still there, on the edge of my mind, but I felt that any trifle would be enough to drive it back into the darkness out of which it had come. It was at this moment that Gioconda exclaimed: "Would you like me to guess what you're thinking about?"

Stung to the quick, I answered: "You won't guess if you try for a hundred years."

"But I tell you I *can* guess.... Now, let's see if I'm right. I say you were thinking about these socks I'm wearing rolled down to the ankle, that match my sweater.... Be truthful, that's what you were thinking about." As she spoke she held out her leg, which was big and red and covered with fair hairs, displaying her foot in its strawberry-coloured sock. I could not help raising my eyes and looking at her foot, and then, all of a sudden, I became aware that the thing had fallen back over the edge, down into the darkness. I no longer felt anything, I no longer understood anything, I was empty, dead, inert, like the stakes of seasoned wood that my uncle kept propped up against the workshop wall. At the thought that I had lost sight of that most beautiful and important thing through the chatter of this stupid girl, I was seized suddenly with an immense rage and I cried out, turning brusquely towards her: "Why did you come here?... You're my evil genius.... Couldn't you have left me alone?" And, since she continued to squeeze my arm, I tore myself away from her and hit her on the head. But she clung to me obstinately, although I beat her on her big blonde head: so then I jumped up, seized her by the hair and threw her down on the gravel and trampled on her with my feet, all over her body and even on her head. Rolled up into a ball with her face in her hands, she groaned and let forth a shriek or two, but made no attempt at resistance: possibly she was pleased. However, when I was tired of trampling on her, she got up and, all covered with dust, went off sobbing. I shouted loudly after her: "You women are the ruin of humanity." Still sobbing, she went off down a track along the gravelly bed of the Tiber and disappeared.

But the thing, by this time, had taken flight, and now, although I was alone, I felt just as inert and dull and empty as when Gioconda had been there. There was nothing to be done, for that day anyhow; and there was no knowing how long it would be before I could find another opportunity like this. Seething with rage and at the same time both undecided and full of eagerness, I roamed the fields the whole morning, cursing Gioconda and cursing my fate, unable to be still, either in mind or body. In the end I realized there was nothing for me to do except go back to the workshop, so back I went. Amongst the piles of bricks Gioconda, carrying a cookingpot, was scattering food to the hens; she greeted me from afar with a smile. I did not respond and went on into the workshop. "Better late than never," cried my uncle when he saw me. I said nothing, but put on my overalls and resumed my work at the exact point where I had left it the day before.

Translated by Angus Davidson

MORAVIA: *The Ruin of Humanity*

1. *Moravia often communicates through mood or atmosphere. What is the mood of the opening paragraph? Of the succeeding paragraphs? Of the final paragraph?*

2. *In what way does Moravia's "ear for mood" remind you of Turgenev's "ear for emotion"? Is it a substitute for plot? What other writers in this collection depend heavily upon mood?*

3. *Moravia also uses the device of "figurative foreshadowing" ("I had gone into the workshop a year before, like a train going into a tunnel") to move his story. Is it plausible that Gerardo should speak in similes? Is the naturalistic surface of the story violated by this technique?*

4. *Why does work become unbearable for Gerardo? Does his boredom seem believable?*

5. *What is Gerardo's attitude toward his uncle? Is it just?*

6. *What does the river signify to Gerardo? Compare its significance to the meaning of the river in "The Judgment."*

7. *If Gioconda had been more attractive, would Gerardo have welcomed her? Does her name have any significance?*

8. *Who or what is "the ruin of humanity"? Does Gerardo know the real answer? How is it revealed to the reader? (See questions 1, 2, and 3.)*

9. *What has Gerardo gained or lost at the end? What if anything has he learned about himself? What is Moravia's point? Is it tragic or comic? What view of society is being projected here?*

10. *What does this story have in common with "Counterparts" and with "The Man Who Loved Islands"?*

Richard Wright
BIG BLACK GOOD MAN

Born near Natchez, Mississippi, in 1908 and brought up in Memphis, Tennessee, Richard Wright has recently emerged as possibly the most perceptive of the black writers on racial relationships in America. After Wright moved to Chicago in 1927, he became politically aware and then turned to writing, publishing Uncle Tom's Children *in 1938,* Native Son *in 1940, and* Black Boy *in 1945, the three books on which his reputation rests. All three are essentially autobiographical, either directly or psychologically. Yet even as he tried to delineate the role of the black man in the United States, to show his systematic exclusion from nearly all meaningful roles in a white society, Wright was also concerned with the whole texture of American civilization and the type of culture it had created. Estranged from his native country by its racism, Wright moved to France in 1947 and attempted to shift his materials to a more philosophical level, as in* The Outsider *and* White Man, Listen! *It is, however, in the three early books that he had his greatest impact, on black writers as different as Ralph Ellison, James Baldwin, and LeRoi Jones, and on American culture as a whole. Wright died, in France, in 1960.*

THROUGH the open window Olaf Jenson could smell the sea and hear the occasional foghorn of a freighter; outside, rain pelted down through an August night, drumming softly upon the pavements of Copenhagen, inducing drowsiness, bringing dreamy memory, relaxing the tired muscles of his work-wracked body. He sat slumped in a swivel chair with his legs outstretched and his feet propped atop an edge of his desk. An inch of white ash tipped the end of his brown cigar and now and then he inserted the end of the stogie into his mouth and drew gently upon it, letting wisps of blue smoke eddy from the corners of his wide, thin lips. The watery gray irises behind the thick lenses of his eyeglasses gave him a look of abstraction, of absentmindedness, of an almost genial idiocy. He sighed, reached for his half-empty bottle of beer, and drained it into this glass and downed it with a long slow gulp,

[423

then licked his lips. Replacing the cigar, he slapped his right palm against his thigh and said half aloud:

"Well, I'll be sixty tomorrow. I'm not rich, but I'm not poor either . . . Really, I can't complain. Got good health. Traveled all over the world and had my share of the girls when I was young . . . And my Karen's a good wife. I own my home. Got no debts. And I love digging in my garden in the spring . . . Grew the biggest carrots of anybody last year. Ain't saved much money, but what the hell . . . Money ain't everything. Got a good job. Night portering ain't too bad." He shook his head and yawned. "Karen and I could of had some children, though. Would of been good company . . . 'Specially for Karen. And I could of taught 'em languages . . . English, French, German, Danish, Dutch, Swedish, Norwegian, and Spanish . . ." He took the cigar out of his mouth and eyed the white ash critically. "Hell of a lot of good language learning did me . . . Never got anything out of it. But those ten years in New York were fun . . . Maybe I could of got rich if I'd stayed in America . . . Maybe. But I'm satisfied. You can't have everything."

Behind him the office door opened and a young man, a medical student occupying room number nine, entered.

"Good evening," the student said.

"Good evening," Olaf said, turning.

The student went to the keyboard and took hold of the round, brown knob that anchored his key.

"Rain, rain, rain," the student said.

"That's Denmark for you," Olaf smiled at him.

"This dampness keeps me clogged up like a drainpipe," the student complained.

"That's Denmark for you," Olaf repeated with a smile.

"Good night," the student said.

"Good night, son," Olaf sighed, watching the door close.

Well, my tenants are my children, Olaf told himself. Almost all of his children were in their rooms now . . . Only seventy-two and forty-four were missing . . . Seventy-two might've gone to Sweden . . . And forty-four was maybe staying at his girl's place tonight, like he sometimes did . . . He studied the pear-shaped blobs of hard rubber, reddish brown like ripe fruit, that hung from the keyboard, then glanced at his watch. Only room thirty, eighty-one, and one hundred and one were empty . . . And it was almost midnight. In a few moments he could take a nap. Nobody hardly ever came looking for accommodations after midnight, unless a stray freighter came in, bringing thirsty, women-hungry sailors. Olaf chuckled softly. Why in hell was I ever a sailor? The whole time I was at sea I was thinking and dreaming about women. Then why didn't I stay on land where women could be had? Hunh? Sailors are crazy . . .

But he liked sailors. They reminded him of his youth, and there was something so direct, simple, and childlike about them. They always said straight out what they wanted, and what they wanted was almost always women and whisky . . . "Well, there's no harm in that . . . Nothing could be more natural," Olaf sighed, looking thirstily at his empty beer bottle. No; he'd not drink any more tonight; he'd had enough; he'd go to sleep . . .

He was bending forward and loosening his shoelaces when he heard the office door crack open. He lifted his eyes, then sucked in his breath. He did not straighten; he just stared up and around at the huge black thing that filled the doorway. His reflexes refused to function; it was not fear; it was just simple astonishment. He was staring at the biggest, strangest, and blackest man he'd ever seen in all his life.

"Good evening," the black giant said in a voice that filled the small office. "Say, you got a room?"

Olaf sat up slowly, not to answer but to look at this brooding black vision; it towered darkly some six and a half feet into the air, almost touching the ceiling, and its skin was so black that it had a bluish tint. And the sheer bulk of the man! . . . His chest bulged like a barrel; his rocklike and humped shoulders hinted of mountain ridges; the stomach ballooned like a threatening stone; and the legs were like telephone poles . . . The big black cloud of a man now lumbered into the office, bending to get its buffalolike head under the door frame, then advanced slowly upon Olaf, like a stormy sky descending.

"You got a room?" the big black man asked again in a resounding voice.

Olaf now noticed that the ebony giant was well dressed, carried a wonderful new suitcase, and wore black shoes that gleamed despite the raindrops that peppered their toes.

"You're American?" Olaf asked him.

"Yeah, man; sure," the black giant answered.

"Sailor?"

"Yeah. American Continental Lines."

Olaf had not answered the black man's question. It was not that the hotel did not admit men of color; Olaf took in all comers—blacks, yellows, whites, and browns . . . To Olaf, men were men, and, in his day, he'd worked and eaten and slept and fought with all kinds of men. But this particular black man . . . Well, he didn't seem human. Too big, too black, too loud, too direct, and probably too violent to boot . . .

Olaf's five feet seven inches scarcely reached the black giant's shoulder and his frail body weighed less, perhaps, than one of the man's gigantic legs . . . There was something about the man's intense blackness and ungamely bigness that frightened and insulted Olaf; he felt as though this man had come here expressly to remind him how puny, how tiny, and how weak and how white he was. Olaf knew, while registering his reactions, that he was being irrational and foolish; yet, for the first time in his life, he was emotionally determined to refuse a man a room solely on the basis of the man's size and color . . . Olaf's lips parted as he groped for the right words in which to couch his refusal, but the black giant bent forward and boomed:

"I asked you if you got a room. I got to put up somewhere tonight, man."

"Yes, we got a room," Olaf murmured.

And at once he was ashamed and confused. Sheer fear had made him yield. And he seethed against himself for his involuntary weakness. Well, he'd look over his book and pretend that he'd made a mistake; he'd tell this hunk of blackness that there was really no free room in the hotel, and that he was so sorry . . . Then, just as he took out the hotel register to make believe that he was poring over it, a thick roll of American bank notes, crisp and green, was thrust under his nose.

"Keep this for me, will you?" the black giant commanded. "Cause I'm gonna get drunk tonight and I don't wanna lose it."

Olaf stared at the roll; it was huge, in denominations of fifties and hundreds. Olaf's eyes widened.

"How much is there?" he asked.

"Two thousand six hundred," the giant said. "Just put it into an envelope and write 'Jim' on it and lock it in your safe, hunh?"

The black mass of man had spoken in a manner that indicated that he was taking it for granted that Olaf would obey. Olaf was licked. Resentment clogged the pores of his wrinkled white skin. His hands trembled as he picked up the money. No; he couldn't refuse this man . . . The impulse to deny him was strong, but each time he was about to act upon it something thwarted him, made him shy off. He clutched about desperately for an idea. Oh yes, he could say that if he planned to stay for only one night, then he could not have the room, for it was against the policy of the hotel to rent rooms for only one night . . .

"How long are you staying? Just tonight?" Olaf asked.

"Naw. I'll be here for five or six days, I reckon," the giant answered offhandedly.

"You take room number thirty," Olaf heard himself saying. "It's forty kronor a day."

"That's all right with me," the giant said.

With slow, stiff movements, Olaf put the money in the safe and then turned and stared helplessly up into the living, breathing blackness looming above him. Suddenly he became conscious of the outstretched palm of the black giant; he was silently demanding the key to the room. His eyes downcast, Olaf surrendered the key, marveling at the black man's tremendous hands . . . He could kill me with one blow, Olaf told himself in fear.

Feeling himself beaten, Olaf reached for the suitcase, but the black hand of the giant whisked it out of his grasp.

"That's too heavy for you, big boy; I'll take it," the giant said.

Olaf let him. He thinks I'm nothing . . . He led the way down the corridor, sensing the giant's lumbering presence behind him. Olaf opened the door of number thirty and stood politely to one side, allowing the black giant to enter. At once the room seemed like a doll's house, so dwarfed and filled and tiny it was with a great living blackness . . . Flinging his suitcase upon a chair, the giant turned. The two men looked directly at each other now. Olaf saw that the giant's eyes were tiny and red, buried, it seemed, in muscle and fat. Black cheeks spread, flat and broad, topping the wide and flaring nostrils. The mouth was the biggest that Olaf had ever seen on a human face; the lips were thick, pursed, parted, showing snow-white teeth. The black neck was like a bull's . . . The giant advanced upon Olaf and stood over him.

"I want a bottle of whisky and a woman," he said. "Can you fix me up?"

"Yes," Olaf whispered, wild with anger and insult.

But what was he angry about? He'd had requests like this every night from all sorts of men and he was used to fulfilling them; he was a night porter in a cheap, water-front Copenhagen hotel that catered to sailors and students. Yes, men needed women, but this man, Olaf felt, ought to have a special sort of woman. He felt a deep and strange reluctance to phone any of the women whom he habitually sent to men. Yet he had promised. Could he lie and say that none was available? No. That sounded too fishy. The black giant sat upon the bed, staring straight before him. Olaf moved about quickly, pulling down the window shades, taking the pink coverlet off the bed, nudging the giant with his elbow to make him move as he did so . . . That's the way to treat 'im . . . Show 'im I ain't scared of 'im . . . But he was still seeking for an excuse to refuse. And he could think of nothing. He felt hypnotized, mentally immobilized. He stood hesitantly at the door.

"You send the whisky and the woman quick, pal?" the black giant asked, rousing himself from a brooding stare.

"Yes," Olaf grunted, shutting the door.

Goddamn, Olaf sighed. He sat in his office at his desk before the phone. Why did *he* have to come here? . . . I'm not prejudiced . . . No, not at all . . . But . . . He couldn't think any more. God oughtn't make men as big and black as that . . . But what the hell was he worrying about? He'd sent women of all races to men of all colors . . . So why not a woman to the black giant? Oh, only if the man were small, brown, and intelligent-looking . . . Olaf felt trapped.

With a reflex movement of his hand, he picked up the phone and dialed Lena. She was big and strong and always cut him in for fifteen per cent instead of the usual ten per cent. Lena had four small children to feed and clothe. Lena was willing; she was, she said, coming over right now. She didn't give a good goddamn about how big and black the man was . . .

"Why you ask me that?" Lena wanted to know over the phone. "You never asked that before . . ."

"But this one is *big*," Olaf found himself saying.

"He's just a man," Lena told him, her voice singing stridently, laughingly over the wire. "You just leave that to me. You don't have to do anything. *I'll* handle 'im."

Lena had a key to the hotel door downstairs, but tonight Olaf stayed awake. He wanted to see her. Why? He didn't know. He stretched out on the sofa in his office, but sleep was far from him. When Lena arrived, he told her again how big and black the man was.

"You told me that over the phone," Lena reminded him.

Olaf said nothing. Lena flounced off on her errand of mercy. Olaf shut the office door, then opened it and left it ajar. But why? He didn't know. He lay upon the sofa and stared at the ceiling. He glanced at his watch; it was almost two o'clock . . . She's staying in there a long time . . . Ah, God, but he could do with a drink . . . Why was he so damned worked up and nervous about a nigger and a white whore? . . . He'd never been so upset in all his life. Before he knew it, he had drifted off to sleep. Then he heard the office door swinging creakingly open on its rusty hinges. Lena stood in it, grim and businesslike, her face scrubbed free of powder and rouge. Olaf scrambled to his feet, adjusting his eyeglasses, blinking.

"How was it?" he asked her in a confidential whisper.

Lena's eyes blazed.

"What the hell's that to you?" she snapped. "There's your cut," she said, flinging him his money, tossing it upon the covers of the sofa. "You're sure nosy tonight. You wanna take over my work?"

Olaf's pasty cheeks burned red.

"You go to hell," he said, slamming the door.

"I'll meet you there!" Lena's shouting voice reached him dimly.

He was being a fool; there was no doubt about it. But, try as he might, he could not shake off a primitive hate for that black mountain of energy, of muscle, of bone; he envied the easy manner in which it moved with such a creeping and powerful motion; he winced at the booming and commanding voice that came to him when the tiny little eyes were not even looking at him; he shivered at the sight of those vast and clawlike hands that seemed always to hint of death . . .

Olaf kept his counsel. He never spoke to Karen about the sordid doings at the hotel. Such things were not for women like Karen. He knew instinctively that Karen would have been amazed had he told her that he was worried sick about a nigger and a blonde whore . . . No; he couldn't talk to anybody about it, not even the hard-bitten old bitch who owned the hotel. She was concerned only about money; she didn't give a damn about how big and how black a client was as long as he paid his room rent.

Next evening, when Olaf arrived for duty, there was no sight or sound of the black giant. A little later after one o'clock in the morning he appeared, left his key, and went out wordlessly. A few moments past two the giant returned, took his key from the board, and paused.

"I want that Lena again tonight. And another bottle of whisky," he said boomingly.

"I'll call her and see if she's in," Olaf said.

"Do that," the black giant said and was gone.

He thinks he's God, Olaf fumed. He picked up the phone and ordered Lena and a bottle of whisky, and there was a taste of ashes in his mouth. On the third night came the same request: Lena and whisky. When the black giant appeared on the fifth night, Olaf was about to make a sarcastic remark to the effect that maybe he ought to marry Lena, but he checked it in time . . . After all, he could kill me with one hand, he told himself.

Olaf was nervous and angry with himself for being nervous. Other black sailors came and asked for girls and Olaf sent them, but with none of the fear and loathing that he sent Lena and a bottle of whisky to the giant . . . All right, the black giant's stay was almost up. He'd said that he was staying for five or six nights; tomorrow night was the sixth night and that ought to be the end of this nameless terror.

On the sixth night Olaf sat in his swivel chair with his bottle of beer and waited, his teeth on edge, his fingers drumming the desk. But what the hell am I fretting for? . . . The hell with 'im . . . Olaf sat and dozed. Occasionally he'd awaken and listen to the foghorns of freighters sounding as ships came and went in the misty Copenhagen harbor. He was half asleep when he felt a rough hand on his shoulder. He blinked his eyes open. The giant, black and vast and powerful, all but blotted out his vision.

"What I owe you, man?" the giant demanded. "And I want my money."

"Sure," Olaf said, relieved, but filled as always with fear of this living wall of black flesh.

With fumbling hands, he made out the bill and received payment, then gave the giant his roll of money, laying it on the desk so as not to let his hands touch the flesh of the black mountain. Well, his ordeal was over. It was past two o'clock in the morning. Olaf even managed a wry smile and muttered a guttural "Thanks" for the generous tip that the giant tossed him.

Then a strange tension entered the office. The office door was shut and Olaf was alone with the black mass of power, yearning for it to leave. But the black mass of power stood still, immobile, looking down at Olaf. And Olaf could not, for the life of him, guess at what was transpiring in that mysterious black mind. The two of them simply stared at each other for a full two minutes the giant's tiny little beady eyes blinking slowly as they seemed to measure and search Olaf's face. Olaf's vision dimmed for a second as terror seized him and he could feel a flush of heat overspread his body. Then Olaf sucked in his breath as the devil of blackness commanded:

"Stand up!"

Olaf was paralyzed. Sweat broke on his face. His worst premonitions about this black beast were coming true. This evil blackness was about to attack him, maybe kill him . . . Slowly Olaf shook his head, his terror permitting him to breathe:

"What're you talking about?"

"Stand up, I say!" the black giant bellowed.

As though hypnotized, Olaf tried to rise; then he felt the black paw of the beast helping him roughly to his feet.

They stood an inch apart. Olaf's pasty-white features were glued to the giant's swollen black face. The ebony ensemble of eyes and nose and mouth and cheeks looked down at Olaf, silently; then, with a slow and deliberate movement of his gorillalike arms, he lifted his mammoth hands to Olaf's throat. Olaf had long known and felt that this dreadful moment was coming; he felt trapped in a nightmare. He could not move. He wanted to scream, but could find no words. His lips refused to open; his tongue felt icy and inert. Then he knew that his end had come when the giant's black fingers slowly, softly encircled his throat while a horrible grin of delight broke out on the sooty face . . . Olaf lost control of the reflexes of his body and he felt a hot stickiness flooding his underwear . . . He stared without breathing, gazing into the grinning blackness of the face that was bent over him, feeling the black fingers caressing his throat and waiting to feel the sharp, stinging ache and pain of the bones in his neck being snapped, crushed . . . He knew all along that I hated 'im . . . Yes, and now he's going to kill me for it, Olaf told himself with despair.

The black fingers still circled Olaf's neck, not closing, but gently massaging it, as it were, moving to and fro, while the obscene face grinned into his. Olaf could feel the giant's warm breath blowing on his eyelashes and he felt like a chicken about to have its neck wrung and its body tossed to flip and flap dyingly in the dust of the barnyard . . . Then suddenly the black giant withdrew his fingers from Olaf's neck and stepped back a pace, still grinning. Olaf sighed, trembling, his body seeming to shrink; he waited. Shame sheeted him for the hot wetness that was in his trousers. Oh, God, he's teasing me . . . He's showing me how easily he can kill me . . . He swallowed, waiting, his eyes stones of gray.

The giant's barrel-like chest gave forth a low, rumbling chuckle of delight.

"You laugh?" Olaf asked whimperingly.

"Sure I laugh," the giant shouted.

"Please don't hurt me," Olaf managed to say.

"I wouldn't hurt you, boy," the giant said in a tone of mockery. "So long."

And he was gone. Olaf fell limply into the swivel chair and fought off losing consciousness. Then he wept. *He was showing me how easily he could kill me . . . He made me shake with terror and then laughed and left . . .* Slowly, Olaf recovered, stood, then gave vent to a string of curses:

"Goddamn 'im! My gun's right there in the desk drawer; I should of shot 'im. Jesus, I hope the ship he's on sinks . . . I hope he drowns and the sharks eat 'im . . ."

Later, he thought of going to the police, but sheer shame kept him back; and, anyway, the giant was probably on board his ship by now. And he had to get home and clean himself. Oh, Lord, what could he tell Karen? Yes, he would say this his stomach had been upset. He'd change clothes and return to work. He phoned the hotel owner that he was ill and wanted an hour off; the old bitch said that she was coming right over and that poor Olaf could have the evening off.

Olaf went home and lied to Karen. Then he lay awake the rest of the night dreaming of revenge. He saw that freighter on which the giant was sailing; he saw it springing a dangerous leak and saw a torrent of sea water flooding, gushing into all the compartments of the ship until it found the bunk in which the black giant slept. Ah, yes, the foamy, surging waters would surprise that sleeping black bastard of a giant and he would drown, gasping and choking like a trapped rat, his tiny eyes bulging until they glittered red, the bitter water of the sea pounding his lungs until they ached and finally burst . . . The ship would sink slowly to the bottom of the cold, black, silent depths of the sea and a shark, a *white* one, would glide aimlessly about the shut portholes until it found an open one and it would slither inside and nose about until it found that swollen, rotting, stinking carcass of the black beast and it would then begin to nibble at the decomposing mass of tarlike flesh, eating the bones clean . . . Olaf always pictured the giant's bones as being jet black and shining.

Once or twice, during these fantasies of cannibalistic revenge, Olaf felt a little guilty about all the many innocent people, women and children, all white and blonde, who would have to go down into watery graves in order that that white shark could devour the evil giant's black flesh . . . But, despite feelings of remorse, the fantasy lived persistently on, and when Olaf found himself alone, it would crowd and cloud his mind to the exclusion of all else, affording him the only revenge he knew. To make me suffer just for the pleasure of it, he fumed. Just to show me how strong he was . . . Olaf learned how to hate, and got pleasure out of it.

Summer fled on wings of rain. Autumn flooded Denmark with color. Winter made rain and snow fall on Copenhagen. Finally spring came, bringing violets and roses. Olaf kept to his job. For many months he feared the return of the black giant. But when a year had passed and the giant had not put in an appearance, Olaf allowed his revenge fantasy to peter out, indulging in it only when recalling the shame that the black monster had made him feel.

Then one rainy August night, a year later, Olaf sat drowsing at his desk, his bottle of beer before him, tilting back in his swivel chair, his feet resting atop a corner of his desk, his mind mulling over the more pleasant aspects of his life. The office door cracked open. Olaf glanced boredly up and around. His heart jumped and skipped a beat. The black nightmare of terror and shame that he had hoped that he had lost forever was again upon him . . . Resplendently dressed, suitcase in hand, the black looming mountain filled the doorway. Olaf's thin lips parted and a silent moan, half a curse, escaped them.

"Hi," the giant boomed from the doorway.

Olaf could not reply. But a sudden resolve swept him: this time he would even the score. If this black beast came within so much as three feet of him, he would snatch his gun out of the drawer and shoot him dead, so help him God . . .

"No rooms tonight," Olaf heard himself announcing in a determined voice.

The black giant grinned; it was the same infernal grimace of delight and triumph that he had had when his damnable black fingers had been around his throat . . .

"Don't want no room tonight," the giant announced.

"Then what are you doing here?" Olaf asked in a loud but tremulous voice.

The giant swept toward Olaf and stood over him; and Olaf could not move, despite his oath to kill him . . .

"What do you want then?" Olaf demanded once more, ashamed that he could not lift his voice above a whisper.

The giant still grinned, then tossed what seemed the same suitcase upon Olaf's sofa and bent over it; he zippered it open with a sweep of his clawlike hand and rummaged in it, drawing forth a flat, gleaming white object done up in glowing cellophane. Olaf watched with lowered lids, wondering what trick was now being played on him. Then, before he could defend himself, the giant had whirled and again long, black, snakelike fingers were encircling Olaf's throat . . . Olaf stiffened, his right hand clawing blindly for the drawer where the gun was kept. But the giant was quick.

"Wait," he bellowed, pushing Olaf back from the desk.

The giant turned quickly to the sofa and, still holding his fingers in a wide circle that seemed a noose for Olaf's neck, he inserted the rounded fingers into the top of the flat, gleaming object. Olaf had the drawer open and his sweaty fingers were now touching his gun, but something made him freeze. The flat, gleaming object was a shirt and the black giant's circled fingers were fitting themselves into its neck . . .

"A perfect fit!" the giant shouted.

Olaf stared, trying to understand. His fingers loosened about the gun. A mixture of a laugh and a curse struggled in him. He watched the giant plunge his hands into the suitcase and pull out other flat, gleaming shirts.

"One, two, three, four, five, six," the black giant intoned, his voice crisp and businesslike. "Six nylon shirts. And they're all yours. One shirt for each time Lena came . . . See, Daddy-O?"

The black, cupped hands, filled with billowing nylon whiteness, were extended under Olaf's nose. Olaf eased his damp fingers from his gun and pushed the drawer closed, staring at the shirts and then at the black giant's grinning face.

"Don't you like 'em?" the giant asked.

Olaf began to laugh hysterically, then suddenly he was crying, his eyes so flooded with tears that the pile of dazzling nylon looked like snow in the dead of winter. Was this true? Could he believe it? Maybe this too was a trick? But, no. There were six shirts, all nylon, and the black giant had had Lena six nights.

"What's the matter with you, Daddy-O?" the giant asked. "You blowing your top? Laughing and crying . . ."

Olaf swallowed, dabbed his withered fists at his dimmed eyes; then he realized that he had his glasses on. He took them off and dried his eyes and sat up. He sighed, the tension and shame and fear and haunting dread of his fantasy went from him, and he leaned limply back in his chair . . .

"Try one on," the giant ordered.

Olaf fumbled with the buttons of his shirt, let down his suspenders, and pulled the shirt off. He donned a gleaming nylon one and the giant began buttoning it for him.

"Perfect, Daddy-O," the giant said.

His spectacled face framed in sparkling nylon, Olaf sat with trembling lips. So he'd not been trying to kill me after all.

"You want Lena, don't you?" he asked the giant in a soft whisper. "But I don't know where she is. She never came back here after you left—"

"I know where Lena is," the giant told him. "We been writing to each other. I'm going to her house. And, Daddy-O, I'm late." The giant zippered the suitcase shut and stood a moment gazing down at Olaf, his tiny little red eyes blinking slowly. Then Olaf realized that there was a compassion in that stare that he had never seen before.

"And I thought you wanted to kill me," Olaf told him. "I was scared of you . . ."

"Me? Kill you?" the giant blinked. "When?"

"That night when you put your fingers about my throat—"

"What?" the giant asked, then roared with laughter. "Daddy-O, you're a funny little man. I wouldn't hurt you. I like you. You a *good* man. You helped me."

Olaf smiled, clutching the pile of nylon shirts in his arms.

"You're a good man too," Olaf murmured. Then loudly: "You're a big black good man."

"Daddy-O, you're crazy," the giant said.

He swept his suitcase from the sofa, spun on his heel, and was at the door in one stride.

"Thanks!" Olaf cried after him.

The black giant paused, turned his vast black head, and flashed a grin.

"Daddy-O, drop dead," he said and was gone.

WRIGHT: *Big Black Good Man*

1. *This story comes from a collection called* Eight Men. *In each one, the central figure is in one way or another misunderstood by the world he knows. How is the American sailor misunderstood?*
2. *How does the first paragraph "set" Olaf Jenson for us? Is this setting of importance to the story or is it simply filler material?*
3. *Why does Wright give Olaf his extraordinary language ability? Why does he make him an ex-sailor?*
4. *What does the black's size have to do with his dreamlike appearance? Why is Olaf so upset?*
5. *Wright's American sailor is virtually mythical—in size, color, sense of command. How does that mythical quality control the direction of the story? How does it contrast with the black in Faulkner's "Dry September"? Who seems to be "inside" the black man more truly, Faulkner or Wright?*
6. *What is involved in the black's encirclement of Olaf's neck with his huge hands? Is the scene dreamlike or literal?*
7. *Why does Lena react to the sailor so differently from Olaf?*
8. *How does Wright make his points about race and racial relationships? Why does the sailor use the expression "man" and "big boy" during the first visit, and the expression "Daddy-O" during the second?*
9. *Why does Olaf break down when the black presents him with the six shirts?*
10. *What does the sailor mean when he says at the end, "Drop dead"? How does this phrase shift the entire meaning of the story?*

Albert Camus
THE GUEST

Most of Albert Camus' fiction (The Stranger, The Plague, Exile and the Kingdom) *is set in Algeria, where he was born in 1913, the son of an agricultural worker. Having attended the lycée on a scholarship, he entered the University of Algiers to study philosophy. He was an active member of the French Resistance during the German occupation of France, emerging after the war as one of the foremost writers of the broad philosophical school known as Existentialism. Through his gift for lucid classical prose, he expressed a stoical, humanistic view of life and the place of modern man in a "benignly indifferent universe." His essays in* The Myth of Sisyphus *are the best expression of his philosophy, although he was to alter his view in later books. Though many people regard* The Stranger *as his finest novel, it was* The Plague *which first brought him to the attention of American readers.* The Fall *and* Exile and the Kingdom *(from which "The Guest" is taken) aroused international interest in his work, and in 1957 he received the Nobel Prize for Literature. He died in an automobile accident in 1960.*

THE schoolmaster was watching the two men climb toward him. One was on horseback, the other on foot. They had not yet tackled the abrupt rise leading to the schoolhouse built on the hillside. They were toiling onward, making slow progress in the snow, among the stones, on the vast expanse of the high, deserted plateau. From time to time the horse stumbled. Without hearing anything yet, he could see the breath issuing from the horse's nostrils. One of the men, at least, knew the region. They were following the trail although it had disappeared days ago under a layer of dirty white snow. The schoolmaster calculated that it would take them half an hour to get onto the hill. It was cold; he went back into the school to get a sweater.

He crossed the empty, frigid classroom. On the blackboard the four rivers of France, drawn with four different colored chalks, had been flowing toward their estuaries for the past three days. Snow had suddenly fallen in mid-October after eight months of drought without the transition of rain, and the twenty pupils, more or less, who lived in the villages scattered over the plateau had stopped coming. With fair weather they would return. Daru now heated only the single room that was his lodging, adjoining the classroom and giving also onto the plateau to the east. Like the class windows, his window looked to the south too. On that side the school was a few kilometers from the point where the plateau began to slope toward the south. In clear weather could be seen the purple mass of the mountain range where the gap opened onto the desert.

Somewhat warmed, Daru returned to the window from which he had first seen the two men. They were no longer visible. Hence they must have tackled the rise. The sky was not so dark, for the snow had stopped falling during the night. The morning had opened with a dirty light which had scarcely become brighter as the ceiling of clouds lifted. At two in the afternoon it seemed as if the day were merely beginning. But still this was better than those three days when the thick snow was falling amidst unbroken darkness with little gusts of wind that rattled the double door of the classroom. Then Daru had spent long hours in his room, leaving it only to go to the shed and feed the chickens or get some coal. Fortunately the delivery truck from Tadjid, the nearest village to the north, had brought his supplies two days before the blizzard. It would return in forty-eight hours.

Besides, he had enough to resist a siege, for the little room was cluttered with bags of wheat that the administration left as a stock to distribute to those of his pupils whose families had suffered from the drought. Actually they had all been victims because they were all poor. Every day Daru would distribute a ration to the children. They had missed it, he knew, during these bad days. Possibly one of the fathers or big brothers would come this afternoon and he could supply them with grain. It was just a matter of carrying them over to the next harvest. Now shiploads of wheat were arriving from France and the worst was over. But it would be hard to forget that poverty, that army of ragged ghosts wandering in the sunlight, the plateaus burned to a cinder month after month, the earth shriveled up little by little, literally scorched, every stone bursting into dust under one's foot. The sheep had died then by thousands and even a few men, here and there, sometimes without anyone's knowing.

In contrast with such poverty, he who lived almost like a monk in his remote schoolhouse, nonetheless satisfied with the little he had and with the rough life, had felt like a lord with his whitewashed walls, his narrow couch, his unpainted shelves, his well, and his weekly provision of water and food. And suddenly this snow, without warning, without the foretaste of rain. This is the way the region was, cruel to live in, even without men—who didn't help matters either. But Daru had been born here. Everywhere else, he felt exiled.

He stepped out onto the terrace in front of the schoolhouse. The two men were now halfway up the slope. He recognized the horsemen as Balducci, the old gendarme he had known for a long time. Balducci was holding on the end of a rope an Arab who was walking behind him with hands bound and head lowered. The gendarme waved a greeting to which Daru did not reply, lost as he was in contemplation of the Arab dressed in a faded blue jellaba, his feet in sandals but covered with socks of heavy raw wool, his head surmounted by a narrow, short *chèche*. They were approaching. Balducci was holding back his horse in order not to hurt the Arab, and the group was advancing slowly.

Within earshot, Balducci shouted: "One hour to do the three kilometers from El Ameur!" Daru did not answer. Short and square in his thick sweater, he watched them climb. Not once had the Arab raised his head. "Hello," said Daru when they got up onto the terrace. "Come in and warm up." Balducci painfully got down from his horse without letting go the rope. From under his bristling mustache he smiled at the schoolmaster. His little dark eyes, deep-set under a tanned forehead, and his mouth surrounded with wrinkles made him look attentive and studious. Daru took the bridle, led the horse to the shed, and came back to the two men, who were now waiting for him in the school. He led them into his room. "I am going to heat up the classroom," he said. "We'll be more comfortable there." When he entered the room again, Balducci was on the couch. He had undone the rope tying him to the Arab, who had squatted near the stove. His hands still bound, the *chèche* pushed back on his head, he was looking toward the window. At first Daru noticed only his huge lips, fat, smooth, almost Negroid; yet his nose was straight, his eyes were dark and full of fever. The *chèche* revealed an obstinate forehead and, under the weathered skin now rather discolored by the cold, the whole face had a restless and rebellious look that struck Daru when the Arab, turning his face toward him, looked him straight in the eyes. "Go into the other room," said the schoolmaster, "and I'll make you some mint tea." "Thanks," Balducci said. "What a chore! How I long for retirement." And addressing his prisoner in Arabic: "Come on, you." The Arab got up and, slowly, holding his bound wrists in front of him, went into the classroom.

With the tea, Daru brought a chair. But Balducci was already enthroned on the nearest pupil's desk and the Arab had squatted against the teacher's platform facing the stove, which stood between the desk and the window. When he held out the glass of tea to the prisoner, Daru hesitated at the sight of his bound hands. "He might perhaps be untied."

"Sure," said Balducci. "That was for the trip." He started to get to his feet. But Daru, setting the glass on the floor, had knelt beside the Arab. Without saying anything, the Arab watched him with his feverish eyes. Once his hands were free, he rubbed his swollen wrists against each other, took the glass of tea, and sucked up the burning liquid in swift little sips.

"Good," said Daru. "And where are you headed?"

Balducci withdrew his mustache from the tea. "Here, son."

"Odd pupils! And you're spending the night?"

"No. I'm going back to El Ameur. And you will deliver this fellow to Tinguit. He is expected at police headquarters."

Balducci was looking at Daru with a friendly little smile.

"What's this story?" asked the schoolmaster. "Are you pulling my leg?"

"No, son. Those are the orders."

"The orders? I'm not . . ." Daru hesitated, not wanting to hurt the old Corsican. "I mean, that's not my job."

"What! What's the meaning of that? In wartime people do all kinds of jobs."

"Then I'll wait for the declaration of war!"

Balducci nodded.

"O.K. But the orders exist and they concern you too. Things are brewing, it appears. There is talk of a forthcoming revolt. We are mobilized, in a way."

Daru still had his obstinate look.

"Listen, son," Balducci said. "I like you and you must understand. There's only a dozen of us at El Ameur to patrol throughout the whole territory of a small department and I must get back in a hurry. I was told to hand this guy over to you and return without delay. He couldn't be kept there. His village was beginning to stir; they wanted to take him back. You must take him to Tinguit tomorrow before the day is over. Twenty kilometers shouldn't faze a husky fellow like you. After that, all will be over. You'll come back to your pupils and your comfortable life."

Behind the wall the horse could be heard snorting and pawing the earth. Daru was looking out the window. Decidedly, the weather was clearing and the light was increasing over the snowy plateau. When all the snow was melted, the sun would take over again and once more would burn the fields of stone. For days, still, the unchanging sky would shed its dry light on the solitary expanse where nothing had any connection with man.

"After all," he said, turning around toward Balducci, "what did he do?" And, before the gendarme had opened his mouth, he asked: "Does he speak French?"

"No, not a word. We had been looking for him for a month, but they were hiding him. He killed his cousin."

"Is he against us?"

"I don't think so. But you can never be sure."

"Why did he kill?"

"A family squabble, I think. One owed the other grain, it seems. It's not at all clear. In short, he killed his cousin with a billhook. You know, like a sheep, *kreezk!*"

Balducci made the gesture of drawing a blade across his throat and the Arab, his attention attracted, watched him with a sort of anxiety. Daru felt a sudden wrath against the man, against all men with their rotten spite, their tireless hates, their blood lust.

But the kettle was singing on the stove. He served Balducci more tea, hesitated, then served the Arab again, who, a second time, drank avidly. His raised arms made the jellaba fall open and the schoolmaster saw his thin, muscular chest.

"Thanks, kid," Balducci said. "And now, I'm off."

He got up and went toward the Arab, taking a small rope from his pocket.

"What are you doing?" Daru asked dryly.

Balducci, disconcerted, showed him the rope.

"Don't bother."

The old gendarme hesitated. "It's up to you. Of course, you are armed?"

"I have my shotgun."

"Where?"

"In the trunk."

"You ought to have it near your bed."

"Why? I have nothing to fear."

"You're crazy, son. If there's an uprising, no one is safe, we're all in the same boat."

"I'll defend myself. I'll have time to see them coming."

Balducci began to laugh, then suddenly the mustache covered the white teeth.

"You'll have time? O.K. That's just what I was saying. You have always been a little cracked. That's why I like you, my son was like that."

At the same time he took out his revolver and put it on the desk.

"Keep it; I don't need two weapons from here to El Ameur."

The revolver shone against the black paint of the table. When the gendarme turned toward him, the schoolmaster caught the smell of leather and horseflesh.

"Listen, Balducci," Daru said suddenly, "every bit of this disgusts me, and first of all your fellow here. But I won't hand him over. Fight, yes, if I have to. But not that."

The old gendarme stood in front of him and looked at him severely.

"You're being a fool," he said slowly. "I don't like it either. You don't get used to putting a rope on a man even after years of it, and you're even ashamed—yes, ashamed. But you can't let them have their way."

"I won't hand him over," Daru said again.

"It's an order, son, and I repeat it."

"That's right. Repeat to them what I've said to you: I won't hand him over."

Balducci made a visible effort to reflect. He looked at the Arab and at Daru. At last he decided.

"No, I won't tell them anything. If you want to drop us, go ahead; I'll not denounce you. I have an order to deliver the prisoner and I'm doing so. And now you'll just sign this paper for me."

"There's no need. I'll not deny that you left him with me."

"Don't be mean with me. I know you'll tell the truth. You're from hereabouts and you are a man. But you must sign, that's the rule."

Daru opened his drawer, took out a little square bottle of purple ink, the red wooden penholder with the "sergeant-major" pen he used for making models of penmanship, and signed. The gendarme carefully folded the paper and put it into his wallet. Then he moved toward the door.

"I'll see you off," Daru said.

"No," said Balducci. "There's no use being polite. You insulted me."

He looked at the Arab, motionless in the same spot, sniffed peevishly, and turned away toward the door. "Good-by, son," he said. The door shut behind him. Balducci appeared suddenly outside the window and then disappeared. His footsteps were muffled by the snow. The horse stirred on the other side of the wall and several chickens fluttered in fright. A moment later Balducci reappeared outside the window leading the horse by the bridle. He walked toward the little rise without turning around and disappeared from sight with the horse following him. A big stone could be heard bouncing down. Daru walked back toward the prisoner, who, without stirring, never took his eyes off him. "Wait," the schoolmaster said in Arabic and went toward the bedroom. As he was going through the door, he had a second thought, went to the desk, took the revolver, and stuck it in his pocket. Then, without looking back, he went into his room.

For some time he lay on his couch watching the sky gradually close over, listening to the silence. It was this silence that had seemed painful to him during the first days here, after the war. He had requested a post in the little town at the base of the foothills separating the upper plateaus from the desert. There, rocky walls, green and black to the north, pink and lavender to the south, marked the frontier of eternal summer. He had been named to a post farther north, on the plateau itself. In the beginning, the solitude and the silence had been hard for him on these wastelands peopled only by stones. Occasionally, furrows suggested cultivation, but they had been dug to uncover a certain kind of stone good for building. The only plowing here was to harvest rocks. Elsewhere a thin layer of soil accumulated in the hollows would be scraped out to enrich paltry village gardens. This is the way it was: bare rock covered three quarters of the region. Towns sprang up, flourished, then disappeared; men came by, loved one another or fought bitterly, then died. No one in this desert, neither he nor his guest, mattered. And yet, outside this desert neither of them, Daru knew, could have really lived.

When he got up, no noise came from the classroom. He was amazed at the unmixed joy he derived from the mere thought that the Arab might have fled and that he would be alone with no decision to make. But the prisoner was there. He had merely stretched out between the stove and the desk. With eyes open, he was staring at the ceiling. In that position, his thick lips were particularly noticeable, giving him a pouting look. "Come," said Daru. The Arab got up and followed him. In the bedroom, the schoolmaster pointed to a chair near the table under the window. The Arab sat down without taking his eyes off Daru.

"Are you hungry?"

"Yes," the prisoner said.

Daru set the table for two. He took flour and oil, shaped a cake in a frying-pan, and lighted the little stove that functioned on bottle gas. While the cake was cooking, he went out to the shed to get cheese, eggs, dates, and condensed milk. When the cake was done he set it on the window sill to cool, heated some condensed milk diluted with water, and beat up the eggs into an omelette. In one of his motions he knocked against the revolver stuck in his right pocket. He set the bowl down, went into the classroom, and put the revolver in his desk drawer. When he came back to the room, night was falling. He put on the light and served the Arab. "Eat," he said. The Arab took a piece of the cake, lifted it eagerly to his mouth, and stopped short.

"And you?" he asked.

"After you. I'll eat too."

The thick lips opened slightly. The Arab hesitated, then bit into the cake determinedly.

The meal over, the Arab looked at the schoolmaster. "Are you the judge?"

"No, I'm simply keeping you until tomorrow."

"Why do you eat with me?"

"I'm hungry."

The Arab fell silent. Daru got up and went out. He brought back a folding bed from the shed, set it up between the table and the stove, perpendicular to his own bed. From a large suitcase which, upright in a corner, served as a shelf for papers, he took two blankets and arranged them on the camp bed. Then he stopped, felt useless, and sat down on his bed. There was nothing more to do or to get ready. He had to look at this man. He looked at him, therefore, trying to imagine his face bursting with rage. He couldn't do so. He could see nothing but the dark yet shining eyes and the animal mouth.

"Why did you kill him?" he asked in a voice whose hostile tone surprised him.

The Arab looked away.

"He ran away. I ran after him."

He raised his eyes to Daru again and they were full of a sort of woeful interrogation. "Now what will they do to me?"

"Are you afraid?"

He stiffened, turning his eyes away.

"Are you sorry?"

The Arab stared at him openmouthed. Obviously he did not understand. Daru's annoyance was growing. At the same time he felt awkward and self-conscious with his big body wedged between the two beds.

"Lie down there," he said impatiently. "That's your bed."

The Arab didn't move. He called to Daru:

"Tell me!"

The schoolmaster looked at him.

"Is the gendarme coming back tomorrow?"

"I don't know."

"Are you coming with us?"

"I don't know. Why?"

The prisoner got up and stretched out on top of the blankets, his feet toward the window. The light from the electric bulb shone straight into his eyes and he closed them at once.

"Why?" Daru repeated, standing beside the bed.

The Arab opened his eyes under the blinding light and looked at him, trying not to blink.

"Come with us," he said.

In the middle of the night, Daru was still not asleep. He had gone to bed after undressing completely; he generally slept naked. But when he suddenly realized that he had nothing on, he hesitated. He felt vulnerable and the temptation came to him to put his clothes back on. Then he shrugged his shoulders; after all, he wasn't a child and, if need be, he could break his adversary in two. From his bed he could observe him, lying on his back, still motionless with his eyes closed under the harsh light. When Daru turned out the light, the darkness seemed to coagulate all of a sudden. Little by little, the night came back to life in the window where the starless sky was stirring gently. The schoolmaster soon made out the body lying at his feet. The Arab still did not move, but his eyes seemed open. A faint wind was prowling around the schoolhouse. Perhaps it would drive away the clouds and the sun would reappear.

During the night the wind increased. The hens fluttered a little and then were silent. The Arab turned over on his side with his back to Daru, who thought he heard him moan. Then he listened for his guest's breathing, become heavier and more regular. He listened to that breath so close to him and mused without being able to go to sleep. In this room where he had been sleeping alone for a year, this presence bothered him. But it bothered him also by imposing on him a sort of brotherhood he knew well but refused to accept in the present circumstances. Men who share the same rooms, soldiers or prisoners, develop a strange alliance as if, having cast off their armor with their clothing, they fraternized every evening, over and above their differences, in the ancient community of dream and fatigue. But Daru shook himself; he didn't like such musings, and it was essential to sleep.

A little later, however, when the Arab stirred slightly, the schoolmaster was still not asleep. When the prisoner made a second move, he stiffened, on the alert. The Arab was lifting himself slowly on his arms with almost the motion of a sleepwalker. Seated upright in bed, he waited motionless without turning his head toward Daru, as if he were listening attentively. Daru did not stir; it had just occurred to him that the revolver was still in the drawer of his desk. It was better to act at once. Yet he continued to observe the prisoner, who, with the same slithery motion, put his feet on the ground, waited again, then began to stand up slowly. Daru was about to call out to him when the Arab began to walk, in a quite natural but extraordinarily silent way. He was heading toward the door at the end of the room that opened into the shed. He lifted the latch with precaution and went out, pushing the door behind him but without shutting it. Daru had not stirred. "He is running away," he merely thought. "Good riddance!" Yet he listened attentively. The hens were not fluttering; the guest must be on the plateau. A faint sound of water reached him, and he didn't know what it was until the Arab again stood framed in the doorway, closed the door carefully, and came back to bed without a sound. Then Daru turned his back on him and fell asleep. Still later he seemed, from the depths of his sleep, to hear furtive steps around the schoolhouse. "I'm dreaming! I'm dreaming!" he repeated to himself. And he went on sleeping.

When he awoke, the sky was clear; the loose window let in a cold, pure air. The Arab was asleep, hunched up under the blankets now, his mouth open, utterly relaxed. But when Daru shook him, he started dreadfully, staring at Daru with wild eyes as if he had never seen him and such a frightened expression that the schoolmaster stepped back. "Don't be afraid. It's me. You must eat." The Arab nodded his head and said yes. Calm had returned to his face, but his expression was vacant and listless.

The coffee was ready. They drank it seated together on the folding bed as they munched their pieces of the cake. Then Daru led the Arab under the shed and showed him the faucet where he washed. He went back into the room, folded the blankets and the bed, made his own bed and put the room in order. Then he went through the classroom and out onto the terrace. The sun was already rising in the blue sky; a soft, bright light was bathing the deserted plateau. On the ridge the snow was melting in spots. The stones were about to reappear. Crouched on the edge of the plateau, the schoolmaster looked at the deserted expanse. He thought of Balducci. He had hurt him, for he had sent him off in a way as if he didn't want to be associated with him. He could still hear the gendarme's farewell and, without knowing why, he felt strangely empty and vulnerable. At that moment, from the other side of the schoolhouse, the prisoner coughed. Daru listened to him almost despite himself and then, furious, threw a pebble that whistled through the air before sinking into the snow. That man's stupid crime revolted him, but to hand him over was contrary to honor. Merely thinking of it made him smart with humiliation. And he cursed at one and the same time his own people who had sent him this Arab and the Arab too who had dared to kill and not managed to get away. Daru got up, walked in a circle on the terrace, waited motionless, and then went back into the schoolhouse.

The Arab, leaning over the cement floor of the shed, was washing his teeth with two fingers. Daru looked at him and said: "Come." He went back into the room ahead of the prisoner. He slipped a hunting-jacket on over his sweater and put on walking-shoes. Standing, he waited until the Arab had put on his *chèche* and sandals. They went into the classroom and the schoolmaster pointed to the exit, saying: "Go ahead." The fellow didn't budge. "I'm coming," said Daru. The Arab went out. Daru went back into the room and made a package of pieces of rusk, dates, and sugar. In the classroom, before going out, he hesitated a second in front of his desk, then crossed the threshold and locked the door. "That's the way," he said. He started toward the east, followed by the prisoner. But, a short distance from the schoolhouse, he thought he heard a slight sound behind them. He retraced his steps and examined the surroundings of the house; there was no one there. The Arab watched him without seeming to understand. "Come on," said Daru.

They walked for an hour and rested beside a sharp peak of limestone. The snow was melting faster and faster and the sun was drinking up the puddles at once, rapidly cleaning the plateau, which gradually dried and vibrated like the air itself. When they resumed walking, the ground rang under their feet. From time to time a bird rent the space in front of them with a joyful cry. Daru breathed in deeply the fresh morning light. He felt a sort of rapture before the vast familiar expanse, now almost entirely yellow under its dome of blue sky. They walked an hour more, descending toward the south. They reached a level height made up of crumbly rocks. From there on, the plateau sloped down, eastward, toward a low plain where there were a few spindly trees and, to the south, toward outcroppings of rock that gave the landscape a chaotic look.

Daru surveyed the two directions. There was nothing but the sky on the horizon. Not a man could be seen. He turned toward the Arab, who was looking at him blankly. Daru held out the package to him. "Take it," he said. "There are dates, bread, and sugar. You can hold out for two days. Here are a thousand francs too." The Arab took the package and the money but kept his full hands at chest level as if he didn't know what to do with what was being given him. "Now look," the schoolmaster said as he pointed in the direction of the east, "there's the way to Tinguit. You have a two-hour walk. At Tinguit you'll find the administration and the police. They are expecting you." The Arab looked toward the east, still holding the package and the money against his chest. Daru took his elbow and turned him rather roughly toward the south. At the foot of the height on which they stood could be seen a faint path. "That's the trail across the plateau. In a day's walk from here you'll find pasturelands and the first nomads. They'll take you in and shelter you according to their law." The Arab had now turned toward Daru and a sort of panic was visible in his expression. "Listen," he said. Daru shook his head: "No, be quiet. Now I'm leaving you." He turned his back on him, took two long steps in the direction of the school, looked hesitantly at the motionless Arab, and started off again. For a few minutes he heard nothing but his own step resounding on the cold ground and did not turn his head. A moment later, however, he turned around. The Arab was still there on the edge of the hill, his arms hanging now, and he was looking at the schoolmaster. Daru felt something rise in his throat. But he swore with impatience, waved vaguely, and started off again. He had already gone some distance when he again stopped and looked. There was no longer anyone on the hill.

Daru hesitated. The sun was now rather high in the sky and was beginning to beat down on his head. The schoolmaster retraced his steps, at first somewhat uncertainly, then with decision. When he reached the little hill, he was bathed in sweat. He climbed it as fast as he could and stopped, out of breath, at the top. The rockfields to the south stood out sharply against the blue sky, but on the plain to the east a steamy heat was already rising. And in that slight haze, Daru, with heavy heart, made out the Arab walking slowly on the road to prison.

A little later, standing before the window of the classroom, the schoolmaster was watching the clear light bathing the whole surface of the plateau, but he hardly saw it. Behind him on the blackboard, among the winding French rivers, sprawled the clumsily chalked-up words he had just read: "You handed over our brother. You will pay for this." Daru looked at the sky, the plateau, and, beyond, the invisible lands stretching all the way to the sea. In the vast landscape he had loved so much, he was alone.

Translated by Justin O'Brien

CAMUS: *The Guest*

1. *How would you classify the prose style? Even though the Camus story is in translation, do you see similarities with Hemingway's prose? What are both men trying to achieve stylistically?*
2. *What is the "feel" or sense of the first few paragraphs? What gives them their physicality?*
3. *How does the presence of the Arab intrude into Daru's life? The conflict referred to is that between the Algerian Arabs and the French colonialists, who considered Algeria to be French. What are Daru's sympathies and attitudes?*
4. *How does the landscape become part of the story? Is it benign or an active participant? How does the Arab fit into the landscape?*
5. *What are some of the political implications of the relationship between Daru and the Arab? Are there sexual overtones as well?*
6. *Is there any possibility that Daru, a French Algerian, can understand the Algerian Arab?*
7. *What is Daru's purpose in refusing to accompany the Arab to the Tinguit police station? What effect does this decision have on the Arab?*
8. *Are the words chalked on the school blackboard at the end a true indication of what Daru has done? What is his reaction to the scrawled words? Through what twists and turns is Camus taking the story? If you see broad political implications, what are they? Do they still apply?*
9. *What is the tone of the title? Is it ironic? satiric? ambiguous?*
10. *In what way does this story recall a very different tale, "The Man Who Loved Islands"?*
11. *In 1972 there appeared a critical study, called* Camus and Sartre, *based on the common interests and subsequent differences between these two great French men of letters. Do their stories reveal common beliefs?*